The Woman of a Thousand Names

The Woman of a Thousand Names

A Novel

Alexandra Lapierre

Translated by Jeffrey Zuckerman

ATRIA BOOKS

New York   London   Toronto   Sydney   New Delhi

ATRIA
BOOKS

An Imprint of Simon & Schuster, Inc.
1230 Avenue of the Americas
New York, NY 10020

First Atria Books hardcover edition March 2020

ATRIA BOOKS and colophon are trademarks of Simon & Schuster, Inc.

For information about special discounts for bulk purchases, please contact Simon & Schuster
Special Sales at 1-866-506-1949 or business@simonandschuster.com.

The Simon & Schuster Speakers Bureau can bring authors to your live event.
For more information or to book an event, contact the Simon & Schuster Speakers Bureau
at 1-866-248-3049 or visit our website at www.simonspeakers.com.

Interior design by Alexis Minieri

Manufactured in the United States of America

1   3   5   7   9   10   8   6   4   2

Library of Congress Cataloging-in-Publication Data has been applied for.

ISBN 978-1-5011-9791-8
ISBN 978-1-5011-9793-2 (ebook)

To the two loves of my life:
To Garance
To Frank

Where she loved, there was her world, and her philosophy of life had made her mistress of all the consequences. She was an aristocrat. She could have been a Communist. She could never have been a bourgeoise.

> R. H. Bruce Lockhart, British consul general and
> unofficial ambassador to the Bolsheviks in 1918

Moura was the most intelligent woman of her time.
> Harold Nicolson, politician and
> husband of Vita Sackville-West

She . . . has become somehow even sweeter. As ever, she knows everything and is interested in everything. A superlative person! She wants to marry some baron, but we're protesting vociferously. Let the baron pick himself another fantasy!
This one is ours!

> Maxim Gorky, author of *Mother* and *The Lower Depths*

And Moura is Moura, as ever. Human, faulty, wise, silly, and I love her. . . .
When all is said and done, she is the woman I really love. I love her voice, her presence, her strength and her weaknesses.

> H. G. Wells, author of *The Invisible Man* and
> *The War of the Worlds*

Note to Readers

A list of characters, an acknowledgments section, and a bibliography can be found at the end of the book.

Invicta
Unconquered

Throughout Europe's torments, from one war to the next, she accompanied them all: Stalin, Churchill, de Gaulle. And Maxim Gorky. And H. G. Wells. And many others who were less prominent, less known.

She was the woman of a thousand lives. The woman of a thousand names. She was Maria Ignatyevna Zakrevskaya for some, Mrs. Benckendorff for others, Baroness Budberg for most. As for the nicknames her nearest and dearest bestowed upon her, she amassed a multitude: she was Marydear to her Irish governess; Mourushka to her mother, of Polish heritage; Marie to her two Baltic husbands; Baby to her British lover; Tyotka or Chubanka to her Russian lover; Moura to her friends, Moura with no last name but always prefaced by a possessive or an adjective: *my Moura, my wonderful Moura.*

As time went by, in Russia, in Germany, in Estonia, in Italy, in England, in France, each of them had—or was convinced they had—a privileged relationship, an intimate and unique bond, with her.

She was a seductress at heart.

All the same, nobody in the myriad relationships she sustained had the same image of her. Of her close friends, her husbands, her lovers, her children, no two shared the same vision, no two deciphered her nature in the same way . . . And not one could take pride in having been privy to her secrets.

Mysterious, secret Moura.

Welcoming, voluble Moura.

The woman of a thousand faces, the woman of a thousand facets: some sang of her tenderness, her unfailing affection, her fidelity unto death. Others denounced her constant lies.

She was the personification of loyalty.

She was the personification of deceit.

She was adored by those she loved. She was hated by those who considered her far from straightforward: as destructive as she was elusive.

Her admirers and her detractors all agreed on one point, however: Moura Zakrevskaya-Benckendorff-Budberg symbolized Life.

Life in all forms. Life at all costs. Life against all odds.

She was a survivor. This sentence recurs everywhere in the accounts and interviews, the word *survivor* encapsulating the imagery of battle and the idea of an ultimate triumph.

She was determined to survive the upheaval of the October Revolution, which eradicated her social class and her peers. This is what Moura strived to be for her entire existence. She was determined to survive—and survive unscathed—amid the rubble of a destroyed world.

But not only that.

I, for one, would not choose her survival instinct as the most unique part of her temperament. There are other traits, more obscure or more prominent ones, that better illustrate her character.

Her freedom of body, her freedom of mind, her freedom of heart and soul, her absolute freedom allowed her to love herself, to love her traveling companions, and, most unexpectedly, to reconcile the irreconcilable by finding an internal unity.

It was this courage, of living in limitless freedom and loving limitlessly, that inspired me to bear witness to her incredible adventures.

What adventures did she go on? The texts devoted to her ever since her death in 1974 have consistently described her as a formidable spy. In the service of the USSR, or Great Britain, or even Germany, according to these authors. Some go so far as to call her a double agent, working for Russia and England at the same time.

To stick to the facts, I should say that in the counterintelligence archives of the three nations she is supposed to have served or betrayed over half a century, I have found no evidence of her activities. The specialists I interrogated on this topic responded that this lack of any trace is exactly the proof I had been looking for: the greatest spies leave behind no fingerprints.

Yet I do have to concur with this employee of the Deuxième Bureau, which investigated informants' reports during the 1930s in Paris: in the margins of the reports discussing "la femme Budberg" he drew a long vertical line, then wrote at the bottom of the file with a red pencil, *Maigre!* Very little!

Too little: that is all her folders amount to. Or perhaps too much. Too much theatricality, too much emotion, too much playacting. And too many gray areas. The British historians who dreamed of forcing her to write her memoirs or, short of that, interrogating her about her past ended up, like the French police, throwing in the towel: *she's too much like a Russian novel!* And rightly so . . . She embodied the novelistic form so thoroughly that she came to belong wholly to legend, myth, and fantasy. Facts and objective reality barely counted for her. She never owed anything to Truth. Except to her own truth.

All the same, the archives' documents underscore that this woman belongs to History.

My quest to retrace her footsteps has led me, over three years, through the libraries of Russia, Estonia, France, England, Italy, and America: all the lands where Moura left behind written traces.

My story relies upon this immense corpus of letters, reports, and accounts, the entirety of which has fed my imagination.

Her letters in English to H. G. Wells have been reproduced here. And her Russian correspondence with Gorky has been translated for the first time in these pages. I hope with all my heart that the tone and the spirit of these two great writers shine all the more brilliantly within their context.

———

The greatest irony is that after all this extensive academic research, I ultimately came back to the form of fiction, the form Moura herself had always instinctively lived through. In my eyes, it is the most suitable tone for slipping into the contradictions of her soul, for striving to bring her back to life.

But readers can presume that all the protagonists, all the places, all the dates, all the words, and all Moura's acts of which I am aware have been rendered with as much accuracy as I can provide within this novel. Any reader keen to learn more may turn to the end of the book to find a brief bibliography covering the Russian Revolution, the works of the writers with whom she spent portions of her life, and the details of international espionage between the two wars.

There is no risk of exhausting the multitude of topics touching on the life she lived and the fate she met.

With her strength and her weaknesses, Moura personifies all the audacities of the twentieth century, as well as its sufferings and paradoxes.

With her strength and her weaknesses, in my eyes she tragically, magnificently embodies the human condition.

Book I

The First Life of Marydear

A Silver Spoon in Her Mouth:
Love with a Thousand Faces

March 1893–April 1918

CHAPTER ONE

Ducky

1892

T he attachment governesses feel for the children they rear may bear some relationship to their past personal disasters. Those of the Zakrevsky children's Irish nanny were the result of a succession of tragedies that nobody in Russia would ever learn about.

Her name was Mrs. Margaret Wilson, or Ducky.

Moura owed everything to her nurse's love: her calmness, her kindness, and her thorough willingness to indulge—which would come to charm so many men.

❖

Ducky had kept her maiden name, Wilson, even though she was married. She wasn't Irish by origin but British. She was descended from a middle-class Protestant family in Liverpool, where her parents owned a grocery shop. They had instilled in their only daughter a grasp of proper conduct, a sense of good manners, and an understanding of upright morals. In all other domains, Margaret Wilson's education was thoroughly abbreviated. She knew how to write, of course, and even how to count. To read, certainly. But she had little acquaintance with general ideas, much less knowledge itself; she never found herself absorbed in novels, much less the poetry that filled ladies' magazines. Still, she was preternaturally gifted with intuition and shrewd common sense. Tall, svelte, instinctively elegant, Margaret garnered the admiration of everyone in the area. Her reserve and her dignity pleased them. Nothing in her childhood dreams had prepared her for falling in love with an Irish rebel—a Catholic, at that—nor for the heartbreak of her father's opposition, the aspersions cast on her honesty, their elopement, and least of all life in absolute penury in Dublin. She had nothing but her passion and her will to live.

Her husband's alcoholism, his frequent disappearances into unsavory bars, and the birth of a child swiftly sounded the death knell for their marriage. One night he did not come back home, and he never showed his face again.

Abandoned, indigent, bereft of any information about her husband—who could just as easily be dead as alive, for all she knew—the young woman fought against catastrophe. After several jobs, and ensuring the education of her little boy, Sean, as best she could, she struck out on her own. She was eighteen years old.

The austerity this "Mother Courage" underwent would have lasted the rest of her time on earth if she had not met the second man of her life: Colonel Thomas Gonne, a soldier of the British army. He had lived in the Indies and in Russia, and he was now living in Dublin. A widower and a father of two girls of marriageable age, as well as a rich man, the colonel was, like Margaret, in love with the land where he had been posted. This last attribute—his passion for Ireland—seemed to be the only commonality he had with Mrs. Wilson. On all other fronts, they seemed to be not of the same world.

Still, Colonel Gonne courted her properly, inundating her with flowers and attention, waiting respectfully and patiently for her to give in. Mrs. Wilson's innate dignity had seduced him. Even if he never had any intention of doing more with her than he might do with a mistress, he saw in her a charming companion with whom he might while away a small portion of his life. And maybe, who knew, even the rest of his time on earth.

Margaret was twenty-two years old at the time. The colonel was thirty years her elder. Unstinting in his affection, generous, courteous, he succeeded in reassuring her. She glimpsed a promise of happiness, and ended up acceding.

Which was a mistake, because this fall reduced her to nothing more

than a loose woman. Their relationship quickly grew complicated: immediately after their first tryst, she learned that she was expecting a baby. He
promised to support the mother and the child. But Colonel Gonne's swift
death from typhoid fever meant that their adventure took a tragic turn.

Margaret only learned of her lover's death and funeral the day after
she gave birth, when, standing in the street with their little girl in her
arms, she saw the shuttered windows of the empty house. The servants
had already returned to England.

She tried to fight again. But in vain. This time, she couldn't recover
from the blow. She collapsed.

Her job, her respectability, her love: she had lost them all. In one last
attempt, she mustered the energy to head to London. The colonel had
a brother there whom he had once mentioned to her, a brother he had
designated as his daughters' guardian. She made the trip to gain some
money, some time, so the baby could survive until she was able to find
work again.

The shame this journey left her with would stay lodged in her soul
forever. The humiliation of hearing others say she was just a liar, a rogue
who deserved to be thrown out the door, the shrieks, the threats . . .

Only by sheer luck did the colonel's legitimate daughter, Miss Maud,
twenty years old, hear the insults her uncle was hurling at the young woman
sobbing in the parlor. Maud had adored her father. She herself had taken
the responsibility of sending the envelope he had entrusted to her on his
deathbed: a letter and a check meant for a certain "Mrs. Wilson." She
knew without a doubt that the newborn being discussed was her half sister.

And so a sympathy of sorts, bound to their memory of the deceased,
was established between Maud and Margaret. As they were now both
in their twenties, the two young women met again. One had inherited a
fortune and offered to care for Eileen, her father's child. The other was
fighting against starvation and obstinately refused to hand her child over
to anyone.

Margaret dug in her heels for six years. Free, but in the bowels of
misery.

When her first child, Sean, had no choice but to start working as a ship's boy at ten years old and she saw that her pride and egotism were ruining any chance her daughter had of a decent life, she came to her senses. Her temporary surrender consisted of accepting employment with a very wealthy Russian family. One year abroad would earn her a sum that would have taken a hundred years to make in Dublin. Her compensation would allow her to reestablish herself and, upon her return, to guarantee Eileen's and Sean's educations. The potential employer was a Ukrainian aristocrat who had known Colonel Gonne quite well when the Brit had come to work in Saint Petersburg. An Anglophile, he wanted his children, who were now living at his estate in the oblast of Poltava, to speak the language of Shakespeare fluently. When he visited Maud, the daughter of his old friend, in London, she suggested an Irish widow she knew. She presented Margaret to him as a deserving person, presently in need, who had been her tutor and lady's companion in Dublin. A perfect nanny. Mrs. Wilson's charm and dignity did the rest. He hired her.

The scope of suffering Margaret endured in being so far away from her six-year-old daughter, the scale of her sacrifice, was immeasurable.

Margaret Wilson's fate seemed to have been banal to the point that making a story of it would have made a melodrama of it, would have framed the personalities of all its protagonists as *larger*, each in his or her own way, *stronger, more enduring than Life itself* . . . like all those who were close to Moura.

And so this Miss Maud, who mothered Mrs. Wilson's child, would go on to be the muse of Ireland's best poet, William Butler Yeats—the famous Maud Gonne, to whom Yeats would dedicate many of his works, who fought alongside him for Ireland's independence.

As for His Excellency Ignaty Platonovich Zakrevsky, who had brought back a practically illiterate governess, during one of his subsequent trips to Paris he would become a friend and accomplice of Émile Zola in his battle to rehabilitate Captain Dreyfus. Senator Zakrevsky, a legal expert at the tsar's court, even took up Dreyfus's defense against the entirety of Félix Faure's government. In all the foreign papers that accepted his articles—most notably the *Times* of London—he attacked France's monstrous treatment of an innocent man.

This act would cost him his career. But it would earn him the respect of the woman educating his children.

The night before Zakrevsky's departure for Ukraine, in those dark hours of December 1892, Mrs. Wilson sobbed to herself . . . She was going to the end of the world. A year's separation from her children, a year in the farthest reaches of the globe—she presumed.

She was wrong. Her adventure would last nearly half a century. Until 1938, the year she died.

❖

During their interminable journey, His Excellency's manservant had the opportunity to teach her about the history of the family she would be serving. His Excellency's family tree led back to a Cossack chief who had been the great-nephew of Peter the Great. Or, more exactly, the nephew of Tsarina Elizabeth and her morganatic spouse, Kirill Razumovsky. His Excellency could thereby claim to be connected to the Romanov family—a distant relation of His Majesty Tsar Nicholas II.

Whether or not this relationship was true mattered little: the Zakrevsky family needed no such legend to prove their nobility. Their ancestors were of such high birth that adding a title to their names hadn't even occurred to them.

The Zakrevskys were not princes, nor counts, nor barons, in contrast to their relatives and neighbors, the Naryshkin, Saltykov, and Kochubey princes. They didn't have to be. In the Zakrevskys' eyes, their lineage was even better.

If these subtleties of Russian nobility went undetected by this daughter of Liverpudlian grocers, Mrs. Wilson still understood, by the manservant's tone, the grandeur of the house of Ignaty Platonovich Zakrevsky. She was thoroughly convinced of it. She would remain so forever.

And woe betide those who would ever dare to question in any way the high standing of Moura and her sisters. Mrs. Wilson would become more of a snob in this respect than the rest of her flock was, more proud of their birth and their family history. She proved herself an unstinting champion of the clan's claims to aristocracy, defending the Zakrevskys' rights up until the most tragic results of the revolution.

The manservant, who had accompanied His Excellency in London for thirty years, spoke English very precisely. He underscored, however, that His Excellency *also* knew French, German, and Arabic. That His Excellency had studied law in Saint Petersburg, Berlin, and Heidelberg. That His Excellency was renowned across all Europe for his articles on the Russian legal system and for the crusade he was leading to institute trial by a jury of one's peers. That His Excellency had been invited to Versailles as a legal scholar after the French defeat in 1871, to help with the negotiations between Chancellor Bismarck and President Thiers. That His Excellency had chosen to trade his position as a justice of the peace in Saint Petersburg for that of a prosecutor in Ukraine, thereby settling not far from his own lands.

Ignaty Platonovich Zakrevsky had inherited all the manors and forests of the villages of Orlivka, Kazilovka, and Pyratyn. He had also inherited the family estate, Berezovaya Rudka. He also owned an extremely lucrative distillery, which produced vodka that was sold everywhere in the Empire. He produced sugar, tobacco, and—even more profitably—saltpeter, which was used to make gunpowder. In short, he was one of the most powerful landowners in Ukraine. Nothing had forced him to lead a legal career, aside from his immense intellectual curiosity and his passion for the law.

At this point, His Excellency would have been in his early fifties. He was tall, thin, with a small birdlike head, which accentuated his too-long neck, oddly round skull, and aquiline nose. His thin, black mustache, which more or less sliced his face in half, brought to mind the feathers of a bird of prey. It was no reproach to say that Ignaty Platonovich was everything but a youth.

Although he was elegant, distinguished, and courteous toward Mrs. Wilson, he was full of haughtiness, disdain, and impatience for those who did not belong to his house. He was a man whose authority Margaret might be able to respect. A man used to giving orders, which she could perhaps appreciate. This did not mean that any hint of seductiveness slipped into their relationship. In this respect—being courted—she was branded for life. She could not bear any other attempt at philandering.

Such was not the case for Ignaty Platonovich. He was attuned to the charms of the weaker sex—indeed, *too* attuned, according to his wife. He had a tendency to get the peasant women of his domains pregnant and to collect mistresses in every world capital.

If he had hoped to distract himself from the ennui of the trip by flirting with the pretty governess, he quickly came to understand that she would hear nothing of it. There was no chance of finding some privacy with this sort of woman, not even by suggesting it directly. As for trying to make a move . . . no question of it. And so he chose to kill time by asking her about her feelings, her memories, her personal life . . . Dublin, her husband, her children, her friendship with Maud, her relationship with Colonel Gonne: he wanted to know everything.

Sitting across from him in the luxurious compartment of the train bearing them to Ukraine, Margaret Wilson, stiff, straining, responded in monosyllables: his insistence on questioning her was painful. The risk of revealing an indiscretion forced her to lie, which she hated. She was keenly aware of how much her employment with the Zakrevskys depended on deceit. What could she teach the offspring of such a character? It was hard for her to be sure even of how many there were . . . A son about twelve years old, whom Ignaty Platonovich seemed to hold in utter contempt; two twin girls who were about five years old; a ward, the eldest of them all? Were there others? He did not say. Nor did he offer anything about their mother, except when he remembered that she was expecting a baby. As for what he hoped Mrs. Wilson might teach . . . that was a mystery. He was happy to reassure her that so long as she made sure the household spoke English at the dinner table, just as in the pantry, she was free to be in charge of the four nurses, the four caregivers, the four tutors, the various French ladies—in short, the whole *menagerie*, to use the senator's word for his wife's former governesses, who were responsible for the nursery.

Terrified at the thought of her ignorance and her accent betraying the plainness of her origins, Margaret tried to hide it all through her silence. But to no avail. As an experienced inquisitor, he did not relent; as a former judge, Prosecutor Zakrevsky was used to playing the interrogator.

She fixed her gaze and rarely spoke a word to him. She was trying to judge him herself. Her new master . . . the "little father" of two thousand souls populating his mansions and his lands. The *barine*, as he was called by the long-bearded countrymen in the stations. They kissed his hand: an homage to the serfs of olden times, liberated barely thirty years ago. This man who, despite his seeming courteousness, blew cigarette smoke into her eyes, got up, sat back down, could not stay put, was always on the lookout, always in motion; this man, endowed with a curiosity, an intelligence, and an energy that was unparalleled, could not be quiet or listen or stop or wait. And his impatience, compounded by his tactlessness, would be his downfall. This was the first impression Margaret Wilson had, a flash of intuition that she tried her best to forget.

There were so many oddities.

As the train plunged into unbroken whiteness, as it carved a path through the forests, she lost all sense of time and all idea of limits.

There were so many images, so many sensations, so many new fears.

The size of the suitcases and the number of domestics serving His Excellency in his train car should, however, have prepared her for the atmosphere of the mansion at Berezovaya Rudka.

❖

As the bells chimed, the long string of sleds slipped beneath the cradle of trees.

Following a well-worn furrow, the path led directly from the hamlet to the mansion. But there were no lights on the horizon, no glimmers in the sky. In fact, despite the lanterns on the troikas, the darkness was total. And if anyone had regaled Mrs. Wilson with the gleam of moonlight on snow, or the glare of sunlight on ice, or the powdery fields drowning beneath a purpled sunset, they would have led her to keen disappointment. As for the silence of those grand spaces . . . The wind howled through the tops of the poplars, the precious poplars imported from Italy, which lined the path. Their branches murmured with the rustling of crumpled paper, of silk being torn. A sharp whistle came through the surrounding woods, shaking the pine trees and the birches, which cracked and screeched over hundreds of versts in an unnerving racket.

The master's sled led the rest. He drove it himself, urging his three horses to brave the elements. Faster, harder . . . At a gallop, with cracks of his whip, His Excellency staked his claim to his lands again.

Covered in a bear fur that had been thrown across her lap, the young foreigner he had brought along was hoping the trip would never end. An aimless journey that would take them nowhere.

Not to have to think of her children, to forget Dublin. Not even to have to imagine the future.

Just to feel the wind, the chill, the life whipping her face. Faster, harder. She, too, needed action, violence, shrieking. The forces pushing through the trees above her slipped beneath her skin, shouting within her and seeking some outlet.

When she saw the white, baroque, abundant silhouette of Berezovaya Rudka abruptly surging forth at the end of the path, she understood that they were nearing their end point.

Every style, every material, every form. A cacophony of columns and arcades, verandas, terraces, loggias adorned with mosaics, balconies of carved wood, balustrades and ramps of wrought iron. Not to mention the grand staircase and the coats of arm that stood a full story high above the porch.

Not to mention the hundreds of people arrayed among the torchlight flames on the front steps: the very particular jingling of the master's bells had alerted his people. Ghostly silhouettes of gentlemen in top hats, tail-coats, and wolfskin greatcoats. Ladies in sable, pillbox hats, and dresses with bustles. Little girls in short white dresses, immaculate muffs in front of their torsos. Old ladies hunched over beneath their Victorian hair-styles, in fur coats, black outfits, and black pearls . . . Young boys in Russian Army uniforms, chambermaids in lace pinafores, peasant women in Ukrainian dress, muzhiks in boots, priests in cassocks. People from all classes, of all genders, of all ages.

And at the very center of the group stood the monumental profile of a pregnant woman: the frivolous and formidable matriarch of this immense family. The progenitor of Moura, the woman on whom Margaret Wilson's fate would depend: Her High Nobility Maria Nikolayevna Boreisha, known among those who she disfavored as the Viper.

CHAPTER TWO

The Viper

1893–1895

She was relatively young: thirty-four years old. Pretty, even deeply attractive, despite the curves she could no longer rid herself of, Maria Nikolayevna knew how to lure those she liked.

She was blond, pale complexioned, green eyed, with a piercing gaze that could chill onlookers. She did not lack for intelligence or ambition or drive or education or, indeed, spirit. Her own mother had been lady-in-waiting to the empress and looked every bit the well-born baroness she, in fact, was. Maria Nikolayevna herself, who had been raised in Poland, only spoke in French. As for the rest, she had a reputation for luxury and for taking revenge on her husband's infidelities by doing the same to him. *A courtesan's mentality*, said her neighbors' wives. She could not have been more lighthearted with the men who visited her. As for the women, she considered them, without exception, to be her rivals.

But her face betrayed no hostility toward the attractive governess who had been brought here from Ireland. Nor, despite her tendencies, any jealousy. She welcomed her, in fact, with grace.

Whispers immediately went around that for the sake of peace and pleasure, the Viper had weighed the usefulness of this newcomer. Because even if she hated the countryside and only recalled the existence of her progeny in occasional flashes, she still knew where her interests lay and how to preserve them.

In any case, between the mother and the governess there was never any conflict.

◈

From the reception hall to the nursery, where "Wilson" presided in the left wing (they referred to her by her last name to preserve some distance), from Maria Nikolayevna's blue-and-pink boudoirs to the pink-and-white quarters where "Ducky" lived—so Margaret was called by the younger generation—harmony reigned. An astonishing equilibrium.

The two women agreed with each other on everything, even the choice of the baby's name when she was born two months later. They called her Mary, an English name, as His Excellency Ignaty Platonovich had wished.

This concession to the master's Anglophilia—the only concession the couple made to each other—did not last long. He ultimately agreed both to baptize his fourth child Maria Ignatyevna, as was custom, and to call her Moura, the common French nickname for Maria.

For her mother, the newborn would be Mourushka—a way to accentuate the Russian diminutive without using Mary, the name her husband loved.

For Ducky, her governess, Mourushka would be Babydear.

Nobody dreamed of arguing with Mrs. Wilson: whether the family liked it or not, Maria Ignatyevna Zakrevskaya had been born Babydear on March 6, 1893, at Berezovaya Rudka. And she would remain Babydear until she turned eighteen, when she was married on October 24, 1911, in Berlin.

Only then did Baby turn into Mary and become Marydear to the end of her days.

In Moura's heart, the word *baby* would always encapsulate all the devotion, all the harmony, all the tenderness of the world. *Baby*: among the nicknames of her array of loves, Baby would only ever apply to the man of her life.

And so Margaret Wilson watched over her wholeheartedly. A heavy burden.

Had she paused for a moment on Her High Nobility Maria Nikolayevna's personality, on her behavior toward her eldest child and only son, her husband's ward, her twin daughters, even Babydear, she would have hated her. Maria Nikolayevna was one of those women who divided in order to conquer. In her eyes, humanity could be broken into two categories: those whose merits or beauty deserved her affections, and the rest, who had no importance or existence in her mind. And happy were those chosen by her heart: they knew they were truly exceptional! For a week? a month? a whole year? they alone counted; all the others mattered little. For the one she favored, Maria Nikolayevna was generous with compliments and indulgences, not stingy of any sacrifice. Her admiration was limitless and her cordiality boundless. As a result, everyone around her argued over who she liked best, hoping to ensnare her with some particular elegance, or a particular spirit or talent.

Among her children, she had liked the boy at first. The heir of Berezovaya Rudka bore the name of his grandfather, Platon; she had baptized him Bobik. Until he was ten, Bobik had struck her as worthy of being among the happy few of her inner circle. He was frail and wan: an angel, with his blond curls and melancholy expression. And then one day she had decided he was sickly, far too small for his age, too weak, too gloomy, too slow. One word summed all this up: she suddenly found him ugly. And from that day on, Bobik ceased to exist. The unfortunate boy never recovered, slowly growing closer and closer to the description his mother had bestowed upon him.

Disappointed by her son, she shifted her affection to her daughters, Alla and Anna, seven years younger than him. She never did accept the two daughters as equals in her heart. One touched her: Alla, the livelier, prettier one. This one, with her long golden-red hair falling down her back from a white bow, was adorable to her. The other, Anna, blessed with the same hair but more reserved, squinted a bit. A defect that wasn't visible enough to ban her from the maternal paradise but that set her far behind, amid the crowd of hopefuls.

The appearance of Mourushka singlehandedly dethroned everyone else. The last-born one was by far the sweetest, the cheekiest of her babies! And Maria Nikolayevna's evident passion for Babydear erased all her other shortcomings in Margaret Wilson's eyes. The governess always restrained herself from voicing the smallest criticism of the mothers of the children she cared for. *The mother*. With that title, Maria Nikolayevna had her respect. Unconditionally.

❖

The ease with which Wilson settled into the rhythms of Berezovaya did not surprise anyone. "This huge family is Russian to its bones, and she's succumbed to their charms," the French tutor said. "She's succumbed to Russian charm and she doesn't even realize how fascinated she is."

Ducky did admire the freedom that reigned among the family's members and their generosity toward their most destitute relatives, the unmarried cousins, old tutors, old nannies. She thought that maybe life on the old estates of Russia might, indeed, provide a few moments of grace.

After a year had gone by, everyone dreaded asking her whether she was planning to return to Ireland, as per her contract. Maria Nikolayevna, however, did not even bother inquiring. For her, it was a given that Wilson was part of her household.

Ducky was losing sleep over it. She missed her children.

To go, or to stay? What decision should she make?

The money she had sent back to Ireland had been used to enroll her son, Sean, in a military academy; he would become a naval officer, as he had hoped. As for Eileen, she was growing up in the private mansion her half sister had bought on the avenue du Bois in Paris. Their letters conveyed some degree of happiness.

Their mother's return to Dublin would mean the three of them would have to go back to living together in the dirty outskirts of the city. The previous year's salary had already been spent on accommodations, and they would not be able to stay for long.

How could she knowingly go back to poverty without feeling like she had backslid, that she had closed off a potential future?

She grew scared. And the prospect of a new separation—leaving Babydear, leaving Alla and Anna, even leaving Bobik—only agonized her further.

But then, one morning, the situation became clear: she had no choice. By staying in Russia, she would pay for Sean's studies and save up for her daughter's dowry. After she had earned enough, she would go back home.

Having made her decision, Ducky found some semblance of peace again.

◈

She enjoyed the blazing summer days and the hours when everyone in the manor was taking an afternoon nap, when nothing disturbed the estate's silence. She savored the moment when she could go around alone to make sure the blinds had all been drawn properly. She would cross the reception hall, the ballroom, the long succession of rooms leading to the second stairway and the children's wing. Along the way, vases full of lilies and roses filled the air with a heady perfume that followed her to the next floor. Upstairs, the twin girls shared a bright, spacious room where the whiteness of the walls seemed to blaze, just like the whiteness of the immense earthenware pots and of the muslin curtains that not a single breath set aflutter. And, later, the table that was set up in the nursery for snacks was completely white as well, with its silverware and its golden samovar making her think of the altar and the ciboria of the church in Dublin. She would take her place there with a sigh of happiness as she waited for the tea to be served. There was no need to go down to the kitchen: an army of domestics would bring treats for her charges. And she certainly did not lack for things to do. She moved around. She checked the laundry, counted the handkerchiefs, put the books in order, put away the toys. She knew she was ill suited to manual labor, so she focused her attention instead on the smallest details of organization. Her indefatigable energy, even at the hottest hours of the day, made for the evening's jokes: Wilson was the only one who could survive the midday heat at Berezovaya!

She had the greatest difficulty, however, enduring the scenes that always played out in the summer during lunch or supper.

In those circumstances, her footsteps rang out sharply on the stones, her voice felt more muted, her tone more impatient. And her Cockney accent came out again. The violence with which she pushed back her chair, not unfolding her napkin or just throwing it on the tablecloth, underscored her feelings: she did not in any way condone her masters' behavior.

It was customary for the entire house to take meals together. At one end of the table under the aegis of His Excellency were the gentlemen—relatives or neighbors of the Zakrevskys. In the middle, under Her High Nobility's watchful eye, were the ladies—tutors or confidantes. And under Ducky's thumb were the children, their nannies, their instructors, the household help. Three chattering worlds that all kept to themselves.

And Ducky hated it when Maria Nikolayevna, suddenly turning to the younger ones, would interrupt all the conversations to pull aside Darya Mirvoda, her ward, to criticize her clothes and humiliate her. Of course, nobody was unaware that this "ward," this stunning fifteen-year-old young lady, was Ignaty Platonovich's own daughter—whom he'd had with a peasant woman from the next village over. And that he forced his wife to accept her every day. And that he was still having an affair with the mother . . . All the same, forcing this poor little girl to leave the room in tears—how shameful! And His Excellency never batted an eye!

Ducky could not stop thinking about the fate of her own daughter. Was Colonel Gonne's family in England humiliating Eileen in the same way even as they offered to educate and rear her? Was she was being forced to leave the table in tears?

She also hated, above all, those drunken soirees, when Maria Nikolayevna would send her to go find Babydear in the nursery and then make the child wake up again at midnight, put on her nicest dress, go into the dining room, get up on the table . . . She paraded the child like an intelligent pet among the glasses and bottles of liqueurs. As a digestif: some entertainment for her guests. An adorable doll, with her huge dark eyes and her brown ringlets, exquisite in her white clothes and her lace collar. A marvel of nature. Then Maria Nikolayevna would ask her darling Mourushka to recite love poems that the great artist Taras Shevchenko had written for the girl's grandmother:

Forget not to remember me . . .
Bury me thus—and then arise!

Shevchenko—singer of national freedom, more acclaimed in Ukraine than even Pushkin—had, in the preceding generation, been a suitor of His Excellency's mother. The poet of love had even painted her portrait. And the face of Anna Zakrevskaya, framed by the curls of her gleaming black hair, adorned the wall of the room. *It's incredible*, the guests whispered to each other: *the latest in her lineage already resembles her.*

And when in freedom, 'mid your kin,
From battle you ungird,
Forget not to remember me . . .

Absolute self-assurance. Not an ounce of shyness. The child wasn't four years old yet, and she already seemed to understand the lines she was declaiming. A prodigious memory. Perfect diction. She took on the role and played it to the last. She imbued it with passion, naturalness, and charm.

The doll knew how to captivate her audience. She liked to seduce. In fact, she loved the light, she loved the attention, she loved the praise.

And maybe it was this tendency in Babydear that Ducky dreaded. This need to please both touched and unnerved her governess.

In order to keep her angel from pride, failure, and outright coquetry, from all the weaknesses of children born here with a silver spoon in their mouth; in order to protect her little girl from arrogance, laziness, egotism, and all the faults of a spoiled youth, Margaret Wilson would have to watch over her with the vigilance of Cerberus.

❖

August 1895 was the month when no rains came to cleanse the air so laden with pollen and dust. The atmosphere was stifling. It was impossible for the children to go out on the lawn, even in the late afternoon, to play croquet or tennis . . . The dust did not go away; it left a chalky taste in their mouths.

So Ducky had decided that tea would not be served in the nursery, or under the dome of the bandstand, or in the shadows of the Chinese pavilion's arcades, but that they would go have a snack with Her High Nobility Maria Nikolayevna in the woods along the river. Out in the countryside: a picnic, as Margaret Wilson preferred.

Swathed in linen cloaks that covered their straw hats completely, their faces hidden behind thick white veils, the ladies sat in the first horse-drawn carriage. It led all the others and was therefore unaffected by the cloud of dust the other vehicles had to move through. In it were the lady of the house, her mother, her sister, her sister-in-law, Cousin Vera, Cousin Katya, and Senator Ivan Logginovich Goremykin . . . the only man sitting in the first car. The beloved guest at the estate, a lawyer and a colleague of His Excellency's at the Ministry of Justice who had spent his summer vacation at Berezovaya for the last three summers. Maria Niko-layevna kept him beside her because of his influence in the government of His Majesty, Tsar Nicholas II.

Several unmarried relatives of His Excellency's dead father, as well as two neighbors who were staying with them that night, followed in pha-etons with the other gentlemen. Then came Countess von Engelhardt's and Princess Kochubey's sons and daughters, six children who were all about fifteen years old, along with their governesses and instructors. Last were the little ones, Bobik and his sisters, too young for the "big ones" to keep nearby. Even though he was a good fourteen years old, *poor Bobik*, as the adults called him, would have to spend the afternoon with Ducky, the twin girls, and Babydear, all squeezed in together beneath the shadows of the huge trees. The help, perched amid the piles of baskets and iceboxes, brought up the rear in three covered wagons.

The only one who was visibly absent was the master of the house, who was said to be in his library, busy working on his magnum opus on the history of Russian jurisdiction.

Nobody was aware that, in fact, His Excellency was in a carriage with a peasant woman. To maintain the decency of their relationship, he had brought along as a chaperone his ward, Darya Mirvoda. Their daughter.

A provocation that amounted to an insult upon the Viper in what she valued most highly: her pride in being well born.

In order to insist that a former serf was a woman just like any other—and even more deserving of respect than some grand dames he knew—His Excellency would take his mistress home by carriage, politely assist her in stepping down, offer her his arm to cross the few steps separating her from her humble abode, and take off his hat to wave to her in front of her door—only after he had theatrically kissed her hand as his farewell for the evening.

This behavior made no sense, either to the people of the manor or to the peasants of the village, who struggled to interpret this profligacy of consideration.

Nobody on either side dared to protest. But on both sides, everyone commented on Ignaty Platonovich's stance in the same way. He tried in vain to present himself as a judge who favored reformation, who only sent the seditious to Siberia sparingly, a master purportedly full of kindness—a *liberal aristocrat*, they were now saying in Berezovaya—who still exercised his *droit du seigneur* as his ancestors once had.

At that moment, his wife was trying to calm her nerves along the river, pacing along the towpath arm in arm with her companion, the all-powerful Ivan Logginovich Goremykin. This picnic in the forest served one purpose alone: so she could complain about her marital difficulties to the friend who, rumor had it, might be the minister of the interior tomorrow.

"Your ordeal won't last forever," he reassured her.

Enjoying some privacy on his vacation, the future minister had traded his uniform for a linen suit. The wind, the dust, all the mishaps of the countryside often forced him to smooth his sideburns, two long triangular appendices that served as his beard.

He gently stroked the hand that his hostess had let fall.

"Believe me, my dear, the week won't end without our new tsar resolving your difficulties. His Majesty is young. His Majesty simply needs to be surrounded by all the brilliant Russian souls that he can gather at the Court. I'm saving a little surprise I've come up with just for you."

A whistling above them and some commotion by the embankment interrupted their conversation: a cavalryman was riding through the woods. Even at a distance, Maria Nikolayevna could see that he had his arm outstretched and he was waving a piece of paper.

"Lord, a telegram! Something's happened . . . My God, my God, I hope nobody's died!"

Above her in the clearing, all her guests had stood up, no longer paying attention to their tea and petits fours on the picnic cloth. Maria Nikolayevna and her companion rushed up the slope to join them.

Princess Kochubey and Countess von Engelhardt were already crossing themselves. They were imagining their homes on fire. They fretted about their eldest sons, their brothers: had there been a duel?

They thanked the heavens when they learned that the message was not meant for them. It was addressed to the master from the county court.

Maria Nikolayevna wavered. She tried to meet the senator's gaze. He nodded, encouraging her:

"In his absence, Maria Nikolayevna, it behooves you to accept."

With a shaky hand, she tore the seal. Even Bobik, even Alla and Anna were quiet. Silence.

Maria Nikolayevna read. The telegram was long.

The twins were holding Ducky's hand and looking at their mother. Babydear, forgotten under the trees, had stood back up. With her wide, dark eyes, she watched the adults without drawing any attention to herself.

Finally looking up, Maria Nikolayevna turned toward her coterie: an amazed face, a Madonna's face, radiating a beauty Ducky had never witnessed before.

As if she were dazed, she simply said:

"His Imperial Majesty has bestowed my husband with the Order of Saint Vladimir. His Imperial Majesty has named my husband prosecutor of the Senate. His Imperial Majesty has conferred upon him the rank of senator in his own right."

Her voice rang bright, rang clear:

". . . His Imperial Majesty is summoning us to the Court. We must leave Ukraine and settle in Saint Petersburg."

There was a hubbub of congratulations. Everybody's arms reached for Maria Nikolayevna to embrace her, and everybody's voices fought to share their well-wishes. Bobik's piercing voice rose above all the others.

"Leave here?" he exclaimed.

He seemed crushed. He loved nothing more than Berezovaya:

"Leave now? Forever?"

"What else should we do, my poor boy?"

To her son, Her High Nobility had recovered her old tone.

But to Mourushka, who, forgotten in the chaos, was now clinging to her skirts, she was tender:

"There you are, my marvel," she crooned as she raised the child up, "our marvel who'll marry a grand duke in no time!"

She turned toward the senator, showed him the little girl, and uttered these astonishing words:

"She has so much of you in her, Ivan Logginovich . . . The same vitality, the same intelligence. She owes everything to you! And she knows it, the little rascal: see how much she wants to hug you. Can't you see, dear Ivan Logginovich, how much she looks like you?"

He leaned forward and kissed her hand again with the utmost gallantry:

"Would to heaven, dear friend, that this charming baby were mine!"

Even Ducky, who had always avoided listening to the gossips and even wondering about Babydear's lineage, could not hide her exasperation.

Exactly what kind of relationship did Maria Nikolayevna have with Senator Goremykin? The prospect that he might have been her lover for several years had not occurred to her. All the same, she would instinctively watch over Babydear all the way to her mother's sitting room when Goremykin or other senators were there. A task made more difficult by the gentlemen always insisting on the child's presence and enjoying her company.

———

She pulled her out of Maria Nikolayevna's arms with almost no resistance from the mother, as usual. Her High Nobility clung to her paramour's arm as she stepped into the carriage. She made Ducky join her with her three daughters:

"We're headed toward real life, my sweet little darlings!"

CHAPTER THREE

The Heritage of
Ignaty Platonovich Zakrevsky

1899–1906

In these final years of the nineteenth century, Senator Zakrevsky gave his children a sterling education. Even though Bobik was a dunce, he was admitted into the Imperial Lyceum near Saint Petersburg. And the twin girls attended the Obolensky Institute, where the daughters of nobility studied before being presented at Court. As for the youngest, given the enormous difference in age—a dozen years separated her from Bobik, and five from her sisters—she remained in the care of her governess for the time being.

At six years old, Babydear spoke three languages fluently: Russian, French, and English. She was studying German and Latin. And contrary to all customs and laws, her father allowed her to devour indiscriminately the world classics she could find in the library. This was an unexpected consensus between her parents: she was free to look at everything, listen to everything, share in everything. But she would have to do all this alone! Neither of them would let her ask any questions.

Ignaty Platonovich may have insisted on reforms in the Senate, but he still belonged to the old school: in his eyes, children had only two rights—that of obeying, and that of silence. And woe betide anyone who interrupted him for an explanation or to contradict one of his theories. He had developed many on justice and law, even though he was rarely to be found in his office. His presentations before the criminality congress in Geneva and his various lunches in Paris at the house of Émile Zola took up so much of his time that he had barely any to spend with his family.

However, he did pride himself in offering his progeny the wonders of Saint Petersburg. Puppet performances and walks through the gardens of the Summer Palace. Skating lessons on the Fontanka and the massive lake of the Tavrichesky Palace. For the little girls, fitting sessions at the ateliers of dressmakers who had been trained in Paris by Worth. Posing sessions at the photography studios of Hélène de Mrosovsky, a former student of Nadar.

Ducky orchestrated this extraordinary ballet with the precision of a metronome. Sleds, carriages, trams: from dawn to dusk, she kept the time of all her charges' countless activities.

Babydear's enthusiasm for this whirlwind of society life astonished and exhausted her. The little girl wanted to be like her big sisters. The fear of missing an outing was the one sentiment that could keep her moving. It was impossible to make her give up any activities. The possibility that she might be too young, too tired, or too weak to participate in one of these pleasures forced her to stop listening to herself, grow up quickly, and always improve herself. This fear kept her, in fact, in the best of health.

Dance lessons—mazurka, quadrille, Polish and standard waltzes—with the esteemed Master Troitsky, who put all future debutantes through their paces. Piano lessons—Glinka, Schubert, Chopin—with Madame Prabonneau, who was the accompanist at the Mariinsky Theater. Singing lessons with Fräulein von Kischkel of the Salzburg Opera. Deportment lessons with Mademoiselle Violette, of the Maison royale de Saint-Louis at Saint-Cyr.

Not to mention the various diversions to which she accompanied Their Excellencies. Visits with Mommy's friends—twelve each day between two and five in the afternoon, ten minutes each. Military parades at the imperial ministers' arena with Daddy's colleagues. Children's treats at the Winter Palace. White balls for grand duchesses' birthdays.

Could anyone have hoped for such a magical childhood along Millionnaya Street, in a private residence along the banks of the Neva?

❖

But now all the promenades and spectacles had come to an end for Mourushka. In September 1899, the thunderbolt of the emperor's ire struck the Zakrevskys. And Minister Goremykin's curses shook the mansion's chandeliers.

"How, just how, could Ignaty Platonovich—senator of the Russian Empire, an ambassador of His Majesty abroad—how could he have let himself be carried away by his passion for scum, for Jews, and for Freemasons with so little regard for the potential consequences?"

Slumping in her chair, her nose in her handkerchief, Maria Nikolayevna shook her head in incredulity, sobbing all the while.

To Ducky's great displeasure, Babydear was watching the scene. The mother had insisted on her presence. She wanted her child beside her during this ordeal, she wanted her nearby, with her: only Mourushka, who was always so happy, so affectionate, had the power to reassure her and steel her against her husband's shortcomings. Even Petit Chéri, her beloved fox terrier, could not do that.

Ducky did not approve. And so she made a point not to let the child out of her sight.

Goremykin was thoroughly worked up as he brandished the article from the *Times* that had occasioned his fury. He now knew those words by heart and recited the most scandalous passages verbatim.

"'France (which claims to be bearing the torch of Civilization) has fallen so far!' Have you been listening to your husband's words? 'France's complicity with Russia has naturally led to its anti-Semitism, its government's arbitrariness—in a word, all the ignominy of the Dreyfus Affair . . .' If I understand Ignaty Platonovich right, he thinks that Russia has contaminated France and that France can thank us for all its vices. Those are the kinds of ideas that get you sent to the labor camps! If he keeps on like this, your husband will be joining his friends in Siberia."

He stopped and stared accusingly. "Do you want me to tell you, Maria Nikolayevna, why he published this polemic in London? Because only an English paper would spread such attacks on France. And on Russia, its ally. Do you understand? Your husband is an agitator! A traitor working for foreign powers, an agent provocateur in the pay of England!"

The minister kept going. Maria Nikolayevna started to protest. She knew her husband was hardly one for tact. That he was arrogant. Certainly rash. But an agitator? Absolutely not!

Mourushka, sitting at her feet, did not move. She stared straight ahead, resting her head on her mother's knees. No tears. No noise. She was trying to be forgotten. Ducky felt she was nevertheless tense and ready to jump at the minister's throat.

But Ducky could not take the girl away, as Maria Nikolayevna had set her hand on her daughter's head.

"All the same," the minister barked, "I don't understand, I don't understand, I don't understand what Ignaty Platonovich's motives are here! He has to know about the commercial treaty we're negotiating with France. And just as France is ready to sign it, Senator Zakrevsky provokes a diplomatic incident that could be the ruin of all this . . . By writing this article, he is doing serious harm to his country, he is wronging Russia! Do I have to spell it out? His career is finished!"

Maria Nikolayevna's sobbing increased. Mourushka stood up in front of her mother as if to protect her, and glared at the minister. Ducky thought Mourushka was about to intervene, and she got ready to stop her.

Paying no heed to the women's reactions, he kept on screeching the worst of the article:

" 'Well, let's leave our sweet France, let's leave it to its great military leaders, to its clergy fanning the flames of Saint Bartholomew, to its vile press that traffics in lies and insults. Let's tell this chauvinist, anti-Dreyfusard France that everything happening in its borders will arouse nothing abroad but disgust. And above all, above all we will not come to its Universal Exposition in the coming year, for we may find ourselves in a very delicate situation there. We would only hear, as we always do, grandiose declarations of Progress and Liberty and Justice. And what would we do then? We would burst out laughing!' Your stupid husband won't be laughing! He'll be crying! And I, the one who nominated that idiot to the Senate, I'll be going down with him. This is the downfall of the Zakrevsky family. And the downfall of my ministry!"

The minister could not have spoken truer words. His enemies were already demanding his head.

As for Maria Nikolayevna, Goremykin's disgrace meant the end of her affair with power, business, and politics. In short, with all the passions of her life.

All this she understood immediately. Oddly enough, Mourushka did, as well.

But despite all Ducky's fears of the child's hostility, Mourushka had restrained herself. Rather than tear apart her father's aggressor, no matter how much she might have relished doing so, she had grabbed the minister's hand and was rubbing her cheek against it like a small cat. She was caressing him.

Ducky knew her baby well enough to know that this act was only meant to redirect Ivan Logginovich's rage from her mother's head to her own. To shift this emotion toward others, toward trust, toward tenderness, toward the affection she herself held toward him. To distract, to sidestep these difficulties to get back to the peace she wanted.

That was how she always was, and that was how she would always be.

She had always avoided direct confrontation with her older sisters, arguments, sulking, all forms of conflict. She could unfurl immense reserves of energy for the sake of maintaining harmony. She only wanted to love and be loved. She put her efforts there and did not succumb to any urge to be cruel or get revenge when she lost a battle. And maybe it was that, Ducky thought, this preference for happiness, that made her such an endearing child.

Despite her many shortcomings.

"Stop worrying so much, Ivan Logginovich," the girl said while stroking his hand, "because Mommy and I both admire you. My father does, too. You are our protector, you're so wise and so good. And our Lord, too, knows how wise and good you are. And He will bring us out of this difficulty."

Rather than curse her, the minister patted her head and let out a sigh: "You don't know what this life is like, my child! If you knew . . ."

This was the miracle: he was talking calmly. The worst was past.

❖

Minister Goremykin and Senator Zakrevsky were, however, forced to hand in their resignations together.

They put their shame behind them, a somewhat bearable setback that had no effect on the children's habits for almost seven years. Winters at the palace in Saint Petersburg, summers in Berezovaya. Ignaty Platonovich's personal wealth allowed them to go on living a life of luxury. Stays in Switzerland, trips to England, Roman holidays . . . A suspended sentence.

Chaos would come later, right around Mourushka's thirteenth birthday.

❖

Catastrophe arrived in the form of another telegram: Ignaty Platonovich was dead. He had been laid low by a heart attack in Egypt. He had passed away in Cairo on March 9, 1906, while he was visiting the Near East with Alla and Anna. A rite of passage for the twins, traveling up this Nile valley that he loved so dearly; a way for him to celebrate the two girls' turning eighteen, far from the Court and the marital hearth.

This escape to the pharaohs' land had taken a turn for the tragic.

❖

Senator Zakrevsky's coffin descended slowly into the pyramid vault that he had had built in Berezovaya Rudka. Like Khufu, he had prepared for his eternal rest.

The priests intoned their prayers in their low voices while swinging their thuribles. The village criers, the old nannies, the former housemaids—all bemoaned loudly, as was custom.

The horde of peasants gathered beneath the trees showed no emotion. No more than did the man's friends, kin, and colleagues huddled in front of the tomb's door. Nor was there any hint of sadness among the deceased's children. Even His Excellency's ward, whom he had wedded to a Frenchman and who had made the trip to attend the funeral, had dry eyes. Only the youngest of his daughters expressed her grief in sobs and tears.

Moura had loved her father. Ever since the day she had heard the minister's insults, she had professed a love that knew no bounds. She now understood the work he had put into details of Russian law, the progressive agenda Ignaty Platonovich Zakrevsky had advanced. She knew his articles by heart, as well . . . At thirteen years old, all she dreamed of was defending his ideals and preserving his memory.

Of course, he had been only a distant presence in her life. But he had loved her more than the others. She knew it. She felt it. Despite his taciturnity, he had never made any mystery of his sympathies.

Harsh and contemptuous to Bobik, who hated him.

Indifferent to the twins . . . Until last Christmas, when he suddenly noticed their beauty: a short-lived realization. In place of celebrating their birthday on the Nile, the pair had to bring their father's corpse back to Russia. From Cairo to Berezovaya was a nightmarish trip of more than a thousand miles.

Maria Nikolayevna, in turn, seemed more astonished than moved and did not bother to pretend to be grieving.

❖

Although Ignaty Platonovich's death at sixty-seven years old had caught his wife by surprise, she hadn't seen the last of it: the reading of his will would give her the shock of her life.

He had left the entirety of his fortune to the Freemasons, with a special endowment for building a lodge in Scotland, the first of its kind.

To his family, he left his debts and a huge apartment in Saint Petersburg. And the realm of Berezovaya Rudka, mortgaged to the hilt. This posthumous betrayal forced Her High Nobility to abandon the city's pleasures and return to the countryside she hated.

The travels and the social calendars were over. She would only come back to Saint Petersburg to sell off everything that could be bought.

❖

Maria Nikolayevna asked everyone she knew for advice, but to no avail; she turned the problem over and over in her mind, but kept coming back to the same conclusion: her only option was to change her lifestyle and live more simply.

She still struggled: Ukraine? Was it really advisable to return there? Hadn't there been rumors that hordes of countrymen had been burning areas around Kiev in the past year? And that they had massacred their masters? There had even been talk of revolution! How could she be assured that those bandits wouldn't return?

Once again, the answers were unanimous: the army had calmed the region. The uprisings had been quashed and the leaders taken care of in Siberia.

If Maria Nikolayevna wanted to resolve her financial complications, she would have to retire to her country estate. And she would have to take her daughters with her. Their exile would not be permanent. Just for as long as it took to regain control of this long-neglected domain.

And who knew what would happen? Maybe Bobik would restore the family's honor by marrying an heiress.

Bobik! He was twenty-six years old now and his career had barely progressed. Him as the head of the family? He would have to do a great deal to get his sisters married.

And what prospects could those girls hope for in this wasteland, without any dowry?

CHAPTER FOUR

Alla and Anna

1908–1909

"How strange that she should have the gift of turning every-thing she touches to ashes," Alla whispered to her sister. "She's no viper, she's a dragon!"

"We're the ones the neighbors are coming to visit and court . . ."

"And she hates us for it."

"If she could, she'd imprison us here until death."

Lying in the grass, the twins hid themselves from their vindictive mother at the far end of the park, under the mulberry tree. They knew that Maria Nikolayevna, leaning over the ledgers with the accountant, would not come that far to find them. And that Ducky and Mouru-shka, well aware of their hiding place, would not betray them. How ridiculous, even so! Twenty years old, and they could only lie down if they had their governess and their little sister promising them dis-cretion. Forced to act like children for a smidge of privacy. Well, the Viper could claim to be working on restoring the family fortune to pro-vide for their dowries and see them married in Saint Petersburg, but nobody here was fooled. Not even Mourushka, who the Viper insisted she was protecting from her older sisters' influence by trapping her within this estate's confines, as well. Not even Ducky, who knew per-fectly well how to work with the prudishness that Her High Nobility affected.

Moura walked up to the mulberry tree where the twins, looking sky-ward with heads propped on elbows, were whispering furiously.

She was tall like they were, but dark haired and more muscular, more athletic. She slipped between the branches to get as close to them as she could. It was summer 1908, she had just turned fifteen, and, despite her traces of baby fat, she carried some measure of her sisters' maturity. Their three identical white dresses stood out against the greenery; it was a miracle that they had gone unnoticed.

Moura could tell by the sisters' hushed tones that they were telling secrets. Alla and Anna refused to let her be part of their conversations, insisting she was too young to share their confidences.

Maybe. But they couldn't keep her from listening. Her best distraction in Berezovaya was listening . . . She loved nothing more than hearing about her sisters' plans to escape, their dreams of fleeing, all their schemes for getting back to Saint Petersburg.

Not that she disliked Ukraine, but there was hardly any excitement here, hardly any men, hardly any parties.

In the kitchens they said that Moura Ignatyevna had too much lifeblood, too much energy, that she was the only young lady in the house who was unable to walk, preferring instead to run.

All the same, the teenager thought, all the same, wasn't there anything else to do in Berezovaya but listen to her sisters, barge into hallways, and live other people's lives? Was there nothing crazy, nothing truly forbidden that she could try to make happen?

The twins spoke even more quietly.

Moura knew what they had to be talking about. They were talking about love! About the handsome, young Count Vladimir Ionov, who had asked for Anna's hand and who Mommy had rejected. Why? Nobody knew. Mommy claimed that his health and wealth were lacking. Mommy also said that Anna was meant for someone else.

The girls discussed the arranged marriage that Mommy was setting up for Anna in Saint Petersburg.

"All the same," Alla said, "I don't understand why she won't let me come to see you get married to this horrid Baron von Bülow."

"To upset you," Anna replied. "She doesn't want you with her: you would steal the show from her in Saint Isaac Cathedral . . . But don't worry: I won't be there, either!"

———

In the Kharkov and Kiev banks, Maria Nikolayevna's careful manage-
ment of her assets was close to bearing some fruit, but her confinement
was making her bitter to the point of insanity. In insisting that she had
to give up her toilettes, her soirees, her paramours to restore her social
status, she claimed she was steering her daughters down the path she had
followed. The correct one.

To her dismay, Anna and Alla had already had a taste of the world's
pleasures; they had already reveled in them. As they were both gifted with
innate charm and uncommon vitality, the Court and the city had her-
alded them as among the most beautiful debutantes of Saint Petersburg.
Their presentation before the tsarina had been a success.

The mothers of fellow debutantes recalled that during the five years
Anna and Alla had stayed in Saint Petersburg, the hallways of the Cadet
School and the Page School had buzzed with poems and songs celebrating their beauty. At every high tea and white ball—those balls strictly for
young ones—Senator Zakrevsky's daughters had caught the eyes of all
their friends' suitors. They had broken up multiple marriages.

Tall, redheaded, well endowed: far too precocious to be proper. And
far too lighthearted. And far too brilliant. And far too ambitious.

The gentlemen—the fathers—understood their sons' passion for Alla
or Anna Ignatyevna Zakrevskaya. Both of them, they said, had "some
temperament." For less wealthy and well-born girls, temperament might
have been a handicap. But these girls had beauty, education, and, above
all, money. What more could be hoped for?

Nobody doubted they would find husbands in the close-knit circle of
the Court. Names were already being whispered, the most respected ones.

❖

Such success, such promises of happiness, belonged to a bygone era. And
the future, with an acceptable husband, seemed centuries away.

Now they were afraid. If Providence did not intervene, they would
end up like the outcasts who surrounded their mother, the tutors, the
cousins . . . All the old spinsters of Berezovaya.

So they worked to maintain a connection to their years in Saint Petersburg, and to help Fate along.

❖

Life was hell.

Maria Nikolayevna kept stirring up drama and terrifying everyone. The confrontations took on cataclysmic proportions whenever she meddled in the twins' affairs, breaking the locks on their writing desks, going through their correspondence, throwing out the trinkets of their past life, burning all the souvenirs Alla and Anna had held on to: poems from their past suitors, letters from old friends at the Obolensky Institute, photos, ribbons . . . She said she was destroying the traces of their poor conduct.

In fact, as she was learning how to manage her household, Maria Nikolayevna was coming to understand how many details she had ignored over the past twenty years. She was making up for lost time: she was sure her daughters maintained dangerous relationships behind her back.

"She's measuring us against herself," Anna sneered.

"She's the one Goremykin compromised. Not us!"

As was her wont, Maria Nikolayevna always tried to divide the two, exiling them to separate wings of the house.

She had found a successful technique for putting an end to their secrets: she made them change bedrooms every eight days. She did her inspections and combed through their possessions during these moves.

The result was that Alla and Anna dreamed more than ever of a man who could take them away from this tyranny, a man who loved them and would carry them far away.

The elder, Alla, the more artistic, fragile one, tried to escape through music. As her frustration and her fears grew, she became an increasingly virtuosic pianist. She dreamed of making it her profession, earning her living and thereby escaping her mother's iron grip.

It was a dead end. Maria Nikolayevna considered such a career debasing and forbade her from pursuing it.

"It's not enough for you to be well born, my dear. You must comport yourself as an aristocrat. You must preserve your rank and remain a noble woman."

"Noble, noble, noble!" Alla shot back. "That's the only word you can think of. What good is it? You're set on snuffing out everything that lives. You're killing music itself with this gloom and doom. Fortunately you're the last of your generation. Fortunately your world has already stopped existing."

Anna, more adept and pragmatic, wanted to catch her mother unawares, and prepared to elope with the young Count Ionov, who had just been posted as ambassador to Berlin.

In this atmosphere, Mourushka always escaped Maria Nikolayevna's wrath. Her mother would not wish to fight with her. She professed to adore her! She was the only one here who might be a normal child: a happy, affectionate, unconstrained young girl.

Mourushka had made sure she would not fall from grace. And she remained her mother's favorite.

By some miracle, neither Bobik nor her sisters held this unfair, unchanging preference against her. The eldest child, a fairly unremarkable secretary to the ambassador to Japan, no longer set foot in what had once been his paradise. The twins knew their younger sister was loyal and would stay both curious and discreet about their loves. Mourushka would not betray them.

They used her as a messenger to Ducky and an ambassador to Maria Nikolayevna. As a diplomat, Mourushka used her skills to smooth over sharp edges and plead their cases, and on occasion she was able to reestablish harmony.

She admired Alla and Anna too much, she sympathized with them too much, she understood them too much not to help and support them. She loved them.

But how could she also love their mother, then? That was a mystery.

Moura was always torn between her affections, aware of lingering sadness, and no longer remembered peacefulness. She, too, contemplated her need to stay in Berezovaya, her future in this world. Even her faith in

God brought her no answers: the day of her fifteenth birthday, the Lord had proven deaf, and blind, and mute to her prayers.

Her escape was books.

Solitude had turned her into a voracious reader. The Berezovaya library overflowed with first editions that Ignaty Platonovich, in his wealthy years, had had bound in red morocco leather. Every genre was present. Every language. Corneille, Racine, Zola, of course, Shakespeare, Tolstoy, Dostoyevsky. And the classics, the Greek and Latin authors: Herodotus, Virgil, Ovid.

Literature. And physical exercise.

She never forgot that outside, beyond the reception hall and the bedrooms ruined by Maria Nikolayevna's inquisitiveness, life had kept on going in the world.

Life was going on everywhere.

❖

At dawn, she rushed down to the park to go up the paths amid the embankments of snow. Here, she could revel in her existence. The reasons for her joy hardly mattered so long as she could be as far as possible from the endless rooms and miseries ensconced behind the columns and walls of the mansion.

When she heard shrieks and doors slamming, she had her gray mare saddled and galloped straight ahead. The cold took away her breath, the air burned her throat. The sun, making the snow shimmer, blinded her. She shut her eyes, she pursed her lips. Leaning against the animal's neck, she only saw the mane rubbing against her cheek, only felt the heat that flushed her face. And then, deep in her lower back, the to-and-fro of the animal's gallop, which set her blood pounding in her veins. Alive again.

Except for the family dramas, so little happened in that house that life there felt nonexistent.

In fact, Anna was preparing for her escape. She had long understood that, fundamentally, resistance was futile. So she had ended up accepting her mother's choice of a husband, on condition that the ceremony be modest—just a few intimates—and that it take place in Saint Petersburg. Two wishes that, for once, were in accord with her mother's hopes.

While her guests were waiting for her at Saint Isaac Cathedral, she hiked up her train, pulled up her veil, grabbed her trousseau, and ran to get married at the other end of the city, behind the walls of a monastery in the church of the orphanage.

Having become Countess Ionov, she followed her husband to his post in Berlin.

❖

Anna's kidnapping and disappearance plunged Alla into despair. Panicked, lost, she allowed herself to be courted by a Baltic baron staying on vacation with Countess Engelhardt, their neighbor.

The man was married . . . And then, to add insult to injury, she became pregnant.

The result was Alla's humiliation as unending arguments raged between mother and daughter. And scandal, this one quite real, reverberated in Berezovaya. A scandal that Mourushka was supposed to know nothing about.

Who did they take her for? She was not unaware of the affair Alla had carried on with the handsome Baron von Biström, nor of its consequences. And her heart broke for Alla.

"My God," she said, trying to talk to her in generalities rather than touch on the drama she was undergoing, "our education has been so strange . . . We wait, wait to live, and this waiting is killing us. We talk about uninteresting things, we go this way, then that way just to seem like we're saying or doing something. But we know that what matters is elsewhere. So we stare at the horizon and keep waiting. The years go by. And nothing happens. Happiness never comes. Nothing comes. We keep waiting . . . And so much patience does our brains no good. If we stare at a void for that long, of course we'll lose our heads. We're going to go completely crazy."

Alla listened to her without replying. Torn between her passion for her lover and her fear for the future, she played Schubert fanatically. But as she struck the last note on the piano, hitting the final chord of the sonata, the fire within her died. She became Alla Ignatyevna again, pregnant by a married man who would never wed her. At least she had experienced love . . . She was sure she would die in childbirth and it would all be over soon.

◈

In the huge white manor where they had grown up among withered poplars, Ducky blamed herself for her protégées' tragic fates. She had failed. She hadn't succeeded in educating her girls, she hadn't succeeded in teaching them how to live, how to hold firm, how to avoid pitfalls and downfalls.

Her charges had fallen, just as she herself once had. History was repeating itself.

Instead of being well-reared young ladies . . . One had slipped away and fled to Germany. The other was pregnant.

At that very moment, Alla's mother was marrying her off in France— far away, for discretion—to a complaisant husband: the youngest son of Countess Engelhardt, whose assistance they had bought by offering him a hundred hectares of forest in exchange for his name and title for the baby to come. The marriage and the birth would be in Nice. The divorce would be, too.

As for Babydear, sunken in sadness and solitude, she was racing her horse to the point of exhaustion. Her face was still pink and childish, her black hair fluttered in the wind. But her gaze was dark and her lips were sullen. No hint of a smile lingered on those pursed lips. To leave this house, to leave, to leave, to leave.

She opened the windows, drew the blinds, pushed open the shutters, and kept on looking toward infinity, beyond the park, the follies, the music hall, the pyramid, beyond the forest itself. To leave.

CHAPTER FIVE

The Perfect Son-in-Law

1910

The five letters that Maria Nikolayevna had open on her lap left her stunned.

Not unhappy, no. For once, the news wasn't absolutely terrible. Just odd.

Indeed, her Mourushka would never stop amazing her.

She had let her child go, what, two weeks ago? How long did it take to travel between Kiev and Berlin? A week? And on the way, she had found a husband. And not just anyone!

Her High Nobility sat upright in the immense medieval chair of her study, where her interminable meetings with the manager of Berezovaya had left her depressed every morning and every afternoon for the last four years.

Her frustration and aggravation had aged her. Fat had altered her profile, filled out her throat, her cheeks. Too much sugar and alcohol had taken its toll on her. Otherwise, it was still clear that she had been a beautiful woman. Her hair, now ash blond, was a gleaming contrast to the dark wood of her seat. And her bun, knotted at the top of her head in the latest style, was still thick, wavy, and curly. As for her eyes, always the same vivid green, they looked on from her heavy lids with all the same sharpness.

At that moment, Maria Nikolayevna's gaze was lowered, considering the five sheets of paper and the five envelopes arrayed over her vast skirt. Like the bluebottle fly that had gotten lost in the room and was hurtling itself against the panes, her spirits were going every which way.

The first letter was from Mourushka, spontaneous and unaffected as ever, telling her all the details of "the meeting of her life."

The second had come from Bobik in Berlin, who got lost in the details and mixed up everything, his sister's reputation, loves, interests . . . everything.

The third, from Anna. Always pragmatic, Anna discussed the advantages of the union Mourushka was hoping for.

The fourth—brief but effusive—was written by Wilson. Maria Nikolayevna knew how she was generally unenthusiastic about the suitors for "her girls." The governess considered Vladimir Vladimirovich Ionov, who had stolen Anna away, to be insipid; Baron von Biström, who had seduced, dishonored, and abandoned Alla, to be odious; and Arthur von Engelhardt, who had married her, to be corrupt.

For all of them, Wilson had registered her disapproval and contempt, refusing to receive them, even to greet them. Maria Nikolayevna could not suspect her to be complicit in their affairs, as Wilson remained hostile from the outset.

Wilson, however, displayed considerable weaknesses and shortcomings. She had allowed her protégées to flee or be dishonored. And just look at the results! Her High Nobility had reprimanded her sharply.

Maria Nikolayevna reflected.

Wilson was permissive, yes. But not blind. Because of her good sense and shrewd judgment, the widow still trusted her. And what Wilson had written here, what she said of this suitor, augured very well indeed.

Mourushka's marriage remained the focus of Maria Nikolayevna's concerns. For her littlest one, she dreamed of a good catch and was still hopeful. Today, she could almost afford it. Even if the "purchase" of Arthur von Engelhardt—Alla's momentary husband—had diminished her forest by a hundred hectares, that madness hadn't ruined her finances outright. When all was said and done, a fake marriage was cheaper than a real one. The twins had chosen to live their love lives without their mother's consent. Meaning: without their dowries. A huge burden had been lifted off her shoulders.

Out of a sense of obligation, she had given them their rightful part of their father's inheritance. But their part prior to the restoration of the family's finances, when there was so little money left.

Anna and Alla had brought their ruin upon themselves. Too bad for them.

Maria Nikolayevna could now be proud of her results. After four years of work, four years of dogged saving, four years of sacrifices, she had now settled all accounts, restored all her property's productions to full health. Her efforts were paying off. The peasant revolts of 1905—"the Revolution," as the late senator, with his usual affectation for modernity, had called those uprisings—seemed distant. She had set her peasants to work. And woe betide those who might throw a wrench into her schemes. The vodka distillery and the sugar factory were now working at full speed; the saltpeter was showing nice returns.

Mission accomplished.

Maria Nikolayevna was thinking of returning to civilization and settling in Saint Petersburg again. Her horrible husband had left her an apartment on the Fontanka embankment; she would live there. The time had come to return to the rhythms of yesteryear, those of the high aristocracy: winters in the capital, for the season of social gatherings and balls; summers in the countryside at her estate. Although her fortune could no longer be called incalculable, the widowed Madame Zakrevskaya now had enough means to be able to maintain her rank.

As for the vacations that Mouroushka had been clamoring for . . .

The mother sighed. Should she have refused?

She had been reading Mourushka's correspondence with Anna ever since the elder daughter had fled to Germany two years ago. And what Anna described, the story of her life in Berlin, hadn't displeased Maria Nikolayevna: "If you come to Berlin," she had told her little sister, "bring your most elegant finery, because there will be many balls."

Tempting, indeed.

How could Mourushka have resisted such a call? Dancing at the kaiser's court . . . Maria Nikolayevna understood her desire. She shared it. She wanted all the best for her Mourushka.

Anna had taken care of her mother's authorization, negotiating with her directly. The conversation around a potential trip for Mourushka had been an opportunity for them to reconcile. The younger one, Anna had assured her mother, would be under the personal protection of her and her husband, Count Ionov. Moreover, she would also be under the protection of Bobik, who had just been named secretary to the Russian ambassador in Berlin.

Under the protection of Anna and Bobik? Who could trust that?

Yet, above all, how could she resist Mourushka, when her voice had been so tender? "Please, Mommy, let me visit them."

Thinking of her youngest daughter, Maria Nikolayevna felt herself going soft. "A few weeks on vacation, please, Mommy, say yes, pretty please . . . So I can practice my German." Mourushka's voice, slightly husky . . . Such an adorable little kitten.

And there she was.

The letter she was holding in her lap, the fifth, was from the officer who had fallen in love with the little kitten during her trip. Asking for her hand in marriage.

Thinking of her other sons-in-law, the mother let out a bitter sigh.

Small fry, the two of them.

But the worst seemed to be behind her. She had been able to maintain what mattered most: appearances. Everyone could say that Senator Zakrevsky had given his daughters to heirs of Russian nobility; the Ionov family and the Engelhardt family had served the tsar for generations.

Of course, in Saint Petersburg these marriages might be considered contemptible. Hadn't there once been talk of her twin daughters marrying two young men of the imperial circle?

But Maria Nikolayevna didn't dwell on her regrets.

In fact, after all these tempests, she felt rather relieved. With her work ethic, she had avoided shame and preserved the family's honor: her two ungrateful daughters were now fairly well off. One was now Countess Ionov, the other Countess Engelhardt. And their children would inherit that title. What more could she ask for?

And yet damage had been done. Anna had already given birth to a girl, who was growing up in Berlin. She was expecting another baby. As for Alla's wanton ways, on July 2, 1909, she had also given birth to a daughter, who Maria Nikolayevna made sure was born in France, in Nice, with the name she had bought for the mother and child.

In order to give greater legitimacy to the bastard, Maria Nikolayevna had insisted that the baby be baptized with the name of her alleged paternal grandmother, their neighbor in Ukraine: Countess Kira von Engelhardt.

A name, a title. The little Countess Kira could easily ignore the secret of her birth: she belonged firmly to this world and would have no questions to ask. Her father's identity was now a moot point. Her patronymic was noble: the matter was settled. That was all she or anyone else had to care about.

Though Maria Nikolayevna agreed that Kira's true father was a handsome man. Baron von Biström had proven to be a scoundrel, yes, but a good-looking one. Just as endearing as the Vladimir Vladimirovich Ionov whom Anna had followed and who was considered in Berlin, rumor had it, the most splendid specimen of Russian beauty.

On this one point, the looks of their gallants, she shared the twins' tastes. And she was grateful to them for it. The gracefulness of the little Countess Kira, who Alla, her mother, had brought to Berezovaya, reassured her. Her entire entourage—Mourushka first and foremost—had sung the baby's praises: a marvel, a love.

At least her grandchildren were pleasant to look at!

Of course, one day or another, she would have to feed and raise them: Maria Nikolayevna had no false illusions on that point.

Anna might still claim to be raising her daughter, but Alla was wholly uninterested in her own. And the more Kira grew, the less Alla seemed to know of her existence. In truth, Alla seemed to be terrified of her baby.

And it was Mourushka who had taken over, chattering with the child, watching over all the nannies' responsibilities with a zeal and an attentiveness that had astonished Ducky. Who could have guessed that Babydear would have such maternal instincts? Never in her life had she played with dolls, much less held a tea party for her stuffed animals. She was always outside, riding horses or playing on the tennis court. The only place she was calm was the library. And even so! She would always read standing up, walking around. Did she ever lean over the cradles in the neighboring houses' nurseries? No, never. Unlike the other girls, she was unmoved by babies.

Only Kira charmed her. The little one resembled her, too. Brunette, like her—not redheaded like Alla—with huge brown eyes . . . The same kind of child. If Mourushka hadn't been so young, she might have appeared to be her mother.

Mourushka's love for her niece touched Maria Nikolayevna. Her baby was all grown up now.

After all these years, she, too, poor Maria Nikolayevna, needed a vacation.

Berlin? The most prestigious ambassador in Europe . . . Why not?

Yes. Mourushka could spend a few weeks with Anna in Berlin. She gave her consent.

So long as she was accompanied by Wilson. And so long as Wilson took along baby Kira, whom Alla couldn't bear in Berezovaya without Mourushka to take her in her arms, rock her, and play with her.

In any case, Alla needed to go back to France with her "husband" to finalize the divorce they had requested in Nice.

Yes, they would all have to go!

And little Kira would stay with Anna. She already had a full family: she could easily rear her sister's child, who she was already godmother to.

Yes. Berlin.

On the condition that Mourushka come back to Saint Petersburg in November: she would need to be presented to the tsarina that winter. As her sisters had. At eighteen, as was customary.

So the young girl had left Ukraine, intoxicated with happiness and the welter of dreams of conquest.

Finery, balls . . .

And hardly had fifteen days gone by when poor Maria Nikolayevna had received these five letters.

Moura said she wanted to marry the officer who had escorted her. A friend of her brother, Bobik, and her brother-in-law Ionov. To marry him tomorrow. Now. Right away. In Berlin! Marry him without her mother, without a dowry.

She was seventeen.

What should Maria Nikolayevna do?

The letters she was holding in her lap answered the questions she might have asked. She read them. Reread them. Pored over them.

All the missives seemed relatively rational . . . Anna and Bobik concluded their notes with the same words: Mourushka's suitor would be the perfect son-in-law for Mommy.

In her own letter, the perfect son-in-law simply proved to have a solid education, an understanding of customs, a deep respect for the memory of the late senator, an even deeper respect for Mourushka. No sentimentality. No big words of any sort. Hard to get a sense of him.

What to do? Maybe nothing. Just wait. Yes, but . . . *When Fortune smiles upon a beautiful young girl in the form of a good catch*, Maria Nikolayevna thought, *her mother ought to seize it*. She had lived long enough to know that Lady Fortune was fickle. Once, yes, but twice . . . was this simply chance?

Maria Nikolayevna dissected what Anna had written:

His family, of Germano-Baltic extraction, goes back to the Teutonic horsemen; it has also been part of the Russian nobility for three generations.

Good.

His grandfather was named governor of the province of Estonia by His Majesty the Tsar Nicholas I.

Very good.

He himself was admitted at twelve years old to the Imperial Lyceum of Saint Petersburg, where he outranked his classmates. He then entered the Ministry of Foreign Affairs before being named chamberlain and private counselor to His Majesty.

Perfect. An excellent start in the world.

*At twenty-five years old he lost his older brother, thereby becoming heir to
the family estate, a vast domain close to Reval, where his three younger siblings
currently live.*

Anna added the calculation that "Mommy's perfect son-in-law" had
about three thousand rubles in income at his disposal.

It was hard to imagine better.

And what about his kin?

*His cousin is none other than the grand marshal of the Court, who you know—the
husband of your friend Princess Dolgorukaya. His other cousin is our ambassador
to London, who Daddy met and spoke well of.*

*He himself followed Count von der Osten-Sacken alongside His Majesty
Emperor William II to Berlin. Count von der Osten-Sacken treats him like his
own son here. He considers him, in his own words, the most brilliant of his
attachés and plans to place him in a diplomatic career in any way possible.*

A favorite of the Russian ambassador to Germany? An officer and
diplomat in Berlin, the most prestigious of ambassadorships?

This, too, was excellent.

The final advantage: his father had just died, leaving him free to make
his own decisions about marriage.

*There is no reticence to fear regarding his family, no father's refusal to
dread.*

This final consideration of Anna's underscored that this marriage was
nothing but advantageous to the Zakrevskys.

Anna insisted. Mommy should not wait . . . A marriage that was suitable in every way.

Maria Nikolayevna did not even dare to think: *a lucky accident.*

Especially since, according to Bobik, Mourushka had already turned the heads of all the young attachés to the diplomatic delegations. And she seemed to have decided to give her hand to the first one who asked. Fortune was that the best of them should have stepped forward first. She had sensed it. She had known it. "But who knew?" Bobik said. "One can always change one's mind at seventeen."

Maria Nikolayevna stifled her impatience. Changing minds? He was one to talk! How many marriages had he let pass him by? He hadn't been able to court anyone, and he was now looking at his thirties! And God knew how many suitable girls he had been introduced to!

Enough with poor Bobik. Here were the final details that mattered: the ones Wilson described.

Reading her words, one might be led to think that Mourushka's suitor was the best of the secretary-officers. More charming even than Anna's Count Ionov. Wilson specifically wrote:

> *I think his heart is as beautiful as his face. This young man seems thoroughly distinguished, thoroughly reasonable, and thoroughly serious.*

Wilson insisted on another particular:

> *Despite his reserved nature, he seems to love Babydear fervently. Over the course of the trip, he has proved himself willing to risk everything, sacrifice everything to have her.*

Wilson did not specify the nature of the acts in question, but she called him *wholly besotted. Madly in love. Worshipful, even.*

This was the only fault in her panegyric.

Adoring of his own wife? Maria Nikolayevna knew that song. And they had seen what had become of Senator Zakrevsky's "passion." He, too, seemed willing to risk everything, sacrifice everything to conquer her. Full of orations as he had asked for her hand! And when he obtained it . . . he had preferred the company of serfs and courtesans. Before leaving all his fortune to the Jews and the Freemason scum. Before leaving her in poverty at Berezovaya!

Her High Nobility had developed a theory that one should never, ever, marry for love: this rule held for both sexes. Her experience was that only marriages of mutual benefit lasted. Clear profit for both parties.

By sheer luck, the perfect son-in-law did not demonstrate great sentiment.

What to do?

On paper, everything seemed ideal. Even their ages. Well balanced: he was twenty-eight, just eleven years older than Mourushka. As for his name . . . it was a nice one. Quite historic. Quite glorious, indeed. He was named Johann von Benckendorff, pronounced *Jon* in the English style: *Djon*.

No title, though.

This Benckendorff belonged to a smaller branch of the family. The other one, that of the Count Benckendorffs, very close to the tsar, would have been better.

But only in the eyes of the bourgeoisie. Maria Nikolayevna knew all too well that in the Russian aristocracy, the noblest families were not necessarily those with titles.

What should Maria Nikolayevna do?

If not to ask for other people's advice . . .

If they all agreed in the five letters she was folding pensively, one by one, tying together in a single packet, carefully putting into a drawer of her writing desk . . . if they all agreed, by the grace of God: she would consent!

CHAPTER SIX

"For Better or for Worse, the Deed Is Done"

1911

On the morning of October 24, 1911, in the small Orthodox chapel of the Russian ambassador to Berlin, the governess of the four children of the Empire's late senator Ignaty Platonovich Zakrevsky stood in for her mistress at the marriage of her youngest daughter.

This time, the mother's absence was not explained by any opposition to her daughter, or by a disagreement with the son-in-law's family over the dowry. On the contrary. Madame Zakrevskaya had given the young couple her blessing, willingly and warmly. But in the complexities of her own return to Saint Petersburg, overwhelmed by so many pleasures she was rediscovering, she was unable to set aside her business for a long trip to Germany.

Such effort would have been in vain. She was not needed.

Bobik would serve as his sister's witness. Anna would bestow her with advice for her wedding night. Wilson would take care of the rest. No, her beloved Mourushka did not need her mommy any longer.

The little girl had turned eighteen in March and had wanted this wedding ever since she had arrived in Berlin, almost six months ago now. She had had plenty of time to prepare herself for the sacrament she would be receiving.

Maria Nikolayevna was not stupid enough not to understand that her dear Mourushka had found this solution—a rushed marriage abroad—so that she would not have to come back to Ukraine. In order to flee her, perhaps?

Anything to avoid coming back to Berezovaya Rudka, indeed.

Alla had not returned from Nice, either. She claimed that the divorce was keeping her in France, that the procedure was dragging on.

Bobik and Anna, in turn, were staying in Germany.

Maria Nikolayevna pretended that she understood them all: for young people these days, cosmopolitans like her children, cosmopolitans as their father had been, Europe had to seem more modern, more stimulating, than Mother Russia. Their old mother's Russia.

So be it, they would live in Europe.

In front of her friends, she did not say: "Good for them, good riddance!" But that was her conclusion.

For her Mourushka, however, it was another story: the girl tugged at her mother's heartstrings. She blessed Mourushka with all her soul, prayed night and day for Mourushka's happiness. For the Lord to grant Mourushka prosperity. For the Queen of the Heavens to keep Mourushka in good health!

As for her dowry, since Johann von Benckendorff had been kind enough to ask for her hand without the usual financial negotiations, why should she be stingy? They would talk about money when the young couple returned to Saint Petersburg.

❖

All the diplomatic representatives posted in Berlin attended the ceremony. British, French, German, and Russian, of course. A thoroughly worldly marriage. The chapel was full.

Officers in buttoned-up gaiters or high-top boots, gleaming epaulets, polished belt buckles; their hats, bicorns, or peaked caps held in place by their right arms. Tightly corseted marquises, countesses, baronesses; bustles, parasols despite the winter season, and huge hats adorned with flowers and birds. Priests with long beards and gold-plated ciboria.

The wisps of incense and the choir's incantations could not mask the attendants' agitation and whispers. The ladies whispered that in Ukraine, the eldest Zakrevskaya girls' reputation had been quite compromised. They wondered about the youngest, as she seemed to have too clear an idea of what life might bring her. They murmured that the answer was a single word: *everything*. To see everything, to do everything, to experience everything.

And the handsome, wise Benckendorff had let himself be caught.

It would take the entrance of His Excellency Count Nikolai von der Osten-Sacken, the Russian ambassador, in his massive white parade uniform, his breast covered with the highest distinctions of the Empire, for some semblance of silence to reign. He advanced with small steps, his face contorted, his leg stiff: the year before, an attack had paralyzed his left side. His advanced age and his infirmities had not brought about his retirement, to the supreme displeasure of the sharp tongues saying that ever since the Japanese war, crises between Russia and Germany called for a subtler intelligence than that of this old reactionary elephant.

But he hardly cared about that gossip. Count Nikolai von der Osten-Sacken had been orchestrating these international relationships between the kaiser and the tsar for almost sixteen years. And the Russian Empire, like the German Empire, was doing well, thanks to his services.

To the Zakrevsky family's great honor, he was to walk the bride to the altar, and in this way to present, introduce, and launch this young woman into the high society of Berlin and Saint Petersburg.

"What youth! What grace! She's adorable!" Their procession was accompanied by such acclamations. "What a beautiful dress! And what splendid lace!"

Behind the mass of ruffles and tulle, Anna—Countess Ionov—every bit as splendid with her red hair gleaming brightly under the white of her picture hat, carried the train.

"How different those two sisters are . . . But how beautiful they both are."

Ducky, turning to the two girls, looked at them both with a gaze full of love.

Babydear had insisted that she sit in the front row, where her mother would have been. Tall, thin, more elegant in her modesty than most of the noblewomen, the governess had certainly learned her good manners from her acquaintance with the aristocracy, as Ionov and Bobik—Moura's best men—whispered while watching her. At forty-seven years old, Mrs. Wilson seemed to have been born in this higher circle: she *belonged*.

She could not stop looking at Babydear.

She felt her throat quivering as she looked at this profile that could barely be seen beneath her veil, at this head held high that did not affect humility or contemplation, at this intense fixed gaze that could have been full of either joy or tears.

When her child had passed by, Ducky focused on the man waiting for her, standing back there, in front of the doors of the iconostasis. Johann von Benckendorff was exactly as she had described him to Her High Nobility: serious and distinguished, tall, well proportioned, his mustache curved in the latest fashion. Extremely moved, despite the impassivity of his expression and his apparent coldness.

No doubt of it: Babydear could not have found a better husband. Even though she was quite young to be getting married—just eighteen.

Ducky felt worry weighing her down. Should she have insisted that this wedding take place later, upon her return to Russia?

Or was her sudden sadness simply because of the nostalgia she felt for Babydear's childhood—*Marydear* nowadays, if not *Marie*, as her husband was calling her—because Ducky missed this era that was nearly gone, when her little girl belonged to her alone?

◆

"Well?" Anna asked, carefully removing the veil and the crown of orange blossoms from her sister's hair.

With the help of Ducky and her own chambermaid, she undid the chignon that the hairstylist had arranged with hundreds of pins. The braid finally fell loose, rippling over the shoulders of the newlywed, who was preparing for her first night with her husband.

Anna wavered. How should she broach the subject of the wedding night?

Did she really need to broach it? To tell Mourushka what her spouse expected of her? To urge her into obedience, as Mommy had said, to insist on patience and resignation?

Anna knew her sister well enough to know that she was not prudish. She had seen her flirting and bantering in Ukraine and Germany. Instinctively, Mourushka was a seducer. Not even aware of her power, she charmed men, fascinated them, tempted them. She loved to see passion in their eyes. She played with fire. She liked to please: not just gentlemen but everything that moved. She did not simper, no, she did not pretend. No playacting. No fussing, no affectations. But she was hungry for attention and worked to garner it.

She cultivated a way to captivate without participating in conversations. She knew how to listen attentively, with a degree of concentration she alone possessed. When others asked her questions, she answered them warmly. The few neighbors of Berezovaya Rudka, like the officers who visited the Ionovs in Berlin—all came to discuss their problems with her. And all fell under the charm of her solicitude. And so they all adored her. *Such a sweet young lady!*

Perhaps. But they should never have taken Mourushka for naive. Alla's affairs and misadventures had made her perfectly aware of what love was about. She knew how babies were made. And—in spite of Mommy, who had asked Anna to instruct her—she also knew very well what her husband would want to do with her on their wedding night.

Anna's own husband, handsome Ionov, kept saying over and over that the little sister was hot-blooded. And Ionov was one to know! His infidelities just kept piling up.

God willing, Anna thought, *Djon's wisdom could tame Mourushka's lust for life. God willing, she would find peace with him. Peace, yes, peace . . .* In contrast to what she was experiencing with Ionov, who was cheating on her. In contrast to what her twin was experiencing in France.

Alla had found one of her old suitors in Nice and started up a torrid affair with him. He was a journalist, son of the late colonel Pierre-Étienne Moulin, the military attaché to the French ambassador in Saint Petersburg, who they had known when Daddy was alive. In her letters, Alla wrote that she would marry him once her divorce from Engelhardt was complete, and she would settle with him in Paris.

She was crazy! This boy, René Moulin, had no name and no fortune.

Married life, or rather motherhood, had given Countess Ionov a taste for conventionality, following customs, and prudence.

Anna did not have to explain anything. Just be quiet, daydream, as she looked at her little sister. Moura didn't need any advice. At her age and in her milieu, she already knew far more than she should.

The newlywed was looking at herself in the mirror. Her face, normally luminous and lively, was inexpressive. She must be tired. Exhausted after such a day.

Moura observed the oval of her face, with the widow's peak at the top of her forehead.

Of her hair, Djon—*her husband Djon*—had whispered that it looked like velvet and silk. That he had loved its fire, its deep fieriness.

Why was she thinking of Djon in the past tense tonight?

He had also said that, in his eyes, she, *Marie*, embodied Ukrainian beauty . . . Robust. Harmonious. Wide hipped. Slim jointed. With tiny feet and tiny hands with strong fingers, incredibly soft palms.

The adjectives of this description were the only romantic compliments Djon had ever allowed himself. A moment of lyricism. Usually he barely spoke, only uttered understatements. He was not effusive. He respected the honor of his young fiancée too much, apparently, to let himself be carried away by his own desire.

She had been ready to give herself over to him completely, body and soul. Was that not love? A gift with no limitations? He had pushed her away. So unexpected for a man! Wasn't it usually the other way around?

No caresses, he told her, certainly no kisses and no embraces, before their marriage.

She considered him magnificently serene. Upright, perfect. She admired him, respected him wholeheartedly. She knew he was full of goodwill, of an intrinsic generosity that she admitted she did not possess. She would try to hold herself up to his standards, to be like him.

Perhaps he was a bit conservative? Rigid in his ideas?

Count von der Osten-Sacken had told her that in Estonia, Djon had been in the regiment the tsar had ordered to punish the leaders of the 1905 uprisings. That he had nipped the revolution in the bud and restored order immediately. That he led the peasants of his domain at Yendel masterfully.

She had frowned. If the ambassador thought this detail was another diamond in the crown that was Djon's qualities, he was sorely mistaken. Crushing peasants and workers underfoot was not to her taste. She considered herself liberal and progressive. Like her father.

Senator Zakrevsky, in his writings, had foreseen the revolts the ambassador was alluding to. He had even proposed the reforms that could have prevented them.

She had read Daddy's final pamphlet out loud to Djon, a sort of moral testament titled *Long Live Common Sense!* Djon had listened to her respectfully. Without hearing what she was saying. She had a right to her opinions, but he would not discuss them with her.

Djon . . . She couldn't think about Djon. Not right now. She had to come back to the sight in the mirror.

Her hair, which Ducky was holding with one hand as she vigorously tamed it with the other, brushing it back with energetic strokes—her hair pleased him and pleased her, as well. Her slightly flat nose, a little crooked from when she'd broken it falling off a horse? No. She hated her nose! The eyebrows that seemed to stretch all the way to her temples; her almond-shaped eyes, drooping just a little on the outside; her thick lips, cherry colored, also drooping at the corners. The whole made her look catlike, as Mommy had said so often.

But at this moment, a burned cat. Sulky. Sad, in fact.

She got a grip on herself, forced herself to smile.

Anna, whispering as if it were a secret, with a warmth that encouraged confession, asked: "Well, my darling? Did everything go as you hoped?"

She nodded: "Exactly as I hoped."

Her own voice, a bit hoarse, came out strangely. It sounded muffled. Or distorted.

Was it the emotion of finding herself in the protective, familiar hands of her governess for the last time? Of her sister's solicitude?

Or was it the unease, the uncertainty of what might finally happen tonight in Djon's arms?

"It's been a magnificent wedding!" Anna exclaimed, mentally comparing the vibrancy of today's ceremony to the darkness of her own wedding at the orphanage's church.

"Yes."

"All of Berlin was there. Did you see? Even the Duchess of Trachtenberg came!"

"Yes."

"Princess von Hartzfeldt has been over the moon. I heard her telling Djon, who is her kin in some way, that she's taking you under her wing."

"She told me that as well. She's a wonderful old lady."

"Are you happy, my darling?"

Moura thought, shrugged, sighed, and let out, quietly, resignedly:

"Well, whatever happens, happens. The deed is done!"

Anna was dumbstruck. She certainly knew how much Moura had wanted to marry Djon. *Whatever happens, happens. The deed is done!* A strange conclusion for someone deeply in love.

After falling in love at first sight, did she feel she had made a mistake? Momentarily suspect she had made the wrong decision? That they had both gone wrong? She hadn't hinted at any such worry before. Or shown any fear. Maybe she had felt forced to forge onward at all costs.

Had she realized it was too late to backtrack?

And now . . . *Whatever happens, happens. The deed is done!*

Such indifference, such lack of concern, such resignation shown in the casualness of the response shocked even Ducky. She protested:

"But Mary, dear . . ."

Noticing their astonishment, Moura stood up as if she would brook no questions.

She did not care to explain. Even if she had wanted to, she wouldn't have been able to. Even in her own mind, her feelings were a mystery that she had no intention of deciphering.

But in case one of them wanted to press the question, she repeated, sharply, as a definitive conclusion to this chapter of her marriage:

"For better or for worse—the deed is done, come what may and *evviva!*"

CHAPTER SEVEN

The Belle Epoque of
Madame von Benckendorff

1911–1913

S he was a member of society now. A triumph everywhere.

She loved her first season as a married woman in Germany. She loved her first season as a married woman in Russia. She loved her first season as a married woman in Estonia.

The family manor at Yendel in the summer, some sixty miles from the Baltic Sea. Saint Petersburg for Christmas, at Mommy's or in the huge apartment Djon had bought at 8 Shpalernaya Street for their visits while he was on leave. And the Russian embassy on Frankenstrasse in Berlin, in spring and fall. She felt like life was finally starting, like she was meeting the finest people and that she herself was the axis upon which the world turned . . . the world of imperial courts.

Anna hadn't been exaggerating when she had told Moura to come to Berlin with her best finery for the many balls she could expect.

In this wholly cosmopolitan society, where aristocrats were intimately connected by blood—like the three cousins Tsar Nicholas II, Kaiser Wilhelm II, and King George V—the circles of gossip and society took up all her attention.

Circles, clubs, clans: Marie von Benckendorff spent her days in company, and filled her hours in conversation with her friends.

She sought out the companionship not of other young women of her generation but of dowagers, loving, philosophical grandmothers whose stories about their pasts fascinated her. They had once waltzed with Senator Zakrevsky at the residence of the Princess of Croÿ in Paris, played bridge with him at the residence of the Duchess of Bedford in London, and prided themselves on having met him around the world.

"Meeting someone in another country who's known my parents," she told Djon, who was astonished by her patience with their ramblings, "hearing them talk about the father I no longer have, always touches my heart."

Touched was the perfect adjective to sum up her feelings toward the former éminences grises of Berlin.

With others, the wives of the ambassador's attachés, conversations grew more intimate—frivolities, gossip, scandals. She chattered passionately about the next ball or the latest brouhaha with her British counterpart, Lady Russell, who had just remarried. Her husband was the son of the late British ambassador, who had been the favorite of Chancellor Bismarck in the 1870s. This old preference now opened many doors for the Russells. And, consequently, for their close friends in Germany.

Marie cultivated a third sort of intimacy with some better-established socialites—there weren't many here—the Parisians who were richer, had more titles, were two decades older than she was, and had been through life. They deigned to teach her about it. Among this type was Madame de Méricourt, the witty wife of Davidov the banker, who the gossips insisted was just like Madame de Merteuil—that is, she had the name, the money, and the social background of a century earlier. She was the only person in Mary's entourage whose influence Ducky thoroughly disapproved of.

As for the rest . . . Hunting parties at the residence of Djon's Prussian parents, afternoons at the Potsdam racecourse, evening galas at the opera, receptions at the estates of friends of the Hohenzollern and Hapsburg dynasties: the waltz of her pleasures never ended.

And if Ducky had once found Babydear's diligence at the children's meals and balls, at dancing and skating and horseback-riding lessons, to be exhausting, she would have been stunned by Moura's energy at "visiting and receiving" friends.

Even Djon, who was obsessed with strictly observing custom and respecting tradition—even he, who needed to follow the smallest rules he had been taught about Russian and German society, sometimes found himself saying with a smile, "God in heaven, Marie, you're indefatigable!" The enthusiasm with which she carried out her social obligations commanded his respect.

He wasn't unaware that she was making up for so many years of loneliness at Berezovaya. And that that stretch of immobility and imprisonment was such a painful memory for her that she summed it up in French with a single word: *enfer*. Hell. These days, having conversations at home would have meant being incurious, not seeing, not living.

But in fact, it wasn't so much the cotillions and waltzes that charmed her as it was the exchange of ideas at the various embassies.

Dinners among diplomats? By far the most cloistered. And yet the most exciting evenings! Veritable obstacle courses for her husband . . . Because even though the officer-diplomats, like Djon von Benckendorff, could whirl on the residences' waxed parquetry, it was still difficult for them to be invited there, to dine with only a few colleagues, before having reached the rank of general.

But that was the one thing she loved. Politics at the top.

Hearing arguments around the table about the "Morocco issue," discussing the "Agadir crisis," talking about amending Cameroon's boundary lines, the question of the Balkan League, the challenges of the Triple Alliance, of the Triple Entente, and weighing the risks of a general war.

Being familiar with both the details and the larger picture. The rumors, the gossip swirling around the States, the ideas their representatives had.

Observing the universe through both ends of the spyglass. And not missing anything.

"Whoever in Berlin or Petersburg wants to learn about the world at large and at small, and its seedy underbelly," Countess Ionov joked, "will have to go through my sister's intelligence services."

In those years, from 1911 to 1913, Moura's mastery of English, French, Russian, and now German, as well as her literary education and her musical upbringing, made her quite a catch. The soothing tones of her voice perfectly suited the imperial language spoken by the plenipotentiary ministers and the chargés d'affaires, the consuls, the legates, the military attachés . . . in short, the diplomatic corps in every capital.

The Count of Chambrun, the French ambassador's right-hand man, called himself her most devoted admirer. And the secretaries of the Russian ambassador swore by her. The American wife of the British ambassador, the old Lady Goschen, was besotted with her "young Russian friend," to the point of keeping her at her side at the top of the main stairway as she received the guests of King George V. His Excellency, Sir Edward Goschen himself, always raised his glass to her at dessert: "To His Majesty Tsar Nicholas, our ally . . . and to the dazzling eyes of Madame von Benckendorff, his most exquisite ambassadoress!"

The intoxication of vanity, the pleasure of existence.

The only question was whether Djon approved of her success. Did he encourage it? Did he merely take note of it? He seemed to find her success in society wholly natural. Never a compliment. No sign of admiration, nor even an indication of the attention she genuinely needed. A politician even at home.

Considering his wife an intrinsic part of himself, he found no need to congratulate her, much less go into raptures. There's no need to show off what's part of you; you don't congratulate it, you don't parade it. Out of propriety, out of modesty, out of good taste, you keep your lips sealed. He would have considered such praise a lack of manners.

With apparent indifference, he would leave her there, at the entrance to a salon, and go off to commingle among other uniforms. He claimed to be granting her free rein to flit about and charm as she pleased, as any refined husband might.

He stayed so distant, so cold, that she could not even imagine just how much he loved that moment when everyone's eyes turned toward her. He, hidden behind greenery, would cock his ear and find himself unable to look away.

Marie's passion for Worth dresses and Fabergé jewelry had made her one of the most fashionable women in Berlin. Djon, personally, had no taste for "fashionable women" or extravagant expenses. But for Marie . . . Tall, thin, utterly elegant. Chic in such a simple way.

Yes, Marie was wondrous. And Djon saw her beauty as only part of the miracle.

She was wondrously tactful. She never made an error in protocol. She had a keen knowledge of precedent. He had found in her an unparalleled hostess, and on top of that a woman of the house without equal, who knew how to manage the help.

She was wondrously kind, as well. She rushed to him every single night, brought him his cigarette case, and devoted herself to his well-being. Her endeavors to prove herself a perfect spouse charmed him. And such a spouse she was indeed: she always rose to the challenge.

In the Ionov family nursery, he had seen her coddling her niece, Kira, taking the little girl in her arms, playing with her, making her laugh, rocking her back and forth. He appreciated her actions around Kira, for whom she served as tutor. Marie would make an extraordinary mother!

As he watched her tonight under the wooden panels of the British ambassador's residence, as she moved from one circle to the next in her orchid-gray muslin dress, he wondered where she had found this light self-assurance, this sense of etiquette, this amiability that delighted the high society of every nation.

He did not let a hint of his amazement show. Not a word.

And if he was overjoyed to hear his relative, the formidable Princess Nathalie de Hartzfeldt, say again and again that she adored his wife, he took care not to say more. Everyone on all sides was singing her praises: even the kaiser, to whom Marie had been presented by Princess Nathalie at the Potsdam court—even Wilhelm II had been seduced. A reciprocal seduction. His Majesty had managed to make Madame von Benckendorff laugh. A rarity for him.

"Being as young and good-looking as you are, don't you ever grow tired of the company of all these old folks?" the British ambassador teased her at the table, where she was sitting to his left.

"On the contrary, Sir Edward, I adore them."

"Really?"

"Really. It's such a rare pleasure to listen to the conversations of elders: they have so much to say and so much to teach me!"

"The worst part, my dear, is that you seem so sincere. Are you telling me what you really feel? In which case, my dear, you may be the only person who tells the truth in all Europe." He looked at her mockingly. "Sincere? You? Let me see . . . How about that handsome officer down there at the end of the table—how would you describe him?"

He pointed out a splendid hussar from Empress Alexandra Fyodorovna's regiment, whose gaze she knew after having seen it land upon her at all Countess von der Osten-Sacken's receptions.

At that moment, the hussar was staring lustily at her. Sir Edward had noticed.

But there were other incidents, other improprieties, that Sir Edward couldn't know about.

During the last gathering, as she'd taken a glass of champagne from one of the waiters, she'd let her dance card fall. The hussar had rushed over to pick it up, brushing her foot in doing so. And, almost accidentally, her ankle. Then her leg . . . up to the knee.

It would be an understatement to say that her heart skipped a beat. She had never felt such sensation before. Such emotion. She was shaking so hard that she left her card and ran out.

It hadn't been enough for her to leave the buffet: she had gone out into the hallway, hurtled down the steps, and, without even warning Djon, without thinking up some sort of excuse, called for a hansom cab. Overwhelmed.

As she was trying to pull herself together on the porch, she saw the hussar running after her.

"Madame, your dance card, you've forgotten your dance card!"

The hansom cab pulled up, and she hurried into its carriage. He jumped in. A bellboy shut the door.

"Get out! You've lost your mind! Get out!"

"Yes, I've lost my head, and my heart, as well!"

"How dare you!"

"I love you madly, I love you to death!"

He tried to pull her into his arms. She hit at him and, banging on the windowpane, shouted:

"Stop the car!"

The hansom cab halted.

"Get out, or I'll have the driver throw you out."

"I'll get out, yes. But first, hear me out—"

As she tried to cut him off, he grabbed her wrists:

"Do you know that I've been in love with you ever since I came to Berlin? You know it, don't you, that I love you to death?"

She wrested herself away violently.

"I don't know you, sir," she said coldly. "And I am asking you to get out."

"Hear me out! There isn't enough time for me to convey what I feel. In a few months, in a few weeks, in a few days, I won't exist anymore . . . I don't have long to live."

He was quite pale and seemed to be blazing with fever.

His head was like an icon's. The oval face of a Byzantine Christ. His eyes were gray, almost slanting, edged with long lashes, so long, so dark that they almost seemed drawn on with kohl. Jutting cheekbones. Round, plump lips.

"Can't you love me a little as well?"

"Get out!"

This time he obeyed. But not without one last line through the window frame:

"To remember you by, I'll keep your dance card . . . With the names of those lucky enough to hold you in their arms . . . As for you, Madame, when I shall be dead, *forget not to remember me!*"

She was astonished. This madman knew the lines of the Ukrainian poet she had recited as a little girl to her father's guests at Berezovaya! Or was it just a coincidence?

Back at her residence, she locked herself in her bedroom, lay down outstretched on the bed, and stayed there in her clothes, her face in the pillow.

Anger, fear, and remorse: the whole night.

And that hand, the memory of that hand under her dress . . . Djon's caresses had never aroused such emotion!

She did not say a word to her husband about the outrage she had felt. He would have avenged the matter with gunfire. And if there was one thing the wife of an ambassador's attaché could not allow in Berlin, it was a scandal.

So she had to be quiet. So she had to forget.

Since then, she had come across the hussar repeatedly.

She had met him here, in Sir Edward Goschen's tightly knit circle, at his table. With that same gaze that undressed her. He had made sure to present himself: Captain Afanasy Ivanovich Gramov. As morally incorrigible as he was physically fit. She, too, had done her research: Afanasy Ivanovich Gramov's eccentricities were notorious.

He had come from the Russian embassy in London, where he had burned the candle from both ends: gambling, alcohol, women. His nomination to Berlin had raised many protests. But what could be done? He was a protégé of the tsarina. Some insisted he was part of the circle of Grigory Rasputin's followers, an affiliation that opened all the Court's doors to him. What could be done? He had fought well in Manchuria, had proven his worth brilliantly in the war against Japan, and was known as a brave man.

They claimed, moreover, that he had a cardiac ailment. What misfortune. One foot in the grave at such a young age. He seemed to have only two years left to live. This fate earned him respect and pity.

She glanced at the person the ambassador had pointed out.

"I'd say, Sir Edward, that your handsome officer doesn't weigh much and isn't long for this world."

The line was so sharp, so sardonic, that the ambassador let out a forced laugh.

"You don't beat around the bush! So direct in your judgment!"

She seemed to have put an end to the discussion.

The ambassador pressed the matter:

"However, Madame von Benckendorff's dazzling eyes are perhaps not so discerning," he added in a whisper. "I believed her to be an intelligent woman, but she let herself be compromised by a good-for-nothing!"

The warning made her flush. She was frozen.

"Your Excellency is mistaken," she let out.

"At least His Excellency is sincere," he concluded with a smile.

❖

"Oh, to be alive on a day like this one," she sighed as she settled into Madame de Méricourt's uncovered Mercedes carriage. "How wonderful it feels!"

Their faces turned skyward, their eyes fixed on the pale Berlin sun, the two women were being driven by horses to the Tiergarten, the park where they would continue their afternoon promenade on foot.

One was brunette, very young, with a stunning sensuousness; the other, slender, blond, with a refinement, a cynicism in every turn of phrase that made her more than merely attractive: they bore no resemblance to each other.

Both, however, knew the world well enough to know that their two kinds of beauty—polar opposites—made them even more attractive.

Under the lappet of their veils, they looked out at the street. In this early spring, the passersby had brought out their boater hats, the matriarchs in lace pushing their strollers.

"In a herd," the countess sighed. "Like maids . . . *Küche, Kinder, Kirche*—kitchen, child, church—oh, how boring Germany is!"

"Boring?" Moura exclaimed. "But I like Berlin! All these automobiles, these trams, these bicyclers . . . They even say that under the Alexanderplatz, they're building a subway . . . . If it wasn't for the spiked helmets and the troops, I'd love this city."

"I do think, my heart, that you're the only person to my knowledge who claims to always, always, always be happy with her life."

"It's because I'm always, always, always in love with my husband!"

"Wishful thinking, my dear!" she replied in heavily accented English. "Your husband is one of the most proper men—in fact, he's everything that a woman, a very old woman like me, could wish for."

"An old woman? You? How can you say that? Men love you and woo you passionately. Even he does!"

"Oh, yes, an old woman. I'm twice your age . . . almost forty years old."

"You're magical, the most attractive person I've ever met!"

"And your husband—the most *magical*, the most attractive one, too, I should know, you tell me about him all day . . . A man of honor. In love with order and discipline. Just between us: horribly Prussian, no?"

"*Prussian?* Djon is Russian to the bone."

"Tsk, tsk, tsk! A Baltic baron in all his splendor, giving his orders in Russian, yes, and thinking in German . . . and, like all Baltic barons, fretting over the gulf between his two homelands. I wonder how your husband can bear to live so torn between Russia and Germany."

"Djon isn't torn. He has sworn fealty to the Romanovs. He reveres the tsar. The Benckendorffs have been Russian for generations." She insisted: "Djon is a chamberlain of the Court, a private counselor to His Majesty. He's Russian."

"But of Germanic culture and tradition. Spare me your protestations, my heart. I am telling you the facts: Peter the Great invaded the Baltic lands and conquered them by folding their aristocracies into the ranks of Russian nobility . . . after all this time—how long? two centuries?—after all this time, the old Livonian Brothers of the Sword considered Russia their chosen land. But Germany remained their ancestral homeland. I'm merely saying that, nothing else! That your husband isn't Slavic . . . That he's in need of your charm, your fire . . . And probably in need—don't be upset, you little fool—of your intelligence. That he might even seem, to those unacquainted with him, somewhat boring . . . Not to say outright dull. And time is passing! And life is short! Take advantage of it, my dear, take advantage of your youth as long as it lasts. Revel in it at every moment. And cherish your memory of it dearly. That's all we'll be left with, we proper women, in our later days: our memory . . . Our memory of happiness. Our memory of love. Our memory of an hour, just one hour, of passion . . . Do you have a memory, just one, with your husband, that you can cherish until you die? I think not! You can sigh *how wonderful* all day long, I won't believe for a second that you feel alive with him. Do you want me to tell you? You're going to grow disconnected from what matters. And yet what matters is there, right by you. Don't try to play innocent: you know just as well as I do that a certain captain acquainted with us both loves you madly and is ready to do anything to be loved by you. Even hasten his own death! As for you, my child, you risk dying without having lived!"

What answer did she have to that? *A memory of passion with Djon?*

The man from their first meeting, the joyful, daring officer who had escorted her between Petersburg and Berlin, had long since disappeared. She actually found herself wondering if he had ever existed! Yes, of course, he had existed, because she was able to pinpoint the moment he had changed. It was the day she had accepted his hand in marriage. Rather than covering her in kisses, as she had hoped would happen at such a moment, he had bowed respectfully, seriously, had tapped his heels and thanked her for doing him the honor of becoming his wife.

From that day on, the day of their engagement, Djon's flame had flickered and practically gone out. Dead. No more spark.

Even their wedding night had been a fiasco. And things had worsened since. He seemed no longer to feel any desire for her; if he did, it was frighteningly little.

When, coming home from a ball, they parted ways for the night, he would lead her to the door of her bedroom, kindly bid her good night, and make his way to his own door. He didn't even try to go into her bedroom. She would always have to go herself to knock on his door before she could sink into his arms. He didn't push her away, he took her in, even warmly. But the motions he made her go through were becoming humiliating.

And disappointing.

Anna insisted that some husbands wanted every woman on earth—

even the meanest and lowest ones—every woman . . . except for their own wife. According to Anna, Djon admired her too much, he respected her too much, he loved her too much.

But what did this ridiculous respect and this icy love matter to her? She wanted to be loved with fire. And especially not to die without having lived, as Madame de Méricourt had put it.

She didn't protest any further. She was silent.

When the carriage brought them to the park fence, when they met Captain Afanasy Ivanovich Gramov there, when he amiably took Madame de Méricourt's arm, when he paid no attention whatsoever to Madame von Benckendorff, she furrowed her brow.

In the maze of passageways, the captain and the countess walked slowly, trading remarks and laughter . . . But with her? Nothing. She had been forgotten, she was a stranger. Invisible.

After everything he had put her through! All those inconveniences . . . the gestures, the glances, the encounters. Not to mention the declarations.

And now? Not a word, not a look. Not from either of them. She was practically a nuisance. She might as well not have existed.

The rules of high society forbade a woman from being seen in public alone with a man other than her husband. So she was their chaperone.

She felt irritation, followed swiftly by resentment. Jealousy wasn't far behind.

❖

Madame von Benckendorff's second season in Berlin fulfilled all the promises of the first. Beyond dazzling. Her husband, on the other hand . . .

He had transformed completely. Mood swings, moments when he was domineering and brusque. Djon, who had once been renowned for his charm and fine upbringing, no longer stayed calm, and he showed his true face.

He wasn't himself anymore. He was disagreeable, even unbearable! It was a shock.

Others explained this change through the loss of his protector, Count von der Osten-Sacken, who had died of a heart attack in the summer of 1912, during a stay in Monte Carlo—a loss that had touched him deeply and threatened his career.

The new ambassador, Sverbeyev, came to Berlin with his own protégés. As he was competitive by nature, he kept on reassessing his predecessor's initiatives. There was plenty to criticize: Osten-Sacken had held his position for sixteen years. Sverbeyev's judgments upon his work in Germany hardly lightened up the atmosphere.

Others thought that Djon's descent was due to the death of his friend and brother-in-law, Platon Ignatyevich Zakrevsky—Bobik—who, too, had died in the summer of 1912 from a shameful illness, the name of which was not uttered in Berlin. He was thirty-one years old. He might already have been forgotten at the embassy offices, but Djon, who was a family man, seemed to still miss him.

Others attributed his anxiety to the tensions of the international situation: Germany wanted war and was preparing for it. And Russia wasn't ready. Everybody here knew that. And Djon von Benckendorff better than anyone else.

And yet others wondered about the disagreement that had arisen between him and the hussar from the tsarina's regiment, the tragic and splendid Captain Afanasy Ivanovich Gramov. A question of honor, went the rumor, that his wife had presumably been involved in. There had even been talk of a duel that the military doctors had stopped at the last minute, sending that hothead Afanasy to look after his heart in Switzerland.

Nobody dared to claim that the refined Madame von Benckendorff had been compromised. Nor to utter other, more unpleasant words. The adjectives *guilty*, *lost*, or the fatal word, *adulterous*? No.

But all the same they feared that in her youth, her inexperience, her spontaneity, she might have committed some impropriety.

At this thought, they recalled the whispers that had ruined her sisters' reputations. Hadn't they once said that the Zakrevskaya daughters were hot-blooded? Often enough, evidently.

In any case, nobody ever did find out the truth.

Nothing ever transpired of the marital drama or comedy that played out in the Benckendorff residence during that year of their marriage. The husband and the wife, each as discreet as the other, did not whisper a word to anyone. And so Marie's many friends were reduced to making conjectures.

Only one thing was clear: this couple that everybody had considered *magical*, this couple that everybody had considered perfectly harmonious, was falling apart.

A year later, matters seemed to have been resolved completely: Madame von Benckendorff was expecting a baby. She would give birth in Estonia, amid her husband's family, at the Yendel estate, as befitted tradition.

When she left Berlin after the imperial races in June 1913 and made her way to her estate with all her baggage, her husband, her British governess, her, niece Kira and her army of Russian servants, it was understood that she would return in the fall for hunting season.

Djon came back alone.

On October 2, his wife bore him a son. Paul . . . A firstborn son he had rushed to have baptized in the Lutheran faith, like all the males of his bloodline.

If he had to have a second child, and that child was a girl, then she would be raised in the Orthodox faith, like all girls born to Russian mothers.

Now sympathetic, now welcoming, he once again became the perfect gentleman everyone had known. He was happy again. Yes—but happy without her. To the great regret of Berlin society, Marie von Benckendorff would not return to Germany.

Not for a long time.

CHAPTER EIGHT

Moura Benckendorff of the Yendel Estate in Estonia

1913–1914

Who could have imagined, six months earlier, that Moura would leave Berlin in such haste? And that she would find, on this Estonian estate, such peace and joy?

Leaning on the balcony of the second-floor terrace jutting out from her bedroom, she took in the beauty of the Yendel countryside.

As her eyes swept across the trees' crowns, the lake's blue stretches, she thought over the years that had passed.

No regrets about Germany.

Bobik's death darkened her final impressions permanently. *Poor Bobik,* she thought. So little known, so little loved. She tried to remember him as a child, but as he was thirteen years older than her, he had disappeared from Berezovaya too quickly. And in Berlin he was already suffering from that horrible ailment, syphilis, which had whittled him down to his bones and eaten away his intellectual faculties. Poor Bobik, who nobody at the embassy had cried over. Nor even missed in Saint Petersburg, where Mommy had been more concerned about concealing the nature of his illness to her friends than about honoring his memory. Only Djon and Ducky had shown any affection, their genuine compassion.

Her thoughts lingered on Djon's behavior, wavered.

Throughout the crisis they had weathered . . .

She stumbled in her thoughts, stopped, turned, returned.

What a hullabaloo he'd raised over this silly affair!

Hadn't he hinted at being more flexible, more open? It had been impossible to explain herself. He had suddenly turned hateful. Vindictive. Locked up in his self-certainties. He had immediately accused her of the worst and sentenced her without hearing her side, with his fury and jealousy turning what had been just a fling into a tragedy.

She had indeed been guilty. But not toward him. Toward herself. She hated thinking about her own behavior, her vanity, her stupidity. What had gotten into her head that last year? Oh, to think of it!

She had wondered at all hours of the day and night: "Is this true love? Is this the man of my life?"

True love? . . . That mad hussar! And the other woman, that Madame de M., who had warned her about how short life was: "You risk dying without having lived!" A friend who had turned out to be a matchmaker who belonged in a Zola novel, among the brothel madams of *Nana*. She had such painful memories of this woman that she didn't even want to name her.

The whole period had left her with the same feeling of shame and disgust.

"Don't admit anything!" Anna had advised her.

Anna was suffering through her husband's affairs. She had recognized the symptoms of her own illness in Djon and knew from experience that for the unfaithful, the best defense was denial.

"Don't confess . . . Anything . . . Not even the smallest bit of flirting. Don't confess!"

Moura had made sure not to.

Grazing fingers, hugs, kisses in corridors . . . She had denied everything completely.

Had Djon, by reacting so quickly to what he had considered, from his first suspicion, as an unforgivable attack on his honor, saved her from worse?

Or had he even, maybe, saved her from herself?

But he had been icy, contemptuous, always busy. It was impossible to talk to him, impossible to reach him. As for regaining his trust . . . So many tears had been shed, so many promises had been made, so many hugs had been cajoled before he finally allowed her to be with him again.

She had only entered his bedroom, his bed, after painstaking negotiations. And even then . . . how much love and dexterity had she had to arm herself with to convince him to take her in his arms? Once again, everything was the wrong way around with Djon: the wife forcing the husband to take her. By sheer luck, their reconciliation had been fruitful from their very first night. And expecting a baby had overturned matters.

She, however, had only been forgiven after her nine months of pregnancy. And this forgiveness had been only partial.

In fact, Djon had shifted the affection he'd once held for her onto their baby. He had only become himself again for the newborn.

Yes, it was impossible to predict what life could bring. Who could have imagined that the birth of Paul at Yendel would touch her less than, for example, Kira's arrival at the Berezovaya nursery?

Not that she hadn't wanted her son.

Unlike Alla, who still showed no sign of wanting to bring Kira to France, where she had remarried, Moura loved her child. She had awaited him with delight, wholly certain of the strength of her maternal instinct.

Nothing, however, had gone as she had imagined. And motherhood didn't bring her the kinds of pleasure she had expected. It was something else. The feeling of belonging to the Benckendorff lineage through blood and flesh. Yes, she belonged to Djon. She belonged to Paul. She belonged to Yendel. Body and soul. The link was now unbreakable.

She leaned over the railing, the better to admire her domain. Yendel, like Berezovaya, covered dozens of hectares. And, like Berezovaya, the outbuildings were a village unto themselves. There was a vodka distillery, a dairy, a kennel, some barns, some stables. Nearly five hundred people worked on the estate in total. A vegetable garden, a park, several lakes, immense forests, and fields that stretched out of view. The area extended to the boundary markers of the common areas, those of the Budberg barons, the Schilling barons, and the Stackelberg barons, whose medieval coats of arms—along with those of the Benckendorffs—adorned the white walls of the Lutheran church of Reval.

Here, the twenty or so families that owned the majority of Estonia's land were protective of the privileges they enjoyed, but they neglected to use the *von*, the German aristocratic particle with markedly Teutonic overtones. They didn't say Djon von Benckendorff but rather just Benckendorff. As for Marie, she was now Maria Ignatyevna . . . Moura to her mother-in-law, her three brothers-in-law, and their inner circle: they all used, as was customary for Russians, her first name and her patronymic. Eventually her diminutive as a nickname. Among the Benckendorffs, some branches had even become so Russian that they had converted to the Orthodox faith. As was the case for Her Imperial Majesty's ambassador in London, Djon's cousin.

The younger branch resisted this particular turn toward modernity. But in other spheres, it charged eagerly toward untrammeled innovation.

Some years earlier, the manor at Yendel had burned down. The structure had been completely destroyed by the fire. It had to be razed.

Rather than rebuild it as it had been, or in the neoclassical style of the other Estonian estates—white, pink, or yellow—Djon had reinvented it with bricks, mullion windows, crenellations, turrets, a donjon: an imposing British manor whose red mass loomed over a hillock at the heart of its wealth of greenery.

In all, there were more than forty rooms, a ballroom, and a grand stairway that would make the Tudors' pale by comparison.

Anybody who considered the building anachronistic—a massive Renaissance castle from the Elizabethan era at the start of the twentieth century in Estonia—didn't understand at all.

On the contrary, Yendel was an ode to the contemporary world. The numerous openings that gave rhythm to its facade, the intricate caissons in its ceilings, the arabesques of its green porcelain chimneys, the smallest details of its architecture and decoration, the mirrors, the furnishings, the rugs bought from the cutting-edge studios of various Berliner or Münchner or Viennese or Swedish artists. The pinnacle of art nouveau. The latest fashion.

Djon, who might have been presumed to be rather conservative when it came to aesthetics—as he was in all other fields—proved to have a spectacular audacity: every rhythm, every color, every decoration at Yendel was Jugendstil.

When it came to modernity, the Benckendorff couple shared the same taste.

They saw eye-to-eye in one other sphere: their love of books.

Like so many men of his generation, Djon was well read. He might have hated the latest authors, such as the socialist writers Maxim Gorky and H. G. Wells, whose novels electrified the crowds and garnered Moura's enthusiasm; he might have paid little mind to theater and poetry; but he was still an intellectual. Works of history and philosophy, essays on political science, treatises on military art covered his nightstand. And after the fire that had destroyed the old house, his greatest disappointment hadn't been the loss of his rifles but of the volumes that his own forebears had read.

None of the books at Yendel had burned. They were, in fact, the only relics presumed to have been saved. But that presumption was incorrect. The fire, indeed, had not touched them—it was the water. The buckets of water and the pumps used to extinguish the flames had damaged the books irreversibly.

And so he had to hunt through the bookshops of Reval and the university town of Tartu for the masterpieces of literature, old editions as well as new: Djon's zeal in this realm was paralleled only by that of his wife. They would rebuild a library at Yendel worthy of its name.

As for the rest, the new manor was the very personification of comfort. The twenty-five bedrooms each had their own bathroom, with hot and cold running water.

As for heating—a necessity during the winters, when temperatures fell below negative twenty degrees—it was "central," with an oil heater in the basement.

The telephone was in the hall. And the train station was a few versts away.

The final advantage of modernity at the Benckendorffs' was the train. The trip from Saint Petersburg to Yendel was a single night by Pullman car. At the other end of the Gulf of Finland, the estate could serve as a weekend home. It seemed to have been built solely for that purpose: receiving numerous guests for wolf hunts, rustic balls, evenings by the hearth . . .

A haven of peace after official ceremonies in the capital.

With her customary energy, Moura managed to bring together those two worlds: Yendel and Saint Petersburg. Two worlds that seemed wholly unlike each other.

On one end, she had to represent Djon in Estonia. To manage, with her mother-in-law and her three brothers-in-law, the property that would be little Paul's inheritance. And keep a weather eye.

On the other, she had to maintain her status among the aristocracy on the banks of the Neva, where the receptions had never been more numerous nor more riotous.

Indeed, in 1914 they reveled everywhere, in Paris, in Venice, in Vienna, in Berlin . . . But in Saint Petersburg, luxury and freedom from care reached their apex. Fresh flowers came from Nice by the cartload. And fattened chickens from Nantes. And truffles from Périgord.

Oh, what a carnival it was at Mommy's! People talked for years afterward about her February 1914 ball, with its rather original theme of the Jewel Ball. Reviving the idea of a celebration at the residence of the Princesse de Broglie, Madame Zakrevskaya had asked her guests to dress up in diamonds, hard stones, fine gemstones: each guest embodied, in keeping with their family tradition or personal whimsy, a favorite jewel.

The Jewel Ball held by Mommy at number 52 on the Fontanka River embankment had become such a fireworks show that the international community deemed it divinely Russian in its excesses. Countess Naryshkina had arrived dressed head-to-toe in ruby, displaying her famous oxblood tiara across her forehead and the twenty rows of pigeon's-blood rubies that were the pride of her family. The old princess Saltykova came in emeralds, caparisoned in green stones from her chin to her navel. As for the charming Madame Benckendorff, she had made the trip from Yendel in pearls. Her diadem, brooch, and bracelets were a contrast to the gleam of Madame her mother; even so, her gray pearl necklaces seemed to be divinely refined. As for her dress—in pearly-white satin, a creation of the Muscovite couturier Lomonoff—it was exquisite.

So said the papers.

Moura shrugged. This kind of entertainment, which had once fascinated her, now merely amused her. The arrogance, stupidity, and blindness of some upper-society people was now starting to shock her.

Whenever she heard whispers among her circle of diplomatic friends— whether the old or newly appointed attachés in Saint Petersburg—that Russia embodied the most civilized society of all time, Moura no longer smiled with such tact and no longer kept quiet.

"But of course," her former admirer the Count of Chambrun—a French diplomat she had met in Berlin, who was now posted in Russia— whispered in her ear. "Look at all these people around us. Your compatriots. Listen to them . . . How they appreciate the arts, music, literature, all the refinements of civilization. You Russians aren't insular in the least, not like the British, nor are you bourgeois at all, not like the French these days. Nor are you imperialist like those darned Germans. Nor are you ostentatious the way American nabobs are. And yet you're far richer than the Rockefellers and the Astors! You alone have managed to perfect the art of living. And you've managed to raise it to a level of sophistication that no other society in the world, in all of history, has ever succeeded in achieving."

"I fear you may be idealizing Russia slightly . . . We don't *all* claim quite as many riches as the Astors."

He didn't notice the irony.

"Practically! Russian society embodies the great miracle of civilization."

"You've only seen a very small portion. And you're only speaking here of an infinitesimally small class. I personally think that this class, all these people around us, as you say, are doomed to perish. And if they want to survive, if *we* want to survive, we'll have to change, well, everything. And very, very quickly!"

He kissed her hand:

"I adore you. Who would have thought, in Berlin, that Madame Benckendorff might be an agent of the Bolsheviks!"

"I'm not a Bolshevik."

"An anarchist, then?"

"The only things I believe in are liberty, fraternity, and equality. You must understand me, you who serve la République."

The Count of Chambrun took in her whole body, with the amused look he gave pretty little women who prided themselves on being well informed and well considered: they were all the same.

He smiled.

"La République doesn't suit everybody, and Russia isn't France. Russia needs to be held, it needs an iron fist . . . Otherwise a revolution will come."

"The revolution is already here, everywhere. I imagine that in Monsieur Poincaré's procession yesterday, nobody pointed out the protestors who were tearing up the French tricolor flag, only keeping the one red strip! You haven't seen the barricades and the general strikes that have paralyzed the city."

"And have you, my dear friend, seen them yourself, perhaps?"

"No. But I know all about it. And I've been hearing 'La Marseillaise' . . . Oh, the accents the Russians have been singing that song with! I can assure you that the men in 1789 would hardly envy these workers' fury!"

Charming. Madame Benckendorff was thoroughly charming!

From a very young age, she had been listening to grown-ups' conversations. The result was that she now claimed to have ideas. She read foreign papers, down to the articles that the infamous Jaurès wrote. Who was sending them to her from France? It was a mystery. Her sister, perhaps? The one who was apparently married to a Parisian journalist? How did these articles get past the censors? That, too, was a mystery.

One thing was clear: she was well informed.

She still took herself far too seriously. But could anyone blame her for it? She was twenty-one years old!

He smiled again:

"Does your husband share your dreadful revolutionary opinions?"

"Do you think he would?"

"Absolutely not."

"Indeed. He's hungry for more authority and considers the tsar too liberal. He would like Her Majesty not to give in to any pressure. For Her Majesty to dissolve the Duma again, this time for good! For Her Majesty to dismiss the deputies, for her to reject the reforms. And for us to return to how things were, to the monarchy before 1905. Absolute monarchy. But what I see all around me—whether here, or at Yendel, or in Ukraine, everywhere—needs to move forward and to achieve a parliamentary system that works."

"When you play the oracle, you're heavenly . . . What about war? You, who can see the future: will we have war or will we not? Yes? No? What does Djon think? What are they saying in Berlin?"

◈

Her husband wrote her:

Berlin, July 28, 1914

My dear Marie,

In the absence of Ambassador Sverbeyev, who has decided the moment is right to leave for the summer holidays, I alone am in contact with the German chancellor Bethmann-Hollweg, whom you know. I find it all quite exciting. The preparations for war, the negotiations: it all fascinates me. I'm ashamed to be so thrilled about the present and curious about the future. I have to scold myself for this almost joyful fever that has seized my body. But this excitement isn't diminishing.

Nothing in the world, however, must force Russia to launch the first strike in such a conflict. We cannot take responsibility here and send out the four horsemen of the apocalypse on earth . . . inflicting conquest, war, famine, and death upon all civilized nations.

But I fear that the devil has already seized our spirits and that hell might be close by.

◈

Berlin, July 31, 1914

My dear Marie,

Our ambassador has just returned from holiday. A storm is brewing around us. The kaiser has ordered general mobilization. The trains full of soldiers are already making their way to Belgium.

But we still have some hope of saving the peace. Deploying our sixty thousand men during the military exercises last week at Krasnoye Selo has had the intended effect: Germany is finally taking the measure of our strength. Germany now understands that we could deploy one million men on its borders, and it is trying to calm the hysteria of its ally, Austria-Hungary, which is leading right into catastrophe.

That said, the two nations are preparing for war, and the world could go up in flames in the space of a second.

❖

Berlin, August 2, 1914

Germany has just destroyed our last hope for peace: it declared war upon us in the night. It's all over. I'm leaving Berlin with the ambassador's retinue. We will be in Saint Petersburg in two days.

May God save us and grace our Holy Russia.

CHAPTER NINE

The War

1914–1915

Nobody was waving red flags anymore: everybody was holding up icons and placards with the face of Tsar Nicholas II. Nobody was launching into "La Marseillaise" anymore: everybody was singing "God Save the Tsar," the national hymn.

Never in the time since Napoleon's armies had invaded in 1812 had Russia seen such an upwelling of patriotism. Never in the time since Alexander II's death in 1881 had the Romanov monarchy seemed more solid and popular. Even the opponents to the regime conceded that public opinion had swung around in the space of an hour. Germany's declaration of war had put an end to all civil strife, and everybody was now thinking only about fighting against the kaiser's soldiers and defending Eternal Russia. The strikes that had broken out in the early summer of 1914 were over. The protests were over. The rumblings of revolution were over. Peasants, workers, bourgeois: all social classes and all political parties had rallied single-mindedly around the white banner and the two-headed black eagle.

Nobody would forget the ceremony on Sunday, August 2, 1914, when the crowd spontaneously fell to their knees in the square of the Winter Palace in front of the tsar's distant silhouette, which had just appeared on the balcony.

"I solemnly promise," he had said to the dignitaries of his court, "that I will sign no peace treaty before the last enemy soldier has left our land. And it's through your intermediary, through you who represent the troops so dear to me, you who represent the Guard and the administrative district of Saint Petersburg, that I speak to my whole army, and that I bless them for the hard work they will have to carry out."

A roar of hurrahs had answered his words.

And now tens of thousands of men, their hats in their hands out of respect, prostrated themselves at his feet, swearing their fealty to him and praying in unison for the safety of their "little father."

In front of such an expression of love, such a powerful fervor around him, how could Nicholas II have doubted the affection of his people and the unity of all Russia around him?

❖

The barricades were now a thing of the past, yes. But the balls and the social gatherings were, as well. They had bid farewell to splendor, flowers, and violins. There were no more elegant noblewomen in carriages on the promenades running along the Neva. If victorias bearing a respectable family's coat of arms could still be seen in the palace courtyards, their owners now had other things in mind than placing their visiting cards, with the corner turned up, in silver receptacles, or having a turn in the waltz with one Imperial Highness or another.

The tsarina, the grand duchesses, all the princesses, and all the high society of Saint Petersburg had left their beautiful garments behind. Wearing nurses' uniforms, with the short brown veil worn by the sisters of Saint George or the white veil with the red cross of international organizations, they were driven each morning to the hospitals where they might have to look after the regiments of their husband, father, or brothers. As well as the common rooms and the operating rooms, the sitting rooms of numerous private mansions teemed with these strange silhouettes . . . Circles of ladies shredding rags for bandages. Circles of ladies assembling packages to be sent to prisoners. Circles of ladies writing letters to the families of wounded soldiers. The world of yesteryear no longer existed.

And yet, in the month of August 1914, the aristocracy's children were still playing with each other in the lanes of the Summer Garden, which had served as a public park for them for generations. And their nannies, with wooden beads ringing their necks and *kokoshniks*—the traditional headdress—crowning their foreheads, were still watching their charges with the same attentive, devoted eyes.

❖

Sitting apart on a bench, far from the group of other British nurses talking loudly about the British Empire's entrance into the war—the news of the day—Ducky anxiously watched Kira running over the grass with little Paul.

She was fifty years old.

Still just as thin, just as elegant, and just as simple. In her long pencil skirt, the skirt she had worn in her youth, she turned her nose up at all fads . . . Her hair up in a high bun and a few tendrils rippling around her face. Her hat with a single pheasant feather stuck in it, tilted slightly over her right eye.

Unchanged. But for one detail: her nickname.

In Marydear's family, there was a habit of modifying each member's diminutive as the years progressed. The second generation of Zakrevskys hadn't escaped this rule: Anna's two children and Kira had felt it best to take in their nanny, and to rechristen her.

In this era when the house spoke English, the cousins found the name Ducky rather unflattering: Ducky reminded them of, yes, a duck . . . a description that hardly conveyed the grace of their beloved governess.

For the younger group, that of 1915, Margaret Wilson therefore became Micky.

The adults had followed the trend. Even for Marydear, even for Her High Nobility, Ducky became Micky. And Micky she would remain, until a third generation came along.

Amid the basins and the statues, behind the garden's gilded fence, Micky saw the ever-flowing Neva, heavy and leaden. Not a breath of wind, not a leaf trembled around her. The air smelled like smoke: evidence of the forest fire that was presently blazing across Finland. And everything—the heat, the burning smell, the imperial flag that hung, limp and unmoving, over the spire of Peter and Paul Cathedral—everything underscored her distress and left her feeling as if a storm, an explosion, might be imminent.

She thought about her son, Sean, who was now a naval officer. Sean, who would be one of the first to mobilize. And she recalled the harrowing words uttered by Djon Benckendorff, who had left this morning as a liaison officer for the staff of the Northern Army. He had said that the war with Germany would bring about the end of Europe as they knew it, and chaos in the years to come.

She tried to reassure herself by thinking about how life went on, how Marydear was expecting a second baby and how she herself would care for that child. Yes, life went on.

She wanted to believe what she had heard everyone repeating at the children's grandmother's: the war would be short. Her High Nobility Maria Nikolayevna Zakrevskaya couldn't be wrong. Micky still admired her intelligence and acumen. No matter her shortcomings, she still esteemed the elder woman.

As the old family friend Ivan Goremykin returned to favor and was named by the tsar as president of the Council, Madame Zakrevskaya's apartment on the Fontanka embankment had become the political salon for the most conservative of the aristocrats. The old-fashioned noblemen came there to sing the praises of the government. They all said that the army, by virtue of its sheer numbers, would essentially steamroller the enemy. And that with the help of the British navy, Russia would win its victory.

The war would be short.

❖

Three weeks with a vague feeling of security, only to end up with this disaster . . . At the end of August 1914, the news had just reached Saint Petersburg.

The mounted guard, the knights, the hussars, the Preobrazhensky Regiment, the Pavlovsky Regiment had all been bogged down and trapped in the Tannenberg marshes in eastern Prussia. Most of the young men

Moura had danced with the previous winter were now dead. Dead, too, was her Berlin lover—that mad Afanasy Gramov. All brought low in a single blow.

By sheer luck, Djon was fighting in the north. But the massacre had taken the officers as well as the soldiers. Not one woman among the Benckendorffs or the Zakrevskys were spared the grief of losing a father, a husband, a son, or a brother.

At Tannenberg, twenty thousand men had been killed or wounded. Nine thousand others were taken prisoner. And all their rifles, all their cannons, all their artillery—eight tons of ammunition—had fallen into the hands of the enemy.

The "Russian steamroller" was now unarmed and immobilized. The tsar's hordes had been reduced to a powerless monster. And Madame Zakrevskaya's friends, who had once called Russia invincible, were at a loss for words.

The enthusiastic demonstrators were now firmly in the past, as were the fanfares and the imperial flags waved during processions. Silence enveloped the city. The only noise that could be heard in the streets was cries of hatred against the Germans.

In their private mansions, the aristocrats became even more fractious: when they talked about the kaiser's soldiers, they used the French slur *les Boches*.

The theaters had already removed Wagner's operas from their repertory, and the rabble had already burned down the German ambassador's residence: the doors broken in, the chandeliers shattered, the paintings ripped, the furniture and pianos and statues thrown out the windows, as in the worst days of the 1905 revolution.

The tsar himself yielded to the Germanophobia that had already befallen his subjects. He could not, of course, suspect his German-born wife of treason, nor his dignitaries who bore Germanic surnames— whether Count Kleinmichel or the grand marshal of his court, Count Paul von Benckendorff—but he worked to rub out whatever sounded overly German in his empire. And that began with the name of his very capital, which he ordered to be Russified.

From August 31, 1914, *Sankt Peterburg* was no longer called Saint Petersburg but Petrograd.

If Nicholas II had been hoping to placate passions and calm spirits with this change, he was sorely mistaken. From the palaces to the farmsteads, everybody saw it as a bad omen.

❖

"Ridiculous!" Moura exclaimed. "We don't cut a city off from its past like that, we don't rip its history away. It's just another whim of the autocracy! This change bodes poorly for us all."

"Would you be an enemy of your own government, Mrs. Benckendorff? Would you be one of these superstitious Russian women?"

Notwithstanding his accent, the purest of Irish accents ever to ring in Moura's ears other than Micky's marvelous brogue, the officer's voice was icy.

In his bloodied khaki uniform, his short brown mustache burned by the smoke of his pipe, General Knox—the British military attaché—loomed over her in the British embassy's rooms. She was working there as a volunteer: a way of participating in the war effort.

In fact, she had been poached by the wife of the ambassador, Sir George Buchanan, who had taken her under her wing, as another British ambassador's wife had done in Berlin.

Under the eyes of the incredible Lady Georgina, who reigned over the international high society in Russia and worked at the hospital she had founded herself for the war wounded, her young and charming friend Moura Benckendorff would be more useful in any office than in an operating room. Her knowledge of English, German, and French, not to mention her mastery of Russian, made her a perfect translator and secretary.

Moura looked up from her typewriter and gave the officer her most charming smile.

He wasn't fifty. And he, too, spoke Russian.

But he didn't like her. She knew it and was cautious. General Knox was infamous for his misogyny: "Women? Damned nuisance!"

In the case of Frau von B.—as he regularly called her behind her back—Knox's antipathy seemed boundless. From the very first day, he had tried to get the ambassador to release her, arguing that a woman of high society, a chatterbox, and on top of that pregnant beyond belief, had no business here.

The embassy served as a channel for all communications between Petrograd and London. Even if this Frau von B. didn't know the secrets behind the codes, she was, through her presence, exposed to the most confidential information of every sort. How on earth could his colleagues take such a risk in involving this person in the most important work of their service! Teaching her how to decrypt and encrypt dispatches? It was an outright error! Sheer madness!

It hadn't been so long ago that the tsar's police had succeeded, through a housekeeper in their pay, in making copies of the nine keys that would let them into the embassy's coffers: the nine keys needed to open the final drawer containing *the code*!

That had been in 1905.

What the Germans wouldn't give, these days, to obtain a wax mold of the nine new locks.

"I am here to help," this lady said. Well, well! She was such a bad typist that the ambassador's secretaries, themselves boys just out of Oxford and Cambridge, officers trained in far more difficult tasks, typed better than she did. Of course, they were understaffed and didn't have a minute to spare. Any assistance, no matter what kind, was welcome.

In the face of Knox's suspicions, Frau von B.'s supporters—the department's six young men—answered with their absolute trust in her devotion: her skills were definitely improving. She was taking classes at the Vasilyevsky Island university, studying international law. As well as typing, of course. In a matter of months, she would be one of their best collaborators.

"Nonsense! She has to be kicked out!"

General Knox had no right, in principle, to make any changes in the diplomatic service's organization. Nor was there any reason for him to fixate on this stranger who was volunteering for England's sake. His protests to the head of the embassy had come to naught. As had his complaint to the ambassador himself.

All he could do now was force this woman to give in of her own accord.

He had caught her by surprise as she was lingering in the office at eleven o'clock at night. The chance was just too good.

Moura was in danger. She couldn't confront this military man. She couldn't explain or justify her presence by saying she was working late. She had to endear herself to him.

As she usually did, she opted for seduction and humor:

"Does the change from Petersburg to Petrograd give me goose bumps? Of course, General! I'm ridiculously superstitious. Names that are bad omens, spells, tarot cards, and fortune-telling are all in my wheelhouse . . . How could I escape that? Aren't I both a lady and a Russian?"

"With a German husband."

She couldn't let such an implication drop . . . This insult was too grave!

The shift in her tone underscored her seriousness:

"You would do well to brush up on your geography, General Knox. My husband isn't German. He's Baltic. As we speak, he's fighting against the *Boches*."

"But he lived in Berlin."

"As a representative of the tsar."

"You must have made many friends back there. After all, you lived in Berlin, as well."

"I may well have spent years there as the wife of an attaché to the ambassador . . . All the same, this is no reason for being accused of spying!" Her voice trembled with emotion. "Just like the poor Countess Kleinmichel, who's rumored to have sent the kaiser the Russian Army's campaign plans in a box of chocolates!"

She was shaking on the inside. Never before had she been attacked like this. *Spy*. This Briton was calling her a *spy in the pay of Germany*!

She had to calm down. Collect herself. Try to be peaceable.

He pressed the matter:

"I'm only surprised that a lady who isn't a subject of His British Majesty could have access to the British ambassador's files."

"I remind you, General, that our homelands are allied."

She wouldn't let him gain any ground. She was now fighting him blow for blow. But he, too, refused to back down.

"The friendship between our two countries doesn't justify a Russian lady, no matter how many languages she speaks and no matter how high the society she comes from, having access to confidential documents."

She was silent for a minute, then attempted to explain patiently:

"Your ambassador himself, Sir George Buchanan, asked me to leave my work as a nurse at the hospital to come and lend a hand. As you can see, your embassy does not have enough staff. It needed a secretary to translate the news from France and Germany into English. As well as the dispatches that arrive each day from the Russian ministries."

He grumbled: "That's exactly why we've hired Mr. Chukovsky, an interpreter who's been sworn in."

"Mr. Chukovsky is excellent. But overwhelmed. Between being asked to write a propaganda brochure on the British army and negotiating the cost of a portrait of the ambassador by the renowned painter Repin, he can't keep his head straight."

She was right. Over the last few weeks, Moura had turned out to be useful. And even indispensable.

Apart from her intellectual capacities, apart from her charm and her good humor, she was the only person in the embassy who belonged to the Russian oligarchy. The British had hired her as an essential connection. A desirable recruit. This she knew very well.

There was no question of letting herself be sidelined by this blinkered military man's paranoia. She wanted to serve. She wanted to work. She wouldn't give up this job for anything in the world.

"England thanks you for your support, Mrs. Benckendorff, but it's late. Considering the state you're in, you should head home and not go out again."

There was no arguing with this idiot: she had too much to lose. She smiled at him a second time:

"You're right, General. It's late. And really, really, you must stop worrying about my health: I'll be leaving the embassy at Christmas . . ." She glanced at her belly: "My child will be born in January."

❖

She was tenacious.

General Knox might have thought he'd gotten rid of Moura Benckendorff, but he barely knew her. Two months after her daughter's birth, she once again had the run of the British ambassador's offices and the men there.

And General Knox remained the only one to complain.

❖

Moura was hardly more touched by Tania's birth on January 5, 1915, than she had been by Paul's in 1913. At least not in the way Djon could have hoped.

As he continued to fight on the front line, he had imagined Moura hugging their little girl with the same tenderness he had witnessed in Berlin as she cared for their niece Kira.

Wishful thinking.

The forced postnatal bed recovery, the stupidity of nursery prattle, the constraints of breastfeeding with the wet nurses, the division of time, the regularity of meals, naps—everything in this stretch of confinement left Moura feeling stifled. Within four walls in front of a cradle, she was dying of loneliness and boredom.

At twenty-two years old, she felt more than ever the need to leave her house, play a role, be part of the world. And live alongside the fighters who protected it from evil Germany.

Motherly love would only come later, at the end of the day, when she had quenched her curiosity and worked off her boundless energy.

Only then would the impatience to return to her family overpower her. She would rush home at night to see her children, listen happily to Micky's discussions of their mishaps, tuck them in, and bless them every night.

Yet right now, Moura had only one dream: to work at the British embassy.

From the family home at 8 Shpalernaya Street to the embassy, she only had to cross the small bridge that overlooked the canal and follow the railings of the Summer Garden. Not even fifteen minutes by foot along the Neva.

In her rush each morning, Moura was reminded of Mommy, who was always so indulgent toward her, her Mourushka, and so hard on the others. Mommy, who hadn't changed over the years. She had even refused to let Anna and her two children stay in her massive apartment, leaving them without a place to live upon their return from Berlin.

Moura had welcomed the entire Ionov family into her home. With Kira. She loved nothing so much as life within a clan, as long as she could step out when she wished.

Poor Anna . . . Mommy never spared her daughter her sarcasm. She kept reminding her that unlike Djon, her handsome Count Ionov wasn't fighting to save Russia. Instead, withering away from syphilis as had that late imbecile Bobik, he would pass away at the Benckendorffs'. Anna would soon be a widow and penniless: this was the future Mommy had predicted long ago.

She was pitiless.

Luckily, Anna didn't just sit around. She had seen one of her former beaus from Ukraine here in Petrograd, a beau who had urged her energetically to return to Berezovaya Rudka: it would be better for her husband's health and easier on her finances than staying in the capital. She was getting ready to leave with her children.

A retreat. Not unlike the one Mommy had beaten a decade earlier.

During her sleepless nights, Moura recalled all five of their lives—her own life, Mommy's life, Anna's life, Alla's life, and even Micky's life—as long trains with lead-sealed passenger cars. A string of watertight compartments unconnected to one another.

For her, there was the Yendel compartment, with Djon, the children, and Micky. Mommy's compartment had her salon and its old courtiers clinging to their privileges, blinded by obscurantism. There was the one with empty streets and deserted embankments: Petrograd in wartime. The women who had traded their nurses' veils for mourners' veils. The doleful gatherings in front of store windows to learn the latest news from the front lines.

Spring 1915, which had been so long in coming, hadn't allayed their dread. The army was withdrawing everywhere. And Germany was advancing. Moura knew this better than anyone, as she had translated and typed up this information from the minister to the Allied nations: Russia no longer had any reserves of ammunition. On the front lines, the men were sharing rifles: one for every six soldiers. Rifles without any bullets that didn't even have their bayonets. Now everybody knew that the war would be a nightmare without end.

And then there was this: the magic of the British ambassador's world.

Moura had come to the corner of the embankment and Troitsky Bridge. There rose up her paradise: the palace on the Neva that the Saltykov family, kin to the Zakrevskys, had rented out to the British diplomats. An immense neoclassical building painted red that faced the bridge and the gilded spire of Peter and Paul Cathedral on one side, and Suvorov Square and the marble palace of Grand Duke Konstantin on the other. The buildings occupied a whole city block.

She felt at home here. And rightly so. She had danced at so many children's balls hosted by the owner, Princess Anna Sergeyevna, her aunt by marriage. The Saltykovs still lived in the back of the palace. And ever since her return from Germany, Moura had made a habit of visiting the old lady, whose refinement, spirit, and sharpness of tongue she adored. She flattered both her better qualities and her shortcomings, seducing her as she alone could.

The floor the British occupied had no secrets for her, either. She had dined there before the war, with all the members of the Russian aristocracy. She had dined there more often than the others, in fact. Her closeness to the former British ambassador in Berlin had brought her to the special attention of Sir George Buchanan, the British ambassador in Russia. She had taken his daughter, Meriel, who was the same age, under her wing, introducing her to the various strata of the Saint Petersburg aristocracy. They had both been educated well; they shared the same love for books, the same taste for literature and ideas. Meriel wrote short stories: one of her texts had just been accepted by an esteemed publisher in London.

The two young women had become friends.

Now, with the war, they hardly saw each other. Each day, one left the palace just as the other arrived. Meriel went off to work at the British hospital her mother had opened on the corner of Nevsky Prospect and the Fontanka embankment, while Moura, with a sheaf of translations in her bag, made her way step by step toward the mezzanine level.

On the right-hand landing were the chancellery offices. On the left were the private apartments of the Buchanans. There, the velvet brocades contrasted with the chintz; the rustle of baroque gildings contrasted with the small flowers and lace doilies; the enormous pendant chandelier contrasted with the Wedgwood lamps and sets. England and Russia at the same time. The two worlds Moura loved, the two worlds Moura belonged to, were unashamedly on display here. And she reveled in the combination.

From the landing, the main staircase wound a double spiral up to the state apartments, the ballroom, and the ambassador's office.

At home, yes. Her domain. She knew the place. She knew the hosts, and she knew the help.

First and foremost, the most important person of all: William the porter, who was responsible for Sir George's security. He welcomed her as the second lady of the house. And then Ivan, the coach driver. And then the Italian chef. Finally, the three secretaries and the two attachés to the ambassador, whose office she shared.

She loved nothing more than the huge chancellery office decked out with hunting trophies and fossilized fish, with its huge Chippendale desks set end to end in a square like a banquet table.

There, among the sweetish odor of tobacco, pipes, and English cigarettes, in the green gleam of the globe lamps, the officers came and went and joked and worked . . . A world of men.

As in Berlin, everybody here adored Madame von Benckendorff's presence, and everybody claimed to be ever so slightly in love with her. And, as in Berlin, she took great pleasure in the emotions she aroused: admiration, a need to hold on to her and keep her for themselves.

It wasn't just the fascination that was mutual. She had the same degree of respect for these boys barely older than herself, the same wish to emulate them, the same need to rise to their level and please them.

In her eyes, they were heroes and gods . . . Every one of them.

Or just about.

CHAPTER TEN

Heroes and Gods

1916–1917

In those years of massacre, the gods weren't thirty years old.

One was named Captain Edward Cunard, the descendant of the founder of Cunard Line, the fleet of ocean liners that carried everybody between Europe and America. The fifth baronet with this name, Cunard had read at Eton and earned his stripes in the Belgian trenches. As a sporting man, he embodied the high-born Briton who joked about the smallness of his milieu and laughed at its conventions. A family trait. His brother, Victor, was openly homosexual. His cousin, Nancy, created a scandal wherever she went. "That Cunard could have had the stuff of a good officer," General Knox wrote in the margins of his report, "but he smokes too much, drinks too much, fucks too much."

Another was named Captain Denis Garstin: he had read at Cambridge. He was so fascinated with Russia that he had traveled there before the war and worked for three years as a private tutor in Crimea. In 1914, Garstin was sent to France. There, he had fought a terrible war before being sent to Petrograd, where the general staff needed his expertise. The ambassador had put him in charge of writing propaganda brochures for the Russian population. Far from enjoying it, Garstin had resented being reassigned from the front lines as if he had deserted. The feeling of having abandoned his men had never left him. With his dog at his heels, a mongrel griffon named Garry who he had found God knows where, Garstin walked with his little mustache and his long profile through the outermost neighborhoods of the city. As an idealist and a poet, he had written a book about Russia already, *Friendly Russia*, to which the famous author H. G. Wells had agreed to write an introduction. Garstin took no pride in his literary success. But he loved nothing more than intellectual exchanges and conversations until dawn.

Finally, a bit older than the others, was Captain Francis Cromie, a brilliant officer in the Royal Navy who had led part of the fleet of British submarines in the Baltic Sea. Stories had gone around of how he had sunk four German boats in one day without losing a single man. It was just one masterstroke of many for him, because Captain Cromie's deeds were countless. The tsar himself had bestowed the Cross of the Order of Saint George upon him, the highest military honor in the Empire. His handsomeness, courage, composure, and mysteriousness enticed many members of the weaker sex. He paid his respects to them all. Even though he was married in England, Cromie collected affairs. In his defense, love reigned everywhere here.

Love and friendship.

The camaraderie the three captains shared was commensurate with the complicity shared by the three young women who haunted the embassy. They called them the Three *M*s: Moura, Meriel, and Myriam. In their eyes the women were three splendors, and they took pleasure in admiring their proportions.

None of them, however, were mistresses to the men. They had other loves.

The ambassador's daughter, Meriel, a tall, distinguished blond woman, suffered an impossible love with one of the tsar's cousins, who the Empire's dynastic laws forbade her from marrying.

Myriam, in turn, was an American from California. She had been adopted at eight years old by her mother's second husband—a Russian count by the name of Artsimovich, who at the time was serving as a consul in San Francisco—whose fortune she would inherit. One of the best matches to be found in all Petrograd. She, too, was tall and as beautiful as a caryatid, and she harbored no affectations. It hardly mattered that she was less of an intellectual than Meriel, because her craftiness and brazenness offset it; she had just gotten engaged to a Cossack who had grown up in London. The man of her life. She had long since granted him what no well-raised young woman should ever give away, and she made no secret of it.

Moura, in turn, made a point of remaining faithful to Djon. Nobody cheated on a husband fighting on the front lines. Her fidelity, however, was no impediment to her feelings of loving friendship. With her warmth and her usual openness, she welcomed the three men with a kindness that would turn into a very special closeness with each of them. She flirted with Cunard, who she called Ed. With Garstin, who she called Garstino. With Cromie, who she called Crow. Even though she was younger than all of them, she harbored a somewhat maternal affection for each one, respecting their tastes, making sure to dredge up the preferred whiskey for one or another: Cunard liked Glenfiddich, which was nowhere to be found in Petrograd during this time of the war, and Moura would always find it for him. She looked through all the bookstores for a first edition of Pushkin, which delighted Garstin. She told a thousand white lies only she could make up to cover up Cromie's continual disappearances with his mistresses, at the risk of arousing General Knox's suspicion of herself.

So much warmth and attention made Moura truly precious to each of them. A wonder, as rare as she was indispensable.

Together, the six youths tried to enjoy life, stealing pleasures wherever they could. They knew death might come for them the next day.

In two years, Russia had lost nearly eight million men.

Petrograd was now under threat. The Germans were gaining ground each day. The downfall of Warsaw in August 1915, then of Lemberg, then of Brest-Litovsk, had spread panic throughout the country. Refugees arrived in the capital by the trainload. Sick, famished populations covered in vermin that Meriel Buchanan and her mother strived to help. In the massive camps built around the train station exits, typhus wreaked havoc.

Morale was so low that the tsar deemed it best to take command of the army. This would turn out to be a grave miscalculation. He became personally responsible for every catastrophe and everyone's despair.

There was no food. Coal was nonexistent. Women trying to buy a heel of bread had to line up in interminable queues. Some waited in front of the stores in the cold, starting at four in the morning. They would end up seeing just one word set on the iron grille: "Nothing."

The fury that had grown before the war surged forth anew. But now it was more bitter, more violent.

The pamphlets attacking the empress for her negligence—the empress who the tsar had named regent because he was serving on the front lines—multiplied. Her supposed debauchery with her lover, the monk Rasputin, was now on everybody's tongue.

And day after day, the rumors grew. Rumors that confused what was true and what was false. What was true was the incompetence and greed of the war minister whose corruption explained the lack of provisions, the dearth of ammunition and equipment on the front lines. Weren't people saying that in the Carpathians, soldiers were fighting barefoot?

It was being said that Germany was sabotaging the army through scarcity, illness, famine, that it was paying the imperial ranks to sell off the Empire.

It was as if the end of the world were nigh.

All that remained was vodka, the cabaret, and Gypsy songs; all that served to help one forget, however momentarily, how imminent death was.

And there remained those holidays at Yendel.

❖

"I see a blue lake reflecting a cloudless sky, a sky that seems infinitely far away," Garstin murmured.

"I see, around the lake, immense black forests of pines and birches," Meriel replied.

Lying every which way on the pontoon, in bathing suits and with their arms crossed behind their heads, the six youngsters were drying off in the sun. Their eyes were only half-closed because they didn't want to miss one bit of the world's beauty; they were trying to retain it in their memory.

"Oh, try to hide your pleasure a little," Cunard said with a smirk.

"Shut up, Ed. I see a stork standing stock-still atop a chimney," Garstin shot back.

"And under the stork, I see a small wooden house with a porch and four wings," Myriam Artsimovich added.

"You're looking at my mother-in-law's dacha, where we'll be having our picnic," Moura concluded pragmatically.

She loved their fantasies, but as the lady of the house attending to her guests' well-being, she had to take care not to get carried away, like they did.

Even so, she encouraged them.

And even though their conversations remained conventional—in Russian or French, with the odd bit of English, always maintaining some formality—Moura encouraged utter whimsy in their remarks and conduct. She would not condemn excess. She herself smoked, drank, and allowed herself to be intoxicated in every way.

Even more so than the others, she saw these radiant hours as overshadowed by the impending sunset. The sense of a decline, the vague, unarticulated impression of fatality that she accepted as a fact, was never far behind. As a result, she was very consciously determined to transform each second into a pleasurable memory. *I must remember the smell of the pines behind me*, she thought. Her desire to identify the smallest sensation, to extract a physical joy from it, was her own deeply inborn survival instinct.

Cunard's eyes were closed as he kept describing the landscape: "I see a Lutheran church with its tall white bell tower, topped with an endless spire."

"Oh, stop spouting nonsense . . ." Meriel whined. "There's no tall white bell tower! There isn't a single village nearby."

"I don't care. I can see it!"

"When you come down to it, Yendel is solid land," Cromie said. "And ultimately, solid land isn't so bad."

"That's an understatement," Garstin murmured. "Every minute we don't spend here is a complete waste."

Myriam Artsimovich chimed in. "How odd it is, then, that we can enjoy such a moment . . . and ever do anything that isn't pursuing it!"

They had gone to the other end of the woods and swum in Kallijärv, a quarter of a mile from the main house. When the building had gone up in flames, Djon's parents had settled by the lake itself, in the old fishermen's cabin. The elder Madame von Benckendorff had stayed there after her husband's death, leaving the manor to her sons. Her daughter-in-law's closeness to these British officers, even as Djon and his three brothers were fighting on the front lines, didn't bother her. Far from suffering in their happiness, far from being annoyed at Moura for sharing the pleasures of Yendel with them, the elderly lady rejoiced in these boys' presence. Their gossip allowed her to believe that life was still going on as it had before the war.

Djon's mother was far more indulgent and intuitive than Mommy was. When she heard these young boys' laughter, when she heard Moura's slightly husky intonation, their voices reminded her of her children's joyful cries on a swing: *See how they want to catch us?* they seemed to be saying. *They can try all they want, but they won't be able to grab us, much less hold us back.*

She had a vague sense that in the battles to come, in the tragedies that awaited them, even in the very moment they would die, they would recall the marvels of Yendel. That just like her sons, whose love for the land she knew intimately, they would remember, at the hour of their death, these swims and these picnics as the very incarnation of paradise.

She was not mistaken.

In the four volumes that Meriel Buchanan would publish on her experiences in Russia during her father's time as an ambassador there, she kept returning to the magic of those moments:

> *Yendel in the summer! Unexpected lakes, which had been hidden under the snow, shining vividly blue between the pine trees.*

In book after book, over nearly half a century, Meriel would return to Yendel:

Long mornings bathing in the cold, clear waters of the lake, long drives through the woods in a queer-shaped cart where one sat cross-legged on a narrow board and held one's next-door neighbour tightly round the waist. Picnics at night when we built fires of sticks, baked potatoes in the red-hot ashes and watched the wavering light of the flames cast weird distorted shadows on the sleeping trees.

Days of peace and idleness that seemed unbelievable in the stress and turmoil that followed, days of laughter and care-free happiness that now are incredibly far away.

Yendel. The leitmotif haunted her memories.

In the twilight of her life, she would write again:

How often I think of the days we spent at Yendel, the comfort of that redbrick house, the breathless stillness of the snow-covered fields and woods, with only now and then the silver jingle of bells from a sledge, bringing supplies from the farm or the distant village. The unhurried movable hours for meals, the disregard of time for getting up or going to bed, the sudden impulsive plans, a visit to Reval, a fancy-dress dance, a picnic in the snow, the gipsy songs Moura sang to us, sitting on the floor with her golden eyes gazing into the fire.

Summers at Yendel might have impressed Meriel Buchanan, but for her it was winter weekends that encapsulated the poetry of a youth on the edge of death.

Every day a cloudless blue sky stretched above the woods where we spent the mornings tobogganing or trying to ski, my own ineffectual attempts invariably landing me head foremost into the snow. In the afternoons we drove in troikas through the woods, with now and then a sledge upsetting into a snow-covered ditch, and a laughing extraction of rugs and cushions, and then we drove home with the sunset casting a pink glow over the white, untrodden fields, the lighted windows of the house shining out a welcome through the falling shadows.

No constraints. No restraints. Moura made sure they had no obligations. She offered them freedom as they had never known it:

> *At Yendel, girls begin the day*
> *In optimistic negligé,*
> *Followed hot-footed, after ten,*
> *by the pajama-radiant men*

Garstin sang, with a pipe held between his teeth, his boots on the railing. He composed the morning hymn, which he intoned to the tune of "Rule, Britannia":

> *Oh God, I must take a train*
> *And go to Petrograd again*
> *And while I deal out propaganda*
> *My nicer thoughts will all meander*
> *Back, back to Yendel,*
> *Oh, to be in Yendel for eternity.*

❖

For eternity . . . Among these friends, Moura was perhaps the one who took the greatest pleasure in, and had the keenest awareness of, these stolen moments.

She had never been able to get up early. But these days, she awoke around dawn. Sitting in bed in front of the balcony, she let the daylight slowly make its way into her room.

As she used to at Berezovaya, she liked to go down to the park on chilly days, the days when the coach drivers couldn't control their horses, when the icy air stung her cheeks. Yendel's light on those days gave the snow a pinkish hue. Even the icy patches on the road, even the lake looked pink. This muted gleam that covered the world reminded her of the sweetness of yesteryear and gave her peace.

Peace was what they all needed.

She thought of Micky, who she had seen go pale and stumble after reading a letter from Ireland. She had gone straight to her bedroom without a word. Moura had understood. The ship Micky's son had been serving on had sunk. Sean was dead. Killed at sea during the first bombings.

This mourning was the reason the governess and children were absent; they had stayed in Petrograd.

The truth was that Moura wanted them—Kira, Paul, and Tania—here at Yendel every morning and every night. She would have liked for them all to be safe around her. She would have liked for Mommy to be in the next room over, and Alla and Anna nearby.

She had no news about Alla. All anyone knew was that she was living in France and that Monsieur Moulin, her journalist husband, was working on propaganda. In her most anguished moments, Moura feared that she would call Kira back. But Alla, true to her nature, gave no signal to that effect.

Anna, however, had cooked up a dramatic turn of events—as was her nature, notwithstanding her seeming orderliness. On February 5, in total secrecy, in the Duma church in Petrograd, she had gotten married again, this time to her Ukrainian suitor—even though she was still married to Ionov. She had not gone to the trouble of getting divorced first, much less waiting until she was a widow. So now she was a bigamist! Her first husband, of course, was in his death throes. It was a matter of days. She cared for him, attended to his well-being. But she had been pregnant for several months and had no intention of falling into disrepute, as Alla had, by giving birth to a bastard. The father of the soon-to-be-born child was a prestigious match for her, a marshal of nobility in the Berezovaya province. He might not have borne the title of prince, but he still belonged to the illustrious Kochubey family and was a direct descendant of the Crimean Tatar Beys. The opportunity was one Anna couldn't pass up. She was penniless and had only herself to count on. She needed protection for her two children, who Ionov's imminent death would leave orphans without any resources. Vasily Vasilyevich Kochubey was mad about her. What assurance did she have that he wouldn't change his mind? So she had done what she had to.

Moura admired her and wept for her. She knew how much Anna had loved Ionov.

As for herself, she felt sympathy for her new brother-in-law. He was so unlike Mommy's reactionary aristocrats! He was a liberal. He had been unanimously elected deputy to the fourth Duma by the sitting members of the provincial assembly. He belonged to the Progressive Bloc, which opposed the tsar's irrational whims.

As she thought about her sister's remarriage and bigamy, Moura told herself that she understood. She, too, was worried for the future. She was afraid for Djon. She was afraid for the British officers. She was afraid for Russia.

In her eyes, Russia was a separate entity: she carried the land within herself. Russia physically belonged to her, she felt it in her body. It was more precious, more essential than her own self. At once her land, her haven, her family, her self: everything that was hers. This was the motherland.

The idea that Russia could be invaded, degraded, wiped out, that it could become German tomorrow, plunged her into terror and shame.

She shouldn't even think of it.

But she thought about it all the same.

Rasputin's assassination in December 1916 hadn't had any effect on the empress's negligence, nor on the idiocy of her government. The murder, carried out by the tsar's underlings, had only underscored the regime's decadence. In Moura's eyes, the situation could be summed up in a single sentence: the Romanov court was now akin to the Borgias'. And the streets of Petrograd had become cutthroat; rioting and pillaging were now commonplace.

She had to take advantage of what the present could still offer.

Even without Micky and the children, the house was full.

In the first half of March 1917, Myriam had arrived with her fiancé Boris Ionin, a diplomat of Cossack heritage. A former secretary to the Russian ambassador in New York, Bobbie spoke seven languages, won every athletic competition, and ordered all his tuxedos from London.

Cromie, too, had just arrived, accompanied by his latest conquest, Countess Schilling, a neighbor of the Benckendorffs and a queen of Estonian society. Garstin and his big dog, Garry, were also there, as well as Cunard, Meriel, and the rest of the British officers posted to Reval.

The capital of Estonia was now serving as a base for the British Royal Navy. The military there was preparing for an offensive: they would sink the German fleet that was advancing in the Baltic Sea.

The battle was imminent. And the stay in Yendel was more momentary than it had ever been before. Everybody present knew it. And they all tried not to think about it.

◈

After dinner, night enveloped the manor in a milky darkness. Through the sitting room's immense bow window, the moonlight illuminated the huge cushions of snow that gleamed at the feet of the firs. The youngsters were standing, gathered together around the chimney, with pipes and cigarettes in their hands. The most uninhibited one this evening, perhaps the most drunken one, was the one who usually drank the least and made no noise except to recite his poems: the one they all affectionally called Garstino.

Acting as the ringmaster, he clapped his hands.

"Everybody, quiet!"

His dog, Garry, jolted. The others turned around.

"Moura . . . 'Now then, niece!'" he cried, quoting Natasha Rostov's uncle in *War and Peace* and bringing her to the center of the room.

She immediately caught the allusion. Like Garstin, she knew Tolstoy intimately. More than him, she understood both the letter and the spirit of his books. He opened up the circle to give her free rein and cried:

"All yours, Moura!"

Playing the role he expected of her, she threw her head back, rolled her shoulders, put her hands on her hips, and broke into the most dramatic song in her Gypsy repertoire.

She began it slowly, as if she wanted to break their hearts. Then she walked up to them, one by one, addressing her lament to each of them. Meeting their gazes one at a time.

She knew better than anyone how she embodied Russian mystery for all these British men. In their eyes, she was that alone: the Slavic soul. She understood this. She understood that Garstin, Cromie, and Cunard were all wondering—as had Tolstoy's characters, in front of Natasha Rostov performing her famous folk dance—where, in what previous life, Madame von Benckendorff had learned just how to sway her hips and just how to sing such words of love!

Just how did she know these words that she sang with a husky voice, so full of violence and sensuality?

Moura, this socialite of a woman with her European education, who was rocking back and forth in the moonlight with the snow and the storm behind her, belonged to a world that was fundamentally removed from their own. They let themselves be enraptured. Their fascination intoxicated her.

But this evening it wasn't just the desire to entice them, her usual need to play a role and seduce them, that gave Moura her drive. It was the sheer emotion of sharing with these foreigners, who had come to protect her homeland, the love they all felt for Russia.

Her lament was hardly finished when she shifted register abruptly. She wound up the gramophone and asked Cunard to take her in his arms. Her face was serious, as if something in the Gypsy song she had sung had taken root, deeper than ever, within her. She no longer seemed to be the impeccable hostess, nor the married woman, nor even the playmate they had all known in earlier days.

She needed a weight to press against her body. She needed to be embraced, to be possessed and carried away. Myriam had Bobbie. Countess Schilling had the man they'd nicknamed Crow. Meriel had her romance with the Duke of Leuchtenberg. But she . . . she had no dreams. Not even memories.

She had recognized long ago that the love she shared with Djon had not moved her soul deeply. She retained no memory of their embraces.

The only thing she was left with was the unpleasant feeling of her immense solitude.

Morally, spiritually, she remained a virgin.

She had to prove to herself this evening that she was still alive.

Cunard, who sensed her fervor, had pressed her leg in between his. Cheek against cheek, he pulled her close, turned her toward him, accentuating the positions of the tango before leaning on her as he swung her back. Other couples came and joined them. Meriel's and Myriam's profiles spun around them, sometimes shot through with a ray of light, sometimes effaced and lost.

❖

In her autobiography, Meriel described how she, along with Myriam and Moura, left Yendel on the night of Sunday, March 11, 1917—February 26, in the Russian calendar—after the boys had left earlier that morning. Cromie and his officers had reached their base in Reval already.

We knew nothing of the events of the past few days, no news having reached us from the outside world . . .

We left the warmth of the lighted hall with its comfortable chairs and blazing fire, and packed ourselves into the waiting sledge. The servants, standing shivering by the lighted door, bowed their farewells, the huge fur rug was fastened firmly round us, the coachman, muffled in his shapeless coat, shook the reins, and with a sudden silver jingle of bells, we started off.

There was no moon, but the deep darkness of the sky was sown with stars, and the pure-white stretches of snow gleamed like sheets of silver on either side . . .

Then, at last, the lights of the little station, the waiting-room full of soldiers and peasants in evil-smelling sheepskins, the hoot and whistle of the engine. The train, coming from Reval, was full to overflowing, even the corridors packed with people sleeping on stools or on the floor, but the head of the district police had reserved us a compartment, and little knowing it was the last time we should be allowed such privileges, we locked our door and settled down for the night.

We arrived at Petrograd the next morning at a quarter to eight, the train being for a wonder only ten minutes late. The big station seemed somehow darker than usual, the few porters who were about wore a somewhat perturbed and distracted air, and the sight of General Knox in full uniform caused me a momentary feeling of alarm, my thoughts swiftly flying to the possibility of something having happened at the Embassy. His first words, however, reassured me on that score. "I have come to meet you," he said, "because there have been riots here the last few days and no motors are allowed in the streets without a pass."

His keen eyes surveyed us sternly as we waited shivering on the dark drafty platform, while William collected our luggage. "Women," I could imagine him thinking, "ought not to be here! Damned nuisance when there is trouble."

Then, when at last we had managed to get ourselves and all our luggage into the car, and driven off, leaving the other wretched passengers hopelessly standing on the steps of the station, he gave us the gist of what had been happening.

Because of the lack of fuel and material, caused by the disorganization of transport, several factories had closed their doors, and the workmen, waiting hopelessly for bread, had started to loot some of the provision shops. There had been skirmishes with the police, the Cossacks had been called out, but had not tried to stop the crowds . . .

It is very often the time just prior to a catastrophe that is laden with ominous warning, and early in the morning of 12th March the storm had not yet broken, but the deathlike stillness of Petrograd was a thing I have never been able to forget. There were the same wide streets we knew so well, the same palaces, the same golden spires and domes rising out of the pearl-colored mists, and yet they all seemed unreal and strange as if I had never seen them before. And everywhere emptiness: no long lines of carts, no crowded trams, no izvozchiks, no private carriages, no policemen. Only, as we turned out on to the Palace Quay, the figure of the one I knew well, who had always held guard at this corner. He had always been so dapper and smiling, but that morning his face was ashen, and as he raised his hand to salute us, I knew as certainly as if the words had been spoken in my ear that he would not live to see the end of the day.

And indeed we had hardly arrived at the Embassy, having dropped Moura and Miriam on the way, when the uncanny silence was broken by the sharp crack of rifles, by an uproar of angry voices and a woman's scream of terror, as a crowd of workmen and soldiers surged across the Souvorof Square, running up the quay towards the

Winter Palace, brandishing rifles and revolvers, shooting in all directions, inflamed with that terrible infection of crowds which spreads like an angry, consuming fire, wiping out reason and sanity.

As the morning went on, new reports reached us, showing that the situation was getting out of hand. The Military Arsenal had been stormed by a group of soldiers and workmen from the idle factories, who were dealing out arms and ammunition to a turbulent crowd. The Law Courts were being burnt and looted. The Central Office of the Secret Police was being raided. Three of the principal prisons had been carried by storm, and all the political and criminal prisoners had been set free.

The soldiers were now refusing to obey their officers and remain in barracks. They wandered about the streets, getting caught up in crowds, swept along in an orgy of destruction, a sudden unreasoning fury against law and order.

In the afternoon, some of the English ladies, courageously facing the danger of the streets and walking all the way on foot, came to the usual sewing party and sat together, talking in hushed voices of what they had seen on their way to the Embassy. One had met a mob of drunken soldiers, which had trussed a policeman up in ropes and were dragging him along the frozen road. Another had seen an officer shot down on a doorstep. Still another had passed a crowd gathered round a huge bonfire, and was told by a grinning woman that they were burning a sergeant of the Secret Police. As a grim accompaniment to their low-toned conversation, the distant sound of shooting, a clamour of voices, the roar of motor lorries, filled with a motley collection of soldiers, sailors, and workmen, thundered down the quay and over the river. Then a sudden burst of cheering took us to the windows, and for the first time we saw the scarlet flag fluttering above the fortress on the other side of the Neva.

Back, back to Yendel,
Oh, to be in Yendel for eternity.

CHAPTER ELEVEN

The February Revolution

FEBRUARY–OCTOBER 1917

T he cries and uproar outside, in the streets, were met with silence inside.

On the second day of what was being called the February Revolution, everybody whispered in the dark, not even daring to light the lamps out of fear of attracting the attention of the rioters and shooters.

Muted complaints, anguished murmurs: the few society women courageous enough to walk outside to meet others seemed to have lost their voices and, once welcomed in, were unable to utter the outrages they had endured and describe the horrors they had witnessed. Only the shrill ringing telephone broke their quiet communions.

At Moura's residence, the device, installed on the hallway wall, never stopped thrumming.

Everyone came to her to learn the latest or to share new rumors. She belonged to so many social circles: that of the aristocrats close to the Court; that of her brother-in-law Kochubey, the liberal deputy to the Duma; that of the Allied ambassadors . . . She was at the center of everything, a veritable fount of information!

As it had when she was a teenager when an incident—a brief illness, a storm, a letter, the twins' romantic crushes—upended entire days and changed everything at Berezovaya, this break in the household's routines enthralled her.

Something, an outside event, had finally happened: she wanted to know what it was. She needed to understand it, accept it, take control of it, and disseminate it. Her willingness to answer questions and exaggerate facts amounted to the same childish feverishness she had experienced when she was a messenger and go-between for Alla, Anna, and Mommy. This role intoxicated her: the adventure became hers.

Even as she was fully aware—more so than all the other women of her social standing—of the scale of the cataclysm, she felt no genuine fear. The only sentiment she had within herself was what Djon had once described in his letters when, living alone in Berlin in July 1914, he found out what was happening:

> *I find it all quite exciting. The preparations for war, the negotiations: it all fascinates me. I'm ashamed to be so thrilled about the present and curious about the future. I have to scold myself for this almost joyful fever that has seized my body. But this excitement isn't diminishing.*

She picked up the little Bakelite horn from the wall twenty or thirty times a day to hear and respond to the thousand contradictory stories her callers had to share. She stayed there and stood right by the phone for hours on end.

The Count of Chambrun, her old friend from the French embassy, called to tell her which roads not to take. Nevsky Prospect was barred, lit only by a marine searchlight on the Admiralty tower. The day before, he'd been hoping that everything would resolve itself. This morning, he was very clearly worried.

Cunard called her to confirm what Chambrun had been saying: she should under no circumstances go to the British embassy. The riots were growing everywhere. The soldiers who had joined the rebellion had had no choice but to shoot their former officers. Cunard himself had seen mutineers pulling the epaulets off an old colonel and spitting in his face. As the poor victim was complaining, the soldiers had shot him through the head, in front of the embassy, right there on the street.

It was open season for the city's policemen. Meriel had just heard that they were chalking numbers on their prey before tying them to one another and gunning them down on the Field of Mars, near the Summer Garden.

Mommy called to tell her what had befallen their relative, Princess Saltykova, who shared her palace with the embassy. As the princess had been sitting down to eat the night before, her kitchen servants had rushed in, distraught: the commoners' door to the palace had been broken open. The old lady barely had time to run down the stairs, cross the courtyard, and take refuge at the other end, in the wing the Buchanans resided in. At eighty years old, bareheaded, in evening slippers, she ran, stumbling over snowdrifts, through a five-degree chill. Through the ambassador's office windows, she was able to see what was happening at her residence: the rioters were ripping her tapestries, shattering her mirrors, and destroying the portraits of the tsar and the empress with sledgehammers. The savages emptied the bottles from her wine cellar one by one before vomiting, dead drunk, on her rugs. A group of women came and joined them to drink with them and fornicate on her own bed. In the morning, they soiled the alcove's pink silk with their excrement. The princess witnessed it all. The monsters terrorized the servants, forcing them to attend to them on their knees, and showed no intention of leaving the residence. The princess didn't dare return, and she didn't know where she could go after this. It seemed that the British ambassador could not host her for long, as he had been ordered by his government not to intervene in Russia's civil turmoil.

"And do you know what they did to my dear friend Countess Kleinmichel?"

"I know, Mommy. They arrested her."

Mother and daughter were cut off from each other by the impossibility of crossing the city, so they talked on the phone for hours. These distant exchanges now seemed as natural to them as a conversation in a salon.

"Is it possible you didn't see what they posted on her balcony?"

"No, I saw. It's terrible!"

"'The revolutionary forces have captured a dangerous spy in the kaiser's service. She will remain under custody until her trial.' They're going to kill her!"

"Of course not, Mommy. She's an old woman. They'll release her."

Something in Moura's tone upset her mother:

"Mind your words, my girl. You'll see when these brutes ransack Yendel! I wouldn't wish it on anyone, of course, but you're going to see. And I have one other piece of advice for you: change your name. They murdered Count Friedrich and poor Stackenberg, only because they—like your cousin Count von Benckendorff—were thought to be in Germany's pay. You're the next one on their list. You fool, how dare you defend those murderers?"

Moura sidestepped the accusation:

"How could *we*—all of us—be so blind as to not see any of this coming?"

"If the tsar abdicates, as they are all predicting, it will be the end of Russia."

❖

There was a new phone call from Mommy at dawn.

"His Majesty abdicated last night!"

The shock was so great that it had reduced Mommy's sonorous voice to a mere wisp. Moura couldn't hold back a sigh of pity. Her mother's world was collapsing.

But all the same, it was impossible for her to disguise the relief and joy this news brought her. She had learned it a few minutes earlier, thanks to a call from Garstin.

"I understand how you feel, Mommy. But it was the best solution, you know."

The old lady was nearly at her wits' end. "Russia is dead!"

"Don't panic, dear Mommy . . . On the contrary, Russia will be reborn."

"Nothing can save us now!"

"Except perhaps for democracy."

"We're going to fall into chaos!"

"Mommy, Mommy. We've already been in chaos for a long time now."

"Are you still endorsing what's happening? Are you? You're the last one, my daughter, the last person in the world who should be happy about this. People like us are going to lose everything."

"What's happening is terrible, yes. But people like us should have understood a long time ago that so much injustice was unacceptable . . . People like us should have known that matters couldn't stay as they had been, shouldn't have lasted this long."

"But it's all happening to me so quickly! I can't get my head around any of this. The tsar's abdication in a matter of hours: between this past Monday and last night, it hasn't even been three days!"

"With a population that's been starving for three centuries," Moura concluded bleakly.

This discussion was one she'd already had a thousand times over with Cromie, Cunard, and Garstin at Yendel. But in another way. They all shared the same ideas and principles. With no equality, with no freedom, there would be no salvation.

Even for Meriel and Myriam, those first days of the revolution embodied that distant dream . . . the promise of a better world.

Even Sir George Buchanan, who nobody would ever have suspected of socialist leanings, knew that regime change could not be avoided. It was necessary. He made sure not to hold such an opinion in public. He also made sure not to provide full official support to the government that had just taken charge. He saw its leader, the ebullient lawyer Kerensky, as an opportunist. Just after he had had the tsar arrested, Kerensky installed himself in the Winter Palace. "Get out of the way so I can climb in!" General Knox grumbled, summing up the situation.

At least, the ambassador repeated, at least this Kerensky seemed to be intelligent. He would reform the army, keep fighting the Germans, and maybe give Russia the keys to victory . . . Kerensky? The lesser of two evils, compared to Lord Lenin and his henchmen, who had just come from Switzerland: they had crossed Germany in a sealed train compartment, and clearly the kaiser had approved of it—and reportedly even paid for it. Those men were known to be extremists and demagogues. They were demanding an immediate end to the war, pushing soldiers to fraternize with the enemy, and advocating peace at any cost: yes, those Bolsheviks were dangerous.

❖

Each night, the roar of an armored car coming and going below their windows awoke Moura, Micky, and the children.

In the nursery, Micky forbade anyone from moving. But in the master bedroom, Moura stood, barefoot in a nightshirt, and hid behind the curtain: she was watching this spectacle that the inhabitants of Shpalernaya Street knew all too well. A huge monster was spitting gunfire and flames. The car was moving slowly and killing at random. Whose side was it on? The horse groomers and coachmen said that the man hiding inside was a tsarist officer determined to massacre the proletariat . . . As many proletarians as possible. The doormen, butlers, and higher ranks of the domestic staff, however, were convinced that the driver had to be Lenin himself, determined to sow fear and terror in the hearts of Petrograd's citizenry.

❖

Little milk, no sugar, no meat—not even for the rich. No more vegetables anymore. The children were getting thinner and thinner.

As the summer of 1917 began, everybody's sickly appearances, Micky's dispiritedness as she still mourned her son, Mommy's ailing in the wake of her friends' deaths, the fear of what was yet to come drove the entire family to move to Yendel.

Like most landowners, Moura had prepared to return to the estate for harvest season. Because Djon and his brothers were away, she had to audit accounts and oversee matters herself. Each year, the whole of

Petrograd's aristocracy, with their retinue of protégés and staff, left the city for their country domains. It was a timeless ritual.

Nobody imagined that this summer sojourn of 1917 would be the final one.

❖

In Estonia, nothing looked the same anymore.

In the port of Reval, Communist agitators had succeeded in undermining the sailors' animosity toward the Germans and transmuted it into a hatred of the upper classes. The Bolsheviks' promises of "peace, land, bread" had been heartily welcomed by everyone down to the British troops. Cromie found himself struggling more and more to maintain his authority over his inferiors. There was an increasingly serious risk that the fleet would be handed over to the enemy without a battle. If that did happen, Captain Cromie would have to sink his ships himself.

It seemed so long ago—though it had only been three months—that he had been dancing a tango with his latest companion in the salon at Yendel. Countess Schilling had had to flee and take refuge in Stockholm with her husband, a former officer of the tsar.

In Cromie's eyes, Yendel still remained an untouchable refuge, a haven he longed to go back to.

How could he have imagined that at this very moment, Moura and her mother were hiding in a barn with Micky and the little ones? Or that as they hid amid the sheaves of straw, covering Paul's and Tania's mouths with their hands, they were listening fearfully to the peasants ransacking the farm? Stealing the horses and cows? Slaughtering the sheep? Chopping up the pigs while they were still alive so they could rip out the lard? . . . That they were listening to the pillagers insulting their masters, threatening them with the same fate that had befallen their animals?

Fear. Moura, unable to move an inch, discovered the terror of dying. They would find them; they would kill them here and now. They would kill her and all her kin.

For the first time, she felt true terror.

————

It was only sheer luck that the peasants were satisfied after they had ransacked the farm. That they didn't think of forcing open the barn's doors, or those of the house itself.

Not this time.

Moura's inability to protect the three children she had been holding close to her had shaken her to the core. Mommy's line—"You'll see when these brutes ransack Yendel! . . . You're going to see"—now seemed utterly prophetic.

CHAPTER TWELVE

The October Revolution

As they weren't under the protection of Djon and his brothers, it was impossible for the women to stay all alone in the countryside even one second longer.

They had to return to Petrograd.

And this time, Moura was to bring back her mother-in-law and the fox terriers she had been keeping to her own apartment.

On the night of November 7, 1917—October 25 in the Russian calendar—she accompanied Mommy to a concert. This wasn't unusual in any way, not uncommon at all: the capital's theaters were packed.

Just to go on living.

But the time when women dressed up to go to the opera now seemed so distant. The mob of unruly soldiers in the imperial lodge was bustling. Workers, seafarers, students, and prostitutes filled the orchestra seats. Mommy couldn't keep herself from whispering in Moura's ear, complaining about "the bedlam that Kerensky and his provisional government have unleashed."

Mommy hadn't seen the half of it yet.

At the exact moment that she heard Shalyapin's poignant bass voice imbuing the grandeur of *Boris Godunov*, the Soviets were diligently working to drive out this bedlam that Kerensky and his government had unleashed.

◈

When mother and daughter woke up the next morning, all they heard was silence. The telephone in the hallway was no longer ringing. Moura picked it up and heard the truth for herself: the lines had been cut.

They would only learn later on just how much had happened. Because at this point, it was impossible to share news. Everybody instinctively shut themselves at home. She did so, as well.

In the night, the Red Guard's regiments had seized post offices and telegraph poles; they had invaded the train stations and commandeered the newspaper offices. The Bolsheviks were now occupying the city.

Only the Winter Palace, where the ministers sat, was still holding out, defended by the last faithful few: very young and inexperienced officers, as well as a battalion of female soldiers that Kerensky had just installed. He himself had fled.

At noon, there was a series of explosions. The palace was surrounded. Some twenty armored cars were arrayed on the square. Under the arch at Bolshaya Morskaya Street, two cannons were shooting directly at the walls of the imperial residence, chipping away at the red paint and leaving gaping white dents. On the Neva, the Aurora cruiser was slowly turning its gun turret toward the windows.

The besieged residents were huddled together at the top of the grand staircase, behind sandbags and stacked logs. They fought off every grenade blow they could.

The bombardment lasted the entire day and went past midnight. The truth was that the young, inexperienced soldiers had no chance. They fell like flies. Outside, word was already going around that three hundred female soldiers had already been killed.

The fate of those who lived until morning would not be worth the fight for survival. Once the immense building was finally breached, the Reds would drag them back to their barracks to rape them before cutting their throats.

As for the ministers hidden in the bottommost depths of the palace, they would be arrested and imprisoned, added to the dungeons that were already full to bursting. Before they were executed in turn.

_____

In the morning, a strange smell wafted across Petrograd. It wasn't the smell of smoke, or gunpowder. The city reeked of wine.

The rabble had pillaged the Hermitage: after destroying the artwork, they'd broken into the wine cellars.

The discovery of tens of thousands of bottles—all the best and most famous vintages from history—had opened the floodgates. It would be one of the most widespread drinking binges ever recorded.

The alcohol fumes reached the farthest ends of Nevsky Prospect.

The crowd grew as people came from every neighborhood. Everybody wanted to join in the debauchery and claim some loot for themselves. Women could be seen running with handbaskets; children staggered under the weight of magnums. Cars full of soldiers drove in from all corners, only to make off with full loads in an immense roar of metal and rubber.

Around noon, the Soviets sent the Red Guards. But it was no use: the crowd was out of control, even for the Bolsheviks. At this point, it was better to let the drunken men stumble into the gutters.

In the evening, among the shards of glass and remnants of bottles, hundreds of bodies slept off their drunkenness. The snow was pink with the bloody tint of burgundy and gold with the amber glow of champagne.

The era of Lenin and Trotsky—each known for their sobriety—began under a citywide hangover.

❖

The Count de Chambrun, the French ambassador's right-hand man, wrote in his diary:

> *Nationalizing the grand estates, arresting suspects, executing the bourgeoisie: I've been talking to Madame Benckendorff for quite a while about the current situation. This little woman entertains me. She knows about everything, absolutely everything. General Knox told me that she borrowed her maid's rags and dressed up as a local woman to go hear Trotsky's harebrained ideas at the Smolny palace. In another era, one might be reminded of Marivaux's heroines. It seems that she has become friends*

with several tovarishes currently talking to the tribune. Knox is beside himself. Personally, I think her curiosity is rather amusing. She doesn't judge. She listens. I've tried to get her to say what it is we're all thinking—that these Bolsheviks are thugs and robbers—but she doesn't let me drag her into this debate. She explained to me that this word, burzhui, *"bourgeois," which they use indiscriminately, doesn't have the same meaning in Russian that it does in French. Here, the term is fundamentally pejorative. It describes or names not a social class but rather elites at every level. The aristocrats, the intelligentsia, the businessmen, the Jews, the Germans, and even the revolutionaries, if they're well off. According to Madame Benckendorff, the* burzhui *are the incarnation of the Enemy. To be precise: the Enemy of the Revolution. In short, going by what comrade Lenin says, anybody who takes a bath, wears a white shirt, and reads with eyeglasses appears to be a parasite that must be squashed. Their goal is to crush every single one. With only a single exception: himself . . . The fact is that he's a descendant of lesser nobility.*

Madame Benckendorff and I have also discussed this unlikely piece of news: three delegates of the Russian Army have signed the preliminaries for an armistice with Germany. How could Lenin dare to propose a peace treaty with the Germans at the very moment when they've invaded a large part of his territory? If the Russians sign a cease-fire, they're betraying the Triple Entente. The position of the French ambassador and the British ambassador in Petrograd will grow untenable.

Madame Benckendorff has informed me that Sir George Buchanan was called back to England. His departure has left her depressed. She hasn't let it show, but I get the impression that she's devastated. I do sympathize with her. If England and the Allied powers abandon Russia, what will the future hold for our friends?

Yesterday, a delegation of twenty officers' wives came to the embassy to ask for our assistance. It was a profoundly emotional experience to see these unfortunate women reduced to begging. They're still wearing fur coats and proper dresses: those are the last vestiges of their past. Their husbands are imprisoned in barracks, where they live as convicts, granted nothing more than a soldier's pay. Their inferiors refuse to let them work elsewhere to earn their living. One of those ladies told me that her husband, a lieutenant in the Guard, managed to escape and that he spent the night unloading bags of coal at the train station. But the tovarishes caught him and confiscated the few rubles he had worked so hard to earn. As for the fates of the other Russians, those hailing from the middle classes, it can't be much more enviable.

The university professors have been forced to accept whatever manual labor they're assigned.

We have to wonder what will become of the burzhui. *All properties have been confiscated, bank accounts seized, salaries and pensions stopped. It's misery everywhere. I went to visit Madame Naryshkina to see a bust of Marie Antoinette that she hopes the Louvre will purchase. It's the only one that exists, all the others having been destroyed in our own French Revolution. It would be preferable if it didn't end up adorning a transatlantic pig farmer's salon sometime in the future. Many aristocratic families are leaving Saint Petersburg. Some were assassinated as they fled. The tsar's minister, old Goremykin—who was rumored to be the lover of Madame Benckendorff's mother—was just murdered in his villa in Sochi with his wife, his daughter, and his son-in-law.*

Madame Benckendorff told me that her mother's apartment, on the Fontanka embankment, has been requisitioned. Armed soldiers and several dozen women are sleeping in the salon, and all she's been granted is the mousehole she has to share with her servant.

Madame Benckendorff is currently housing her mother . . . But that will only be until her own apartment is confiscated. She doesn't harbor any illusions on this point. Soldiers have already come three times in the night to conduct searches of her place.

Several days ago, I saw a general and an Orthodox priest—all of Russia as it used to be—shoveling snow in front of the Winter Palace. That's the only work they're allowed to perform so they won't die of hunger. A group of young soldiers was watching them and snickering.

If Sir George Buchanan takes his entire embassy with him, we may be able to hire Madame Benckendorff for our own purposes.

Her background would be extremely useful to us in our negotiations with Ukraine. The war and the Revolution have encouraged separationist tendencies. The Ukrainians aren't holding out hope anymore for freedom and a progressive regime under Russian sovereignty, whether monarchist or Bolshevik. They're demanding the right of the people to dispose of themselves: the self-determination Trotsky has been banging on about.

Yesterday, their representative came to see the ambassador to confirm the Ukrainian people's ardent wish to obtain autonomy as they wait to gain full independence. They will look to France for how to organize their army, their finances, and their education system. Ukraine is the breadbasket of Russia. The fertility of its lands is proverbial. The effect its reorganization would have on our economic and intellectual standing shouldn't be underestimated. Madame Benckendorff would serve as liaison to the young republic.

Her marriage into the Baltic aristocracy may also be of some use to us in our communications with the Estonian patriots. They're fighting bitterly against the double threat of Germanization and Bolshevism. Our ambassador has promised them that once the Triple Entente has won the war and imposed its conditions for a peace agreement, the French government will pay special attention to smaller nations and their interests.

I don't dare tell Madame Benckendorff all the details just yet. For now, it's more than enough to simply trade the latest gossip with her.

❦

On December 25, 1917, on the eve of Meriel Buchanan's departure with her parents, the British ambassador received the members of his staff, the chancellery, and the military and naval missions—the entirety of the British community in the city. As well as his closest acquaintances in the Russian aristocracy. The farewell soirée, their final reception at the Saltykov palace.

It was only by sheer luck that the electricity had not been cut off that evening and that the crystal pendants of the chandeliers adorning the state apartments were shining in full illumination. As in the past. As before the war. As before the two revolutions.

The only dissonance was the sandbags that covered the windows all the way to the ceiling. And the strips of adhesive paper sealing the ballroom windows to keep German gas from wafting in: the White Army had seized that toxin. The monarchists were now fighting against the Bolshevik Red Army and using chemical weapons.

Another difference was that all the guests carried revolvers. Browning guns were visible in the pockets of the men outfitted in tuxedos or tailcoats. And the women's handbags hid small pistols with loaded cylinders. Behind the curtains it was possible to make out the silhouettes of rifles ready to use. And enough cans of food to outlast a siege.

As they held glasses, the officers took care to hide their sadness with social niceties.

The most despairing men of all were the lonely ones drinking heavily by the buffet: Captain Francis Cromie and Captain Djon von Benckendorff.

The Reval harbor had fallen. Cromie had had to sink his own fleet to keep the Germans from capturing the British submarines. He had been forced to send his troops home. It was a defeat he could not bear.

Moreover, he had just acquiesced to Sir George's requests, albeit unwillingly. While Cunard had left Petrograd already and Garstin was soon to follow, he would stay here at the embassy as the naval attaché.

As for Djon, his regiment, like all those of the Russian Army on the northern front, had been dissolved. The separate peace the Bolsheviks were negotiating with the Germans had compelled a general cease-fire.

On this Christmas night, he had put on the Guard's white uniform. He was determined to go on parading his officer's helmet and the red-and-gold insignia sewn onto his gray military jacket in the city's streets. It was a bravado that could result in being shot in the head at any moment.

Three years of war had aged him, leaving him stiffer and even more brittle than he already was.

The imperial family's future obsessed him. His fidelity to the monarchy was still unwavering. He repeated the reactionary sayings of Mommy's friends over and over.

As Moura heard him despairing over Russia's fate and mourning "the world of yesteryear" incessantly, she couldn't help but feel that his nostalgia was growing unhealthy.

In the time they had been apart, she had written him twice a week, as any good wife would. Even if she didn't tell him all the details of her life at the embassy and at Yendel, she still kept him fully apprised of who she spoke with, gave him the smallest details of what was happening with their children and to his mother, Madame von Benckendorff, and his three brothers, and updated him on the particulars of his property. Djon had replied with polite letters in which he revealed practically nothing . . . There was no personal news about his life on the front lines. The regularity of their exchanges, however, had granted them the illusion of genuine intimacy. The infrequency of Djon's military leaves had not jarred this impression of closeness in the slightest. Being at a great distance, with contact limited to the written word, they thought they got along.

But since the moment they had finally reunited, their differences had never been starker.

She often recalled the conversation she'd had with Madame de Méricourt in Berlin, when the countess had asked her how her husband, of Baltic origins, could bear to be torn between the tsar and the kaiser.

Torn was how Djon could be described now. Germany would soon occupy Estonia, the same Germany he hated and had fought against. The Germany he wanted to go on fighting against . . . but also the Germany he believed needed to triumph in order to quash the Bolsheviks.

He struggled amid a welter of contradictory emotions and impossible choices. On the one hand, his fidelity to the Romanovs and to the wage-it-all against the invader. On the other, his hatred of the Reds and his need to hope for the Germans' victory.

The evening, which they had all thought of as a final celebration, dragged on. How could they laugh? How could they even dance?

In her long, gray, satin dress, Moura seemed to be floating. She was wearing, pinned to her corsage, an orchid brooch that Garstino had given her, and she drifted from one circle of guests to the next with a faint smile on her lips. Like Djon, like Cromie and Cunard, she was drinking heavily. It was a habit she had acquired at Yendel as she had entertained her guests. She could hold her alcohol.

But this time, unlike in the past, she did not participate in the various conversations. She kept quiet, listening to everybody as they made promises to one another and traded thoughts on future prospects—*we'll see each other in England, we'll all meet up in London after the war, we'll dine together at the Ritz*—with seeming interest. Something in the sadness and steeliness of her gaze, however, made it clear that she wasn't really listening . . . that she was simply trying to capture in her memory the features and voices of her departing friends.

At midnight, Bobbie, the Cossack fiancé of Myriam Artsimovich, sat down at the Steinway piano and began playing the first notes of the national anthem of yesteryear, the tune that had accompanied so many of the greatest moments of Russian history: "God Save the Tsar."

The conversations died down. The entire group stopped moving. Everyone present was trying to forget the past that this music evoked.

But the pain in Djon's eyes, the suffering that devastated his face, revealed the extent of the despair they all felt.

❖

Meriel recounted how, two weeks later, on the dawn of Monday, January 7, 1918, she and Moura met again at the Finland train station of Petrograd:

> *No red carpet now, no bowing officials, no bouquets of flowers! Only a little group of friends collected on the platform, stamping their feet to try and keep warm, their faces pinched and white in the sizzling light of the gas flares high up in the roof. Miriam and Bobby Yonin, Moura, her lovely eyes a little sad. The Italian Ambassador, the Dutch and Danish Ministers, Captain Cromie, Dennis Garstin, Colonel Thornhill, and one or two members of the British colony.*
>
> *Moura's cheeks were wet with tears when I kissed her. . . . Dumbly, because I also could not trust my voice, I said good-bye to them all, and got into the train, and with a shrill whistle and a sudden jolt it started slowly on its way. Standing at the window I caught a last glimpse of Captain Cromie's clear-cut features, of Bobby Yonin in his Cossack uniform . . . Then the train gathered speed . . . Petrograd with all its memories was left behind.*

CHAPTER THIRTEEN

Something Entered My Life . . .

JANUARY–APRIL 1918

January 1918
Citizen Trotsky
People's Commissary for Foreign Affairs

DEAR COMRADE,

The bearer of this letter, Mister Robert Bruce Lockhart, has left for Russia.
Mr. Lockhart has been assigned by his government to a mission the specific aim
of which we are still unaware.
I know him personally and consider him an honest man. He is a gentleman
who understands our position and who is sympathetic to our cause. As such, I
consider his stay in Russia as beneficial to our interests, and I recommend him
to you.

The specific aim of the mission, which the author of this letter—
Maxim Litvinov, the Bolshevik chargé d'affaires in London—claimed to
be unaware of, could be summed up in two sentences: Stop Russia from
signing a peace treaty with Germany. And stop it at all costs.

Yes, but how?

Sir George Buchanan's return and England's refusal to recognize
Lenin's leadership had deprived the British government of a diplomatic
relationship with the Reds.

The only solution was to send an unofficial agent to Petrograd to keep up the conversation with the Soviets. The challenge was immense. If Lenin signed the armistice, Germany would withdraw its troops from the Russian front line and send them to the western front. And if they did, no army would be strong enough anymore to fight them off.

Convince the Bolsheviks to continue the war, even though their popularity was premised on the possibility of peace. The order was clear enough.

But the real question was: how?

Mr. Lockhart had carte blanche.

At the Foreign Office, the choice of such an emissary had brought about interminable conversations. A wager, a gamble that the politicians were hardly relishing. But fundamentally, at this stage, what did they have to lose?

All things considered, Robert Bruce Lockhart, notwithstanding his youth and his reputation as an adventurer, presented many advantages. First of all, he spoke Russian. He was known to be very literary and well connected to the left-wing intelligentsia. He had met Lenin's great writer friend, Maxim Gorky, and chaperoned H. G. Wells during his trip through Russia in 1914.

In Moscow, Lockhart had spent more than six years as vice-consul and then consul for England. Ambassador Buchanan was very visibly satisfied with his services. He had even recommended him warmly to the ministries, arguing that he had a larger-than-life intelligence, energy, and acumen.

Upon further scrutiny, his origins (he was Scottish, from a lineage of many rather belligerent clans, including the McGregors), his age (he was thirty years old), his health (he was an excellent rugby and soccer player, known to have an unparalleled physical strength), his taste for risk, and his charm all proved to be considerable assets.

He was married, but rumor had it the couple was struggling and his wife had not been happy in Moscow. Perfect! He would go alone. God only knew how things would work out . . .

On Monday, January 14, 1918, a week after having accompanied the Buchanans to the train station, Garstin and Cromie were pacing back and forth down the platform again. They had come to welcome the consul—their old Moscow comrade—and celebrate his return. The three men greeted each other with sturdy handshakes.

They were the same height, the same strength. All three were tall, athletic, with dark hair parted on the side. But what was most striking about Lockhart wasn't the regularity of his features, his sheer beauty (as was the case for Cromie), or his kindness and distinction (as was the case for Garstin), but his extraordinarily youthful look. With his slightly protruding ears, he could have passed for a kid. But a kid with an athlete's shoulders, more used to running than walking. With an effervescent, excited bounce to his step.

And then there was his voice: the singularity of this Scottish brogue, which they could have picked out of a thousand others. A rapid-fire yet precise diction, a register that was at once arrogant and self-mocking, self-assured and modest. It was a perfect mix of boundless pride, humor, daring, and whimsy.

"Garstin has reserved a room for you next to his own at the Hotel Astoria tonight. But as of Sunday, you and your men will have your own apartment on the Palace Embankment, right by the embassy."

"Moura was the one who found it. She negotiated the lease with the owner, who needed it to survive."

"Madame von Benckendorff," Cromie added. "Do you know her?"

"No."

"Of course you do! You met her at the embassy."

"That's possible."

"In any case, she knows you for sure! Moura knows everybody, even the Bolshevik ministers you came to meet . . . Don't tell Garstin you don't remember this woman, he'd have a fit. She's the love of his life," Cromie said. "He's not going to say a word about it, but he's bankrupting himself with orchids and dying of lovesickness. And all she's doing in return is taking care of his dog."

"You'll find the city's changed," Garstin cut in as he lugged the suitcase onto the seat of the military car.

Cromie got into the driver's seat.

"You missed the best of the festivities: the October Revolution. A drunken party at the Winter Palace."

The two officers weren't unaware of why Lockhart had had to leave Moscow in September. Buchanan had unilaterally sent him back to London to cut short the affair he had been having with a Frenchwoman, a lady hailing from the theater world who the ambassador considered to be of ill repute. A forced homecoming in order to quash the affair.

Lockhart was well used to this sort of scandal. When he worked on a rubber-tree plantation in Malaysia, he had taken the liberty of abducting the daughter of a Malaysian chief. He had lived with his princess for nearly a year before malaria and the diplomatic services had forced him to break camp.

Petrograd was indeed unrecognizable. Gone was the time when men in fur hats and white coats took shovels to deal with the snow. Now it was black and icy, piled up in scattered blocks. It covered the corpses of dead horses that littered the avenues. The car veered between the mounds and skidded across Nevsky Prospect. Its progress was slowed even further by pedestrians walking in the middle of the street, themselves trying to avoid the patches of ice slipping off the roofs in entire sheets.

"All these people are dying of hunger," Garstin mentioned.

"And all these people are afraid," Cromie added. "The Bolsheviks have been bleeding the city dry."

"The anarchists, you mean," Garstin said.

"The Bolsheviks! A hamstrung government that's leading a reign of terror with all the tricks of a mob boss . . . And Lockhart, do I understand right that you've come to help them?"

The "consul" sidestepped the question:

"If the Allied powers don't recognize the Soviet government, if the Allies don't help Lenin, then he'll sign this damned armistice. The only way for us to win the war is to accept the revolution's legitimacy."

At those words, Cromie couldn't help jerking the steering wheel:

"Nonsense, Lockhart! You don't know what you're talking about . . . You haven't seen those bastards at work!"

❖

On January 14, 1918, Djon Benckendorff was also on the platform at the Finland Station, hoping against hope to catch the last train for Estonia. He was leaving behind his wife and children, as well as his mother and mother-in-law. The peasant revolts they had narrowly missed being targeted by that summer had only worsened, and the violence they now wreaked was unprecedented in the Yendel area. Many of the neighboring estates had been ransacked and set on fire while their owners were tortured. Djon was determined to retake control of the peasants and, once he had tamed them, bring his family back at Easter.

It was with a heavy heart and no small measure of bitterness that he was leaving. His disagreements with Moura—who he no longer called Marie—now seemed far more serious than anything that could be easily resolved. Oh, she still showed him that same perpetual graciousness she was famous for. No household arguments, no screams: neither of the two Benckendorffs would ever stoop to insulting the other. But the lack of overt fighting hinted at the futility of any explanation.

On all fronts, she seemed to avoid any confrontation. "Wait and see" remained her motto.

As if she hadn't seen with her own eyes what those thugs were capable of! But it was impossible to get her to confess any antipathy, impossible to get her to criticize how they acted.

By affecting not to judge how the Bolsheviks acted and to respect their ideas—the "struggle for a more just society"—she was pushing him to his limits.

How could she betray her kind this profoundly?

He needed her to share his indignation, to understand his fury. But she didn't. She would only advocate for half measures. She would concede that this chaos didn't do the Bolsheviks any favors, but she refused to acknowledge the dishonor and shame they were bringing down upon Russia.

It was true that he had once found her too easygoing. Too young. But thus far, he'd never stopped respecting her. Even though he'd felt, for a long time now, that she was a terrible mother.

Oddly, ever since he began esteeming her less, he'd somehow desired her with a violence, even a brutality, that he'd never experienced before. During their last reunion in Petrograd, at the start of his discharge, he had loved her with some measure of passion. And Moura had met him with equal impulsiveness.

For a single moment, they were reunited . . . or rather, unified. A brief unification.

Now, if he wanted to possess her, he would have to beg her or force her. And he had no taste at all for rape. Neither pleading nor assault felt right to him. However, oddly enough, the more foreign his wife seemed to him, the more he hungered for her.

As for the rest, Moura's visible boredom, the forbearance with which she listened to his complaints about the Reds and his sighs when he grew overwhelmed by his horror for the present, was exasperating.

Whose side was she on? The Soviets'? If only she'd come out with it! What did she think? Was she a Communist? Was she or wasn't she?

She had a way of somehow not hearing the question, of looking away just as the question was being asked, that drove him mad. As if saying "yes" or "no" was so uninteresting that neither word warranted the air into which it was uttered.

She was just impossible to pin down.

Djon didn't understand her anymore.

"You need to keep the ball of thread in your hands," his grandmother used to tell him over and over when, as a child, he would untangle the mess of threads for her to sew with. "Hold it tight . . . Otherwise it gets all tangled up."

When it came to Moura, it had indeed gotten all tangled up. All he could make of it was his doubt and his confusion. There was no direction, no discipline in her that he could figure out . . . No decency whatsoever.

What he did give her credit for was her courage. She went out of her way to ensure her family's survival. She was indefatigable as she went down into the courtyard ten times a day, carrying up bucketloads of snow, bringing back wooden poles she had stolen from God knew where.

There was nothing to scold her about there. On her own, she did the work of five maids from yesteryear. If she took pleasure in it, so much the better: she could thank Comrade Lenin for that!

During this month in Petrograd, the only person he had taken any comfort in was Mommy, who unashamedly told everyone that she was pinning all her hopes on the German forces' arrival. She went so far as to say she was overjoyed that they had invaded Ukraine and that they had installed a dictator they kept under their thumb—who was a distant relative of her son-in-law Kochubey. That was the end of all the Bolsheviks in the Berezovaya region. The only thing that still troubled her was her frustration at having had to give Anna the estate and all its land so that the property, which would now be considered Russian, wouldn't be confiscated by the kaiser's armies.

She prayed every night for the Prussians to oust the Reds in the Yendel countryside and reestablish order in the same way they had in Ukraine.

Her High Nobility remained faithful to herself.

Physically, however, she was no longer the same. The murder of her former lover, Goremykin; the loss of her apartment on the Fontanka embankment; and the sale of Berezovaya to her daughter had left her a shell of herself. She had once been a voluptuous woman, but now Mommy was merely a little old lady who could never stop trembling. Her weakness was pitiful to see. Moura, who watched as she wasted away, could not stop worrying about her health.

Djon's mother wasn't in much better shape. The world was growing darker with each day.

❖

Djon was disillusioned with his marriage, but what did Moura feel? Her husband's departure had been a relief, if nothing else.

Djon's bitterness, his habit of rehashing the past over and over while refusing to understand that the past was firmly past, that it would never return, distressed her. It was hard enough to live in the present, and she needed to at least try to believe in the future.

She was struggling to keep her faith and told herself that with just a little imagination, everybody could understand the workers' and peasants' plight.

What could be more natural than the factories belonging to those who worked there and the land belonging to those who tilled it? What could be more reasonable? The horrors resulting from the lower class taking possession might be nothing more than the turbulence of a necessary current.

And, notwithstanding what Djon felt, the monarchists were no more civilized than the Soviets. The White Army turned out to be even more abominably cruel than the Reds. The two camps practiced the same methods . . . Heaven help the peasant Djon would punish!

She often thought of her father, Senator Zakrevsky. Hadn't he predicted the revolution in his writings? She remembered hearing him say over and over that Russia, with its superstitious aristocracy, blind and blinkered Russia, was headed straight for disaster. He had said that catastrophe was imminent, unless there was a complete regime change.

She recalled the urgency in his voice as he argued for installing a parliamentary monarchy in the British model. Or even a republic with institutions akin to France's, even though he didn't like the country . . . It still would have been better than the obscurantism the turn-of-the-century Russian aristocracy was then championing.

Starting in her teen years, she had supported his progressive ideas. And the war, which had laid bare the negligence of the tsar's functionaries, the corruption of his ministers, and the incompetence of his generals, had only underscored for her the necessity of such reforms.

She had cheered the democratic ideals of the February 1917 socialist revolution, wholeheartedly accepting, as did so many other young liberals—whether nobles or enlightened bourgeoisie—the tsar's abdication and his replacement by the lawyer Kerensky.

Kerensky's government had turned out to be a mess. Incapable of running the country and continuing the war.

Oh, *the war* . . . Moura did share Cromie and Garstin's faith in the need to win it—the necessity of stopping the Krauts, of fighting off Prussian imperialism—but she also shared the desire for peace that Jean Jaurès, whose articles she had once read fervently, championed.

Who wouldn't be willing to extol peace, this universal peace among peoples that the Bolsheviks claimed to strive for?

She understood, deep down, the interpersonal drama that the terrible Soviets had unleashed as Lenin led them to victory and power. The death, the grief, all the pain the men and women of her social circle suffered.

Her peers aroused her sympathy. She worked to help them and tried to secure them the protection of the Red Cross and England.

As for herself, she tried to avoid tragedy.

But she couldn't stop thinking about how the values of men like Djon Benckendorff were premised on selfishness and inherently led to injustice.

Lenin's ideals, at least, might revive hope and spark enthusiasm.

But there was no room in her mind for triumph or joy. Nor for hatred toward anyone, or intolerance, or contempt.

She only had room for the necessities of surviving each day, of caring for Mommy, who now had to rest a hand on Kira's shoulder just to make her way to her bed.

And above all, the conversations she had with her British friends. It was the last pleasure she took, the last miracle she could count on.

But for how much longer?

The peace talks at Brest-Litovsk meant that the Allied forces would soon have to break ranks with the Bolsheviks. England had been shrewd enough to call Sir George Buchanan back on account of his poor health. But nobody was unaware that the French and the Italians were also in a rush to shutter their embassies. The departure of all these diplomatic corps was only a matter of days.

Soon enough, Russia would be cut off from the rest of the world.

In material terms, Moura could bear anything. She could bear hardship and discomfort. But how could she survive cut off from the rest of the world?

❖

To hell with sadness and fear! To hell with misery and hunger! Tomorrow she would go sell what silver she had left, pawn the samovar and the candelabras. But that would be tomorrow. Today, January 30, 1918, she intended to prepare a birthday lunch for Cromie that would be equal to the celebrations they had had at Yendel. There were still so, so many things to appreciate. The thirty-six springs that Cromie had lived through, first. The promotion Garstino had just received. The return of their comrade Lockhart . . . *Life all the same*, as Anna, who had buried her first husband in Moscow and given birth to her second husband's daughter, said while expecting her fourth child at Berezovaya. Yes, life had to triumph.

Micky would take out the last embroidered tablecloth, the last bucketfuls of ice, the last pitchers of water. And the last box of caviar, the only thing Mommy had been able to hide when she had fled her apartment. And the three bottles of vodka hidden inside the children's toy chest.

Lockhart wrote:

It was at this time that I first met Moura. She was then twenty-six. A Russian of the Russians, she had a lofty disregard for all the pettiness of life and a courage which was proof against all cowardice. Her vitality, due perhaps to an iron constitution, was immense and invigorated everyone with whom she came into contact. Where she loved, there was her world, and her philosophy of life had made her mistress of all the consequences. She was an aristocrat. She could have been a Communist. She could never have been a bourgeoise. Later, her name was to become linked with mine in the final drama of my Russian career. During those first days of our meeting in St. Petersburg I was too busy, too preoccupied with my own importance, to give her more than a passing thought. I found her a woman of great attraction, whose conversation brightened my daily life. The romance was to come afterwards.

———

"So what do you think of the old consul?" Myriam Artsimovich asked as the two women went to the Saltykov palace, where they were helping pack files into boxes.

The allied ambassadors were evacuating Petrograd and moving to Vologda, a small town nearly three hundred miles east of Moscow, which would let them flee Russia should it fall under German occupation. This way, the foreign legations weren't completely leaving the country. *All the same*, Moura thought, *it's the end of an era.*

In the offices, she was dragging suitcases and Myriam was sealing boxes of papers: so many responsibilities that depressed the two of them.

Of all these jobs, burning the documents that the officials couldn't take with them and couldn't safely leave behind was the most painful. It served as an unshakable reminder of how abandoned and isolated they would be after the British had left.

"What about you?" Moura asked. "What do you think of him?"

Myriam gave her a sidelong glance.

"At Cromie's birthday celebration, you two seemed to be thick as thieves."

"He's smart."

"He was just eating you up with his eyes."

"He's the kind of man who eats up every woman with his eyes."

"Oh, of course, but you know it takes two to tango. You were just torturing poor old Garstino."

"Oh, stop it! Garstino has nothing to worry about . . . Lockhart is just a wild little thing."

"An old wolf, I'd say."

"He's certainly aware of the effect he has. But does he know what he's walking into?"

"Cromie said he has a high opinion of himself."

"Cromie is jealous."

"Don't be silly—Cromie likes him quite a lot, he actually admires him! Going by his words, Lockhart is a hothead, but that head is squarely on his shoulders. He's a phoenix who's always being reborn out of its ashes. He went back to London a diplomat who was done for. Dead of shame and broken. There was such a scandal around his committing adultery with someone the higher-ups didn't approve of that it practically cost him his career. He had only himself to blame. He thought he'd never get to see Russia again. But here he is, the sole representative of England, with the goal of influencing Lenin's decisions and changing the course of history . . . He's been reborn from the ashes, I tell you."

"But he's all alone: England will disavow him if he fails."

"Well, that just goes to show what kind of stuff he's made of. He's an adventurer . . . Clever and dangerous."

Moura held back from pushing the conversation further along. Every time someone talked about Lockhart in front of her, she was utterly unable to disguise her investment. Her curiosity was becoming obvious. She even started to feel a sort of lightheadedness at the mere mention of his name.

Was Myriam trying to warn her? Did she know they'd met up already?

Of course she had to know! How could she not have noticed that since Cromie's birthday, they had met up twice at Kuba, the last French restaurant in Petrograd, the last open restaurant . . . So expensive that only a foreign agent or a Soviet commissioner could go.

They had dined there together and greeted the dandy of the regime, the diplomat Lev Karakhan, who would be leaving in a few days for Brest-Litovsk to conclude the peace talks with Germany.

Being of Armenian extraction, Karakhan bore no resemblance at all to his Bolshevik colleagues. Sharply dressed, his hair thoroughly pomaded, his black beard trimmed thin, he affected a bygone foppishness. He never spoke out of line. His slickness had won him the mockery of his political adversaries. A lover of fine wine and cigars, he seemed to be the embodiment of the perfect diplomat. Which meant he was cunning and had no scruples.

Lockhart, who had been visiting his office at the Smolny Institute all that week, had invited him to join them at their table. Shooting back at the idea of Russia signing a separate peace with Germany through offers of aid from England, he had prolonged their discussion in this informal setting. Offers of financial and military support: the two mediators went through several rounds of negotiations in a lighthearted tone. But the conversation only lasted a few minutes and wrapped up with Lev Karakhan making Moura Benckendorff an invitation: would she like to come tomorrow, along with Mr. Lockhart, to the committee meeting on the conditions of the armistice?

Moura accepted on the spot, just as quickly as she'd accepted Lockhart's second invitation to have dinner at Kuba. Without Myriam and the other British officers watching them warily. The old world might be gone at this point, she thought, but this, at least, was one upside! All the stifling social conventions had gone out the window. A woman could spend an evening out with a man who wasn't her husband without anyone raising a fuss, or even paying any mind.

But she would come to realize that she was sorely mistaken on this point.

Her one-on-one meetings with the agent of His Majesty King George V were quite the talk of their British friends. They were all laughing up their sleeves . . . Lockhart, the same as always! They wondered: had he somehow managed to catch mysterious, elusive Mrs. Benckendorff in his net?

"Oh, it's clear she's smitten," Cromie muttered as he took a drag on his pipe. "That's all she's ever wanted to be!"

The most surprised one, however, wasn't Cromie or her devoted admirer Garstino. It was Captain William Hicks, Lockhart's close friend and co-conspirator.

Hicks had been to Yendel in the past. Over the two years he had spent in Petrograd, he had taught the tsar's armies, then those of the Bolsheviks, how to shield themselves against German gas attacks. It was thanks to him, Captain William Hicks—a world-renowned specialist in counteracting chemical weapons—that the ambassador of England had had all his windows sealed against drafts on that Christmas night. Hicks had gone back to the United Kingdom on the same train as the Buchanans, and upon his return to London he had fallen in again with his old friend

Lockhart. And when Lockhart was sent out on his second mission, he had asked for Hicks to come along as his right-hand man: the war minister had given his consent.

So Hicks was back, to Moura's great pleasure.

She used to lavish the same attention on Hicks that she had on Ed, Crow, and Garstino, and she had come to affectionately call him Hicklet. This nickname wasn't a jab at his shortness or thinness. Hicks looked every bit an athlete, after all, even though his beauty wasn't quite as striking and his health wasn't quite as hearty as those of his friends. He was a wiry whipcord boy who lifted weights and went running every morning. His endurance was notorious. His demeanor, too. He did have a sense of humor, yes, but honor was no joke to him and he was quick to call out any flimsiness on his friends' part. In short, Hicks was a prudish fellow wholly at odds with the charm, daring, and nonchalance of an adventurer like Lockhart, who was the perfect exception to all his moral stances.

As far as women went, he sneered at flirting, hated coquetry, and could not make heads or tails of the rules of seduction.

His upbringing had been too prim and proper and Protestant, so he had taken Moura's warmth as an advance and mistaken her friendliness for something rather more. Presuming himself to have hit gold, Hicklet had fallen in love.

His disappointment upon learning the truth had been crushing.

Now he was in love with someone else. And even though he was still sympathetic toward his former inamorata, he kept his distance. Fundamentally, Moura remained a mystery. She had escaped him: she escaped them all.

He considered her as generous as she was interested. As spontaneous as she was calculating. Because ultimately, the privileged relationships she had ingeniously established with the British embassy's officers protected her from the new regime's persecution. Thanks to Cromie's and Garstin's friendship, she could expect many, many benefits: a reference so she could take her mother to the best doctors at the former British Hospital . . . a double ration from the American Red Cross . . . In his head Hicks was counting off the examples. He did concede that she hadn't asked for any of this explicitly. And certainly, none of it was for herself. But he was clear on the main point: she cultivated the relationships that served her best. Under her cover of affection and hospitality, she was maneuvering.

The interest that his boss, his friend, had for this strange animal, something between a sly cat and a high-flying bird, this inscrutable sphinx that Moura remained in his eyes, worried him. He wasn't worried at all about her survival, however. The only person he was worried about was Lockhart.

According to Hicks, Lockhart had only one weakness, but it was a very serious weakness: women, pure and simple.

It was true that he had made plenty of them cry. And his wife's tears were still flowing fresh. But ultimately, he was the one who had suffered the most because of his liaisons. His Malaysian princess, his French actress, his many Muscovite trysts had all earned him, if not the distrust of London's politicians, at least that of the other military missions in Petrograd. It was out of the question to let him commit, here, now, the same errors all over again! Hicks was well positioned to know what his former superior, General Knox, who Lockhart had had to battle on other fronts, thought of Mrs. Benckendorff.

Hicks took care not to broach the topic with him, but merely made it clear that this Russian dame, with a husband who was rather too German, would amount to a conquest of zero value. An easy target.

He might have thought he had put Lockhart off, but he would soon learn just how sorely he was mistaken.

It was impossible for a puritan like Hicks to realize just how fast the former consul carried out his business. It was difficult even to imagine how swift his assaults were.

His manner of wooing wasn't discreet and gentle, as Moura was used to seeing. Rather, his approach was just as direct as it was sentimental.

In a more general way, Lockhart spoke, Lockhart acted exactly as he felt. Utterly sincere, but in the present only.

Even though there was no question that he was too absorbed by his negotiations with Lenin's government to grant Mrs. Benckendorff "more than a passing thought," he had already talked to her about the emotions that overwhelmed him in her presence. Already, after their first conversation, in the sleigh that was carrying her down Shpalernaya Street, he had attempted to kiss her.

She had pushed him away, pretending to laugh about it, accusing him of having had too much to drink, calling him an absolutely devilish skirt-chaser and a cheap seducer.

The gaiety, the clear nonchalance with which she handled his occasional attempts—every one of them failures—allowed them to remain good friends. He laughed right alongside her. And promised not to try again.

Thus far he had kept his word, which gave her the freedom to steer their relationship. Conferences in Smolny. Books loaned to each other. Endless discussions about Pushkin's poetry as compared to Lermontov's. Future plans for Russia, around Lockhart's samovar.

Of all those moments spent together, she retained the memory of shared delight, a slightly different kind of conspiratorial pleasure than she'd enjoyed with Garstino. But she stayed calm. She believed she was serene.

There was no use in Myriam trying to alert her to the very evident danger ahead. At first blush, Moura had understood exactly who and what she was dealing with. She would never have a tryst with such a character. Not even a vague romance.

Lockhart struck her as interesting, yes . . . Fascinating when he led her down the hallways of Bolshevik power so that, thanks to his efforts, she would better understand the events that were threatening the world.

Intellectually: a force of nature. A pretty boy, to top it off. Courageous. And well read. What more could be hoped for?

As for the rest . . . Lockhart's diligence, his declarations, his gallantry all counted for very little. For her, and for him, it was a small moment of bliss. A smidge of lightness, a dollop of humor in the tense, sad, and chaotic normalcy of daily life.

No more. No less.

Lockhart wrote that on Sunday, March 3, a month and a half after his arrival, the Russian delegates signed the preliminary peace at Brest and that the formal ratification would take place in Moscow on March 12.

The separate peace with Germany wrested away all the territories it had conquered: Ukraine, the Baltic countries, Belarus, and Poland. So Lockhart's mission had been an utter failure.

Earlier on, he had written that he was staying at his post for two reasons. The first was that as long as the Bolsheviks had not yet signed the peace terms, the situation could still prove advantageous to him. And the second was that he felt it wise to maintain contact with the Bolsheviks as long as they continued to control the government.

And so he was swept up by the party's movements.

Lenin left on March 10, and the political center shifted to Moscow. Five days later, Trotsky informed Lockhart that they would be leaving the morning after, as he had just been named the commissar for war.

When they reached Moscow, what Lockhart saw was wholly new to him. Few of his Russian and English friends were still there, and even fewer of the rich merchants' residences—they had been commandeered by the anarchists, who had gone even farther in Moscow than in Petrograd. But the entire city was remarkably vibrant. Everyone seemed to be eagerly awaiting the Germans, expectantly looking forward to their salvation. The cabarets were open all night, even the one in the Hotel Elite, which was serving as the men's headquarters.

During that early period, Lockhart and his colleagues had little difficulty meeting with Trotsky or speaking with Lenin. Lockhart also strove to stay in touch with his men in Petrograd. And with a woman, as well: Moura, who he realized was the best informed about goings-on in the former capital. The letters they exchanged would become a necessity for him; he awaited her words with increasing feeling.

Petrograd
March 20, 1918

Dear Lockhart,

Thank you for your kind little note, the kindest one anyone's ever addressed me. I do miss you dearly, and while this is a cliché, it's a cliché that does convey my genuine feeling.

The last of your compatriots left the city today: your departure seems to have stolen away what courage they had left! Joking aside, however, nobody's left here. Even Garstino has packed his bags. As I write, he's already reached you in Moscow. As for Cromie, he's in Oslo. Tell me, please, what your plans are: to leave, or to stay in Russia?

I wish you the best of luck and I hope, perhaps, to see you soon.

Moura Benckendorff

Petrograd
March 28, 1918

Dear Lockhart,

As I seem to be poorly these days, I don't know if I'll be able to come down to Moscow next week, as you suggest. What would you say to the following weekend?

Send me a telegram, please, to let me know if that would be too late for you, or if you've already left the country.

I doubt it. Why would you leave? But who knows?

Petrograd has become a provincial little town. I imagine Moscow is hardly any better.

And how are you doing? Have you managed to resist the advances of the feminine species peopling the Hotel Elite? Or have you already fallen under the lure of the sirens' song?

I hope my stay in Moscow will be possible and that it will raise my morale somewhat.

Until soon.

My warmest wishes.

Moura Benckendorff

❖

In alluding to her morale and her poor health, Moura glossed over the reality: that Djon had opened Yendel to the Germans, and that he had called for his family to join him there.

She also passed over in silence the fact that her mother, whom their doctor had just diagnosed with cancer, could not undertake such a trip. Which forced her to stay in Petrograd to take care of her.

But most important, she did not say that on this Lutheran Easter Sunday, she had sent off the three children—eight-year-old Kira, four-year-old Paul, and three-year-old Tania—on the stagecoach to Reval. Her plan was to join them as soon as Mommy was able to move. Until then, Micky would watch over them. It was a dangerous trip for the elder Mrs. Benckendorff, as well, made even more difficult by her two fox terriers, whose barking could very easily catch the guards' attention.

The risks were equally great on both sides of the border. It was terrible.

In the eyes of the Bolsheviks, this family was nothing more than a group of aristocrats fleeing the country. In the eyes of the Germans, a group of Russian spies. Micky was forbidden to say a word. Should anybody in Estonia hear her English accent, she would be shot down immediately as a citizen of one of Germany's enemy nations.

In any case: the firing squad for the adults. Prisons and orphanages for the children.

The last detail that Moura didn't mention: her sleepless nights waiting for news. Her fears for all their lives.

She held back from telling Lockhart that she was so anxious for the children's safety that she would pace up and down the interminably dark corridor, her hands clasped over her chest to hold together the two ends of her nightdress, but really to calm her heart's furious pounding. She came, she went, she wandered from one room to the next, from her bedroom to the nursery, only ever stopping to listen to Mommy's snores behind the shut door. The thought that she might have done the wrong thing gnawed at her endlessly.

Should I have said no to this journey? Yes, yes, no question of it. I shouldn't have let them go! But how could I have turned down Djon's orders for Paul and Tania to come?

He said they'd be safer in Yendel than in Petrograd in the end! But was he right about that? Or was he wrong? Should I have made the trip with Micky so I could protect them all? Yes, yes, no question about it: I should have done it all differently! But how could I have abandoned Mommy all alone here?

She listened to her mother's breathing as it occasionally stopped behind the wall . . . Mommy was now mortally sick, Mommy was defenseless in this apartment, which could be requisitioned at any moment.

Should she have . . . ? No question about it! But what would she have forbidden, what would she have allowed? What should she have done?

Her worries about her family's safety had driven her past the point of reason: she had lost her famous intelligence so admired by Garstino and her English friends, who were now working in Moscow. Her English friends? Only the memory of their close friendship during their stays in Yendel and the prospect of making that closeness, that magical experience, happen once again, one last time, gave her the strength to hope for the future.

She didn't linger on what she hoped might happen if she stayed with the British legation. But going down to Moscow seemed like a dream that needed to become a reality so she could confront what might come next . . . All the tragedies she sensed would be coming.

What words were there for the relief she felt upon receiving Djon's telegram?

No sooner had he confirmed that the children had safely arrived than she rushed to orchestrate this escapade she had promised herself and to set the particulars of her trip to Moscow in motion.

❖

Lockhart wrote:

Since saying good-bye to her in St. Petersburg at the beginning of March, I had missed her more than I cared to admit. We had written to each other regularly, and her letters had become a necessary part of my daily life. In April she came to stay with us in Moscow. She arrived at ten o'clock in the morning, and I was engaged with interviews until ten minutes to one. I went downstairs to the living room, where we had our meals. She was standing by a table, and the spring sun was shining on her hair. As I walked forward to meet her, I scarcely dared to trust my voice. Into my life something had entered which was stronger than any other tie, stronger than life itself.

BOOK II

The Second Life of Moura Benckendorff

A Romance of Destiny: From Bedazzlement to Shadows

April 1918–October 1918

CHAPTER FOURTEEN

The Great Adventure

APRIL 15–23, 1918

Waht Lockhart had wished for, what she had probably dreamed of without daring to say so, had come to pass.

And now, on the return train bringing her back to Petrograd, she tried to understand.

When he had embraced her tightly in the middle of the Hotel Elite's salon, she had frozen in fear. It was a shock that had left her dizzy.

A week later—the weekend had lasted seven days and seven nights—her daze was still overwhelming.

But of all the feelings she had felt, the one that still lingered was one she could name easily: joy.

◈

The train. The return . . . She had climbed onto the third berth of the compartment, the uppermost one, meant as a luggage rack.

Just as on the train she had taken to Moscow, Lockhart had reserved her this place above the crowd that also served as a bunk. It was a favor: in the regular trains, first and second class had disappeared. All that remained was the "special car" for police chiefs, the cattle cars packed to the gills with peasants and refugees, and the car for usual passengers. The berths in that car were reserved for foreign press correspondents and semi-official members of the regime. They were off-limits to the *burzhui*.

She lay there a long while, stiff like a mummy, her hands crossed over her belly, her eyes wide open. The narrowness of the luggage rack kept her from moving at all, and she barely had any air beneath the car's ceiling. Just as on the train she had taken in.

But my life now is nothing like it was when I was coming here!

Yet just as on the train she had taken in, she stayed awake the whole night. The grind of the axles, the racket of the wheels braking at the train stations cut through her thoughts. And each stop entailed crowds that always went through the same motions. The men and women jostled around the hot-water fountain right under her head. She could hear their kettles clanging against the pipes, their arguments at the tap over who should go first, the hiss of their tea after they had gone back and sat down on their bales of hay. The babies crying and the soldiers jabbering. Some were whining about how hungry they were, others about how much everything cost, and still others were discussing whether peace was possible and what Germany's intentions were. The stench of sweat, the smell of damp fur-trimmed coats, the odor of sheepskins all nauseated her. What a far, far cry all this was from the Pullman cars of her trips to and from Yendel!

But this was an even farther cry from her own thoughts while she was on the train there.

What *had* she been thinking? She pondered the question that night. When she had left Petrograd, going down to Moscow on Friday—*my God, was it only Friday? It felt like a century had passed!*—had she had any idea what would come next? She tried to remember.

Fundamentally, from the outset, nothing about this trip had gone as expected.

First, Myriam was supposed to go with her. What were the plans they'd had? To go visit Lockhart, yes. But also Bobbie, Myriam's fiancé—the Cossack officer with Anglo-Russian roots who was working for Lockhart—as well as Garstino and Hicklet and all their British friends. They had gotten the same pass, booked two rooms on the third floor of the Hotel Elite. But at the last minute, Bobbie had let them know that he would be coming up to Petrograd himself. And so Myriam had canceled her ticket.

Another change in plans was that Garstino and Hicklet were supposed to come pick her up. But they, too, had left the city.

Just as she was stepping down onto the train station platform in Moscow, Captain William Hicks was headed toward Vladivostok to conduct an inspection in the Soviet East. Lockhart had ordered him to go see if Trotsky had been telling the truth when, in a fit of rage and insanity, he'd insisted that the Allies—especially the Japanese—had landed in Siberia . . . If so, the countries of the Triple Entente had broken their commitment to the Bolsheviks. If so, they had broken the word that Lockhart himself had given to Lev Karakhan in promising him that the Allies would never fight the Germans on Russian lands without Lenin's authorization, that England would never intrude upon Russia without the consent of the Bolshevik government.

If so, if Trotsky was telling the truth, then all his efforts would have been for naught. A catastrophe. And not just for the relationships he had forged with the Reds.

So he had dispatched his other colleague, Captain Denis Garstin, to Vologda—the tiny town nearly three hundred miles from Moscow that the Allied ambassadors had retired to—to understand his government's latest plans. Garstin would have to get General Knox to explain the changes in England's strategy—changes that Knox, who hated Lockhart, hadn't bothered to alert him to.

And so, amid all these crises, he had forgotten to warn Moura about their friends' absence from Moscow.

But was it really a mere oversight?

In any case, he had taken care not to warn her with a telegram, had taken care not to make it possible for her to postpone her stay. As she recalled this, she smiled to herself. Lockhart knew that she would end up alone with him. He had wanted it that way.

But he hadn't come to fetch her any more than Garstino had: he had dispatched a police car and a driver to the train station. It was a favor that Felix Dzerzhinsky, the director of the Cheka, was doing for him because he and Lockhart were on very good terms. This same car had shown him the night before just how Trotsky got rid of his enemies.

Trotsky, who had just been named war commissar, was working to clear all the thuggish anarchists out of Moscow. He had drawn on their own methods as he had sicced the Cheka's men on thirty-six of their cells. Hundreds had been shot down on the same day, at the same time, in their hideouts throughout the city. This butchery had essentially beheaded the majority of the movement in a single go.

The day after the massacre, the director of the Cheka had invited the agent of Her Majesty the Queen of England and the head of the American Red Cross to go around and see where the carnage had happened. They had visited the apartments, looked at the blood-spattered walls, returned, and inspected the corpses. A warning to everyone else. For their convenience, Dzerzhinsky had sent along his own assistant as a guide, as well as his personal car.

With his usual cockiness, Lockhart had asked to make use of the car himself the next day.

Standing in front of the dressed-up chauffeur—though it wasn't really a uniform: helmet, black leather boots and jacket, a large Mauser gun in his holster—Moura had wavered.

But she had no choice.

Moscow, like Petrograd, was falling to pieces. There was no transportation. *Izvozchiks* no longer existed: most of the coach drivers had died of hunger, as had their horses. The trams had stopped running. As for crossing the city on foot, the spring thaw had turned the roads into impassable bogs.

But that wasn't what she wanted to remember.

As she opened her suitcase on the bed in her room at the Elite, as she hung her clothes in the armoire, took a bath, applied her makeup, did her hair, did she know what would happen next? Did she want it? Had she come *for* that?

In all honesty: no.

And yet, standing in front of the mirror that morning, her heart had pounded in excitement.

Indeed, ever since January—she did the calculations: she had known Lockhart since January 30, 1918, exactly two months and three weeks—

their exchanges had given her the same sensation of lightness, a delight she now felt was premonitory.

Let's see, let's see . . . Let's not exaggerate. Let's just wait and see . . . See what happens.

When she had come down to the dining room at the Hotel Elite, what had actually happened?

She had seen the silhouette of a person, taller, straighter than she'd remembered, rush at her. The force of his rapid footsteps underscored the directness of his advance.

She had seen, above the bow tie and the starched collar, a face with slightly protruding ears that was flushing with emotion, the uncertain face of a very young man. His plain gaze, fixed right at her, took her in with such visible admiration, such unrestrained desire, that she had been quite taken aback.

But even so, nothing could have prepared her for the feeling of his skin against hers, his smell, his softness as he had pulled her tight in an embrace. She hadn't moved. All she had done was simply close her eyes.

With her eyelids lowered, she had felt the blood boiling in their veins. She had felt their fusion. The same blood.

In fact, the pounding of her heart had grown so violent that she was scared she might faint.

And if she had extricated herself from this embrace, taken a step back, it wasn't, as he had been convinced, because she remained in full control of her faculties, in full mastery of herself—*solid Moura*—but because her head was spinning. This dizziness had forced her to reach out for a chair and sit down.

It was sheer luck that none of their friends had witnessed this moment. And especially not the unusual scene that followed. This meal, punctuated by no gestures, no words. Wholly at odds with the laughter they had enjoyed in Petrograd and the gossip they had traded at Yendel. Wholly at odds with the conversations at Lockhart's apartment, their discussions on the most complex topics. This time: nothing. They were unable to talk, or even to move.

This remove from reality, this silence that was so unlike them, this inability to even look at each other, belied the tumult of their feelings and the violence of their desire, underscored it far more clearly than any factual declaration could have.

For minutes on end they stayed seated at the table like that, facing each other, unmoving, their throats dry, straining toward one another, conveying nothing but the emotion that paralyzed them both. Even though they had lost all their clear-sightedness, they were still attentive, keenly aware of their mutual presence. Each detail stood out. As if she could smell the aroma of his cologne. As if she could feel the skin on his neck where it met his collarbone. He was thinking about this mouth he hadn't gotten to kiss yet, that he wanted to claim for himself, as he did with this throat.

He slowly got up and leaned forward, his elbows on the tablecloth as if to reach over the table to her.

She quivered and looked down, staring at her plate so as not to shut her eyes, so as not to completely lose herself in the astonishment that was blinding her.

Moura shook herself on the luggage rack: she wanted to get a grip again on the bigger picture, the other people in the room. She couldn't let herself get too quickly to the core of what was haunting her memories. *The core?* She couldn't put it into words.

The bigger picture? A black hole. She tried, to no avail, to recall a color, identify a shape, a noise.

In her defense, she had never come back there and sat down; they had taken all the rest of their meals in private, in Lockhart's suite.

A padded existence. Before. Almost heartsick with desire.

Then there had been the walk up to his room . . . And this happiness.

Her discovery of love with Lockhart had been so intense that she couldn't even bear to recall the memory of their kisses, their words. It was a physical, moral, emotional upheaval that had overcome her to the point that she couldn't give it language.

Enough!

Now, in the train, she needed to find, if not some sort of balance, at least some degree of calm.

Calm? But why should I need to find that? The situation's simple enough.

In fact, she felt completely serene. What was unbelievable was exactly that: this peace that wasn't fleeting. While she knew she was profoundly moved, that everything in her, the past and the present, was aquiver, that she was still trembling deep down . . . she had no doubts, no fear. No regret whatsoever.

No pain. No remorse.

She tried to think about Djon, but it was useless . . . She tried to think about her children. Her mother. What would they say? What would they think?

They wouldn't think anything.

Because they wouldn't know anything. And even if they did learn something, she would deny it. "Always deny!" Anna had once urged her.

She had tricked her husband, that much was true. *An adulterous woman.* But the reality of the fault she had committed, the wrong she had done and that she was sure she would repeat, had no effect at all on her happiness.

Her memories were too wonderful.

Let's forget Djon. He's an obstacle. She almost let herself think she hadn't loved him. She had respected him, yes. She felt affection for him. A kind of empathy ever since he had left for the war; a compassion she had sustained ever since he returned. But never this emotion she had just discovered—nothing even close to that!

Was she guilty of something? What, exactly?

She didn't see herself as guilty. Much less criminal. She had waited her whole life for this moment.

She had grown up, become an adult, learned how to live solely to be able to experience the moment when Lockhart had crossed the room and walked toward her. She even felt that she had been born the moment he had embraced her.

She felt the certainty of having always belonged to him. This man embodied her fate.

Without Myriam, without Garstino, without Hicklet, maybe word wouldn't get out about what had happened.

In any case, their adventure would be brief. They had to relish, to savor every precious second. As for later, they would just have to wait and see. The future didn't matter.

She knew he wasn't any freer than she was. He, too, was married. And she knew the clock was always ticking for a British agent in Russia.

What was surprising, though, was what she had discovered of Lockhart's character: how emotional he was, how incredibly fragile this man she had believed to be so direct, so audacious, turned out to be. But the truth was that he was still direct and audacious. Not many men were brave enough to describe their weaknesses, acknowledge their shortcomings, name their regrets and fears. He went so far as to list his failings, to show himself to her exactly as he was, without any false modesty.

In the span of a week, they had placed their full trust in each other. Bound by this mutual agreement between them, by all the memories and affinities they already shared. As close as they could have hoped to be had they known each other for years on end.

Lockhart maintained that his love for her hadn't arisen just yesterday. That he had realized it during Cromie's birthday, but, once burned by his previous mistakes, now he felt twice shy and had resolved not to think about how deep his feelings ran.

But their separation and their absence had crystallized matters. Fear had been overpowered by truth and erased completely. Now all bets were off. There was no going back.

She wanted to believe him; all their feelings seemed to lead toward this end point. Toward the one truth, the one certainty she had ever felt.

He confessed that he was awestruck by the sight of her, astounded by the sheer miracle of seeing her there next to him, waking up, falling asleep. Amazed by the wonder of being loved by her.

But did she love him? He never stopped asking her. He had a way of always fearing that he might lose her, of clinging to her the way a child might its mother, which touched her far more deeply than her son or daughter ever had. He was her tender, vulnerable little darling.

And she was far more at home within the circles Lockhart ran in—of politicians, intellectuals, the underworld—than any other milieu.

As she spent days and nights with him, she came to understand the extent of his obligations in Russia, the breadth of his activities on the international spectrum, how important and extraordinarily complex his work was.

She loved his courage, she loved his delightfulness, his intellect, his craftiness. She loved his need to charm her and to be loved by her. And when he begged her for compliments, when he needed her to reassure him, she confessed outright just how much she admired him. She trumpeted it. She felt so certain of her own existence, so removed from all fear of the future, that she felt utterly free in declaring how enraptured she was.

Nothing held her back from granting him what he needed from her. She was never scared that she might be exposed and might lose hold of herself, nothing hinted to her that she might be losing herself within him in letting herself be so enthralled. And for good reason: she was treading familiar ground. They were so much like each other.

Like her, Lockhart could live on multiple levels, within multiple spheres, could exist here and elsewhere at the same time. Like her, he was able to dance on a tightrope and catch himself just as he was about to fall. Like her, he was everything and its opposite. A man of action and indecision. He could work ten days in a row while barely sleeping or drinking or eating. He could also linger and complain, do nothing, and sleep, then play and drink and fornicate for the next ten days.

He didn't simply go back and forth; he was two men in one. Both rash and restrained. Sly and sincere. Harsh and gentle. Akin to the thousand-armed Shiva: as one arm slapped, the other stroked.

Like her, he could seem confusing to those who wanted to pin him down to a single set of characteristics, a single kind of morality.

At his best, he was a human being full of charm and fantasy. At his worst, he was a weather vane easily swayed by any passing breeze, an undisciplined subordinate, an immature colleague.

But one aspect remained constant: he was gifted with an energy, a vital force that allowed him to never simply be what was expected of him.

She instinctively understood his mental frameworks. He never needed to explain matters to her.

He, in turn, had realized with a magisterial certainty that no life was possible for him outside one with this woman. That without this woman beside him, he couldn't go on fighting. Or even living.

He truly loved her mixture of light and shadow. He loved her generosity and her reserve. This keen understanding of the world, her clear-eyed assessment of people, her calm judgments, her impartial conclusions. Her way of never raising her voice, and the passion that blazed in her always warm, often hoarse timbre.

He also loved how she never talked about herself, except to tell him that she loved him. Nothing about her personal life, about her memories. She told amusing stories, yes: the waltz she had danced with Wilhelm II in Berlin in 1911, or her meeting with the horrible Rasputin at the residence of one of Montenegro's princesses. She told those stories with devastating humor and absolute charm. She could make him laugh.

But her thoughts, her feelings, her fears remained a mystery. She never mentioned the relationship she had with her husband, nor the absence of her children, apart from a vague allusion to the nightmares they had had during their flight to Estonia. They were safe, all was going well, and there was no use revisiting the subject. What about her mother's health, which seemed to have been such a source of worry for her at the beginning of April? She shrugged as if she didn't know anything. Or as if she was resigned to whatever the future might bring. She didn't explain further. Did she get along well with her family? What sort of woman was Mrs. Zakrevsky? And what had become of her sisters? She smiled at his questions and did not answer.

Not a word about the difficulties she had faced in Petrograd, either.

The cold and hunger of last winter warranted no discussion. Nor did the poverty she must have endured.

He had seen the state of the apartment on Shpalernaya Street. He had been able to judge, in the disrepair that was present now, what must have been the luxury of the past. The traces of mirrors, the gaps of paintings, rugs, curtains: all those objects that had been sold or stolen.

He knew that Lenin was working to rub out the class she had been born into. And that with her famous name—an early Benckendorff had been the captain of the police force under the Iron Tsar, Nicholas I; another Benckendorff had been Tsar Nicholas II's favorite dignitary— she was a very easy target. At any moment she could be expelled from her home. At best, she'd be on the streets. At worst, she'd be arrested and locked up for being rich.

She said nothing about her fear of dying. And nothing about her grief at having lost everything. She did not pity herself. She didn't even hint at regret over the carefree nature of her past.

But here and now, he was astonished at how open she was to pleasure!

He loved the sensuality of her womanly body with its heavy breasts, its wide hips, its powerful legs, which knew how to be gentle and supple in love, sinuous and caressing, as light and unpredictable as a cat.

Moura or balance.

Moura or harmony.

He had never met such a partner before. This intellectual prodigy, this voluptuous marvel. When he talked to her, when he kissed her, it was the same kind of headiness. With her, the line between the mental and the sensual, the thought and the gesture, simply vanished. Intellectual excitement mixed comfortably with pleasure.

She attracted him, she absorbed him. Ever since the world had come into existence, she had been meant for him. He had finally found the love of his life, the companion he had always dreamed of. His soul mate.

In the absence of Hicks and Garstin, Lockhart had also found the best possible colleague. The sharpest one. The most efficient one. During their week together in Moscow, she had translated dispatches for him, typed up his responses.

They loved nothing more than sharing these tasks, which allowed them to go on being together in daily life.

In the real world, that of action, they had so much to do.

Events kept happening, faster and faster, and history swallowed them all up.

In the second half of April 1918, the peace treaty between Trotsky's armies and the kaiser's was signed. It called for installing a German ambassador in Moscow: the very Prussian Count Mirbach. The Bolsheviks had set him up with his officers in the nicest part of the city: the Hotel Elite. Lockhart didn't take the news sitting down. Germans on the same floor as Her Majesty's agent? He exploded! It was an insult. How dare Trotsky's government force him to meet the enemy in the very hallways of his own legation?

In light of Lockhart's fury, Trotsky pulled back: he was still trying to be careful. Who knew whether the shameful Brest-Litovsk peace treaty, in which Russia had accepted all Germany's conditions, would last? Better not to get on the wrong side of the British. Another residence would be found for His Excellency Count Mirbach. The matter was dealt with.

But Lockhart was still furious . . . Now that the Russians and the Germans were working together hand in hand, he had nothing left to lose. And so he made an about-face and took the opposite tack with his politics.

Now here was no use trying to convince England of the Bolshevik regime's legality. There was no use trying to supplant the Krauts in Lenin's affections. And above all, there was no use arming and helping fund the Soviet regime so it could wage war.

It was too late for all that.

Of course Lockhart would keep fighting against the Japanese army's advances; their presence in Siberia had been confirmed by Captain Hicks. He would keep pretending to rebel against General Knox's tactics, which Captain Garstin was grappling with on his behalf in Vologda.

It was all a bluff.

The truth was that he had sent Garstin to Vologda for another reason:

to convince the British general staff that he hadn't given himself over body and soul to the Bolshevik cause. He needed to contradict what Knox had been telling the war minister and the foreign minister—Lockhart, a Communist!—in order to undermine his reputation and threaten his career prospects back in London.

Lockhart fought back by framing Knox as a reactionary who was too blinkered to properly understand the Russian reality: wasn't he still trying to depict Lenin and Trotsky as two mercenaries in the pay of Germany? The way Knox put it, the people at the head of the Soviet regime were actually German officers bankrolled by the kaiser.

Rubbish, absolute rubbish!

The Reds hated Germany as much as they hated England, France, and Italy: all those nations were capitalists.

And Knox was still a pest and an idiot.

Nonetheless, Lockhart would back up his strategy. He would help the Japanese. Which would be part of their plan to secretly undermine the Bolsheviks.

On the one hand: he would stay persona grata. He would retain his access to Trotsky and, for the Soviet hierarchy, continue appearing to support the regime. It wouldn't be very hard for him to maintain that cover. The Bolsheviks were able to decrypt some of his dispatches. He'd make sure to let the code slip into the hands of an agent so they could read his finely crafted sentences supporting their cause and their interests. So they could see how he advocated for them in the West.

On the other hand: he would discreetly prepare for the Allied forces' military invasion. A large-scale assault. Unbeknownst to Lenin, they planned to maintain a front that would keep the Germans within Russia and prevent them from marshaling their troops elsewhere.

And consequently, he would fund a resistance network that would work to undermine the infrastructure here. Derail trains. Destroy telephone and telegraph lines, and any other means of communication. Set fire to factories. Disseminate propaganda that would demoralize Trotsky's soldiers. Attack those running the regime.

In the end: he would topple Lenin, arrest his henchmen, clear out the

Soviets. Replace the Bolsheviks with a party better suited to the Allies. And wipe Communism off the world map. Nothing less would suffice.

And so Lockhart set to work.

He might not have revealed the full extent of his secret plans and activities to Moura, but he encouraged her to remain vigilant: to look around, to listen carefully. Were rumors swirling in the former capital? Was there any new knowledge? What were people saying, what were people thinking in Petrograd? She needed to keep her ears and her eyes wide open. She needed to pay just as much attention to their friend Cromie and the last few officers at the British embassy as she did to the expats from neutral countries, the only foreigners who still lived along the Neva. How did the Swiss and Swedish ambassadors react to Lenin's peace treaty with the Germans? She needed to gather intelligence for him within the many circles among which she moved, anything that could be useful for him. Everything that she considered important about Russia's future.

On the Bolshevik side of things she wasn't so well positioned, of course. But who knew? Maybe she'd be able to cultivate her relationship with the handsome Lev Karakhan. His position in the Ministry of Foreign Affairs made his friendship valuable. He often traveled between Moscow and Petrograd: who knew, indeed, whether Moura might see him on the train one day.

Lockhart didn't push her further. He didn't insist. There was nothing aggressive about his demands. He didn't go into any detail.

Just this: she needed to get a sense of the current political temperature. And keep him posted.

She never attended Lockhart's work meetings or his conversations in room 309 of the Hotel Elite. She disappeared to the third floor, behind the door to her own room, and never met any of his visitors.

Even so, she was well positioned to be fully informed on the conversations with the agents from London's intelligence services, who she saw coming at the end of the hallway, going inside, and mysteriously disappearing. Along with the spies and agents provocateurs from the liberal parties. Along with the generals' emissaries from the White Army, in which her own brother-in-law Kochubey and his counterparts in the tsarist aristocracy served. Along with all Lockhart's old friends, his friends from before the Revolution, from when the British consul mixed with the Muscovite aristocracy and danced at the balls that the biggest families threw.

She took care not to ask questions. She simply watched, listened, paid attention. And what she learned fascinated her.

On all fronts.

◆

For each of them, their fates had been decided: the grand adventure had begun. The extraordinary adventure of their lives, which Robert Bruce Lockhart called—drawing on the words of his Scottish compatriot Robert Louis Stevenson—"a romance of destiny."

CHAPTER FIFTEEN

Double Agent?

APRIL–MAY 1918

"What's come over Mrs. Benckendorff? Has she got Saint Vitus's dance?"

General Knox was droning on and on, his rump perched on his desk, his leg hanging in the air. Stuck in the center of the train car the British diplomats were using as an embassy in the Vologda train station, Captains Garstin and Cromie stood in front of the general. They weren't at attention, but at least they were stock-still and silent, as they were expected to be before the head of the British armed forces in Russia.

They had been well acquainted with Knox's habits since 1916. He insisted on deference as he pontificated. His lectures on the most idiosyncratic topics could stretch on for hours. So they let him talk.

". . . We find her in Moscow on Friday . . . then on Monday in Petrograd . . . then in Moscow again on Friday . . . Back and forth . . . North then south. By God, she's relentless! I feel for Mr. Lenin's poor functionaries who have to secure tickets every week! What am I saying? Every week? More like every day!"

Garstin and Cromie traded a glance: news traveled fast here. They had only just learned the details themselves: Lockhart had claimed a new victim. Moura Benckendorff, *their* Moura, was now yet another notch on his bedpost. And Knox knew it. Just like everyone else here.

Moura, Lockhart's mistress? Garstin was shocked. And Cromie had won his bet. Stupid Lockhart—that was all it took to destroy his reputation in Vologda! Not to mention his career back in London.

"This dame seems to have a special gift for being everywhere," General Knox continued wryly as he took a drag on his pipe.

He walked around his desk to sit on the wheeled chair with its throne-like back that kept his spine ramrod straight.

Of all the staff offices, the British general's was the most run down.

The US ambassador had just granted himself the former residence of the province's governor—America, which had been at war with Germany for six months now, had recently joined the Entente. The entente seemed to be in name only, however: President Woodrow Wilson didn't agree with any of the other nations on the strategy to take here. He was opposed to the Japanese landing in Siberia and wouldn't sign on to the plan for an Allied intervention in Russia. And even so, his ambassador was the oldest and most powerful diplomat here. Their tribal elder. Through his window could be seen the five crosses topping the five golden domes of Saint Sophia Cathedral.

The French ambassador, with his wife at his side, had taken up residence in a school for young ladies. Through his windows could be seen the other forty onion domes of Vologda's churches.

England hadn't deemed it necessary to replace its own ambassador, the sorely missed Sir George Buchanan, and so through the windows of its embassy could be seen railroad siding.

Behind General Knox, Garstin and Cromie could see the railroad tracks leading to a warehouse. And in the distance, the sharply angled roof of the train station's small log structure. They needed to be patient. The secretaries and attachés were working to furnish two semidetached dachas along the river's banks, one for the head of the diplomatic mission, the other for the head of the armies. They needed to be patient. In this railroad car, they had what they needed. The flag of the Union Jack; the portrait of His Majesty George V, who looked the spitting image of his cousin Tsar Nicholas II, who had just been transferred to a new prison; a rug with the British royal family's coat of arms; the maps on the wall; the flat desk; the chair; and the case for the general's pipe—the seven elements of English decor.

"Ah, Vologda!" From his room at the Hotel Elite in Moscow, Lockhart laughed: Vologda! To understand Russia's political life and keep up to date on the events that were shaking Europe, the Allies had outdone themselves;

they couldn't have found a more remote, disconnected corner of the world if they'd tried. They might as well have headed to the North Pole!

The city was perfectly tiny, thoroughly sleepy. It had more churches than inhabitants; five convents; a fourteenth-century monastery that stood alone and loomed over the vast expanse just past the fortifications. The only distractions were the Orthodox services that followed one another, notwithstanding the local police chief's diktats; the power struggles among the French, British, Americans, Japanese, and Italians, who were all jostling for the attention of Lenin's representatives; the officers' mess, where anti-Bolshevik paranoia held sway; and the endless poker games at the old American ambassador's, who sneered at the Russians and unburdened his allies of their minuscule wealth.

General Knox smoothed out his mustache; he was trying to look amiable and debonair. But he pointedly did not invite the two captains to take a seat. Garstin's new job with Lockhart in Moscow had authorized him to meet Knox as a civilian. Garstin had put on his uniform again anyway. Tall, thin, with an oval face so narrow that he looked perpetually down, he seemed like a teenager who had gone to seed. His equally thin mustache only accentuated this apparent youth . . . but looking like a romantic boy dying of consumption didn't detract from the fact that he was a fine officer. His seriousness, bravery, and honesty raised him to the level of the men on the front lines.

As for the handsome Captain Cromie, who Knox suspected and bitterly, he had just come from Norway. The trip had been to discuss the future of the Russian fleet in Oslo. Lockhart had negotiated the scuttling with Trotsky. He had even managed to convince him that destroying those ships was of critical necessity. It was quite the success on his part, because the Brest-Litovsk treaty had given the Germans the Russian fleet in the Black Sea practically on a silver platter.

Cromie was taking over for Lockhart in handling the negotiations with the representatives of the neutral powers. Their agreement to continue this systematic destruction was of interest to every level of the Royal Navy's hierarchy.

But Cromie's mission and the Russian fleet's fate didn't seem to be on the agenda here.

". . . Maybe Mrs. Benckendorff, who's so fond of trains, will happen upon us here?" General Knox muttered. "Will she be paying a little visit to her old friends from the Saltykov palace? What's a few hours to get to Vologda compared to her nights in third class between Petrograd and Moscow? A third-class berth, my men, just think on that: isn't it just a disgrace for an aristocrat like her? I have to admit that given her social status, our Mrs. Benckendorff keeps a taste for the finer things in life: in all of Russia, this boy seems the only one who's still respectable. Or at least he's the nicest-looking of the three guys from the Foreign Office. This Mr. Lev Karakhan—"

"Karakhan!"

"Are you really so surprised, Captain Garstin? You seem aghast. Yes, Karakhan and Moura von Benckendorff dine together in Petrograd. They go to the ballet together—apparently theaters haven't suffered too much from the Soviets' bad taste—they go to the public committee sessions together. And God alone knows what else they do together at the Smolny Institute . . . Or someplace else!"

"They met one time at a restaurant," Garstin stuttered. "In the company of Robert Bruce Lockhart."

"At Kuba, perhaps? You're right: they eat there after performances, just like back in the good old days."

"Lev Karakhan was one of Lockhart's main contacts in February, before they both followed the government to Moscow," Cromie cut in. "Karakhan is still his best contact within the Party. But—"

"Oh, yes. Lockhart," said Knox. "Lockhart, Lockhart, our dear friend Lockhart. Let's talk about him. I think I've been made aware, Captain Cromie, that before you left for Oslo—if I'm not wrong, it was almost a month ago—you felt it was wise to send an 'urgent and confidential' note to the Royal Navy's secret services. And the note said this, more or less: 'A well-informed person has let me know that the Bolsheviks have possession of all the codes for the Allied legations and ambassadors.' Is that right?"

"Well, my general—"

"And you also added this: 'Consequently, the dispatches Mr. Robert Bruce Lockhart sent to the prime minister in London and the war minister and His Majesty's foreign minister were read by Lenin, Trotsky, and Karakhan.' Is that right?"

"Yes."

"May I ask you who exactly this 'well-informed' person was?"

"Forgive me, my general, but I cannot answer you on this point: I am not permitted to divulge the names of those who help us."

"Your sources . . . whether they're men or women . . . Fine. I understand."

General Knox didn't press the point. He knew that Captain Cromie, a career military man who had come from the Royal Marines, had been asked by C. to stay back and observe matters in Petrograd. C., in this instance, meant Commander Cumming of the Royal Navy, who was now the head of British domestic security. So Cromie was working for MI5: Military Intelligence, Section 5. And the intelligence services didn't divulge the identities of their sources to officers of the regular army. At least, not directly. Captain Garstin, who was in fact part of the same mission for Lockhart, was bound to the same code of silence.

The two men, who had no love for such discretion, hated this role of secret agent that the war forced them to accept.

"I understand," Knox repeated. "Let's forget that telegram from earlier in the month, Captain Cromie. Just know that the foreign minister in London received a second telegram of the same kind as your own. And that this second telegram came from your boss, my friend Admiral Hall, who agreed to send me a copy with the minister's response. Go ahead and read this for yourself . . ."

Knox held out the dispatch:

"Out loud, if you please, for the sake of Captain Garstin."

"'May Foreign Office be informed of the following. The employment of lady clerks of foreign nationality by missions in Russia now occupied on confidential work is considered dangerous as they deal with work of a secret nature leakage of which would prove useful to the enemy. In my opinion these women should not be used in cyphering or decyphering telegrams.'"

"How interesting," Knox said. "For two years, that's exactly what I've been saying! Captain Cromie, would you be so kind as to let us know what Captain Edward Cunard, currently posted in London, had to say? Cunard, the former secretary at Sir George Buchanan's embassy. A friend of yours, I believe? What did he scribble in the margin of the paper you're holding?"

"'This evidently refers to Madame Benckendorff and Miss Artsimovich who with other ladies were employed in semi-official British organizations in Petrograd.

"'I did not know that there were other ladies besides Mme. Benckendorff. I think all our missions should be warned against employing them.

"'There are certainly ladies employed as clerks in the British Consulate at Petrograd. But I cannot say if they were ever employed in ciphering or deciphering.'"

General Knox cleared his throat, then said:

"Good. The Bolsheviks are now in possession of our codes: there's no question of that fact. You, Captain Cromie, have this knowledge from a well-informed person. If the Bolsheviks have our codes, it's because someone gave them to them. So I must ask you: in your opinion, who could it have been?"

Cromie didn't beat around the bush. He went straight to the point:

"It would seem, my general, that if Mrs. Benckendorff and Miss Artsimovich were working for the Russians, they would have been far more discreet."

"In such a scenario, the best cover is always to be absolutely visible. But there's still one question: which of the two women had access to the codes and enough time to copy down the keys? I'd say it's your source, Captain Cromie, the woman who's keeping you informed, who's also informing Mr. Lockhart and informing Comrade Karakhan."

Garstin exploded.

"Moura can't be a spy! That's unthinkable, my general!"

"But why would that be *unthinkable*?"

"Mrs. Benckendorff is an aristocrat," Cromie cut in. "No Bolshevik would trust her. For her entire life she's been the personification of the *burzhui* they want to bring down."

"That doesn't rule out the possibility that before bringing her down, they'd take full advantage of her resources. Even more since she's believed to be one of them."

"Moura's an idealist . . . not a Communist."

"What's the difference, Captain Garstin? And what won't people do out of ideology? I have it on good authority that this dame was especially attracted to Mr. Lenin's theories: land to the peasants . . . factories to the workers . . . What balderdash. She's a doctrinarian. An extremist. I'll say it again: what won't she do out of ideology? And in this case, what won't she do in her own interest?"

"Mrs. Benckendorff's origins make her part of the interests of the White Army's officers, my general. Not those of the Reds."

"I agree with you completely, Captain Cromie: the Whites, the Reds, the Allies . . . she's got a finger in every pie."

Cromie couldn't stifle his snicker:

"So she's a triple agent, then?"

"Why not?"

"You're forgetting the Germans, my general!" Garstin joked.

"So that makes her . . ." Cromie paused sarcastically. ". . . a *quadruple* agent!"

Their irony went over Knox's head.

"The Germans, too. The Germans were the first ones . . . The Russians—Red or White—only came later. The Germans, however, hired her first. Probably before 1914, in fact: who knows what she was doing in Berlin with her husband? The proof is that right now, the Benckendorff husband is collaborating with the Prussians in Estonia. So your pretty little friend, my boys, will stay close to *each* of these parties, no matter who wins the battle and no matter how the war ends."

Knox's tone deepened as he concluded coldly:

"Put an end to this. Am I clear? I don't want to see this dame flittering around the embassy, or around any of you. I don't want her in touch with a single British officer or any of the Allied officers or any of the representatives of the neutral powers. Not in Petrograd, not in Moscow, not anywhere . . . Make sure Lockhart gets this message from me. Make sure he kicks her out the second he hears it—otherwise he's going right out with his little Mata Hari!"

❖

Petrograd
May 28, 1918

My beloved Locky,

I got your two telegrams safely. And now this wonderful letter that's just arrived by the messenger from the legation. He's waiting in the hall for my answer and I'm writing as quickly as I can. To cut a long story short, I want to tell you the most important thing: that my present and my future are yours. That I'll be frank and honest with you, no matter what. Do not worry. You can't imagine how much I loved the words you've written to me, Babyboy, and yes, yes, we'll talk seriously about everything when I come to Moscow on Friday. We'll talk, we'll wait, we'll find a solution. All shall be well. Because I want only two things above all: your happiness and your peace of mind.

I only hope that you'll come to me when you're weary and need me to support you. That I'll be your mistress when you're looking for passion. Your haven when you want calm. And later on, too, I want to give you a little boy who we'll raise on Scotch whiskey and steak tartare so he'll be a rugged footballer.

Here, Petrograd is dying of despair. I am, too. Even though you think I'm so even keeled, so hard to dishearten, I'm utterly incapable of shaking off this leaden sadness that's weighing on me, crushing me. The future seems so dark . . . But no matter. Let's hope that Providence looks kindly upon us and that it offsets this terrible period with wonderful days to come for my land.

The bourgeois—our burzhui—*aren't calling the Germans for help getting rid of the Bolsheviks anymore. Ever since the armistice was signed at Brest-Litovsk, they've figured out that the kaiser is working hand in hand with Lenin.*

They don't expect better days with the Krauts. On the contrary, they'll end up on your side, hoping for the Allies to come. Nobody's talking yet about the possibility of your landing, nor of a massive military intervention. It's better this way. The news of the British victory on the western front, however, has come out.

That's all the news I can give you.

Cromie is back from Oslo. He went by Vologda. Do you know the question he asked me this morning?

He asked me: "You love Lockhart dearly, don't you? You're hoping nothing will befall him?"

My answer was: "Of course! What a silly idea!"

"Then stop it with all this back-and-forth. Don't come back to Moscow anymore! Lockhart has plenty of enemies . . . in Russia and everywhere else. And your continual presence at the Hotel Elite isn't doing him any favors!"

What did he mean by that?

We should talk about that, too, because I don't have the least idea of what Crow's getting at. Clearly, when I'm put on the spot I've got the psychological understanding of an ostrich!

I love you, Babyboy.

Moura

PS: Whatever happened to the flower Garstino was supposed to bring back from Vologda? Did he leave it behind with Knox by accident? If he did, that's not like him at all.

PPS: Has Hicks, my dear Hicklet, come back from Siberia without any trouble? Is he still saying bad things about me? Is he still trying to convince you that I'm not the woman I seem to be? The one you believe me to be? The one you see me as being?

Sitting at her small bedroom desk, Moura stopped writing. Her pen hovered, she wavered. Should she keep going down this path? Of course not. She'd had it with this dillydallying! It was a minefield—even though she'd been trying to joke about it, to suggest that it was just idle gossip. She shouldn't go any further.

She would see Hicks in Moscow this weekend. She would get to the bottom of all the insinuations and implications Lockhart had nonchalantly told her about. She was going to make Hicklet confess; she would go confront him if she had to.

But the truth was that the mere thought of her British friends suspecting her of being a double agent—that they might presume she was a spy who was betraying Lockhart—was such a torturous prospect that she couldn't bring herself to even say it.

She had, however, realized that they were keeping their distance. Had she, in becoming the mistress of one of them, fallen from her pedestal? Yes. There was no question of that: in their eyes, the aristocratic Mrs. Benckendorff had gone and joined the harem of Russian women who got in bed with Allied men. Moura knew how the world worked well enough, how men worked, and she wasn't the least bit disillusioned on this point. She didn't even shrug at it.

But that wasn't the worst of it!

Her dear Garstino hadn't forgotten the orchid that he'd promised her and brought back for her at great cost. He was knowingly overriding his chivalric stance from years past. He was following someone else's rules.

As for Crow, he wasn't talking as cryptically as she'd made it sound in her letter. He'd told her—with a great deal more specificity than she'd indicated to Lockhart—about Knox's orders and the serious penalties the British officers risked if they continued to have any contact with her.

She had to ignore the offenses. She had to hide the wounds she had been dealt. She had to ignore all the annoyances.

Lockhart, she thought, shouldn't ever realize just how many aspersions were being cast upon her. Nor should he ever realize how much pain she was enduring in the face of such unfair coldness. He pretended to ignore Knox's warnings. She would tread the same path and choose to react just as coolly as he had. She simply had to stick to the straight and narrow and stay lighthearted, nonchalant. She sighed. Yes, innocence at all costs! Otherwise she would just be digging herself into an even deeper hole.

And she'd dug herself into enough holes already.

———

The sleepless yet snowy night bathed the room in a milky light. A brightness that revealed just how run down the place was.

In the bedroom, which had once been so comfortable, there was only the bed, this tiny desk, and, on a shelf in the corner the icon of the Virgin, with her red light. Moura clung to her small sanctuary at all costs and went to great trouble to dig up candles—which were nowhere to be found in Petrograd now—to burn in front of the Queen of Heaven.

She had always believed in God. But ever since meeting Lockhart, she had become somewhat mystical. As if the love she had for her Lord had gotten mixed up in her soul with the love she felt for this man.

She thought a bit longer, wavering between sealing the letter and continuing it. She had already put too much on paper.

The letters between Petrograd and Moscow were probably intercepted and read. Even a missive like this one, which would be delivered in person by a messenger employed by the Allies and faithful to Lockhart, could be opened by the Bolsheviks. Or the British.

Of course, she didn't doubt the integrity of brave Miller, who ferried all the love letters that Lockhart wrote her every day. Miller, with his reddish face, coming and going from the Hotel Elite and the British embassy, where Cromie was staying. Miller, whose trips up and down Shpalernaya Street she looked forward to with so much impatience!

Trustworthy. But who was she to say?

In any case, what she wanted to tell him, the true subject of her letter, couldn't be set down in ink. It could only be shared in person.

And even in person, should she share the news: her secret, her joy? And the immense terror that came with it?

Talking to Lockhart about *that* . . . Adding to his burden? He was already so weighed down by life, the decisions he had to make, the actions he had to carry out.

Should she talk to him right away? Or delay the subject until later, when circumstances would be more amenable?

Yes, later . . . *But when?* she thought. Time wasn't on their side, and the vise was tightening.

Cromie had said explicitly that Lockhart's situation in Moscow had become untenable. The signing of the armistice that had given a third of Russia to Germany—and the honors Lenin had bestowed upon the Prussian Mirbach, the kaiser's ambassador—had made his position even shakier, with the Bolsheviks just as much as with the Allies.

His wife in London was telling him the same thing over and over. In her letters, she informed him of the rumors that were going around at the Foreign Office and the War Office about him. He was said to be sympathetic to the Communists. She begged him to come back home before he was discharged dishonorably.

Moura had to concede that this advice was wise.

She loved Lockhart enough to want to try to protect him and to urge him to break camp. And yet this obligation to leave—and to separate— felt like the sword of Damocles that would fall on her. He shared her fear.

And the more she urged him to leave Moscow, the more he saw his love for her mix with his love for Russia. The more she insisted that he abandon the Party, the more he insisted that he couldn't live without her.

Failing that, she encouraged him to at least undertake a trip to Vologda. To meet Knox and explain himself, face-to-face with the Entente's ambassadors.

He was planning to take her advice. And God alone knew how long his absence would be.

Should she talk to him before? After? Never? The question obsessed her.

Should she tell him *that*: that she was expecting a baby by him?

A son, she was sure of it! An adorable little boy with a bow tie who would look just like his father. He'd have his slightly wide-set eyes and his glimmering, sharp gaze that was so full of life.

Deep down, she had already given this baby a name. He would be Peter.

How would Lockhart react? As a career diplomat, he couldn't allow himself a new scandal. He was married. She was, too. Passion was one thing, but the arrival of a bastard child was another.

They had been in love for less than two months. Would he ask her to get an abortion? The prospect terrified her. What if he insisted on it?

And what about Djon? How would Djon react? They'd parted ways in January. Unless she went and saw him again very quickly, he'd know that this baby wasn't his.

Of course, she could ask for a divorce. The Bolsheviks had made that procedure commonplace.

But Lockhart? Divorce in England was a complicated thing, and it was far more shameful and drawn out there than in other countries across Europe. He himself had brought that up during their first weekend together. To the best of his knowledge, his wife would never grant him such freedom.

And that wasn't the only question, either . . . Djon, too, wouldn't be any more accommodating.

He didn't consider himself Russian anymore; he was now Estonian. And in the Baltic nobility, one did not get divorced. In any case, the adulterous wife didn't. One simply banished her from polite society. She was rejected. At worst, she was killed. At best, she was exiled. In any case, she was forbidden from seeing her children.

She sighed.

Fundamentally, she was now in exactly the same situation that Alla had been in: pregnant by a man who wouldn't marry her.

Having seen her sister suffer and having felt the loneliness her niece Kira, the illegitimate child, endured, she knew exactly what awaited them—her and little Peter.

Mommy, who was already so sick, would never recover from this new downfall. She wouldn't forgive her for this dishonor. She might even die of it. The pain she would inflict upon her mother bothered her, quite possibly, more than any of her other fears did.

She pushed away those dark thoughts . . . One problem at a time. Come on, keep a stiff upper lip!

Anna, her other sister, who had similarly expected a baby out of wedlock, had gotten out of it. And quite nicely: She had risked becoming bigamous in order to protect the future of her children. Now Anna ruled over her land in Ukraine, surrounded by Germans and her vast progeny.

Moura knew herself well enough to know that she would have the strength, as Anna did, to find a way out. But what would that way out be? For now, it was a mystery.

For the moment, the question was whether she should share responsibility for the baby with a father who wouldn't recognize him . . . Or be quiet. To leave Lockhart alone. Absolutely free, as he needed to be during this time.

She would make her decision this weekend in Moscow.

Moura screwed on the cap of her pen again, sealed the envelope, and made her way to the hall, where Miller the messenger was waiting.

CHAPTER SIXTEEN

Little Peter

L ying naked beside him, she listened to the passion trembling in the voice of the father of her baby. She didn't move, kept her eyes shut. The questions she had asked herself, the insurmountable problems in Petrograd, had been resolved with a single gesture from a man unburdened by any constraint of prudence or pettiness.

When he learned the news, he had simply fallen to his knees.

The news . . . She hadn't even told him: he had guessed it.

Something had clicked for him the minute she walked through the door to room 309, something in her smile, in her gait, or perhaps within her body. An instantaneous realization. Was that even possible?

Lockhart knew women intimately; he loved them. A glance, a presentiment, a question was all it took.

"Are you pregnant?"

She nodded.

He fell to his knees. He buried his head in the folds of her skirt, clutching her thighs, enclosing her. His mouth against her belly, he stammered thanks, a thousand incoherent words of gratitude and love.

She had never seen him as proud, as excited, as in this moment, when he was at her feet.

Once he had overcome his emotion, he whispered to her that when he had been a consul, his wife had been expecting a baby. The birth had gone badly. Their little girl had died two hours after she was born. He had held her coffin tight against him in the consular car all the way to the

German cemetery here in Moscow. He often went to visit her grave. He was left disconsolate by this tragedy.

How could she have imagined that he wanted a child so much?

He confessed it to her today.

And now, in the huge bed of room number 309, they made love with a new tenderness.

"We'll call him Pyotr," he declared. "Like the man who built your city, Saint Petersburg."

She smiled. "I chose the same name, but in English. In my head he's not Pyotr but Peter . . . I've been thinking of him as Little Peter for fifteen days now."

"If that idiot General Knox manages to get me sent back to England, you're coming with me. We'll settle into my grandmother's house in Scotland. Or at the end of the world. I'll make you into a cocoa-plantation owner in Chile."

"But for that to happen we'd have to be married to each other, Babyboy. If there's no ring on this finger, your comrades Lenin and Trotters won't let me out. They're more conventional than all our *burzhui*."

"I'll kidnap you!"

She didn't think for a second that he might not be capable of such a thing. He'd find a way to extract her from this country.

"What about my children, though?" she whispered "Kira, Paul, and Tania? I'm not the perfect mother for them, of course, but I can't, I won't, lose them!"

"So you won't lose them. I'll be the one who stays."

He was just as capable of this: of giving up everything and staying in Russia. He'd go all the way for her.

But she had no intention of letting him sacrifice everything for her.

Their faith in their shared fate—whatever it might be—liberated her from any fear she had for the future. This trust allowed her to bring Lockhart back to the present.

"You should see Karakhan. During the last dinner I had with him, he struck me as very suspicious. From what I understand, an incident broke out in Siberia, some kind of altercation between some Red Army officers, some Czech prisoners, and an Allied contingent."

"That's exactly right. The French had a bit of a brushup with the Soviets. And Karakhan had the entire Czech delegation, who were protected by diplomatic immunity, arrested in Moscow. This way the Bolsheviks have of just throwing diplomats in prison is unacceptable! I went to yell at everyone I could. I threatened to have exactly the same thing done to the representatives in London. Karakhan had never seen me anywhere near that angry, and he fell over himself trying to apologize."

"Be careful! You're defending the Czechs, who the Soviets consider their enemies!"

Moura's voice, her advice in the darkness, delighted him. What did he care about Hicks's warnings? This woman was the mother of his son; she was, absolutely had to be, the woman of his life!

Ever-suspicious Hicks would have to accept Moura's presence here, at the Hotel Elite, and in all the places they had been when they were younger. That devil could understand passion well enough! Hadn't he even succumbed to a Russian woman's charms? Hicks had had his own little affair with a niece of the former mayor of Moscow, a charming divorcée by the name of Lyuba. He was madly in love with her. He had been planning to marry her and bring her back to England. So he knew better than anyone else here what importance such an encounter could hold in a man's life.

As for Knox, he could go to hell! How dare he go around saying that Moura, this marvel of kindness and bravery, somehow presented a danger for England?

Lockhart felt a need to protect her, a desire that was as strong, as pressing as that of being supported by her.

She was instinctively reassuring. Even her body opened up with a generosity he hadn't seen in any other woman.

She watched over him, she watched over his career, she watched over his security. She had no more ideological certainties than before. Only the conviction that she loved Russia. And the conviction that she loved him. She would accept all the consequences of those feelings.

Whatever Moura loved would be the world she protected.

He hugged her tighter. She whispered:

"And from what I've heard, Karakhan is ready to use every means he possibly can to get rid of the Allies in Vologda."

He loved when she talked about danger in bed.

She wove together adventure, politics, and love, yoking their two fates to the forward march of history as well as to sensual pleasure.

And this, too, he loved.

❖

Petrograd

July 7, 1918

Baby, my Babyboy,

I'm mad with worry. Cromie has just told me that Count Mirbach, the German ambassador you hate, has been murdered in cold blood.

Nobody here has any doubt that you're the one who ordered the crime. Everyone's saying that the murderer lived in the Hotel Elite. That he'd made his way up the ranks of the Cheka, but in reality he's one of the revolutionaries opposed to the infamous peace that Lenin signed. And that he killed Mirbach to provoke Germany's fury . . . To start up the war between the kaiser's armies and Russia's all over again.

Mirbach's death will have grave consequences! The Germans can't just sit by and let themselves be killed en masse in Russia without a fight. They're calling for the heads of various Bolsheviks. The Cheka police are at the top of the list, and they'll clear their names by pointing their fingers at the Allies. That is—at you!

. . . . You've worked so hard against the signing of the armistice treaty. So hard against Karakhan and Trotsky, to keep the fighting going.

Don't you think the time has come to get out of this hornet's nest and escape the country? Don't you remember the fate that awaited the Czech delegation rotting in prison? You are in danger, Babyboy. Please, please, think about getting ready to leave. If you don't fear for your safety, at least think of what this means for me. I wouldn't urge you to leave if I thought you could still be useful to Russia. But I don't think that. And Mirbach's assassination will only make matters even more unnecessarily risky for you. No matter how I look at your position, I can't find an angle that will allow me to get some sleep.

> *Shpalernaya Street*
> *Evening of July 7, 1918*

I'm returning to this letter I began this morning. I was interrupted by the doctor's visit. The news about my mother isn't good. But I don't want to make you sad. So here I am, so close to you again.

In your message yesterday, you asked me what my intentions were. My plans haven't changed.

You who know me so well, you cannot even imagine just how much the action I'm going to take against my husband upsets me. I detest the idea, believe me.

Compounding the indignity of what I'm going to do is the horror I feel at just how soon you'll be leaving: you'll probably have to leave Russia before I see you again.

And compounding that—*the pain of losing you for a long time—is my disgust at the prospect of slipping back into the ruts of the past.*

I'll have to return to the life I led in years past, the settings of years past, the people of years past, the world of years past, even though I'm no longer the same woman. When the best of myself, my soul, my heart, my body, belongs to you. When my future, my fate is yours.

I love you, Babyboy. More than life. And God knows how I love life! I will be faithful to you through all the difficulties that await us. You must believe me. You absolutely must.

I can't delay my departure for Estonia much longer. The man who will take me over the border and drive me to Reval keeps saying that he has to leave tomorrow. He has Swiss nationality, and without him I'll never be able to reach Yendel. Even with the Russian permit that Karakhan secured for me. Even with the permit of the German general on the other side, my husband's guest, who's occupying our house.

Love and courage: *I'll remember your motto every day, Babyboy, until we see each other again.*

Until then, I'll have to play this nine-month-long pantomime with Djon. I know you can't bear the thought that he'd touch me.

I'll be honest with you, and I'll tell you what I've already said: I love my children, and the prospect of losing them tears me asunder.

I might not have the "maternal instinct" that society expects of me. But I love my children! Putting them into such a situation and not being able to see them anymore is unbearable to me. I'm trying to find the way—if not the easiest or best one, then the least painful one—to leave them . . . without abandoning them.

This is how I would like to act toward all the beings who bear upon our love. I'm thinking of my mother and my husband.

Trying not to make my nearest and dearest suffer too much still doesn't change the decision I've made to live with you. I've never wondered, not for a single second: "Would it be wiser to cut myself off from him? Would it be better to go back to the life I've always led?" It's impossible! Going back would mean abandoning light, giving up water, forgoing air. It would mean saying no to life.

Stop tormenting yourself, my love. You can't imagine everything you embody in my eyes. I'm still able to bear anything, to brave all risks, to be with you. You have no reason to fear losing me, Babyboy. No reason to be jealous. No reason to think that one day I might regret this decision to follow you.

But I shouldn't neglect the details that affect others, especially my children. I need to do things correctly.

And so, for now, I need to preserve appearances, play this ridiculous pantomime, with all the consequences that entails.

I've gone through all this in my head again and again, and I don't see any other solution.

We're both of us married. You have to leave Russia. And the world is at war.

Pretending to reconcile with my husband and maintain our entente for nine months: that's the only way to spare Paul and Tania, and to spare our little Peter.

Deep down, your love has made me a man. Isn't that strange? By that I mean that I now know who I am . . . what I want. And I also know how to get it. My determination is absolute. Yes, sir!

So I'm leaving tomorrow. Think of me, Babyboy, because I'm afraid. If

I'm arrested at the border, I'll have to go back, I'll head to Moscow, I'll fly to you! I'll have tried. And I'll have failed. And I'll be the happiest woman in the world.

Enough for today. Good night, my love.

Know that I will always be with you, that I will write to you, that I will join you again,

Yours forever.
Moura

◆

She felt Djon's heavy hand weighing on her neck. The time for respect was gone. He no longer held his arm out to her, whether to go down the street or up the hallway leading to their bedroom.

The redbrick house that Moura had loved so dearly, with its crenellated tower, its mullioned windows, and its terraces, brought her no comfort.

As July 1918 was winding toward its end, everything seemed to have settled into order. The park was blossoming. The peasants were working the land. The harvest season was approaching. The children, under Micky's watchful eye, were learning how to swim. And the elder Madame von Benckendorff received her four sons and their families at the fishermen's cabin on the edge of the lake every afternoon for the tea ceremony around the samovar.

From the tennis courts just past the communal spaces there could be heard the muted noise of balls being struck and young men yelling at each other over a match. Through the trees, the silhouettes of players in white outfits could be seen. But instead of the English words *out* and *play*, they were yelling in German: *Aufschlag, Einstand.* And on the lake's pontoon, instead of Cunard, Garstin, and Cromie there were groups of Prussians, their chests bare in the sun.

Yendel now served as the base for the staff of the German officers occupying Estonia. Their general looked forward to the honors their hostess might bestow upon them: that Moura would receive them according to their rank and play some small piano recitals for them.

She felt ill suited to the role she needed to play. She was Russian. And the Germans were occupying her land. She belonged to the other camp. That of Lockhart and Hicks, who had been fighting against the advent of the kaiser's hordes, the enemies of England, the invaders . . . the Krauts, who were at the root of so many evils. They were, in her eyes, responsible for the greatest massacre in history.

Here, in Estonia, they lorded over the land. Their ambition, their arrogance, and their brutality were all calculated to bring the locals to their knees.

Djon, who accepted their laws and was collaborating with them, had let himself be sidelined by the hatred he felt toward the Bolsheviks. She didn't consider him weak so much as blind. He acted like a lord, but in fact he was serving them.

As for her, she avoided talking to them whenever possible. When Djon invited her to sing lieder for them in the moonlight and play Wagner on the salon gramophone, she did so with visible unwillingness. The revulsion she felt, however, was nothing compared to the disgust that rose up in her throat when she carried out her other wifely obligations.

Djon was wholly unaware of Moura's betrayal and the immensity of her failings as his wife. He was wholly unaware that she was cheating on him with a British agent and that she had been spending more time in a hotel in Moscow than in Petrograd with her sick mother, as she had claimed to justify her absence from Yendel. He was wholly unaware that she was associating with the regime's dignitaries. That she was dining with Lord Karakhan, one of Lenin's ministers.

As for imagining that Moura's arrival in Estonia was only thanks to the protection of a Party dignitary: that was inconceivable! The idea that she would never have been able to cross the border without Karakhan's approval didn't cross his mind.

No, Djon had no idea whatsoever that she was lying to him about everything. And yet their political arguments had lowered her in his estimation; he deemed her guilty, he condemned her. Guilty, in his eyes, of being insensitive to the unhappiness of other people, of their friends, all their nearest and dearest. Guilty of indifference to the future of their families and the survival of their children . . . She was monstrous in her coldness, such a monster that she barked with the wolves and spat in her soup. Contemptible.

The result, then, was that he treated her like a courtesan and wanted her more than ever.

Djon's leaden touch on his wife's neck at all hours of the day was only a prelude to his other gestures at all hours of the night.

Under the weight of this palm, Moura jumped and stiffened. She had to learn how to calm her nerves, all the same. Hadn't she undertaken this trip to Yendel specifically for this: to carry out her marital obligations?

She had to acknowledge that she had overestimated her abilities.

The journey between Petrograd and Reval had probably worn her out. She shouldn't think about it anymore. The tension, the walks, and the searches that the Russian, German, and Estonian soldiers had all carried out weren't much compared to her daily life.

Mentally, she went back over the interrogations . . . Worse than all that was the disgust she felt today for her husband.

She had discovered that she was incapable of bearing contact with Djon.

When sundown came—and everything that followed—her heart broke and her fears won out.

As for the rest, it was an abyss of absence.

Even though she had been so eagerly looking forward to hugging Paul and Tania tight, she couldn't feel anything but embarrassment when she looked at them. Not a whit of pleasure. Just this: the feeling of her guilt toward them. And this feeling took shape within her, a gulf, a sadness, a fear.

She knew, as she hugged them, that she was planning to leave them. In nine months, in a year, she would go. She would follow Lockhart.

But even so, empathy remained. Her behavior made her feel bad.

Despite everything she said, everything she did, however, she wasn't able to express anything.

Her passion for Lockhart and little Peter had more or less cut her off from all her other affections.

She hated herself. She forced herself to playact.

It was only sheer luck that Paul and Tania were still too young to be aware of her detachment. And to suffer from it. But Kira, her sweet Kira, was now nine years old. In her dark eyes, Moura could sense her expectation, her need, her worry. And Moura couldn't answer it.

She was unable to give Kira anything. Unable to give anything to anybody.

Worst of all were the direct questions.

When Kira asked her, looking right into her eyes:

"You won't leave, will you? You're going to stay with us here in Yendel, right?"

When Paul, playing hide-and-seek in her skirt, had mimicked her:

"You're my mommy and you're going to stay with me!"

She had blushed with shame and stayed silent.

"Where do you want me to go, my darlings?" She could have smiled at them and sworn to them that she would remain a constant presence at the family estate. She could have explained that her obligations might perhaps bring her back to Mommy in Petrograd . . . but that she'd be back the week after, forever.

Inventing pretexts to gain time had never been a problem for her.

But with them: it was impossible! Something in her revolted at the thought of telling them made-up stories. In front of her children, anguish strangled her voice to the point that she couldn't get out anything more than broken words, as if she had run too far and was wholly out of breath.

What did she know of their future together? She had tried, but to no avail: she couldn't imagine anything! She had made a terrible mistake coming here. She had barely arrived, and now she wanted to flee this house.

She couldn't wait nine months. She couldn't even wait one. As soon as she could, she would go join Lockhart in Moscow, in London, anywhere. Djon's subservience to the Germans, as well as his brutality in bed, had been the last straw for her. The tenderness he showed Paul and Tania, his patience with the three children, had made him a completely unfamiliar man to her, and in a way, this had been her liberation. He was a wonderful father. And she, an incapable mother.

She left Kira and the little ones, telling their governess to take them for the afternoon.

Strictly to Micky, she added a sentence that was utterly unlike her: she asked her to care for them should anything happen to her someday. It was a request that she knew was superfluous, but all the same it was reassuring.

Thank goodness Micky would watch over them. Thank heavens Micky would stand guard and protect her children! She was the pillar, the heart of the Benckendorff family in its entirety: the haven for all her Marydear's nearest and dearest.

Between the two women, there was no question of confession, nor of outpouring or confidences. Moura kept her silence. Micky didn't ask. She simply furrowed her brows to see Mary so unhappy with herself.

When Micky saw her in the morning, pale and ghostly in front of the breakfast she was unable to swallow, she understood that Mary had just come out of a nightmarish evening. And that her relationship with Djon was the reason.

But not the only one.

She knew there was something else. Someone.

Micky sensed the presence of an affair, a passion.

Moura was quite aware of this realization. But she didn't worry, she didn't fear any judgment. She was grateful for this intuition. The presentiment that Micky had of Lockhart's existence was the only complicity that could in any way fill the void of her loneliness at Yendel.

❖

Yendel
July 20, 1918

Babyboy,

I've done all I can, I've tried my best, but I just can't get over the despair I feel at not seeing you again.

　How can I explain what I felt as I crossed the boundary line under German escort? The shame of having gone over to the occupier's side. An officer asked me: "Sprechen Sie Deutsch?" I looked at him as if I didn't understand. He asked me: "Russkaya?" I almost yelled my answer at him: "Da."

　Here, we speak only German. It's even worse than I imagined. I feel like I've dirtied myself by coming to Yendel. I'm morally cut off from you. Morally cut off from your country and from Russia. I'm trampling all over my dignity, I have no more respect for myself.

　I'm not sure I can weather the storm, even to protect our baby.

　I feel lost.

　All I can think about is you. I wonder how you are. I pray to heaven to let me see you again before you go. I'm unhappy and pathetic.

Moura

❖

Five hundred miles away, Lockhart felt exactly the same way. His memoir is crystal clear:

The next few days were the most miserable of my whole stay in Russia.

　Moura had left Moscow some ten days before in order to visit her home in Estonia . . . I could not communicate with her. It seemed any odds on my having to leave Russia without seeing her again . . .

Lockhart decided that Knox's arrogance and idiocy were making him a public danger. But he held out hope that Knox was getting ready for the Russian forces to set out, rather than underestimating the Bolsheviks simply because he hated them.

Trotsky had reorganized the Red Army, which knew the land, unlike Lockhart's side. Only a formidable arsenal and the rapid deployment of numerous contingents would give his people an advantage. Lockhart doubted that Knox had any idea what he was doing. In fact, he feared the worst for the British soldiers with such a leader.

There was no question in Lockhart's mind that Karakhan would have him arrested for the smallest reason, and he knew he needed to leave Russia. But he refused to do so before seeing Moura one last time. He waited for her to call.

But there was nothing but silence.

He phoned her residence in Petrograd with no luck. On his first phone call, he reached her mother, who immediately hung up on him.

❖

Each day that summer seemed to Moura to be yet more oppressive, yet more hostile. The dust on the roads, the wasps' buzzing on the terrace, the crickets' chirping in the fields. She was suffocating. Only her desire to flee and return to Moscow kept her going.

She impatiently walked to the fence around the park. She waited there, in the sun, staring at the train station, waiting for any noise from outside, imagining stupid things, dreaming that Lockhart would somehow appear with his suitcase at the corner of the street.

She saw the peasants looking for shade during the noontime break and heading toward the forest in small groups. A few of them, older ones, were lying down at the edges. But the youngest ones went deep into the woods.

She knew what they were going to do there.

She noticed a boy just then following a girl. Her gaze was alert as she watched the couple disappear amid the trunks. They made their way forward, one behind the other, the girl always ahead. Their path toward a thicket off to the side, their slow progress, so seemingly calm, reminded her of the trek she always made up the stairs toward room 309 at the Hotel Elite.

They had disappeared. What did it matter? She knew that right that second, the girl would be slowing down.

She's stopped. There it is . . . She turns around . . . She looks at him . . . He approaches . . . His face is red, his look is serious, cruel, just like every other man full of desire, every man driven mad with love. He's going to catch her. He's going to push her down. He's going to turn her over in the grass . . .

She herself was standing up, unmoving, so overwhelmed by her memories of Lockhart's embraces that she felt her nipples tensing beneath her shirt.

. . . They're lying down in the shade. She's resting her hand on his neck . . . This almost childish neck that belongs to Lockhart. She feels the prickle of his close-shaven hair growing back thick beneath her fingers. She feels Lockhart's palm under her back, stroking her gently, slowly. He holds her close. She feels her breast being crushed under his torso. Her belly against his. Her knees against his. Her face a little lower than his, she presses her head into the hollow of his shoulder. She touches her lips to the beating artery.

When the boy and the girl, their lips reddened with kisses, came back out of the woods to return to the fields, she ran away from the fence in a rush. She abandoned the sun and slipped past the closed shutters of her bedroom, feeling as if she'd just been cut off from everything that life had to offer. Of everything that fate could still give her. Deprived of what mattered, of the miracle of the perfect union that Lockhart had helped her discover. It wasn't just a matter of sensuality. Pleasure, to her, was simply a sign of miracles.

It was at that exact moment that Djon chose to enter, put his hand on her neck, and bend her over.

Yendel
July 20, 1918

Babyboy,

I'm so close to collapsing. I can't write anymore. I think I'm falling.
The only thing I know is that I love you.

Your Moura

❖

For four days and nights I never slept. For hours on end I sat in my room playing patience and badgering the unfortunate Hicks with idiotic questions. There was nothing we could do, and in my despair my self-control left me and I abandoned myself to the gloomiest depression.

Then on the afternoon of July 28th my telephone rang. I picked up the receiver. Moura herself was speaking. She had arrived in St. Petersburg after six days of terrible adventure, during which she had crossed the no-man's land between Estonia and Russia on foot. She was leaving that night for Moscow.

The reaction was wonderful. Nothing now mattered.

If only I could see Moura again, I felt that I could face any crisis, any unpleasantness the future might have in store for me.

CHAPTER SEVENTEEN

Gypsy Waltzes over a Nest of Spies

July 31–August 31, 1918

On the night of July 31, 1918, the Gypsies of the famous Strelnya cabaret performed for the final time. This charming glass palace, which rose up among the dachas in the outskirts of Moscow, was known for being a temple of *burzhui* pleasures. Petite women, champagne, music: the physical manifestation of all their vices. Tomorrow the Cheka would close the place down forever, the same way it had shut down all the other cabarets.

What miracle had made it possible for the Strelnya to escape the police's sights for eight months? It remained a mystery. Had the owner, Queen Maria Nikolayevna, the sweetest of Gypsy singers, managed to touch the hearts and bring tears to the eyes of enough Party members? She must have, because if the people of the past—as the aristocrats and bourgeoisie were now called—had disappeared from her place, the men of the Revolution, most especially Karakhan and his friends, had replaced them at her round tables. In winter and spring, the circle of commissars from Foreign Affairs came religiously to drink from her *charochki*. Oh, the *charochki* that everyone drank from to the music of violins, to the queen's health: silver cups that were tall enough, big enough to contain half a bottle of champagne. The men drank down the full cupful in a single go, like they were goblets of vodka, before clanking them back down on the plate with a silvery tinkle.

In any case, the champagne was now done with! The Strelnya, Lockhart's favorite cabaret and the place where he usually met Moura, was not long for this world.

Tonight it was empty. Ever since the warning sign had gone up, even the regime's dignitaries hadn't dared go there.

All that remained was the music. For the last time.

Despite the warmth of the July night, which should have brought the musicians out to the garden, they had all set up their chairs inside so as not to draw too much attention.

With a black wainscoted wall behind them, the six men in traditional Russian garb—white shirt buttoned on the side, pants tucked into boots—stood as they played. Two violins, two guitars, one balalaika, one accordion. Facing them, sitting together at tables, were the six great admirers of their art, their faithful patrons: Lockhart and Moura; Hicks and his fiancée, Lyuba, the brunette with bright eyes who he was planning to bring back to England; Garstin, who had just been called up to active service and was spending his final night in Moscow.

Last of all was a character who was well known to Queen Maria Niko-layevna: a regular customer by the name of Mr. Constantine. Of average height, thin, his hair black and his complexion swarthy, divinely elegant in his Savile Row–cut smoking jacket, Mr. Constantine had reappeared at the Strelyna last May.

And Moura was meeting him tonight, for the first time.

So much for prudence.

Mr. Constantine: alias Sidney Reilly, the absolute master of infiltra-tion and sabotage. The spy who had made off with, among other things, the German Navy's plans in Berlin in 1913. His colleagues, the other British agents, called him the Ace of Spies.

So much for precautions!

Ever since Moura's abortive trip to Estonia, the disastrous journey she had taken to protect herself and her children from the consequences of her affair, she had let herself go.

Now a fatalist, she didn't try to control the future anymore. She didn't make plans anymore. She didn't scheme anymore. Her fate lay in the hands of God alone. And she was determined to live the little bit of time she still had with Lockhart in full, honestly. Yes, so much for the sacrosanct circumspection driven by fear!

Lockhart had the same sentiment. They were only going to be together a short while longer. The storm of emotions caused by Moura's brief leave-taking, her return, and her settling back into Moscow had redefined his priorities.

He didn't want to hide anything from her anymore.

He introduced her to his contacts as his collaborator, drawing openly on her secretarial skills. She served him as an assistant, all the way up to the letters he exchanged with Trotsky, whose personal secretary was, similarly, the mistress of a British man, the *Daily News* correspondent in Moscow.

To Hicks's great consternation, Lockhart introduced Moura everywhere. He shared and discussed with her the most trifling contents of their folders: his work on official tasks. And his involvement in others.

So she knew everything there was to know about Sidney Reilly. That he was of Russian extraction, born in Odessa, and that he had been working for England for more than eighteen years. That he drove women crazy everywhere, that he had lavish taste and the personal means to satisfy them. That he had lived in New York, where he had made a fortune selling weapons. At the same time he'd orchestrated, with considerable success, the bankruptcies of German businesses that had been trying to gain a foothold in the United States. As well as America's entrance into the war.

He answered to the name Signor Massimo in Petrograd, where his talent for languages and his skill at disguise allowed him to appear as an Italian diamond merchant. He was Mr. Constantine, a Greek businessman, in Moscow. He was Captain Sidney Reilly, in a stiff British army uniform, when he was asking for an audience with Lenin, claiming to bear letters of introduction from the British prime minister Lloyd George, who had sent him as a delegate to the Bolshevik leadership to verify the accuracy of Lockhart's reports.

Moura also knew that in London he answered to the code name ST1. And that C., the chief of the British intelligence services, had sent him to Russia so that he could prepare the secret Allied invasion.

As he went from one hideout to the next, from one outfit to the next, from one mistress or wife to the next—Reilly was "married" everywhere—Agent ST1 was crisscrossing the country. From west to east, he was building and financing counterrevolutionary networks. He worked closely with his colleagues, Captain Cromie and Captain Hicks . . . and under the control of his boss: Robert Bruce Lockhart.

Moura also knew that Lockhart admired Reilly's indifference when it came to danger, that he adored his guts and his incredible cheek.

She knew, most of all, that Lockhart was suspicious of him.

But tonight she didn't care about any of that.

She did not glance at the newcomer.

That an adventurer like Sidney Reilly aroused no intellectual curiosity in her was, in and of itself, the sign of a sea change in her temperament: the proof that passion had consumed her completely. The newcomer's doings only interested her to the degree that they affected Lockhart: the dangers that he himself was risking.

And he alone.

On the final night here, they went to listen to the Gypsies. Their final night together in this Russia of the Gypsies they both loved passionately.

The voice of Maria Nikolayevna, with its deep inflections akin to sobbing, drowned Moura in a melancholy that was impossible to control.

Nothing could distract her from the face of the queen, a little old woman whose immense gold hoops gleamed through her long gray hair. This silhouette, so heavy as it rested, became the very embodiment of grace when she sang.

The two women never stopped looking at each other. The Gypsy seemed to be singing only to Moura and Lockhart. She had foretold their future. She had read, in Moura's palm, the tragedies that awaited them.

The violin's tremolos, the balalaika's vibrations, and the guitars being strummed simply accentuated the sadness of her song, bringing out a feeling of sensuality that submerged the two lovers in pleasure and worry.

> *They say my heart is like the wind,*
> *That to one maid I can't be true;*
> *But why do I forget the rest*
> *And still remember only you . . .*

The words seemed banal, but as they rang out in Maria Nikolayevna's voice they trembled with passion, with desperate need.

> *But why did I never, never forget*
> *Why did I never forget to remember you . . .*

Lockhart looked at Moura. She seemed to be on the verge of tears.

Deep down within her heart, the fear welled up again around their separation, the uncertainty of their future together, the feeling that her fate would go unfulfilled. And, already, a sweet nostalgia for their love.

However she thought of their situation, the fact remained that their adventure in Moscow was drawing to its end. He couldn't stay in Russia . . . Unless he gave up his family, his country, his career. As for her . . . How could she follow him to London, married to someone else and utterly penniless? By abandoning her children? By leaving behind her mother suffering from cancer in a world that was falling apart? The music was telling them the facts plainly enough: this night might be their last one.

Lockhart, in turn, shared the same impressions in his memoirs: those of a swan song, a final moment of grace on the brink of nothingness.

> *Maria Nikolaievna, our gipsy queen . . . wept over us copiously, sang a few of our favourite songs to us in a low voice, which was scarcely louder than a whisper, and, kissing me on both cheeks, begged us to remain with her. She saw tragedy ahead of*

*us. She would disguise us, hide us and feed us, and arrange for our departure to the
South. Her advice, as sound as it was well meant, could not be taken. She came to
the gate to see us off, and we said good-bye beneath the giant firs of the Petrovsky
Park with the harvest moon casting ghostly shadows around us. It was an eerie and
emotional farewell. We never saw her again.*

*. . . When the dawn broke, I sent the others home and drove out with Moura to
the Sparrow Hills to watch the sun rise over the Kremlin. It came up like an angry
ball of fire heralding destruction. No joy was to come with the morning.*

◈

AUGUST 1918

Public Reports and Secret Relationships
Headlines and Coded Dispatches

MOSCOW, AUGUST 1

Events were happening one after another. The rhythms had been broken,
the tones changed: history was hurtling at full speed.

Two pieces of news were making all the newspaper headlines.

First, the ambassadors of the Entente had rejected the Party's friendly
invitation to set up shop in Moscow. They had left Vologda in haste for
the port of Arkhangelsk on the White Sea. Were they getting ready to flee
by sea? Or were they preparing for an Allied attack?

At the same moment in Ukraine, the German governor, a representative of the kaiser, was killed by a bomb in Kiev: it was a murder
intended, just like that of Ambassador Mirbach, to break the Treaty
of Brest-Litovsk. Nobody doubted the Allies' complicity in this new
crime.

◈

On August 1, Lockhart received an encrypted report from one of his informants with the detail that the police's first question to the German dignitary's assassin had been: "Do you know somebody in Moscow named Lockhart?"

The noose was tightening. The days of every Briton in Russia were numbered.

Lockhart sped things up.

As matters progressed, he worked to shore up more support in the counterrevolutionary parties and poured yet more money into Russian movements that were pro-Allies. Moura helped him however she could in all these activities.

MOSCOW, AUGUST 3

The spy Sidney Reilly introduced two officers of Lenin's praetorian guard to Lockhart. The two men informed him that the Latvian regiments were ready to betray the Bolsheviks and fight for freedom alongside the British.

Lockhart was suspicious.

He was worried that he might be dealing with agents provocateurs and insisted on meeting their boss, Lieutenant Colonel Berzin, whose artillery protected the Kremlin.

MOSCOW, AUGUST 4

A thunderbolt: the Allies docked at the port of Arkhangelsk!

Moscow was overcome by panic. Rumors swirled that the invaders were marching toward the capital with a hundred thousand men. The Party's leaders were losing their heads. They packed up their archives and got ready to flee.

Lockhart went to the Kremlin to meet one of the men in Foreign Affairs.

Karakhan told him the Bolsheviks were lost.

MOSCOW, AUGUST 5

The Soviets broke off all relations with the countries in the Entente. In their eyes, the invasion of Russian territory, in contempt of all international laws, justified such drastic measures. The Cheka invaded the consulates and arrested the representatives of the foreign nations.

Lockhart escaped those roundups: he still had carte blanche to move as he wished, thanks to Trotsky, whose permit had for the last six months guaranteed diplomatic immunity for him.

The British legation, however, was expelled en masse from the Hotel Elite.

From room 309, Lockhart carried his personal effects up to the fifth floor of 19 Khlebny Lane, in the Arbat district: the marital apartment he had occupied during his time as a consul. He brought along his colleague Captain Hicks and his secretary, Mrs. Benckendorff.

Having been denied their passports, the two Englishmen were now hostages of the government. Their departure had been delayed indefinitely.

At once worried about and delighted by this situation, which kept the man of her life nearby for a few more days, Moura personally saw to the well-being of her guests on Khlebny Lane. This much Hicks was willing to let her do. As he was preoccupied with his own romantic relationship, he was quite happy to let her take charge of handling day-to-day matters.

He admitted that she was tactful. This woman had a particular skill for smoothing out difficulties. She made life a lighthearted affair, on the whole. And she couldn't be unaware of the doubts he had once voiced about her, but she didn't give him any grief about it. Any reproach. She made no assumptions about his motives. He continued to be suspicious, but for the moment he had laid down his weapons.

She adroitly dealt with their new existence as the lady of the house, hiring a cook for them as well as a manservant. As the base for the British mission—which she now called "our ménage à trois in the little hermitage"—the apartment had to maintain all the trappings of prestige in the Bolsheviks' eyes. This suspended sentence gave her the illusion that both her past existence, with hired help, and her future, alongside Lockhart in a diplomatic post, remained possible.

She took immense pleasure in this simulacrum of conjugal life, and she tried to retain every impression she had . . . For after.

MOSCOW, AUGUST 10

Lockhart wrote:

> *On August 10th the Bolshevik newspapers splashed their front page with headlines announcing a great Russian naval victory over the Allies at Archangel. I regarded this report as a joke or, at best, as a feeble attempt on the part of the Bolsheviks to stimulate the courage of their own followers. But that afternoon, when I saw Karachan, I had misgivings. His face was wreathed in smiles. The dejection of the previous days had gone, and his relief was too obvious to be put down to play-acting. "The situation is not serious," he said. "The Allies have landed only a few hundred men."*
>
> *. . . Later, I was to discover that his statement was only too true. The naval victory was a myth. The Bolsheviks had sunk an Allied barge in the Dvina. But the account of the strength of the Allied forces was literally correct. We had committed the unbelievable folly of landing at Archangel with fewer than twelve hundred men.*
>
> *It was a blunder comparable with the worst mistakes of the Crimean War . . .*
> *All my worst fears were speedily justified.*
>
> *. . . The consequences of this ill-conceived venture were to be disastrous both to our prestige and to the fortunes of those Russians who supported us. It raised hopes which could not be fulfilled. It intensified the civil war and sent thousands of Russians to their death. . . . To have intervened at all was a mistake. To*

have intervened with hopelessly inadequate forces was an example of paralytic half-measures which, in the circumstances, amounted to a crime. . . . Whatever may have been the intentions of the Allied Governments, our intervention was regarded by those Russians who supported it as an attempt to overthrow Bolshevism. It failed, and, with the failure, our prestige among every class of the Russian population suffered.

MOSCOW, AUGUST 15

One of the two Latvian officers who had already been introduced to Lockhart came back to the "little hermitage." He was accompanied by the head of the Kremlin's artillery, Lieutenant Colonel Berzin, who Lockhart had insisted on meeting.

As a guarantee of sorts, Berzin brought him a letter signed by Cromie, the friend and agent who Lockhart trusted completely.

Cromie wrote that he recommended these two men: Lieutenant Colonel Berzin could be of great assistance to the Allies.

Lockhart was still suspicious. There was no question at all that the letter was in Cromie's handwriting. It alluded to a private conversation, a correspondence they'd had around their departure, when Cromie had said he wanted to "bang the 'dore' before he went out."

"It was unmistakably from Cromie," Lockhart realized.

The handwriting was his . . . the spelling was his. No forger could have faked this, for like Prince Charles Edward, Frederick the Great, and Mr. Harold Nicolson, poor Cromie could not spell. The letter closed with a recommendation of Smidchen as a man who might be able to render us some service.

Lockhart, reassured, asked his visitors what specifically they wanted from him. Lieutenant Colonel Berzin told him that he needed safe conduct to be introduced to the generals of the Allied staff at Arkhangelsk.

He said everybody knew that the Allies were going to win the war against Germany. And consequently, Latvia wanted to help them.

Lockhart wavered. If Latvian regiments were defecting, that could certainly deal a fatal blow to the Red Army.

I arranged for them to call on me at the same time the next day.

MOSCOW, THE EVENING OF AUGUST 15

Lockhart summoned the representatives of the Entente to his place, the few diplomats who had been freed by the Cheka. They decided unanimously to encourage Lieutenant Colonel Berzin in his endeavors and to give him safe conduct to the Allies. Lockhart's secretary noted down the terms of their agreement.

MOSCOW, AUGUST 16

The two Latvians received the documents they had asked for. They also received, from Lockhart's own hands, a sizable amount of money, which would allow them to finance the revolt of the regiments in the Kremlin, as well as those out in Riga and in the other Baltic countries.

MOSCOW, AUGUST 17

At the Foreign Affairs office, the departure that all the Allied powers' nationals were hoping for was still up in the air.

Karakhan was playing the fool.

Of course he'd give them back their passports, of course. But where ever were these good sirs planning to go? The Germans still held Finland and Estonia. The Turks had Constantinople. Did Mr. Lockhart perhaps wish to take the path that crossed Afghanistan, by way of Persia?

Karakhan was joking.

And Lockhart took pleasure in it: the longer he was kept in Russia, the happier he was. He saw this inability to leave the country as a blessing that allowed him not to be separated from Moura.

But there was no news at all from Cromie or Reilly.

MOSCOW, AUGUST 25

Under the aegis of the Americans and the French, the representatives of the Allied intelligence services met at the US consulate to coordinate their actions.

Reilly was present. Lockhart wasn't.

That same night, one of the participants, the French journalist René Marchand, informed the Cheka of the meeting. He warned the Bolsheviks that the Allies were planning to topple the government. He added that the agent Sidney Reilly was determined to skin Lenin and Trotsky alive and to frog-march them up and down Moscow, to the boos and jeers of the Russian people.

The coup d'état was planned for September 6, the day of the Party's meetings at the Bolshoi.

René Marchand's testimony touched upon the entirety of the intelligence services, which were now caught in the Bolsheviks' nets.

All of them. With the sole exception of Lockhart, who hadn't been named.

MOSCOW, AUGUST 26

At the Cheka headquarters, Comrade Yakov Peters—the right-hand man of the creator of the secret police—was sitting at his office at 11 Bolshaya Lubyanka Street as he welcomed his agent provocateur: Lieutenant Colonel Berzin.

Berzin showed him the permit that Lockhart had written and signed on behalf of the Allied invaders: the proof of his complicity in anti-Bolshevik activities.

The Latvian regiments' betrayal had been a ploy. The Englishman had fallen into the trap.

Berzin also handed his boss a list of names and addresses of the majority of the spies working in the country. He had obtained this list by going through the apartment of Signor Massimo—Sidney Reilly—in Petrograd.

As for Reilly himself, he had vanished. But several Russians in touch with the British were arrested.

The Cheka decided not to bother Lockhart for the time being.

Until September 6, the date planned for the coup d'état against the Party, he could still be used as bait himself.

Berzin would have to maintain their relationship.

PETROGRAD AND MOSCOW, AUGUST 30

In Petrograd, the head of the local Cheka was felled by three gunshots. His assassin tried to flee through an apartment that the British had occupied: their club on the Neva embankment. The Soviets deemed the British responsible for this new crime.

In Moscow on the evening of that same day, Lenin, too, was the victim of an attack.

As he was leaving a meeting in a factory, he was shot down. A bullet punctured his left lung; another went through his shoulder. The Party feared for his life.

His sniper was a woman by the name of Fanny Kaplan, a member of the Socialist Revolutionary Party, the party of Mirbach's executioners. An anti-German and anti-Soviet movement that was reportedly funded by the Allies, even though it was Marxist.

This time, for the Bolsheviks, the crisis had peaked.

❖

At 19 Khlebny Lane, Lockhart and his two colleagues tried to assess exactly how immense the catastrophe was.

They had had no involvement at all in the attack against Lenin, much less that of the Cheka's head in Petrograd.

But if Lenin did die tonight, all his opponents would go down with him, as well. The foreigners and the *burzhui* would be the first to go.

The Red Terror had begun.

❖

"Our Ménage à Trois in the Little Hermitage"

On the evening of August 31, 1918, in the kitchen of the "little hermitage," the atmosphere was gloomy. The servants had all been sent home. Nobody had much of an appetite at dinner.

Around the table, the attacks the night before were the subject of a hundred questions.

Where had this Miss Kaplan, who had shot Lenin, come from? And where, too, had the assassin of the Cheka head in Petrograd come from?

"Whatever the facts may be," Lockhart grumbled, "Kaplan and the other one have pulled the rug out from under us."

"That's no understatement!" Hicks said. "They've beaten us to the finish line."

"And they're going to take us along for the ride," Moura joked.

The two men knew that the assassination attempt on Lenin would be the death knell of their adventures in Russia. This time, Trotsky's blank check would be no help to them. Karakhan would have the military forces expel them tomorrow. At best.

After the torrent of questions came silence.

It was impossible for them to imagine the future now, and so they spent the evening putting their affairs in order, making sure to clear away every trace of their clandestine activities, burning the codes and the last papers they still had. As for the rest, their personal effects, the two British men's suitcases were open and ready.

Lockhart and Moura dealt with matters wordlessly. Like two robots, they went from one room to the next, methodically and almost mechanically checking over everything to make sure that no compromising document had been forgotten in one drawer or another. But neither of them was giving serious thought to what could result from a search of their apartment. Their thoughts were too preoccupied by other matters.

Their separation. It hung over everything, it swallowed everything up.

Like the day they had first embraced, during that meal at the Hotel Elite when they hadn't been able to eat or drink a thing, their tension was now so palpable that they didn't dare exchange a gesture, much less a word.

What they had feared every morning since April was finally going to come to pass in this dawn. The guillotine blade, which they had sensed hanging over their heads at every moment of their love affair, would fall tomorrow. The closeness of the end left them with a bottomless exhaustion that drained them of their passion. Of their emotion, and even of their fear.

Lockhart went to bed first. He fell asleep immediately.

Hicks and Moura were too tense to fall asleep, so they set to packing their bags.

None of them had any idea that the building was already in the Cheka's crosshairs.

In his autobiography, Pavel Malkov, the leader of the team that had come to arrest Lockhart, described the activities carried out on the night of August 31, 1918, in these terms:

> With the Cheka man, we turned into Khlebny Lane and drew up a few yards before reaching No. 19, the house where Lockhart lived. It was then about 2 a.m.
> We easily found the entrance to the building but had to use our lighters on the

stairway, where there were no lamps and it was pitch dark. We climbed up to the fifth floor.

My colleagues stood to the side so that when the door of Lockhart's apartment opened they would not immediately be seen. I knocked hard on the door (the bells of most Moscow apartments were out of order in those days). Two or three minutes passed and I knocked again. Someone could be heard shuffling along the passage. A key was fitted in the lock, there was a click as it turned, and the door was opened a crack. There was a light in the vestibule and through the crack I recognized the woman secretary who had accompanied Lockhart on the journey from Petrograd to Moscow.

I tried to pull open the door, but the woman had taken the precaution to leave the chain up.

I moved closer to the crack so that the light from the vestibule shone full on me and gave the woman a good view. I then greeted her as politely as I was able and said I must see Mr. Lockhart at once.

Without batting an eyelid the woman feigned not to recognise me and in broken Russian began to enquire who I was and what I wanted.

I put my foot in the door so that she could not shut it in my face and firmly repeated that I must see Mr. Lockhart. I would explain to him the purpose of my late visit.

The woman refused to give way, and showed not the slightest intention of open-ing the door. There is no knowing just how this verbal conflict might have ended, but just then Lockhart's assistant, Hicks, walked into the vestibule. When he saw me, something in the nature of a smile flickered over his dull features and he flipped the chain off the door.

"Ah, Mr. Mankoff!" he said, that being what the Englishman always called me. "What can I do for you?"

I gently pushed Hicks aside and entered the apartment with my colleagues. I gave him no explanations but insisted he take me to Lockhart.

"But that's impossible, Mr. Lockhart is sleeping. I shall have to warn him first . . ."

"I'll warn him myself," I declared in such a resolute tone of voice that Hicks evidently realized what was going on. He stood aside and pointed dumbly to the door leading to Lockhart's bedroom.

The four of us went in and Hicks switched on the light. The bedroom was small and narrow and furnished with two comfortable armchairs, a Karelian birch wardrobe and matching chest of drawers and dressing-table. The latter was covered with elegant trinkets and toilet articles. A broad ottoman couch covered with a beautifully designed carpet reaching the floor completed the furnishings, except for the second luxurious carpet on the floor. There were no beds in the room. Lockhart was fast asleep on the ottoman and did not wake up even when Hicks switched on the light. I had to shake him gently by the shoulder before he opened his eyes.

"Oho! Mr. Mankoff!" he exclaimed.

"Mr. Lockhart," I announced, "by order of the Cheka, you are under arrest. Kindly get up and dress. You will have to come with me. Here's my warrant."

I must say Lockhart showed no particular consternation and made no protest. He did not trouble to read the warrant, but merely glanced at it. Clearly his arrest had not come as a surprise to him.

Not to embarrass him and to save time, I informed him I would have to search his apartment while he dressed. I took a swift look round the bedroom and then went to the next room with my two colleagues and Hicks. It was Lockhart's study. . . .

I searched the study myself while my colleagues went over the other rooms in the apartment.

I found numerous letters, personal papers, a revolver and cartridges in the desk drawers. They also contained a large amount of Russian tsarist and Soviet money in large denominations, quite apart from money of the Kerensky issue. I found nothing else in the wardrobe or anywhere else. Nor was anything found in the other rooms, though we made a thorough search, feeling in the seats and backs of the armchairs, sofas and divans, knocking on the walls and floors in all the rooms. We made an assiduous search but, as Peters had cautioned us, we worked carefully. None of the mattresses or upholstering was ripped apart.

Lockhart's account of the scene differed from Malkov's. The spy added that he was woken up by a rifle barrel pressing against his temple. And that his questions for why such an assault was happening were answered with orders to be quiet and follow the policemen. He had then been shoved, along with Hicks, into an armored car.

Moura wasn't with them. Other policemen held her back, in the apartment.

A second car was waiting in the distance.

This car would take her as well to the horrible prison in the Lubyanka building that served as headquarters for the Cheka.

CHAPTER EIGHTEEN

The Lockhart Plot

September 1–10, 1918

The room was dark, sparse, as narrow as a hallway. The only furniture was four small chairs set on both sides of a table, where a lamp burned.

It was Sunday, September 1. Midnight. Moura's first interrogation after a sleepless night and a long day in jail spent waiting.

They hadn't let her wash herself, much less do her hair, to look presentable before Comrade Yakov Peters.

With his black pants tucked into his boots, his white shirt buttoned up in the Russian style, his holster that a huge Mauser rifle hung from, Comrade Peters seemed to be the very personification of Chekism, aside from a few differences. The waves of his thick head of hair were pushed back, and his high forehead and his paleness made him look like a poet. And the gleaming watch strapped around his wrist gave him the trappings of a nouveau riche, or at least a modern man who didn't scorn the latest things.

It was a deceptive look. Peters lived frugally and was reputed to be incorruptible.

As for his robust body, it betrayed his peasant origins.

And finally, the one unlikely trait that summed up his character: his charred fingernails, which were clear evidence of the torture he himself had undergone. His pride. Yakov Peters took great care to show them to the suspects he interrogated, in order to remind them of the tortures the tsar's police had inflicted upon him.

Despite his family name, which seemed fairly Anglo-Saxon, Peters had Latvian heritage, like his agent provocateur, Lieutenant Colonel Berzin. And his reputation was well established: he was one of the cruelest executioners of the Cheka. He was infamous.

And young, too. Barely thirty years old.

The last detail was that he spoke perfect English after having lived in exile for ten years in London. He had even left behind a British wife, who he said he was very fond of.

Yakov Peters had just sent away the two soldiers who had informed him that they had seized the "secretary," and he glared at her without a word, with a steely gaze.

Fear had made her seem both cold and dignified.

Moura was indeed terrified, and took care not to meet his gaze. She bore a resolutely neutral expression. She stood up straight: it was a posture that was if not natural, at least composed. As she stared at the table, she looked as if she were awaiting her interrogator's goodwill.

The lamp's ray of light fell across Peters's hands, which he had pressed flat against his other firearm. He held a card-stock folder closed.

He sighed, turned away from his prisoner, and started reading the dossier. He flipped through the pages slowly. As he read, his despair became more evident.

"It's a serious matter," he finally said in crisp English. "I'm rather disappointed to find you mixed up in this scheme."

He spoke politely. But his tone didn't allow for any ambiguity about his conclusions.

"Such acts! Rather serious. The Party should have been thoroughly informed! Why didn't you come here and tell us what you knew?"

"I didn't have anything to report. I'm nothing more than Mr. Lockhart's secretary. And I only accepted this work because the Party held Mr. Lockhart in very high esteem . . . He was invited to Moscow by Comrade Trotsky, and both he and his team enjoyed the privileges of a diplomatic mission."

"Is that true?"

Yakov Peters seemed wholly absorbed by his reading again:

"According to my sources—which surely must be mistaken—you have lived conjugally with Mr. Lockhart . . . since April 15, to be exact. Five months."

"I've known Mr. Lockhart since the time he was a consul. For five years. And I do not live conjugally with him. I remain, alas, the wife of a Baltic man I was married to at the age of seventeen. A man I disdain. I went to Estonia to tell him exactly that. I could have stayed there, but I came back to my home in Russia . . . Nothing required me to do so."

"Nothing, apparently."

"Apart from my loyalty to the Party."

"What else, if not loyalty, could have brought an aristocratic woman by the name of Benckendorff back to Moscow?"

"Comrade Karakhan will affirm to you that this 'aristocratic woman by the name of Benckendorff' fervently admires Comrade Lenin, that she has read all his writings, and that she has supported the October Revolution from the very beginning. I do ask you to telephone him."

"Comrade Karakhan is the author of this folder I hold here. He's saying exactly the opposite of what you're telling me. Who should I believe?"

She stayed silent. Yakov Peters continued:

"Comrade Karakhan writes: 'The aforementioned Maria Ignatyevna Benckendorff, née Zakrevskaya, has no political conviction. Only her personal interests drive her. And, quite likely, her emotions. Both have led her toward England. And specifically toward Lockhart . . . She would be ready to betray Russia at any cost."

"Comrade Karakhan could never have written any such thing: he knows how intensely I love Russia!"

"You are probably not speaking of the same nation."

"I am speaking of Eternal Russia."

"And I am speaking of Bolshevik Russia, which your lover, Mr. Lockhart, is trying to destroy."

"Mr. Lockhart is not my lover."

"Oh, yes . . . And what do you make of this?"

Yakov Peters held a photo up in front of her eyes. Moura was frozen there in Lockhart's arms on the Sparrow Hills.

It had been taken on August 1 as they had left the Strelnya. The dawn, with its red sun, had made it possible for the photographer to take the shot without a flash.

They had never suspected that they had been followed.

Yakov Peters silently savored the expression on the face of the woman he was interrogating.

She wasn't calm anymore.

He allowed himself the further pleasure of showing her a second photo, where she appeared naked in Lockhart's lap in room 309.

She had become so pale that she seemed about to pass out.

But she wouldn't yet.

Yakov Peters still had many questions to ask her. He unhurriedly gathered up the images without pressing the subject. He simply sighed and continued the interrogation in another tone, switching from English to fluid Russian.

"Last name? First name? Patronymic? Date and place of birth?"

"Zakrevskaya. Maria Ignatyevna. March 6, 1893. In the province of Poltava in Ukraine."

"Ukrainian? I should have guessed. I love Ukrainian women, personally: they're real, hot-blooded women! So you're twenty-five years old . . . The same age as my British wife. She's stayed behind in London . . . I do miss her, you can't imagine just how dearly! Oh, beauty, youth! Who were your accomplices in the assassination of Comrade Lenin?"

"I don't have any accomplices. And I haven't plotted against Ilyich . . . I admire him! I simply cannot believe that Karakhan might have told you otherwise. I've gone with him to many meetings of the Party. He knows that what I feel is far from hostility."

"You're a very good liar. But if you keep trying to lie to me, you won't be any help to your lover. You're forcing me to consider him guilty. Do you know this woman Kaplan?"

"No."

"Where did Sidney Reilly go?"

"I don't know."

"But you do know him?"

"No."

"You're still lying! We saw you with him at the Strelnya cabaret a month ago."

"I did have dinner at Strelnya. There were six of us. It was a farewell dinner for a friend of Mr. Lockhart, one of the British officers who was leaving Moscow."

"And Sidney Reilly wasn't there?"

"Not as far as I know . . . There was Hicks's fiancée and there were the British, and then there was a Greek man."

"And what was this Greek man's name?"

"I don't remember. I didn't talk to him."

"But Lockhart talked to him?"

"It's possible."

"What did they say to each other?"

"We were listening to the Gypsies. It was very noisy there."

Yakov Peters leafed through his papers briefly. He extracted the permit that Lockhart had granted Berzin to see the generals of the Allied staff.

"Do you know this handwriting?"

"I can't see anything without my glasses."

"Stop beating around the bush! Is this Lockhart's writing or isn't it?"

She did not answer. He stared at her a long while:

"It would be better *for him* if you told me the truth."

She looked down and stayed silent.

He rang the small bell on his desk. The two guards entered. He ordered them to take her down to the basement, where the women were sent. A solitary cell until further notice.

As she walked through the doorway, he yelled behind her:

"It would be better *for him*: you'd be able to avoid Captain Cromie's fate."

She turned around. He smiled at her.

"Oh, you didn't hear? He died. Slowly. We were forced to kill him like the dog he was."

Cromie, dead? Her Crow . . .

Her grief was so intense that Yakov Peters was certain she would faint.

He hadn't expected this news to come as such a shock to her. That it would impress her, yes. But not that it would strike her dumb.

He gestured to the guards to lead her back, sit her down again, and give her a glass of water.

She had lost all sense of what was happening around her. Her dizzy spell hadn't ended. One of the guards splashed the glass of water in her face.

Cromie . . . She barely heard what Peters was saying. A distant voice mentioning an attack on the English ambassador in Petrograd. Peters gave her a full explanation. Cromie: killed a few hours before she and Lockhart had themselves been arrested.

It was too much detail.

He told her how Cromie had resisted the Cheka's search at the Saltykov palace. How he had appeared on the first landing, a gun in his hand, to defend his home from those scoundrels, claiming that it was British territory. How he had shot down two unfortunate policemen without any warning. How the others had fired back with a blitz of bullets. How he had fallen and rolled down to the foot of the stairs.

How the comrades had recognized a disgraceful tsarist decoration on his uniform, how they had crushed the cross flat beneath the heels of their boots, digging it into his chest all the way to his heart. How Cromie had taken more than an hour to die.

"He's rotting back there, at the foot of his grand staircase. And he'll go on rotting there until I send him to the mass grave, like all the other spies and traitors."

More than prison, more than fear, more than all the emotions she had felt over the past few days, Cromie's death cut deepest to her core.

Yakov Peters had achieved his goal.

He changed his tone, speaking in a more measured, conciliatory way that strained toward politeness.

"You're telling me, Comrade Maria Ignatyevna, that Mr. Lockhart isn't guilty. Prove it to me. If you know, that's all I'm asking for! To believe in his innocence . . . To believe *you*, Maria Ignatyevna . . . Personally, I find your Lockhart to be very sympathetic. We've met each other several times. I brought him out to see all the corpses after the anarchists were executed in April. We had a great laugh, the two of us, as we turned over the bodies. We even admired one, a prostitute who was completely naked, as death had caught her in the middle of an orgy . . . I won't go so far as to say that we became friends. But close to it. I even loaned him my car the next day: he needed it to go pick up one of his lady friends at the train station . . . Honestly, I would hate to have to sign the order for his execution. You can't imagine how sick it makes me to sign a death warrant. Help me avoid it. Tell me what you know. Collaborate with me . . . And save him."

She was still trembling with nausea.

Yakov Peters waved to his soldiers to take her away again.

❖

No window. No electricity. The guards had unscrewed the lightbulb from the ceiling. They had darkened the hallway. Their eyes met every so often through the peephole, but the doorframe didn't let through any light.

The sanitary bucket next to her hadn't been disinfected after the suspects who had stayed in this cell before her. It reeked. They hadn't been taken upstairs to the office where Yakov Peters handed down judgments. Rather, they had been taken to the lowermost cellars to be killed with a bullet to the neck.

The stench was the sole link Moura still had to reality.

No doubt Yakov Peters felt a welter of emotions every time he signed a death warrant; even so, he must steel himself to do it. He had to push aside his sentimentality. His romanticism . . . And if he did, then she could be assured she would be shot in the head, as well.

She wondered what the bullet would leave behind. A small hole at the bottom of her skull? Or a splattered brain?

What part of her would be left behind?

As Moura lay curled up on her straw mattress, she saw Cromie again, dancing a tango at Yendel. The embodiment of beauty, youth, and courage. She knew quite well exactly which medal the chekists had tortured him with. His Saint George's Cross. He had received it for his deeds in 1915, when he had sunk multiple German submarines that were crossing the Baltic Sea off the Estonian coast.

What mattered was that Lockhart was safe . . . And alive!

Once again, she tried to suss out the lies within Yakov Peters's interrogation.

What proof did he really have?

The Cheka wouldn't dare touch him. The Cheka wouldn't dare torture him. The Cheka wouldn't dare execute him. Yakov Peters can't do anything to him: Lockhart represents England, he's still a diplomat . . . But Cromie was a diplomat, too!

Lockhart . . . Was he here? Locked up in the men's wing, the hallway upstairs? She tried to remember. Yakov Peters wouldn't have missed the chance to interrogate him, as well. Who knew if she'd see him tomorrow?

She needed to talk to him, tell him, warn him. Above all, he had to keep his mouth shut!

She shivered.

Deep in her heart, the past and the present were blurring together. *Don't confess, don't confess anything . . .*

She was feverish. Or maybe those were already labor contractions?

But that was impossible.

She was only a few months pregnant.

Little Peter?

A hot liquid dripped down her legs.

She didn't understand right away.

It was quite some time before she realized she had blood on her fingers.

She didn't let out a cry. She didn't move. She had heard so many women screaming during the previous night, screaming in vain, that she didn't even try to call for help.

She stayed there, unmoving, stripped of all clothing, stripped even of any sense of space or time. Without a name. Without an age. Without a future.

She felt her life dripping out of her.

She slipped.

◆

"You gave us a nice scare there!" Yakov Peters exclaimed as he welcomed her to his small office a week later. "Don't stand up. Sit down . . . Why in heaven didn't you tell me you were pregnant? We would have done what we needed to. A more comfortable cell . . . Well, here we are now, that's better! Tomorrow your cheeks will be rosy again and you'll be frolicking again. The doctor is very happy with your progress: you've got a spine of steel, he says . . . You're young, my darling. Yes, yes, I know, your health is the least of your concerns: you're much more worried about the fate of Mr. Lockhart. Rest assured, he's doing quite nicely, too. And you can have plenty of other babies together, as many as you'd like.

"It's a nice love story you've got here! In a way, it's the same story as my marriage in London. But the other way around. She's British, I'm Russian. Two halves coming together to make a single whole. Two souls merging together, the kind that somebody can hope for only once in his lifetime. Do you want me to tell you more? Mr. Lockhart is very attached to you. I'd go so far as to say that he's mad with love for you . . . And Mr. Lockhart's passion touches me so dearly. You should know that the day after you were arrested, or maybe the next day after that, I released him. The truth was that I had nothing against him in my files. So I let him go free, as he wished. He came back to his apartment around noon on September 1, along with his colleague Hicks, who I released, as well. Hicks went to be with his fiancée again as quick as he could. But your friend Lockhart—our friend—had no idea what had happened to you, and as he couldn't find you in your little hermitage, he lost his head completely. He had his suspicions that you had been imprisoned . . . But where? In which prison? He took the police chiefs' offices in the Kremlin by storm for three days and set off a scandal everywhere. He was, I think, sick with worry over you. He even forced open Comrade Karakhan's door so he could plead your case as powerfully as he could.

Karakhan—who is softhearted and loves you, Maria Ignatyevna, dearly, yes, he loves you so, so much—gave me a quick phone call to convey Lockhart's request to get you out of here immediately. Lockhart came to this building to find you. And in this building, unfortunately, I had to have him arrested a second time. The order had come down from above earlier that morning, all the way from Comrade Trotsky himself. You should have seen the wardens and the way they watched Mr. Lockhart make his way up my stairs, four by four! They were determined to find him, no matter where he was in the city . . . And he was right there. His return saved us so much trouble. I have to confess that I'm grateful to him for this almost spontaneous surrender . . . From the prison here at Lubyanka we transferred him to one of the Kremlin's apartments, which we reserve for high-level prisoners. Not a single one, up to this point, has come out alive. Who knows if Mr. Lockhart might, thanks to you, be the exception that proves the rule? Once again, you mustn't worry: he's doing well . . . All is going well. Oh yes, before I forget, incidentally: the doctor told me to let you know that the fetus was well formed. A boy."

She couldn't hold back her sobbing. Her despair was undeniable.

Her week in the infirmary had been morally and physically grueling. She was pale. During her miscarriage, she had lost a great deal of blood. Yakov Peters could claim she was in good health all he liked, she could even pretend to appreciate the compliment, but she was coming out of this ordeal severely diminished.

She looked down. She tried to hide her frailty. He continued:

"Mr. Lockhart, in turn, is in good shape; you can go and see for yourself. I'm going to give you permission to write to him and—who knows?—even to go visit him in his apartment in the Kremlin. If . . . ."

Her reaction was remarkable: a look that betrayed wild hope. But she remained silent.

He continued: "If . . . Well, my condition wouldn't be hard to fulfill. All you'd have to do would be to tell me everything you'd been witness to, in the past . . . And everything you'll see, everything you'll hear, *in the future.*"

She looked up. "You want me to betray him!"

"It's not a betrayal, is it, to help the Revolution and save the man you love? You do love Russia, after all. And you love Lockhart . . . But do you love him as much as he loves you? At least, I should hope so! Because this man, out of love, threw himself right into the lions' den. And he didn't hesitate. He could have fled. Vanished into thin air, just like Sidney Reilly and the others. No . . . Like Orpheus in the underworld, he came to bring you back. His fate is now in your hands. Will you let him die?"

She did not respond. But each sentence had been a solid blow; he could sense it.

He pressed his advantage:

"What I'm offering you to do for me—what am I saying, for me? *For Russia!*—What I'm suggesting you do is nothing compared to letting Mr. Lockhart live . . . Don't make that face at me, or else I'm going to think you're still lying to me. I'm going to think you're still a servant of *the people of the past* who set out to kill Comrade Lenin. Would you prefer the *burzhui* to win out over the Russian people? . . . Which army do you serve? That of the oppressors or that of the oppressed? The moment has come for you to choose! The past or the future: which side do you belong to?"

"I belong to Russia."

"And what is it I am proposing you do for Russia?"

"To serve as a rat and a spy!"

"Such big words all of a sudden. I thought you were smarter than that, Maria Ignatyevna. *Spy?* If your feelings for poor old Mr. Lockhart are too weak to protect him, then I can at least call on your sense of duty and your patriotism: protect Russia from an Allied invasion. All I ask of you is what your love of Russia asks of you. The ball is in your court."

"The ball?" she scoffed.

"Oh, don't mince words with me. Ball, spy, rat, betrayal . . . Are those words such a shock to you? 'Spy!' you say, and you purse your lips in contempt . . . But, my dear"—he broke into English, driving the point home—"you're already a spy! You're up to your neck in this mess. The trap was sprung on you ages ago. What did you think you were doing at Kuba when you were picking Comrade Karakhan's brain? When you were running to the Strelnya just to tell your lover what Karakhan had whispered to you? When you came back to Karakhan to tell him what the Englishman thought? Half our men think you're working for us. The other half think you're working for the Allies. It was exactly the same thing for all the men in the British office . . . Oh, you should read all General Knox's reports! I don't doubt that the French are convinced, too, that if they could pay you more than the others they'd have you working for them. A spy. Even a double agent, even a triple agent. Not to mention the Germans. They saw you coming to your husband's house in Estonia just when all the lines of communication with Russia had been cut . . . Then they saw you leave and return home, as calm as Saint John the Baptist, going back exactly the same way! So what do you think they concluded about you?"

"I wasn't spying on anyone! And certainly not my husband!"

"It doesn't matter. That's what they believed. They think you're protected. Meaning: *protected by the Party* . . . And on that point, they're not wrong: without Comrade Karakhan's protection, you would never have been able to cross the border."

"If I'm to believe you, my cover has been blown everywhere. Seen by all the intelligence agencies all over the world . . . I wouldn't be much of an agent when it came to intelligence! So there's nothing I can do for the Party."

"You can't *do anything*, no . . . Except help your mother, who apparently has nothing but you to keep her going. However will she survive if you choose to abandon her? And that's not to mention your children! You've already lost one boy. That was last week. By disappearing tonight, by disappearing for good into the basement of this building, you'll end up making your little boy and your little girl orphans. You can't *do anything*, no. Except save the life of your lover: it's in your hands . . . But I don't want to force you into this. You are perfectly free to agree to help Russia and save your lover, or not . . . And it's true that you have nothing to lose. Because if you haven't yet realized just how massive a plot you've been embroiled in—*already* up to your neck!—read this article on the front page of *Izvestiya*. It'll be of great interest to you."

Yakov Peters slid the paper across the table to her, taking care to turn it around so she could read it:

THE LOCKHART PLOT
THE IMPERIALIST ALLIES' CONSPIRACY
AGAINST SOVIET RUSSIA

On September 2, a plot hatched by British and French diplomats was foiled.

It was run by the head of the British mission, a certain Robert Bruce Lockhart, and his underlings.

This plot was designed to exile the People's leaders, assassinate Comrades Lenin and Trotsky, blow up the trains that supply Petrograd and Moscow, and reduce the population to famine. They would then erect a military dictatorship in Russia.

The conspirators were acting under the cover of diplomatic immunity and on the basis of certificates signed by Mr. Lockhart, many copies of which the pan-Russian Cheka now holds.

It has been established over the course of the last ten days that Lockhart transferred the sum of 1,200,000 rubles to a man named Sidney Reilly, one of his agents sent out with the mission of corrupting the Red Army.

The conspiracy was unmasked thanks to the loyalty of the Latvian garrisons and the courage of their superiors, who had been offered extraordinary sums of money by the perpetrators. The investigation is moving quickly.

"I'm sure this whole report is just a heap of exaggerations," Peters declared as he took away the newspaper. "And probably a long string of lies. But to prove it, I'll need further information."

Moura looked down again. The article she had read had been yet another shock.

She needed to buy herself time. She needed to think.

She hadn't known that the Soviets had given the whole story around their arrest the horrible name "the Lockhart Plot." But she very much did know what was happening on the outside. A decree had been laid down calling for all the class enemies of the Soviet Republic and every individual involved in the White Army's organizations, in the revolts, or in the riots to be shot on the spot.

Over the week she had spent in the infirmary, the nurses' aides serving as her wardens had also informed her of the details and the numbers.

She knew that the day after Lenin's assassination attempt, 1,300 bourgeois hostages had been killed en masse in the Petrograd and Kronstadt prisons. That five hundred others had been executed in the following three days. That in the six days after, the Cheka was planning to execute nearly fifteen thousand people of the past. And that the number of executions planned for the month of October would be two to three times greater than all the death sentences handed down by the tsar's regime . . . in a century.

That was what the founder of the Cheka, Felix Dzerzhinsky, and his right-hand man, Yakov Peters, had decided.

"Don't presume that Mr. Lockhart's status protects him in any way: he doesn't have the rank of ambassador. He doesn't bear any such credentials. He ceased to be consul, in fact, in 1917. England was careful there: an unofficial diplomat that it could disavow and abandon should there be any problem . . . A spy, as you say, a vulgar *spy*! The truth is that he's on his own. He has only one card up his sleeve now, and that's you.

"If you want to stay close to him, Maria Ignatyevna, you don't have many choices. And I would say the deal I'm offering you is certainly to your advantage. All I need from you is some forthrightness and some honesty for Russia . . . Could Mr. Lockhart be guilty toward your motherland? But of course! It's patently obvious. But between the two of us, that's not the real question. So what do I want of you, then? Proof that England, that every single level of its government is guilty. I want proof of England's interference in Russia's domestic affairs. I want proof that Lloyd George, his ministers, and his king ordered all these acts that the papers accuse Lockhart of plotting. I want proof that the capitalist West is guilty of a whole series of political crimes that no country in the world would dare confess to! And in exchange, I will guarantee that your mother lives in safety. I do not mention your own life, since you don't seem very interested in it. Although . . . Life *with* Lockhart? Get him to say that he wants to stay in Russia. He loves you enough to do that. And you love him enough to make him happy here! That would be quite the coup, wouldn't it? Quite a coup for you, for Russia, for the Revolution, if Robert Bruce Lockhart, the British diplomat, should freely *choose* not to return to England! In any case, there's no life for him back there in London: his career's over. What would you say to him settling in Moscow? And that's not all: I'll make the offer a sweeter one . . . Sweeter than the imperialists were ever willing to be with me . . . Here's a pen, some ink, and some paper. Reassure him, because I'm telling you that he's somewhat depressed. Tell him that you're doing well and that you love him. In Russian, please, so I can seal and stamp your letter in front of you. He'll get your message in the afternoon. Go on: write."

She took the pen he was holding out to her and leaned over the sheet of paper. How to confess, under Yakov Peters's eye, that she lost their baby? How to apologize for not being able to give him the baby he had so dearly wished for? Her throat was choked with sobs. She wavered.

Yakov Peters was impatient. He stood over her, watching her words of love as if they were meant for him.

"Write, or you'll never see him again!"

CHAPTER NINETEEN

In a Bind

SEPTEMBER 10–OCTOBER 3, 1918

She had been released.

At the end of that afternoon, Moura found herself standing in front of the door to 11 Bolshaya Lubyanka Street, Yakov Peters's office, just steps away from the Kremlin, where Lenin resided.

The truth was that most of those buildings were occupied by the Cheka services. It was an extensive complex: not just number 11 but also numbers 2, 7, 9, 13, 14, 18, and 22. They were immense structures, the nicest of which had formerly been home to insurance companies.

Dazed by the light, exhausted by the preceding ten days of terror and mourning, she stayed there for whole minutes, hardly daring to believe it, hardly daring even to move.

She ended up heading toward number 2, the largest of the buildings, a palace in the neobaroque style that served as both prison and torture site and where executions would be carried out. It was right off the square.

The neighborhood, once a din of automobiles, was deserted. It was proof that the area had a bad reputation. Nobody got off the few trams, which were all crammed full, weighed down by human bodies, and went along without stopping.

She hopped on to one at random, the first one with space for her. In her daze, she didn't see until the very last stop that she was going in the wrong direction. It took her nearly three hours to get back to the apartment on Khlebny Lane by foot. Night had fallen. She had to grope around as she made her way up the five floors.

On the landing, she found two guards. They'd been assigned, she learned, to defend the apartment from robbers. They let her by and then stood at attention again. The slightly ajar door had no lock on it.

She pushed it open, quickly closed it behind her, and tried to keep it shut with what was left of the lock, but to no avail. She switched on the light . . . And she saw the mess.

Yakov Peters might have asked for the first search to be "discreet," but he had clearly changed his mind with Lockhart's second arrest. It was a full-on police raid. This time, his men had ripped up all the cushions, torn out all the wallpaper, rummaged through all his books. Even the telephone receiver was hanging off the wall, like a spider at the end of its thread. The first thing Moura did was hang it up.

And then pick it back up. An old reflex . . . to stay connected to everyone.

She wavered. She knew her calls would be listened to now. That ever since she had moved here, not a single conversation had escaped the Cheka.

But it didn't matter: she needed to call Mommy!

Call her mother, reassure her. Moura still had the same reactions as before. She hadn't quite realized just how great these changes to her life had been.

Poor Mommy, she must be terrified! Unless she had no idea of the danger her daughter had just escaped. Did she think Moura was still in the Baltic provinces? Did she not know that her daughter had fled Estonia and returned to Russia?

Quite possibly.

Moura hadn't let her know that she was coming to Petrograd at the end of July. Rather than have to explain how her marriage was falling apart, she had gone straight to Moscow without seeing her mother. And for all of August she had been silent. There was no use telling Mommy this good news: that her Mourushka was cheating on Djon and cohabitating with a married man.

She sighed. She would call Mommy tomorrow. She didn't have the energy tonight to tell her about her stay in prison.

She put down the phone and headed toward Lockhart's bedroom. The chekists hadn't held back at all here, either. Not a single piece of furniture was still upright. Even the parquet wood slats under the Oriental rug had been pried up.

Another reflex was for her to tidy all this up. To pick up the objects strewn across the floor. To put all the things in order. To get all her thoughts in order.

Ever since she had been imprisoned, she'd had only one obsession: to save Lockhart.

What else could she have thought about?

As she gathered up the books, she tried to set her memories straight, organize her impressions, recall everything that had happened over the last few weeks. And understand them.

What had Yakov Peters asked her during his interrogations? What did he need?

She had heard him perfectly well: she was supposed to bring him "documents" that proved to the Bolsheviks that the capitalists had been engineering a coup d'état against Lenin.

But Yakov Peters already had the proof of England's interference in Russia's internal affairs. He himself had set the trap of the Latvian regiments that were supposedly ready to betray the Kremlin for the Allies' benefit. He even had the permits Lockhart had signed for his spy Berzin. He knew the most intimate details of their life in this apartment. The smallest details of their relationship.

He knew that Mommy was ill, the names of her children, the dates she had traveled to and from Estonia. He had probably read all her letters. He even knew the tone of the dispatches that Knox was sending to London, the encrypted telegrams expressing the Briton's doubts about her morality.

She fell to her knees in front of the bookshelves, then right to the ground: she now realized just how much she was at the mercy of Yakov Peters and the Cheka. She stayed there, her legs bent, her arms outstretched.

Followed and spied on by the police for months! Probably ever since the first revolution. Maybe even before . . . by the tsar's police, who knew? Hadn't she passed for a liberal back then?

But that wasn't the worst of it.

The worst was not that the Cheka had been trailing her, but that the Cheka had been *protecting* her.

All Moura's actions during her affair with Lockhart—her comings and goings between Petrograd and Moscow, her stays at the Hotel Elite, her move here—she had carried them out with Yakov Peters's consent. She recalled his words: "You're already a spy! You're up to your neck in this mess. The trap was sprung on you ages ago."

She laughed bitterly. How could she have hoped to slip through their nets? To stay pure, untouched by the war, unaffected by the Revolution?

Not a judge but an impartial arbiter of history.

How could she have believed she would escape all this? Hadn't she been shaped for this: to obey Peters's interests, to spy and betray?

General Knox would be delighted. Reality had proven him right. He had been on the nose on every point. Yes, Mrs. Benckendorff was a double agent working for both the British and the Russians. Yes, her husband was a collaborator with the Germans.

Djon, too, would be delighted: hadn't he kept insisting that she choose one side or the other? The Whites or the Reds? Yakov Peters had uttered those same words: "Which army do you serve? That of the oppressors or that of the oppressed? The moment has come for you to choose!" She had been so sure she didn't belong to any army!

She had genuinely believed in the Bolsheviks' ideal of fraternity. At the beginning.

Now, the idea of assisting them made her nauseous. The massacres of the last few weeks had only exposed their barbarity. They were executioners. How could she "choose" to be an informant for their police? How could she "choose" to belong to the Cheka?

But *did* she have a choice?

Before freeing her, Yakov Peters had made her come to his office for a few poetic thoughts.

The interrogations were over; now they could speak as *comrades*.

He had told her the most romantic story in the world. That of his own return to the revolutionary ideal. He said that while he was exiled in London, he had found himself in the same situation she was in now. Comfortably settled in life as a young married man, madly in love with his British wife, father to a little girl he adored. All his dreams of equality and fraternity had disappeared. And then, one day, he had woken up with a start, ashamed of his selfishness and weakness. He had decided to leave his job, abandon his family. And take up the fight again beside Lenin. Since then, he had been battling for peace and for the good of human- ity . . . She couldn't imagine that this battle had been an easy one! He, too, had been a victim of the Revolution. Far more so than the *burzhui* and the people of the past! Far more so than all the counterrevolution- aries he had executed!

He had pointed out his pistol on the table and asked her:

"Do you know how to shoot this thing?"

She had answered:

"I think I do."

"But have you used one before to kill a human being?"

"No."

"You're a lucky, lucky person, Countess Maria. I swear on the head of my little girl that I would much rather, myself, never have to use it."

He had gone on with his lecture, telling her that personally, he was against the death penalty. As was Lenin. And all the Bolsheviks. He had added that when Trotsky had the idea at the beginning of the Revolution to build a guillotine, the Party had revolted.

But these days . . . Now, in September 1918, Russia was strangled by the machinations of all the conspirators who wanted to bring about its downfall. The comrades were forced to accept that they were in a state of siege. And the Terror was their only defense. Once the land was secure, life would resume its normal course.

Moura, still lying on the floor among the books, tried to decipher the meaning of all these details. The man behind Yakov Peters eluded her.

He had spared her. He had freed her. He had promised her that she would see her lover again. He had even suggested that Lockhart could get authorization to stay in Russia and follow a career that befitted him. His words had given her senseless hope.

She couldn't bring herself to hate him.

She even trusted him. She felt he was sincere.

But she wasn't so naive as not to realize that he would use her as bait. And the Briton as a propaganda tool.

She had to resist the temptation to drive Lockhart into the Party's arms. She had to resist the dream of settling in Moscow with him.

She also understood that with those sentimental phrases, Yakov Peters had been trying to justify his cruelty and make it easier for her to come over to his side.

But to take such great care wooing her, recruiting her, he must have believed she would be very useful to him.

A thousand questions buzzed in her mind.

Why had he called her *countess*? Was he *that* fascinated by the aristocracy?

She wasn't *Countess* Benckendorff, and he knew it. Why had he given her that title she didn't have any right to?

She tried to recall his words.

He had said she was one of the only women in her milieu he had heard express any sympathy toward Lenin's ideals . . . one of the only noblewomen who hadn't been set on fighting against the Revolution.

But that didn't protect her from the possibility of a bullet to the head at any point.

Why had he let her life be saved when he'd killed the others? Did he really need informers among the *burzhui*?

He had shown her the heap of execution orders.

"It's my obligation to make sure that the prisoners are eliminated in a swift and humane manner. I've carried out this task, which is so repugnant to me, with a diligence that those who have been sentenced should thank me for. Because there's nothing worse than an executioner whose hand is shaking and whose heart is torn. Believe me, Countess, as I've already told you, I don't take any pleasure in signing even one of these papers. I only do it because stamping out these traitors who conspire against Russia is essential to the survival of the state."

With that allusion to Lockhart's guilt, he had led her to the door of his office, like a dancer politely guiding his partner to her chair after a waltz has ended.

Moura had collapsed at the bottom of the bookshelves at Khlebny Lane, and all her limbs were trembling. The tension had snapped. She knew she had fallen to the bottom of the pit. She was afraid.

She tried to get ahold of herself.

Who could get her out of the Cheka's sights? Who could save Lockhart?

The Ace of Spies—the infamous Sidney Reilly?

The few surviving members of his network were being judged and sentenced at this point. He himself had disappeared.

What about Hicks?

Yes, she needed to find Hicks!

During her miscarriage, she had learned from the wardens that unlike his superior, Hicks had evaded a second arrest and taken refuge in the American residence, which had become the Norwegian legation after the Allied forces' diplomatic relations with the Bolsheviks fell apart. At this moment he was still shut away there, along with all the other diplomats who had been threatened with death for their involvement in the Lockhart Plot.

It was impossible to go see them. The building was sealed. Trotsky, who had been embarrassed by the international scandal around the murder of Captain Cromie at the British embassy, was reluctant to order an attack. He was planning to force Hicks and the others out by starving them.

If not Hicks, if not the Allied diplomats, who could save Lockhart?

Moura started mechanically shelving the books on the shelves again. Her mind clicked through the possibilities.

Well, who?

The representatives of the neutral powers.

They alone had the power to put pressure on the Bolsheviks. The

Swiss representative, the Danish representative, the Swedish representative. She knew them all: her years living among high society in Berlin, Petersburg, and Moscow hadn't been in vain. During the war, she had continued dining with them. They would welcome her, they would listen to her. She could plead the case of her British colleague to them.

She would also make sure to see the representative from the Red Cross: Allen Wardwell. The mere thought of this tall American whose wisdom, courage, and sympathy she knew well reassured her. Wardwell . . . she had to call Wardwell. She went to the telephone but then stopped herself.

No . . . Her plan would be useless if she got Yakov Peters's attention. What was he waiting for, if not for her to lead him to Lockhart's friends? He wanted all the accomplices.

If not Wardwell, who else?

A member of the Party. She had to aim higher . . . Karakhan? Of course it would be Karakhan! Hadn't Yakov Peters said that Karakhan loved her dearly? He had had enough meals with her that she knew as much. She would try to ensnare him tomorrow.

Who else?

She had found her fighting spirit again. She forgot about the watchmen standing guard on the landing.

Tomorrow she would draw on her connections. Tomorrow she would go all over the city, tomorrow she would see the dignitaries in every building, she would convince every group, she would urge the global powers to step in and save Lockhart from certain death.

The best thing, tonight, was simply to take a bath and go to sleep. She went to find her nightgown in the heap of clothes that had been cast aside.

When she picked up her peignoir, she felt a weight in its pocket. Her notebook.

My God!

The chekists had searched the entire apartment from top to bottom. She herself, along with Hicks and Lockhart, had destroyed all the papers that might be compromising. But none of them had thought to go through their pockets.

She flipped through the little notebook. Her blood ran cold . . . The details of every one of their meetings! She had set down in ink the letter and spirit of everything, all the way down to the conversations that had played out here. The declarations of British, French, American diplomats, the names of White Army agents, the maps of various opposition networks. And even Lockhart's instructions and warnings to ST1, Sidney Reilly, the Cheka's most-wanted man.

This was exactly the "proof" Yakov Peters wanted.

Stunned by this discovery, she took it with her to bed and slipped it under the pillow. Her heart was pounding and her eyes wide open as she thought.

What should she do?

She tried to recall all Lockhart's advice . . . her father's advice . . . her sister's advice . . . Yes, Anna, who had always been so pragmatic: How would Anna act? Would she hand this notebook over to Yakov Peters, proving with that gesture that she belonged to the Party and submitted to it, thereby saving herself and her lover but sending dozens of people to certain death?

Or would she refuse all compromise of that sort, keeping the information close to her at the risk of having her throat cut and letting the man she loved be executed?

No, no, I'm not thinking properly! I'm not asking myself the right questions.

She sat up in bed. She turned on the light.

Think about it differently. Not yes *or* no *. . . I have to avoid the moral dilemma at all costs.*

Look at the particulars.

The notebook . . .

Hand it over or destroy it?

Of these two possibilities, which will save Lockhart's head?

Neither of them!

If I hand over these statements, he'll go straight to his death. If I don't, he'll go there, as well.

She shivered. All answers led to death.

Casting aside the sheets, Moura moved away from the bed . . . The front door was open: Yakov Peters's men could come in at any moment. She had to burn this notebook, and fast!

But before she burned it, she needed to copy it.

She had to create a second version with the same dates, the same names. She had to reproduce in minute detail everything Yakov Peters already knew. And add some revelations for him. Feed his curiosity and give him a welter of specifics. Blur out the dangerous parts, scrub out the riskiest confessions.

And give him a false notebook.

She rushed to the desk.

There had to be a clean notebook amid the writing utensils. Once she found one, she spent the night creating this false copy that she had the secret to: a set of half-truths and lies that would satisfy everybody.

She had to reassure Peters and save Lockhart.

When she finally finished her work, she made her way to the kitchen. The mess there was as bad as everywhere else. She looked for a lighter, then a match, but was unsuccessful. All she had now was water: she turned on the tap and soaked the original sheets of paper. As the manuscript grew soggy, the ink ran, but the dangerous words were still legible.

She went to the bathroom, ripped out the pages one by one, tore them into small strips, threw them into the toilet, and pulled the chain. The flush made a hellish racket. How could she get rid of an entire notebook without arousing the suspicions of the two chekists behind the door? She carried bowls of water over and poured them into the toilet.

By dawn, she had erased all trace of the original notebook.

By dawn, she had all the answers.

She would make herself useful to the Party's leaders, and as valuable as possible to Karakhan and the superiors at Foreign Affairs. She would relay to them the gossip, the rumors, the atmosphere of the international circles she ran in. She would listen to what was being said there, she would repeat what people were thinking.

And she would still take care to pass along only rumors. Never the facts.

The "facts"? Yakov Peters would know them better than she did!

With him, she would negotiate the only service that a "Countess Benckendorff" could offer him, as an aristocrat belonging to this world that a chekist like him had no way into. She would be his eyes and ears in high society . . . What remained of that social class. She would watch which way the wind was blowing for the powerful. Those from before the Revolution, and those from after.

She wouldn't shut any doors. She'd be able to save her Babyboy.

❖

Interviews with Asker from Sweden. Wardwell from the United States of America. Peters from Latvia. Karakhan. She had always been capable of compartmentalizing her friendships. Of establishing a hierarchy for her relationships. Of positioning her partners carefully. And of sparring with multiple people at the same time. Once the student, she had now become the master in these games of seduction on every terrain.

Going from one man to the next, describing for them what was happening elsewhere, telling them what they wanted to hear and staying silent on what she didn't want them to learn: all Moura's education had prepared her for this.

Contrary to the accusations that would fly much later, she didn't sleep with any members of the Party. Not with Yakov Peters, not with Lev Karakhan. The former insisted on his purity, his sentimentality. The latter turned out to be barely interested in sex.

Her closeness to many men in the Cheka, however, was a far more compromising situation than any kiss or embrace could have led to.

Even though she hadn't become a mistress to any of them, her complicity dirtied her all the same.

Her lack of hatred toward them wasn't feigned: in her eyes, they still had the power to spare the man she loved. She invested her hopes in them and tried to please them. Intelligence, humor, personable warmth: she made full use of her arsenal of charms with them. She didn't realize that by establishing ties with them, she was getting lost. It didn't even occur to her that saving Lockhart could mean selling her soul.

And rightly so! She didn't disobey any of the rules she'd set herself, and, against all odds, she stuck to the dictums of her morality.

Relay news, but do not betray people. Repeat words, but do not name their speakers. Do not share any information that might put someone in danger.

She fixated on this obligation: to never cross the line separating gossip from betrayal, the line between life and death.

Such mental gymnastics required that she stay vigilant at every instant. How could she draw a distinction in the heat of the moment, how could she decide with certainty what was mindless prattle and what was fatal detail?

She navigated by sight, she held steady. But she was tiptoeing on the razor's edge. And she knew it.

She sometimes dreamed of Djon: there was no question that he would have scolded her for not choosing a side. She could easily hear him yelling: "Even now, you're still trying to please everybody when you know it'll please nobody!" And deep down, she agreed. Yes, she was trying to keep both sides happy. But what choice did she have? Was there any other way for her to spare everybody?

She didn't want to admit that aside from Lockhart, she was unsure how she felt about anyone . . . When it came to Yakov Peters, was she disgusted or sympathetic?

If she had genuinely hated him, if she had been consciously playing a trick on him, she might have been able to see more clearly the difference between her own hypocrisy and her sincerity. But as she had to juggle what was true and what was false, she ended up mixing it all up. And thereby losing herself.

So much for the flourishes of her conscience!

Only instinct mattered. Everything boiled down to a single word: survival.

———

The notebook she had delivered to the Cheka did its job: it proved her good faith. Now, as September drew to a close, Moura had, if not free movement to and from the Lubyanka, at least easy access to the cruelest of her torturers.

❖

Lockhart wrote in his memoirs of how Yakov Peters came to visit him after his first week, telling him that he was likely to be put on trial.

He had, however, released Moura. What was more, he had given her permission to bring me food, clothes, books and tobacco. . . . He was in a magnanimous mood. Lenin was now well on the way to recovery. The news from the Bolshevik front was excellent. The Bolsheviks had recaptured Uralsk from the Czechs. Kazan was on the eve of capitulation.

. . . That afternoon I had concrete proof of Moura's release in the form of a basket with clothes, books, tobacco, and such luxuries as coffee and ham. . . .

The books I read during my three weeks in the Kremlin included: Thucydides, Renan's Souvenirs d'enfance et de jeunesse, Ranke's History of the Popes, Schiller's Wallenstein, Rostand's L'Aiglon, Archenholtz's History of the Seven Years' War, Beltzke's History of the War in Russia in 1812, Sudermann's Rosen, Macaulay's Life and Letters, Stevenson's Travels with a Donkey, Kipling's Captains Courageous, Wells' The Island of Doctor Moreau, Holland Rose's Life of Napoleon, Carlyle's French Revolution *and Lenin and* Zinoviev's Against the Current. *I was a serious young man in those days.*

. . . After my first week in the Kremlin, Karakhan came to see me. He was reticent about my own case. He, too, hinted that a public trial was inevitable. . . .

He had come to ascertain my views regarding the terms on which England would be prepared to abandon her intervention and to make peace with Russia. The Bolsheviks were prepared to offer an amnesty to all counter-revolutionaries who would accept the regime, and a free exit out of Russia to the Czechs and to the Allies. Obviously, if the Bolsheviks were ready to discuss peace terms with the Allies, they were not going to shoot me. . . .

The next day I received a surprise visit from Peters. He brought Moura with him. It was his birthday (he was thirty-two), and, as he preferred giving presents to receiving them, he had brought Moura as his birthday treat. In more senses than one this was the most thrilling moment of my captivity. Peters was in a reminiscent mood. He sat down opposite me at the small table near the back wall and began to talk of his life as a revolutionary. He had become a Socialist at the age of fifteen. He had suffered exile and persecution. I listened only fitfully. Moura, who was standing behind Peters and in front of me, was fiddling with my books, which stood on a small side table surmounted by a long hanging mirror. She caught my eyes, held up a note, and slipped it into a book. I was terrified. A slight turn of his head, and Peters could see everything in the mirror. I gave the tiniest of nods. Moura, however, seemed to think that I had not seen and repeated the performance. My heart stopped beating, and this time I nodded like an epileptic. Fortunately, Peters noticed nothing or else Moura's shrift would have been short. Although he gave me no news about my own fate beyond saying that preparations were being made for my trial, he treated me in every other respect with great courtesy, questioned me several times about my treatment by my sentries, and asked me if I were receiving Moura's letters regularly and if I had any complaints to make. Then, excusing himself on account of pressure of work for the shortness of his visit and promising to bring Moura again, he left me. Moura and I had hardly exchanged a word, but already I felt a new hope. It was as if I had left the world and come back to it again. As soon as they had gone, I rushed to the book—it was Carlyle's French Revolution—*and took out the note. It was very short—six words only: "Say nothing—all will be well." That night I could not sleep.*

The next day Peters came again. His second visit explained his first. This time he was accompanied, not by Moura, but by Asker, the Swedish Consul-General, a man of great charm and high ideals, who had laboured night and day to secure our release. Peters went straight to the point. The neutral diplomatists had expressed concern about my fate. They had been much perturbed by rumours that I had been shot, that I was being subjected to Chinese torture. He had, therefore, brought the Swedish Consul-General in order that he might persuade himself by the proof of his own eyes (1) that I was alive, and (2) that I was being well-treated. My conversation with Asker was restricted. We had to talk in Russian, and his knowledge of the language was limited. Moreover, he was not

allowed to discuss my case with me. Having satisfied himself that I was not being
starved or tortured, he managed to say that everything possible was being done on
my behalf, and then he left.

◈

She dissembled. She affected optimism. But the fact was that she was lying: she had never been more worried.

The day after she was freed, she had learned from Yakov Peters that Lockhart was going to be sent to a revolutionary tribunal. To be judged as a spy and a traitor. The news was horrifying.

Peters appeared to be apologetic. The notebook she had given him, the information she had dredged up for him, didn't change matters: their friend was a dead man walking. His fate wasn't a matter of how generous the Cheka was feeling but of a trial with an all-but-assured outcome. He was certain to be shot dead.

In a panic, she had run to the residence of the Dutch legation. There she convinced its representative to telegraph the news to 10 Downing Street: Lockhart's execution was imminent.

The British government replied with a telegram of its own: a threatening note addressed to Lenin. If Russia shot Lockhart, England would do the same to the Bolshevik consul in London, as well as all the members of his legation.

Lloyd George backed up his threat with action and took hostages—an act that shut England out of the civilized nations. He had a dozen people arrested and thrown in jail, including Maxim Litvinov, the man who had introduced Lockhart to Trotsky during his departure for Petrograd.

Now the two nations had to come to an agreement about a trade: Lockhart's life for Litvinov's. But where? And when? And how? The negotiations resulted in a stalemate.

England was fighting the Bolsheviks on the Russian lands north of

Moscow; the country considered Lenin and his men to be bandits. It didn't want to be the first one to give up a pawn and show its hand.

Russia, humiliated by such defiance, talked about ending matters quickly. The idea of a trial by a revolutionary tribunal was abandoned: it would take too long. But the idea of summary execution in the basements of the Cheka headquarters, just like the hundreds of other executions Peters's men had carried out, was still under consideration

At Moura's urging, the representatives of the Dutch, Swedish, Danish, Norwegians, and Swiss—all the neutral powers—argued with Lord Balfour in London and Lev Karakhan in Moscow to find a solution.

And despite their efforts, the two sides were still unwilling to move.

Moura went to the Kremlin twice a day. She constantly feared learning of the execution of "the spy." The Party's members groused at learning he was still alive: wasn't the line plastered everywhere in Moscow and Petrograd *Better to shoot a hundred innocent men than to let one guilty man live?* And in this case, the man's guilt was beyond question.

He was still alive in the morning. He was still alive in the evening.

She would be momentarily reassured; she would urge the neutral powers again, urge Karakhan again, urge Peters again. She refused to relent. She was unshakable, she besieged them all, she harassed every single negotiator, although she took care not to attack or anger them. It was hard to strike the right balance.

She would calmly, eloquently propose new ideas, suggest new compromises.

She influenced them. She encouraged them. She energized them.

But she was never able to just think: *all will be well.*

Lockhart described his next meeting with Peters, a week after Moura's visit:

> *Peters came in this evening dressed in a leather jacket, khaki trousers, and an enormous Mauser pistol with Moura. There was a broad grin on his face. He told me that I was to be set free on Tuesday. He would allow me to go home for two days to pack.*

Moura explained the situation to Lockhart. The Swedes and Norwegians had taken charge of the exchange of prisoners: Lockhart and his colleagues were to be exchanged for Litvinov and other Bolsheviks in England. The Englishmen would be allowed to cross the Russian frontier as soon as Litvinov and his party reached Bergen. Then Yakov Peters resumed the conversation.

He confessed that the evidence he had been able to collect against me was not very damaging. I was either a fool or very clever. "I don't understand you," he said. "Why are you going back to England? You have placed yourself in a false position. Your career is finished. Your Government will never forgive you. Why don't you stay here? You can be happy and make your own life. We can give you work to do. Capitalism is doomed anyway."

I shook my head, and he went away, wondering. He could not understand how I could leave Moura. He left her alone with me.

. . . After the first joy of relief had evaporated, my feelings changed to a deep depression. My whole future seemed without hope. My nerve had gone. Now that I was to be set free, or rather to be sent out of Russia, I did not want to go. I found myself coming back again and again to Peters's proposal that I should remain in Russia with Moura.

◈

From that moment on, from dawn, when the doors were opened, to sunset, when they were shut again, Moura and Lockhart didn't leave each other. For two days.

They had never been so happy. Within the prison's walls, she had him all to herself.

Yakov Peters even granted them authorization to leave the apartment of the former maids of honor, where Lockhart had been locked up, and walk through the Kremlin's gardens together: a short path between the ramparts lined with boxtrees.

As two guards escorted them, they talked to each other quietly, walking in one direction and then the other, going slowly toward a small chapel dedicated to the Virgin Mary. In a section of wall hung an icon that the Bolsheviks had neglected to take down. It was called Our Lady of Unexpected Joy.

They smiled at having found their patron saint here of all places, and gave their thanks to her. But they took care not to think about the future.

They turned their eyes, rather, to the past. They recalled their first meeting in Petrograd, at her apartment during poor Cromie's birthday, the Strelnya evenings, the beauty of all the moments they had spent together. And the weeks apart from each other. She told him how their American friend, Allen Wardwell, had been a hero. That he hadn't left the Bolsheviks alone for a single second, that he had negotiated the smallest details of Lockhart's liberation. That he had fed her, as well as Hickie and all the diplomats shut away in the Norwegian legation, with rations from the Red Cross. She told him how Yakov Peters wasn't the monster he appeared to be. That in England, Lockhart would have to go to Peters's wife and daughter, share his news with them, and give them the letters Peters had written for them.

❖

The day Lockhart was freed, Moura came to the apartment he had been kept in to help him gather his books, his cards, all the letters she had written him on the Cheka's letterhead.

In fact, she was sick. She had a fever of 102 degrees. But she set to work without any complaint, packing his bags, locking his suitcases.

Lockhart sat gloomily on the bed as he watched her. After having been so close to death for so long, he keenly understood the price at which happiness came. He couldn't accept the inevitable.

He jumped to his feet and took her in his arms:

"What if I didn't take the train? What if I stayed here?"

She gave a weak laugh:

"I would love that, Babyboy! But it's impossible. You can't renounce your obligations to your country at the very moment when every tele-graph in the world is relaying the news of your freedom."

"No, I can. I can do what the French did, what Captain Sadoul and Lieutenant Pascal did by choosing Lenin. Those men weren't traitors."

"No, but those men were Communists." She was trying to make light of the situation. "And I've spent enough time with your dear friend Yakov Peters to be able to tell you one thing: you don't have what it takes to be a Bolshevik!"

"But if I don't have you with me, I won't be able to live."

"It's only a few months apart, baby . . . Just enough time to settle everything in London and put your affairs in order."

"I need you, Moura, I need you to know one thing: the second I cross the border, the revolutionary tribunal will sentence me to death in absentia . . . I'll never be able to come get you in Russia again."

"Whenever you call me, I'll come to you."

"In two weeks, then: *before* the end of October, before I return to England, as soon as I've been exchanged in Bergen . . . As soon as I'm a free man again!"

The words brought her perilously close to tears. *If only leaving with him could be so simple! If only . . .*

He kept going:

"Once I've reached Sweden, I'll write to you and give you a way to find me in Stockholm. Will you follow me there?"

At a loss for words, she nodded in acceptance. He repeated his question:

"Will you come? At any cost? Even if your mother is sick? Even if you have to leave your children behind? Will you come? Swear it!"

"I swear that I will belong to you my whole life."

"You're my wife, my partner, forever!"

◈

Karakhan came to see me and to say good-bye. He told me that we were to leave the next day. At three that afternoon I was released and taken back under escort to my flat.

. . . Liuba Malinina, the niece of Chelnokoff . . . informed me that she had become engaged to "Hickie," who was still beleaguered in the Norwegian Legation. Could I secure his freedom for an hour the next day in order that she might marry him?

I promised to do what I could, and later in the evening, when Peters came in to say good-bye, I put the question to him in the half-joking, half-sentimental way which I knew would appeal to him. He was amused. "No one but a mad Englishman," he said, "would make a request of this nature at a time like this. Nothing is impossible to such a race. I'll have to see what I can do." He did, and "Hickie" and Liuba were duly married the next day.

Moura, in turn, was authorized to go back to see her mother. Yakov Peters would give her the permit needed to return to Shpalernaya Street. Under normal circumstances, an arrest compounded by a stay in the Lubyanka would call for—at the very least—house arrest far away from any city and a yellow-hued identity document that underscored the disgrace of its holder and the boundaries of his or her space. But for Moura, no mark besmirched her papers.

Nor would there be any obligation anymore to present herself at the Cheka in Petrograd.

These favors Peters had granted Moura would come at a great cost, so great she did not dare think about it.

Lockhart's departure was planned for midnight.

At six in the evening, four cargo vans from the Red Army came to pick up the diplomats embroiled in the Lockhart Plot from the Norwegian legation and in Moscow's prisons. They drove those thirty people to the train station.

At nine in the evening, the courageous Swedish representative, Mr. Asker, came to drive Lockhart in his own car. Moura accompanied them.

They met Allen Wardwell on the train platform. And Lyuba's Russian family, who had come to bid farewell to the new Mrs. Hicks. They also met Lockhart's colleagues, who greeted him coldly. All of them deemed him responsible for the suffering they had endured over the previous weeks. The small group was silent and tense.

Moura and Lockhart went down the platform. The train was waiting for them under the arches, on a distant track. Regiments of Latvian guards were patrolling the area.

It was pitch-black. They walked side by side, not touching. She stumbled several times as she crossed the tracks. Once they reached the train car, they saw that the convoy wasn't ready yet. They stood there, outside, waiting.

They waited until well past midnight. Nothing . . . No sign that they would depart. Anxiety was all too visible on the faces of Lockhart's travel companions. Had there been a counterorder? Were they going to be imprisoned again?

For a second, Moura found herself feeling hopeful again. Just one more day with him . . . But she knew Russian trains well enough to know that this was just the usual delay.

It was now nearly two in the morning.

She couldn't bring herself to say anything more than the usual niceties to Lockhart: how cold it was at night in October in Moscow, how soon winter would arrive . . . Soon there would be snow, which would tinge the Kremlin's walls pink; soon icicles would frame their small chapel with its small icon of Our Lady of Unexpected Joy.

She shivered, her teeth chattered, her cheeks were flushed with fever. She was even more ill than she had been the night before.

Lockhart finally waved to Wardwell on the platform. "Moura isn't doing well . . . It's no good for her to wait here in the cold. Could I ask you to accompany her home?"

She didn't resist. Her emotions, her weaknesses were great enough that she didn't protest. Or even say good-bye to him.

All she did was give him a brief hug.

"When we're apart from each other," he whispered in her ear, "remember this: every day that goes by is one day closer to the day we see each other again."

She couldn't bring herself to smile anymore, nor could she bring herself to cry. She simply nodded.

Wardwell led her away by the elbow.

Lockhart stood and watched her for a long while, as she walked farther and farther away over the tracks.

Once she had disappeared, he climbed into the train car.

Book III

The Third Life of Maria Ignatyevna

De Profundis, but No Matter

October 1918–May 1921

CHAPTER TWENTY

One Day Closer to the Day
We See Each Other Again . . .

Even though she had been aware all this time of how imminent their separation was, even though she had feared it all this time and prepared herself for it, Moura hadn't expected this. To have been wrenched apart so painfully.

When the American friend, Wardwell, had brought her back to the apartment on Khlebny Lane and left her all by herself in the little hermitage, she didn't collapse or fall into bed in tears. But as she trembled with sobs and fever, she sat down at the desk, right there, immediately, at three in the morning, so as to stretch out on paper the moment of saying farewell on the platform.

My first hours without you. They're already interminable.

But don't think for a minute that I'm just letting go. On the contrary. I haven't stopped telling myself what you said to me at the train station: that now, every day that goes by is one day closer to the day we see each other again.

All that remains of me now is a husk. My soul has gone with you.

I just can't let myself see the scope of your absence. Nor can I let myself imagine what my existence here, my life without you, will be like.

I'll go back to Petrograd right away to take care of my mother's papers and try to get her out of the country. I'll be there, waiting for your signal from Sweden. When you call me from Stockholm, I'll be ready.

Don't let yourself worry about me, you're already nervous enough as you are! You know quite well that I'm not defenseless, that I've always gotten myself out.

I'll find a way to keep my mother safe in Finland. I'll find some sort of solution with Djon so I don't lose my children. Yes, I'll take care of matters in one way or another . . . Maybe with Asker and the neutral powers as a go-between.

The truth is that I'm simply tired, very tired. And that will pass.

Once you've written to let me know that you're doing well, that you're not suffering, that the exchange of prisoners in Bergen went as planned, that you're finally a free man again . . . all will be well then. And even now things aren't so terrible because you're healthy and safe, because you love me, and because your letter will come soon.

Safe travels, my love, and good night for now. May God watch over you and keep you safe.

Moura

❖

In this letter, the first of a hundred to come, each one more dignified than the last—and eventually, each one more heartrending than the last—she would repeat those words meant to reassure him.

Don't let yourself worry about me.

Modestly, generously, she would keep up this aristocratic image of herself, a fiction framed around the bravura, intelligence, and loyalty that she credited Lockhart with. The belief that she needed to meet the difficulties that life offered her with élan was rooted in the feeling that she was lucky. Sharing such passion with such a man was a divine gift.

Convinced above all that she needed to not add to his grief, she erected—without his realizing—a bulwark of tenderness to protect him. She was clever; she had guts. She was able to fool him.

Moura's suffering, by contrast, was physical and moral: it was total.

You know quite well that I'm not defenseless, that I've always gotten myself out. That was false.

No matter what she wrote, Lockhart's leave-taking had undone her in every way; his absence laid her bare on every front. And not only in terms of her feelings.

She knew this.

Now she no longer had any diplomatic privileges, any rations from the Red Cross, any of the numerous advantages she had enjoyed thus far. The last Englishmen had left, and so she was sent to suffer the same fate as all the other Russians. Like her mother, like her sister Anna, like all the women of her social circles, she belonged to the people of the past. Without the protections of the international community, she became an anonymous member of a dying class all over again.

Even so, she had no way to expect what awaited her in Petrograd.

On October 5, 1918—two days after Lockhart left—Lenin, who was now up and walking again, published a decree forbidding anyone to sell even the smallest bit of food to any *burzhui* unable to claim a job of their own. Only the workers had any right to ration cards, not the people he called parasites. Those parasites—the *burzhui* between fifteen and seventy-five years old—would have to stoop to the drudgery of public usefulness, clock in every month at the Labor headquarters, and produce booklets stamped by the committees. Anyone unable to furnish proof of the work they had done would lose their ration card and, consequently, all prospect of survival.

As for the rest, a *burzhui* could only live in one of the rooms in their apartment. Apartments—with all their contents—now belonged to the state and to the proletarian families who moved in. Woe betide those class traitors who didn't wholeheartedly make their property available to the Soviets. They would be thrown out and banned from settling anywhere else. Without a roof, without a work booklet, without a ration card: that was essentially a death warrant.

Petrograd
October 23, 1918

If you could see me, Babyboy: a headless chicken running back and forth through a ghost town. The streets are empty. The stores are shuttered. Iron grilles, locks, bolts. Condemned buildings.

There's no more gunfire like there was last year, no more clanging cars weighed down with armed Bolsheviks . . . Which makes sense: there isn't anybody left in the streets to shoot down. And there isn't anybody left to yank your coat off your shoulders: they've all already been yanked off or sold off. There aren't any horses, either, not even dead horses: they've all been eaten.

In this silence, which is so heavy that I can hear my ears ringing, I'm looking for work. But I don't know how to do anything. Typist? I'm still such a bad typist that nobody wants me . . . So I go to the university to take classes in international law. And that's where I find a sense of myself again. Yes, yes, law, I love it! And I'm also learning how to cook with the former chef of my aunt, the Princess Saltykova. And I'm reading, I'm reading, I'm reading Plato, Nietzsche, and Kant, to become a bluestocking as learned as yourself. So, Babyboy, when you see me again, I'll be a sensational woman. A lawyer, a philosopher, and a cook: not bad at all, yes?

Joking aside, you can't imagine what's happening here. Petrograd was already a graveyard back in the spring. But that was nothing compared to the mass grave of this autumn! The roundups and police searches have become a daily occurrence. In just two months, the Bolsheviks have arrested nearly thirty-two thousand people. And don't presume that I'm exaggerating! Those are the numbers Yakov Peters published in the Red Sword, *the Cheka paper. At first, he also published the list of people who were sentenced. Not anymore. In Petrograd, the executioners are feeding animals in the zoo with the corpses of those who have been shot. When someone is taken away, he disappears completely. We don't know who's alive and who's dead anymore. Not to mention the epidemics killing everybody. Myriam was driven down to Peterson with thirty other women to dig graves for typhus victims. After that, the guards took her to their barracks to clean out their latrines. As for her mother, she's had to be at Finland Station until dawn, clearing away all the coal that fell on the railroad tracks . . . The work is just as exhausting as it's absurd, because there are no trains leaving from there and the coal has already been burned. The drudgery they're forcing us to do is pointless, for the most part. That's almost actually the point: to humiliate us and break us. I say "us," but you shouldn't worry about me. It's by sheer luck that my mother forgot to pay her property taxes, and even the rest of her personal taxes, last year. The result is that we don't show up on any register. And the Shpalernaya Street apartment hasn't been requisitioned or even noticed yet. Unfortunately, she also forgot to do her work of sweeping in front of the building yesterday.*

And that . . .

That, Babyboy, doesn't make matters easier for us.

Oh, to hell with it! I'm worried that my letter will only end up making you think of Oscar Wilde's De Profundis. *Don't linger on it . . . I'm just feeling sad, that's all. I've had a somewhat complicated day.*

And I miss you so much, Babyboy! Your absence makes each day even more painful than it actually is. Without you, sad things seem sadder and nice things only moderately so.

Once I've gotten your letter, you'll see, I'll go back to being the incurable optimist you always insisted nothing could bring down.

Tomorrow, I'll go argue so my mother doesn't lose her ration card.

❖

It was much easier said than done. The city had never had so many layers of bureaucracy, nor so much corruption.

First, she had to negotiate with the former doorman who controlled the fates of his sixty inhabitants: he was the building's committee chief. He was the one who guided chekists during their searches, picked out the apartments to go through, watched over the seizure and removal of objects. In the past, he had been a nice man, but now he had turned out to be a terrible monster.

It was sheer luck that Moura, back when she had been rich, had been kind to him. She had always offered him small presents that he sold off on the black market.

"It's the law, Comrade Maria Ignatyevna. What can I do? Your mother hasn't done her requisite three hours of sweeping. I have to report her."

"What if I swept on her behalf?"

"That would be irregular: you've already done your time."

"My mother is elderly, Pyotr Ivanovich. She's suffering from cancer, and she doesn't always remember things."

"Is that my fault? Go see the men at the headquarters in the former Koenig sugar refinery."

"Without your stamp in her work booklet, they'll confiscate her ration card. She'll die of hunger."

"Well, she's already lived five years too long at this point."

The stupidity and the abuses of power were only just starting.

Moura knew what to expect: an unbelievable administrative stee-plechase, interspersed with under-the-table negotiations and bribes that would bleed her dry.

She wavered. Presenting herself at the Koenig headquarters? That would probably be a mistake. The underlings who dealt with minor infractions would take her money without even trying to solve the problem.

She needed to go higher.

Who among her acquaintances would know the right person? She thought logically, the way she had back when she was working to ensure Lockhart's survival. Who?

The Petrograd police had two prison headquarters: the terrifying Cheka general headquarters on Gorokhovaya Street and its annex at 25 Shpalernaya Street, only a few feet away from her home. Both of them were run by women. If she had to deal with those wardens, Moura knew she wouldn't stand a chance.

Could she call Yakov Peters in Moscow? That would be madness! She wasn't going to overplay her hand like that, certainly not by asking him for privileges to be marked in a work booklet. Who else? The Foreign Affairs minister, Lev Karakhan? That would be just as insane.

At this point, the least dangerous thing would also be the riskiest one: not to present herself anywhere.

It was the only way not to draw attention to herself. And to a thousand other infractions. Djon's coffers, whose keys she hadn't given to the new directors of the bank. Last year's taxes, the apartment . . .

She had heard talk of a network that trafficked in work booklets, doc-tored ration cards, even forged passports.

❖

"Well? Do you have it?"

"Yes."

Mommy had welcomed her in the vestibule as she returned from yet another day of exhausting administrative procedures.

Poor Mommy. Without a lady's maid to help, she had no way to do up her hair or get dressed. She was completely lost. And her hatred of the Bolsheviks didn't augur well for her survival.

With her long fur coat that served as a housecoat, her loose hair with its gray strands, she was a depressing sight who caught Moura off guard. She was sixty years old today. She seemed two decades older than that.

Moura took off her shawl, giving herself a few seconds to think. What should she tell her? What could she share with her? Nothing.

Mommy was at her wits' end, and she complained about her misfortune to anyone who would listen. It was impossible to tell her the truth, impossible to explain false papers to her.

And it was also impossible to hide all these difficulties from her and claim that all was well.

Moura came down the hallway:

"I've secured an authorization for a visa request."

"We're finally going to get out of here!"

"It's not a done deal, Mommy."

Moura sank into a chair. She sighed:

"We need to get seventeen others."

"Seventeen other what?"

"Authorizations. To emigrate to Finland, we need eighteen in all. Not to mention medical certificates. Gifts to doctors, and bribes for the other people who can help us with these eighteen things."

"Gifts? We don't have any more . . . They took everything we have. We're going to die of hunger, we're going to die of cold!"

"If I manage to get these authorizations . . ."

"You'll get them, Mourushka, you'll get them, I trust you. Otherwise, we'll leave without them."

"The borders are shut, Mommy. Even if we managed to escape the Reds, the Finns wouldn't let us in. We need proper visas."

"I don't care! We've got to get out of here, we've absolutely got to get out, and I don't care what it takes!" She was shouting. "We have to get out, even if we have to leave everything behind. Even our money, even our past. I don't care if we're naked. As long as we're headed somewhere! I don't care if they exterminate us at the border or in the prison at the end of the street. It doesn't make any difference. No matter what, the Bolsheviks are going to shoot us like dogs. They're not imposing the death penalty, they're just scrubbing out vermin. *Comrade Lenin is purifying society of all the cockroaches sequestered in it*: that's what they've written down in the courtyard. It's a convenient way to justify their crimes! We're not human to them anymore, we're just lice. Your husband was right about everything . . . Djon saw it all, he understood who the Bolsheviks were!"

Moura looked down. Mommy's rants were endless; each day she got closer and closer to hysteria. The best thing was for Moura to stay quiet, to wait, not to try to reassure her. When she was in the throes of panic, she couldn't be convinced by anybody's reasoning.

Her anxiety finally got through to Moura.

"Look at me," she said. "I'm unrecognizable! It's not my cancer. Look at my belly—it's so swollen that I look like what I actually am: the victim of famine. And Europe doesn't care! Nobody even thinks about saving us. The Allies less than all the others. It's almost as if they'd lost all sense of honor. Lenin has taken all the embassies by storm, Lenin has killed all their diplomats. And what have they done? Nothing. They let it happen! How can they possibly accept what's happening here? They can't say they don't know about it: they saw it all! Even the nice captain, the one whose dog you're feeding—yet another stupid thing you're doing!—that boy who wrote poems and who you said was so idealistic that he sympathized with the Bolsheviks . . ."

"Denis Garstin," Moura said.

"Even *he* saw what was happening! Do you want me to tell you? Your friends the British men don't care one bit what happens to us. What do they think of Russia nowadays? It has to be something absolutely simple, the same way they think about the Indians dying of hunger: it just doesn't seem serious to them. It's actually normal in their eyes! And the other man, your consul in Moscow who you said was so smart? He's, how do you say, persona grata in Stockholm. Why doesn't he write to you? Why doesn't he call you? The telephone line hasn't been cut, as far as I know! And why doesn't he send you a visa for Sweden?"

Mommy had met Lockhart, along with all Moura's other friends. Because she read the papers, she knew all about the plot he had been accused of, the story of his imprisonment, his departure. But she had no idea of all the chaos her daughter was living through. She didn't even suspect the passion that connected her daughter and him.

And yet, in her own unthinking way, with her unwavering instinct, Mommy had seen the truth, she had hit the nail on the head without even realizing it.

Forgotten? Abandoned? Moura rejected the thought.

It was impossible.

❖

Well, what did she know about him after a month?

The exchange of prisoners in Bergen had taken place without incident: that was what the representative from the Swedish legation had told her.

That was October 9.

Lockhart had gone to Stockholm quickly: that, too, she had learned from the legation.

That was October 15.

When he'd arrived in Sweden, he'd made a deal with the representatives of the neutral powers so his letters could reach Petrograd through Scandinavian hands. Moura would be notified of the arrival of letters bearing her name by the staff of one legation or another, notified not by telephone but by messenger. Out of caution, she would need to come get them in person, read their contents then and there, and destroy them each time.

But there hadn't been any *each time*! Only two times.

In his two wonderful letters, both of them written the day after they had separated, Lockhart had poured out his love to her. Not a single word failed to express his inability to live without her. Not a single sentence failed to express the vastness of his distress, failed to imagine their future together, their plans for finding each other again. And his impatience, his need to hold her close against his body again.

Unfortunately this couldn't happen immediately, not *the very minute*, not *as soon as he was free*, as he had hoped.

Harried on all fronts, forced to explain himself quickly to his government, he had to rush home to England. He was a bit nervous, he had joked in the second letter, a bit suspicious of what he might have to deal with back home.

He had arrived in London on October 19.

This had been confirmed by Asker, the Swedish representative.

Three weeks.

And since then: nothing.

Why wasn't any other news forthcoming?

Had he been arrested the minute he set foot in England, as Yakov Peters had predicted? Sentenced and thrown in prison?

No! The neutral powers would have told her. They wouldn't have withheld such information. All the more so because at this point, in Russia, all anybody ever talked about was "that traitor Lockhart."

In Moscow, on October 28, 1918, the trial of the conspirators in the famous plot that bore his name began. Each day, each second, Moura was terrified of seeing her own name mentioned in the accounts. All the papers made the British agent's crimes their front-page headlines. Derailing trains . . . Starving people . . . Murdering leaders.

After a week of court arguments, Lockhart had been sentenced to death in absentia, as he himself had predicted. His effigy had been hanged and burned after having been soaked in a barrel of oil at the entrance to the courthouse. His accomplices, Sidney Reilly and two Frenchmen, had attended the meetings at Khlebny Lane, and so they were also sentenced to death in absentia.

Their Russian counterparts who hadn't been able to escape the country had been gunned down or sent to the labor camps.

However, not a mention was made of "the secretary." In the records of the trial, there was no hint of her existence. It was some kind of miracle that Mrs. Benckendorff, a bourgeois woman who outclassed the bourgeoisie, hadn't been named. How? Why? Moura was puzzled, but she wasn't going to complain. And yet she wondered. Did she owe this unlikely silence to Karakhan's protection? To Yakov Peters?

She would rather forget Yakov Peters's clemency. As they'd said farewell to each other in the capital, he had merely promised her a courtesy visit during one of his trips to Petrograd. A friendly meeting, between two appointments.

And then: nothing. No more news. She could let herself believe Yakov Peters had forgotten her. Hope for it, in any case. Did he feel that she had fulfilled her end of the contract by giving him her notebook? By sharing with him the news from the neutral powers?

She didn't believe it for a second. But life was hard enough without giving more thought to Yakov Peters.

She knew he had most likely gotten her out of this mess.

She absolutely, absolutely needed to not think about what he would ask of her in exchange.

One problem at a time: that was how she should deal with this.

In international circles, the whiff of scandal around her gave her enough trouble!

It could be that nobody in her family knew about her adventure with Lockhart, but the representatives of the neutral powers very much knew the details of their liaison. They even had proof of her marital infidelities in their files. They now saw her as the mistress of a spy who had been sentenced to death: everybody was whispering about it. Adultery and espionage were still in bad taste.

Little Mrs. Benckendorff's reputation was absolutely ruined! Her comings and goings to pick up letters started to upset people. She was no longer persona grata in the Scandinavian legations.

"Be careful of the Danish," Lockhart had told her in the first of his two letters. He didn't elaborate on the reasons, but Moura was well positioned to know that the wife of the Danish representative, a highly respected woman who, according to the people of the past, had goodwill, devotion, and peerless courage, now called her Dishonorable Mrs. B. Moura shrugged. No matter the circle, the Revolution hadn't made anyone less cruel.

In other times, these rumors might have wounded her. Now, she couldn't bring herself to care. As long as they didn't reach the children or Mommy, she scoffed at those whispers. Her love for Lockhart had freed her, she thought, from any fear of degradation. He had made her a being capable of overcoming fear. Freed from all prejudice, her own as much as others'.

She felt this change deep in her heart. She was less of a hypocrite. Less of a coward . . . Their time together had transformed her and made her a better woman. Didn't Lockhart tell himself, as well, that he was no longer the same man? That alone was what mattered.

She was wrong to be impatient. She herself had never believed, deep down, that their separation would be only a few weeks. The two of them had too many obligations to handle before they could find each other again and be together.

So she shouldn't let herself be influenced by Mommy's fear. She had to keep trusting.

She counted the days. If Lockhart had gotten to London on October 19, his silence wasn't unusual at all. It would have been impossible to get any letter from him before now . . . New calculations. A month. Yes, a month at minimum.

No reason to worry.

CHAPTER TWENTY-ONE

The Thousand Degrees of
a Descent into Hell

WINTER 1918–1919

Her neck bent, her gaze steady, Moura caught her breath on the Palace Bridge.

The university's vice rector had been arrested. And through some underling's mistake, the unfortunate man's body had just been delivered to his widow. The face was so disfigured, the body so tortured that the poor woman who beheld the bloody corpse couldn't stop screaming. The widow's shrieks had brought out a full battalion of policemen. The lecture halls were buzzing with chekists. As she pushed the door open, Moura finally understood. She would no longer be taught international law; she would no longer have the prospect of this career. Lenin was far too suspicious of intellectuals to let the students enjoy their education. Their bourgeois background inherently made them class enemies, the personification of the "social traitor."

All classes had been canceled for the day. Tomorrow the university would be shuttered. Gone was her hope of finding a job and escaping. Gone was her ultimate pleasure.

Along with her classmates, she had left the room and run straight out.

She was now panting all alone on the bridge. She looked at the Neva as it ferried the earliest blocks of ice. The image of these floes brought forth a thousand other clichés: her nostalgia for what this place used to be; her need to flee.

A river that flowed toward the sea: this was what remained of freedom in Russia, along with the clouds that raced across the sky and the wind that blew in from the shore.

As for the rest, all the beauties of Petrograd rising up around her, the gilded dome of the Admiralty, the spire of the Peter and Paul Cathedral—those now merely housed torture sites, and the only images they offered were those of nightmares.

She shook herself out of her thoughts. *I'm getting morbid. I'm going to end up depressed, just like Mommy.*

Crying over one's lot in life when one had been lucky enough to experience a love as precious as what she and Lockhart had shared was unacceptable. She didn't have the right to complain, much less to go weak.

She shouldn't ever lose sight of this gift she'd received. Among all the men and women laid low by misfortune, she knew that fortune had smiled upon her, no matter how briefly. And that gift would last her whole life.

❖

Petrograd
November 10, 1918

My darling Babyboy,

A messenger from the Dutch legation has let me know of a large envelope's arrival. Finally, news from you! You can't imagine how light life suddenly seemed to me. I took my shawl and I went. The poor man who took hours to find my delivery almost got killed.

The letters did come from England. They were all from Meriel and Lady Buchanan. Except for a little note from Cunard, where he briefly mentioned the death of Garstin.

Cunard told me that Garstin was killed a few days before Cromie . . . Snuffed out in August, as the Allies were invading Arkhangelsk.

I didn't know, Babyboy, I didn't know that he was dead! But you knew, didn't you? You must have wanted to spare me.

My heart is absolutely broken now. I loved Denis Garstin so dearly. I just can't bear the thought.

I'm going to try to send along his manuscripts. He gave them to me, along with Garry, his dog, when he left to go fight. Three manuscripts. I've typed them up over the last few weeks and set them in order. Would you be able to take care of publishing them? Please, please, Babyboy, don't let Garstino die completely! Maybe his manuscripts need an introduction, a short text articulating just how much of a scholar, how much of a gentleman he was . . . How much of an officer he was, as well. Could you take care of it? Or ask that this preface be written by his friend Walpole? Or Hicks or Cunard? Garstino's books are very good. I beg you, please do everything you can so that their author doesn't fall into obscurity! He's always behaved toward me with so much class. And I, in turn, haven't been that kind to him.

Meriel's last letter is from eight days ago. She attaches several newspaper cuttings in it. Your return seems to have stirred up quite a bit of interest. Was it a triumph in the end? What a delight it was to see photographs of you! In every one of them, you're absolutely wonderful. I love the one where you're getting into a car. Who's the person just out of sight in front of you? With your cane under your arm, your cigar in your mouth, and your bow tie, you look quite important . . . quite distinguished!

Here the snow is still falling, as it was when you came to Petrograd last year.

Soon it'll be ten months since you showed up at the house for the first time. We were celebrating Crow's birthday then.

Why don't your letters reach me anymore? These days, I feel terribly gloomy. And stuck.

But I love you, Babyboy.

❖

With her eyes shut, as if her eyelids could protect her from pain, she gently stroked Garry's head. The dog had set his muzzle on her lap. The animal, too, had shut his eyes. "You loved your master so dearly."

Garstino was dead.

She shouldn't blame Lockhart for having forgotten to tell her. He'd had so much to do. He had needed to make a report of his mission to Lord Balfour. To Lloyd George. And probably to the king of England . . . Write so many explanations. Give lectures. Publish articles.

She could think of a thousand excuses, a thousand explanations for his silence, each one more logical, more rational than the last.

What did she know of everything that was happening in the world? All she had for information was the sheets of propaganda full of lies. The other papers had been scrubbed out. She didn't know anything! Except that the war in Europe was still going on. And that the civil war between Trotsky's Red Army and the White Army was intense.

Another thing she could be sure of: the Allies supported the Whites. But what were their real intentions?

On the street, some people were insisting that the British were advancing, that they were only a few hundred versts away, that they would come and free Petrograd from the Bolsheviks. Rumors contradicted other rumors . . . Some people were absolutely certain that the British were beating a retreat, that they had even left the country.

Rumors, rumors, rumors everywhere.

And what was happening in Ukraine? In Berezovaya? Anna hadn't shared any news recently. Was she still alive? Moura took care not to broach the topic with Mommy. She had heard that Kiev was going up in flames, dripping with blood, caught between the Prussians, the Reds, the Whites, the separatists, and the looters.

And what was happening in Estonia? The Germans had apparently evacuated Reval, leaving the city open to the incoming Russians, who reclaimed the territories they had given up in Brest-Litovsk. They were confiscating all the properties there, massacring the *burzhui*, gunning down the Krauts' collaborators and the accomplices of capitalist powers by the thousand.

Where was Djon now? All communications with the Baltic countries had been cut off. Where were Kira, Paul, and Tania?

Moura was paralyzed with fear, and she couldn't even bear to think about Yendel.

And what was happening in London? What was *really* happening there?

Since the envelopes from Meriel Buchanan and Edward Cunard had arrived, she had seen how fast mail came by the legations. Could it be that they were censoring Lockhart?

She couldn't understand why he wasn't talking.

Is he upset at me about something?

She was losing sleep over it. She would fall asleep, yes, only to awake two hours later and lie there, unable to shut her eyes.

Did someone warn him not to talk to me? Has he been hearing gossip of some kind about me, horrible stories about my behavior, anything that could have made his life more complicated?

Who knows what Hicks has been telling him about my connection to Yakov Peters?

Over the course of the weeks spent in their little hermitage, she had been sure that Hickie had resumed the friendliness of old times. But on the platform, the night they had left, he had uttered that odd thought . . . A line about the Cheka that she couldn't quite remember.

But what she did remember of their farewells was that there had been a disagreeable tone to it all. Hicks certainly hadn't been singing her praises. Had he been telling Lockhart some variation on the lectures Knox had given Cromie: *a rat in the pay of the Bolsheviks?*

She needed to stop asking herself these questions.

Enough of these lamentations.

When she was scared, when she was heartsick, she wasn't supposed to bother people. She was supposed to hide her anguish. She was supposed to keep quiet. She was supposed to bury it within herself. And she was supposed to do what she could to live—not with her pain but with every-thing else.

She needed to stop pestering Lockhart by telling him about fears that didn't concern him. She needed to give him courage again, in fact! She needed to support him as he soldiered on.

She leaped to her feet. Yes, that was enough! She had a thousand bat-tles to fight herself. She needed to make sure nobody opened Djon's coffers at the bank. Make sure nobody moved families into the apartment. Make sure, make sure, make sure . . .

Petrograd
November 14, 1918

My darling Babyboy,

Hurrah: peace has come to your land at last! The papers here have just published the terms of the armistice!

Just between us, I think they've been extremely hard on Germany. Even given my Germanophobia and my dislike of the Krauts. I can't feel too sorry for them, however—they've set the world on fire and spilled blood everywhere, so I won't pity them. But such a strict and humiliating punishment strikes me as a dangerous, ill-considered stance on the Allies' part. I've been told that the peace conference will take place in Paris. If by any chance you're attending, my Babyboy, do go and see my sister Alla for me. She lives at 11 quai d'Orsay and she is known these days as Madame René Moulin. That's all I know of her.

Tell her that she's overdoing it with not answering my letters! Tell her that I miss her, tell her how much I love her . . . And do tell her that her daughter, Kira, is in Estonia with my children. But do be careful, my dear, not to fall in love with her! She's too beautiful, with extraordinary red hair that she does up masterfully. So take great care: I can be very, very jealous. But please, I beg you, please tell me her news, tell me how she's doing.

What a change in fortune it is to be writing to you on this old paper with the British embassy's letterhead! These days, the palace is nothing more than an idea, nothing more than a lonely house with all its windows boarded up. You wouldn't recognize the interior at all . . . or what they've done to it. And that's not even the worst part: on the carpet at the foot of the stairs, the huge bloodstain has congealed. It's Cromie's blood. They're still bragging about having tortured and killed him.

The Bolsheviks' methods are atrocious.

You know that I've never shown myself to be hysterically aggressive toward them, nor blindly opposed to Marxist principles. In the beginning, their arrival actually seemed like a spark of hope. A revitalization. I thought they'd strip us of all our hypocrisy, our corruption, our injustice, all the dysfunctions of our past era. But that was a mistake. Rather than freedom, they impose a morality rooted in fear, envy, and denunciation.

　And now they sicken me. I want them out and gone!

　Even you, Babyboy, who know so well the writings of your friend Trotters, even you can't imagine how utterly untenable the situation has become.

　They're giving me horrible, absurd ideas.

　If I hadn't lost your child, our love would have been something else for you. I would have had this joy, this pleasure to offer you. Forgive me, Babyboy, forgive me for having interfered in your future and not being able to give you anything in return.

　But remember that I love you. And my uncertainty about your fate, my not knowing the latest about you, is perhaps the worst of all things.

Stop! No need to be maudlin. And especially no scolding. There's no need to describe every step of this interminable descent into hell.

She wouldn't talk to him about the winter and the cold. She wouldn't tell him that the pipes in the house had frozen and then exploded. That it was only a few degrees above freezing in her bedroom, that her teeth were chattering and she could write to him only while in her bed.

That in other rooms of the apartment it was even worse. That the kitchen and the hallway were veritable skating rinks. That she had had to pull out the woodwork and floorboards to burn them and try to keep Mommy warm as her illness got worse and worse. Her doctor was talking about operating on her.

She wasn't going to overwhelm him with all these complaints about her daily life.

And she wouldn't say anything about how hungry she was. She wouldn't say that today, she had seen a long queue in front of a small sign that said:

DOG MEAT: THREE RUBLES PER POUND.

MOUSE: TWENTY KOPEKS.

Rather than that, she would tell him stories, all the touching details about the people nearby, the idle gossip that might if not amuse him, at least interest him.

She always ended up sitting up again, striking a match for her candle, leaning over at the foot of her bed, picking up her notepad, and writing some more to him.

Her life had been reduced to this: her moments of closeness with him. Her consolation. Her torture.

She would take these letters to the legation tomorrow morning. The trams, like the telephones and the electricity, didn't work anymore. She would walk along the banks of the Neva to the other end of the quay. Five miles in negative five degrees. With no coat and no shoes.

Petrograd

December 14, 1918

Baby,

At last! I'm holding your letter open in my lap. The third one. And I'm reading it, and I'm rereading it, again and again, with a delight that you can't even imagine. I was so afraid you had stopped loving me. Forgive me for having doubted you. And forgive me for making you suffer so much.

　Oh, baby, I am so, so sorry to be a source of trouble for you. The idea that our affair might hurt or hinder your career just eats at me. That you're having so much difficulty in London, all because of my existence . . .

　Don't sacrifice anything for me that you might regret later on!

　But I don't have the courage to tell you to leave me. I'm not afraid of anything when I'm with you, but the mere thought of a future without you strikes such overwhelming terror into my heart.

　When I received your letter this morning, I broke down sobbing . . . But all is well, those tears were tears of joy!

　As for the rumors that you mention, that gossip I'm just not able to stamp out: I wasn't set up with you by the Cheka, set up the way you suggest, to spy on you in Khlebny Lane. I'm sure you never thought any such thing!

　I didn't know Yakov Peters at all when I met you. And I didn't have the least connection with him, with anybody in the secret police, before you were arrested . . .

Not before. And not since. What I did to save your life is what any woman in love would have done in my place. And it doesn't matter.

As far as the day-to-day difficulties: what you've heard is true. But on that point, as well, you shouldn't worry on my behalf. I can bear poverty relatively well, and I don't need any comforting. All I need is luck! That makes things easier for me than for other people.

As long as I know that you love me, nothing can hurt me.

I've just been interrupted by a visit from Korney Chukovsky: do you know who he is? The former interpreter for Sir George Buchanan and General Knox at the embassy. He's now working for World Literature, the publishing house Maxim Gorky has founded. It's quite the wager. Gorky has gotten it in his head to make Shakespeare accessible to the masses. He wants to publish all the foreign classics in Russian. He's looking for translators. Chukovsky has just asked me if I could take up the works of Stevenson and Ruskin. He'll argue my case in front of the master. Cross your fingers: it would be a dream come true!

See, I always manage somehow, and I'm right not to lose hope!

Tomorrow I'm going to play bridge at the home of the old Princess Saltykova. What a spectacle that'll be! Do you remember her? The owner of the building of the British embassy, who lived on the noble floor at the back of the palace. She's quite a character . . . She only ever goes out to listen to Wagner. Yes, yes, concerts are still being performed here. When I'm with her, I laugh and I tremble. She's a bit deaf, and she describes all the wrongdoings of the Bolshevik personalities she sees in the room while yelling . . . There's no shutting her up about the writers who have sold out to the regime. About Maxim Gorky, of course, who's her favorite scapegoat. She detests him. I'm taking care not to let her know that it's my great wish to work for him. But she probably knows it already. She knows everything. She even knows that I love you. How? It's a mystery. Yesterday she shut her copy of the Izvestiya*—which was always full of false rumors about your crimes— and she told me, in French: "Well, my little darling, from what I can see, you're becoming* legendary*!" The truth is that she's a terror, but I adore her. Her eighteenth-century spirit delights me. At eighty years old, she's living in a house with three Red Guard families who she's ruling with an iron fist even as she lives in the pigsty of her former housemaid's lodging. She prefers animals to human beings.*

And I always bring her Garstino's griffon, purely so that our former doorman won't eat him behind my back. Garry struts around her residence with a huge bow tie—a Scottish one in your honor, Babyboy. And as for me, I wear my pearl-gray dress that you love so much; it's the last one of its kind.

And yes, all the same we try to live, as my sister Anna might say. And I've found my place again among the people of the past, the place I had back when I didn't know you.

But I don't feel like I belong there anymore. No matter how much they move me. They still don't understand that the world of yesterday is gone. The facts go into their heads, but not their hearts.

We will all pretend we're dressed up as we should be to play bridge among friends in good company. We will all pretend to be elegant, and for just a few seconds, time will seem to have stopped.

But today really does seem to be an important day in history: the neutral powers are leaving the country.

How will we be able to go on communicating, Babyboy?

They're all leaving. The Danes, the Swedes, the Swiss, all of them! Russia will be left without any foreign representatives.

Without any witnesses.

CHAPTER TWENTY-TWO

Among the People of the Past

JANUARY 1919

"Will you stay in this desert of ugliness and meanness when the others leave, my little friend? You'll keep me company for a little while."

Unlike Mommy, whose misfortune had reduced her to nothing, Princess Anna Saltykova seemed more imposing than ever before.

She had been a dowager with an impressive bosom and a stentorian voice. Thinness, which had altered all her features, had transformed her into a majestic matron. And the rouge on her cheeks, the lipstick on her lips, the kohl on her eyes, all these cosmetics she made liberal use of, did not make her look any more feminine.

She had formerly been famous for the extravagance of her hats, and even now she still paraded strange headpieces that she adorned with doilies and the moth-eaten feathers of her headdresses. If not for the bearing of her head, the authority of her gestures, and something noble in her gait, in an earlier time she might easily have been mistaken for a madwoman.

Now, her willingness to maintain some semblance of decorum had made her the personification of all that was chic.

It was hard, however, to say the same of her apartment, an emptied-out, filthy skeleton. The successive raids had emptied her salons of all their objets d'art.

"Oh, it's just a boring old little thing," she sighed. "Nothing we haven't all faced already."

But in her home, all the palatial decorations had been removed, down to the smallest ornaments. In addition to the paintings, the rug, all the chimneys, the moldings, and even the locks, doorknobs, curtain rods, and rings had been carted away.

This was a catastrophe for Anna Sergeyevna, who had stashed away the last of her money and hidden the pearls she hadn't yet sold in the curtain rods.

All of it was currently piled up at the other end of the courtyard, in the former galleries of the British embassy, which now served to warehouse all the state's possessions. A veritable Ali Baba's cave. All the splendors extracted from the *burzhui*'s homes and seized by order of the committees were stashed away there, in an immense shambles that the regime's leading light, Maxim Gorky—yes, him—was determined to organize and inventory.

The princess loved to tell how that infamous Gorky, and the so-called connoisseurs plucked out of the proletariat, didn't know anything about what they were looking at! Because these louts had left behind the most valuable of her antiques: a parrot that had been owned by a close confidante of Catherine II.

The bird, a plucked thing that Anna Sergeyevna claimed was 140 years old, had stopped talking. But it went on singing the hymn that the poet Derzhavin had composed in honor of the tsarina—singing to her glory. Its horrible voice could be heard all the way out in the courtyard.

It was the only possession of the Saltykovs that Gorky had refused.

Such a snub only served to increase the princess's ire. And woe betide anyone who might praise the writer's talent. "Oh, so you think your Gorky might be an aesthete?" She pursed her lips in disgust. "He's an uncultured monster. I'd even say that he's *incapable* of culture. They say he steals anything he likes, just for his own personal collection. He's said to love Chinese jade and porcelain. The ugliest little trinkets, of course: he has absolutely no taste. And that's no surprise! How could this *muzhik* possibly understand anything about Ming-era art?"

It was a painful topic: her late husband's Ming vases had been the glory of the Saltykov palace.

The other spoils of the apartment, among what hadn't been carted off already—the coal stove, the kitchen utensils—had been repurposed or sold on the black market by the eighteen people who hung their laundry to dry in the ballroom.

The room that the princess had retired to, along with the parrot, was no exception to the disorder and dilapidation of the rest. All she had was a trundle bed, a portion of a mirror, a welter of icons, and the massive birdcage, which took up nearly the entire room. The space—at the end of the hallway, far from the common rooms—did offer her the advantage of relative privacy. The way in was through a servants' door, and she could shut herself away, far from the "whining masses." Its proximity to the kitchen allowed her to heat up water for tea without having to go down the icy hallways.

It was there, under the painted depiction of the Virgin Mary, that the princess's final guests gathered around a wicker suitcase that served as a bridge table.

It was still the same old four or five people.

Count Paul Benckendorff, the most respected man in the tsar's court, served as the evening's master of ceremonies. He had once been famous for his cheek and his appetite, and now, despite the ongoing famine, he was a hefty man who groaned endlessly about the lack of food.

Accompanying him was his wife, the unfortunate Countess Marie Benckendorff—her name oddly close to Moura's own—whose two sons from her first marriage had just been arrested and probably shot dead.

General Mossolov, the former head of the Imperial Chancellery, was also there. He was working on a manuscript about the descendants of Nicholas II, a "capital testimony" whose first chapters were already being circulated under the table.

These three survivors—the three pillars of the circle—braved the potholes in the streets, the climbs up dark stairwells, the groping descents from floor to floor every week. And they braved the constant risk of being assaulted, in one of those all-too-common attacks against the *burzhui* in which the bandits left the victim without a stitch of clothing amid the wreckage. They confronted all these difficulties devotedly in order to appear, if not elegantly, at least diligently at the princess's "Wednesdays," to trade the latest news with her and to play cards together.

The other players came and went, depending on what tragedies might have befallen their families recently. But nothing was more important than the "big day" at the residence of Anna Sergeyevna, nothing apart from force majeure.

With empty stomachs and emptier minds, their thoughts fixated on what they would be eating that night, the size of the oat ration that would serve as their dinner and the price of the tiny potato they couldn't have, they went on playing cards at all costs.

They had known each other for eons, so they bickered with one another often and accused one another of not paying attention.

Then they gossiped and came back again and again to the privileges they had once enjoyed and that now belonged to the people of the future.

Their exchanges could be summed up as a litany of everything they missed. And idle, increasingly bitter talk about how their new masters conducted themselves. Despite their efforts to sound detached when discussing their misfortunes, what one might say and what another might say amounted to yet another stone added to their Golgotha. And their evenings together always turned to the latest indictments.

The great subject, the one that always seized everyone's attention, that offered both premises for discussion and consensus on answers, remained this horrible Maxim Gorky: the princess's bête noire, who was apparently both a close friend of the police commissioners and their loudest critic. A paradox. The man's ambiguity allowed them to talk about the regime without directly discussing Lenin's decrees ordering their extermination; without enumerating Yakov Peters's cruelties as he tortured their nearest and dearest; and without detailing the tortures that Grigory Zinoviev, the new tyrant of Petrograd, had exacted in thoroughly exploiting their city. In short, it was a way to criticize the Bolsheviks, through the literature they had all loved so much.

"The other day," thundered the stout Paul Benckendorff, "my doctor, who is also *his* doctor, told me that when he went to Gorky's home to ask him to intercede on behalf of my son-in-law, he was unlucky enough to come upon him as he was eating lunch. On the master's table were meat dumplings, fresh cucumbers, cranberry sauce. Would you believe what *he* granted my doctor? Oh, you can imagine! Not only did Gorky refuse to lift a finger to help Sasha, but he granted his dear doctor the mere privilege of seeing him eat!"

The truth was that hunger was getting the better of their sense of humor. In this icy room where the wind gusted, it was impossible for them to keep up their grand tradition of wry conversation that they had always practiced here by the fireside. They might still try to maintain the appearance of dignity, but they had already given up when it came to the art of conversation.

Every other week, Anna Sergeyevna invited a member of the younger generation: usually their common favorite, the wife of dear Djon Benckendorff, her cousin by marriage and her host's relative.

Moura, their wonderful Moura, livened up the rote gatherings with her good humor and her indomitable energy. Because of the close-knit quarters and the wide difference in generations, she called them all "my aunt" and "my uncle." They loved her. She, *Moura, their wonderful Moura*, was the one they asked to sell their last rags on the black market. She was the one who got their ration cards checked at the commissariats. She was the one who struggled with the chekists down the street at the Shpalernaya prison and got the latest news about those who had vanished from their lives. She was the one who protected them and did them a thousand favors.

Over time, she became indispensable to them.

Some of them insisted that *Moura, their wonderful Moura*, was hardly the innocent lady she seemed to be. That within other circles she was notorious, that her reputation was rather questionable, that all the local gossips were saying . . .

Those who cast aspersions were immediately silenced by the princess. And should any of them keep on criticizing her *dear little friend*, she showed them the door right away. Nobody dared say a word against her kin. Nobody apart from herself had any right to besmirch the Benckendorff family.

Not as the lady of the house, but as the girl of the house, Moura helped her receive them all.

She came and went down the icy hallway, her dog, Garry, nipping at her heels. She opened the door, escorted Aunt Marie or Uncle Paul down to the room at the end, offered them a box that served as a chair, gave them a shawl, served them some tea, and distracted them with a hundred little anecdotes that she had heard God only knows where. And on top of that, she was a peerless bridge player, which only raised the stakes and increased the others' pleasure.

The entirety of this regular ceremony took two hours. When the lady of the house started to get tired and announced that her "Wednesday" was drawing to a close, it was Moura who took care of leading all the visitors to the door. The hostess brandished a bit of broken English at those moments: "No sticky departure, please." No overstaying their welcome.

After having locked the service door behind them all, Moura returned to the sanctuary, where the princess was waiting for her.

Like a latter-day Madame Récamier, Anna Sergeyevna had lain down, surrounded entirely by her pillows. With her Roman nose and her feather-adorned hair, she bore a striking resemblance to her parrot, which, in its cage above her head, was marking time with its crooning song in honor of Catherine the Great.

Their final ritual was their one-on-one conversations. The princess loved nothing so much as this moment when she had "the younger generation" to herself, and she allowed herself, as the two looked at each other, a welter of small indiscretions. Her favorite subject remained love. But she broached it carefully, setting out from the words that had wrapped up the conversation the previous visitors had left off.

"That said, your mother is right: we've gone well past the limits of what can be borne. Just last year, we still believed there might be a limit to all this horror. But there isn't! And even so, we should still be pinching ourselves at our luck. We haven't reached the point where we're eating leather. It will come. There are so many pairs of gloves I love. I could gulp down my butter-soft morning gloves or my plum-colored peccary evening gloves. And then my long white dance gloves. It's a shame that all my silverware was stolen: I can imagine twirling them tight around one of my forks, as if I were enjoying some spaghetti . . . But let's come back to talking about your mother. She shouldn't be putting on these airs:

what does she think she's doing, talking about emigrating at her age? She would do best to follow my example: to stay calm. What in heaven could she possibly do in Finland when she's sick and penniless? In any case, the two of us will both be dead come this spring. And it's far better to die in one's home. You, however . . ." The princess furrowed her brows here. "You're nothing more than skin and bones at this point." She was looking at her, at those prominent cheekbones, those feverish eyes. "You're headed for trouble! Indeed, my little girl . . ."

As she sensed more uncomfortable questions coming, Moura hastened to cut the conversation short. "But, my aunt, I'm doing perfectly well! And I so love gossiping in French with you."

"Oh, don't take that ridiculous tone with me. I know quite well that you'd be far happier talking in English with someone else."

She did not reply.

"Am I right in thinking that this is the first time you've fallen in love?"

Still no answer.

"How old is he, then?"

"Thirty-one years old."

"And you?"

"In two months, I'll be twenty-six."

"Oh, you're nothing more than a kitten! You have your whole life ahead of you to relive this experience. But I must offer one piece of advice: next time, don't let your lover leave for distant lands without another man ready at home."

Moura tried to smile:

"I didn't really have any choice."

"And how long has this little affair been going on?" The princess didn't give her any time to answer. "It hasn't even been a year, if I understand correctly. Do you want to know what I think?"

She was silent again.

"He'll write to you less and less. Until he stops writing to you completely."

Moura picked up her metal tumbler full of tea and tried to sip a little bit. But it was no use. She set the cup down with a shudder. She trembled so much that the goblet's metal clanged against the pot that served as a samovar.

"Why are you telling me this?"

"Because I love you. And seeing you in such a state is so depressing. Please, Moura, please stop trying to play Madame Butterfly. Stop waiting for him. Stop gnawing at yourself. Stop wringing yourself dry with all this to-ing and fro-ing across town to see if you've gotten any letters that were never sent in the first place."

"But he's writing them and sending them."

"You're thinking like a lady's maid! Listen to me, my darling. Do your best to look at this whole story with a bit of distance. You're carrying out an affair with an ambitious diplomat who's already married . . . Are we in agreement on those facts? He's an adventurer. A man who's dead set on changing the course of history in a country that isn't his own . . . Are we still in agreement so far? . . . Who has fallen in love with a native woman, the prettiest one, the smartest one, and the best-positioned one: a mistress who has assisted him in all his projects and who has gotten him out of bad situations over and over. And at this point, circumstances have forced him to return back home. Not as a man who's triumphed . . . but a man who's lost."

"He didn't go back as a man who's lost! He's settling his affairs in London."

"And however did this hero go back home, if not with his tail between his legs? He wasn't able to stop the Brest-Litovsk treaty from being signed; in fact, he created a major diplomatic crisis. It wasn't just a failure. It was a disaster! Believe me, at this moment he's far more concerned with shoring up his reputation in England than with setting up any kind of reunion in Sweden. And while he might very much have a broken heart, which I do believe is the case—he was terribly sad to have to leave you—he's already letting himself focus on far more practical considerations. He's suffering from being away from you, yes: he's a *sincere* boy. But he's forging onward, he's rebuilding a life for himself. He's settling his affairs, as you say. Let me ask you one question. Doesn't your relationship—a unique one, of course, with him—sound so much like another one? That of a young British plantation owner who got married to a Muslim princess in Malaysia? Who loved her madly? Who wooed her, who stole her away, who lived with her, who fell sick? A young British man who came back to London, having been exiled by the Bolsheviks? I'm sorry, by malaria . . . Now let me ask you another question, my little friend: what happened to the Malaysian princess after that? After he left, did he ever give another thought to the future she had ahead of her?"

"I understand what you're trying to tell me, my aunt."

"I'm not trying. I'm telling you. Sentimental men like your dear Lockhart are the worst! He's gone back to, or he's going to go back to, married life. And you really should do the same, as well. Do your best to go back to your husband. And don't tell me that it's impossible to abandon your mother here. For her and for me, it's all over. Get a visa for Estonia from those savages. I've been told they're satisfied with your work. They'll happily send you on to Yendel."

❖

After Moura came out of the Saltykov palace, she went back up the embankment, running along the banks of the Neva. Evening had fallen. The moonlight on the river's ice floes was enough to light her way. Her shawl was wrapped around her head, and her chin was buried in her bosom as she sank into the night's darkness. Nothing set her apart from a woman of the people. Except for the presence of Garry, who, stretching the leash to its limit, immediately marked her as a bourgeois woman walking her dog.

She was alert to the least noise as she rushed along. It was possible she was being followed, that she might be attacked at any moment. Even arrested. *It is forbidden to go out after 8:00 p.m.* She had only a few minutes left until the curfew. Already, there were no passersby. And not a single light in any of the windows. So much the better. If the electricity had been working in any of the buildings, there was no question of what it would have meant: the Cheka police were busy doing a search of the premises.

In general, those events took place around midnight. The victims, caught by surprise in their sleep, would panic and tell the truth more quickly. The night made them far more vulnerable. It made it possible to make them disappear without any witnesses. But there were no real rules. It could be anytime, it could be anywhere.

The methods, however, stayed constant. The policemen circled the neighborhood, surrounded the house, fanned out across the floors, broke down the doors with pounding fists. They entered the apartments in groups of four or five men, holding revolvers in their hands, ready with insults on the tips of their tongues, keeping their eyes open for any goods they could fence on the black market, banknotes, gold, jewelry, and old clothes. Among them, there were often children: in general, they were the best bloodhounds for seeking out what had been stashed away . . . The most audacious ones would climb on top of the armoires and the stoves, the most meticulous ones would take keen interest in the contents of the chests of drawers and take great offense at the *burzhui* presuming to hang on to anything at all.

Most of the time, the chekists weren't looking for something specific or somebody in particular. But they still had to be careful: a list of telephone numbers could become a list of guilty people. They always landed on someone. A suspect, ten suspects. By chance . . . The vans were always waiting outside.

From a distance, Moura could immediately see what was going on at number 8 on her street. She started running.

As she reached the entryway, the trucks were starting their engines, bearing away their load of men and women who would never see the light of day ever again. She climbed the steps as quickly as she could.

She opened the first door. There was nobody there. An unruly mess faced her. Which was to be expected after this sort of visit. The final things in the salon had vanished. A second door. "Mommy?" she asked in English. She heard no response. In English again: "Where are you?" She was screaming now, in the language of all her emotions: ". . . Are you here?"

The room was empty. All the rooms were empty. Every single one. All she had left was the nursery.

Mommy was there, sitting on the floor, her look crazed, holding one of Tania's stuffed giraffes in her hands.

Moura's relief at seeing her mother alive was so great that she couldn't say anything. She simply got down to pick her up. But to no avail. The old lady refused to move.

So Moura busied herself with picking up the baby clothes and toys that had been flung everywhere around her mother.

As before, when she had returned to Lockhart's place in Moscow, she collected all these belongings methodically, putting each thing away in the drawer where it belonged. She was inexhaustible as she arranged the dozens of slippers in pairs. She smoothed out the vests, spread out the bibs, put away the undergarments, folded the tiny dresses that she had once dressed her children in.

And all of a sudden, as she came across a block beside her mother, she collapsed.

Hunched over upon herself, her face buried in Paul's navy-blue clothes, she stayed put for the rest of the night. She was inconsolable. She cried and cried.

It felt as if Moura would never be able to stop crying.

CHAPTER TWENTY-THREE

World Literature

FEBRUARY–MAY 1919

A t the office of World Literature, the publishing house Maxim Gorky ran at 64 Nevsky Prospect, the conference room was full. In addition to representatives of the regime, all the biggest names Petrograd boasted of—writers, philosophers, and dramatists—thronged there.

There was nothing elegant in the decor. The room was dilapidated, barely heated by a coal stove. The only vestiges of decoration from earlier eras were the nineteenth-century mirror, the stucco friezes, and the moldings on the ceiling. The paint was peeling everywhere. And the chandelier's lightbulbs gave off a murky gleam.

"I broke our back door. Forgive me, please."

Gorky, "the singer of the people," "the bard of the proletariat," as the press and his millions of readers called him, had just hurtled in. He was at home in this space: the rooms had once served as offices for his newspaper, *Novaya Zhizn*, which was now shuttered.

"And I seem to have wrecked the doorbell. Forgive me, forgive me! But it's unbelievable: I've come here from the paper supplier, it's just unbelievable!"

As he climbed up to the dais, he took off his immense black felt hat, tossed aside his coat and his gloves by his spot, opened his satchel, and took out a pile of manuscripts, a handful of cigarettes, some matches. But he wasn't able to sit down or overcome his fury.

The meeting was supposed to define the official program for publications: the list of foreign authors he deemed worthy of being published anew. What was his dream? To make the classics available in the vernacular language: to put the best writers of all time and all countries in the hands of the common Russian. But the exasperation he felt upon leaving the previous meeting risked undoing the entire gathering here.

Two of the greatest contemporary Russian poets—Alexander Blok and Fyodor Sologub—were standing beside his empty chair. The first had just finished giving a lecture on the translations of Heinrich Heine, which he had revised himself. And the second had done the same on the translations of Stéphane Mallarmé and the other French symbolists.

All these personalities from the world of letters, seated in the first rows below the podium, got to their feet. The small fry—the translators—were standing up, as well, in the back rows.

Leaning against the wall, Moura simply listened. She never took her eyes off the speakers. She had never before experienced what she had been feeling for days now, even weeks. What pleasure! What intoxication.

She was still stunned by the intelligence, the sheer energy of Blok's and Sologub's speeches she'd just heard. How could Princess Saltykova have dared to call the group of poets surrounding Gorky barbarians and philistines? The princess was sorely mistaken on this point. Clearly she was working from extremely poor faith: "a gang of monkeys fallen straight from the tree"? In fact, they were absolutely brilliant!

And as for the star himself, who the people of the past had called an uncultured, corrupt peasant . . .

Too tall, too thin, his eyes set slightly apart, his cheekbones prominent, Gorky could indeed seem just that: a Russian and a *muzhik*, pure and simple.

As his faded blue pupils scanned the room, shifting swiftly from fury and despair, his drooping eyelids, giving him both an interrogative and a gentle look; his high forehead, offsetting his unruly, stiff, thick hair, which he pulled back; and his mustache, which covered his mouth and which he chewed, all gave his onlookers a thousand contradictory impressions.

He was first and foremost a physical presence, a vital force that nobody could possibly miss, even a hundred yards off. He was handsome, far too handsome, with the looks of a young man who life had marked deeply and was starting to bend down. He was fifty years old.

He was emotional and theatrical as he pulled himself upright, grumbling under his mustache, whining to himself, cursing everyone around him, and smoking cigarette after cigarette. His seemingly internal monologue was actually very much aimed at his audience.

In short: he was a great actor who put all his indignations on display and who calculated his effects brilliantly.

"Goddamn them! Those idiots are claiming that there's no paper left for any of our books. And I told those stinking bureaucrats that they were wretches, that it was shameful for them to act that way! And they told me that of the thousand tons of paper Russia had available, the Ministry of Education needs two thousand. Those monsters don't even know how to count, there isn't two thousand in one thousand!"

He held a cigarette butt between his long fingers as he paced back and forth, coughing his way through his words.

"If we want to get one little thing from them, we have to fill out fifty forms for these bureaucrats, a hundred certifications, five hundred requests. And I'd wager that they have no trouble at all losing those cursed forms. And after all that rigmarole, they'll just tell us that there isn't a single sheet of paper left anywhere in Russia! Those imbeciles!"

Moura leaned over to whisper to Chukovsky, the ambassador's former interpreter, who was standing next to her along the wall. The violence of Gorky's words astonished her. She murmured:

"I thought he was a Bolshevik?"

"Oh, not exactly, Benckendorff. Not exactly Bolshevik!"

Over the two months that they had been collaborating, they had become close friends. In many ways, Chukovsky—who she now affectionately called Chuk—reminded her of Garstino. He was similarly tall, with a similarly small brown mustache and a similarly slender profile. And he had the same gentle humor and generosity.

Korney Chukovsky was ten years older than her and married with children. He earned his living as a literary critic and a children's book illustrator. He was remarkably gifted, remarkably spiritual, and remarkably well read. He knew all the major personalities of contemporary literature in Russia and England. His friendship with the intelligentsia had won him a nomination to head the Anglo-Saxon department of World Literature. Moura was now a member of his team. She wasn't the best of his translators, not really. But she was the fastest, the most enthusiastic, and above all the most flexible. Benckendorff, as he so readily called her, accepted criticism with aplomb and rewrote her texts without complaint. Working with her was a pleasure.

There was no special closeness between them, however. Their relationship was limited to intellectual exchanges.

He vaguely knew the concerns she had about the fate of her son and daughter, but he had no idea of the situation she lived in. He was wholly unaware of the scope of her financial difficulties and the sheer depths of her emotional exhaustion. She took care to hide those details from him.

It's better to be envied than pitied: that was the old adage she went by, and so all she showed the world was a smile on her lips and a regal mien. She did not confess anything.

The result was that Chukovsky deemed her a mysterious woman, a thoroughly charming one.

He heard a new whisper in his corner of the room:

"But," she whispered, "I thought Gorky was part of the regime? If he hadn't already sold his soul . . ."

"He's torn. He lives for the values of the Revolution. He believes in the prospect of a better life. But he's horrified by the methods being used to get there."

"At the education commissariat," Gorky continued, "they're saying that our World Literature is full of bourgeois men and women. But I do wonder somewhat whether the policemen going around in cars with their wives aren't themselves *burzhui*, as well."

"That's quite daring of him," she said in a shocked whisper. "Is he really attacking Zinoviev?"

With a thrust of her chin, she gestured to the thick head of hair atop a massive man sitting in the first row. With his wife sitting beside him, he seemed to embody power, even from behind. Zinoviev, the man everyone called the dictator of Petrograd. And whose Rolls-Royce, of course, was parked in front of the building.

The rivalry between Zinoviev and Gorky was widely known. The two of them were close friends with Lenin, who they'd known for a long time and were in the habit of calling simply Ilyich, and they often fought for his favor. But that was one thing; directly attacking each other really was another. . . .

This time, it was Chukovsky who leaned over to say something to Moura:

"The guys taking paper away from us and keeping us from printing anything are under Zinoviev's thumb. He disdains intellectuals. He would love nothing more than to have Gorky's head, and so he tries to get in his way however he possibly can . . . This little speech against all the bureaucrats and the commissioners is going to cost us more than a million rubles. But even so, you should enjoy this spectacle, Benckendorff: Gorky's fury is worth a billion rubles! I don't think I've ever seen him in such a state."

"Why," he was asking the audience mockingly, "why, oh why, my dear friends gathered here today, why don't our commissioners have the right to love beautiful cars? And why can't they take any pleasure in wearing magnificent coats and washing themselves with refined soaps every morning? Their children, at least, don't catch lice or spread typhus! And it's all very well . . . In Russia, everybody should be permitted to wash properly and dress themselves suitably. And everybody should be allowed to drive a car. And everybody, above all, should be able to read fine books!"

On that note, he finally reached over to his chair, pulled it out, and decided to sit down and preside over all his colleagues, whose faces were impassive. He stubbed out his half-finished cigarettes in the three ashtrays set out in front of him.

The truth was that he was still in a bad mood, but he needed to catch his breath. A suicide attempt when he was younger had cost him a lung, and smoking cigarettes back-to-back hardly helped matters.

He was lost in his thoughts for a minute, and then he changed his tone.

"At the headquarters I've just come from, I was asked not to talk to you about foreign authors. Just about Gogol and Dostoyevsky. But I personally would much rather talk to you about literature from around the world. And about Victor Hugo . . . And on the topic of Victor Hugo—who, just between us, I don't like more than Dostoyevsky—I must allow myself to recommend that we do a limited edition of his works . . . Just two or three volumes. I wouldn't choose *Les Misérables*, which strikes me as a sermon on patience and humility. We'd be better off to publish *The Toilers of the Sea*, which is an ode to man's victory over the elements. What do you all think?"

The question was a mere formality. It was possible to discuss those choices, of course: he knew how to listen, he sometimes changed his mind. But that was rare.

The truth was that Gorky essentially served as minister of culture. An omnipresent minister.

He had created this World Literature publishing house and made it his focus to preserve the patrimony amid the rubble that had been heaped up in the former British ambassador's residence. But he had also founded the Committee for History and Theater, which he envisaged as producing nothing less than stage adaptations of all the crucial events of world history. The House of Arts was intended to bring together all the representatives of every artistic field. And the House of Scholars was intended to bring together all the scientists and all the academics. These immense undertakings might have seemed utopian to anybody looking at this city that was dying of hunger. But not to him. *We have to believe in this* was his motto. And his charisma was enough that he could instill this faith in the most skeptical men.

But even so, it was impossible to imagine that this man, who had read everything and who remembered everything—authors, titles, dates—this man, who could quote entire pages from novels off the top of his head, could be self-taught.

This was the only detail that betrayed his humble origins: his absolutely fantastical way of pronouncing the names of foreign writers. The fact that he didn't speak English or French or any other language that wasn't Russian clearly showed how he had been raised. In fact, he hadn't spent even six months on a school bench. And so what he knew was thanks only to his own efforts. His own physical energy, his own intellectual curiosity, his own passion for books, and his own memory. All four of which could be qualified as prodigious.

And above all, his faith in humanity and his unshakable belief in man's ability to redeem himself through knowledge.

His real name was Alexey Maximovich Peshkov. He had been born in Nizhny Novgorod to a father who had died of cholera when he was three years old. His grandfather had beaten him. After his mother had died in turn, he had fled the house to earn his living at twelve years old. At first he had been a baker's apprentice, then a newspaper boy, then a stevedore, then a tramp and vagabond—in short, he had lived out his youth in rough areas of every kind. And this pseudonym of Gorky—the Russian word for "bitter"—that he had chosen when he was twenty-four years old as a nom de plume for his first texts perfectly relayed all his fury and all his determination to declare the bitter truths about the injustices and brutality of a life in Russia. Six years later, in 1898, he published *Sketches and Stories*, the collection that made him a famous author. And since then, he'd never stopped writing. The success of his play *The Lower Depths*, then the publication of *Mother* as an insert in a New York–based magazine in 1906, had made him a prominent figure on the international scene. The novelty of his subjects, his forms, and his perspectives had led people to compare his genius these days to that of Tolstoy himself. The two men had known each other well, in fact. Each of them looked at literature as a political act that could change the world.

His determination to get books off the shelves of the privileged classes and make them a common good within reach of as many readers as possible was part and parcel of this belief.

In the room, one of the intellectuals from the literary committee had just suggested replacing Victor Hugo's works with another French author, who nobody present had ever heard of.

Gorky shot back: "Yes, of course, you're right. In *The Relaxations of a Man of Feeling*, Baculard d'Arnaud, that brilliant unknown author, wrote something interesting about the relationship between the author and his critic. But his prose is weak. However, in Madame de Staël's *On the Spirit of Translations* . . . Ah, yes, that's a special text, we should have it retranslated and published in its entirety! Who among you might want to take it on? In accessible language? A woman, perhaps? Chukovsky, my friend, while I'm thinking of it: do keep an eye on this point . . . When you assign a text to a translator, think about his elective affinities with the writer in question. Who's the one working on Ruskin and Stevenson? That translator is absolutely terrible with dialogue. No sense of poetry to speak of. But maybe that translator's style could be a good match to these essays . . . Does that person speak French, as well?" He pulled out his small glasses, looking through the pile of translations that he had already annotated, edited, corrected, some even rewritten wholesale, for the name of the person he had in mind. ". . . M. I. Benckendorff?"

❖

Moura returned to her home in a state that felt if not strange, then at least uncommon.

It had been a revelation.

Gorky seemed to her like a door that led toward potential freedom. A key that would unlock her survival. A savior she hadn't expected.

Her head and her heart pounded furiously in excitement, unwilling to slow down for even a minute. Her enthusiasm was all-encompassing.

Of course, her admiration blurred somewhat into her hope and her own self-interest. But her careful calculations didn't in any way detract from the spontaneity of her feelings. Careful consideration, in her mind, only served to amplify the fervor of her sympathy.

Wasn't everybody already saying that Gorky had the power to change Lenin's mind? And that he never refused to help those who asked him for something? Perhaps he could secure a visa on Mommy's behalf for Finland. An authorization for her to emigrate. It was true that there was no shortage of people who sought his favor and who flattered him: everybody crowded around him relentlessly with these sorts of requests.

But still—who knew what could happen?

———

She had to work. And work. And work.

She would do translations one after another. She would become wholly immersed in them. She would drown in them. In this way, she would belong to the world she had just discovered, this ever-expanding realm of World Literature that teemed with projects, overflowed with ideas, and stood in stark opposition to all the nostalgia and regret in which the people of the past stewed.

◈

Dawn found her sitting in front of her old typewriter, an Underwood that the former doorman—now the committee head, who occupied the nobles' floor on the same landing as her—could hear clicking away all night. He wasn't unaware of his neighbor's slowly developing relationship with the renowned Maxim Gorky: this connection, even if it was vague or distant, increased Maria Ignatyevna's prestige in the building.

She now had a career, a proper job. She was earning 300 rubles for each translation she did. It was a paltry sum, especially considering that a tiny sack of flour cost eight. But it was enough: the twenty volumes of Charles Dickens's works she was translating would allow her to pay Mommy's doctor, who had been saying that an operation was absolutely essential. It was now scheduled for this month.

With the melting of the ice floes that had freed the Neva's powerful currents, with the return of the spring sun and the earliest buds on all the trees, the city's daily life was becoming a little less gloomy.

On a practical level, she was starting to find her way out.

On another level . . .

She often thought about how Princess Saltykova had been wrong to accuse Gorky—in which case she could also be wrong about the judgments she had cast upon other situations, upon other people.

Even so, Lockhart's silence remained deafening. But it could possibly still be explained by the neutral powers' leaving.

We have to believe in it: She hadn't forgotten Gorky's adage as he continued to believe in the Revolution, that it was good and wise, even in spite of the acts he had borne witness to.

Gorky.

The letters from his readers came to him from every corner of the world. He himself corresponded with his readers abroad. Was it possible that he could serve as a go-between and make it possible for her to receive mail from England?

At the least, at the very least, she could hope for letters from Yendel!

After the armistice of 1918, Estonia had kept fighting for its independence: it wanted to be a sovereign nation. Free from all interference and all administrative supervision. So the country was fighting against both the Germans, who still staked a claim to ownership of all the Baltic countries, and the Bolsheviks, who had invaded it. The "war for its freedom" was far from over. A provisional government that simply hoped for democracy had managed to seize power, all the same. And ever since April 1919, the separatist regiments had been winning the majority of their battles.

Did these victories on the Estonian side signify that peace and security might be in the cards for Djon and their children? Had he been able to keep them safe all this time?

We have to believe in it.

She had regained her faith in the future.

◈

"Maria Ignatyevna Benckendorff?"

As she was stepping out to take her month's worth of work to the World Literature building, a man accosted her on the street. She thought he was about to snatch her purse. She tried to wiggle away. He held her in place.

"Are you indeed Maria Ignatyevna Benckendorff?"

His fingers were tightly gripping the strap across her back and trying to pull her onto the entryway. He was small and sturdy, and he pronounced her name in a strangely familiar way. His profile seemed to be telling her something, though she couldn't quite figure out what.

"Are you indeed Maria Ignatyevna Benckendorff?" he asked again, sharply, for the third time.

She stared at his face for a moment.

"Yes, I am."

"I have a message for you . . . From Estonia."

She stopped struggling. Her blood ran cold; she could feel her heart tensing. Her face went pale.

Her voice trembled with barely suppressed emotion as she asked:

"Are you bringing me news from Yendel?"

"I was just told to come and tell you this: he's dead."

She seemed not to understand his words. He explained:

"They came and murdered your husband. Djon Benckendorff is dead."

CHAPTER TWENTY-FOUR

Free Fall

T he shock was so violent that she didn't even think to ask the messenger the hundreds of questions that would come to mind later on.

She did learn, however, that Djon had been killed at Yendel on April 18 or 19. And that the murderers had hit him with three rifle blasts in the forest, training their sights on him from the small bridge that straddled the path. Her husband had been walking under the wooden edifice at that moment, on the walkway between the estate and the lake that they had all taken so often in the past when they went to swim.

To be precise, Djon hadn't been heading out for a swim: he was going back home, to the old fishermen's cottage on Kallijärv. In January 1919, the day after his mother had passed away, he had made the decision to settle there with his children, their nannies, and the cook. Given its modesty, the dacha had felt more secure to him than the immense manse. In any case, it was less attractive to thieves and robbers and thus less dangerous. During this tumultuous period, Yendel had been ransacked several times and picked to the bone by heavily armed rioters connected to the Reds. Djon wanted nothing more than to keep his family safe and sound while he was gone. Because he was already packing his bags: he was going to join the "Benckendorff regiment," which was fighting Latvia's Reds for Estonia's independence.

Two months later, in March 1919, he had returned home only to find the entire area around Yendel a burning, bloody battleground, carved up by the regiments of the Baltic nobility that had tried to hold on to their land and their privileges, the republican militants hungry for power and intent on nationalizing the manors, the roving bands of peasants on the hunt who were all too eager to seize whatever they could lay their hands on.

What he saw was extraordinary violence that he was determined to set right.

And it was at that moment that he had been killed.

Why? As the messenger had put it, nobody bore the man any ill will. Except perhaps the son of a former sharecropper, a boy by the name of Rudolph Rosentrauchy, who Djon had once punished with thirty lashes of his *knout* for attempting to rape one of the servant girls who worked in the house. That had been before 1914. But the Rosentrauchy boy had a long memory. He had come back from the front lines with his head full of Bolshevik ideas, swearing that he would get his revenge on the tyrant and make him pay for every one of his thirty lashes.

As the prime suspect, Rosentrauchy had immediately been arrested and sent to Reval to be judged and sentenced. But nobody had been able to furnish any proof of his guilt. *Was* he the murderer? That was a mystery. In prison, he had attacked one of the wardens and managed to escape. Djon's three brothers were all determined to find him again. The messenger worked for them.

By searching all Petrograd for the widow of the man who owned Yendel, by informing her that the eldest Benckendorff son had now been under the ground for nearly three weeks, the man was dutifully carrying out the family's orders. His mission had been accomplished. He had said everything he had to. He left her standing there, under the awning, as he went down the street and disappeared just as quickly as he had first appeared.

What now?

Now she had to keep to herself. She had to stay quiet. She had to hide the news from Mommy. It was two days before her cancer surgery, which was planned for that Wednesday at the hospital. She had to go say hello, reassure her, and give her a smile.

Ever since the winter night when she had dealt all on her own with chekists carrying out a police search, Mommy hadn't been the same. There weren't any more scenes, any more bouts of panic. There weren't any more struggles or shrieks. All that remained was silence.

But even so, it wasn't peace. Not as much as it was a muted fear, an unending fear that paralyzed her completely.

This passive, oddly gentle old woman was such a change from years past that nobody could have recognized the Viper in her countenance. Mommy had loved her son-in-law dearly. She wouldn't have the strength to survive such grief. The news would kill her.

◈

"Give me your hand, Mourushka, stay with me, talk to me . . . Tell me happy things, please."

In the hospital waiting room, behind the screen that separated her from the other sick patients, Mommy's eyes were shut as she prepared herself for the ordeal.

Moura had changed her clothes in the latrines, pulling off her veils and crapes in a rush so as not to alert her mother to the misfortune that had descended upon them. She stuffed her black blouse and skirt into the bottom of her handbag. Even in these times of upheaval, custom dictated that she wear mourning clothes. She had no choice but to present herself to Princess Saltykova and the Benckendorff family in a widow's garments to convey the news of her husband's death. They wouldn't have been able to bear the scandal of her behaving otherwise.

Under the nurses' gaze, she made her way into the building in red. She was elegant and regal. She crossed the room with a decisive step, not even glancing at the other beds, all the way to the corner where Mrs. Zakrevskaya lay.

Sitting beside her bed, she now tried to hold back her tears.

The truth was that Moura, like Mommy, was afraid. The surgeon had claimed that there was no alternative but to remove her breast . . . A quick glance at the other patients in the room, all of them groaning in the nearby beds, portended the worst for her.

The worst. She couldn't help but think of Djon. Her thoughts returned to him day and night. His loss had stirred up a sorrow within her that was equal parts remorse and shame. A bottomless sadness.

She took her mother's hand and stroked it. The memories rose up. She recalled their wedding ceremony, under the thumb of her sister Anna as well as Micky's. The blessing in the small chapel of the Russian embassy in Berlin. And Djon, standing in front of the iconostasis. He had seemed so reassuring to her back then.

She was well positioned to know just how terrible a wife she had been for him, a companion who barely loved him. But even so, she had believed they could come together. That was after Paul was born, when they had both dreamed about rebuilding Yendel. Then the Great War had come, putting an end to this small bout of intimacy.

In her regret, in her compassion, even in her tenderness, there was another feeling, a less certain one, a feeling that she barely dared to articulate because of the shame it brought. What she felt was a sort of relief. Djon's death freed her. As a widow, she could no longer be an adulterous wife. As a widow, she could stop being an unworthy mother, and she no longer had to face the potential scandal of a divorce. She could love Lockhart with impunity; she could even marry him without losing Paul and Tania.

And as she thought this, a third emotion rose up and choked her throat, a feeling that was far more pregnant with potential than all her hopes and regrets, more overwhelming than pity, more harrowing than remorse: a terror for her children's survival. Where were the little ones at this moment? Now that they were bereft of Djon's protection, they were three orphans.

The messenger had said that the governess was with them at Kallijärv. But what could Micky do without Djon, without money? What could Micky do while she was alone and poor in a land that was at war? She didn't even speak the language there!

Sensing her daughter's anguish, Mommy whispered, "Your husband must be working at the moment to secure a passport for you. Once a provisional government is elected in Reval, you'll have the right to Estonian nationality. Djon will send you the papers, no question of it. He'll do everything he can to bring the two of us to Yendel."

Moura tried to hold back her sobbing. "Yes, Mommy. He's working to take care of it."

"Give your Djon all the love you have. If anything should happen to me . . . Love your husband, my darling, take care of him and take care of yourself. If I should somehow not wake up after the operation . . ."

"Mommy! Don't say things like that!"

"If I should somehow not wake up, I want you to make sure my body is cremated . . . Don't be too sad for me, Mourushka, life has been excruciating."

"But everything will be okay. Dr. Milyutin is the best surgeon in all Petrograd. And you were recommended to him by Gorky himself."

"In my final moments, I'll be thinking of you, my darling, assuming that we can think all the way to the end. And I'll be thinking of Djon. And I'll be praying that the two of you can stay happy together forever. I love the two of you so, so much."

◈

Mommy didn't die right away. She came back to her apartment on Shpalernaya Street, where she spent the summer convalescing.

And as she did so, Moura took on more and more work. She was now a secretary for Korney Chukovsky at the Studio, the organization Gorky had established to develop screenplays for the cinema. This second job gave her a way to feed and care for her mother.

But it was a losing battle.

Mommy ultimately passed away at the hospital during another operation. It was the month of September, 1919, a full year since Moura had lost Little Peter in the Lubyanka prison.

◈

When the nurse brought her the few belongings of the late Mrs. Zakrevskaya, Moura took them without saying a word.

The loss of Mommy, the murder of Djon, the silence of Lockhart . . . After so much tragedy, she had no tears left to cry. Bent low by pain, her head hung, the bundle under her arm, she made her way out, determined to get back home so she could shut herself away. She practically ran across the Trinity Bridge.

"Papers!"

A young chekist had stopped her:

"I said, your papers!"

In her daze, she hadn't been paying attention.

How could she have been so unaware? She, Moura, always in control of herself, always attentive to her surroundings . . . This time, her instincts hadn't alerted her. And she hurtled further toward danger as she committed an utterly absurd, unbelievable mistake.

Rather than presenting the certificate her employer, Chukovsky, had signed—a work permit fully in order and authorized by Deputy Commissar Greenberg of the People's Commissariat for Education—she rummaged through the bundle of her mother's possessions.

She took out Mommy's false work booklet and her false ration cards.

The two sets of documents, with their owner's age wholly at odds with Moura's, drew the policeman's attention. It took only a slightly longer examination for him to recognize that they were counterfeit.

"Where did you buy this shit? On the black market? Are you a seller? Go on, get in there . . . You're going with the others!"

He hit her with the butt of his rifle and forced her toward the prison van parked on the corner of the embankment, right in front of the former British embassy.

She was being taken straight to the terrible prison on Gorokhovaya Street, where the Cheka was headquartered.

❖

"Call Comrade Yakov Peters in Moscow," she begged of the two prison guards leading her through the hallway of the lower basement.

"Of course not!"

"Please, I beg you . . . call him. Call Yakov Peters!"

"Why not Lenin, while you're at it?"

"Yakov Peters will tell you that you're making a great mistake."

"What of it?"

"He will tell you to free me!"

"Shut your mouth, or I'll punch you a new one. Go on, get in there. And shut it!"

The cell wasn't small, like the one in the Lubyanka, nor was it empty. Women were sleeping everywhere. Some were even sleeping standing up, leaning against the walls in each corner, while others were stretched out on the floor and the pallets. In that space, former bourgeoisie were pressed up against prostitutes, aristocrats, thieves, and sellers on the black market, women young and old alike. She could see that some were filthy; their misery clearly evinced just how long they had been here. Months, in fact.

The iron door slammed shut behind her.

She stayed there, staring through the peephole, unable to believe what was happening to her. She clutched her blanket and her mess kit. The lightbulb in the ceiling, which was perpetually on, radiated a gloomy light over the dozens of bodies below and their faces pressed against the ground. Their heads, barely visible beneath their hair, remained hidden so they would not be disturbed by the light.

She was devastated. She couldn't bring herself to move. She could feel all sense of reason flooding away. Her moral distress was such that she didn't even think to look for a place among the detainees where she could lie down.

She was shaken out of her consternation by a new jangling of locks and keys. Two female wardens in gray shirts opened the door and barked out:

"Maria Ivanovna Cheu."

The bodies gave a vague shudder, twitching like a heap of maggots before shifting around and pulling away to let through the unfortunate woman whose name had been called. The prison wardens only ever yelled out the first syllable of their family names—never the entire name—so that nobody in the neighboring cells might learn the identities of the women who were in such close proximity to them. This was a tactic Moura had learned about during her stay in the Lubyanka prison in September.

All her reflexes as a detainee came back. She didn't need to be told what to do. The prison experience remained engraved in her body. She knew the rhythms of life and death intimately. She knew that in prison, the interrogations always happened at night. As did the executions.

"Your hands behind your back."

The woman whose name had been called moved automatically. The jailers' faces were impassive and their eyes unmoving as they tied her up and ordered her to move.

Moura heard the three women's footsteps fade away and then disappear in the hallway.

"So what are you in here for?" One of the captives, her fitful sleep disturbed, had gotten up and was whispering in her ear.

Moura knew this, as well: in prison, one needed to keep secrets from the stool pigeons.

"No reason . . . What about you?"

"Same thing. No reason."

In the week that followed, three obsessions kept coming back to the fore of her mind: Getting out of there. Making her way to Estonia. Being with her children again.

Only three men had the power to make those three thoughts reality. Yakov Peters. Lev Karakhan. Maxim Gorky. And they absolutely had to be informed of her imprisonment.

None of the functionaries processing her file had taken the trouble to meet with her. She felt like she had been forgotten about outside. And inside.

Each night, however, the contingent of prisoners changed. Some were called for interrogations and came back. Others vanished without anyone knowing whether they'd been freed or executed. Yet others came in from other prisons and replaced them. Yet others were never called . . . And she was in that latter category.

❖

"Maria Ignatyevna Ben. Your hands behind your back!"

At last! She jumped up and let herself be taken away, rushing toward a meeting that had terrified all her companions.

The interrogation chiefs were hunched over their folders. The chekist in charge of her case had been busy carrying out other interrogations until dawn. He was exhausted and had gone to sleep. He would come back in the late morning.

There was no use taking the prisoner back underground. So she had to stay and wait.

Six hours standing in front of the interrogation room's locked door drained Moura of all her energy and took what little fight she still had out of her.

As in Moscow, in Petrograd the Cheka building was a former private mansion. Its state rooms had been divided up into offices, but the grand staircase, the neoclassical friezes in stucco, the garlands of knots and flowers on the ceiling provided a striking contrast to the specks of blood staining the walls and the shrieks that could be heard now and then on the other side of the walls.

The clock over the chimney had stopped. Still, she was able to calculate that it had been noon when she was shoved into her interrogator's office. He must have gone down the other hallway, because she hadn't seen him come in.

The space reminded her of a room she knew well. A table, a lamp, a chair. And two photos of Lenin, high up on the wall above the two seated men: the two functionaries who were going to grill her.

The chekist at the table in front of her was young and thin, with round glasses. The one who went and stood behind her seemed older and heavier.

The other detainees in the basement had told her how the interrogation would play out. The younger one would ask the questions and pummel her with insults. The old one would be a calm, reassuring presence. They would trade off, taking turns being threatening and welcoming. They might also trade roles. The goal was to catch her off guard until she signed her "confessions" at the end of the interrogation.

The young one lobbed the first question at her:

"What were you doing on the Trinity Bridge with false ration cards?"

"I will only answer your questions with the consent of Comrade Yakov Peters."

"Do you know what the penalty is for false ration cards? The firing squad . . . Or, well, let's be optimistic: maybe just ten years in the labor camps. If you cooperate: then five. Who made those false papers for you? Give me the name of the forgers, and I'll get you out of here."

"Call the Lubyanka."

"I've heard she says that all day long," the old man whispered behind her. "She wants the Lubyanka, and she wants Yakov Peters."

"Do you think she's just feebleminded?" the younger one asked. "Or do you think she's stupid?"

"Well, it's her lucky day today: he's coming to Petrograd."

She shuddered . . . Peters, here!

"He should actually be in the building this afternoon."

"Quite likely . . . At some point."

The younger chekist turned and looked at Moura again:

"If you're really his friend, we can ask Comrade Peters to come here. But I must warn you: he's thoroughly humorless. If you've bothered him for no reason, it'll be the end of you. I can't negotiate for your flesh."

For the hundredth time, Moura spat out the same three words:

"Call Yakov Peters!"

❖

He was wearing the same boots, the same leather jacket, the same Mauser pistol in its holster. But in just eleven months, he had gained several pounds and aged twenty years. Was it the weight, the cramp, of his signature at the bottom of hundreds of death warrants? She looked at him, and she knew he had changed. And he saw the same thing in her. Neither of them dared, however, to broach the question.

"Leave the two of us alone."

The two chekists, flabbergasted, got up and headed toward the door.

"And bring in a cup of tea for Comrade Benckendorff. With some biscuits."

They left. Yakov Peters turned back to Moura and took his place in the chair facing her.

"You're dying of hunger, aren't you?"

She smiled, quickly putting on the half-sentimental, half-teasing tone that he was so fond of. "I do believe that in such circumstances, you're the only man in the world who would think about such a thing."

"Are you telling me, Maria Ignatyevna, that you think I'm kind?" he said wryly.

She thought for a long moment. "I think that you're a good person, Yakov Khristoforovich."

The answer caught him by surprise. He let out a great burst of laughter and then changed the subject. "What news do you have of our dear friend Lockhart?"

It was her turn to laugh.

"Meetings, gatherings, honors: the entire capitalist world has just swallowed him up whole. I do suspect that he wasn't really made for life with us."

"That's too bad for him. Poor Lockhart. You really should have seen him during his interrogations. He was like a donkey wavering between two bales of hay: Russia? England? Which of the two stables would be better for his creature comforts? Which of the two carrots would be better for his appetite? It really was pathetic. Not at all what he recounted after the fact!"

"Well, I must say, I thought you were a good person, but here you are, pouring water on a drowning man!"

"Oh, are you still in love with him? You women, oh, you women. Fine,

fine, the matter's over and dealt with. As for your false ration cards . . ."

"They weren't mine. And I didn't know they were false."

"But you were carrying them with you."

"They belonged to my mother, who just died while she was in the hospital. And she was cremated back there. They gave me her belongings so I could incinerate them, as well. She had been in contact with people suffering from typhus. I hadn't been planning to keep anything."

"Good, good. Now, you know Maxim Gorky, don't you?"

She frowned.

"Vaguely."

"Comrade Grigory Zinoviev would like for you to be better acquainted with him. I do believe Zinoviev's not going to be pleased with what you'll tell him. Gorky's a massive pile of filth whom I would love nothing more than to lock away forever. But Zinoviev is hoping that you'll tell him a bit about what's being said by the great man himself. Who he's seeing. What he's working on."

"I don't have access to Gorky. I work for the World Literature publishing house. And I'm just a plain translator, among twenty others."

Peters changed his tone. His stare became glacial.

"You seem not to have understood me properly, Maria Ignatyevna. You listen to things marvelously, you understand things marvelously, you explain things marvelously. And you keep secrets marvelously: you really are a remarkable woman. But you seem not to have understood me properly . . . Which really does bother me. Because I've always held you in high esteem. And if I had been in the place of that donkey Lockhart, I wouldn't have hesitated, not even for a second, between my two stables and my two carrots: I would have chosen both of you, you *and* the Revolution . . . And in any case, those would have been one and the same thing! Haven't you been one of ours from the beginning? At the very least, that was what you reassured me in Moscow last fall. Did you change your mind in Petrograd? Keeping in mind all your particular merits, I really have done you a great many favors. I don't think I really should go so far as to recall exactly how many, exactly how sizable those indulgences have been. But, at heart, you're right: *kind* and even *good* is what I've been

to you. The time has now come to prove to me that our affection is reciprocal."

"It is!"

"That reassures me. Because it's not a new friendship that I'm suggesting you strike up, but an alliance that I'm asking you to deepen. Or
rather, to begin. Do you remember? An agreement signed . . . How long
ago? A year?"

"I do remember. Although I'm not sure how—"

"You do remember quite well how. If you want to see your children
again one day—and, more immediately, leave this room alive—you'll go
each week to Comrade Zinoviev and provide him a summary of what
you've seen and heard among your new friends at World Literature."

There was a knock on the door.

"Ah, here's your tea at last, along with your little delicacies to enjoy."

❖

She was trapped.

And this time, she was trapped for life.

In the end, General Knox and Captain Hicks had all been exactly
right. She had become what they had all accused her of being. A spy. An
informant. A snitch in the pay of the Cheka.

Or, in the slang of those who had been betrayed and arrested, a *seksot*.
A secret collaborator.

❖

But she had no choice. She had to please, she had to lie, she had to survive.

At the same moment, while she was locked up and Yakov Peters was
making his way to Grigory Zinoviev's residence in Petrograd, the Cheka
was executing sixty-seven people in the Lubyanka and twenty-nine on
Gorokhovaya Street. The majority of them were university professors,
scholars, and members of the intelligentsia.

In September 1919, Moura's friend, the great literary critic Korney Chukovsky, wrote in his diary:

I've just seen Gorky crying. . . . I followed him . . . to ask for his help with Maria Benkendorf (my assistant at the Studio), who has also been arrested. He started in on a long reply, but it disintegrated into gesticulations. "What can I do?" he finally managed to come out with. "I told the bastards—I mean, the bastard Zinoviev— that if [my friend] wasn't released this very minute I'd make a scandal. I'd break with them, with the Communists, for good, damn them!" His eyes were moist.

CHAPTER TWENTY-FIVE

The Two Animals

S he was completely alone. Without her husband, without her lover, without her children. Without her parents. Even the old Princess Saltykova had died earlier that year, died of hunger, exactly as she had predicted she would.

Myriam Artsimovich had been arrested in May. And her fiancé, Bobbie Ionin—accused of having worked for the British—had just been sentenced to five years in one of the worst labor camps.

And while she was in prison, other citizens had settled into the Shpalernaya Street apartment and kicked her out.

So she had taken with her what she could of her memory—at least, the family's memory: the portraits of her father and of Djon—and put it in the maid's quarters of General Mossolov's residence, where she had so frequently met with Princess Saltykova. Even though he himself was being threatened with expulsion, she was determined to stay there until the next catastrophe came.

She had even lost her dog, Garry. He had disappeared while she was gone, and had most likely been eaten.

It would have been remarkably difficult for anybody to accumulate so many misfortunes in so little time and to feel more vulnerable.

She had to hold it all in.

❖

On this afternoon in September 1919, Moura crossed the Trinity Bridge again and went back through the checkpoint where she had been arrested.

This time she was accompanied by her employer, Chuk, who was taking her along to have tea with their mentor, who she wanted to thank for his assistance with the Cheka.

Gorky had played no role in her liberation; she knew that quite well. But her colleagues at World Literature all believed that he was her savior. And she didn't want any of them to suspect her of having any connection to Zinoviev. So she would go and express her gratitude to the master.

The wind whistling sharply past the bridge's lampposts tugged at the ends of her immense coat—a relic of Lockhart's—and undid her hair. Her thinness, accentuated by the men's hat, and the few locks of hair falling into her eyes made her look like a young woman. Prison had made her emaciated. Her eyebrows seemed to jut out even more, and her cheekbones seemed even more prominent.

She made her way forward at a quick gait, so quick that even Chuk, with his long legs, struggled to keep up. He kept on talking as he described the world she was about to set foot in. A world that was thoroughly fascinating to him, as well. Gorky, he warned her, lived among many friends. "You'll see, Benckendorff: he's surrounded by an incredible court, and he only ever goes out when he's surrounded by his courtesans."

They had made their way to one end of the avenue, where the former private mansion of the ballerina Matilda Kshesinskaya, a special mistress of Tsar Nicholas II, had once stood. It was the first palace where the revolutionaries had planted the red flag in 1917. She remembered having seen it, high up, from the other side of the river, from the windows of the British ambassador's residence.

And from there, they turned left onto Kronverksky Prospect.

The apartment that Gorky occupied, at number 23, had become a mythical place. The translators for World Literature described it as a labyrinth filled with legendary creatures: all those that Russia considered the most intelligent and gifted. The three arches, built out of blocks of black stone, that broke up the building's three porches made her think of the Minotaur's lair. And the ancient Greek theater masks that overlooked the central door's pillars only added to this distinct impression. The whole space seemed to be the cutting edge of modernity. The archaic maze of courtyards and the narrow, crumbling staircase, however, were a testament to Petrograd's impoverishment.

The building's ambiance changed on the fourth story, where the smell of tobacco and the muted hum of a thousand conversations gave unexpected life to what had seemed deserted spaces.

Chuk pushed open the door without bothering to ring the bell, threw his hat on the coatrack, and strode easily from the entrance all the way to the kitchen. She followed close behind.

The first thing that Moura saw was the samovar right at the center of the tablecloth. Massive, heavy, golden . . . a samovar just like the ones of the past. And then, all around it, the people in half darkness, standing and sitting, far too many for the table: some twenty people who were trading the latest news, joking, and arguing with each other. In this happy hubbub, she could hear bits and pieces of what people were saying: both low-class gossip and cleverly articulated philosophical ideas. It was impossible for her to make out the features of those talking. Their faces blurred together in the pale haze of cigarette smoke as they lit one after another. There were men and women of all ages who she had already seen milling around World Literature; they struck her as being as oddly dressed as she was.

The decor was simple, however. Here, as elsewhere, the electricity wasn't working anymore, and the room was lit only by a massive petrol lamp that hung from the ceiling. The notes of a clock ringing five o'clock and the buffet seemed to have come straight out of a nineteenth-century bourgeois interior. The knickknacks lined up higgledy-piggledy on the shelves would have driven Princess Saltykova into a rage: a collection of blue porcelain Chinese vases.

Hung on the wall between the rows of shelves, a Pushkin mask and a Nietzsche portrait peered knowingly over the master's chair. It was empty, and the guests pushed it aside to make some room for the latest newcomers. How could they resist tasting the delectable tea that was being served here? It bore no relation to the infusion of dried carrots that everybody elsewhere in the city drank. At Gorky's place, the tea was markedly weak, but it was real tea—like the people milling around the table: real human beings, wholly unlike the Cheka's henchmen.

The door of the semidetached cabinet opened. Gorky's tall profile came into view. He was wearing an old Chinese dressing gown cut from red silk and a Chinese officer's cap on his head. He was flanked by two of his best friends, who were just wrapping up a long conversation with him. Moura recognized the commissar of the education ministry, as well as the singer Shalyapin, who she had met several times before the war at various receptions. The three men were still talking to one another as they sat down.

"No, what matters to me," Gorky was explaining to them, "is the birth of a new, cultivated man . . ." He lit a new cigarette as someone poured him some tea. "What matters to me is that a worker at a sugar refinery be able to read Shelley in the original."

Everybody had gone quiet so they could listen. He seemed not to realize it.

"I know, I know, you're all going to tell me that I'm being an old romantic, a dreamer, one of those cursed utopians! And yes, yes, yes, I'm a utopian: if we believe in illusions with all our heart and mind, I'm firmly convinced that they'll come true . . . Even if it's only because man is a god unto himself, and he can do anything and everything that he sets his mind to. Why? Because he is endowed with reason! And reason is omnipotent. All man has to do is develop it, care for it, nourish it; and then it can make the world better on all three levels that touch on human needs: that of intellectual development, that of moral perfection, and that of economic prosperity."

Carried away by his theories, Gorky was smoking, coughing, and paying no attention to anybody but the people right beside him. The finely proportioned Shalyapin was making just as much noise as him, refuting his generalizations about Reason and grousing with him about what he called the Bolsheviks' idiocy.

Moura, sitting far off from the stars, was in no position to approach them. Or even wave to them. Much less thank Gorky and express her gratitude to him for his phone call to the Cheka. In any case, for her to do so here would be unremarkable: more or less everybody here around this

table had gotten out of prison . . . That afternoon, she wasn't even able
to catch the master's eye.

But her first visit to Kronverksky Prospect wasn't in vain. The other men
appreciated her presence. Her neighbor the painter Rakitsky, a small
forty-year-old man with a mustache who was kind and had no taste for
seduction, told her about his arrival here the previous year. He had set
his bags down in this apartment, half-naked and nearly dead of hunger.
They had fed him, bathed him, dressed him here. He hadn't left since.
Now he saw, in this young woman who clearly knew how to keep her
silence and listen, the symptoms of his own fascination. He could sense
what she was feeling that very instant. This combination of enchantment
and well-being. This desire to engage with each of the members of the
community. The need to belong to this reassuring crowd of bohemians.

The long walk back in Chuk's company offered her all the details she
could possibly want about the world she'd just managed to glimpse.

He was just as charmed, just as entranced as she was, and there was
no stopping him as he waved his long arms and kept talking about the
man who bore the name Gorky. The subject offered so many facets ripe
for scrutiny.

"Did you hear them, Benckendorff? They call him *Duca*, the duke . . .
Doesn't that just take the cake for a champion of class struggle? Using
the Italian word for duke, that's nothing if not classy. It's an allusion to his
years in exile on Capri and his instincts as a leader of the pack. The truth
is that the pack nipping at his heels just gets bigger and bigger every day.
Did you understand what I was trying to say there when I mentioned his
pack? The number of people living off his largesse is just unbelievable! I
don't know if you took the time to count. There's his chosen family first,
all his closest ones: his first wife and their son, Max; his former companion; his current mistress; his closest friends, their wives, and their children. He spends every moment of his daily life with them. And, just as an
aside, he's housing them all in the apartment you saw. What I think is that

he's far too trusting of his friends. Just between you and me, he's naive: some of his good friends are nothing more than bandits!"

Night was falling: a serious risk for walkers. Neither Chuk nor Moura gave it any thought, however. Their two profiles stood out on the bridge between the sky and the water.

This September day had been sublime, with a crystal-blue sky, the last glimmers of which the Neva was still reflecting back. Behind them, the spire of the Peter and Paul Fortress had taken on a shade of gold that was darkening with each passing second. In front of them, the facade of the former British embassy rose up, with its long row of barricaded windows. This time, Moura didn't even glance at it. She was looking at Chuk, with his hat tight on his head, his too-long hair covering his eyes as he waved his hands and kept talking. She listened to him and did not interrupt.

"Do keep in mind that his loyalty to his loved ones does not prevent him from making other connections. Gorky likes nothing so much as love at first sight and new encounters! As long, however, as the latest comers please the older ones already there. If his circle deems acceptable whoever arouses his curiosity, if the circle welcomes this person, then he throws himself into that friendship, he commits himself body and soul to amiable companionship or a love affair. So be careful, Benckendorff: his magnetism and power of seduction become irresistible at that point. On the other hand, if his colleagues turn out to be hostile to the object of his desires, he will put an end to his enthusiasm. The thing is to please his friends: if you fail, it's the death of your prospects! To those people, he's maybe not so much a despot as a clear-sighted leader. He might try to behave in a democratic way, to speak simply, to joke good-naturedly, but his behavior weighs upon each of us as a form of tyranny. We love him, no question of that. We admire him. But we also fear him. This goes for the most powerful ones there, as much as for the most humble ones . . . If anyone dares to contradict him and discuss his ideas, woe betide anyone who still opposes his decision after opinions have been exchanged. He remains the leader. A middle-aged duke whose lungs are in bad shape, who's not all that worried about his appearance . . . But even so, a duke who's elegant in a particular way, charming to an unmatched degree.

He's a great seducer. As I said, Benckendorff: watch yourself, he has a way of arousing passion. I do assure you, however: he's a sentimental man, he's not the sort to collect mistresses. But the women who have accompanied him in his adventures are still a part of his life, and they carry great weight. He loved them dearly, tormented them dearly. Not out of cruelty but out of a stubbornness, an unwillingness to accept reality when it gets in the way of his ideals. Despite the difficulties, we must believe. Despite the Bolsheviks, we must believe in the Revolution. Despite so many disenchantments, we must believe in love. I think he's unable to abandon his dreams. So he cheats with his feelings, he lies to himself, and he tortures the mistress he does not want to hurt directly ten times more by being subtle. And he, in turn, is perfectly able to unleash torrents of tears when one of them threatens to break up with him: for him, *break up* is a meaningless concept, one that does not belong to his vocabulary. And because for him everything begins with emotion, and because for him everything ends with emotion, he cannot bring himself to leave or abandon anyone.

"The result is that with time and success, he's become overwhelmed with so many people that he's starting to wear himself out trying to support them all. You saw for yourself: it's just an endless parade . . . All the representatives of his huge workshops—not just us, the collaborators at World Literature as well as his House of Arts, but also from his House of Writers and his House of Sciences—they all settle down at his table at any given moment to discuss their latest plans. And of course they are! Gorky's projects are meant to allow them to create and to survive: they have the scope of a Tower of Babel, and they'll take thirty years to accomplish . . . His fight with that horrible Zinoviev to save the intelligentsia is only just getting started!"

As he spit out those words, Chuk stumbled and narrowly avoided falling into one of the holes that now dotted the path along the Kutuzov embankment: it had become a veritable bog where it was all too easy to break one's neck, as a result of the previous winter's raids: as there hadn't been any wood left to stay warm, the inhabitants of Petrograd had dug up the streets in order to get at the wooden planks that supported the cobblestones.

She grabbed him by the arm in the nick of time. Once they were steady, they made their way around the crevasse. Chuk continued his monologue, almost as if he hadn't noticed the interruption.

"And as if that weren't enough, Gorky's welcoming workers, sailors, even *burzhui*, who all beg him to put in a good word for them. They ask him to get them food rations, clothes, medicine, tobacco, dentures for the older ones, milk for the babies . . . And the most incredible thing is that he listens to all their stories, writes a thousand letters of recommendation for them, and never refuses to help any of them. I do wonder where this man, who's half-dead from tuberculosis, has managed to find such energy . . . I really do wonder how he finds any time to work on his own manuscripts. He's perfectly happy to pick up his phone ten times a day to ask for this son or that daughter of this aristocrat or that *burzhui* he doesn't even know to be freed—the same way he did for you—and to yell into the contraption about the sheer stupidity of a particular arrest or to hurl complaints at Party members. Only to hang up on them in a fit of anger."

Moura didn't miss a word of the portrait that Chukovsky was sketching for her.

How could she get the attention of such a man when so many people were already clamoring for his time? How could she get close to him? And how could she embed herself in his milieu enough to satisfy Zinoviev's rancor?

She needed Gorky to survive. He needed everything except her, a survivor of a society he had denounced.

It was a reminder of just how skewed their relationship was.

"But on the other hand, he can burst out laughing and slap his knees when something delights him. I've seen him revel in the stupidest jokes. Just between us, the best of his intellectual faculties is his memory. Among the others, his capacity for logic is a disappointment. As for his political vision and his theories, they aren't markedly better than any teenager's ability to generalize."

❖

Chuk left her at the entrance to the Mossolov building. She went in and found herself back in the solitude and desolation of her bedroom, even as she was still overcome with wonder. She had found the energy again tonight, a hundred times stronger, of the first meetings at World Literature.

But where in this world buzzing with powerful personalities, where in this world of such well-ordered disorganization, where in this world that so seduced and fascinated her, could she find a place for herself?

A way to devote herself, body and soul, to the beings who peopled this world?

◈

She had to prepare for the reading committee meetings at World Literature, type up the agendas at the Studio, write up the minutes, attend to the well-being of the attendees, heat up the room, and reheat the tea. She had to show interest in each member of the group.

On all fronts—material, moral, sentimental—in every way, she had to prove that she was indispensable.

And she showed herself to be a master at this game. She was well versed in the intricacies of being diplomatic, being organized, and being a secretary. The role she had played as assistant to Lockhart had perfected her skills.

With Gorky's circle, there was no need for her to flaunt her talents. Nor was there any need for her to exaggerate her enthusiasm. She felt boundless admiration and sympathy for the man. She instinctively wanted to please him, to be attached to him, to be first in his thoughts . . . Throughout the disaster that was her life, he had been the very embodiment of hope for her. In her heart of hearts, she called him My Joy, an expression that revived in her mind the image of Our Lady of Unexpected Joy, the icon of the Virgin Mary at the Kremlin that she had gazed at with Lockhart.

Even so, she moved carefully and made sure not to raise a fuss. She was navigating a minefield, and she had to watch every step she took.

She harbored no illusions: Gorky's lovers were powerful women, with secure positions as eminent Party members and significant connections as acquaintances of Lenin. They were all on the alert and quick to take offense.

Over time, she had met those rivals. At least, the most formidable ones.

First and foremost was the legitimate wife he had left fifteen years earlier, Yekaterina Peshkova. She practically ran the Political Red Cross in Moscow—she had to work with the Cheka's founder, the terrible Dzerzhinsky, and apparently succeeded in standing up for his victims without losing his trust. As the mother of Gorky's son—the young man Max, who worked in the Lubyanka with Yakov Peters—she still had near complete sway over her husband. Gorky had never formally divorced her.

Moura had also met his second companion, who was the passion of his life: Maria Andreyeva, a voluptuous redhead, a widely acclaimed actress whom the Bolsheviks had just named commissar of the theaters. She shared Gorky's apartment, and she also lived with Gorky's secretary, who was her lover and who was seventeen years younger than her. She had already turned fifty, but somehow she still looked far younger.

And finally there was Gorky's current mistress: sweet Varvara Tikhonova, the wife of one of the master's closest friends, who had given her leave to be with Gorky so that he could seek out love elsewhere.

The first woman hated the second, who refused to say a single word to the third. How could Moura manage to replace them all without burning any bridges with any of them?

For once, Moura was in an enviable position. She realized that Peshkova would be happy if she could oust Andreyeva, who had once deposed her. Andreyeva would be happy if she could dethrone Tikhonova. Tikhonova would be happy for a new favorite to come along and make it possible for her to disengage from a cumbersome adulterer. And so Moura worked to establish a special friendship with each of them and endeavored to charm them.

The women's personalities all attracted her. She found them all sweet, and she respected them. Once she had ensured that they would be welcoming, she would finally be in a position to try to shower Gorky with the warmth of her devotion.

With the huge bag he carried everywhere, his immense felt hat tilted over his eye, his mustache darkened by countless cigarettes, and his long fingers that tapped on the table or creased a sheet to make a paper fortune-teller when he was bored, he touched Moura deeply.

❖

In the fall of 1919, the people watching the whole affair were keeping track of the stages of Moura's relationship with Gorky and tallying up the points. Her progress was measured, yet assured.

In his diary entry for September 24, Chukovsky described an editorial meeting devoted to scripts:

> *Gorky, though he did not say a word to [Moura], said everything for her, fanning out his peacock's tail in its entirety. He was very witty, loquacious, and brilliant, like a gymnast at the bar.*

Chuckling to himself, Chuk saw how things were playing out on November 14:

> *Gorky turned out to be very considerate to Maria Ignatyevna. He offered her his place to stay in. Yesterday [he said]: "Because you must come to Kronverksky Prospect, Maria Ignatyevna, wait until five. I'll take you. I have an automobile."*

Two weeks later, on November 27, Chuk wrote:

> *A meeting at World Literature the day before yesterday. And Gorky asked Maria Ignatyevna: "Where do you find the time to pursue such trivial matters?" His tone was rather harsh as he set her this question, but with a charming smile: "Yes, yes, Maria Ignatyevna, such trivial matters!" He was alluding to the fact that she had*

sent him to see a doctor and that this doctor had ordered immediate bed rest so that he could recuperate.

Christmas:

At four I went to Gorky's . . . Maria Ignatyevna [and all Gorky's friends] were there, talking at their leisure. . . . Lunacharsky tells a funny story about some boys in Moscow who ate their friend. Chopped him up and ate him. . . . "Oh, and last year a man cut up his wife—now that I can understand . . . See how bad you women are, Maria Ignatyevna? You go on being spoiled even after you're dead. I think Maria Valentinova is next. It makes me lick my lips just to look at her."

The sweet-talking was in full swing.

❖

Sofas, divans, and chaise longues were crammed into Gorky's apartment, serving as makeshift beds: it was widely understood that the guests lingering after dinner would stay and sleep. The reason was simple enough: there were risks to going back home on foot at night in this city, which had become increasingly dangerous.

The only problem was that there was already a crushing crowd on the furniture. The massive space that Gorky owned on Kronverksky Prospect housed not only his guests but also those of other members of his tribe. He could provide for a dozen people, who themselves welcomed their own friends. And the end result was reminiscent of Rabelais's Abbey of Thélème, where each inhabitant was given a nickname. At this point, nicknames had become hallmarks of the residence . . . Not unlike Moura's habit with her own friends.

And she herself had to play the same game here. To the other occupants of "the duchy," she was now Tyotka, the Russian word for "little aunt," perhaps because of her genial yet protective attitude. No matter that she was fairly young, half Gorky's age: she mothered him.

It was a sight to witness her looking after his well-being. She was mischievous, lighthearted, always smiling, and unwaveringly efficient, and she lavished no end of attention upon him without him or his colleagues even noticing. The things she did were small but had an outsize effect on the ambiance, and so he fell under the spell of her charm and enjoyed her kindness.

Tyotka's protectiveness of the Duke, who everybody called *Duca*, applied to both the public man and the private writer. She knew and understood his books better than anyone else. She shared his tastes in literature and his belief in Man's greatness. She even came to see Russia's future the way he did.

Or, at least, that was what he thought.

Gorky loved nothing more than asking her endlessly what she thought about the foreign authors he was considering translating, or discussing the list of British and French authors she had drawn up for him. He also kept her by his side so he could gossip while he was shut away in his office: they both took great pleasure in exchanging ideas, both invested great energy in the art of fine conversation.

Moura, in turn, was now thoroughly familiar with every nook and cranny of the apartment. The layout of the space was simple enough: on each side of the long hallway were rooms in a row. On the left side, first was Gorky's office, adjacent to his own bedroom. Then that of Varvara Tikhonova, his official mistress. Then the bedroom of the medical student he had taken in: the daughter of one of his friends who had been assassinated by the tsar's police, a woman he had nicknamed Molecule. And at the end was a guest room.

On the right side, facing Gorky's personal quarters, were those of the flamboyant Maria Andreyeva, his former companion: a bedroom as luxurious as a salon. It included a room to sleep in and an office, which she currently shared with her lover, Pyotr Petrovich Kryuchkov, whose name everyone shortened to Pepekryu. Next was the studio of the painter Diederichs (everybody called him Didi), which was also used by his wife, herself also a painter: Valentina Khodasevich, more generally known among this crowd as the Merchantess. And still farther down was the studio of a third painter, the one Moura had met on her first visit: Ivan

Rakitsky, whose constantly rumbling stomach had earned him the moniker of the Nightingale.

In the evenings, they all came out of their rooms to gather under the immense gas lamp in the shared dining room.

Andreyeva was still the lady of the house. She would appear at seven o'clock to receive their friends. Shalyapin, Chukovsky, and the others all made a hubbub as they arrived. And Moura would be with them. By now, she had a particular chaise longue at Gorky's place, the same way that others had their usual corner of the table.

She loved the atmosphere of those dinners at Kronverksky Prospect: those magical moments where laughter and intellectual debate shunted aside the tragedies of the day. Fantastical stories, charades, poems . . . It was a heady mixture of silliness and swiftness.

Everyone stayed at the table after dessert, for endless debates around the samovar. The tea would be followed by a card game, which Gorky always lost. He was a bad loser and always ended up going to bed furious.

But his departure wasn't a curfew warning. The younger ones— Tyotka, Molecule, the Merchantess, and Max, Gorky's son, who wasn't thirty years old yet—would go on chatting late into the night.

In the morning, Moura—Tyotka—didn't linger long. But when Maria Andreyeva left to deal with the theaters and Molecule for classes at the university, and the Merchantess was painting in her atelier, she came and took care of the housekeeping, supervising the two old maids, planning the menus, and balancing the books.

Before she herself headed out to World Literature, she spent a short while cleaning up Gorky's desk. She also took it upon herself to organize his papers, and over time she came to type up his mail and translate his answers to his admirers abroad into English, French, and German.

In a word, she made it her business to simplify everybody's lives. And now nobody could do without her, not at World Literature or at the duchy on Kronverksky Prospect.

And Gorky least of all.

◈

He was fascinated by her vitality, which he sensed was on a level with his own. She was like a cat. She had the strength of a cat, the suppleness of a cat, the gracefulness of a cat.

He knew nothing about her. Just a few details: that her husband had been murdered, that she had been separated from her son and daughter.

Whenever he asked her to tell him about her childhood, to describe her golden days, she remained reticent. It was impossible to get three words out of her about her past. Even though he could sense the emotions and memories stirring beneath her silences, she refused to be forced into any kind of nostalgia.

She could show herself to be endowed with unparalleled drive and pragmatism. She could also seethe in silence and sink into motionless thought.

She seemed to take life as it came, as if she had nothing to prove. She lived in the moment, giving her all every day. But nobody could pretend she wasn't withholding something.

He always spoke to her politely, respectfully: he never used the nickname everyone else in the house had given her. In his eyes, she wasn't Tyotka. Nor was she even Moura. He always called her by her first name, to which he added her patronymic as a sign of respect: Maria Ignatyevna. And she did the same for him. In her eyes, he wasn't Duca. Nor was he even Gorky. She always called him Alexey Maximovich.

She was imperial yet resigned, and so she remained an enigma to him. And this enigma captivated him. In some way, she incarnated this bygone world that he had never had access to. The world of the aristocracy.

She was the inaccessible Lady. The Contessa.

She was something else, too: the very embodiment of youth.

She was going to turn twenty-seven years old; he would turn fifty-two in March. He could feel in his bones the gaping abyss of the years separating them. He was an old man. A worn-out, sickly man who coughed up blood.

What could he offer this triumphant image of Life? He was afraid of his own feelings. Of this attraction that drew him close to her. He resisted with all his strength the affection she lavished upon him and forbade her from using any word of tenderness. He himself made sure not to show the least physical or sentimental gesture toward her. He pretended not to even be dreaming of making her his mistress; he kept her at a distance. The truth, however, was that he was suspicious of his own feelings, and he was trying to protect himself. Like her, he was navigating a minefield, and he had to watch every step he took.

❖

On a late afternoon in January 1920, when Gorky was in Moscow arguing with Lenin, the actress Maria Andreyeva, who had come home earlier than usual, summoned all the occupants of the apartment to sit around the table. The only exception being her rival, Tikhonova. It was a council of war.

"It has just come to my attention," she explained, "that the former head of the Imperial Chancellery, General Mossolov, is going to be executed by firing squad. Not to put too fine a point on it, but Tyotka, who is staying at his residence, will find herself on the streets tonight. What shall we do? Shall we offer for her to come live with us indefinitely?"

The Merchantess murmured: "Duca already suggested that last month. She didn't respond favorably."

Molecule weighed in: "Tyotka is discreet. She's tactful. She would never ask for anything herself. Her involvement is limited to helping her cohort, most especially her dear friend the daughter of Count Artsimovich, who she cares so deeply about."

Nightingale added: "Her company is a pleasure for us all."

"She is indeed an interesting woman," Andreyeva said. "Very intelligent. She could stay in old Tikhonova's room, considering that all that silly woman wants is to go back and live with her husband again."

The conversation around the table grew animated, everyone chiming in all at once.

"Why not ask her directly? No matter her social class, Tyotka is one of us now. She's come to understand that the Revolution is here to stay."

"Gorky is trying to get her to come around to our more fundamental principles. He doesn't have any doubt that she shares the same ideals we're all fighting to achieve."

"But there's quite a difference between sharing the same ideals and sharing the same apartment!"

"Didi's not wrong."

"And that really would be just the cherry on top for Zinoviev if we decided to shelter, well, a *contessa* under our roof. All his underlings are already insisting to him that we're traitors to the Revolution."

"And that World Literature is festering with *burzhui!*"

"My feeling is that there isn't an immediate rush here. Just because Mossolov's going to face the firing squad doesn't necessarily mean she's going to be put out on the streets there and then."

"So let's wait for the Duca to return."

"If you do ask him that question, though," Maria Andreyeva said wryly, "then the jig's up!"

❖

On February 9, 1920, Chukovsky summed up this bout of flirting that he had been witness to for the entire winter:

Maria Ignatyevna Benckendorff has settled for good at Gorky's residence. They're great friends. She pretends to hit him on his hand and he shouts: "Ach, how hard she hits!" Well, now she has a room in the Kronverksky Prospect apartment. She's settled in there with all her ancestors. (The portraits of the Benckendorffs, and other people whose names I forgot.)

❖

Chuk and Nightingale had helped her move. On that icy February evening, one hammered in the nails while the other held the ladder against the party walls of the Gorky apartment.

Standing solidly on the uppermost rung, Moura hung the paintings above her bed: her father, Senator Zakrevsky, in a black tailcoat; her mother, Countess Boreisha, in a pink silk bustle; her late husband, Djon, in the white uniform of a tsar officer. They hung in a row, staid in their gilded frames. The photos of Alla and Anna, in tiaras and court dress, were placed on the nightstand.

◈

The ultimate irony of history and the Revolution was that depictions of the Russian high aristocracy were now peering over the home of the Bard of the Proletariat.

CHAPTER TWENTY-SIX

The Duke and the Contessa

FEBRUARY–OCTOBER 1920

In Tikhonova's former bedroom, Moura was unable to fall asleep. If she had been hoping that Gorky's hospitality might protect her, she now knew she was sorely mistaken.

Zinoviev was expecting her the following week for their meeting on Gorokhovaya Street. The fifth one since she had been freed. And each time, she had been loose with the truth, overwhelming him with stories, embroidering details endlessly, and in her special way only ever giving him explicitly the rumors and facts that were already publicly known. Nobody was unaware of Gorky's curses against the atrocities carried out by the Bolsheviks. She repeated those to him knowingly, willingly.

It was all smoke and mirrors.

Zinoviev was uncultivated, but he was shrewd, and even quite intelligent. He had immediately seen that she was toying with him, fooling him, lying to him.

And so his gray eyes grew steelier, and his threats grew sharper. His verbal violence was only a prelude to the blows he would land.

Moura had never known how to hate anyone, but now she hated Zinoviev. In her eyes, he was the ne plus ultra of those personalities the Party deemed the most brutal, the most bloodthirsty, the most envious. He wasn't "a fanatic and a pureblood," as she might have been willing to say of the executioner Yakov Peters. No, he was a tyrant, and every bit the bastard Gorky had said he was.

The idea of meeting this man yet again and telling him all the criticisms, complaints, jokes, and general conversation that came up around the table on Kronverksky Prospect horrified her viscerally. The thought of this massive body swollen with fat nauseated her, as did this immense head topped with thick, filthy hair, this wan face with its bloodless gaze . . .

How could she extricate herself from such a hornet's nest?

Zinoviev was now the third-highest member of the Party, right behind Trotsky. As a member of the Red Terror, he kept insisting that out of the hundred million Russians that Lenin governed, the Party should be able to win over ninety million of them with the Revolution's arguments. *As for the others, the remaining ten million, we don't even have to say it: they should all be rubbed out.* In his eyes, Gorky and his clique belonged to that set of ten million people he wanted to blot out completely.

Zinoviev's methods ranged from bloodthirsty attacks to the smallest acts of pettiness. He didn't think twice about stealing clothes, rations, and permits, and repurposing all the passes that Gorky had fought so hard to obtain for his friends. This writer risked great danger in working to help out one or another of them. He would draw Zinoviev's attention to the protégé in question, who would then become the target of all his persecutions: a man to overpower. "The Benckendorff woman," who was a member of both the aristocracy he hated and the intelligentsia he sneered at, seemed like the perfect weapon to hunt down the *burzhui*. A valuable tool. And, in the end, a privileged victim.

In the war that had Zinoviev and Gorky on opposite sides, Lenin played the arbiter. The truth, however, was that he gave Zinoviev free rein. They had come together from Switzerland in the sealed train car the Germans had chartered in the middle of the Great War to bring them back to the Russia of the tsars. Their friendship had had some difficulties as Lenin was seizing power, but it now seemed to be on solid footing. Lenin was even thinking about adopting one of Zinoviev's sons, since he himself was unable to have a child with his companion. He did bear some degree of respect for Gorky's evident genius. But he clearly thought far more highly of the work Zinoviev was carrying out as a revolutionary. He needed the latter. Not the former. And Ilyich would never forget that. Gorky was always pushing back on all fronts and criticizing him: at heart,

Lenin knew he wanted to be rid of him. And he was still trying to do so tactfully, by purporting to be worried about his health. He suggested that he leave the country to get some fresh air and be looked after in a good sanatorium.

Lenin's medical advice always exasperated Gorky. He could very clearly see, and rightly so, that Lenin was trying to shut him out.

Moura was tossing and turning in her bed. She could hear Alexey Maximovich—as she was still calling him—on the other side of the wall, his irregular breath broken every so often by bouts of coughing. Was he reading? Or writing? He, too, often suffered from insomnia. And yet he was wholly unaware that he was sheltering under his own roof, only a few paces away, the *seksot*—the informant—who would be his downfall.

How could she possibly undermine such a man?

He was her joy. He was her hope. The man she had met who was most worthy of his dignity. She wasn't in love with him the way she still was with Lockhart, but she cared for him. Tenderly, gratefully, respectfully. How could she accept his hospitality even as she betrayed his confidences?

How could she resist Zinoviev without getting shot as a result?

❖

Among the many mysteries of Moura's life is a specific journey that she has always refused to explain: her escape from Gorky's place, less than a month after the miracle of her being brought to live on Kronverksky Prospect. It was in March 1920.

What event, what scruples, could have driven her to make such an attempt? It was a shocking disappearance. A poorly thought-out escape.

Of course, nothing was forcing her to stay in Petrograd. Her mother was dead. Her older sister, Alla, was living in Paris. Her other sister was now in Yalta and doing her best to make her way to Constantinople: Anna was hoping to emigrate to France with her entire family. Lockhart was living in England. And her own children had vanished to some corner of the Baltic countries.

Of all her misfortunes, perhaps the worst was this one: her absolute lack of knowledge about how Kira, Paul, and Tania were faring.

In February 1920, a week before she had settled into Tikhonova's bedroom, Estonia had won its independence. The recognition of its government had been made official, ratified by the entirety of the international community and even Russia. The country was now printing its own money and issuing its own passports.

But Moura didn't have any legal means to join Djon's family at Yendel. In 1918, just when she was in a relationship with Lockhart, she had missed the chance to declare her Estonian nationality and paid no attention to the deadlines that would have allowed her to return to her husband's home. Her arrest for false papers in September 1919 had put an end to any prospect of receiving a visa from the Soviets. To make matters worse, during one of the numerous police searches of her Shpalernaya Street residence, the chekists had stolen her marriage certificate.

So it was impossible for her to return to Estonia. But even so, she kept thinking about it, dreaming about it every night and every day. And her worries about the safety of the three children kept her from enjoying the refuge she had been granted by Gorky.

And there was one more matter: Lockhart's abandonment, which she couldn't bring herself to believe. The time they had spent together in love had been perfect. She couldn't have been completely wrong there! What she had felt and experienced with him couldn't all have been in her head, not the way Princess Saltykova kept insisting.

She knew that Lockhart's silence wasn't out of cowardice. If her feelings weren't worth anything, if they had been an illusion, she needed concrete proof of that. She needed to confront the mirage. Or at least understand it.

If she stayed here, she wouldn't learn anything new.

From Estonia, she would have the freedom to continue onward to England. And to learn the truth . . .

But that was one matter. Leaving Gorky, leaving Russia, abandoning them all, to disappear into the wild and exile herself with no prospect of returning? Doing such a thing was wholly unlike her.

And yet she needed that chance. She would give it her all.

◆

Her friend Myriam Artsimovich—who Peshkova, Gorky's wife, had managed to snatch out of the Cheka's grips—knew the name of a guide. That was the only thing the survivors of the Red Terror talked about in Petrograd: the Finnish networks that would handle the border crossing for cold, hard cash.

Moura, accompanied by Myriam, went to find the guide.

After a pat-down on par with the police's efforts, the smugglers took them into a small room full of other people like them, who had made the same request. The guide was willing to take them over, yes, but he didn't give them much time to think it over.

"If you want to leave, it has to be now. Right away . . . It's March, and we're still able to cross the frozen gulf by foot. Meet me tomorrow night at five o'clock at Finland Station. You're going to be dressed in rags, with a peasant's shawl wrapped around your head and felt boots on your feet. You need to be ready to walk a dozen miles. Bring crampons and carry two old gunnysacks on your shoulder, one in front and one in back, so you'll look like what you're claiming to be. You'll all travel separately, and none of you will open your mouth —everybody would recognize your *burzhui* accent immediately. After about an hour on the train, you're going to get off at the first station. You're not going to look left or right; you're going to take the path straight ahead of you into the woods. You'll continue on down in the space between the trees. By then, night will have fallen and the snow will be heavy. But once you've come out of the forest, you'll reach a bay of the gulf. You'll walk across the ice. On the other side, you'll find a sled and several guides."

The two young women came out of the meeting shaken.

"It's impossible for me to leave tomorrow!" Myriam said. "My father is still in prison. I can't leave my parents behind."

"We'll have to wait until next winter. If I understand right, tomorrow is our last chance. So it'll be another year."

"You should go on ahead!"

❖

On March 4, 1920, Moura came to the end of her journey across the ice and was met not by a sled nor any guides but by Bolshevik border guards, who seized her along with four other fugitives and brought her back to Petrograd.

The worst had come.

❖

Moura was in rags, and her wrists and ankles were shackled as she went up Shpalernaya Street. Having lived there for nearly ten years, how many convoys had she seen passing under her window, how many fugitives stumbling, as she now was, toward the prison? As she walked past number 8, she couldn't help but look up toward the noble floor, to the balcony that overlooked the porch, where the head of the building's committee, her doorman, was sweeping the snow. Their eyes met. She could feel his eyes boring into her back as she continued on to the massive iron door of number 25.

❖

Moura would never find herself willing to describe the horrors of her third arrest.

Many years later, she could bring herself to share only a few details . . . images that nobody could believe. She would say that when her former doorman had recognized her among the prisoners, he had run out to alert Gorky, in hopes of getting a reward. She would also say that among her numerous stays in the Cheka's prisons, this one had been by far the most terrible.

She was locked up for more than a month. The only companion she had in her cell was a rat that she later claimed to have taught how to sing.

In an interview she gave to a journalist at *Vogue* fifty years after the fact, she added that she had felt so alone in the prison that she had waited for her rat "as one would wait for a lover." She concluded with these words: "If there is anything extraordinary about me, it is the fact that I took prison as I did. I learned what people were like, and I learned what life was about, which before had simply been unreality."

It was plain that she was trying to prepare herself for death. She thought about Lockhart. She thought about her children. This time, she wouldn't escape execution. She knew it.

But she hadn't counted on her friends on Kronverksky Prospect.

❖

On April 3, 1920, Maria Andreyeva, commissar of the theaters and a truly consummate actress, wrote a long petition to Bakayev, the new head of the secret police in Petrograd, who was far more infamous than his predecessors for his use of summary liquidations.

She swore to him that she would shoot a bullet into her own head if he, yes, he, her beloved Ivan Petrovich, didn't release her special friend Maria Ignatyevna. She was shrewd enough not to call her Benckendorff, far too famous and noble a name.

> *Maria Ignatyevna Zakrevskaya was headed to Estonia to find her children, who were living in terrible conditions with an uncle. But, for her as for us, the time for such quixotic adventures is gone! She has promised never to do such a thoughtless thing again. And I can assure you, my dear, that as she has now been informed that I was willing to put a gun to my own head, she will never do so much as raise a little finger without having informed you first.*

Gorky and Peshkova, in turn, harassed the Party's dignitaries in Moscow. Moura-Tyotka was released to them in May 1920.

❖

Never had the climb up the four stories leading to the apartment been more exhausting.

As she pushed on the glass door overlooking the stairway, she had seen her reflection.

She had already been thin in February. But now she was simply skin and bones. The oval of her face had sunk in so much that it had become triangular. She was a ghost. She felt so weak that she had to stop on every landing, lean against the wall, and catch her breath.

The truth was that she wanted to delay the moment when she would have to see everybody. She was ashamed. She was afraid. How would the inhabitants of the Duchy of Kronverksky Prospect welcome her? Her actions must have caught them by surprise, and hurt them. Wasn't it true that she'd readied herself to flee in secret, disappearing behind their backs without warning anyone?

But she couldn't have expected the astonishment that her entrance provoked. Was it her deterioration that surprised them so much? Even Maria Andreyeva was left speechless.

Gorky didn't give any of the witnesses to this scene the time to ask her any questions: he took her and led her immediately into his office.

"Well, now, Maria Ignatyevna," he said as he shut the door behind them. "Well, now, whatever came over you? Doing something like that!"

As was his habit in moments of heightened emotion, he had started pacing back and forth. He was walking between the piles of books and manuscripts over and over.

"It's sheer madness, I tell you: trying to walk straight across the Gulf of Finland! Crossing the border in the middle of the night!"

The office had become a shambles all over again. The boards of the towering bookshelves were about to break, and a morass of papers blanketed the table she used to tidy up so diligently.

"What a truly ridiculous thing to do!"

She stayed where she was, not moving, in the center of the room. He stopped waving his arms for a minute to get a better look at her.

"Are you not happy here?" he asked despairingly. "Are you not at home among us?"

She met his gaze and answered calmly, warmly:

"On the contrary, Alexey Maximovich, I love it here. I'm so happy. And you can't imagine just how grateful I am to you! But I needed to see my children again."

"I understand, your children, I understand." He sighed. "But why didn't you tell me? You've been keeping all these secrets! You never tell me anything! All the same, all the same: we might have been able to organize . . ."

"I wasn't able to talk to you about it."

"Why?"

She paused, looked down, looked back up, and then stared right at him.

"Zinoviev positioned me here to spy on you."

"What are you trying to say?"

She caught her breath, and then explained:

"Grigory Zinoviev and Yakov Peters planted me close to you so I could report everything you were doing." She was talking quickly, in a tone of voice she wasn't accustomed to. "When I was arrested in September, Peters saved my life, but that was the price he made me pay. And Zinoviev only freed me again this morning on the condition that I continue."

"And you dare to come back here?" He was so taken aback that he couldn't keep himself from yelling. "You dare to come back here and tell me such a horrible thing!"

"I couldn't not tell you the truth," she said.

He was silent for a minute, trying to assess just how much she had betrayed him. He couldn't.

"That's vile!" he declared. "Lying to me! Tricking me! That you would do something this horrible to me." His glasses were fogged up. He took them off to wipe away his tears. "And to think that I actually respected you the most of everyone here!"

She, too, was trying to hold back her tears. They ran slowly down her cheeks. She didn't make any noise, she didn't let out any sobs. He had never seen her cry before.

"Forgive me for having hurt you, Alexey Maximovich."

"There is nothing to forgive you for: you are beyond all hope."

He couldn't bring himself to believe what she had confessed.

"I'm asking you, Alexey Maximovich, not to think that!"

Nor had he ever seen her beg before.

"What else am I supposed to think? You're the one who decided to do it. You came into this room, you looked me in the eye, you told me all this."

"Forgive me!" she pleaded. "Forgive me, I had no other choice! I owed you the truth. I love you, Alexey Maximovich. That's why I left the first time. That's why I have to leave you again and go away for good."

She started to head toward the door.

"No!" He grabbed her by the wrist and pulled her close. "You didn't understand me!" he stammered through the locks of her hair. "I'm getting it all wrong. I'm grateful to you for what you've just done. I admire you for having had this much courage. Nothing obliged you to do it. You could have moved back into your bedroom, taken your place beside me all over again. After being in prison and going through so many ordeals, you would have been well within your rights to do so. You're all on your own, you have nowhere to go. If you left this place, if you went somewhere else, without any friends, without any work, without any ration cards . . . In your state of exhaustion, that would be certain death, and you know it. But somehow you summoned up the strength to tell me the truth, you made that decision yourself. At the risk of being kicked out. At the risk of losing everything, you still dared to do it!"

They stayed there, holding each other tight, crying over all Russia's misfortunes. And over all the betrayals, all the compromises, all the unspeakable acts the Revolution had forced each of them to carry out.

◈

That night, Maria Andreyeva, Pepekryu, Didi, Molecule, the Merchantess, and the Nightingale had dinner without them.

Around the table, not one of them dared to say a word about what was happening in the adjoining room. But they all understood: on this warm night in May 1920, the Duke and the Contessa were making their peace and bonding with each other.

"She's won," as Maria Andreyeva declared: Tyotka had become the muse, the lover, the mistress. It was official.

Max confirmed his father's new relationship with a terse line. The next day, he wrote to his mother, Peshkova:

> *We finally have a manager. No more laziness!*

❖

Manager. Secretary. Muse.

With his usual need to dream, Gorky even claimed to believe that Maria Ignatyevna had been very much a muse from the outset: it was in her blood.

Hadn't divine Pushkin, whose face reigned over the dining room, dedicated several of his poems in 1828 to Countess Zakrevskaya, whom he had called at that point "the bronze Venus"?

A century later, her granddaughter would continue breathing life into the dream shared by those poetically gifted beings. She had the same strength, the same beauty, she had all the unchanging features that had so charmed the Prince of Poets. But in this modern era, she now embodied "the iron Venus."

Moura smiled and ignored these arguments. She was well aware of the weight of legends and the value of symbols. She refrained from underscoring that she belonged to another branch of the family tree and had nothing in common with that particular Anna, Agrafena Fyodorovna Zakrevskaya, the Venus of Pushkin's poems.

And in turn, this October of 1920, the greatest of the contemporary poets, the delightful Alexander Blok, had just offered her a copy of his latest collection. At one of the old desks in World Literature, he inscribed it to her with these words:

To Maria Ignatyevna Zakrevskaya

You weren't fated for me.
So why did I see you in my dreams?
It was one dream of many.
The paladin sees his lady,
The wounded sees his enemy,
The exile his homeland, . . .
But my dream was different,
Inexplicable, singular,
And should it come to me again,
My heart would fail me.

I don't know why
I don't keep this dream a secret,
Nor why I can't leave these words
And these lines to be forgotten,
By you and by me, in their uselessness.

❖

A new life had begun, one that would place Moura among the greatest inspirations of literature.

CHAPTER TWENTY-SEVEN

The H. G. Wells Intermezzo

OCTOBER 1920–MAY 1921

" 'On Sunday, Gorky ate four herrings . . . The vodka for Monday's dinner came from Fyodor Ivanovich Shalyapin's personal stores.' Are you trying to pull the wool over my eyes, Comrade Benckendorff? This is nonsense! You're always giving me nonsense: a sprinkling of the truth, a heavy dollop of invention, a silly detail, a plausible revelation, and then you're all done. I can't believe you're coming here just to feed me this balderdash you're not even trying to sugarcoat. Lies, lies, lies! What do you want me to tell you? Gorky didn't eat *four* herrings, he ate two. And it wasn't *Sunday*! The others, at least, try to be honest when they inform to me. I might not speak English, but I know how to read the Russian between the lines: 'See if you can fool this Zinoviev pig.' You two must just be in stitches from all the laughter. Have you two been concocting all these stories you're telling me? Did you put your heads together to come up with these spiels?"

Zinoviev had a feeling she had told Gorky the truth.

Of course, with her *burzhui* origins and her three arrests, she was in no position to let him down on Gorokhovaya Street. Nor was she free to refrain from giving him her monthly summary. But before her meetings, she had to be discussing all the details with her benefactor.

Even though Zinoviev wasn't entirely sure about that, the prospect was likely enough. *Ah, they had to be having a great laugh as they thought up their twaddle*, he mused. This hussy deserved what she had coming! He wasn't the kind of man who let his prey go free. By getting close to Gorky, she was giving him his weapon of choice. Through her, he could now hit Gorky where it would hurt most.

In October 1920, Zinoviev's fury was concentrated on 23 Kronverksky Prospect, fourth floor, apartment 5. He ordered a police search.

The Cheka at Gorky's place? Unthinkable! Zinoviev's order shocked all those in the literary circles of both Petrograd and Moscow. His message came through clearly: nobody, not even a writer for the regime, not even a friend of Lenin's, was safe from his apparatus.

His policemen had been told to rummage especially zealously through the room adjacent to the master's quarters. The armoires, the chests of drawers . . . Everything there would have to be emptied out. The laundry, the dresses, the undergarments—everything would be inspected. The books and papers would be leafed through. Here, too, Zinoviev's message came through clearly. Mrs. Benckendorff was at the heart of it all. He had chosen a day and time when nobody would be at the house. Except for her.

As she heard the hammering at the door, this rapping of rifles that she recognized so clearly, was so familiar with, Moura felt her face, her entire body, break out in a cold sweat. At first, she didn't believe it. She wavered. But the orders being yelled from the landing left no doubt.

The chekists, with their Mausers in their fists, flooded the apartment in an instant. As they had studied the floor plans already, they went straight for her bedroom.

She tried to follow them calmly, pacing softly down the hallway.

She stood and leaned in the doorway. She did not move; she was silent as she watched the carnage unfold. Long minutes went by as she saw them throw out, tear up, and trample over the little that was still hers. The mere prospect of a fourth arrest made her blood run cold. She tried to control her trembling hands, lighting cigarette after cigarette and smoking furiously. But to no avail. Every single one of her limbs was shaking.

The vise she had felt tightening on her life loosened only once they came out of her room, opened the buffet in the dining room, ran through Molecule's room, paused for a moment in the Merchantess's room, glanced quickly over Maria Andreyeva's room, and finally left. Only then did she realize that the search had been perfunctory and pointedly personal.

It was a warning.

Maria Andreyeva and Gorky were still powerful enough that Zinoviev didn't dare to attack them directly and seize their personal belongings. And so his men hadn't taken anything with them. Not even from her room. The portraits of her parents lay on the floor, ruined. But the paintings themselves hadn't been confiscated.

It was only getting started.

Gorky understood that.

He was seething with fury over Zinoviev's actions toward Maria Ignatyevna, and he immediately went to Moscow to make his rage clear to Lenin. The latter proffered excuses. The Party acknowledged that this time, Zinoviev had gone too far.

Then Gorky called from the capital to remind those in Petrograd that he was returning the next day to welcome a special guest.

There was a general panic among the residents of Kronverksky Prospect, and a commotion among the women living on the fourth floor. In the morass of anger that Zinoviev's search had set off, a rather important detail had been forgotten: that an invitation had been sent the previous month to an illustrious foreigner.

Even though the apartment was already full, all the beds and all the sofas were taken, and food rations were increasingly difficult to obtain, Gorky had invited an extraordinary character, his English counterpart, the most powerful of the British intellectuals: H. G. Wells, the author of *The Island of Doctor Moreau, The Invisible Man,* and *The War of the Worlds.*

In Russia and in practically every other corner of Europe, Wells was more or less a god. Everybody here had read his books. And everybody knew him by reputation. He was a great writer. And a great libertine.

Before the war, his escapades had been the talk of every literary circle. Even though he wasn't much of a looker, he loved ladies and was always eager to add yet more notches to his bedpost. He was rumored to have a seraglio of mistresses whose scenes of jealousy rivaled, in violence and sheer numbers, those of all the couples that came to the French Riviera.

Like Gorky, he refused to divorce his wife, who he had abandoned but still remained deeply fond of. He now lived with another writer, Rebecca West, whom he hadn't married but who had borne him a child.

He came with Gip, his legitimate son, who was nineteen years old. Gorky's own son, Max, was twenty-three. Wells had forced Gip to study Tolstoy's language, going so far as to convince a British secondary school to offer a Russian class for that purpose. It was the first of its kind.

How would they be able to welcome such an esteemed guest amid such difficult circumstances? A world-class star for more than a week!

It was eventually decided that Moura would let him stay in her room, and that she would sleep on the chaise longue in Molecule's room. That young Gip would stay in the back room. That all meetings would take place at World Literature, the House of Writers, and the House of Arts—all events that might interest their visitor would happen in one of those buildings.

The truth was that Gorky had only invited Wells to stay with him out of patriotism. He was worried that the lack of comfort at the Hotel International—which was the only open hotel in Petersburg, but didn't have any electricity, bedding, customer service, or food—would leave him with a bad impression of their country.

He himself might have a right to criticize the Bolsheviks, but he wanted to give the West the impression that Communism had been a success and an inevitable stage of history.

As they were nearly the same age—fifty-two for Gorky, fifty-three for Wells—they shared the same ideals and both believed in the Revolution. On his part, Gorky had written one of his most favorable letters ever to Mr. Wells to congratulate him on the publication of *Mr. Britling Sees It Through*, Yakov Peters's favorite book of his.

Gorky and Wells had, in fact, known each other a long while. They had first met in the United States in 1906, during a round of conferences. Then in London in 1907. Then in Moscow just before the war. At that time, Wells was on his first trip to Russia: his guide there had been the young British consul, a certain Robert Bruce Lockhart, who had served as a translator for his conversations with Gorky. Wells had negotiated this, his second visit, with the *Sunday Express*, which covered his costs: a dispatch from the Soviet lands and an interview with Lenin. He had left London on September 15.

❖

Over the course of the seven short chapters of his 1920 book on Russia, Wells described his impressions. He made only glancing allusion, however, to Moura.

In the autobiography that he would publish later, there wasn't a word about her.

But in 1984, four decades after his death, his son Gip published *H. G. Wells in Love*, Wells's romantic confessions. There, the writer revisited the very first scene of his stay in Petrograd. It was a vision that would continue to haunt him until his death.

It was the very morning he came to Kronverksky Prospect. He was sitting in front of Gorky in the office. His searching gaze took in the room where his colleague was writing . . . A beautiful mess. The only exception to this disorder was the writing desk. It was impeccable. There was no ink on the blotting paper. But dozens of pens and hundreds of pencils in every color, well used, were sticking out of numerous containers. A pad of blank paper with lined sheets awaited the master's writing.

The conversation moved slowly, limited as it was to exclamations and friendly gestures, since neither of them knew the language of the other. There was a knock at the door. Gorky's assistant came in.

Wells wrote:

> *She was wearing an old khaki British army waterproof and a shabby black dress; her only hat was some twisted-up kind of black—a stocking I think—and yet she had magnificence. She stuck her hands in the pockets of her waterproof, and seemed not simply to brave the world but disposed to order it about.*

❖

Wells, a small, plump man with sparse hair parted on one side and a mustache almost as thick as Gorky's, got up.

Moura walked over and greeted him.

"We've met before," she said in English, recalling her instincts as a society woman and offering him her hand.

"I have to confess, to my great shame, that I don't remember it."

She smiled. "Oh, but I remember you. It was during a reception here, in Saint Petersburg, in 1914."

Was she right? Or wrong? If Wells had ever laid eyes on such a resplendent woman, he wouldn't have forgotten it.

She insisted, in her particular, slightly hoarse voice, with that charming Russian accent that always made him think. "There were many people there, you were just surrounded. At the time, one of my Benckendorff cousins was taking you to a session of the Duma, which was taking place at the Tauride Palace . . ." She smiled again. "You see, Mr. Wells: I do remember you."

He had indeed gone to the Duma with a Count Benckendorff.

With befuddlement, he whispered in a falsetto, which with its sharply rising inflections was just as unusual as Moura's own voice: "Oh, I do recall it now . . . You were wearing a pearl-gray dress!"

He had said that off the cuff. He knew that this kind of praise always worked.

Gorky interrupted them, saying a few words to her. She translated, "Alexey Maximovich is asking me to accompany you on your visits, and to serve as your guide."

"Please thank him on my behalf. And tell him how much I'm looking forward to it."

She was now my official interpreter. And she presented herself to my eyes as gallant, unbroken and adorable.

Wells did not have enough experience of the regime to realize the irony of Gorky's gesture in providing him with Moura as a mentor. Mrs. Benckendorff, as the official guide for a man of his stature in Bolshevik

Russia? Gorky was thumbing his nose at Zinoviev! It was a small but undeniable comeuppance. The commissar of Petrograd would be absolutely beside himself over the matter. He had planned to surround Wells with reliable men. Spies in his own pay. Apparatchiks of the Party. Wells was only going to be shown what he was supposed to see. Parades and brass bands and speeches would be his entertainment. He would be blinkered by an unending sequence of ceremonies and performances . . . All of which would keep him from talking to the *burzhui* and realizing just how destitute the city was.

Moura's presence beside him—the personification of the class enemy, who Zinoviev dreamed of crushing—would drive him insane. He would insist that she be shoved aside. Dismissed. Arrested.

But Lenin, who had just had to deal with Gorky's screeching in Moscow, wouldn't allow any such thing to happen. Gorky knew this very, very well. His complaints about Zinoviev's mandated police search—specifically in the bedroom that Wells was supposed to stay in—were too recent. Ilyich wouldn't take the risk of arousing his ire yet again.

So all Zinoviev would be able to do was be quiet and sit back.

❖

H. G. Wells could immediately see that unlike his cicerones in Moscow, his official guide in Peter the Great's city wasn't inclined toward political judgments and didn't spout any propaganda.

She did seem disappointed when, as he beheld the gutted streets and palaces, he drew comparisons between the beauty during his previous stay and the leprosy of the city now.

"Is that," she asked him, "Mr. Wells, is that what you're going to tell your readers: that Russia has suffered a defeat that it will never recover from?"

"What I'm going to bring back to the British, my dear lady, will be this. First, that the ruination of Russia isn't due to the Bolsheviks but to the corruption of the imperialist, capitalist, tsarist regime—a

regime that had rotted to the core so thoroughly that it simply collapsed with the smallest push from the war. Then I'll tell them about
how Lenin is now the only bulwark against outright anarchy. And
finally, that a Communist government strikes me as the only system
that could keep your country from sinking into chaos. Will that be to
your satisfaction?"

She smiled. "Thank you."

Later on, Wells would confess his suspicion that if he'd specified in his
articles the sheer extent of the destitution he had witnessed everywhere in
the city, his guide would have suffered the consequences.

Among his stories from the trip, he also described how he hadn't felt
like he was being followed by the police, which was an indication of the
freedom of thought and action available to those living in Russia. And
that the day he had to speak to the Soviets in an official capacity, Mrs.
Benckendorff had handled the matter adroitly.

When he started worrying about the thought of her having to translate the entirety of his speech, she told him she wouldn't be doing it.

"Tomorrow you'll have an accredited interpreter."

"Oh dear! The one they gave to the British philosopher who came
here before me took the liberty of changing around his sentences. He
made everything seem more flattering to Russia than what my compatriot
actually said to the assembly . . . The *Izvestiya* published the translator's
version. And the international press reprinted it everywhere. The result,
apparently, was that they printed exactly the opposite of what the orator
had been thinking!"

"Write your speech, Mr. Wells. I'll translate it tonight. You'll give *your*
translation to the interpreter so he can read it out loud. That way, nobody
can meddle with your words."

*I read it, and when Zorin rose to paraphrase what I had said into the usual
glorification of the new regime, I passed him her translation. "That is what I said:
read that," and Zorin could do nothing else on the spur of the moment. So Moura
saved me from being labelled a red convert, and that I thought a very courageous thing
for a woman already suspect to do.*

❖

She took him everywhere. To Falconet's Bronze Horseman statue in the Admiralty garden, and to the Cheka's headquarters. There, she stayed outside. But he was able to visit the palace on Gorokhovaya Street, which had now been divided up into offices with yellow partitions, the noise of typewriters recording the depositions of various "traitors" being interrogated there. She took him to the government stores—the only shops that were still open—where he was able to buy plates as souvenirs. He offered her a bouquet of chrysanthemums, marveling along with her at how florists could still be working. They went to the opera together, a production of *The Barber of Seville*, where they heard their friend Shalyapin, who Wells considered the greatest of all actors, the greatest of all singers of all time. And they went to the theater together, where they saw *Othello*. With Mrs. Andreyeva in the role of Desdemona.

Receptions, conferences, visits to schools, canteens, saunas, and churches: accompanying Wells around Petrograd was a constant torrent of tourism, politics, history, and culture. He was fascinated by everything. She shared his curiosity. A hint of carelessness. A succession of pleasures.

Hunger and fear no longer existed. All tragedies ceased. Life became light again. Even his wooing was lighthearted. His compliments on her beauty, his flowers by the armful, his kisses . . . Wells's tributes brought her back to the gallantries of yesteryear. She could laugh at it all and brush it aside with a joke.

She loved his especially British sense of humor. She loved his understatements and his ironic declarations. Wells was on a level with Lockhart. He served as a bridge between Petrograd and London. Between the past and the future. He embodied England. He embodied Literature. Above all, he embodied Freedom. His presence in Petrograd intoxicated her, and she nearly lost her head.

And he, in turn, was obsessed with the curves of her body beneath her thin black dress. He was certain that the attraction was mutual. She pretended not to notice his advances, but she did.

Just one doubt niggled at him, however: he couldn't be sure whether she was Gorky's mistress. He had seen them together and yet hadn't been able to detect any degree of intimacy between the two of them.

The thought of leaving this woman without having made love to her tormented him. He could only think in terms of possession. But his chances seemed slim. His scheduled interview with Lenin would bring him back to Moscow, and she would not be following him. A condition of her previous arrest was that Moura had to stay within the confines of Petrograd.

He left the city feeling sick at heart.

His meeting with Lenin was far shorter and far more disappointing than he had hoped. The master of the Kremlin was only interested in talking to him about the electrification of the Soviet Union. It was an instructional conversation about the network of cables he was planning to install across the country.

Wells rushed back up to Petrograd for the few days he had left in the country.

The rather boozy farewell dinner that Gorky gave in his honor at Kronverksky Prospect was the perfect way to cap it all off. The two literary titans kept on drinking to each other's health and launched into speech after speech, which Moura took it upon herself to translate.

When Gorky, Andreyeva, and the others got up to get some sleep, Wells lingered behind to gossip with her on one of the dining room couches. The gas lamp above their heads was dimming. His final night . . . They whispered as they recalled the pleasures of their time together. They also discussed the future of Russia and its relationship with the West.

Wells took a long drag on his cigar, the red glow of which tinged Moura's face briefly.

She was holding her vodka well. She seemed to be thoroughly in control of herself. He, by contrast, was fairly tipsy. Well, he was leaving the next day . . . He had nothing to lose by broaching the question that had been nagging at him.

Still, he came around to it carefully. "Mrs. Andreyeva has been an unstinting hostess."

"She's the lady of the house."

"So is Gorky still living with her?"

"As he is with us all."

And then he cut to the chase: "Is he your lover, Moura?"

She opened her eyes wide. She didn't seem upset, only caught off guard. "I do say, you're being quite indiscreet, Mr. Wells!"

"Forgive my brusqueness. But I wouldn't want to be impolite to him, nor inconsiderate to you. I just need to know if Gorky loves you."

She smiled. "What is your opinion on the matter?"

"I don't know. That's why I'm asking you the question."

"I think you can judge for yourself: I'm sleeping on the chaise longue in Molecule's bedroom."

"And Molecule isn't there tonight."

"No, she's gone to stay with her fiancé."

"So you're alone in her bedroom?"

"Yes. And I do believe it's time for me to head there. Good night, Mr. Wells."

And with that, she got up and went down the hallway, leaving him frustrated and lost in thought. He hadn't dared to take her into his arms, since any of the many inhabitants might have come into the room at an inopportune moment. Finally he went to bed, as well.

I think from the outset I had a very clear feeling that there was much about Moura that I had better not know. I did not want to hear her history or know what alien memories or strands of feeling her past had woven into her brain.

Later that night, once he was certain that his son and the rest of the household were solidly asleep, he carefully snuck out of his room and crept through the darkness.

If he should happen upon someone, he had a pretext: he was looking for the bathroom and had gotten lost in the labyrinth of this immense caravansary.

He tiptoed to the far end of the apartment, wavered between the door on the left and the door on the right. He decided to try the left one and went in without knocking. Moura, in Molecule's bed, woke up immediately.

She presented herself to my eyes as gallant, unbroken and adorable. I fell in love with her, made love to her . . .

   I believed she loved me and I believed every word she said to me. No other woman has ever had that much effectiveness for me.

◈

Oh God, she thought. How could she have behaved so abominably? Stepping out of the bedroom in the morning, Moura asked herself that question gleefully. She didn't have any regrets about the experience. On the contrary, she felt like celebrating.

The experience had been nothing like the communion she had had with Lockhart. She hadn't ever wavered then. And yet the experience had been nothing like the love she shared with Alexey Maximovich.

Gorky had told her not to be over the top, had insisted she was exaggerating about how much she needed him, how ecstatic she felt when he touched her. He was rather reserved. In a muted way, their intimacy still bothered and worried him. He kept telling her that he didn't have the right to enjoy her youth, that he was far too old for her. Their nights together were filled with tenderness, but they were infrequent and hardly passionate.

Wells, who was nearly the same age, had no such scruples. His impulsiveness in bed, his enthusiasm, and his vigor made him a wonderful lover.

That he had appeared in pajamas at the foot of her bed when the clock was chiming three in the morning hadn't taken her by surprise at all. She hadn't dreamed even for a second of resisting his advances. Nor even of arguing with them. She had welcomed them as a concrete fact, the natural result of their shared closeness.

Those two weeks beside him had been exactly this: a rediscovery of pleasure. A wonderful exploration of what her body, her life had to offer.

The proof that bursts of freedom, moments of joy were still possible in this miserable city.

There had, of course, been that horrible visit to the British embassy, when Gorky had wanted to show Wells the spoils of war claimed by the Bolsheviks, which he himself was still busy inventorying. The furniture ripped out of the palaces of Petrograd, the thousands of statues of Venus and Diana, the chandeliers, the tapestries, the rugs, the paintings. All these marvels piled up in a single place had awed Wells. For her, it had been an unbearable spectacle. Cromie, Garstino, and all her other friends of the past were still so present here! The space seemed haunted by ghosts.

And then that tragic moment during a banquet at the House of Arts, when the writer and journalist Amfiteatrov, unbuttoning his shirt to show Wells just how thin and ragged his clothes were, told him that everybody had been lying to him. That everything he was eating at this table, this bread, these meat dumplings, and these little cakes, everything he saw here, was just a decoy. A horrifying trompe l'oeil!

Amfiteatrov's honesty about the poverty that was commonplace here and the horrors that had become ordinary here had left Gorky absolutely livid. He would never forgive Amfiteatrov for having ruined this moment that he had put so much store in: it had been meant to be a delightful meeting with artists and scholars from the proletariat around so many overflowing plates.

But Amfiteatrov had been telling the truth. Wells's stay in Russia was nothing more than that: an illusion.

And her night with him? It was as much an illusion as the rest. An unimportant diversion that was to be sealed off this morning.

Now, only one thing mattered: that Wells keep his word.

As he left Kronverksky Prospect, he had promised to look into the matter of her children. He was going back to London via Reval. He had sworn to write to her from Estonia with all the information he was able to glean. He had also promised to ask after Lockhart in England. And after her sisters in France.

The romance was over and done with, and now the adventure really did seem to be over.

◈

The "Wells Intermezzo," however, remained deeply imprinted in the household's memory. Each one of them was rather nostalgic about it. Each one of them had seen the foreshadowing of emergency.

Their conversations with the British writer about freedom of expression in Europe, the threats that Zinoviev's mandated police searches constituted, and the decline in Gorky's state of health, which hadn't been helped by the tensions of October, had all served to underscore the fact that danger was imminent.

The bohemian life on Kronverksky Prospect was barely hanging by a thread. The end was alarmingly near. Did Duca need to listen to Lenin's insistences that he go seek care in another country?

Ilyich never stopped underscoring the necessity of his doing so. He wrote:

> *You're coughing up blood. And you haven't left. Do you realize how dishonest, how irrational that is for you? In Europe, in a good sanatorium, not only will you be able to recuperate, but you'll be able to do three times as much work. It's true. And right now, right here, you're unable to do either the former or the latter. All you're able to do is tremble. And tremble for no reason. Leave, recuperate. Don't be stubborn, I beg of you.*

Nobody was so naive as not to realize that he was trying to hasten Gorky's departure and doing everything he could to speed it.

Had the moment come for Gorky to leave?

◈

Soon enough, Maria Andreyeva was presiding over a new war council around the table. This time, it was with Gorky present.

"Ilyich is right," she said. "This is the most reasonable solution. In Germany, you'll be ten times more effective in helping Russia. You're the only one who can create a famine relief committee and find financial support abroad. The harvests here have been disastrous, and thousands of men are going to die of hunger this winter. You're the only one who can bend Europe's and America's ear to their fate!"

"I don't want to leave the country when things aren't going well. And I have absolutely no interest in going to Germany!" Gorky protested.

"You don't have any choice: you need to care for yourself."

"What about you? All of you."

"We do, too!" the Nightingale exclaimed. "You mustn't let yourself be mistaken, Duca, and think we'd let you go there without joining you!"

"But if I agree to leave Russia, that will ultimately be another exile."

"Not necessarily," Maria Andreyeva said. "You can negotiate an official position. I personally have been asked to be the Soviet commercial representative in Berlin."

Moura did not say anything. Her restrictions as a result of her arrest forbade her from ever leaving Petrograd.

Gorky thought for a minute before returning to the point. "I guess we've all come to an agreement here, then? If I go, you'll all join me?"

"Of course!"

"Even Maria Ignatyevna?" At that question, Maria Andreyeva remained silent, but Gorky didn't relent. "If we leave without Maria Ignatyevna, Zinoviev will put her in front of the firing squad immediately."

Maria Andreyeva nodded.

"You're quite right there. She needs to leave first. In fact, that's the first thing you need to negotiate with Lenin. *Her* immediate departure. You can always argue that you're going to send your secretary ahead of you so she can prepare for your stay. Not only for you to be brought and settled into a sanatorium, but also to help the Russian people so dear to your heart. She speaks four languages, which makes her perfectly suited to this international work."

Moura held back from adding to the conversation. Her heart was pounding. She was terrified of showing her excitement too openly, out of fear that such a trip might not come to pass. Because even if this project were to come about, how much time would it take for everything to be squared away? Months, maybe even years!

How could Gorky abandon World Literature, the House of Arts, the House of Sciences, all his endeavors, all his programs? How could he give up the project of publishing the 1,500 translations currently underway?

She tried to stay levelheaded. Not to mistake her hopes or wishes for reality. Not to think to herself that she might be able to see her children again. Or live with Lockhart again.

But it was too late. Her heart was full to bursting with hope. All she could dream about was leaving.

◈

On November 19, 1920, Chukovsky wrote in his diary:

I saw Amfiteatrov on Nevsky Prospect: "Do you know that Gorky's going out of the country?" he asked me. ". . . He, Andreyeva, and [the others. They're going to] stage a café-concert: Andreyeva will sing and Gorky will be the security." . . . There's no better illustration of how Amfiteatrov's hatred of Gorky simply leads him bewilderingly astray.

◈

Six months later, the Party accepted the first of the conditions that the writer had set before his own departure. He then set numerous others. But out of all his requirements, that first one had struck him as the most unrealistic.

In the spring of 1921, Moura received a letter from Moscow: a permit signed by the commissars at Foreign Affairs authorizing her to cross the Estonian border.

It was a miracle!

And sheer luck had it that at the same time, another miracle came about: a second letter meant for her. This one had the return address of H. G. Wells. He wrote to her about the nostalgia he felt for the moments they had shared together, and told her that her children were alive. As far as he could tell, they were still living right by the lake she had told him about.

Wells's mail also included his latest publication, *Russia in the Shadows*, the little book that bore witness to what he had seen with her in October 1920. As she read the inscription, she smiled: "To Marie Benckendorff, on the occasion of her return to the capitalist world." Even if the country was isolated, the news was traveling fast across Europe!

She had already gotten two letters, so she knew that a third one bearing her name would have to arrive at Kronverksky Prospect before she departed.

As she sorted Gorky's international correspondence, Moura's face went pale and her knees trembled . . . This envelope, too, had come from England. Written in blue ink, in a particular scrawl: she recognized the handwriting immediately.

The day was May 18, 1921, the eve of the day she thought she would be leaving Russia forever.

It was the first letter from Lockhart in more than two years.

CHAPTER TWENTY-EIGHT

Crossing to the Other Side
of the Mirror

MAY 1921

Her forehead pressed against the window's glass as she sat in the train slowly crossing the birch woods, Moura thought about how she had already begun this trip west, that she had even gotten through the first part, standing in a cattle car . . . only to end up in solitary confinement at the Cheka. That was last year.

Around her, the fields bore the traces of massacres. The remnants of fire were still inscribed in the earth. Trees with long white trunks were now twisted and burnt. Timber split by artillery shells. Lopped-off cupolas like onion bulbs. Churches and cemeteries desecrated. Crows everywhere, in the holes and along the knolls. The Allies' cannons had carved up the land. As had the Russians'. Four years of civil war. Four years of battle and unrelenting atrocities between the White Army and the Red Army. How many millions had died? This winter's famine had been the coup de grâce, killing several million more people.

There was no trace of life anywhere. Even the peasants had disappeared.

These bombed-out landscapes, these stony-gray and ashy-black plains, were perfectly suited to her heart. They were still so familiar, so intimately known to her. The sky's gray light over the divided lands and the lakes were nothing more than a reflection of her torn heart.

It had been so difficult for her to leave Russia . . . And even more painful to leave Kronverksky Prospect.

The idea of abandoning Alexey Maximovich and his nearest and dearest—she felt the same affection for every one of them—cut deep to her core. This sadness, this difficulty in leaving wasn't new to her. But Lockhart's letter had turned this departure into a rupture.

After she had buckled the two clasps on her luggage, then set her suitcase by the front door, she wandered from one room to the next for a long while, unable to bring herself to go. What would happen to her once she was no longer under the protection of the duchy? This apartment had been such a haven. She collapsed into the leather armchair in the office, her usual spot in front of the master for more than a year.

With Gorky, there had been no goodbye. Of course, this separation wasn't definitive, and she understood that: he would join her again outside this country, later on. But would he be able to tear himself away from Petrograd? He barely wanted to. Right that moment, he was still in Moscow. Should she have waited? Taken care to only leave the country accompanied by him?

No.

She needed to learn from the past: she had already made the mistake once of ignoring the deadlines that would have allowed her to join her children in Estonia.

She had to stick to the plan.

If she had to break herself away from Russia, it had to be now. Right away. When Zinoviev was also in Moscow. His absence made this an opportune moment. The second he got back to his office, he would block every way she had to the West.

But who knew for sure whether, at the end of the day, Alexey Maximovich would keep his promise to go into exile? He was so Russian! Would she see him again someday?

The possibility of a permanent break with Gorky was unbearable to her.

She imagined him appearing at the apartment tomorrow, now that she was absent. He would kiss the clock in the dining room, as he did every time he returned from a trip. Then he would take a bath. He would soak there for a long while, pondering the thousands of problems on his mind, before hurriedly climbing out of his bathtub. She wouldn't be there to make sure he dried off. He would go to his office, barely dressed, and risk catching a cold. He would go over to his table and rummage through the mail, which she had already sorted for him into small piles. Among the envelopes, he would find the letter she had left for him. In it, she confessed her fear that he would forget her. She hadn't clarified that "you might forget me the way Lockhart did." Just that "you might forget me, the way you alone know how to forget."

She kept talking to him in her head, repeating what she had written to him, adding other phrases she would have liked to tell him. *Let me be sweet and affectionate with you, Alexey, at least for now. If only you knew just how much I need you! I'm leaving, and I'm very afraid . . . I know that by leaving here, I'm going to lose what little in my life is still logical. And I want to tell you how grateful I am. I know you don't like it when I thank you. So, instead, let me thank God for having met you. Yes, for having spent time with you, I offer my thanks to the Lord I believe in. My Joy. You truly are my great joy . . . You drive me mad so often in telling me that the love I have for you is made-up. I wonder why you keep trying to prove that my place isn't beside you. And why you also try to prove that my place isn't anywhere else. You manage to be so convincing in both instances that I end up doubting who I am.*

But as I go back over the experiences of these last few years, I think that the time I spent in the Cheka was a very necessary and useful education. It was irreplaceable for learning how the world works, how life works. Now I know only one thing for certain: that you are the best thing that has happened to me. And that nothing as wonderful will ever, ever happen to me again. I have no idea how you will be affected by my absence; I haven't seen you for a month. But I can't keep myself from thinking that there'll be moments when I'm in your thoughts, when you want, just as much as I do, to hold hands and hold tight. That there'll be moments when we need to look each other in the eye, to offer each other this mysterious tenderness that holds us together more concretely than any other feeling ever has.

She didn't dare go further, not even in her thoughts. The truth was, it wasn't the sadness of leaving Gorky that gnawed at her. Not only that. But the despair of a different reality.

Her miraculous escape from the Bolshevik hell no longer meant that she was running frantically toward freedom, but rather that she was walling herself up in solitude, bitterness, and jealousy.

Jealousy especially, which was now so deeply rooted within her as to arouse nausea.

She was talking to Lockhart, as well, in her head. But she resisted the urge to write to him.

Exit Lockhart, she forced herself to think. *It's over!* she repeated to herself with just as much grief as stubbornness.

The past was past. She needed to turn her gaze to the present now.

As she saw her reflection in the mirror, she realized that she was a sorry sight. Thoroughly passé. It wasn't that fashion was unimportant to Benckendorff women. But propriety was certainly important. As were outfits. And all the outward signs that they belonged to a particular class.

She didn't have any gloves or hat: all she had on her head was her hair, like a common maid. As for her old military waterproof and her men's watch on a bracelet, she was fairly certain they wouldn't meet with approval in the eyes of her sisters in-law. She instinctively brought her hand to the nape of her neck, trying to pull back up the hairs that had fallen. *There aren't even hairpins to be found in Petrograd these days!* Unlike the other women there, she hadn't cut her thick head of hair, and she wore it in a low chignon. Darn it! Her "return to the capitalist world," as Wells put it, was filling her mind with ridiculous thoughts that she hadn't considered in eons.

Because it was all a matter of *money*, of course. Apart from the clothes she was wearing right then, her black dress and her ragged undergarments, she had nothing. In her suitcase, stored above her head, she had brought only books, the ones she cared about, the works of Gorky, Wells, and Blok, that had been signed for her. As for the rest—the paintings of her ancestors—the Cheka's last search had made short work of them.

How could she ensure her children's education?

For the umpteenth time, she calculated their ages: Kira was nearly twelve years old; Paul was eight; Tania was six. She didn't know them well enough to be able to imagine their faces, and she didn't have enough experience with children to be able to imagine their heights. How would they welcome their mother after such a long absence? What would Micky say about her desertion? And her stepfamily? How would Djon's brothers welcome her?

The devastated landscape took her back into her memories. How many times had she crossed those lands, these Russian plains between Saint Petersburg and Reval? In a sleeper car with Meriel, the daughter of the British ambassador, with a flute of champagne in each hand behind the compartment's closed doors . . . Oh, that had to be a century ago! Back then, it took six hours to cross those two hundred miles. These days, wood-burning locomotives soldiered on with an endless clanking, as if the nails and bolts of their wheels were going to pop and the rails were about to break. It was a two-day trip with many, many stops. They never stopped at the train stations. But there would be abrupt halts in the middle of nowhere. For no discernible reason . . . A group of looters on the horizon? A rebellion in the ruins of the next village? Or maybe the train, like an old beast that quickly ran out of breath, just needed multiple stops to keep going.

It was interminable.

She tried to think about what would await her at the end of this journey. But to no avail.

The car was nearly empty. The hot-water tap for tea was leaking, and nobody came to fill their cup there. The memory of her trips from Moscow to Petrograd, fresh from Lockhart's embrace, roused her spirits momentarily. Those nights on the train when she could still feel his arms on her skin.

She pushed the memory out of her thoughts. For good measure, she reminded herself of that Balzac character, an arriviste, setting out for his new life: "And now, Reval, it's me against you!"

But even that allusion didn't make her smile. Even irony couldn't bring her any comfort.

Lockhart's letter . . . what she had read yesterday still chilled her to the bone. The lack of imagination, the lack of empathy, the lack of desire contained in it had been breathtaking. But she caught hold of herself: best not to think about it anymore. She now had the answers to every one of her questions. She no longer had to make her way to the other end of Europe to ask anybody.

The voice—far more than the words—the tone, this flatly pragmatic, utterly unromantic perspective on their situation, had taken away all her bearings, all her convictions. She wasn't even sure anymore what she felt. Apart from the sensation of being completely lost. For all these years, she had lived in anticipation. She had sometimes been discouraged, of course. At moments, yes, she had been uncertain. But at others, she had been able to find a thousand different reasons to live . . . She had held out hope. Even in the most horrible moments. Even in the cold, or when she was hungry, even in front of the meanness, the cruelty, the fear that had overrun her country, even in her darkest hours, even as she sat in prison. She had never stopped believing that this run of ordeals was a step on the way to something else. That Lockhart's love still existed somewhere. Far off. But real.

This was the only thing she had believed in: the strength of her instinct, of the instinct they both had. What they had felt and shared in 1918 could not disappear. It was this truth that had allowed her to go on fighting. And now she felt like a dying woman who, at the end of a long battle with cancer, was discovering on the very hour of her own death that there wouldn't be an afterlife. No resurrection. No ascent to heaven. No reunion with all those she loved. The pain she had endured over the past years hadn't been a stepping-stone to something else. Rather, it had been her millstone, and she would die with it still around her neck.

I don't know, my Baby, if I'll ever send you this letter.

And if I do, it'll still be a mistake. Because in cases like this, it's best not to write. That's what every romance novel insists. Better to grind your teeth and bear it.

After two years of silence, I received your news the night before my departure. It's quite a stroke of luck, isn't it? Just twenty-four hours before I went. I'm so naive to the end that I would have bombarded you with telegrams. That would have been silly, wouldn't it? And embarrassing.

There's no use asking why you've stopped loving me, is there? How? When? *There's no point to any of those questions.*

Of course this entire stupid letter serves no purpose. The fact of the matter is that what you've written to me is so painful that I can't help but want to yell back at you . . .

So you've had a son, you say?

A wonderful little boy?

Do you know that as I write these words, I feel like I won't be able to live with this thought? I'm ashamed of my tears. I thought I didn't know how to cry anymore. But I carried Little Peter in my belly, as you know.

I fought against my wish to write. And now it's done.

So there you have it. Good-bye. Be happy, if you're able to. But I don't think you'll ever be able to.

My feelings for you haven't changed over time. And my love won't ever change. Not that that makes any difference.

But if we should ever meet each other again in this godforsaken world, how should I greet you?

❖

She was pulled out of her despair by the train slowly coming to a stop. Yamburg: the first Russian border post. She saw four chekists through the window, all of them in boots and leather vests, coming out of a barrack and getting close.

If she had thought for even a moment that she was indifferent to her fate, she now felt, suddenly—and very precisely—just how much she cared about her freedom and her crossing to the West.

Moura was reminded of the police search on Kronverksky Prospect. Now she felt her forehead break out in sweat, and she couldn't help but pull back. The woman in charge of the train, a fat woman dressed in gray like the wardens at the Lubyanka prison, ordered her not to move. "And don't look outside!"

This woman, too, could not hide the tension she felt as the policemen approached. They made their way down the aisle.

"Passport."

Moura opened her bag and extracted her permit. She held it out unemotionally, taking care not to meet the chekist's eyes. For a long time, she hadn't been able to describe those men in detail. She knew them too well: the only face they had, in her eyes, was that of her own fear. And they could sense that fear immediately.

He barely glanced at the paper. But he folded it up, put it in his pocket, and went off with it.

As she watched the only trace of her identity disappear, she couldn't help but turn around. She had come back to reality; she knew that he was leaving to call the warden's station.

The woman running the train came over immediately:

"I told you to look straight ahead!"

She tried to obey, but in vain; she took in everything . . . The dozens of broken-down convoys, all the small red boxes that were train cars on the tracks leading out of the garage: the trains that had stopped there. Just like all the others, hers would not be leaving again.

The wait was interminable. She was now so afraid that she didn't dare even to breathe.

When she saw the policeman coming out of the barrack with a steely look, a whip in his hand, she had no doubt that her arrest was imminent. Zinoviev had caught her.

The man came down the aisle and stopped at her seat. "Get out . . . You and the others!"

The same as when she had made her failed escape attempt, there were five people here determined to cross the border. He made them all get up.

She reached up to get her suitcase. He stopped her:

"No! Leave that there. And get out."

She joined the other passengers from the other trains on the platform.

The small group crossed the tracks and reached a small path between two barriers that encircled a set of sentry boxes and watchmen in Red Army uniforms.

The now-empty train started up behind them, very slowly.

They walked several yards, at the same speed as the locomotive, to a second border post.

There, the train and the people stopped again, and everybody's passports were rechecked. They were told to go back into their train car and sit down in their seats again. Then their bags were searched, their contents emptied out. Moura's books were not remarked upon. Her papers were returned to her. But two of her fellow travelers were stopped. A random catch. A quota for manning the work camps.

She didn't look at them as they filed out. Like she did, the other travelers kept their eyes lowered when the unfortunate ones walked past them. Each of them knew it could just as easily have been them walking out.

The convoy left again, slower than ever. Nobody said a single word, but they were all asking themselves the same question: What fate were they being led to? Toward freedom, or toward the slaughterhouse? The train went another twenty miles, heading toward what seemed to be a no-man's-land delineated by barbed wire.

As they came to the third border post, there was another set of barriers. Another stop. Another regiment of soldiers. This time, Estonian policemen who spoke Russian. They were better trained, however, and more pleasant.

They got back onto the train and stayed together by the entrance. The convoy continued on to the final border post: Narva.

There, as on the Bolshevik side, an officer—a lieutenant—checked their papers. He took Moura's and disappeared.

She noticed several carts on the station platform. Luggage from other trains had already been loaded into them. She had the feeling that this train, the Russian train, wouldn't be going much farther and that the passengers would be taken by horse-drawn cart to another convoy. An Estonian one. The porters were getting to work.

She could see, in the station office, the profile of the officer, who was making a call. The papers she had been given were all in order: this time, she had nothing to fear when it came to verification. She was coming back into Estonia by legal means, with the temporary permit that had been sent to her in Petrograd by the Commission for Estonian Emigration. She even had a second document, delivered by the Forty-Fourth Emigration Organization of the new government in Reval. She could stop worrying about arbitrary officer judgments, about reigns of terror.

She suddenly realized, by how relieved she was, just how afraid she had been. A panicked fear that Zinoviev's long reach extended even to here.

She got up and went to the entrance. This was another change: the woman running the train, whose route ended here, didn't stop her. The contrast between these two worlds was evident even in the smallest details.

On the Russian side, the train station was an old wooden dacha, hastily painted red. Under the primer coat, it was still possible to make out the black-and-white traces of the tsars' eagle. On the Estonian side, the post was a solid yellow-and-white building adorned with stucco columns. The undeniable symbol of a border. Even the sentry posts and the barriers were painted yellow and white.

She took long gulps of the evening air, looking at the immense gray mass of the Narva Castle: the sentry post that, since time immemorial, had stood guard and symbolized the doorway into Europe.

She started to feel more and more excited. The West . . .

Off in the distance, she could see the sharp bell towers of the medieval churches topped by spires that nearly pierced heaven.

The customs officer came back, with six men at his side.

"Everybody can get off the train and go to one of the sleighs."

She jumped down onto the platform.

"Except for you!"

He was talking to her in Estonian. She understood the language but didn't know it well. She kept going, pretending not to have heard him, and followed the group. He caught her by the arm and pulled her aside.

"I said: not you!"

This time, he was talking to her in Russian.

"Why?"

"You're staying in Narva."

"But my stop isn't Narva! I'm going to Reval."

"We don't say Reval anymore. We say Tallinn."

"Very well. I'm going to *Tallinn.*"

"For now, you're not going anywhere."

Recalling her aristocratic reflexes, she looked down her nose at him:

"I must ask you to change your tone with me, Lieutenant! I am Madame von Benckendorff, an Estonian citizen, the widow of an Estonian citizen. And I will be continuing my journey to meet my family."

"You're not an Estonian citizen. You're a Bolshevik spy!"

She was at a loss for words.

Moura hadn't accounted for that: the fact that the world had changed everywhere. And that in Europe's eyes, anyone who could cross the borders of Lenin's Russia could only be an agent in the pay of the Soviets. A *Bolshevik spy*, as this officer had just called her.

Nor had she accounted for the fact that Estonia was now a democracy. That the nobility, which had owned eighty-six percent of the land before the war, now had nothing to their name. And that the Reds' Communism displeased the republic just as much as the Whites' despotism had.

She tried once again to make use of the previous era's codes, when one's heritage and name could still open doors everywhere.

"You are mistaken, Lieutenant. You do not know the bloodline I belong to. My coat of arms can be seen on the walls of the cathedral of Tallinn, with the arms of the Shillings, the Budbergs, and all the Baltic barons. I am Madame von Benckendorff, of the estate at Yendel."

"You are Maria Ignatyevna Zakrevskaya, of the Cheka of Petrograd."

This time, she was worried.

"Call Mr. Alexander von Benckendorff. He will tell you that I am the widow of his older brother. Call him."

She was using the same words she had with the guards on Gorokhovaya Street, when she had insisted that they call Moscow: "Call Yakov Peters."

"Call Alexander von Benckendorff!"

"He knows. It's the Benckendorff family that warned us."

"So you're well aware that the Benckendorffs know me and are await-ing my arrival."

"That's correct, they know you. As for awaiting you, however, I'm afraid they're not hoping to see you. I'm afraid, in fact, that none of them wants to meet you again, ever. At least, not before you've answered a few of our questions."

"Questions? About what?"

"Your revolutionary activities during these last three years."

She sighed, as if these preliminaries were a genuine burden:

"I've gone through hell, Lieutenant: the only activities I've carried out have been trying to survive it and to escape it. So I could find my chil-dren, who need me."

"Your children don't need a chekist mother who's an accomplice to the executioner Yakov Peters and a mistress of the agitator Maxim Gorky."

"How dare you! What right do you have?"

"I have the right of all policemen to stop spies who are sneaking into their country . . . You will need to follow me, lady. Don't force me to handcuff you for the interrogation. Kindly step into this van without giv-ing us any trouble. Here."

The prison van's door slammed shut behind her. She heard each of the three locks turning five times on the other side.

The other side of the mirror.

BOOK IV

The Fourth Life of the Signora Baronessa

Welcome to the Capitalist World

May 1921–August 1934

CHAPTER TWENTY-NINE

Children on the Lake's Banks

MAY 1921

I n the fishermen's cabin on the lake's banks, behind the closed doors and the bay windows of the veranda, the men who had been lords before the war, the former masters of Yendel, were holding a meeting and whispering:

"We can't let this woman rot in Narva Castle for more than two days."

"But we can't let her live here in Kallijärv, either!"

"Or even come into this house."

"She shouldn't be anywhere near the children. They absolutely mustn't be allowed to see her."

"All the same, she's their mother."

"Barely."

"All the police have to do is send her back to the Bolsheviks in Petrograd."

"Yesterday, in Tallinn, Contessa Manteufel was telling the noble marshal, Count Ignatyev, that she sold out everybody back there!"

Micky stood behind the windowpanes, watching the Benckendorffs discussing and arguing around the table, paying them no attention as they kept muttering. There was only one piece of news she cared about: after three days imprisoned at the border, Marydear was coming! What state would she be in? It hardly mattered. Mary would be coming down on the slow train from Narva today.

As for the rest, Mary's activities among the Communists and the indecision about welcoming her back—so much for the Benckendorffs! Micky didn't want to hear them anymore.

The children, however, were crouched beneath the windows, trying to eavesdrop.

It was impossible for her to deal with the little ones today! Between her excitement and her uncertainty, Micky had grown irritable and was losing her patience.

"Go play somewhere else!" She waved her hands as if she were trying to brush away some birds, spouting off sentences with no rhyme or reason. "Off you go, everybody go outside now. Go play in the garden. Out into the woods. Go pick some mushrooms. Your mother would love to have some mushrooms! Get some flowers, too. Pick her a nice bouquet of lilacs. Off you go, off you go, scoot!"

Micky, in turn, walked off into the house, went up the hallway, paced in the kitchen, and headed to the other veranda, the one in back. Every time she thought she could hear sleigh bells tinkling, she thought: had Marydear arrived?

The train between Narva and Tallinn stopped once a week on the platform of the small Yendel train station. Micky had sent the farmer's son there with the horse-drawn carriage. The boy had been down there since this morning and hadn't returned yet.

Three years. And Marydear was coming back!

◈

Over these three years, no specific news had made its way to the lake. Apart from that of the famines, the abuses, the tortures, and the massacres. Nobody among the Baltic nobility had been lucky enough not to lose any of their kin and goods in Russia. Djon's three brothers, like Djon himself, had married Russian aristocrats whose relatives had been on the tsars' court. Most of them had been executed.

Bolsheviks: from the salons to the kitchens, the mere word summoned forth nightmarish visions.

Micky tried to preserve her flock from all this fear and hatred by keeping mum on the horrors of the Revolution. She never said a word on the matter; she never commented on the stories of rapes and murders that circulated here. It was a steely silence. The atrocities carried out by the Reds, however, constantly haunted her imagination. Any time she heard the name of her dear Mary, whom she considered both a heroine and a victim, mentioned amid these abominations, she was horrified.

She had to stay quiet.

But the more she stayed quiet, the more the children sensed just how terrifying their mother's world was.

Ever since Djon's death, life in Estonia hadn't been easy for anyone. The bourgeois democracy, which had been trying to rid itself of the feudal nobility, had nationalized and redistributed the land, and their former owners were left with only five percent of the possessions they'd had in 1914. The estate of Yendel had been no exception to this mandate: it no longer belonged to the Benckendorff family. The distillery, the brick-yard, the shared spaces, the woods, the fields were all the property of the republic. The immense redbrick house, a replica of the Renaissance-era Elizabethan estates, was now a governmental institution for agricultural education.

The family, however, had been left the place on the lake's shore and the adjacent gardens for their personal enjoyment.

Now the Benckendorffs were poor, although they didn't deign to notice it, much less complain about it. They lived frugally and refused to ask for anything. The Revolution had wrested away everything they once had a right to: they weren't going to sink down to everyone else's level and beg. Such a prospect was too vulgar for them. Their pride forced them to settle for the essentials. Money only had value if one knew how to spend it, which required savoir faire. Which was now in disrepute.

At their home, as at all the surrounding manors, the splendors that had been the backdrop to their youth no longer existed. The objets d'art had been seized or burned during the peasant revolts of 1917. And during the German and Russian extortions of the Great War. And the Civil War. And the War of Independence. Now all that remained were a few menacing paintings of ancestors, now hanging along the wainscoted hallway of the cabin. And the books, the relics of the library that Djon had loved so dearly, that he himself had taken and shelved behind the glass panels of the dining room when he had moved the children into his mother's house.

Djon's bravery during the fight for freedom—his feats of glory against the Reds in Latvia between January and March 1919—had conferred upon the Benckendorff children a form of respect: the authorities didn't dare to even think of taking away their sanctuary.

But then again, nobody dared to think of giving them their estate back.

The cabin at Kallijärv wasn't much to look at. No electricity. No running water. It was a small wooden house with four wings that jutted out over the lawn like the arms of a star. The charm of the site lay in the beauty of the landscape, and this lake that the black mass of the forests framed: a gray zone, a blue disc that changed its color as clouds came and went.

And it was there, under this mercurial light, that Micky did her best to protect Marydear's children. It was there, in the heart of the small world where they lived in self-sufficiency, far from any town and any school, that one of Djon's cousins, a well-educated spinster obsessed with the memory of her privileges, had come to instruct them.

In Micky's eyes, she was a guard dog; she had no love, no grace, no dreams. She was the last descendant of the Teutonic knights, a woman the Irish governess felt no affinity for.

This intruder was named Baroness von Rennenkampf. The children called her Aunt Cossé, a diminutive of her first name, Constanza. What she did have was a sense of honor, a preference for work well done, and a passion for discipline.

A military salute every morning for Paul, a hand on his cap and his heels clicking together. Deep bows for Kira and Tania. And punishment for everybody if the least mistake was made.

Micky hated her and made no secret of it.

Kira, Paul, and Tania, too, hated her and made no secret of it.

With her gray chignon, her light mustache, and her stentorian voice, the wonderful Aunt Cossé had absolutely no interest in any of their feelings. She hardly cared about what flitted through anyone's soul. She considered herself to be above all emotion. She cared only about Work and respected only Virtue. As a consequence, she didn't hate anyone. With two sole exceptions: Vladimir Ilyich Lenin and Maria Ignatyevna Zakrevskaya, who her cousins kept on calling Marie von Benckendorff, as the unfortunate Djon had very aristocratically named her.

The reappearance of "that woman"—Aunt Cossé didn't even deign to say her name—would be a fatal blow to all her principles of morality.

Of course, this woman was still the widow of a Benckendorff, the one who had given birth to these little ones. But this woman was a little late in remembering her obligations! Why hadn't she followed her children to Yendel in the spring of 1918, when her husband had asked her to? And three months later, in July 1918, why had she come and joined them, only to abandon them again and return to Petrograd alone?

Aunt Cossé knew the dates well and recalled them every so often. She also knew the answers. This woman had gone back to Russia that August so she could care for her sick and aging mother—or so she claimed. But Aunt Cossé wasn't fooled! That was merely a pretext. If she really had wanted to care for the late Countess Boreisha, why hadn't she brought her here during her visit that July? Or later on? Why hadn't she taken her to Yendel when Estonian citizens were still able to leave Russia and return to their homeland?

Those questions were what the family council was trying to answer this morning. Aunt Cossé underscored that Kira, Paul, and Tania were doing quite well without this woman they had no need to see again.

Their tutor, Alexander von Benckendorff, who the children called Uncle Sasha, had just come in from Tallinn. He was a former cavalry officer, rather quick-tempered and sentimental by nature, despite the stiffness of his posture and the sharpness of his waxed mustache. He was presiding over the meeting.

The Baltic barons—like the inhabitants of the Kronverksky Prospect apartment—lived in a group and argued over all the grand questions their circle cared about. Uncle Sasha listened to their suggestions, but he made his decisions alone. And woe betide anyone who dared to ignore his verdict.

Counter to all expectations, Sasha—the youngest of the Bencken-dorff brothers and, after Djon's murder, now the head of the clan in Estonia—seemed to be the least worried one there. In any case, he was the least hostile to "that woman."

He explained to his outraged wife, his sickened cousin, the other hor-rified aunts, all the family's grandes dames, that he couldn't bring himself to leave the widow of his older brother to rot in solitary confinement.

Yes, it was he, Sasha, who had gotten her out of prison after two days, confirming her identity with the police and guaranteeing that she would be under house arrest in the residence on the lake. There was nothing to fear. She would be watched there. And her stay in Kallijärv wouldn't be for longer than the summer, as the Estonian authorities had only granted her the right to visit for a few weeks. Then she would be expelled and returned to her kind: *to her Bolshevik friends*, as Cossé insisted.

And so he confirmed that Marie would arrive at the station today, at noon or at midnight, depending on the train schedules. With his consent.

"She is still a Benckendorff, cousin Cossé . . . I can't sentence her if I haven't heard her case."

"With all due respect, my dear Sasha, your romanticism is bewilder-ing: you say you want to hear this woman make her case? What an inge-nious thing for you to say! But what defense could she possibly have? She has nothing!"

She has everything! Micky responded in her head.

Over those three years, not a day had gone by when Micky hadn't prayed for her dear little girl's return. She, who barely believed in divine mercy, had put her hands together in prayer for her child's life.

The heavens had heard her pleas: Marydear was returning!

And now Micky had to prepare a room for her, a bed with fresh sheets, yes, the sheets from her trousseau—the linen ones that had been embroi-dered with her monogram. Micky also needed to iron her nightdress and several personal effects that she had been able to save in the move to the cabin. Micky needed to cook her a meal. Something solid, a delicacy that would be filling. She herself had never been a good cook or a good lady of the house. But she knew what Mary would need after her arrest on the border and so many years of misfortune. She needed fresh bread, a pat of butter, a jug of milk.

She set to work. Food at Kallijärv was still scarce. It didn't matter: Micky knew every one of Aunt Cossé's hiding spots and secret reserves.

If so much emotion had caused the governess to lose her composure, what was there to say about Tania's impatience? She was dizzy with excitement. Her mother was coming! At six years old, Tania had no memory of the woman. *My mother*, she kept saying out loud, *my mother, my mother*. She thought of her dressed up like a fairy, a hennin on her head, a wand in her hand. Like the illustrations in her children's books.

She, too, was expecting *everything*.

The little girl ran across the lawn, her brown braids wrapped around her head, and she started spinning under the veranda, chanting:

"My mother's coming, my mother's coming, my mother's coming . . . And my mother's going to get rid of Aunt Cossé. Come as quick as you can, come as quick as you can, and kick out the big fat cow!"

Even though she was the youngest one, Tania was clearly the trickiest. In other words, the least docile. As a result, she was Micky's favorite, even though she took care not to show this preference in any way. But how could she help feeling that way? Tania had all Marydear's charm, all her energy and her joie de vivre.

Paul, in turn, was more like his father. And Micky had loved Djon dearly.

Like him, Paul was modest. Silent, secret, closely attuned to nature . . . He was rather big for seven years old. And he was extraordinarily handsome.

And then there was Kira. Countess Kira von Engelhardt. She was almost a young woman now. Kira had nothing in common with the Benckendorffs, and she only lived with them because Marydear, many years earlier, had decided that she would.

Micky had to acknowledge that in this particular aspect, there was nothing to scold Aunt Cossé for. She had never drawn any distinction between the Engelhardt girl and the other children she had taken it upon herself to rear.

Rear Kira? That was absurd! She could think of nobody who was inherently more grateful. More generous. And probably more unfortunate. Ah, Kira on the threshold of adolescence: perhaps the most touching of the three, Micky thought.

Kira, who was far away from everyone's eyes. Kira, whose face was turned toward the train station, who was waiting all by herself down in front of the doorway, listening to the noises from outside, imagining the arrival of "Auntie-Mommy" around the curve of the road with her heavy suitcase . . . Kira, who, without realizing it, was acting exactly the same way Moura had when, at the zenith of her passion for Lockhart, she had stood motionless, dreaming about seeing him coming around the bend.

All three of them had to go to sleep before they could see their hope or their fear coming down the powdery roads of Yendel—the one all of them were awaiting. Moura. A monster to some, a wonder to others.

The governess stayed up and waited on her own.

❖

Micky saw the gleam in the distance between the pines, the cart moving beneath the wooden bridge over the clearing. It was now riding over the patch of land where Djon had been assassinated. She could distinctly hear the clinking of its bells drawing near with each passing second: it was coming around the lake.

Micky rushed to the bottom of the steps outside. She reached out with her arms as if to grab the reins and stop the horse. A figure stood up in the carriage. She stepped down slowly. Micky pulled her into her arms.

Without a word, without even trying to look at each other, the two women hugged. It was impossible for them to say anything. It was impossible for them to even look at each other. Their eyes were shut as they clutched each other tightly. Emotion choked their throats and took away their breath. They stayed there, in an embrace, for a long while.

The feeling of their bodies, their lives, entangled again, overcame them.

Micky, carrying Moura's suitcase, was now leading her down the hall-way where all the bedrooms could be found. The darkness was complete. As was the silence.

Their tall, thin silhouettes blurred together. They walked cautiously.

"They're there," Micky whispered.

"Here? Behind this door? All three of them?"

Moura's voice seemed to be practically gone. Hoarser than ever under the stress of so much feeling. She was almost gasping.

"Here?" she repeated.

"Yes. They're sleeping."

"Can I see them?"

The governess carefully pushed open the door, pulling back to let Moura through.

Moura stepped forward hesitantly. The tiny room was pitch-black. She groped ahead until she reached the children and didn't move any farther.

She listened to the light sound of their breaths, contemplating them one by one. She couldn't make out their faces. The boy, flat on his back, had his arm across his eyes. The girls, flat on their stomachs, had their heads buried in their pillows, their faces lost beneath their brown hair.

Moura stayed there, not moving, not seeing them.

She stayed there, hunched over the three forms, for so long that Micky was afraid she was crying . . . Just as she herself cried silently in the night, thinking about Eileen, the daughter she had left behind so she could come care for the Zakrevsky children, her daughter whom she had not seen since.

Sensing that she needed to console her other daughter, to tell her something reassuring about all those years that these children had been growing up without her, Micky whispered, "They're wonderful, wonderful children."

"Even with a spy for a mother!"

The bitterness of such a sentence was so unlike Marydear that Micky couldn't help but reach out in compassion. She stepped forward, caught her hand, and pulled her close.

Moura stiffened and pulled away from her.

That, too, was unlike her.

Micky shut the door again behind them, grabbed the suitcase, and continued all the way to the bedroom at the end. A gas lamp was glowing on the night table, shining a golden light over the quilt. The sheets were pulled back, the nightdress laid out.

The two women faced each other.

For the first time since they had met again that night, they looked at each other, trying to take the measure of their respective states. Morally, physically.

Moura's feverish eyes interrogated her governess's face. Even through the drama and all the hardship, there wasn't a single gray hair in Micky's chignon. She kept it pulled up high, a bun on the top of her head, as she had in 1900. Her back was straight, as it usually was. She was fifty-seven years old, but she seemed a decade younger.

Micky fixed her eyes on Moura.

There wasn't a single gray hair in Marydear's chignon, either. Her locks were drab and uncombed, yes. But her skin hadn't aged. She was twenty-eight years old: still young. She would recover quickly. Not a single blemish, not even a wrinkle, despite the unhealthy pallor of her complexion, her hollowed cheeks, and her strained features.

The relief was mutual. They recognized each other as, if not indestructible, at least unbreakable.

They had survived: the world wasn't all for naught.

What about the rest?

As they came out of their contemplation, the conversation grew difficult. Micky realized that there was something distressed in the way Marydear moved, something halting in her motions. An untamed restlessness. She was usually so firmly rooted in reality, but here she seemed absent. Elsewhere, in a waking nightmare. And she was trying to get out of it, to say something sensible.

"Where would the children be without you, Micky? You've saved them."

"I haven't saved anyone. You found a way to get out of there, that's the only thing that matters . . . And you've come back."

Moura's eye was fixed on Micky as she stood straight. She couldn't bring herself to move. Not even to sit down. "If you could only imagine . . ."

"You're exhausted, my darling. It's time for you to go to sleep."

"I think they got me at Narva . . ."

"Time to sleep now."

"Yes, that's it . . . With all their suspicions and their vile questions, they managed to get me."

"You can tell me tomorrow."

"After interrogations like that, there's no way to know what you're supposed to think anymore, what you're supposed to feel, you don't know how to sleep anymore . . . I don't know how I could possibly thank you enough, Micky."

"Oh, but you know, you know very well. You just have to go ahead and lie down. That's all."

"I can't stay in the darkness."

Marydear's voice had always seemed a bit broken. But Micky could see that something in her had broken this time. Or shattered.

Could it be possible that they really had "gotten her," as she was saying in this incoherent way, at Narva? She was keeping her fear so close to her heart, there was no doubt about that.

"Just leave the lamp turned up, my dear. Dawn isn't far off."

"The prison, just when I was so close . . . It was just . . . The cell in the fortress . . . The isolation at Narva. It was just . . ."

She was trying to say something, and then Micky realized what it was. "A bridge too far?"

Moura nodded hesitantly. "Yes: too far, too hard . . . The final straw . . . After everything else . . . They shouldn't have."

"No, the Benckendorffs shouldn't have. But it wasn't for long. And it's over now . . . You're here, you're at home. With *your* children. At home, Mary, where nobody can take you away without your consent. Don't forget that, Marydear: Kallijärv is *your* home. Not theirs. Yours. It's your inheritance from your husband."

Micky had opened the suitcase and put Moura's underclothes away in the drawer. She set the books on the chest of drawers, organized by author, in alphabetical order, just so. She was setting them up for a good long while.

And a smile finally came into Moura's eyes: the expression she had when she was little, back when she hugged her old governess so she could have some lace, some ribbons.

"Stop, Micky, stop . . . Stop bustling around!"

Micky came back to the bed, and this time Moura didn't resist. She let her unbutton the old blouse, she let her help her pull off her skirt, give her her nightdress, help her lie down, tuck her in.

Before falling fast asleep, she whispered, as she had when she was a child:

"I didn't do anything, Micky. I didn't do anything bad."

❖

More than sixty years later, in the book she wrote describing her years in Estonia, Moura's daughter, Tania, would describe more thoroughly the impressions she had of Moura's return in May 1921:

> *I can remember wondering what my mother would be like, but I have no memory of her actual arrival at Kallijärv. She must have come at night after we had gone to bed.*
>
> *But on the morning after her arrival Micky took us to meet her, as far as I was concerned for the first time.*
>
> *It is curious, when I think of it now, that the moment was so unemotional. I have a very clear picture of the room and of a woman sitting up in bed. I remember thinking that she was larger than I had expected and that this rather healthy-looking person did not correspond to the stories of hunger and privation we had been told.*
>
> *But I was also aware that this woman was a total stranger and I felt at that first meeting nothing of what one might expect.*
>
> *I suspect, looking back on it, that there was a great deal of embarrassment on both sides which prevented any closeness between us straight away.*

Micky, while fussing around Moura, very soon ushered us out of the room again, telling us that she must be left to rest as she was very tired.

That was my first real meeting with my mother and yet it is remarkable only for its ordinariness.

For that week I think that she remained in bed more or less the whole time. It is true that she had gone through a series of great ordeals and must have been exhausted, both physically and emotionally.

Tania also described how—against all expectations—the members of the Estonian nobility came to pay their respects to her, even sitting beside her bed. The men did, at least.

It was incredible. Moura would ask to see such and such an old friend, and he would come. Micky was always the one to introduce the visitors, announcing each of them in turn. The procession would last until lunchtime. Tania also mentioned that, true to her reputation, her mother waited for each of them to pay homage to her, notwithstanding their wariness about her rumored doings in Petrograd.

There was an aura of mystery about why and where she had been all this time.

It was inevitable that people who firmly held these beliefs should be suspicious of Moura and that they should want to have some answers about her activities during the past three years.

The setup where Moura might perhaps entrust one of her guests with a story about her adventures on Soviet soil was characteristic for her. She had transformed the room at the end of the hallway—which had been spartan and bare when she arrived—into a sort of oratory. Shuttered windows. Flickering flames. Gilt-bound books, wall hangings, icons, votive candles, and perfume vaporizers.

It wasn't a particular design she'd wanted to flaunt, just an ambiance that the Baltic barons were no longer used to.

The youngest daughter of Senator Zakrevsky, a former servant of the imperial court, embodied the spell of an eternal Russia. The values of the tsar's aristocracy and the Estonian nobility.

Tradition was first; the Orthodox faith was second. And the charm was last of all. The message was clear: anti-Bolshevism in all its splendor.

Her admirers might have been rushing to her bedside, but their wives, their sisters, their daughters all refused to say a word to "the Benckendorff woman." They treated her as a pariah as much as a courtesan.

Moura harbored no illusions: she was an adventurer, a lady of the night, a spy. The men gathered around her the way they used to seek out the company of courtesans.

She thanked the heavens that not one of them, not even Micky, seemed to have heard about her affair with Robert Bruce Lockhart. By all appearances, her life as a woman in Moscow alone with the British consul had slipped through the cracks of history.

Nobody, she thought, nobody could ever hear about this liaison, ever! The rumors about her relationship with the Communist figure Maxim Gorky were dangerous enough and had given her enough trouble that she couldn't bear the thought of yet another indignity.

❖

She was the center of attention in a mere matter of hours.

She had already reclaimed her place, the only one she'd ever accepted among the Benckendorffs: front and center.

There was nothing artificial about this role; she instinctively, easily remained the lady of the house. The mother of the children. The widow of the landowner. Here, in the house on the lake, just as before, in the estate at Yendel, she ruled with an iron fist.

Aunt Cossé was ejected and relegated to the end of the table, even though she had tried to keep her seat. But it was useless to try. *That woman* held sway up by the samovar, serving the tea and handing out the cups. *That woman* had put her foot down, and now *that woman* was in charge.

The strangest thing was that Cossé, who had once been the watchdog, was now trembling in her corner, not even daring to protest.

Micky had triumphed. No more were Paul's military salutes and the girls' courtly bows. Marydear had taken the reins of the house and was naturally attending to the education of her children.

She balanced the accounts, planned the menus, checked her son's knowledge, corrected her daughters' work. She even planned to go back to Tallinn—notwithstanding her house arrest—to get official confirmation from the government of Paul's and Tania's rights to Kallijärv with a property deed.

She was, in short, putting both her life and the future of her offspring in order.

❖

A future with *them*? There would be no future. Everybody here knew that: Moura's seizure of power was just a game. In a matter of weeks, the Estonian police would be taking Moura back to the border.

She herself never forgot that, not even for a second. The time she spent here, lying on her bed or sitting at the head of the table, was merely a momentary distraction. One last respite, one final cigarette, before she was killed.

At the end of the summer, she would be in Zinoviev's grip.

How could she avoid that? The question haunted her.

❖

The truth was that she felt uneasy.

Uneasy everywhere.

Her sovereignty was just a facade that hid the sluggishness of her senses and the emptiness of her soul. When she saw her children again, however, she had been convinced that her heart would burst, that she wouldn't be able to bear the immensity of her joy.

Then the excitement had gone.

And now they were here, they were running around her, they were making noise. She knew she was close to them, but to no avail: she couldn't actually be *with* them.

Am I really a terrible woman? she wondered. *Yes, yes, I'm a terrible woman. An unnatural mother.*

The only realm in which she didn't constrain herself was her involvement in their studies. She was obsessed by the need to teach Kira, Paul, and Tania the lessons that would allow them to survive in the modern world.

She needed to get them out of Kallijärv quickly and enroll them in proper secondary schools, in Berlin or London. Meaning: she needed to find work, she needed to earn money to build a life for five people—the three children, Micky, and herself.

But in her situation, how could she avoid being separated from them?

These questions kept her awake at night. She was at an impasse. She couldn't see a way out.

The only thing she was certain of was that her "repose" on the shores of the lake was tantamount to suicide. She was losing valuable hours. She needed to move, to act. To get herself to Tallinn, consult a lawyer, find a way to get Estonian nationality.

But she didn't have the energy anymore.

❖

Despite her uncertainty, she was still sure of one thing: that she was able to fool people and instinctively figure out what was expected of her. Had Gorky, Andreyeva, or any of the other inhabitants of the duchy seen her ruling over Kallijärv, they wouldn't have recognized this magnificent diva as their Tyotka of Kronverksky Prospect.

Between Tyotka, "little aunt"—with such charming tact, such discreet efficiency—and the imposing Marie von Benckendorff lay an immense distance: a thousand lives, a thousand worlds that she alone was capable of traversing, that she alone was able to understand, and that she alone could master.

Moura's reincarnation as a grande dame, an aristocrat used to giving commands, to being obeyed, and to being served, was a return to a role that she had never really abandoned, though the metamorphosis had taken everyone else by surprise.

If they had doubted in any way the authenticity of one or the other of the two characters—Tyotka and Diva—they would have been mistaken. She remained their muse, their inspiration, their instigator, their co-conspirator. The prima donna of all their lives.

But a prima donna on the razor's edge.

CHAPTER THIRTY

On the Razor's Edge

On a June afternoon, Moura's forehead was pressed against the window of the slow-moving train as it covered the last few miles separating it from the city. She had hoped that by leaving the secluded world of the house on the lake, she would breathe better; that by jolting herself out of inaction, she would be able to shrug off the unease that still niggled at her, this feeling she had of being absent, this distance that undermined the love she felt for her children. But it was in vain.

Over the course of the trip, the feeling of emptiness had lasted. She hadn't been able to distance herself properly from the past; the nightmares of her life in Russia were still unnervingly near as she took in the normalcy of life here.

She looked at the flat countryside broken up by lakes reflecting the sky. Always the same lakes, always the same sky.

Always the same white trunks of close-knit birch trees that reminded her of cliffs closing off the horizon.

There were few animals. A cow here and there. A few occasional sheep. Nothing, really. Just storks atop the water towers. And the last few geese migrating, whose flight was hidden at moments by the sun.

There was no life in the fields. Nor was there any in the train car, apart from the distant shape of the plainclothes police officer watching her. He had followed her from Narva all the way to Kallijärv. He would be nipping at her heels up to the capital. The man's presence had become so familiar to her, even though he wanted to be invisible, that she didn't give it any thought anymore.

She tried to fight against her apathy. But without Lockhart's love and her dreams of a shared future, the universe seemed dead to her. She did not move, despite the train's jolts. And she was unable to feel anything now that Gorky wasn't nearby. Without his sound, his furor, and his convictions. *Enough, enough,* she thought: best to concentrate on the landscape.

She tried in vain to take interest in the world around her . . . But it was impossible for her to focus on anything.

And yet the scenery was beautiful and familiar.

She didn't hesitate as she stepped out of the station and got into one of the hansom cabs that awaited the travelers. The policeman rushed into the next one. She knew that they'd have to go around the sea and bypass the town before they could enter it by car.

Tallinn, a city Moura hadn't thought about even once over the past three years, rose up again in her memory, intact. She recognized everything about it, even the pale light of these first summer nights on the shore of the Baltic Sea.

As always, the road along the fortifications was empty.

The massive medieval towers with their red roofs broken up by defensive walls. The arched doors open within the ramparts. The church bells soaring up to the heavens and their towering spires piercing the clouds.

She could recall, down to the smallest details, all the houses of the lower city: narrow, medieval, still owned by merchants. And the neoclassical palaces of the upper city inhabited by the Estonian barons. And then there was the enormous Russian church crowning it all with its white facade and its golden domes.

Once they had crossed the archway and started up Pikk Street, Moura was met with a shock. The memory she retained was of a sleepy place. What she saw, however, was a teeming anthill.

A riotous, motley crowd thronged on the sidewalks, women in short skirts and cloche hats, men in brightly colored suits and shiny shoes. Everywhere, laughter and booming voices could be heard. It wasn't seven o'clock yet, but the bars and cabarets leading up to the grand plaza already seemed packed. Jazz rhythms rose up from former cellars. It felt like she was in one of the liveliest neighborhoods of a major city capital—

apart from the two black hansom cabs dating from the nineteenth century, braving the postwar crowds and lurching over the cobblestones.

At the top of the hill, under Toompea Castle, the atmosphere felt different. There, she couldn't see any more cafés, any more nightclubs. But just past the pastel-toned walls of the private mansions, behind the straw-yellow facades, the emblazoned pediments, the porticos and the colonnades, she could still hear the rumblings of celebrations and the tunes of tangos.

In front of the Orthodox church, all the lights of the building that housed the club Djon had once belonged to were lit. Groups of men in tuxedos were smoking on the balcony and sipping cocktails. The need to live at all costs seemed to have reached even the most conservative aristocracy in Europe. Although they were also one of the farthest fallen.

After ten centuries of oppression, freedom had seized Estonia.

Moura stepped out into one of the few alleys off Toompea, behind a palace transformed into a boarding house for women. She had managed to reserve a room there, where, far from Aunt Cossé's prying ears and the suspicions of her sisters-in-law, she might be able to convince Djon's three brothers of her innocence and of the injustice she had been victim to.

❖

"You must understand and realize this, my dear Sasha: I simply *couldn't* leave Petrograd . . . It's impossible for anybody at all to leave there! I tried once, walking across the ice of the Gulf of Finland. And I was caught. Do you know what that cost me?"

The head of the Benckendorff clan was sitting in the only armchair that furnished the room. The Second Empire decor seemed frozen in time: old rugs, old upholstery, and old beaded chandeliers. Moura had tried to make a show of receiving them here, as she might have in one of the salons of the past.

Unnerved by this one-on-one conversation that would have cost him his head if anybody learned about it, Sasha remained wary. His two brothers hadn't shown up.

"There's nothing for me to understand," he said in a serious tone. "Nothing to realize. I only replied to your invitation to give you some advice." He was speaking to her formally. "Take care of your children. Then go back to Russia, as the police insist. Don't make any waves. Go back home *before* you're expelled."

"But I *am* home! And I'm taking care of my children, as you're so kindly suggesting. Further, to that point, I've just seen a lawyer to formalize their inheritance from their father."

"Don't do that. Don't ask anything of the republic. Don't attract any attention to yourself!"

As she answered, she affected serenity:

"On the contrary, my friend. I believe the time has come for justice. For my children. For myself. For you. For all us Benckendorffs."

"Justice? You want justice?" In his anger, Sasha had dropped his icy formality and was talking to her with the closeness they had always had as family. "Well, the Budbergs were right. I don't see any solution other than this trial!"

"A trial?"

"A court of honor . . . The Budberg clan, the Manteufel counts, the Schilling counts, all the old families want to send you to the Ehrengericht. The tribunal of the Baltic barons."

She couldn't hold back her sigh of exasperation. Setting aside her usual grace for a moment, she asked sharply: "And why would we do that, my dear friend?"

"Don't make me repeat the activities you've been accused of. They're so scandalous that it behooves us both to absolve you of them or disavow you."

"You mean sentence me." She forced herself to smile. "And what penalties do I face?"

He paused.

"Infamy, if you're judged guilty. You'll be expelled from our ranks, you'll no longer belong to our nobility . . . to any nobility in the world.

But if you're found innocent, you'll come out of the Ehrengericht with a clean slate. Nobody will dare insult you anymore. You'll have been rehabilitated and restored in everybody's esteem."

"A court of honor? In the twentieth century? That's absurd! It's ridiculous!"

"Honestly, my dear, no, I don't think the court of honor is ridiculous. Honor is the only value that still carries weight in this land. And in your situation, you have everything to gain by submitting to this tribunal."

"If I accept, will you guarantee that you'll help me obtain Estonian nationality? I'm owed that by rights, as I was married to Djon."

"If the Ehrengericht absolves you of these accusations: of course."

"Give me your word that I'll be free to take my children wherever I think is best."

"Free? But Marie, who among us is free today? What I can guarantee you is that you will be one of us again, and that you'll belong to our family forever."

She stayed silent. There was nothing pleasant about such a promise. Nothing reassuring.

What was Sasha's advice worth? Should she submit to this archaic practice, this mockery of justice?

She knew the barons' conservatism, their hatred of change well enough—especially after the Revolution—to know what they thought of her relationship with Gorky. She didn't have a chance. And the idea of being judged by these men, who proudly upheld their honor when they themselves were incapable of surviving and had lost practically all reason to live . . . These men were incapable of overcoming the loss of the land that they'd been all too happy to inherit over the centuries, incapable of conducting themselves with dignity today and living off the products of their work. The prospect of such a trial exasperated her.

Sasha, despite his goodwill, belonged completely to this caste that was still standing only thanks to the privileges it still enjoyed. He could talk about his peers' moral laws all he wanted, but he respected them in appearance only: at the same time, he collected mistresses and behaved toward his children as his parents had toward him. His gaze was fixed stubbornly on the past.

He was full of hatred for the Communists and dreamed of confronting the Bolsheviks.

No reasonable dialogue could come of this.

She kept thinking.

Even if the Ehrengericht turned out to be to her advantage, would she be able to obtain Estonian nationality? A passport was the only thing that mattered.

The visa she had been granted at Narva would expire in a matter of weeks. And any deferral she might be able to secure through her legal representative still wouldn't solve the fundamental problem. At best, she could buy herself a bit more time . . . But then what?

She had not heard anything from Gorky. The Estonian papers were saying that he was expected in Finland sometime soon. Should she believe them?

If the police sent her back to Zinoviev just when Gorky had finally left Petrograd, that would be the end of her.

❖

Tallinn
June 11, 1921

My very dear, very close friend,
My dear beloved,

Hurrah, letters, letters, letters! Ah, Alexey Maximovich, how funny you are, how much I just want to laugh with you. Above all, I want to tell you just how much I miss you. I left your place with my eyes shut, because you had convinced me that my departure would make yours easier. My eyes are still shut: I'm staying here and I'm waiting for you. But you haven't come.

The truth is that I don't feel well, Alexey Maximovich. I claim to have mastered my life. But I haven't been able to.

I've adapted, of course . . . You know just how easily I learn to accommodate everything. But my head is still empty, empty, empty.

Forgive me. You must be unaccustomed to my quibbling like this, moving back and forth, going off on tangents so far that I don't know how to get back to the subject. You wouldn't recognize me anymore: I don't do a single thing the entire day. And yet I have reasons to be busy, with my three children.

Don't get mad, don't furrow your brow. I think that what I need at this point isn't my children but a friend. That is, you. Oh, don't laugh! Every kind of love, even the most devoted kind, conceals some measure of selfishness, and mine consists of exactly that. The desire to share everything with you, the slightly sadistic desire to tell you everything. And, too, the desire to say sweet nothings to you, to be tender with you. Exactly what you've forbidden me to do.

No matter what, keep writing to me, okay? I do worry so, so much about your health!

All right, I'm going to try to answer your questions . . .

In one of your letters, you ask me if I'm living gaily and if I'm celebrating.

Gaily, no.

Celebrating? Yes.

Well, if drinking, drinking, and drinking means celebrating. Rest assured, I'm not drinking to excess. But I do need to forget myself a little to keep going.

You'll understand, Alexey Maximovich, once you've spent a bit of time on this side of the border.

My "return to the capitalist world," as Wells put it in his inscription in my copy of his book, can be summed up as my increasingly frequent visits to bars in Tallinn. I'm drinking champagne, listening to the latest ragtime music, and telling myself that there's a man in Petrograd whose presence here could have turned all of this into a slightly more exciting adventure.

Without you, I feel old moods coming back, old desires. The desire, for example, to be wild . . . To prove myself frivolous, frivolous, frivolous to the point of idiocy . . . To top up my glass of champagne with, I don't know . . . the most precious, most unprocurable things, like ripe peaches or strawberries. But my need for excess goes away quickly and leaves behind a disagreeable taste in my mouth.

At the end of your third letter, you ask me about my life here. Let's say that it's a bit complicated. I've tried in vain not to sidestep difficulties and not to struggle with obstacles, but I can hardly bear narrow-mindedness and stupidity.

Even with the absurdity of my situation, there are still funny details to be found. I'm constantly followed by a policeman who tracks who I meet. I'm suspected, of course, of being a spy. I'm accused of having a relationship with the Cheka and of complicity with the Bolshevik powers. People look at me as if I were going to pull two or three bombs out of my pocket and throw them at their buckets of champagne.

Everybody's interested in me. I can't complain: I could go to the fairs and make a bit of money that way. I'll have to hurry up, because the barons are starting to not be afraid of me: I go to social evenings at the club for former noblemen and I don't lob grenades at them.

Like before.

For the Russians of my "social class"—if we want to use that old cliché—a trip to the West can mean one of two things. Either it means a return to our old way of life, or it means a clean break with it. I still haven't been able to decide which I want.

Something in me, something that seems like a habit, a childhood memory, can even make me feel like I'm supposed to be here. But only momentarily. The reality is that here doesn't belong to me anymore.

Enough about me, however.

I'm going to try to get rid of what you call my "depression." I'm going to replace my ragged underwear, which always bothered you so much—remember those?—with frilly lace things. And I'm going to agree to submit my life to the immutable laws of society.

In short, I think I'm going to do even more stupid things, and then I'll land on a solution. What I mean is: a job. I'm thinking about looking for something in Berlin.

But for that, I have to belong to a nation and hold a passport.

For that, I have to be free.

◈

"'Free, free, free.' You say that word like it's a diamond that will burn your lips . . . The solution is easy enough: marry me!"

Moura didn't even try to feign surprise.

She raised her glass up to her eyes and looked at her wooer through the bubbles. She offered him a mysterious, sphinxlike smile.

Around them, the bourgeoisie who had just risen to power were thronging at Danyjazz, a former theater that had served as headquarters for Cromie and the British marines.

Unlike the other couples, Moura and her beau had chosen to sit not at a table in one of the boxes or in front of the orchestra, but on two stools at the bar. The din forced them to sit shoulder-to-shoulder just to hear each other.

The old waterproof and the men's watch were long gone. Tonight, she was wearing a drop-waist dress dotted with jet-black tears. A headband decorated with a plume covered her forehead. And, whether she was being chic or cliché, she had a cigarette holder in her gloved hands.

She had sold the few jewels that Micky had managed to save from her box in Yendel to update her wardrobe. And even though she refused to cut her hair and wasn't wearing pearls on a string, as was the style, she still embodied the fashionable woman. As for her companion, in a tux and bow tie, he was identical in every way to the men who frequented the Tallinn cabarets. The only detail setting them apart from the others were several open carafes of vodka, as well as a magnum lolling in a bucket of ice.

Moura had been careful not to describe the extent of her excesses to Gorky. Her stay in Tallinn had become a bacchanalia. She could hold her alcohol, yes, and she didn't stop at champagne. She now added liqueurs to the mix and downed dozens of those trendy cocktails.

She had kept silent, as well, about the men who accompanied her to these bars. She certainly tried to protect her reputation by taking care not to bring them back to the boarding house, but even so, she was at risk of setting tongues wagging.

How old was Baron Nikolai Rotger von Budberg-Bönningshausen? she wondered, examining him through the prism of her crystal flute. Far younger than her usual suitors. Younger than she was, in any case. Twenty-five years old, even though he was bald? His scalp was completely bare, and his physique was unremarkable: rather small and unsteady. But he was spirited, and in the end not as boring and conventional as most of the former officers of his milieu, who hadn't been able to find a place in the new republic.

She had known him for a long while. Several marriages connected the Benckendorffs to the Budberg family.

Nikolai, who everyone called Lai, had been born on the family estate of Vanamõisa, the sixth and youngest child of Otto Bernhard von Budberg-Bönningshausen, a marshal of the Baltic nobility. A far older and far more powerful lineage than the Estonian branch of the Benckendorffs. On the walls of the Tallinn cathedral, his coat of arms, with its great helms, its crowns, its feathers, and its flags, was three times bigger than Djon's escutcheon.

Lai had fought as a lieutenant in the tsar's cavalry before being deported by the Bolsheviks to the Krasnoyarsk work camp in 1918.

Having been repatriated after the signing of the armistice, he had set out again, this time in the cavalry of the Baltic regiment that was fighting the Red Army for its country's independence. In January 1919, he had been sidelined close to the Kautjala estate. With a serious wound to the shoulder, he had been taken in for several days by Djon, before returning to service and continuing the crusade until victory in 1920.

Even though he was courageous, he was apparently in disgrace. He was known as a lady's man, drowning in debt, an alcoholic, and a gambler, who was quick to take offense. He courted scandal, sneering at the pro-German society he belonged to. He kept fighting duel after duel, doing his best, in his own words, to rid the aristocracy of its most reactionary offspring.

Moura had welcomed him at Yendel in the past. The young Lai's lack of discipline, his impertinence, his coarseness—his despair, perhaps?—had made her smile at the time. But she'd never been interested in him.

Now, squeezed in next to him in the darkness of Danyjazz, she was listening to him.

He repeated his proposal:

"Marry me! What do you have to lose?"

"So you're offering me a deal, Lai. I'm all ears. What are the terms?"

"They're simple enough. Some money."

"Oh, surely you're joking?"

"As surely as I can see you at this bar, I can tell that you're sitting on a heap of gold."

She mimed getting up to inspect the velvet upholstery. "That's good news, then!"

"Your hoard goes by the name of Maxim Gorky, and it's a sizable one."

She changed her tone and said icily:

"Your vulgarity is equaled only by your stupidity, Baron von Budberg."

"Your intelligence is equaled only by your hypocrisy, Mrs. Benckendorff. Let's be frank: I need you to pay my debts and help me move out."

"Your debts?" She looked at the magnum of champagne. "From what I've heard, they've already cost your father the little the government left him."

"I'm simply counting on you to take care of the rest."

"You know quite well that I don't have any money."

"But you have something else. You know the entire country. All the elites in Germany, and probably all of Europe."

"You're dating yourself! The war decimated my friends."

"Your close friendship with Gorky will open new doors for you."

"That's what you think."

"I'm just saying that by marrying me, you'll be able to get a nationality and a passport. Become my wife, and I'll take you to Berlin."

Moura set down her glass and looked him in the eye. "Are you in love with me, Lai?" she asked mockingly.

"It's to my regret that I must tell you the truth: not one bit! And yet, God knows I love women of the demimonde. But you aren't at all light enough or silly enough to be my type. We can, however, be very good friends. Let's get married."

"I'm still not sure I understand how I can be of help to you."

"What does it matter? I'll give you my name, my title, and the possibility of traveling."

"I understand quite well what worth it has for me, Baron . . . But what about for you?"

"Think a bit longer and you'll see."

◈

She didn't want to think about this Nikolai Budberg. It was one thing to flirt with him and tell him everything she had had to endure while drinking. It was quite another to give the least bit of weight to his drunken suggestions.

The latest newspapers were trumpeting Gorky's arrival in Helsinki on August 23. She absolutely needed to find a way to see him in Finland.

The trip over the sea from Estonia would only take a few hours. But how could she get out of the country without any papers? The only person who could give her the right documentation was the commercial representative of Bolshevik Russia in Tallinn, a certain Georgy Solomon. She had known him back on Kronverksky Prospect and had no doubt he would help her see Gorky again. The writer was still a key figure for Lenin's propaganda efforts. The Party wouldn't refuse to make his life easier by allowing his "secretary" to join him.

The problem, however, was that Solomon's support would give the Benckendorffs the proof they needed of Moura's collusion with the Communists. And grist for the Ehrengericht mill that they were already setting up.

But she had no choice!

She went to find Solomon.

Once he had furnished her with the necessary papers, she set off on the ferry for Helsinki.

For two days, Moura ran across town. She checked every hotel. But to no avail. Gorky was nowhere to be found in Finland. If he had indeed reached the border, he had had to backtrack there. Contrary to the rumors, he had gone back to Petrograd to take care of himself, and he wasn't talking about leaving anymore.

Had he changed his mind in the end? Pulled back once he'd seen the border? Decided not to cut himself off from Russia?

Moura was suddenly seized with panic.

By leaving Estonia without succeeding in joining Gorky, she was running a great risk. Who knew if the authorities would use her escapade as a way to get rid of her and forbid her from returning to her children?

She rushed to catch the ferry back to Tallinn.

This time, luck was on her side. Solomon's papers allowed her to return without any trouble.

❖

A week later, Max—Gorky's son, whom the Bolshevik minister of foreign affairs had named diplomatic courier to Germany—wrote to his father that Tyotka had come to welcome Duca to Helsinki and had gone looking for him everywhere. Matters in her family weren't going well. And so Max had invited her to come to Berlin, and she had told him she would.

❖

The failure of Moura's escapade, however, would turn out to have serious consequences for her. Her trip to Finland only reinforced the international intelligence services' suspicions that the Benckendorff spy was protected by the highest Communist authorities. And on a personal level, the newspapers she had been able to look through during her failed trip had informed her of crushing news.

Her friend at World Literature, her admirer, the wonderful poet Alexander Blok, had died at forty years old, driven to despair by the Bolsheviks' persecutions.

Another great poet by the name of Gumilyov, whom she had known well and loved dearly, had been arrested in July by the Petrograd Cheka. Gorky had gone in person to Moscow, to Lenin's office, to ask for his pardon. He had gotten it. But as he was coming back to announce the amnesty, Zinoviev had rushed to have Gumilyov executed.

And since then, Gorky had been coughing up blood.

And the list of catastrophes didn't stop there.

In a letter dated July 13, which awaited her upon her return and confirmed the news she had read in Finland, Alexey Maximovich wrote:

> *Famine is widespread across Russia. I'm writing to you . . . to ask you to help as much as you can to collect donations [in Europe] and to help me in transferring them as quickly as possible into Russia. . . . Go and do it! There's no need to tell you how to work. You know better than anyone else how.*
>
> *I'm planning to go abroad in August to campaign on behalf of all the people dying of hunger. There are nearly twenty-five million of them. Almost six million of them have already been displaced, abandoned their villages, and gone off somewhere. . . . Cholera and dysentery are rampant. . . . We're making stews out of old leather, drinking the broth, and making gelatin out of animal hooves. . . . We're killing all the animals because there's nothing to feed them with . . . The children—the children are dying by the thousands.*

Gorky's anguish was growing so extreme that they now feared for his health. His state worsened with each passing day. The doctors refused to let him travel.

What use was it for him to say that he would come *as soon as possible*? God alone knew when he might be able to leave!

And if the horrors of history weren't enough, there was another detail that Gorky had taken care not to mention: he was again in love with the mistress who had preceded Moura in his affections. His bed on Kronverksky Prospect was now being shared with his former lover, the wife of one of his best friends: Varvara Tikhonova, whom Moura herself had once unseated.

◈

She was jealous.

Moura had already become well acquainted with the torments of that emotion in learning of the birth of Lockhart's little boy in London. But nothing in her relationship with Gorky had prepared her for such torture.

She wasn't naive; she knew he needed a companion. But she hadn't imagined that she could be replaced so quickly.

Of course, of course, Tikhonova had the requisite qualities: sweetness, youth, even beauty. But she didn't have what truly mattered. She didn't have what, in Moura's eyes, was at the heart of her own relationship with Gorky: literary taste, intellectual camaraderie, sentimental complicity. These affinities, she had presumed, were necessary for him as much as for her. The thousand links that she believed had been decisively tied.

Consumed by fear, she considered just what the appearance of a rival meant for her and her future. What place could she claim beside the writer if another woman accompanied him to Germany?

Not only had he invited Tikhonova to follow him to Berlin, but he had urged her children to come along. Tikhonova had a son and daughter.

Like her.

The threat was even greater because Gorky was working to obtain papers for Tikhonova by calling her his secretary.

Gorky's abandonment, in point of fact, put her own survival at serious risk.

As was her habit, Moura didn't let any of this show. No questions, no reproaches, not even a glancing mention. She was absolutely silent on the sufferings that such a renunciation had brought upon her.

Do you want, Alexey Maximovich, for me to reflect on this trip abroad that terrifies you? But that's all I'm doing! And believe me, I'm not doing so only for selfish reasons.

This, then, is what I would advise: you should go. Yes, of course, "abroad" is a terrible place. But it's worst for those with a storm in their hearts, like myself.

You, however, have nothing to fear. Nothing could separate you from Russia.

You speak so lovingly about those among us who are dying of hunger. You ask me so forcefully to alert Wells and all my acquaintances in Europe, to go to Berlin and London to collect funds to fight the famine that's raging around us. I will go, of course. I will do what you ask.

But you must come, because without you I am powerless! Come . . .

She was in a rush to send off this appeal. Would it reach the one it was meant for? Their correspondence took weeks to cross the few hundred miles separating the two countries, and she couldn't discount the possibility that their letters were being opened and read by the police. And that on both sides of the border, the intelligence services were keeping some for themselves.

❖

She needed to buy herself time. She needed to rejoin society. She needed to accept the pariah Baron Budberg's offer: what did she have to lose? She could always change her mind once she had seen Gorky and learned his plans. For now, without his support, she needed to survive.

She didn't stay in Tallinn any longer; she headed back to the house on the shores of the lake.

❖

"Don't make that face, Micky. Baron Budberg isn't the monster you think he is."

The governess didn't deign to reply. She was in a bad mood. Her gaze was gloomy. Her lips were pursed. She pretended to be focused on methodically putting the laundry in piles. But she couldn't hide the violence of her gestures as she hit the planks of the armoire.

The news of Marydear's engagement to Baron Budberg outraged her. She couldn't get over it. She refused to discuss even the possibility of such a marriage.

Standing behind her, Moura tried to justify herself.

"Do you really think he's that disagreeable?"

Micky couldn't stay quiet any longer. "When you've been the wife of a man like Mr. von Benckendorff, you don't commit to that sort of man after."

Moura frowned.

"You are judging him—you're all judging him—by his appearance. Lai is not who you think he is."

Micky shrugged. Moura insisted:

"He's a perfectly modest man. Oh, do you want me to say it? He's an honorable man!"

"I won't be told such balderdash!"

"He is trying to make my life easier and to resolve my situation. He is doing so calmly, in his own way."

"The children deserve a better kind of father than that drunken gambler!"

"Who says he'll be acting as their father? That's not the case here!"

"Oh? And what is the case, then?"

"It's the case of a brave young man who likes me and needs me."

"And why in heaven would he need you?"

"To save him from his demons."

"That's a heavy burden!"

"Micky, listen to me: Baron Budberg's cynicism is just a pose. He's just as lonely, just as sad, just as lost as I am."

That line, the first time that Marydear had truly shared how she was feeling, assuaged the governess's fury momentarily.

She herself had never stopped sensing Mary's unease at Kallijärv. She knew she was struggling to stay afloat, that she kept her true feelings to herself, that she was trying to fool everyone. But that her bravado was disguising a void. And that she was wavering.

Micky, however, did not lay down her weapons just yet.

"*Sad?* Baron Budberg? *Lonely? Lost?* That's not what they're saying in the gambling dens."

"You know just as well as anyone else that what people say isn't always what's true. Lai can claim that he wants to marry me out of self-interest all he likes, but he's trying to protect me."

"And what about you?"

"It takes two to tango. He wants to defend me from the others. And I want to defend him from himself. And in this desert all around me, he's the only oasis I have left."

Micky was furious. "What about your children? Do you think about them even once in a while?"

"They can only benefit from a marriage that will allow me to take all of you to Berlin."

"Paul and Tania hate him!"

"They don't know him. And besides, Micky, I don't have a choice. It's only through marrying an Estonian that I'm able to stay here longer. This man is offering me a bulwark."

"A bulwark? He'll be your downfall. He's going to gamble away everything. He's going to drink away everything."

"So what if he does? I have nothing."

"Just like him. And I do wonder what it is he's hoping for."

"A bit of kindness, probably."

"If I were you, I wouldn't bet on that."

"And what should I bet on, then? Do you have other prospects for the future up your sleeve?"

"You should prepare your defense for the Ehrengericht. So you can walk out of there with your head held high."

"If you have nothing better to suggest, then this conversation is over."

Moura couldn't help slamming the door shut behind her.

On the landing, she had to catch her breath.

She had been telling the truth when she said that Baron von Budberg was behaving chivalrously toward her. Her humiliations had been multiplying. And he had pulled off his gloves three times, challenging to duels the officers of his club who had insulted the honor of Marie von Benckendorff. Wives were no longer the only ones to cast aspersions upon her morality. Even the men who had formerly been her admirers now publicly called her a spy.

Luckily, Lai's reputation as a killer preceded him. And his new status as a fiancé permitted him to take offense. Which meant he could choose the weapon. He wasn't much to look at, but he had a steady eye and hands, which made him better with a gun than with a sword.

Up to this point, Lai's duels had ended with apologies from the offenders. No blood had been shed.

And she, in turn, didn't ask anything of him. Especially not to defend her! On the contrary, she tried to keep a distance and only reluctantly accepted his help. But the farther she moved away from him, the more keenly Budberg—through the rules of seduction that she herself had mastered thoroughly—rushed to her aid.

The truth was that the baron's involvement in her affairs ended up compromising her. And bringing them together.

He could present himself as her champion, but she wasn't the least bit charmed by him. And as Micky lectured Moura, she was simply giving words to the feelings that overcame Moura.

In any case, her governess wasn't the only one revolted by the prospect of such a marriage: the two families proved just as hostile. Lai's parents were wholeheartedly against a union with a chekist; the Benckendorffs were against one with a drunkard drowning in debt. Not to mention Paul and Tania, who threatened to run away into the woods if their mother married again.

They could object all they like, Moura thought, but only Budberg could resolve her stateless status, could give her an identity, could extricate her from the threads of this spiderweb she was flailing within. Unless . . .

Unless, with his influence, with his fame in Europe, Gorky could secure a passport for her and take her with him. To Germany. Or elsewhere, to France, to Italy.

He alone had the power to save her from this horrific union!

She had to see him, she had to talk to him. She hoped with her whole heart that he would come to the West.

◈

In the fall of 1921, there were new headlines. The writer's departure was making all the papers: Gorky was leaving Russia.

The papers even gave the details. They wrote that from Petrograd, he would be taking a car to the border. They also said that he was very sick, but that his faithful secretary, Varvara Tikhonova, was caring for him.

This time, the information was correct.

Accompanied by Tikhonova, Gorky came to Finland in mid-October.

Moura rushed to the Soviet commercial attaché. And from Solomon's office, directly to the port of Tallinn.

On October 18, 1921, armed with a second set of papers, she got on the ferry that was raising anchor for Helsinki.

CHAPTER THIRTY-ONE

Gorky versus Budberg

OCTOBER 1921–JANUARY 1922

"Did you find him in Finland? Did you see him this time?"

She did not respond. Lai Budberg asked again:

"Did you talk to him about our plans?"

He had come to pick her up when she returned and had been waiting for her at the end of the gangway as she got off the boat.

Behind her was the gray, unruly Baltic Sea, seeming more sinister and dangerous than ever. Even on the quay, the late October wind was gusting with enough strength that they had difficulty breathing. She shivered. She was frozen to her bones. After such a crossing, seeing a familiar face— even this young baron's clean-shaven face, his bald scalp—gave her a strange feeling of safety. Tallinn could almost feel like a haven.

Budberg, at least, had come to welcome her back. He was wearing his gloves and hat; despite the cold, he took them off to greet her.

His presence was now the only promise she had of any future.

She suddenly felt a blind rage toward the two men she had loved—and still loved. She was angry at Lockhart for having forced her, through his abandonment, to wed this rogue and pleasure seeker. She was angry at Gorky for driving her, through his rejection, to marry this offspring of the society he had rejected, this embodiment of the idle, self-congratulatory aristocracy that she herself had wanted to escape. After such geniuses as those, she had to end up with a man like Budberg!

But this person was fundamentally the only one to show her some degree of devotion and courage.

A self-interested courage, to be sure, but still, weren't they *all* self-interested, her just as much as him?

As she considered this dark silhouette waiting for her, she felt for the first time a surge of recognition and sympathy.

Maybe she really could help this boy conquer his demons of alcohol and gambling? Maybe they could work together to escape their own despair?

She looked down, burying her chin in her collar. Budberg took her by the elbow and led her to the hangar.

He repeated his question:

"Did you tell Gorky that you're planning to marry me?"

She nodded.

"Well?"

She shrugged.

"Well, nothing."

❖

The truth was that the meeting with Alexey Maximovich had amounted to that: nothing. The absolute minimum.

What a sad, disappointing exchange it had been!

Gorky's Finnish friends had booked an entire floor of a family boarding house for him in Munksnäs, a neighborhood on the periphery of Helsinki. This isolation was meant to save him from the fatigue of too many interviews. But to no avail: a crowd of admirers thronged at the famous writer's door.

As for the coterie that comprised his court, it was still impressive. Along with Tikhonova and her children—her daughter Ninochka, eleven years old, bore such a striking resemblance to Gorky that some did wonder if she was his—he was traveling with another couple, accompanied by their three daughters.

The rest of his troupe was waiting for him in Berlin. The actress Maria Andreyeva, his second wife, was already serving as the Soviet commercial representative there, assisted by Pepekryu, her lover. His son Max, who had just gotten married, had been living there with his young wife since the summer. The painter Nightingale was looking for an apartment that would house the other members of "the duchy"—Molecule, the Merchantess, the entire group.

But right now, in October 1921, Gorky's frailty seemed so serious that he had to stay in Finland for a few days before continuing on to a German sanatorium. He was thinner than ever; his lips were pressed together beneath his mustache, and his eyes were reddened from exhaustion and insomnia. He was only able to receive his dear Maria Ignatyevna while lying in bed, his back propped up with cushions so he wouldn't choke as he coughed.

And his thoughts were elsewhere.

Tikhonova, as a good lady of the house, was busy with the samovar: she served the tea amiably, even kindly. But she didn't leave the room . . . It was impossible for Moura to shift the conversation to more personal topics. And Gorky was still distant. She couldn't reach him. He was absorbed by the only subject he cared about: saving the millions of peasants starving back in Russia.

"I've forwarded the Anti-Famine Council's call to the American secretary of commerce, Herbert Hoover. And to the elites in Chicago, New York, London, Berlin, Madrid, Paris, and Prague. But that's not enough! I've asked for the help of the Clarté group, I've written to Anatole France, I've written to Romain Rolland. What about you, Maria Ignatyevna, have you gotten an answer from H. G. Wells? Is he planning to do anything?"

"Mr. Wells has not yet responded, my dear friend. But don't worry: he will act." She smiled. "I've notified all my acquaintances in England. Do you remember Sir George Buchanan, the British ambassador in Saint Petersburg? And his daughter, Meriel, who was one of my closest friends? She's published several books on Russia, and she knows just about everybody in the world of London letters. She will endeavor to make sure your manifesto runs in the *Times*. I've also told her to reach out to your admirer, Mr. Lockhart, the former English consul who you met in Moscow before the war."

"Good, very good. You've always been so kind. So remarkable."

Gorky looked at her feverishly. This woman was the incarnation of intelligence. She took interest in everything! What a miracle she was, a marvel of diligence and generosity. She never asked anything for herself. But she was always ready to help him and those who needed her.

She seemed thinner to him, very elegant in her high-heeled shoes and her fur coat. He liked seeing her that way.

But in some way he couldn't be sure of, she was starting to intimidate him again. He was starting to feel as reserved with her as he used to. This sort of suspiciousness harked back to when they had first met. A fear of sorts in the face of her energy, a guilt in the face of her youth.

To be sure, she seemed more poised, more self-assured than when they had first met at World Literature. She had only become even more impressive.

At the time, he had hoped to win her over. Now, in his deep exhaustion, he couldn't summon up the strength or the desire to charm her.

The truth was that now that the first flush had faded, this reunion had become more and more difficult for both of them. Over the five months that they had been apart, life had set them at a great remove from each other.

"You should get some sleep, my dear friend. You have to be reasonable. You can't imagine how much your health matters to me. How much it does to everyone! If you should die, that would be the end of all those of us suffering in this world who need you."

The conversation was halting. She waited for him to ask her about the new government and the political atmosphere in Estonia. About her material life in Tallinn . . . She waited for him to express some interest in her future. But Gorky seemed completely fixated on the tragedies he had witnessed over the last few months in Russia.

She tried to get his attention by sharing some news about her children, about Kira, Paul, and Tania. Back when they lived on Kronverksky Prospect, he had always been curious about what they were like. But now he was surrounded by other children. And even though he was keenly interested in their education, he now had more urgent worries on his mind.

And she tried to broach the topic of her impending marriage:

"If you can believe it, an Estonian baron wanted to come here to ask you for my hand in marriage. Would you have granted it to him?"

She had taken on that teasing tone they had used so often to whisper secrets to each other. But Gorky wasn't in a state of mind to follow her down this path. She kept on joking:

"What would you have told him?"

He furrowed his brow and mumbled, "If a baron is rich enough and adventurous enough to marry you, tell him to make a hundred-thousand-ruble donation to the Anti-Famine Council!"

She left him, heartsick with disappointment. Once she was back in her own hotel at the other end of the city, she broke down in tears on her bed. She wrote in the night:

Dear Alexey Maximovich,

I've grown so accustomed to sharing my thoughts with you in writing during our separation that I'm going to keep doing so tonight. Our meeting affected me so much that I seem to have lost all my resources. I felt stupid in front of you, unable to talk to you. You can't imagine just how much seeing you, my dear, was magical for me. And hard, as well. During our year together on Kronverksky Prospect, I grew accustomed to being close with you. Close on all fronts. And so the gap that still remains frustrates me. Do you think I'm exaggerating? That I'm bitter in my love for you?

Don't worry. Seeing you was a wonderful delight for me. I saw your dear face and I told myself that I would never leave you, no matter what. Because there's something priceless about our relationship.

For four days straight, she went to see him in Munksnäs. She lavished her love upon him, listening to everything he might have to say and doting upon him endlessly.

Through her attentiveness, she was able to regain some modicum of the influence she'd once had. She became indispensable to him again. Even irreplaceable, he said, as much on a practical level as an intellectual one.

He suggested that she keep translating his correspondence. He went so far as to say that she should take care of the publication of his books abroad. Why not? She could negotiate his contracts with the publishers. Serve as his literary agent, because she spoke so many languages.

He made her promise to answer his call immediately once he had settled in Berlin.

But he did not give her any way to carry out the least of his projects. No help, no offer, no solution for joining him. Nor even a way to follow him to Germany.

She had thrown him all the lifelines she could, but he refused to grab any of them and reel her in.

The papers Solomon had provided her were nearing their expiration date. It was impossible for her to wait any longer. It was impossible for her to stay in Finland until Gorky left on October 29. She had to go back to Tallinn.

❖

Baron Budberg met her on the quay as she got off the boat.

❖

"You never answered me . . . What did your illustrious protector say about our marriage?"

"I've told you, Lai: nothing."

"But what does he think?"

"What do you want him to think? He's counting on me to come when he calls me."

"When he calls *us*. Surely he's imagining that you'll travel with your husband."

"I'm not sure he took that prospect seriously. I'm also not sure that he would get along with you."

"Don't be silly. I can be very amiable. As amiable as you, when it comes to my survival . . . And just like you, I'm remarkably good at landing on my feet."

"Let's be honest: I can't reciprocate anything you give me, you know that. I can't on any front, not with feelings or money. What do you want from me?"

"You're reminding me of that refrain the Gypsy singers always came back to before the war: *My heart is cold and my purse is empty* . . . All the more reason, my dear, for me to open them both up."

"Oh, enough of your stupid jokes. In exchange for your name, your title, your hand in marriage, what do you want?"

"For Gorky to free you of a burdensome husband and pay for that husband's fare to South America."

"That's enough, Lai!"

"I'm not joking. Book me a first-class cabin on one of the nicest Cunard Line ships. If the price is trifling for Gorky, or for one of your other friends who can pay, it should be easy enough: didn't I meet, back at Yendel, a certain Ed Cunard? As soon as you've put me on a boat for Rio, you'll never see me again!"

"Is that all?" The look on her face was incredulous. "A fare to Brazil? You don't want anything else?"

"If I could pay for it myself, I wouldn't be going to the trouble of marrying you."

"But if I marry you, you'll go?"

"I'll go the minute I can."

She asked again:

"Will you go the very second I've bought your ticket?"

"Oh, don't be so plain in your impatience, my dear. And do let your illustrious protector know about the marriage that will allow you to leave Estonia with a passport so you can work for him in Germany."

❖

Gorky had barely reached Berlin before writing to the Merchantess, who was supposed to join him at Christmas:

In Finland, I saw Maria Ignatyevna, who was wearing sturdy boots and a warm fur coat. . . . She wants to marry some baron, but we're protesting vociferously. Let the baron pick himself another fantasy!

This one is ours!

◈

On November 13, 1921, almost exactly a decade after her first wedding, Maria Zakrevskaya, the widow of Djon Benckendorff, married Baron Nikolai Rotger von Budberg-Bönningshausen in the Alexander Nevsky Cathedral, the cavernous Russian church in Tallinn.

As in Berlin in 1911, the rumble of Gregorian chants filled the choir. And the audience, the witnesses, the family all belonged to the highest nobility. The entire aristocracy had ended up supporting this socially acceptable marriage. In terms of birth, education, interests, fortune—and even lack of fortune—the couple was well matched: what more could be wanted for two people about to be joined in holy matrimony? Only Micky and the children still complained.

The governess, flanked by the three children, sat determinedly in the back row, as far as possible from the open doors of the iconostasis, from the patriarch covered in his golden chasuble, and from the Orthodox priests swinging their thuribles back and forth.

Micky had a lump in her throat as she compared the gnome in a black tailcoat holding Marydear's hand to the tall silhouette of Djon, who even she had deemed worthy of her little girl.

She could see Mary at eighteen again, her chin raised, her back straight, beautiful, her pride visible beneath her lace veil.

Now she wore a light outfit, but no veil or train. Just a modest ecru mantilla, a plain, straight skirt that came down to her calves, and a fitted jacket. Apparently in traveling clothes, it seemed she was practically ready to leave, despite the golden coronet that the priest had just blessed and set upon her head.

As Micky saw her drink the wine from the chalice, walk three times around the altar, kiss the cross, honor the icons, and let her husband kiss her in public at the end of the ceremony, she tried to make sense of her face: serious, unyielding, expressing merely a form of concentration.

Mary had always been pious. Was she praying?

The governess had to acknowledge that she seemed collected. Calmer, in any case, than she had been over the summer.

In the face of the last protests against this marriage, she hadn't even slammed the door behind her. She simply shrugged: "Well, this man isn't the one I would have dreamed of. But *c'est la vie!*" She was as calm as always. "*C'est la vie*, Micky, that's life and that's beyond me!"

She seemed to have returned to the fatalism of her younger years.

Whatever happens, happens . . . Micky recalled those words Moura had said in front of her bedroom mirror in Berlin as Micky had readied her for her first wedding night.

Those words still rang true ten years later: *Whatever happens, happens. The deed is done!*

The newlyweds sat next to each other at the center of a long table in the banquet hall facing the Russian church. As was customary, the toasts kept coming and coming. Lai and Moura answered each one gracefully. They might have been physically at odds with each other—she tall, healthy, and powerful; he thin, bald, and prematurely old—but nothing in their behavior hinted at any dissonance. There was even a complicity of sorts between the two.

Uncle Sasha, who was hardly curious about anything—least of all female psychology—wondered whether Baron Budberg was her lover already.

As Moura granted her new husband a waltz, she showed a serene face. On her lips there floated the mysterious Mona Lisa smile that unfailingly seduced every man she met. Had Lai fallen into the trap she had set?

He pulled her close. "Baroness Budberg came into the world this afternoon," he whispered teasingly in her ear. "How is she doing tonight?"

"And how are you, Lai, surviving this ordeal?"

"This farce of a wedding is just giving me a foretaste of the revelries awaiting us next week."

He was telling the truth: the Ehrengericht would hold court in this room, the banquet hall. The same place, the same actors, the same witnesses: the court of honor would be made up of those who would come to pass judgment. On her side would be Pyotr Petrovich Zubov and Ernest Arnold Friedrich Turman. On theirs would be Baron Jesper Ernestovich Stackelberg, along with Alexander Alexandrovich Benckendorff, the dear Uncle Sasha who was tutoring her children. Not to mention the master of ceremonies, the marshal of the Russian nobility: Count Alexey Nikolayevich Ignatyev, who had served in General Yudenich's White Army.

Tonight, the count and the barons were raising their glasses to the health of *the baroness*.

But tomorrow, all of them would be judging her.

She accepted their simulacrum of justice just as she had submitted to the ritual of her marriage, as a gambler wagering her own future.

With each step of the waltz, Moura's gaze met her family's. The Budberg brothers-in-law, the Benckendorff brothers-in-law, each of them in uniform; the sisters-in-law in finery, plumes on their heads and pearls on their necks. Just like before. Everything was *just like before*. The dozens of servers were pouring champagne into the glasses. The children were chasing each other between the tables. Kira and Tania, with massive white bows holding back their hair, were trying to dance with their cousins. Paul had never seemed more lighthearted, more delighted than during this meal. They had all forgotten their grief.

She had no doubt that she had to submit to the Ehrengericht. It was an absurd gesture. But it was necessary.

She had nothing to lose.

If she managed to convince everyone of her innocence, she would be symbolically free of the matter. And if not? The barons' verdict—no matter how unfavorable it might be—wouldn't keep her from leaving the country. As the legitimate wife of an Estonian citizen, she didn't depend on their judgment for her legal existence.

Lai had said as much: Baroness Budberg had come into the world this afternoon.

Armed with her passport—so new that she could still smell the fumes of its adhesive—she could take the train tonight, tomorrow, the day after, meet Anna in Nice, Alla in Paris. Gorky in Berlin. Lockhart in London.

Of course she was running the risk of a moral execution. But that was no worse than being deported to Zinoviev's Russia. And that was all that mattered.

Or so she thought.

❖

A week after the wedding, on November 20, 1921, the French counterintelligence agent wrote the following note to his colleagues in Paris:

> *The Soviet services have a formidable secret agent here in Tallinn: Countess Benckendorff, who, over the last few weeks, has been busy with the Ukrainian organization Kussakov.*
>
> *This Countess Benckendorff is also a member of the Cheka in Petrograd and has just wedded Baron Budberg in Tallinn. The couple is preparing to leave for Poland very soon.*

The agent reiterated this information—which proved to be partly incorrect, but was still unnerving—with a second coded message:

> *The Soviet intelligence service is still working tirelessly to collect more information both about the Estonian military forces . . . and about the activities of anti-Bolshevik organizations in the Baltic countries. The Reds are especially interested in the activities of foreign missions in Tallinn, with emphasis on the Polish and Japanese outfits.*
>
> *Countess Benckendorff, who we already know is a chekist and who is currently living in the vicinity of the capital with her new husband, Baron Budberg, may have told her friends (Count and Countess Manteufel), who have scolded her about the rumors swirling around her, that she was never affiliated with the Cheka—only*

with some chekists—and strictly so that she could provide information about the
Reds to the Germans, who her late first husband, her own mother, and her entire
family supported.

❖

At the end of 1921, the Baltic barons didn't seem to be the only ones interested in the revolutionary activities of the new Baroness Budberg.

❖

In the great hall, seated around the horseshoe-shaped table that had been used for the banquet, were the nine judges who would have to rule on the reputation—whether it was ruined—of their own Marie Zakrevskaya-Benckendorff-Budberg. They had all put on their uniforms again, and they were all solemnly bearing the colors of the regiments in which they had served His Majesty the Tsar during the war. Even Sasha, with a saber at his side, was wearing the white outfit of the cavalry's officers, with its gold epaulets and its gleaming froggings.

Moura stood in front of them, between the three trestles that delimited an arena of sorts. The light of the immense beaded chandelier high above her head underscored the harsh, pale day reflected on her features.

With her hair pulled back into a complex knotted chignon at the back, she had chosen a look that suited the circumstances well. Not too elegant, not too slipshod. A light blouse. A dark skirt. A jacket.

She was tense as she listened to the charges that the esteemed Count Ignatyev was enumerating.

He had been the final governor of Kiev, a fiftysomething military man who Lai said had just founded a secret society of Russian monarchists in Tallinn. The son of Princess Golitsyna, Ignatyev was living in exile here. He lived with some distant relatives of Moura's sister—the Kochubey princesses—and was seen by the republican police of Estonia as an ally of the former Germany.

He was the most esteemed of the anti-Bolshevik prosecutors.

He was standing with a shaved head and a hooked mustache as he intoned his indictment in a loud, clear voice without looking at any paper. Nothing would be consigned to writing. Today's meeting would remain, if not hidden, at least discreet. No trace would be left behind. Apart from the stroke of a pen, a line of blue ink that might cross Baroness Budberg off the Corporation of Estonian Nobles—the Estländiche Ritterschaft.

She had no knowledge of any file of papers about her, because it didn't exist. There had never been any investigation. Much less a lawyer to argue her case for her.

She tried to keep track of each point that Ignatyev accused her of so she could offer a defense.

It was difficult. The list of grievances was so long that she lost count.

"In Russia, between March 1916 and May 1921: member of the Communist Party; pro-revolutionary activities; affiliation with the Cheka; complicity with the regime's torturers; support of Marxist ideology, through the writer Maxim Gorky . . . In Estonia, between May and December 1921: propaganda in favor of Russian expansionist policy; spying on the tsarist aristocracy in Tallinn; in the pay of Soviet intelligence services."

Ignatyev concluded with a question:

"What answer do you have to that?"

She didn't move for a minute. Then:

"Nothing . . . *Everything!*"

She shut her eyes and pulled herself together.

She had freely chosen to undergo this trial; she needed to come out on top.

She had to regain her position in the West, at the top of the social ladder, once and for all.

She had to remember her children. By defending her honor, she would protect them from the humiliations to come. So they wouldn't ever have to be embarrassed by how their mother had behaved. So they could rightfully claim a place in Djon's world. And, in the future, in whatever realm they chose.

It was now or never. Sink or swim. She took the plunge.

"I must specify that, first of all, I have never been a member of the Communist Party. That, second of all, I have never campaigned for the Revolution. That, third of all, I have never belonged to the Cheka. Further to this point, I must remind you that I myself was imprisoned three times in Moscow and Petrograd under horrific conditions: the first time in the Lubyanka prison in September 1918; the second in the Shpalernaya prison in September 1919; and the third in the Gorokhovaya in March 1920."

"And you came out alive, which raises the question of how you did so!"

"How I did so, Count, was through friendship, through compassion, through mutual aid. I owe my salvation to the great actress Maria Andreyeva—"

"One of the pillars of the Party, as much a stooge of Lenin as your employer is!"

"On the subject of my work with the writer Alexey Maximovich Peshkov, known as Maxim Gorky, my presence and my work for him allowed me to save a dozen people. And I take responsibility for that. I take pride in it! Above all, I must underscore that ever since the Revolution, Maxim Gorky has opposed the Bolsheviks in every way possible. I am not making any of this up. All this is public knowledge. As is the fact that he called on Lenin to save the four grand dukes—"

"Who were killed in the Peter and Paul Fortress in January 1919."

"He even protected, he even harbored Prince Gabriel Konstantinovich of Russia, a relative of His Majesty the Tsar, in his own home. He helped the prince to flee. As for me, thanks to him, I was able to save our cousins from numerous arrests, most especially Count Paul Konstantinovich Benckendorff and his wife, Princess Maria Sergeyevna Dolgorukaya. I myself interceded, at risk to my own life, to get Alexander and Vasily Dolgoruky out of the work camps they had been sentenced to. I was not able to succeed. That, too, I must make clear to you! Their mother can tell you how hard I fought to help her save her sons. She is now in Tallinn; ask her! She will tell you how I fed and cared for our relative, Princess Saltykova, for all of the year 1919. She will tell you that the princess held me in high esteem. She will tell you that the princess died of hunger when

I was absent because I was in prison. And that only my imprisonment kept me from helping her in her final moments."

"You've taken advantage of your circle and your relatives to fool everyone: Princess Saltykova, like Princess Dolgorukaya—and I will note here that you did not save her two children from being executed by the Reds—were naive to think that because you belong to the aristocracy, you cannot be a Bolshevik agent. That by virtue of your birth and your education, you cannot serve the Communists. A classic traitor's trick! A classic rat's smoke and mirrors. The reality is that you are spying on your own kind! The reality is that you are denouncing them!"

This horrible accusation left her speechless. Ignatyev kept going:

"And we don't say the word *spying* lightly."

Her voice trembled as she interrupted him:

"A sorry excuse for a spy! The truth is that the intelligence services of every nation have been tracking me closely! You should know that for nearly ten years, the British, the Germans, the Russians, and the Estonians have all been accusing me of working for the others. Who would take the risk at this point of trusting me with any information? I'm not even talking about showing me military maps or revealing plans for battle! Who would be stupid enough—seeing that I'm so untrustworthy and so heavily scrutinized by every country's police—as to entrust any information of any kind to me?"

"That's your cover: a good spy is never where you expect to find one. You seem so visible, you seem so noticeable that nobody would think to suspect you!"

She shrugged. "'Nobody would think to suspect me'? Surely you must be joking. Look for yourself! Ever since I've arrived, you've never stopped being suspicious of me. A policeman has been following me this whole time, and every little thing I've said has been reported—no, *distorted*—by agents from all over the world . . . and even so, I believe my actions speak for themselves. Whether in Russia or elsewhere, I challenge you to find one person, just one, who can contradict what I've told you . . . I've tried to survive without hurting anyone. No more, no less . . . Was it wrong to survive? Clearly."

She paused and caught her breath before concluding:

"I thank you for your attention."

Without giving them any time to ask further questions or to decree a sentence, she left the room.

She walked out of the hall with a determinedly calm pace and unhurriedly shut the door behind her, so unhurriedly that it seemed to take several seconds to close completely.

The truth was that she was shaking all over, and she needed to keep her palm on the handle. On the landing, she lost her composure and nearly fell.

Baron Budberg caught her.

From the balcony that was normally meant for musicians, he had been watching the scene. He was still laughing.

"I take my hat off to you, my dear. You were magnificent: so pure, so innocent, so courageous."

She tried to smile in return. But it was no use. Her distress was too great for her to hide it. She looked down:

"I'm done for, aren't I?"

"Your bit about the old Princess Saltykova *dying of hunger*: that was a masterpiece. Dead? That poor woman dead because you were locked up in the Shpalernaya prison and couldn't feed her? Not to mention the Dolgoruky son executed despite all your battles! Was all that true?"

She nodded.

"Sasha interrogated their mother. He knows the truth."

"Magnificent, I have to say: the little doe has made short work of nine wolves. Listen to them. They're eating each other alive. They have no proof against you, baroness of my heart."

❖

The case was dismissed.

Her honor, just like her reputation, was bruised. But now she could go out on the street and present herself at social gatherings of the aristocracy with her head held high. No stroke of the pen had crossed her name out of the Corporation of Estonian Nobles.

The society ladies might still refuse to greet her, but she knew from experience that they would ultimately follow the social rules that their husbands, their brothers, their sons imposed upon them.

She had been cleared of all accusations.

She had won this round.

But now there was another, more dangerous, more subtle gambit she had to play: telling Gorky about her marriage without losing him forever.

She knew that this union would make him suspicious and likely furious. He wouldn't be able to bear the thought of her being with another man. He wouldn't be able to understand how she, his darling, his muse, could bind herself to such a bland aristocrat, such a mediocre husband.

Despite his kindness, Gorky didn't joke about his obligations as a great writer. He needed his work and his being to be respected. Even if he didn't consider himself a genius, he still saw himself as greater than the run of men. A despot in his own way, a master, a duke who needed to be first in the hearts of his nearest and dearest.

There would be jealousy.

There would be class rivalry.

There would be emotional disappointment.

There would be a bitter fight to win him back.

And the others, Maria Andreyeva, Max, Molecule, the Merchantess, and so on, would struggle just as much to understand . . . They would see it as a betrayal. Their Tyotka had gotten *married* behind their backs? Their Tyotka had *sold out* behind their backs?

And Gorky was supposed to buy her back by using his royalties to offer her husband a ticket that would send him to the end of the world?

No matter how they were told the news, it would be upsetting. A very bitter pill.

An especially difficult pill for a former lover now living with another woman to swallow!

———

She ended up writing to him from Kallijärv on December 16, 1921:

My dear friend.

First of all, believe me that it's a misunderstanding that I wrote to the Nightingale about my wedding before Munksnäs.

I wrote to him and you as soon as it became even remotely possible, and you must believe that between me and you there is only absolute truth. I want to explain everything to you. . . .

My kind, dear friend, Alexey, I've fallen into such a web of complications, where, believe me, even someone much stronger than myself would have lost their bearings

I think that over the year and a half that we lived together, you saw how little so-called public opinion can affect me. . . .

But isn't it odd that there can be circumstances stronger than we are?

When I came here in the summer, I immediately found myself in a nest of conflict that went well beyond me. I talked to you about this a little in Munksnäs. But I haven't told you about all the purely personal insults to me in public places, where I was accused of having committed numerous provocations in Russia.

It is hard to live like this.

I know you want to tell me: you have to take the children and leave.

Duca . . . my children bear the last name Benckendorff. If I had ripped them out of their world to run away from the humiliations I didn't want to confront, would my actions toward them have been fair? I would have been tearing them away from the clan they belonged to by blood. I think I would have been wrong. In any case, I wouldn't have been able to decide on their behalf. I wouldn't have known whether they genuinely wanted to leave.

For me, yes, I did need to flee. But did they?

And so I had to go on living there.

On the one hand, I had to keep my respect and not lose myself in what the people around me were saying of me. Like, for example, criticizing you in the Estonian papers; expressing my horror of Bolshevism during meetings.

And on the other, I had to fight in silence, fight constantly, go on existing despite the insults. I'm not going to go into the details: they're too horrible.

And that was when Budberg came.

He tried in his own way—calmly, quietly—to make my life easier and to resolve my problems. I knew that it was pointless, I asked him to stay out of my life and my affairs. I told him that there was no need to compromise himself for me, that his involvement would obligate me to repay him with something I didn't have. But to no avail.

After three duels, which thankfully ended without any bloodshed, there was a fourth while I was with you in Finland. And in that one, he killed his adversary.

I don't know what else I should explain to you, Alexey. I leave the decision to the God in which I believe . . . And not you, my Joy. Do you remember? I've written that to you before.

When I came to see you in Munksnäs, I hoped that you would force me to abandon everything, to leave with you, to follow you. But you were indecisive, hesitant, preoccupied. In any case, you did not make that decision. And I could not weigh down your already weary heart with my own worries.

Again: don't think for a minute that as you received me at your bedside, I was lying to you! Your previous relationships with women who weren't sincere have made you suspicious of this kind of deceit. My feelings, on the contrary, have never and will never change.

Write to me with your news, write to me, Alexey, I beg of you. And don't presume that when I receive your letters I'll raise a fuss! Don't believe that you'll bring me unhappiness. What could I accuse you of?

Of being indifferent? As if I didn't please you enough?

As if you once said, lying in your bed in your beloved bedroom on Kronverksky Prospect: "I wanted to love you, I tried—but I couldn't"?

No, my dear friend, rancor and accusations and drama aren't worthy of us.

Just know that I can run toward you with all my heartbreak, with the good, with the bad, with all my doubts, with my heart in pieces: what we've shared has remained intact, hasn't it?

My letter must strike you as very disjointed—I'm having so much trouble writing to you.

I'm waiting for your call from Germany, my friend. No matter where, no matter when . . . Know that I will come as soon as I can leave Estonia.

I'm waiting.

◈

The waiting? That was just a figure of speech now. Moura had definitively stopped waiting. Patience was passé for her.

The moral isolation she had experienced, the suspicion old Europe felt toward her, the accusations, the humiliations, the theatrics of the Ehrengericht, the absurdity of her marriage had given her, over the last six months, a full measure of her loneliness.

She now understood that she couldn't depend on anyone. She especially understood that she didn't want to.

This realization hadn't brought about any rupture in her affections, any questioning of her feelings. She wasn't giving up anything, she wasn't abandoning anyone.

She was attached to her children, attached to Micky, attached to Gorky; attached to her sisters, who she dreamed of seeing again; even attached to Budberg, who she wanted to protect. And attached—above all—to Lockhart, who she hoped to be with again.

She was passionately faithful to every love of her life.

Passionately bound.

But she had not been sacrificed. She was not imprisoned. Or even limited.

◈

At the moment that her dear Alexey Maximovich, sitting in a tuberculosis sanatorium deep in the Black Forest, received her reassurance that at the very second she could leave Estonia, she would join him *no matter where, no matter when*, a train from Tallinn came to a stop at the train station in Berlin.

Baroness Budberg stepped down. She was alone. She crossed the platform and got into a taxi that would take her across the German capital she knew so well. The city seemed unrecognizable to her. She was only there for an hour, the time she had to reach the other train station.

But she didn't go to see Gorky.

She got onto a second train and kept going, embarking upon one of her swift escapades that defied time and space. The first of her escapes across Europe.

These journeys across terra incognita would become her trademark: lightning-quick sojourns that she alone knew the reason and purpose for. These were mysterious trips with endpoints that she hid from everyone, systematically lying, without any shame or regret.

"I'm doing what I think best. I'm saying what I feel best. And my heart will stay pure."

❖

Questioned many years later about her dreams that January in 1922, she confessed:

"I had to go to London, I had to *see* London! Whether I found the people I was looking for or not wasn't important. I might be seeing friends from the past there, I might be making new connections there.

"But what mattered, what truly mattered, was the city! I couldn't wait any longer!"

She was twenty-eight years old.

As her husband had said: Baroness Budberg had come into the world. And Baroness Budberg was planning to live on her own terms.

In the half century to come, she lived in such instinctive, such total freedom that she never needed to justify it to a man or take responsibility for it in any way.

She would revel in it in secret, in silence. That was her mantra here: *Never explain, never complain.*

❖

She didn't see Gorky on the way to London. Nor did she see him on the way back.

Evviva la libertà!

After all these years of being closely watched, the idea of coming and going as she wished intoxicated her. As she flipped through the pages of her passport, she felt lightheaded in a way she hadn't since the excitement of her first days at World Literature.

Her passport was her trophy.

Not the Nansen passport, those papers the Swedish had invented for stateless persons, which resulted in questions from the customs officers and suspicion from every police force. It was a stigma for Russian émigrés who had been stripped of their nationality through exile.

No. A real passport. She inhaled the scent of its binding in deep breaths, the odor of its glue, which made her head swim. She ran through the names of her husband, through his titles. She savored her freedom.

She harbored no illusions about her dignity, revealed no snobbishness about her social status: she didn't believe she was owed any respect. Not for a second. That was just window dressing. Just a bluff.

But she knew she was highborn enough not to be deemed a usurper.

It was a ploy, however. A duplicity, all the more brazen because Lai had just been stricken from the Corporation of Estonian Nobles.

Owing to his debts, his duels, and other unsavory matters she was unaware of, the members of the court of honor had invited him to face the Ehrengericht, as well. As he found this whole rigmarole to be a farce, he hadn't presented himself. The result was that on February 7, 1922, three months after the wedding, Nikolai Rotger von Budberg had been judged unworthy of belonging to the aristocracy, excluded from the Ritterschaft.

Irony of ironies: the man Moura owed her position to no longer had any position!

But what did it matter? Who outside of Tallinn cared about the Baltic barons' diktats? In every other European capital, the prestige of having married into the Budberg-Bönningshausen family opened every door to her and guaranteed her autonomy.

As for the rest, her next step? Moura hadn't given it any thought. Should she leave the children in Kallijärv? At first she had thought she would. It was out of the question to make them live under the same roof as Lai: she was in agreement with Micky on that point.

But it was also impossible to take them to Alexey Maximovich while he was struggling with a hundred difficulties, especially his health, which he was trying to restore in Germany's sanatoriums and hotels. At this point, she had no idea where to take them.

She had been so tense since her escape to the West that she couldn't think about the future. Only one thing was certain: her Estonian papers meant she could decide as she went along.

And the old bohemians of Kronverksky Prospect wouldn't be calling her Tyotka but Chubanka: "the woman with soles of wind."

CHAPTER THIRTY-TWO

The Woman with Soles of Wind: "Your Chubanka, Who Loves You"

December 1922–December 1924

Three days in France. Fifteen in Germany. Ten in Estonia. Back to Germany. And after? God only knew where . . . Italy, where the climate might be beneficial to Gorky's health?

At night she kept on dreaming about journeys and trains, as she had when she was young. She saw her future divided up into airtight compartments, her existence fragmented into a thousand small cars.

A thousand lives that light, speed, space, and time had subdivided. Gazes multiplied in the windows of cars, smiles split along the beveled edge of the glass.

A thousand faces. A thousand facets. A thousand possibilities. So many places, so many worlds, so many roles.

And so many women all at once.

In Kallijärv, she was a caregiver, a teacher, a mentor. She shaped her children's intelligence, won over their hearts. She chose what they read, oversaw their homework, decided what they learned, listened to their thoughts. Moura was attentive. Moura was authoritative. Moura was omnipotent.

In Berlin, she was a literary agent, a financial adviser, a representative to European publishing houses for the greatest Russian writer alive. The one in charge of his translations, the negotiator of his contracts, the manager of his author's rights . . . Moura was hardworking. Moura was organized. Moura was deft, worldly, driven.

In the Black Forest, in Sankt Blasien, in Bad Saarow, in Heringsdorf, in Marienbad, and in all the other resort towns where her *dear friend* tried to recover from his tuberculosis, she was the lady of his home. Moura was his nurse. Moura was his governess. Moura was his secretary and his lover.

Tikhonova, her rival, hadn't been able to hold out for long. She was amiable, yes, even touching, but she was incapable of managing the complexities of an international career. Incapable of translating his correspondence, of answering it on a typewriter with a German keyboard. Incapable of choosing hotels in other countries; reserving rooms in other countries; welcoming friends, settling visitors, ensuring the well-being of the small group living abroad. Moura was cosmopolitan. Moura was efficient. Moura was sweet, attentive, reassuring, funny, joyful, brilliant. Moura was the exchange of ideas. Moura was the art of conversation. Moura was the spirit of Russian joy, which she radiated everywhere she went.

In Paris, in Nice, she was the guardian angel of her exiled sisters in a society that had not granted them any space. Moura was worried. Moura was protective. Moura was full of compassion for their pillaged lives. She cared for Alla, who had become an opium addict and was getting divorced for the second time; she was moral support for Anna, her husband, and her children, who were struggling to survive.

And elsewhere? She was the wife of a wreck who spent his days at the casino, drinking away everything she earned and sleeping with everything that moved. Bounced checks, gambling debts, lady friends, political transgressions. Moura was sickened. Moura was contemptuous. Moura was determined to fulfill her end of the bargain by sending her husband to the other end of the world.

But with what money? That was the question. With what money?

She never had any to spare. She always felt ashamed about her finances.

She thought, with some measure of frustration, that if she had just been the spy so many countries' police forces claimed she was, she might have been paid! And even paid well, even paid threefold by the intelligence services of the three nations she was supposed to have served!

But she lived off the fees Gorky paid her, and the translations she did one after another. Taken together, they provided her with a decent income. But it was hardly enough to pay for the people who depended on her work: Budberg, Kira, Tania, Paul, Micky, Alla, Anna . . . and Moura herself.

The truth was that this lack of means drove many of her decisions.

This lack of a fortune explained her decision to let the children grow up under Micky's watchful eye in Estonia: the result of endless calculations and sad assessments. The cost of life in Berlin ruled out the prospect of sending her children to good boarding schools. The schools in Rakvere, the town adjoining the Yendel estate, were considered the best in the country: they would suffice for everything up to secondary education.

This lack of money also went a long way in explaining her need to earn her bread elsewhere, and her practice of never playing all her cards at once on the casino table of her future.

"There's so much to do when you're as poor as you are!" Lai joked. "'Don't abandon anyone. Don't give up anything.' What an agenda for an émigrée who's broke. My dear, you really are a Slav to the core!"

Slumped across the bed of the studio they shared on the Zimmerstrasse in Berlin, the baron watched with his arms crossed behind his head as she packed her bags.

He knew this tune all too well: every Christmas, every Easter, every August she would go back to Kallijärv. She would put the bottle of Guerlain Jicky cologne for Micky in her bag. Silk stockings she had brought back from Paris for her sisters-in-law, colored pencils for her children, a collection of postcards, stamps, a lace slip, a little white outfit for Kira . . . Even a phonograph in a box, the cutting edge of modernity.

Lai knew quite well how "Moura the Magnificent" looked to them down there when she stepped onto the empty platform of the Kallijärv train station with all her suitcases. She had a gift, several gifts, for each of them: she didn't forget even the cook or the farmhand. She was so determined to please everyone.

He also knew how much trouble they would go to in welcoming her. In showering her with affection. In proving their love for her.

Micky would have *her* room, the little room at the end of the hallway, tidied up so it was beautiful again. The oil lamp and copper candlesticks would have been polished, the icons and the books would have been brought out of the cabinet . . . Micky would have a sink, ewer, and portable bidet set up for a personal washroom, where the napkins exuded an aroma of lavender. She would also have had the round table brought into the garden and the veranda's chairs placed in the shadow of the huge pine, Marydear's favorite tree, for her conversations with visitors.

The children, excited by the general frenzy, by their governess's raptures, by the fury of Aunt Cossé, Aunt Zoria, and the other aunts, would be wild with joy at the thought of seeing their mother again. They would draw beautiful pictures for her, compose sweet poems for her, and gather stunning flowers for her.

And they would cry at the end of her stay a week or a month later, once she left them to go back into the world again.

She, however, did not cry. But her heart was torn, her gaze was despairing, and her voice was somber as she blessed them, drawing a cross on their foreheads. Then she made them sit in a circle around her, shut their eyes, and take a minute of silence to wish her luck on her travels.

As they sobbed again, she got into the carriage. The farmer would take her back to the station in the moonlight.

Standing on the platform with her empty suitcases, she would catch the night train headed south.

"Oh, the staging of your arrival," Lai snickered. "And then your pathetic departure! What emotional acrobatics . . . You really do have an art for manipulation. No matter how fatalistic and stoic you are, life just isn't worth living without some drama. So much emotion! So much theatricality! So much romance! It really was you that Dostoyevsky was talking about in *The Idiot* when he described the quintessential Russian woman! Your friend the British consul must have said as much to you."

For Baron Budberg, irony was a favored weapon. His sarcasm, which had amused Moura in Tallinn, wore her out in Berlin. He never stopped snickering. His black humor swallowed up all conversation.

"What would you know about anything the British consul might have said, Lai?"

"The two of you barely knew each other . . . Just enough that he knew what a hornet's nest it would be to get close to you. And just enough for him to backtrack quickly . . . Did you see Mr. Lockhart again when you went to London?"

"As far as I can tell, he doesn't live there anymore."

"Did he answer your letters?"

"Why do you care?"

"Because I care deeply about Mr. Gorky's honor: cuckolds are never mild mannered. I don't want you to indispose him to my journey to Brazil by arousing his anger . . . Were you at least able to reassure him, to give him some news about Mr. Wells? You were hoping for his help in collecting funds for the victims of the famine . . . So did you see him in London?"

"H. G. Wells wasn't there."

"He wasn't, either? Oh, to hell with it! What a disappointment all this is. What about Cunard? Did you see Ed Cunard?"

"I saw him."

"Did he agree to grant you a reduction on the cost of a trip to Rio? I must remind you that you are obliged to put me on one of his liners. I must also remind you that I have been waiting two years now to take this trip! For the last two years you've been hopping all over the world without me. Just between us, my dear, you're wearing me out! You've got so much enthusiasm! So much energy!"

"I'm doing what I can, Lai. I have children. I have sisters. I have friends. And I have a husband who's gambling away my money!"

"That, my dear, is your problem. As well as Mr. Gorky's."

"Oh, you're drunk! Go get undressed and go to sleep."

"Without you? Of course not! Aren't you my woman with soles of wind? My beloved Chubanka, who I can screw whenever I like until she's paid me back for the name and the title she bought from me?"

"These vulgarities are beneath us, Lai, beneath you and beneath me."

She wasn't so naive as to think that he hadn't loved her, or at least desired her . . . Wanted her, in any case. Coveted her, to the point of finding a pretext in her personal interest—in their common interest—to marry her and possess her.

And he had been claiming all the marital rights of a husband. She had granted him that. And even though their nights together were generally a failure, she had steadfastly maintained the fiction of a happy union for a few months.

At heart, in her heart of hearts, she still considered him "a brave boy," exactly the character she had described to Micky much earlier. Lost, yes, and so weak! Unable to live upright, without any support.

He had clearly believed she could be that: a support he could lean on. The support that would make it possible for him to escape drunkenness, gambling, debauchery, all his disorders and demons.

She, too, had believed that, in a vague and confused way. As she had believed that helping Lai, saving Lai, could give her a reason to live. He had come into her life just when Lockhart and Gorky, the men she had loved to the point of devotion, had abandoned her. And so she had attached herself to him in hopes of being useful to a man.

But how could she help someone or save someone she didn't love?

Between indulgences and insults, their relationship had become so unclear that Lai himself couldn't bear it anymore. He could tell that she felt only pity for him now. At best, a kind of compassion. But no real tenderness or sympathy. And Moura's false kindness to him, her sangfroid around his excesses, ended up driving him crazy.

This disappointment had been followed by fury and a wish for revenge. He tried to cast scorn upon her, to attack her in the same way she had him. He was always drunk, and each day he grew cruder, more unwilling to respect their agreement.

Instead of the quid pro quo of a marriage of convenience, their relationship turned into a drama.

"Want me to tell you something, sweetie?"

"No."

"I'm going to tell you anyway . . . Of all the whores I've been with, you're the most dishonest, the most deceptive, the most untruthful of all . . . In other words, you're the most professional one!"

She shrugged. She wouldn't let herself be baited. She was going to ignore the battle he was trying to start. She hated these scenes. She buckled her suitcase and left the room.

This was exhausting!

How could she handle such a drunkard's despair? And how could she get rid of him?

She had tried to save up, but what she earned was barely enough to take care of Lai. As the months passed, it proved impossible to pull together the money she needed.

As for begging Alexey Maximovich for the money to buy a ticket, that would be just as impossible.

Bringing her husband to Berlin with her had upset Gorky enough that she couldn't risk exasperating him again.

Maybe later.

But time wasn't on her side. Lai grew more frustrated, more bitter, more choosy with each day. The cost of his passage was no longer enough. Now he wanted her to pay him a pension. He declared that he wouldn't leave for Brazil until she had signed legal papers to that effect. He would be paid for life.

Lai's extortions were doubled now with threats of getting himself arrested for illicit political activity and gambling debts.

Baron Budberg in prison? That would be a new stain on the reputation, the name, the title, the respectability that Moura had bought at such a steep price, as he took great pleasure in reminding her. A ruination that she couldn't allow! She herself was being monitored so closely by the German police that she couldn't risk any scandal in Weimar Republic Berlin.

She had to get Lai out of Europe. And send him far away.

She had to find a solution. And fast.

He was intuitive enough to realize the importance of her British network. Moura's friendships, the society connections from her aristocratic years, were now the only relationships she had with people who were sufficiently established, powerful, and wealthy to secure him a berth on a British ship.

During a quick trip to London, she had indeed dined with Ed Cunard in the sumptuous rooms of the Savoy Hotel. It had been a wonder, a pleasure for them both . . . To see darling Ed, who she had known from the Saltykov palace during the war, who she had welcomed at her mother's on the Fontanka embankment, at her place on Shpalernaya Street, and at her husband's estate at Yendel . . . What warm memories she had!

They had tenderly recalled their friends who were now gone, heroic Cromie, Garstino with his sensitive poems . . . What tragedies they had suffered!

She had also shared—in another tone, in a more lighthearted way— several bottles of champagne with Victor Cunard, Ed's brother, and their cousin Nancy, the heiress to the Cunard Line.

And she had dined with Lyuba Hicks in a Russian cabaret in Chelsea: *her dear Lyuba*, Hickie's mistress, hurriedly wed just as he was leaving for England . . . Moscow. October 1918 . . . *My God!* It hadn't been years. It had been a century.

The Hicks couple was now assigned to Vienna, running the Austrian office of the Cunard Line.

The truth was that the two women had barely discussed the cost of cabins on the liners headed to Rio. They had been too busy talking about the adventures of their lives.

"What about Lockhart?" Moura had finally, cautiously asked.

"You're not going to believe me: he's turned into a zealot and a banker!"

Lyuba had burst out laughing. Her blue eyes gleamed in amusement. She continued:

"He's just become Catholic, and he's working for the Anglo-Czech bank in Prague. But at heart he's still the same man. His wife and his son are living in London while he's chasing floozies and spending a fortune in Gypsy nightclubs."

❖

Lockhart wrote in his memoirs:

It was at this moment—on July 29, 1924, to be precise—that I was rung up on the telephone from Vienna. Will Hicks, who had been my assistant in Russia and who was now head of the Cunard office in Vienna, was at the other end. We exchanged one or two rather pointless remarks. Then, just as I was beginning to wonder why he was wasting his money on a long-distance call, he broke off with a sudden "there's some one here who wants to speak to you" and passed the receiver to some one else.

It was Moura. Her voice sounded as if it came from another world. It was slow and musical and very controlled. She had escaped from Russia. She was in Vienna, staying with the Hickses. . . .

Now after a separation of six years I was speaking with her again—and on an accursed telephone. "Let me speak to Hickie," I stammered at last. Quickly I shot my questions at him. "May I come in for the week-end? Can you put me up?"

When everything was arranged, I walked out of the bank and went home in a stupor of uncertainty. . . .

The next night I left for Vienna, my mind still not made up. I arrived at 6:30 and went straight to Mass at St. Stephen's. After Mass I walked to my hotel. I was to meet Hickie at his office at eleven. I did not know if Moura was to be there or not. We were to go out to Hickie's villa in the country for the week-end. I sat in the hotel, drank my morning coffee, smoked a chain of cigarettes, and tried to read a newspaper. At half-past ten, I began to walk slowly down the Kaertnerstrasse. The sky was cloudless, and the sun beat down fiercely on the pavement, turning the asphalt into a soft putty. I looked into the shop-windows to pass the time. Then, as the clock struck eleven, I turned into the Graben, where above a large bookshop the Cunard Company had its office on the first floor.

Moura was standing at the foot of the steps. She was alone. She looked older. Her face was more serious, and she had a few grey hairs. She was not dressed as in the old days, but she had not changed. The change was in me—and not for the better. In that moment, I admired her above all other women. Her mind, her genius, her control were wonderful. We walked up the stairs to the office where Hickie and his wife were waiting for us.

"Well," said Moura, "here we are." It was just like old times.

We collected our suitcases and took the little electric railway out to Hinter-brühl, which lies in the beautiful Brühlertal, flanked with rugged rocks and hills and pine-forests, and bedecked with vineyards and ruined castles, about twelve miles to the South of Vienna. We all talked at once and laughed at every word. Yet it was rather a nervous laughter. Hickie, good, gentle, and very English, was, I knew, a little uneasy. As we were leaving the office, he had mumbled something about being careful and I knew exactly what he had meant.

Liuba Hicks led the conversation, talked very quickly, and jumped from subject to subject, recalling episodes from the revolution and picnics in the country and games of rounders . . . Moura was the only person who seemed completely self-possessed. For myself I was tongue-tied with that dread of anticipation, which is so much worse than the actual ordeal. I knew—we all knew—that this thing had to be talked out, and after luncheon Liuba and Hickie left us alone, and Moura and I walked out to the hills behind the villa.

❖

She could feel her heart beating so hard that she was afraid Lockhart might see it pounding beneath her blouse. It wasn't because of the steep path rising up the hill, or the sun at its apex beating down. The truth was that all her nerves were on edge, her very soul was on edge.

She suspected that he had no idea what this walk with him meant to her, the mere act of walking together. He was leagues away from any idea of the tension she had been suffering since that morning, since the night before, since the very second she had learned she might see him again.

She took off her hat and held it close to her left side, against her stomach, to hide her anxiety.

He was focused on the upward climb. The heat was sweltering. He hated that she was seeing him like this, panting as they pushed onward. His shirt was soaked, his forehead was dripping, and his hair was plastered to his scalp. He knew he had put on some weight and that he was no longer the athlete he had been.

But it wasn't such a serious matter. He was still alluring. He still charmed ladies and dogs and cats and everything else that moved. He was even enjoying a rather spectacular affair, an ongoing tryst back in London with the wife of an English lord. He had converted to Catholicism out of love for her. A papist lady who would never get divorced.

Despite what she had been through, Moura still seemed to be in better shape than him.

"Go on ahead, if you like."

She outpaced him easily. She was wearing a calf-length white canvas skirt. He could see her legs, and especially her ankles, which he had always considered well turned.

But he didn't lust after her.

It wasn't that the weather was too hot for this kind of passion. The truth was that the weight of his guilt had stolen away all his fervor. The prospect of a scene, of grief and judgment that would inevitably come into play, filled him with apprehension. And there was another matter: Hicks's suspicions about Moura's role in their arrest by the Cheka.

Hickie was, of course, less certain about the matter than General Knox, who told everyone in London about "the Benckendorff" having been "planted" there by the Bolsheviks from the very outset. And that she had been the one to inform Yakov Peters in September 1918 about the British agents' designs to bring down the regime. Even if Hickie granted Moura the benefit of the doubt, even if he believed that she had been cornered and seduced by Lockhart, he still refused to rule out the possibility that she had indeed been a spy.

Hickie's whisper to Lockhart to be careful wasn't a new warning.

Lockhart, however, didn't believe for a second that Moura could have betrayed them. Their trysts certainly hadn't been ordered by Lenin's intelligence services, contrary to what several diplomats in the Foreign Office believed. Not only had she loved him, but she had most likely saved him from the firing squad. He was certain that he owed his life to her . . . And so he owed her every ounce of gratitude he had. Their adventure, indeed, remained the greatest memory, the most exciting moments of his life.

The passion he had had during the war for a Russian woman many described as a Mata Hari had cost him dearly upon his return to England, so dearly that he couldn't contemplate the possibility of another affair with the same frivolity.

And besides, he thought, and besides, he was still a married man! He was a family man. The lover of a respectable lady he loved in turn. And Catholic, to top it all off.

It was out of the question to be unfaithful in any way to his wife . . . or to his mistress.

Absolutely out of the question to get carried away here!

As he watched her forging onward ahead of him, as he contemplated the way her back and her hips moved, he recalled her nude body, this body she had offered him so freely. He had always been struck by her grace: Moura didn't walk, she *floated* . . . Even on a mountain path. Six years after the shock of first meeting her, this woman proved to be just as dazzling as she had been when she was young. He felt no regret at having loved this woman. At having loved her this intensely!

And yet he had no intention now of loving her anew.

The landscape around them was nothing but sunshine and beauty. The gilded leaves of the vineyards gleamed down below on the hillsides. And the thickets of birches on the edge of the forest above them glittered with silvery glints.

Once she reached the peak, she waited for him. He arrived and leaned against the massive rock she was sitting on. She had crossed her legs and held her face in her open hands. Her eyes were contemplative, staring straight ahead. She did not speak. Lockhart felt embarrassed, but finally broke the silence:

"How was Petrograd after I left?"

"It wasn't much fun, Babyboy."

If he thought she was going to describe what she had endured, he had another think coming. Her answers were terse, scant on details, merely underscoring the literary aspects of her life. She knew he was well read and curious about matters of the soul. She told him about what interested him: her meeting with Gorky, her work as a secretary, her translations for World Literature.

He let out an admiring sigh:

"Your strength is unparalleled, Babygirl!"

"Oh, Babyboy, you're exaggerating. You always are!"

They had found their old tone, their old rhythm again. Lockhart observed her with the old amusement he had felt before. "I know what I'm talking about . . . And I'm going to say it again: your wisdom and your intelligence are unparalleled."

"It's my luck that's unparalleled."

"No, it's not just that. The Revolution crushed men and women by the thousands. The Revolution wiped out an entire social class. The Revolution destroyed the lives of everyone you were close to. Some died, and the rest will never recover. You alone, you and nobody else, managed to come out victorious."

"Victorious? Oh, no!"

"*Moura* is the soul of Eternal Russia, the one who adapts and survives!"

"Don't be silly. I haven't survived, not entirely. So many things within me have died. But what about you? You, my Babyboy? Tell me about you."

"Me? There's nothing to say. Coming back to England was difficult. And I haven't done anything remarkable since . . . Not in London, not in Vienna, not in Prague. I'm drinking too much, I'm smoking too much, I've accumulated debts that have brought me to the brink of bankruptcy several times. And I'm the one who brings misfortune to every woman I'm with."

"*Every* woman? Are there really that many?"

He didn't answer the question. But he regaled her with anecdotes of his excesses—his taste for alcohol, his love of luxury, his weakness for gambling. He exaggerated his faults and spun such fine stories that she couldn't help but laugh and yell at him:

"Did you really do that?"

"My word . . ."

"Really? My God!"

As he looked at her sitting on the rock, he almost hoped that she would criticize him, that she would disapprove of him and furrow her brows. That she would tell him to get hold of himself, that she would beg him to summon up a bit of courage, that she would urge him to start a new life with her.

But no reproaches nor propositions were forthcoming.

She leaned forward, her chin still in her hand, and gave him a vague smile while she stared at the bottom of the valley half-hidden in a haze of heat. He knew quite well that she couldn't see the vines on the hillsides, the torrent beneath the waterfall. Was she listening to the roar of the water in the ravine?

Her silence both bothered him and touched him. In the form before him he could see the mysterious, indulgent woman he had once loved.

She finally spoke and gave him a sermon. "You will be thirty-seven on the second of September," she said gently. "The anniversary of Sedan and of Omdurman. You see, I remember the date. At thirty-seven one is not the same, men are not the same, as at twenty-seven. Don't let us spoil something—perhaps the one thing in both our lives—that has been perfect. It would be a mistake, would it not?"

The blood was pounding violently in Lockhart's temples. A lust that he had thought was gone drew him to her again. She was irresistible.

He saw himself again in Moscow. He heard again the voice of his jailer, Yakov Peters, who had given him every encouragement to remain behind and deny his country and marry Moura.

He reached out to take her into his arms, to pull her close. He would whisper to her, swear to her . . . She got to her feet.

"Let's not spoil it." She looked at him, this time peering straight into his eyes. She took both his hands. "Yes, it would be a mistake."

She said each word carefully. Her tone made her words irrevocable.

"It would be a mistake to spoil it. The one thing that has been perfect."

She did not say anything further. She got up and started down the path. They made their way back to the house.

The two of them had to return the next day. The one to Czechoslovakia, the other to Germany. But the nostalgia they felt for their love, the magic of their passion still weighed on them. They felt dizzy. The past had come back. How could they separate again now?

At the last minute, Moura changed her plans. She wouldn't leave from the Vienna station. She would take the train to Prague with Lockhart. And then she would decide on her next step.

❖

They sat next to each other among the others, trading stories. They talked the whole night, speaking in Russian so as not to be understood.

"Do you remember Karakhan? His dandyish outfits? His trimmed beard that reeked of cologne for miles around?"

"And remember Peters with his steel watch, the height of American fashion?"

They laughed as they recalled the details of their experiences with the Bolsheviks: Trotsky's rage, Radek's wit.

"Do you remember, in the Kremlin, when you slipped your message into my book behind Peters's back?"

Lockhart concluded:

At six o'clock in the morning I said good-bye to Moura at the Masaryk Station in Prague. She was going on to Berlin and to Reval. I had to be in my bank at nine o'clock.

Months before, when we had had a slight altercation about a question of principle, Moura had described me as "a little clever, but not clever enough; a little strong, but not strong enough; a little weak, but not weak enough." . . .

It seemed then, it seems to-day, a fair definition of my character. And now I had left her. My cup of unhappiness was full.

❖

She watched for a long while as the silhouette of the man she had dreamed of for so long disappeared into the crowd. He was elegant despite the heat wrinkling his pants; svelte despite the excesses, the alcohol, the fatigue of a sleepless night.

She had been waiting six years for this moment. For him to explain himself . . . She had moved heaven and earth to make this meeting happen.

By all appearances, it had all gone well. Neither of them could have hoped for a more harmonious meeting. They had laughed together, drunk together. They had traded ideas, shared impressions, recalled memories. They had not scolded each other. Not a single detail had blemished the magic of their reunion.

They were still close at heart. The emotion that had brought them together was intact, as well. And the understanding they had come to wasn't merely an agreement about the past.

Lockhart's humor when he tapped his belly to underscore his short-comings still charmed her. His sincerity touched her. Even his weaknesses, his failures moved her. And their discussions about Russia's future still delighted her.

A thousand shared interests united them. As did the physical instinct to let go and sink into each other's gaze. The effort it took to resist their desire, to not hug or kiss each other on the rock . . . She knew just how much he had wanted to take her into his arms.

She herself had struggled to repress her passion, fought to resist this surge of tenderness and love that overwhelmed her, worked not to show anything so that he could remain free with his words and his actions.

After those two days of battle, she felt wrung dry.

Powerless.

And sunken into the lowest depths of despair.

She had tried to keep what mattered. But her defeat had been complete.

They should have talked to each other as if the world could give way beneath their feet. Yet Lockhart hadn't said anything. Lockhart hadn't felt anything. Lockhart hadn't understood anything.

A gulf separated them, and she knew it could not be crossed.

In the heat of the moment, thanks to the sun, the beauty of the countryside, he could have reestablished a relationship with her like his other trysts. She knew him well enough to know how emotional, how impulsive he was. The romanticism of his nostalgia, the memory of his great adventure in Russia . . . An abrupt blaze of passion.

He would have loved her for, what, an hour? It would have been delightful, but empty. And pointless.

In stirring the embers again, all she had found were ashes. The ordinariness of this reignited flame would ultimately have burned away the rest of the beauty of the memory. She hadn't wanted to say anything else in declaring: "Let's not spoil it."

Because the flame in his heart had gone out.

And now she had to let it go. She had to pull herself together and keep going.

◆

Three months after this meeting, on a wintry morning in Sorrento, Italy, the friends from Kronverksky Prospect were discussing the latest news that the end of 1924 had brought them.

"Apparently she was able to get her stupid baron shipped off to Brazil," the Nightingale reported.

"But what if he comes back?" Molecule asked.

"Brazil is an entire ocean away!"

"Still!" Pepekryu insisted. "She put him on a boat last year. But he woke up in his cabin one morning with the realization that she had scammed him. That she'd promised him a monthly payment, but she wasn't going to keep her word. He got off at Antwerp, or Cherbourg, I don't know where, to come right back to Berlin. He forced her to sign other papers and tortured her in every way possible. So it took him six months to leave for good!"

"What about her?"

"She's never talked about any of her problems to anyone. I had no idea she was having trouble with her husband."

"Was she hiding them from Gorky?" the Merchantess asked. "Really?"

"Who knows? She was always telling him, 'Don't you worry, Alexey, I always land on my feet. I'll find a way to get the money.'"

"Well, I never! He was the one who paid for the whole trip in the end. Both the ticket and the monthly allowance for that monster."

Moura could hear them from the balcony. She was taking long breaths of the sea air coming off the Gulf of Naples. The view from her window was breathtaking. On one side, she could see the rows of tall black cypresses on the promontory leading toward the white crosses of a cemetery. On the other, in the haze, was the rocky mass of Capri, the heavenly island where Gorky had spent six years in exile back during the years of tsarist persecution.

The view was indeed magnificent.

But Il Sorito, the villa she had rented from the Duke of Serracapriola to house Alexey's Russian cohort, wasn't meant for winter stays. It was a summer home, really. Built to stay cool during heat waves.

What good was the damp of its airy rooms for Gorky's lungs? The building felt utterly cold, utterly empty. Moura was worried. Had she made a mistake in abandoning the Villa Massa, where the group had stayed last spring? No, that house was worse. Far less comfortable. Far more cumbersome. But still, here, the wind gusted through gaps in the windows, and the water from the bathroom taps was tepid. She dreamed of the boiler that needed to be fixed, of the chimney that had to be swept, of the curtains that needed to be dealt with.

One thing at a time.

What mattered was that now that he'd been in Italy for six months, Alexey was doing better. Far better than in those somber sanatoriums in Germany where he had stayed for two years.

No question of it: this climate was better for him.

From her second-story bedroom, she considered the last bougainvilleas clinging to the arbors. Even though it was December, some things were still growing in the garden. That, too, was incredible. It was warmer there than inside.

She could still hear the Nightingale, Pepekryu, the Merchantess, and Molecule as they took their morning coffee, sitting around the table in the pergola. Soon, other visitors would join them.

The Peshkov family—Gorky, Max, and Max's wife—as well as the painter Nightingale, the uncle and poet Khodasevich, and his companion, Nina Berberova, lived here permanently, while their close friends who were visiting stayed across the road at the Hotel Minerva. The Merchantess, her husband, Didi, and Molecule would be spending Christmas at the villa.

Pepekryu—who had broken up with the great actress Maria Andreyeva, who as a result was no longer coming to Sorrento—and the Nightingale, who needed visual inspiration to keep going, were summing up the last of the gossip for the Merchantess. All four of them were murmuring to one another.

"She can get divorced at last and settle in with us. Move here for good. Gorky spends his whole life waiting. He suffers so much whenever she's gone."

"Well, that'd be quite a change!"

"Max showed me a note that was sitting on his father's desk. She was teasing him: 'All right, all right, I won't marry any more barons. You say they're all drunkards. But what about you? You're a marquis and a duke, and you drink your weight in Chianti!' She's got Gorky laughing, she's got him giving in. She got him to cough up the money."

"Of all the women he's loved, I think she's the companion he's the most besotted with. He thinks of her as his wife."

"Their relationship has changed. He needs her for everything! To discuss his ideas, to read his chapters, to help him with his articles. Lenin's death in January was a serious blow for him. She urged him to write his eulogy. It was a beautiful ode where he declared his respect, his admiration. To hear him, Ilyich was the greatest political thinker of all time. And the regime he established was the only one possible for Russia."

"And after Ilyich forced him out into exile!"

"After his death, Gorky set aside all their differences. He misses Russia. And Comrade Stalin, who's working to oust Zinoviev, keeps inviting him to come back home."

"What's her opinion on the matter?"

"She's taking care to avoid influencing him there."

"That's the right thing."

"She has very good judgment. She would make an excellent counsel."

"That's what Gorky thinks, in any case."

"Or, to be more specific, that's what she wants Gorky to think! She's fooling him. Do you know she saw Lockhart again?"

"What? Say that again. The consul?"

"I don't believe you!" Molecule bleated. "You're wrong!"

"It's true! She went and met him in July. Just after we settled into the first house. She was busy moving everything from Marienbad to Sorrento, she found the villa, she rented it, she had it furnished. She could leave us, just as she has every summer, to visit other lands. To spend August at Kallijärv with her children. And that was what we thought she did. But in fact she was meeting up with her old lover."

"Unbelievable. She's been wanting to see him again, and she's gone and done it. Hats off to her. She never lets go, does she?"

Moura shut the window again. She had heard enough already. Even at the tip of the Cape of Sorrento, news traveled fast! And a life lived in a vacuum did nobody any good. Poets, novelists, painters, all the representatives of Russian art and literature living here ended up behaving like petty bourgeoisie on vacation. Rivalries, gossip, rumors . . .

What could her old friend the Nightingale—the first one to welcome her to Kronverksky Prospect—know of her feelings toward Lockhart? Only what little she had confided to him.

The truth was that the conversation she had overheard upset her. Not because these rumors showed her a distorted image of her gratitude and compassion for Baron Budberg, her immense tenderness for Gorky, and her love for Lockhart. But because she herself hadn't realized just how important what had happened between Vienna and Prague had been to her.

Since then, Lockhart had been writing to her constantly. They had agreed to see each other again. She dreamed of those new reunions.

Despite her feelings about his weakness, her thoughts about his mediocrity, he was—he remained—the passion of her life.

She accepted the facts.

She felt bad now; she was even angry at herself for not having taken the opportunity to lie in his arms when they had seen each other on the steps of the Cunard office. Or on the rock above Hicks's country home. She should have kissed him, she should have loved him.

Their time together would have been fleeting, and then what? What did it matter? Yes, what did it matter that he was in love with another woman? She would disappear like the sick princess had and like all the other women to come would.

She knew how to change their relationship, how to bring about a new degree of closeness and pleasure. How to stay the first and foremost in his affections. The only one, when all was said and done.

She knew how to become his lodestar.

As for the rest, the departure of Baron Budberg, who everyone under the pergola had been talking about, had freed her from a burden whose weight she hadn't, until that moment, realized had been bearing down upon her for the last three years.

As the friends of Kronverksky Prospect had been talking, the Nightingale's comments underscored another, far more disturbing, reality that the tension of her relationship with Baron Budberg had hidden—a reality she hadn't wanted to see, that she couldn't control, that overwhelmed her, that displeased her. There was no more peace or harmony between her and Alexey Maximovich.

He suffered when she was gone and scolded her for it, accusing her of not paying him enough attention, of neglecting him, of fundamentally abandoning him both professionally and emotionally. He declared that he was wounded three times over. Hurt as a person. Offended as a man. And humiliated as a writer.

She defended herself, showing him how she continued to work for him in Berlin, Paris, and elsewhere, taking care of his contracts with his publishers, negotiating his rights, collecting on them.

On that point, her arguments were unassailable, as she was offsetting her absences with yet more energy, effectiveness, and devotion.

But the truth was that for the last few months she had been trying to stifle this need for independence that kept driving her out of Italy, out of the Villa Massa, out of the villa Il Sorito, this spirit that she called *her baser instincts* . . . Only to see this need grow and blossom.

The shame of torturing the man she admired, the man she respected more than anyone else in the world, the regret, the fear, the horror of not being in love with him, drowned her.

Alexei, my dear, my Joy, she told him in her mind, *I've struggled with myself for so long, trying to convince myself that this wasn't serious . . . There he is, I've been telling myself every time I see your dear face, there he is, the man I love and need . . . The man who needs me just as much, who loves me, who is so near and dear to me, who I feel just as tender to now as I did before . . . But not ecstatic anymore. You can't imagine how much I've hated and still hate myself for that.*

Had she undone so much good by seeing Lockhart again?

Moura's feelings were tangled together, and she had no idea how to move forward.

CHAPTER THIRTY-THREE

Crisis

July 1925–July 1926

O n a July evening in 1925, Micky cautiously crossed the road winding down the Cape of Sorrento. She had just left the Minerva boarding house, where she had gotten the little ones washed and dressed and had their hair done after spending the afternoon by the sea.

Even though Gorky had invited them to come stay with him in Italy that summer, Micky and the three children slept at the boarding house. But they all took their meals across the street at the villa Il Sorito and spent time on the terraces and in the immense garden of the Serracapriola dukes, full of fig trees and rosebushes. Or on the rocky beach farther down. To get there, they had to go through a delightful orange grove that was practically on top of the waves. And Micky hated climbing back up this slope in the worst of the heat wave with the towels and beach balls. The afternoon rest at the Minerva boarding house for the children's bath was a welcome respite before the evening.

Kira, who was now sixteen, was already waiting for them in front of the villa's fence, between the two ocher posts of the entrance. But Paul, who was almost twelve, and Tania, who was ten, were practically beside themselves with the excitement of seeing their friend Alexey Maximovich. It was out of the question to let them run across the road, so Micky clutched their hands firmly. There was no sidewalk here. No visibility. Any truck or car or motorcycle with sidecar, like the one young Max drove at breakneck speed, threatening to overturn with all its passengers on one of the Amalfi Coast's hairpin turns, could come zipping around one of the curves in the road framing the house.

Micky was still exhausted from the trip. She had been certain that she wouldn't survive this interminable journey across Europe, not with so many train transfers between Kallijärv and Sorrento.

The truth was that she wasn't young anymore. She had just turned sixty-one, and she was starting to suffer from more and more small ailments that she didn't dare mention. As for the others, when they stepped down on the platform of the Stazione Roma Termini where Marydear had come up to welcome them, Paul and the girls were hardly any more hale and hearty than she was.

What kind of energy did Marydear have to be able to brave such a trek in both directions multiple times each year? Micky was especially fixated on that question today. She considered just how long the journey had been. She didn't relish the prospect of going back in August.

In the end, however, they had made it, and they had been here for nearly a month now. And Micky had never seen Kira, Paul, and Tania so happy.

They were excited to see their mother again. Even more excited to spend time with Alexey Maximovich. Gorky played surprisingly well with the children, and they did him good. Tania had grown absolutely besotted with him. The old man and the young girl were inseparable.

Oddly enough, the life they led in Sorrento reminded Micky of the rhythms of vacation months in Berezovaya Rudka long before, back in Senator Zakrevsky's time.

Even this massive Neapolitan villa built in the eighteenth century, even Il Sorito with its baroque facade, its intricate windows, its tiny wrought-iron balconies, its oculi, its terraces and stucco walls, reminded her of the Zakrevsky residence in Ukraine.

Even down to the help, who only referred to Marydear as the Baroness, a title she heard echoing in the halls twenty times a day with just as much respect every time.

Buongiorno, Signora Baronessa. Subito, Signora Baronessa. Scusi, Signora Baronessa.

Micky knew perfectly well that Mary's position within the Corporation of Estonian Nobles was hardly to Gorky's taste. But she could see just how much the revival of the Zakrevsky family's mythology charmed him. He laughed just as hard as the three children did whenever Mary held a lock of her black hair under her nose to imitate Tsar Peter the Great's mustache. Her resemblance to him at such moments was so striking that nobody doubted she was a descendant of his. Maria Ignatyevna, a great-great-great-granddaughter of the most audacious tsar of Russia? The thought delighted Gorky endlessly.

Moura didn't reject the idea; rather, she encouraged the legend.

As for the actual Italian duchesses who were their neighbors—the villa owner's two daughters, who would live in a corner of the estate until they were married—they remained the beloved regents of the Cape of Sorrento. The peasants of Massa Lubrense, the adjoining village, saluted them whenever they walked by, uncovering their heads, bowing down low, and murmuring incomprehensible words of praise. To everybody living in the region, the two thirtysomething damsels would always be *le Signorine Duchesse di Serracapriola*.

The lord of the house, *l'illustrissimo Professore Massimo Gorky*, could have been a god. His Neapolitan readers were so devoted to him that his rare journeys outside the villa set off crowds and even mobs.

Micky had taken in his unlikely popularity during their visits to Sorrento's churches and Naples's museums. Everybody rushed up to the car, hoping to kiss his hand. And at Capri, where Gorky hadn't lived since his exile during the reign of the tsar a decade ago, fishermen repeatedly made the trip in their boats to bolster their presence in his memory and to ask for his blessing.

In the twenties, Gorky's fame was matched only by two writers who had come before him, writers who, too, had been politically engaged: Victor Hugo and Leo Tolstoy. Like them, Gorky was the guide, the master, *Il maestro assoluto*, revered by the people.

But even more than these markers of respect, these titles of nobility, and the charm of this region, the strange parallel between Marydear's present and her stately past—this similarity that struck Micky between Il Sorito and Berezovaya—was rooted in the atmosphere. The mix of generations and genders, the picnics, the trips to the countryside, the tennis matches. The charades, the rhyming games, the rounds of bridge, the endless meals, and the freedom of wide-ranging intellectual exchanges.

In Estonia, the Benckendorffs' psychological rigidity, deepened by the shame of their present financial difficulties, the stiffness of social conventions, the harshness of the climate, all the challenges of living in a land tormented by invasions, had left her unaccustomed to such lighthearted gaiety.

Even if luxury didn't really exist here, either. Comfort was a relative term. But there was beauty everywhere.

And the table, sagging under the weight of so much incredible fruit that had not been seen in Kallijärv for decades, welcomed a constant stream of visitors from abroad. Most had been born in Moscow or Saint Petersburg. Some considered themselves Bolshevik. Others had emigrated.

The visitors—artists, musicians, poets, or simply cadgers—were welcome to stay for lunch. They could also stay the night, sleep there for a week, a month, a season at Gorky's place, as the summer vacationers of the past had done at the home of Mary's father. And as at the home of Mary's father, each saw to his own business, worked on his piece of art, or took some leisure time before coming back together in the evening to discuss ideas and dreams for hours on end.

Here in Italy, in the villa of the Revolution's supporter, in the house of Lenin's friend who was a forceful defender of Marxist thought, Micky ended up having, to her great surprise, all the same impressions she had had during her earliest summers among the members of the Russian aristocracy.

At least, that was what the old Irish woman thought of the circle in which her Marydear ran.

❖

The day had been torrid, and the cicadas refused to quiet down. Micky, the Nightingale, and Timosha, Max's beautiful wife, who was seven months pregnant, were sitting side by side on the bench in the courtyard.

Moura was sitting at the top of the front steps. Everybody was watching Gorky playing tag with the children and yelling louder than them while perching on the stones bordering the flower beds. His little dog, Kuzka—the terrier Moura had given him—was barking happily and following him from one perch to the next.

Alexey Maximovich wasn't the only one running around and climbing up everywhere, even on the cactus pots, in order not to get tagged. A dozen other adults—including Max, the Merchantess, and the two friends currently visiting, a Russian soprano who was performing that summer at the Teatro La Fenice and the set decorator for the Teatro alla Scala in Milan—were also trying to stay away from Tania, who was chasing them around the palm tree with gleeful cries. She was merciless: whoever got tagged by her would have to hop all the way to the front door.

And Gorky always got caught. He bounded all the way to the pillars and yelled down the bend in the road the words that Tania made him recite: German phrases that he mangled on purpose with a heavy Russian accent so as to make the little girl laugh even harder. This was their ritual before dinner at Il Sorito. A ritual that would be followed, after dinner, with yet more games, until Moura and Micky finally decided that it was time for the children to go to bed.

Notwithstanding the master's whimsies and the festive atmosphere that hung over the house, life at Il Sorito was ruled by the creative process.

There was more discipline than anybody would have guessed. Alexey Maximovich was early to rise and early to bed. With or without Moura's help, he wrote until late afternoon in their second-floor quarters. And she translated his articles, typed up his mail, or attended to her obligations as lady of the house, ensuring that things ran smoothly at the residence. She handled accounts, the servants' wages, the ordering of food from the village. The couple only showed themselves once the temperature was cooling down, around six o'clock.

At that point, all the shutters were opened: Moura knew how best to weather heat waves. The truth was that she, along with Gorky, was the only one not to wallow in the general *farniente*; she was always hard at work.

As she saw them come out together through the frame of the front entrance, Micky gave no thought to the ties that bound them together.

The idea that her Marydear could be anything other than the collaborator of an esteemed writer simply didn't occur to her. Her marriage to Baron Budberg had upset Micky far too much for her to imagine Marydear cohabitating with any man at all. Like Kira, Paul, and Tania, who were too young to consider such a question, she didn't let her thoughts meander too far in this particular direction. It was impossible for her to even think of Djon's widow, Baron Budberg's wife, and these children's mother to also be Maxim Gorky's mistress.

It wasn't that Alexey Maximovich's charisma hadn't won over Micky . . . On the contrary, she was spellbound!

She was astonished by the sheer size of the mailbags that the postman delivered to the doorstep every day, all these letters coming from every corner of the world just for this master. She was actually fascinated by this fame, which extended to Marydear and the children, to the point that even she could bask in its glow.

She was indeed fascinated by the writer's success, even though she hadn't read anything of his. And she was seduced by the man's humaneness. She adored Gorky's amiability. His intensely kind blue eyes, which glittered when they landed on Tania. Her raven hair, tied off with massive white bows, and her hazel eyes so full of life gave her a striking resemblance to her mother.

Micky especially liked Gorky's laugh, an unstoppable laugh like a little boy bursting with happiness at whatever delighted him. His childlike sense of wonder, his habit of slapping his knees or crying in admiration when a bit of music or a performance was especially affecting. His fervor whenever he looked at the black mass of Mount Vesuvius in the evenings from his terrace, his passion for the cozy glow of the hundreds of lanterns lining the path up the volcano's slope.

She adored the emotion in his voice, which grew slightly muted whenever he declaimed poetry, halting and angry whenever he defended his ideas.

But she saw him as a man of her generation, unable to read without

putting on his glasses, suffering from arthritis in his joints, with drooping shoulders . . . An old man whose stomach sagged under his gray
coat.

As soon as Alexey Maximovich's long silhouette appeared on the front
steps, his guests ran up to greet him. Some immediately halted their tennis match, others took a break from their walk around the garden, and
yet others set aside their sketchbooks. They all needed his thoughts—
whether on intellectual, sentimental, or practical matters—and each was
determined to charm him with stories about their day. Even here and
now he was still their *Duca*, their Duke. He was the soul of this little coterie at Il Sorito. As for the children, Tania, Paul, and Kira, words didn't
suffice: they literally jumped onto his back. He understood them instinctively. And he felt deeply understood by them.

The pleasure that their youth brought Gorky commingled with another
feeling, that of immense relief: Maria Ignatyevna's children weren't a
myth. They existed in reality.

It wasn't that he believed she had made them up to justify her silences
and get away from him. It was that he had so often seen her being particularly withdrawn on Kronverksky Prospect and had asked her over and
over again: "Now, now, what are you dreaming about?"

To which she had replied over and over again: "Oh, nothing at all."

And he had pressed the question over and over again: "No, really,
what are you thinking about?"

And she had answered over and over again: "About my children."

The sadness of this line had tinged their relationship with a genuine despair that Paul's and Tania's presence had relieved him of. Seeing
just how alive they were, discovering just how energetic, how joyful, how
beautiful they were, realizing just how endearing, how objectively well
raised they were, had assuaged his heart.

He couldn't stop thinking that Maria really shouldn't be cut off from
her family anymore. Fate had been fickle for her; the separation she had
endured was one no mother should ever have to suffer.

But all was well now. Her children were here. They were playing all around her at Il Sorito.

Seeing her like this, sitting at the top of the steps, as a mother who ensured their education, who looked after their health, who attended to their well-being—seeing her sitting this way at the center of their circle nearly brought him to tears. As she played this role he hadn't known she had, he found her even more respectable, even more extraordinary, even more touching. It almost scared him just how much she was flourishing. He didn't dare look directly at her.

She was a thirty-two-year-old woman, and she was just as energetic and joyful as her offspring.

He loved nothing more than when the setting sun turned her hazel eyes to gold, as it was doing right this moment, and when she let out a laugh as she took Kira, who had just been taken out of the running, into her arms. He loved the way she hugged the girl, holding her neck and her waist close to her own body, motherly and protective. Their white cotton summer dresses merged into a single pool of light against the ocher background of the wall.

The truth was that he took just as much pleasure in slipping away from the little dog and Tania's chases as he did in making a spectacle of himself in front of her: in letting Maria Ignatyevna discover him as a man who could still run, shout, laugh, and play. An indefatigable character.

He would have loved to charm her . . . Did he still charm her? He wasn't so sure. She seemed rather distant these days. Sometimes she was outright impatient, annoyed by his quirks. This muted frustration, which he hadn't seen before, seemed rather foreign and even hostile.

She still supported him as she alone was able to do. But she no longer treated him the way she had before: as a fellow traveler, a lover, a husband. She treated him as a sickly man a quarter of a century older than she was.

This new condescension drove him mad. As did her other shortcomings. Why was she always flitting off? He wanted her to stop living bits and pieces of various lives and wash her hands of all these treks from one world to another! He wanted her to no longer feel torn between her various loyalties and her numerous obligations! Torn between what she owed him, what she owed her children, what she owed her sisters, what she owed herself . . . And what she owed to God alone knew who else! Maybe to their neighbor?

This jealousy was torturous.

That anti-Fascist lawyer from Sorrento? The young, handsome Carlo Ruffino—in any case, younger and handsomer than *him*—who claimed to be defending the Neapolitan resistance against Mussolini's tyranny? Would she end up slipping away with this man? No. Of course not. No woman like her ever left a man like him for an Italian shark, even one who was anti-Fascist. She wouldn't abandon Gorky himself, with his magnificent name, for a grandiloquent Carlo Ruffino, whose very existence she minimized by calling him simply "R." But still . . . the wife of Alexander Blok, the subtlest of poets, had abandoned him for an actual circus clown!

When Maria was away in town for too long—apparently to talk with this lawyer she called R. about the proceedings of her divorce in absentia from Budberg—he wondered, was she cheating on him? She probably wanted to. At moments, Gorky hated her.

Notwithstanding what she thought of herself, Maria Ignatyevna wasn't a diligent woman, he said to himself, much less a levelheaded woman. She was simply an instinctive human being. The kind that Schopenhauer had described so clearly when he argued for the superiority of instinct over reason . . . Just like the flies, the frogs, the guinea pigs, all the little wild animals whose purely sexual behavior shocked him.

And he, in contrast, was thoroughly bookish! *Wordy*, as she now declared whenever she was arguing with him.

Was he cerebral? But of course! And that was what she took offense at. It was a fundamental difference.

He still trusted her, as ever. But when he happened upon her in the middle of writing letters and she hid them hurriedly in a drawer or under a book, she hurt him. Why did she have to hide anything? He wasn't asking her to give up anything, after all! So why was there all this mystery? Why this silence?

And why wouldn't these children be staying here and living with her? Why wouldn't they be growing up here in Italy?

He had asked her that question once.

She had evaded the subject, changed the topic.

Yes, it would be nice for her not to have to make the journey from Kallijärv to Berlin and then Sorrento, she conceded . . . Why not? Yes, that would be lovely.

But the conversation about eventually choosing a school here in Naples had stopped there. The topic was abruptly cut off like so many evening games and courtyard chases were, by a terrifying asthma attack or a coughing fit that left Alexey Maximovich bent in half over his blood-stained handkerchief.

He wasn't a mature lover so much as an ailing tuberculosis patient whose doctor had forbidden him these evening activities.

Moura watched him from the top of the steps. She loved seeing him play like this with Tania. But she was unable to relax. She knew the risk he was running.

She also knew she shouldn't get involved. She had to stay quiet. To go on smiling like a sphinx and waiting.

He hated it when people pitied him for how he had turned out. He especially hated when embarrassing realities—like his poor health or the news of yet more atrocities carried out by chekists—crushed the hopes and dreams he held dear. He had a nearly superhuman ability to ignore the facts that displeased him and a supernatural capacity to deny them.

It was out of the question to talk to him about the one lung he had left. As soon as he sensed that the topic might come up, he closed off completely. His fury mottled his neck with red blotches . . . And his pain worsened. He always left the room gesticulating angrily.

And otherwise, he always talked about his ailing health and the cruelty of Zinoviev's men with the same words: "Those pigs!" he grumbled when he saw specks of blood on his handkerchief or when he read reports that had just come in from Russia. "Those thugs, those monsters!" And that was how he put his revulsion and his astonishment into words.

Deep down, he refused to listen or even to see what bothered him. He left it to Moura to deal with those problems.

But she was supposed to deal with these embarrassing, unpleasant realities only by appearing unaffected by them, by taking everything in stride—the same way she wrapped up games of tag or blindman's bluff, by jumping up to tell the cook to ring the dinner bell and serve the meal on the second-floor terrace overlooking the sea. The maestro's terrace with such a wonderful view.

❖

The days grew stiflingly hot. The children did not allow them any rest in the summer heat. There was no respite for poor Micky.

But the temperatures had laid the adults low. Even Max had stopped taking his drives in his motorcycle sidecar so he could doze beside his wife. Timosha was extremely pregnant and anxiously waiting to give birth.

Leaning against the balcony railing, Moura looked out over the coast and smoked as the purple evening sun tinted her whole body. She loved this blinding light that shimmered in the garden and over the Gulf of Naples, this light that seeped in everywhere, even here, even as it set.

The honeysuckle clinging to the wall behind her exuded its ambrosial smell, which the night breeze would soon carry toward the beach. *Melancholy waltz and languid vertigo*: she recited Baudelaire's lines to herself as she thought about how, after the dinnertime discussions, after she had kissed her children good night, waved goodbye to her friends, settled Alexey in his bedroom, she could rejoice in this silence, this peace she was owed.

Heaven knew how much she hated being alone! But she was sick of all these visitors' compliments, all the courtesans' bows, and all the hangers-on lingering here.

The waves rose and fell in the distance. She was breathing slowly, matching the rhythm of her breath to that of the swells. Everything seemed perfect.

Everything *was* perfect, yes. And yet . . .

Where had this odd unease coursing through her veins come from?

She didn't understand herself. She knew how magical this summer was. She loved it. She knew she would keep it forever as a special memory. As would Tania. As would Micky.

And yet . . .

She would wait until the sun had dipped below the horizon before considering what was troubling her heart.

The truth was that nothing was going well for her.

Moura looked back at the house briefly. Night had already fallen over the facade.

Apart from one window that still let some light through its louvered shutters, the entire place was already asleep. Except for him, except for Alexey, who, like her, was suffering from insomnia.

Moura sighed . . . Her inability to assuage Alexey's jealousy saddened her.

She could hear him moving around in his bedroom. He was getting out of bed. Opening the shutters. Did he also feel this anxiety she wasn't able to control anymore?

She had to spare him what could be spared him. His life in exile was already leaving him with enough struggles; he didn't need to suffer from others. And he was right to push away what upset him. He had enough weight on his shoulders.

There was no use explaining to him the difficulties she faced in handling his affairs. There was no use telling him again that Lenin's death the year before had meant the Party was no longer making payments into his account at Deutsche Bank in Berlin. Meaning that serious financial difficulty was now imminent.

By the way he had started tapping his fingers on the table whenever she broached the topic, she knew that this information belonged in the category of *unpleasant facts*.

It was also impossible to tell him that these bags of mail that had him believing he was still a worldwide success were practically an illusion, the last remains of glory that masked the reality. Ever since the war, the print runs of his books across Europe had diminished dramatically.

Paul could easily read *Mother* until dawn with a small light; Tania could devour *My Childhood* in bed, and Kira *The Lower Depths* while Micky's back was turned: outside Russia, these three titles would soon be the only books of Gorky's anybody knew about.

In Berlin, she was fighting every step of the way to support his work, and she increased her conversations with international publishers. The prospect of Alexey's reputation being eclipsed upset her: he had never been greater than he was now! She was convinced that *The Life of Klim Samgin*, the novel he had been working on since March and that she typed up every morning, was his masterpiece.

But even so, sales were down in every country, except for Russia, where his popularity was only growing.

But the money Gorky was earning over there was now blocked. And if sales continued to drop here in Europe, Alexey Maximovich would be done for. How could he take care of the needs of his son, daughter-in-law, and forthcoming grandchildren? And all the visitors staying here in Italy at his expense? How could he go on renting Il Sorito and living in Sorrento?

Of course, he had no reason to take into consideration these threats that she tried to warn him about. Stalin kept insisting that he adored Gorky. Unlike Lenin, who had driven him out, Stalin had invited him to return and live in luxury.

But that was in theory. In practice, Stalin was making sure Gorky would have no control over his Russian royalties and rights so long as he was abroad, and so, having been frozen out, he would be reduced to rags and tatters in Europe. In practice, Stalin was ensuring his death by a thousand cuts. One way of proving his friendship: forcing him to return home.

Moura shuddered. If he kept on refusing to look at *frustrating realities*, Alexey would end up going completely blind!

Returning home? Oddly enough, Gorky was dreaming of it. He had been away from Russia for just about four years now. He missed his motherland. All this time and distance had made his journey to the West start to feel like a betrayal of his core values.

The grief he felt for Lenin's death had almost made him forget the barbarities he had witnessed, the violence he had denounced so angrily.

Now, he hated receiving letters that attested to the Bolsheviks' cruelty. They deprived him of his hopes for the future, the hope that he could return to a more just society. He didn't want to hear about the horrors and excesses anymore.

He even started to think that he had been wrong, that the violence the Reds had resorted to had been a necessary weapon.

How could the slate be wiped clean when it came to the past, how could anyone transform a society from the ground up, if they didn't rip out the roots of *burzhui* evil? The vermin had to be exterminated.

That such a thug, such a pig as Zinoviev had been allowed to rise to the top of the Party was, of course, a mistake. But mistakes were human. A mere bump in the road that did not in any way diminish the excellence of Marx's thought and the purity of Lenin's system. His successor, however, was determined to set things right again with remarkable speed as he worked to oust Zinoviev and Trotsky from the hierarchy. Stalin knew what was best for the Russian people.

Peshkova, Max's mother, who often stayed at Il Sorito, was urging Gorky to accept Stalin's invitation. She argued that Alexey was wasting his time in Italy. He was squandering his talent.

In her eyes, Gorky was a member, in flesh and blood, in heart and soul, of this race of new men working to establish the Soviet Union. Gorky needed to reclaim his rightful place among Russian writers. Reclaim his people. Reclaim his readers.

He had to accept the invitation of Comrade Stalin.

Max echoed his mother: he, too, wanted to play a role in his homeland. Pepekryu, Molecule, and the Merchantess were in full agreement. He should go back.

Moura lit a cigarette. There was still time. "Wait and see," she decided. The deadline was still far off.

She, too, wanted to ignore other people's words once in a while.

The fact was that the prospect of Alexey returning to Russia terrified her.

She stubbed out her cigarette nervously, lit another one.

If he left, that would mean a separation for the two of them. Worse: a break. Should she prepare herself for that?

Ultimately, he would be forced to go. If he couldn't live off his sales here and support the twenty-odd people who depended on him, what choice did he have?

She could feel anger rising up within her, an old anger that would always be simmering. She was upset with him over his thoughtlessness and his selfishness. His perpetual, ever-so-kind insistence that she bring her children here from Estonia and have them live in Naples . . . When he himself had no idea whether he would still be in Europe next year! Alexey's hypocrisy exasperated her.

And there were still other problems looming on the horizon.

The Sorrento lawyer, Carlo Ruffino . . . It was a stupid temptation she was trying to resist.

But to no avail.

She loved this foolishness. And she understood how Blok's wife could have been seduced by that circus clown Gorky sneered at. A bit of silliness, nothing more! She was sick of all the drama, all the doubting, all this weight.

She lit a third cigarette. Judging by the number of butts in the ashtray, she was smoking too much. And she was drinking too much. But she could hold her alcohol, and Gorky didn't notice her excesses.

Now she heard his footsteps approaching on the balcony. Alexey's interminable shadow darkened the paving stones, the railing. His shadow covered her whole body.

He was wearing his old purple dressing gown, his Chinese mandarin gown that she had loved so much back on Kronverksky Prospect.

He had forgotten to put his dentures back in. She could tell by his voice.

"What are you thinking about, Maria?"

She didn't turn to him.

"Nothing."

"No, what are you really thinking about?"

"About the trip next week . . . About school starting again in Tallinn."

"So you're thinking about your children!" he declared with a bitterness that was unlike him. "You're thinking about your children, the way you always are when you're lying to me!"

"I'm not lying to you."

"You're doing nothing but that!"

She remained silent. He kept going:

"Does my presence upset you that much? Am I being difficult?"

"Not at all!"

"Rejecting the truth: that's always been your philosophy, hasn't it?" He was shaking with fury. "You don't even bother to look at me anymore when I talk to you!"

She looked up. He was mad with rage! The very picture of frustration and wrath.

Under his close-cut gray hair, which was like a heap of silver on his head, his brow was furrowed with anxious wrinkles. The ridges framing his mustache made his stare menacing.

She feared he would explode.

Alexey could refuse to face matters quite easily. But she knew quite well that when someone or something didn't agree with him, his anger would become uncontrollable.

He was going to make himself sick. They would both end up bedridden.

She had to avoid a confrontation.

"I understand what you're telling me, darling. Please forgive me."

"No, you don't understand me. Of course you don't: you don't care . . . You don't care about me as a man, and you don't care about me as a writer!"

"I do realize that sometimes I'm not as attentive to you as I could be, but—"

"Even now you're talking to me like I'm an idiot . . . Nobody should treat a Russian writer with the kind of condescension you're showing me!"

She couldn't hide her frustration. She needed to explain herself. He didn't give her the chance:

"It's painful to see you—a person better educated than myself, *you*, Maria Ignatyevna—lose yourself like this. This lack of human respect doesn't become you. It's degrading. Both for you and for me . . . You're looking down your nose at me like an officer snubbing his lackey. And now the people who observe us feel like they can gossip about how a baroness doesn't want anything to do with an upstart like me, an upstart with a big head who takes himself so seriously that she has to put him back in his place!"

At this, she burst out in crass laughter:

"I have no idea who these *observers* you're alluding to are, who these fools talking about a difference in education between the baroness and the upstart are! I don't believe such words have ever been uttered in connection with the two of us. I don't have the impression that anybody has ever been led to believe there's a social barrier between us . . . My God, Alexey, my God, this is all just ridiculous!"

At this point, she was trembling with bitter indignation. He responded in soothing tones.

Her anger had calmed him down. He was quiet for a minute before whispering:

"You never tell me anything. You never tell me about your worries. I can tell, I know, just how hard life still is for you. But the truth is that I don't know *why* it's hard! Max knows more about your personal life than I do. And that tells me I've become a total stranger to you."

"You? A stranger? Oh, Alexey, if only you knew!"

She sighed, thinking about what she didn't tell him. About what rattled her so deeply that she couldn't even put it into words . . . Her inability to assuage her sisters' despair, to make their lives bearable.

Her impotence in the face of Anna's decline in morals and health as she stretched herself thin trying to raise her four children in Nice . . . She was running all over town to teach piano lessons, singing lessons, English lessons, German lessons. Her husband, Vasily Kochubey, the former marshal of Ukrainian nobility, was hitching together trains at the station and delivering sacks of coal all night: the work was wearing him down, as well. Exile and poverty were killing them both. It was a slow death.

And Alexey—in his haven here in Sorrento—didn't have the least idea of this kind of emigration, of this sorry reality!

What could she tell him, besides, about Alla, who was succumbing to drugs in Paris?

"I am hiding my worries from you, dear Alexey, so as not to burden your life with the weights bringing down mine. They're trifles that we should shrug off so they don't trouble you. Little obligations to be dealt with. They're of no interest to you. That's why I don't mention them to you . . ." She stroked his hand. "Now, my dear, let's go back in, shall we? No matter what you think, I care about you too much to let you catch a chill tonight."

He smiled now and took her in his arms. "Oh, I've never doubted your fear of my catching a chill . . . But you're right: let's go back in." He couldn't help adding: "I'd forgotten that our days were numbered. I'd forgotten you were leaving so soon to take your children back next week and that I don't know when you're coming back."

❖

Gorky to Moura, Sorrento, August 2, 1925:

I've written to you so much lately, Maria, but I haven't sent you any of these letters out of fear that you might take them the wrong way. Or not understand them at all. I still fear that. . . . Our last conversation—where you were sending me your thanks from Nice, in the telegram you sent me from your sister's home (a gratitude that is absolutely unnecessary and silly on your part!)—hasn't changed my feelings.

Why?

Because, when I asked you the night before you left: "Are you all right here? . . . Are you content here at Il Sorito? . . . Are you happy with me?" you replied unthinkingly, without even considering just how broad these questions were: "Probably."

With that simple word, I could feel your exhaustion. And nothing else. No love. No compassion . . . Just that: exhaustion.

. . . Again, you must understand me! I'm not asking anything of you, I'm not

insisting that you feel anything. I'm only telling you about me, about my fear of losing you because you are the most important, the most special person in my life. Of all the ordeals I've overcome in my short existence, losing you would without a doubt be the most impossible one to surmount.

But, honestly, I have to confess that you're not leaving me much hope about any change in plans. . . . I don't know if this letter will reach you in Nice. Maybe it would be better if it didn't.

Alexey

Moura to Gorky, Nice, August 5, 1925:

My dear Alexey Maximovich,

I just received your letter, and I'm crying.

. . . I didn't want to explain myself in Sorrento, because I was hoping to come back having recovered. To come back to Il Sorito having calmed my nerves and gotten hold of myself.

And I wanted to push you to calm your nerves as well.

But I know I have to answer your letter. Alexey Maximovich, my attitude toward you hasn't changed, not at all!

. . . I think you may have misunderstood my reply when I told you that I was "probably" happy with you: my "probably" has never indicated any indifference on my part.

I also suspect that you may have sensed the truth when you heard in my voice the same weariness that sometimes bothers you. A world-weariness that weighs on me and crushes me like concrete. Alexey Maximovich, God knows I'm not a hysterical woman, and you know that as well. But even so, there are moments when I want to die.

There you have it.

All the same, I want to remind you, my love for you, my "fusion" with you, my need for you—none of that has changed. Those golden days when we were all passion, all loving feeling that made our lives so light, are long gone, that much is true. Am I guilty of that, my friend? I think not.

. . . When you receive this letter, write me back at least a few words in Berlin. Please. It hurts so much. And believe me, I love you dearly.

Maria

Gorky to Moura, Sorrento, August 8, 1925:

I suspected that you might not realize the fear that drove me to write to you. A very simple, very human fear. To be honest, I'm crushed by the prospect that you, my dear, the exhausted and wearied person inclined to swift—unexpected, even for you!—responses might want to leave me. Is that clear? There you have it. With my letter, I was shutting the door so I could stop suffering.

. . . I can't write to you anymore because I'm afraid of writing even worse. I love you, pure and simple. When you're with me, I don't know how or I don't dare to tell you that.

Alexey

Moura to Gorky, hand-delivered to the Continental Hotel in Naples, where they try to explain themselves, October 23, 1925:

I want to confess everything to you, even though I know my words will influence what you think of me.

By way of introduction, I want to reassure you that at no time, not even for a single second, have I forgotten this "higher obligation" that your love imposes upon me. These are not simply words. You know quite well that I don't like big words. And I think I've damaged many things in our last conversations: I should have decided to talk right away. I wasn't able to, and later you'll understand why.

Listen to me, my dear friend. The situation is as follows: I hope you don't have any doubts, you can't have any, about this powerful, all-encompassing love that I felt for you at the time. In Russia. And this strong sentiment lasted everywhere, in Saarov, in Freiburg. Everywhere. But then I felt—little by little, I think, because I don't remember exactly when—that I was no longer in love with you. That I would always care about you, yes, but that I was no longer in love.

. . . *This made me very scared, very scared—I remember it—so afraid that I couldn't say it.*

. . . *Do understand that this wasn't out of a wish for a sexual relationship with someone else—no, I know those feelings well, it wasn't that—but the need to see my life illuminated anew by this incredible love for which life is worth living, this love that gives everything and asks nothing in return. I experienced it with Lockhart, I experienced it with you. And "this love" is now gone.*

But is life over?

. . . *Understand me. This isn't some sort of instinct, this is just my inherent incompatibility with a life drained of magic. You know well enough that I'm not accustomed to "apologizing," but this much I know about myself: I need only one thing—this joy. And without it, what use am I to this world, as well as to you?*

Ultimately, I would find it humiliating to accept the rapture of your love and to not tremble with delight at your embrace. To be unable to sing in harmony with you.

My dear friend, God knows that if I've made you suffer, I've repaid the price over and over with my own pain. I struggled with myself and I'm still struggling.

I thought I could escape this state—because I know all too well what I have to lose in you. This is why I didn't want to talk . . . I felt that putting these thoughts into words would only worsen them. But I see that I was wrong to stay quiet, that I should have talked sooner. I don't know what to do anymore. . . . Because, despite the difficulties I've just confessed to you, my love for you has grown more solid, more sincere with each passing day. Do you think that what I'm writing doesn't ring true? That I'm saying these words just to "console" you? No, no, it's plain to see that I'm laying myself bare for you, that there is no room here for any lies!

Believe me, my dear: I haven't lied to you about anything, and I'm not able to play any tricks on you. You've alluded to my wish to establish "another relationship." Your suspicions wound me, because I've always forbidden myself from developing any such attachment and I've pushed away other relationships in order to save you from the least bit of tawdriness. My ambiguous situation with Baron Budberg weighted heavily on me and I've put a swift end to it. No, you can't scold me about that.

And now I'm afraid. . . . And I'm terrified that I've set all of myself, my weakness, my ordinariness, my unworthiness of your love down on paper. I'll never be able to forgive myself this unworthiness.

Maria

Gorky to Moura, Naples, December 30, 1925:

My friend,

. . . The letter you sent to me at the Continental Hotel is replete with fatal truths for me. But you are finally, finally, finally telling me The Truth!

. . . You know that I've been dreading for years what is now happening to us . . . that I haven't stopped telling you that I'm too old for you. I kept saying it in hopes of hearing an honest "yes!" escaping your lips. You didn't dare and still don't dare to say it. And so you've put us—you and me—into an absolutely unbearable situation.

Your attraction to R., a younger man—and therefore more worthy of your love—is wholly natural. And it's not worth hiding, as you do, the voice of your baser instincts beneath the fig leaf of your fine words. What use is that? You're not trying to "overcome" your thoughts, are you? Because you never will! And besides, why ever would you try?

You can't live "without magic," as you put it, and I can understand that as well. But this is where our irreconcilable difference lies. The magic that the cruel law of sex drives you toward is wholly at odds with my perspective. As for myself, I endure it as a monstrosity of nature and I feel the relationship Blok's wife has established with her clown as a personal insult. You can see just how sharply our visions diverge! . . .

In your last letter, the only honest one, you ask me what is to be done. And I am telling you again: we must separate. Perhaps temporarily; that call is one you must make. But from my point of view, such a rupture is necessary. . . . You won't have to show two faces anymore, to slice your life into segments, you won't have to tell me these little lies that just keep on multiplying, "for the sake of my well-being," to desecrate and denature yourself.

. . . As for the rest, my work is dependent upon more fundamentally peaceful

conditions. And to be with you, given where our relationship is, a peaceful heart is impossible. Because, as you know, I love you, etc. And so I am jealous, etc., etc. Maybe I shouldn't have reminded you of that? . . .

In practical terms, I would suggest this: Gather up as much money as you can, take half of it, go to Paris, Nice, London, go and celebrate wherever you are—I don't care.

That's all the advice I can give you. . . .

A.

Moura to Gorky, Paris, April 29, 1926:

If I understand right, I haven't been able to reassure you all through the winter. Do you say that I haven't tried? Well, you should concede that, on this point, you haven't been entirely fair with me . . . I do think, however, that you'll concede this: I've devoted my life to preserving your inner peace, a peace that you write I don't care about.

I told you that I decided not to see R. anymore. And I've been true to my word.

With every fiber of my being, I, too, have been trying as best as I can to find calm again. And I'm not necessarily seeking out what I can instinctively, contrary to what you say. I don't even claim to be wringing what would please me from our lives . . . just what is needed for me to breathe.

And, thank heavens, this path that leads to peace is starting to become clear for me!

❖

Peace for Moura? What wishful thinking!

What she didn't tell Gorky in this exchange of letters was that the French intelligence services, drawing on messages they had received five years earlier from their correspondent in Tallinn, had been watching her from Paris.

That the British intelligence services, too, were watching her. And after her brief visit to London under her new name as Baroness Budberg, she hadn't been able to return to England. Her visa application had been refused repeatedly, without any explanation.

The only thing she knew was that she was being followed everywhere.

What she also didn't tell Gorky, what she would explain to him only much later, was that by leaving him to stay in Nice with Anna in August 1925, she had suffered the humiliation of a forceful search by the Fascist police. The customs officers hadn't been satisfied with the contents of her luggage. They had also gone through the children's belongings and Micky's bag.

It was sheer luck that they had found only the nineteen packets of cigarettes Moura was sneaking through. The fine had been astronomical. But nothing in comparison to the prospect of a new arrest!

She was released for lack of any proof—a miracle: the Fascists rarely bothered with such particulars—and so she had kept going, without making any mention of the incident. Only the children made any kind of allusion to it in their short letter to Gorky from the château, telling him about the experience and thanking him for the lovely vacation.

But that was far from the end of the matter.

A month later, on September 17, 1925, a horde of Blackshirts tore through Il Sorito.

The police searched the entire villa, taking special care to rummage through every corner of Baronessa Budberg's room and to empty out every bit of her desk, her armoires, her drawers. They took away everything.

It was the same scene as on Kronverksky Prospect, with Zinoviev's chekists.

Gorky was furious and filed a complaint about this invasion with Stalin's ambassador in Rome.

The ambassador raised such a fuss with the Italian government that Il Duce, fearing a diplomatic incident with Soviet Russia, made a special phone call to offer his apologies to *l'illustrissimo maestro Gorky*, his guest.

It was a mistake, of course. All the papers that had been confiscated would be returned to him. And his collaborator, Signora Baronessa Budberg, wouldn't be bothered anymore.

Gorky wasn't satisfied with that answer.

This investigation, which had directly threatened both his safety and Maria Ignatyevna's, had only convinced him that it was time to leave Italy and return to Russia.

The danger of such a "visit" thoroughly deterred him from any prospect of breaking up with her. This woman needed his help and his protection.

All the more so because three months later, in December 1925, Moura would be searched again by Mussolini's men. And this time, taken away.

Her fifth arrest in seven years.

At that point, she was traveling alone toward Estonia—on the way to her usual Christmas holiday at Kallijärv—and had been planning to go through Austria. The customs officers had decided to take her aside for an interrogation. So they had removed her from the train. Taken her into the station. And locked her up there.

Their questions centered on a report made by Fascist police informants in Sorrento—a former cook at Il Sorito whom Moura had fired for theft and the cabdriver Gorky had used for his trips into town.

These two moles had given the intelligence services a list of all the visitors to the villa, with their names, their occupations, and their political opinions. The administration had rounded out the document with their dates of birth and their genealogies.

The paragraph about her was the longest one.

General Directorate for Public Safety and Security. Concerning Gorky, Massimo, Russian writer and notorious Communist, . . . born in Novgorod 26-5-1868.

BARONESSA BUDBERG ZAKREVSKYA, MARIA. Daughter of Ignazio Zakrevsky and of Maria Boreisha. Born in Poltava 3-3-1892. Estonian nationality. Suspected of espionage and monitored by the National Defense.

Takes many trips abroad, most especially to Paris, . . . Berlin, and Estonia, where her children live. But we do not know the real purpose of her many travels.

This time, too, nothing was found. Nothing at all. No compromising evidence. And this time, too, there was a miracle: Moura was released. But she wouldn't be able to escape the Fascist prisons a third time. She knew that. As did Gorky.

Mad with rage, incensed at the surveillance she had been subjected to, he complained to the Russian ambassador in Rome again. The treatment they had been subjecting his colleague to was unacceptable!

Whether the ambassador relayed his anger to Il Duce is a question that has been lost to history. The only known fact is that Mussolini did not pick up his telephone a second time to apologize for his conduct toward Baronessa Budberg.

And Gorky did not calm down again.

He was suddenly aware that without his support, Maria Ignatyevna would suffer—would be disappeared. That without him, she literally would not survive. That without him, her personal safety was just as endangered as her social and financial safety.

Literary Agent and International Representative of Maxim Gorky.

Those eight words alone would guarantee her safety.

They were her bread and butter, they justified her trips, they opened the doors to the intelligentsia in every capital of Europe. They offered her the opportunity, for example, to be welcomed by André Germain in Paris—who published and supported Gorky—and Montherlant, Soupault, Drieu La Rochelle, and Romain Rolland.

Literary Agent and International Representative of Maxim Gorky.

Those eight words alone would allow her to serve him; to share his view of the world with other celebrities and younger writers; and to make his work visible abroad.

He had always thought he was insignificant in her eyes, but now he saw that he was very much essential to her—necessary, in the most fundamental sense—and that she was, herself, just as much so to his work as a writer, to promoting his work, and to giving his books a long life.

And that at the end of the day, even though personal interest had some role in the friendship of their two souls, the affection they felt for each other was so deeply rooted that neither of them could live without the other.

❖

That summer, in 1926, the jig was up.

Both of them conceded that their love had fundamentally changed, but they knew that they were bound together.

Indispensable to each other's emotional stability. Indispensable to each other's mental well-being.

Inseparable, no matter what.

The Italian, French, Estonian, British, and Russian police forces had brought about this miracle: allowing them to overcome the crisis that had torn them apart and nearly destroyed them over the course of three years.

❖

Maxim Gorky dedicated the three volumes of his novel *The Life of Klim Samgin*, his final work, to Maria Ignatyevna.

BOOK V

The Fifth Life of Moura Budberg

Master of My Fate and Captain of My Soul

April 1929–September 1934

I am the master of my fate
I am the captain of my soul

William Ernest Henley

CHAPTER THIRTY-FOUR

Between Two Seas

1929–1931

"H G!"

In the crowd, the voice, a woman's voice with a Slavic accent, had yelled somewhat hoarsely: "Aige-Gee." Wells jumped.

It was an evening in April 1929, in the wings of the Reichstag lecture hall where he had just given his speech "The Common Sense of World Peace," and everybody in Berlin was descending upon him to thank him. Albert Einstein, the man who had welcomed him onstage and introduced him, was part of the group of pacifists thronging around him.

After the audience was done congratulating him, his German compatriots—the ambassador to Britain and his army of attachés and secretaries—would toast to his success with an elaborate dinner in his honor at the Hotel Adlon. Indeed, with his ideas on establishing universal peace and creating a new world free of nationalisms and borders, Wells was at the peak of his glory in the most progressive society in Europe: the intellectual Berlin of the late 1920s. In less than four years, Hitler would have seized power.

"Aige-Gee!"

It was a melodic—charming—deformation of "H. G.," the initials his friends used: shorter for everybody than Herbert George . . . *Aige-Gee.* That sound, that voice, seduced him.

It was in Petrograd . . . In that woman's bed . . . During their one night of love. A whisper in his car: *Aige-Gee* . . . It had been unforgettably sensual.

That wonderment had cost him nearly everything once he had

returned to England, when he had been stupid enough to confess the shock of this brief encounter—and his one-night stretch of infidelity—to Rebecca West, the writer he was sharing his life with at the time.

Now he was living with another woman. And he didn't entrust anything to her.

He knew that Moura was now in Berlin. She had left a brief note for him at the Eden Palace, where he was staying, to let him know that she would be attending his lecture. He had tried to find her face in the audience. In vain. The amphitheater was too dark: it was impossible to identify anyone.

He peered through the crowd again.

And now he saw her, tall, powerful, striding boldly toward him. The same face, the same slightly flattened nose that had been broken when she was young. The same protruding cheekbones. The same hazel eyes dotted with specks of gold that narrowed into almond curves when she smiled. The same expression that was simultaneously luminous and serene; and the same raised chin that announced she could conquer the entire world. All that had changed was her hair, which had once been straight and dark but was now crimped into waves and shot through with streaks of gray. And her clothes, while modest, were almost stylish.

Now she was a made woman, a thirty-six-year-old woman.

"Moura! . . . Is that you? . . . It's you! Oh, come here, my dear!"

They held their embrace for longer than perhaps was necessary.

He was struck again by the simple, direct way she had now, as she'd had before, of simply sinking into his arms. And this way that she alone had of answering his excitement with warmth as she pulled him tight against her body.

"Well, there's no question of it, none at all: it's you, my adorable guide from Petrograd! Let me look at you . . . You're still magnificent. It took me nine years, my dear, nine years, to see you again. And I've been counting every single one of those years."

"As have I, Aige-Gee, I've counted all the years."

"The last time we were at a meeting together, it was at the northern Congress of Soviets in Petrograd, remember that?"

"Yes, when we walked out we were all singing 'The Internationale'!"

"Come with us. And don't tell me you're not free tonight, I'm not letting you get away. Do join me and Einstein for the photographs. Then we can toast to seeing each other again at the Adlon. A car's waiting to take us there. You'll dine with us at our table, with me."

"You think so? I'm not dressed for a reception."

"You're perfect! Although I'll allow that you're missing your British waterproof, your little black dress, and your huge men's watch. But as for the rest . . . You're my splendid Moura!"

He took her by the elbow and immediately led her away to talk, without even thinking about it, in his excitement, as his hosts—the director of the Reichstag and the German minister of education, who could hear everything they were saying—looked on. He still had that falsetto voice with too-high intonations that carried a great distance:

"And how is our friend Gorky doing?"

"He's doing well enough."

"Is he still enjoying himself in Sorrento?"

"He still is."

"I heard he was thinking about going back to Russia . . ."

"He spent the summer there."

"And?"

"And he came back all excited . . . He's planning to go back there next year for a few months."

The two of them paid no attention to the people around them as they picked up their conversation where they had left off, trading thoughts as if they had left each other only the night before.

They had so much to catch up on. Wells directed them past the journalists and the photographers without ever letting go of her arm. His voice rose over the crowd:

"Knowing him, he wants to see everything that's happening over there."

"Of course. After seven years away, he thought the country had made great progress!"

"And maybe Stalin's a proper gentleman."

"That's what he says. According to him, Stalin is the best leader possible: he developed the educational system, had schools built. And now people all the way down to the Caucasus are reading books. At every station, Gorky's train was mobbed by his readers. There were huge crowds begging for him to come. It was such a heartwarming welcome."

"And what about you?" Wells asked.

"As for me, I'm translating his books and taking care of his business across Europe. I live here. My agency is named Epokha Verlag. It's also a small publishing house. I wrote to you about it in my letters."

"I loved your letters, my dear. They're so happy . . . So intelligent and well considered . . . What did you think of my talk about peace? Did you like it?"

"It was visionary, Aige-Gee!"

"Could everybody hear me okay?"

"Perfectly!"

"Even in the back?"

"Everywhere. Look at the crowd: your listeners were rapt."

◆

The first counselor to the British ambassador in Berlin—Harold Nicolson, the husband of Vita Sackville-West and a close friend of Robert Bruce Lockhart—wrote to his wife the next day:

> *I went to H. G. Wells's lecture in the Reichstag. One simply could not hear a word. Not a single word. It was rather a disaster.*

He also noted in his diary, in April:

> *I dined with H. G. Wells and Moura Budberg. Towards the end of the evening, Wells ceased to flirt with the lady, and talked intelligently. . . .*
>
> *He is a wrong-headed but amusing little man. He believes in the new world very thoroughly, I think. He did not think very much of Lenin as a personality, but*

realized that he must have been one. What was funny was that he was embarrassed
about going out to pee. We teased him about it, and he admitted that this was one
of his conventions.

There was no need for Harold Nicolson to seek any further proof. There was no need for him to write that Wells—whose reputation for loving women was notorious; who was a great seducer, despite having seen sixty-three springs go past, despite his diminutive stature, despite his too-high voice—didn't leave the bedroom, whether Moura's or his own, after this dinner and stayed shut away in there for the remaining five days of his stay in Berlin. The reunion with his "adorable guide from Petrograd" wasn't merely sentimental, after all.

But it was an affair that had to remain discreet, all the same.

❖

They had the same sense of humor in bed. The same voluptuous playfulness. The same fancifulness. The same sensuality. The same freedom.

They had a great deal of fun lying beside each other. They had just as much fun standing up.

They had the same intellectual interests. The same political opinions.

Wells might have been a good two years older than Gorky, but his soul and his body were remarkably young. The pleasure she had gotten a taste of in Petrograd blossomed into full fruition in Berlin.

On the dawn of April 20, 1929, their second adventure drew to its end. Sitting next to each other in the massive bed at the Eden Palace, their backs propped up by a pile of cushions, they were smoking together. He was taking drags from his pipe. She was lighting the last cigarette from her last packet, with the ashtray resting on her belly. The two of them were thinking about the car that would come pick up the writer at the end of the morning to take him to the train station. God alone knew when Wells might come back to Berlin.

He felt somehow guilty. Forced, if not to justify himself, at least to explain himself.

He broached the subject gingerly, trying to get her to bring it up first.

"Have you had many affairs, Moura?"

"Very few."

He laughed. "Now what does 'very few' mean?"

"Fewer than you."

"I'm not quite as voracious as you might believe . . . I'm actually unable to sleep with a woman I'm not charmed by."

"It's the same for me. The idea of just falling into the arms of a man I don't like . . . It's impossible! I've never given myself up to someone I wasn't passionate about."

"Have you often been passionate about men?"

"No."

"How many times?"

"I don't know. I've never counted."

"*Who* were your lovers?"

"The father of my children. Lockhart. Budberg. An Italian man in Sorrento. You."

"And now?"

"Nobody."

"Gorky?"

"Never."

"I would have thought . . ."

"And you would have been wrong . . . Everybody knows that. In Russia, everybody talks about it: Gorky has been impotent for years."

"But he has a cast of your hand, I saw it on his desk at Kronverksky Prospect. That's some evidence he cared deeply for you, isn't it? He writes with your hand in sight!"

"It's true that we were very close."

Wells paused before taking the bull by the horns.

"What you're giving me, Moura, makes me so happy!"

"As it does me, Aige-Gee . . ."

"But you have to know that I'm not able to offer you a love that's worthy of you. We've met each other far too late in life," he said wistfully, "far too late for me to muster the courage to destroy everything and start all over again."

She didn't blink. The memory of their meeting in Russia had stayed fixed in her heart as a magical moment. And what had just happened over the last five days comforted her. Everything seemed to be in harmony.

She wanted Wells's love with all her heart.

She loved the honeyed smell of his skin. She loved his weight, this slightly thick body so full of energy. She liked his strength. She liked his joy.

And now he was pushing her away, telling her that they weren't meant for each other. As Lockhart had, as Gorky was doing.

She stroked his cheek. "What would you like to give me, if not what we've just experienced?"

"I'm all tied up in matters you can't even begin to imagine!"

"So what? We're two adults who are coming to each other with a past. You and I each have a life of our own, maybe several lives, apart from what connects us. For now, let's share what we're able to share."

He insisted, afraid that she didn't understand:

"Bad timing, my dear, bad timing . . ."

He had already told her that his wife had died from cancer a year and a half earlier, and that he was still grieving. He called her Jane. Even though he had had other companions for the last twenty years, he still felt very tender toward her and hadn't wanted to divorce her. She was the mother of two of his sons.

Her death had left him at sixes and sevens. And the welter of his feelings went far beyond simply mourning his wife. He also had a mistress in France, the same one he'd had for five years, a jealous, passionate lover who often threw fits. Her name was Odette. And she had been hoping to marry him. As a widower, he wanted to satisfy her. He wanted to take the plunge.

"I have no plans to leave her, Moura. I love the home that we've built together, in Grasse. I'm working there, I'm writing so much. And I love my hefty angora cat who lives there. The house is called Lou Pidou, and the cat—"

"Nobody's asking you to separate from her, darling."

"I don't want to lose you. But I can't keep you to myself any longer, either! You have to build a life for yourself without me."

"We're in agreement there." She took a long drag on her cigarette and slowly exhaled the smoke, which rose to the ceiling. "Hic et nunc. Here and now. Nothing more, nothing less . . . I'll take it!"

"But you deserve more than that. . . ."

"We'll see each other again when we can, when we want to, exactly where and when we think best."

"Will you come to see me in London?"

"London, hmm. That could be a bit difficult . . . But we still have Vienna and Paris and Prague and Berlin!"

"Why would England be difficult?"

"Your government doesn't want anything to do with me. Every time I've applied for a visa, they've refused. Even though two British army officers have vouched for me. The visa office didn't even bother to contact them. That's how it's been for seven years or so."

"I'll take care of your visa when I get back. A residence card for the old, old, old friend of the esteemed H. G. Wells. It's the easiest thing, in fact, for me to get! A visa for the very respectable Baroness Budberg."

"Oh, I'm not so old as that!"

"And you're not so respectable . . ." He took her into his arms, kissed her, then let her go. "As for the rest, I think you should get married again, to a man worthy of you. A lord with a seat in Parliament. You deserve a husband who can protect you, serve you, and adore you."

"What horror!"

"That would be a nice thing, wouldn't it?"

"Not at all. I've already had two husbands; marriage doesn't go over well for me . . . And it hasn't gone over well for them, either. I'm not made for that."

"So what are you made for, then?"

She shrugged but did not respond.

He wasn't deterred:

"I'm going to tell you what I want you to have: an easier life."

"You know I'm not interested in that."

"All the more reason to seek it out!"

Wells, like Gorky, had been born into modest means. He had experienced, if not hunger, at least deep poverty. His character and qualities—his narcissism, his need to please, his drive to shine, his crusades for peace, and his battle for a more just world—were all part and parcel of his fundamental stance: against this society that had nearly killed him by not giving him what he needed to grow and develop. He considered his short stature a consequence of the deprivations he had suffered as a child.

In forty years of work, his social ascent had been a conquest. And his fortune was a victory. He took pride in it.

Even though he was neither a snob nor a socialite, and though even in the most conservative salons he still argued for militant socialism, he was only happy these days among the rich and powerful. His peers.

The great hostesses of London, Lady Cunard and Lady Colefax, were his close friends. He stayed with Charlie Chaplin when he traveled to America.

His successes in bookstores—*The Time Machine*, *The Island of Doctor Moreau*, *The Invisible Man*, *The War of the Worlds*—had brought him international renown, in both literary and scientific circles.

The undeniable master of the futurist novel, he thought about new ways humanity could be organized, played a role in politics, wrote about whatever he wanted to in the papers. His curiosity was limitless: he waxed poetic on every subject.

As a pillar of the PEN Club, which he was determined to be the world president of, he insisted that writers have freedom of thought and speech, since without them they would not be able to create. He fought fiercely for ideas to be able to circulate between nations.

As for himself, he demanded the right to move between numerous worlds at any moment, to spend time with whomever he wanted wherever he wanted, to say what he thought, and to change his mind if he wanted to.

———

Nobody was more appreciative than he was of how gracefully Moura was able to move between social circles, between different strata of the upper classes, always making an impression.

Even though this woman lived in a tiny studio on the Koburger Strasse (which Wells found far too uncomfortable to spend more than a night with her there), even though she didn't have anything to her name, not even a ring, a jewel, not even an evening gown for a dinner at Pavilion—the restaurant at the Eden Palace, where a strict dress code was enforced—the maître d's bent over backward to please her. She was a star. The bell-hops, the concierges, the chambermaids—they all adored her.

He loved her nonchalance. She was at home wherever she went. She didn't go from place to place: she *sailed* from circle to circle . . . Exactly the same way she moved around the bedroom: she didn't walk so much as float.

She was the opposite of Odette at Lou Pidou, he thought. Odette, who was so heavy, who mistreated her chambermaid, who wasted so much money at Parisian couturiers.

Wells wrote in his erotic autobiography:

I felt a great tenderness and solicitude for her. The fact that she was manifestly very poor hurt me. Directly I returned to England I settled a small annuity (two hundred pounds a year) on her, love masquerading as pseudo-camaraderie.

I thought it quite possible I should never see her again and I thought she was one of those careless people who might easily come upon extreme want.

I schemed for some further provision for her in my will and I kept up a correspondence with her and arranged presently to see her when she came to England.

There again we were lovers. But I told her plainly that I should keep Odette going at Lou Pidou; that we must not have a child; that I would not exact fidelity from her. . . .

I told her I counted our meetings no more than happy accidents—that I held myself to be free—and that she was free.

"Very well, my dear," said Moura. "As you will. If I happen to be faithful to you that is my own affair."

They saw each other again in Berlin that July. And again two months later, when Moura came to celebrate Aige-Gee's birthday in northern London, at his wonderful Easton Glebe estate on the Countess of Warwick's lands, a former vicarage in red brick that was now covered in ivy.

How could anyone describe the magic of such a secret celebration, just the two of them in front of a blazing hearth? It was September 21, 1929.

As he had promised, he had supported her application for a visa, helped fate along a bit. He had influence. Now she wouldn't have any trouble crossing the Channel anymore.

And, as she had promised, she came back to Easton Glebe the following year, again on his birthday. For them it was sheer pleasure: they stole kisses and loved freely.

And then again in his London apartment on September 21, 1931.

They also saw each other in Salzburg and Dubrovnik.

But at that point, Wells knew what she didn't yet: Moura Budberg was the woman of his life. He wanted her to himself. For her to be wholly his. Body and soul.

And that was a mistake.

Bad timing, my dear.

In London, she had met other men.

❧

The diary of Robert Bruce Lockhart:

Saturday, 4 October 1930

Lunched with Moura at the Savoy. She leaves today for Genoa [to see Gorky] and then Berlin. . . .

Discussed Gorky: now . . . poor, has given all his money away, makes about £300 a year, cannot get foreign currency from Russia now, sells 2,700,000 copies a year . . .

Tuesday, 6 January 1931

    Letter from Moura . . . She writes cheerfully and kindly. She is a big-minded and a big-hearted woman.

Friday, 6 March 1931

    In the afternoon met Moura at the Wellington. Sat there till 8.30 drinking sherry.

    Then went on to the Hungarian restaurant where we remained till two a.m. I felt very ill after drinking so much. She—as usual—never turned a hair.

    Naturally, we discussed Russia the whole evening. Moura thinks we are all wrong about the Russians. She thinks, like Wells, that the capitalist-finance system has broken down and that Russia will succeed with her Five-Year Plan—not necessarily in five years, but in the sense that she will make rapid progress towards becoming an industrial nation like the U.S.A.

    She saw Gorky a few weeks ago. He is now ultra-Bolshevik, has returned to his own class, believes implicitly in Stalin, and justifies the terror from which formerly he shrank.

❖

That was Moura's masterstroke: in a single year, 1931, Wells, Gorky, Lockhart . . . She had pulled it all off.

Connected with the three loves of her life.

Kept each one of them.

Not given one of them up, not now, not ever.

The first had no idea about the second. The second had no idea about the first. Only Lockhart knew the facts. But all of them could easily have used the line Robert Louis Stevenson wrote about the surprises his wife had had in store for him: "the most . . . direct of women will some day, to your dire surprise, draw out like a telescope into successive lengths of personation."

What her three lovers could not understand, however, was that Moura still respected the terms of the compact that, at one point or another, each had imposed upon her. *Here and now. No more, no less.*

◈

During Aige-Gee's escapes from his villa at Lou Pidou, she ate with him, she laughed with him, she slept with him, she spent the night with him. She was his beloved lover who accompanied him everywhere, even before he made his way back to Grasse, without thinking too long about how she was his first port of call.

She didn't complain, didn't explain. She was always happy, always whimsical and easygoing when they were together.

Wells wrote:

> *She is not a feverish lascivious woman like Odette. She has no sensuous initiative, but she loves to be made love to and she is responsive.*

But she furrowed her brows whenever he brought her gifts—at least, expensive ones—and refused the sums of money he offered her. Or rather, she spent it all in one go, blowing through it with a spectacular lunch or a vintage wine.

The truth was that she cared about her independence.

There was no question of his treating her like Odette.

He didn't understand. It was simple enough: he was rich. She wasn't. So she should get something! So she should accept his payments into the Deutsche Bank in Berlin. At least to update her wardrobe, or to take care of her children's education.

She smiled as she told him that he was very useful and helpful on other fronts. She didn't specify which.

She liked to accompany him to nice hotels, yes. To spend time in classy neighborhoods, to travel in first class. She liked the rhythm of life with him. Their nights of love and their long conversations in the morning. The delight of time together, trading ideas.

Their meetings with so many intelligent minds: listening to Einstein talking endlessly at their table; attending the first of George Bernard Shaw's plays; laughing, especially when all of them were together, to W. Somerset Maugham's caustic witticisms.

She had always striven for excellence. To find the very best in life—the best on every front—had been a matter of instinct for her. Gorky: the best living writer in Russia. Wells: the most famous one in England. Each of her friends, each of her lovers, was at the pinnacle of his art. Each embodied genius and power. Each played a role on the international stage.

She was drawn to their orbit so she could be part of their world and bask in their glow. There was no denying that.

But she didn't care about luxury. She didn't even want to look for comfort, for any of the basic commodities of material life without which Aige-Gee wouldn't be able to exist. His excesses—this financial generosity that she couldn't offer him—was an imbalance in their relationship that detracted from all the risk, all the poetry of their adventure.

Their secret meetings struck each of them as a fumbled romance, a succession of leisurely pleasures that they were both impatient for and excited about. They were now closer than ever.

Even if Wells still insisted on being able to live with another mistress, he was certain that Moura loved only him. It was true that he had given her every opportunity to sleep with other people. But she seemed to be devoted to him . . . Faithful, even? Hadn't she said that the choice was hers?

Well, it would seem that this wasn't the case.

❖

Whether by chance or necessity, the fourth man in Moura's life lived in London, as well. And this man was from her past: his name was Benckendorff. He was, in fact, the only Count Benckendorff in the family, the son of the tsar's last ambassador in London. He was married to a famous Russian harp player and was a distant cousin of Djon's.

Konstantin Alexandrovich Benckendorff, who was thirteen years older than Moura, was a liberal aristocrat. He had served, successively, in Nicholas II's marines and Lenin's Red Army, and had vacillated endlessly between the two fronts.

Just like Moura.

He still believed in the Revolution. Even today, even in spite of what he knew about the Soviet Union, he couldn't reject those dreams he had had of equality, fraternity, and justice.

Just like Moura.

The White Russians were suspicious. They were convinced he was a spy working for the Bolsheviks, a traitor to his class.

Just like Moura.

And more important: Konstantin Benckendorff had been Russia's representative in the negotiations for Estonia's independence. He had even been one of the writers of the treaty that had liberated the country. He had lived in Tallinn. He knew Yendel and Kallijärv well. He had even spent time with the Budbergs.

But he had never met her there. This Benckendorff had already left the Baltic countries by the time Moura was making her way to the West.

He had already emigrated with his wife in 1924, settling in London, where his mother still lived. "Cousin Moura" had stayed with them during her second trip to England, using their kinship as a pretext to stay under their roof for several days before she went to see a friend in Essex: *an acquaintance* who lived in Easton Glebe.

One evening when his wife was giving a concert out in the countryside—she would be the first harpist to perform at the Glyndebourne Festival—Benckendorff invited his relative to dinner at the best Russian restaurant in London. Their affair began on the sofa once they returned from this delightful, inebriated evening out.

Their trysting, which was just as discreet as all Moura's other assignations, would last two decades.

"I loved Gorky and Wells," Moura confessed during one of her rare interviews. "For Konstantin, I felt a physical passion."

❖

"Her name is Baroness Budberg," Konstantin's unhappy wife declared, "but it ought to be Baroness *Bedbug!*"

Odette, Wells's official companion, repeated those same words. She had snooped through his correspondence and learned of her rival's existence.

"I've been talking to our friends so much about you," she said, "and I've been telling them the most atrocious things. About you and your Moura. . . . Do you know that I've picked out a new name for her? It's already making the rounds in London . . . Such a funny name. All England is going to have a good laugh at your expense. I'm not calling her Budberg but Bedbug . . . Baroness Bedbug. It's funny, isn't it?"

CHAPTER THIRTY-FIVE

Baroness Bedbug: Engagement, Fidelity, and Compromise

1930–1932

S hut away in the phone booth of a seedy restaurant by the Parc des Buttes-Chaumont, Moura was reluctant to pick up the receiver. Just outside the booth, the door to the restrooms was constantly banging, and the customers eyed her as they walked past. She was the only woman here.

With its bare walls, the place bore no resemblance to the modern cafés of the Roaring Twenties; it didn't boast the ambience of La Coupole or Le Boeuf sur le Toit. Rather, it was emblematic of the dirty Paris of the barricades, the working-class Paris of Zola's novels.

She pressed her forehead to the wall for a moment and shut her eyes. The ruckus she had just escaped, a bout of hysteria at Alla's place—exactly like so many of her other bouts—had been too much for her.

Usually, she took great care to make sure that nobody could see her during these stretches of discouragement, when she was overwhelmed with exhaustion. This exhaustion that Gorky had scolded her for in Sorrento; that Wells had never seen and would never see on her features.

This time, she knew she couldn't do it on her own. There were too many problems on too many fronts.

She needed to call Anna.

She still hesitated to dial the number; she would have loved to spare Anna this new ordeal.

Poor Anna! In Nice, living on the rue Rossini, she had already lost a little girl. And if she had thought her life would be easier after she'd come up to Paris, she had thought wrong.

Unlike the other aristocrats who had come before him, her husband hadn't been able to find work as a cabdriver. He'd had to go back to working for the railroads. It was night work, enervating, embittering. He was still hitching trains together and carrying sacks of coal back and forth. But this time, at the Gare du Nord, Vasily had lost all his love for life.

Anna, in turn, was running all over the capital, stretching herself thin with all the classes she had to teach. She was just as pragmatic and organized as always. But she was tense, always staring straight ahead, pinching her lips together. She hadn't smiled in years.

Now, the only future the couple saw for themselves was a return to their previous life, at Berezovaya or on the Kochubey estate in Ukraine. Anna and Vasily's hatred for the Bolsheviks, their need to recapture those lands and get revenge, was their only way of keeping hope. Like most White Russians, they lived only in the past. And like so many emigrants whose exile was causing them unbearable suffering, they were foundering.

Moura's compassion for her siblings was endless. She never passed any judgment upon them, and her inability to help them was the source of an anguish that verged on obsession.

She made sure to see them several times each year. Every trip she took to France meant being scolded by Alexey Maximovich, who accused her of choosing to crisscross the decaying continent rather than discover the great sites of Eternal Russia beside him. Gorky had been invited back by Stalin and had spent the last few summers in the Soviet Union. What he had seen there had confirmed his anti-Western sentiments, which were a far cry from his earlier tolerance. Of all Europe's capitals, Paris struck him as the most decadent. He was disappointed in Maria Ignatyevna for abandoning him to enjoy herself.

Her visits, however, usually ended up being nightmares.

She had always believed she would be able to save Anna and Alla. She never flinched; she kept on fighting. But she was losing more ground with each passing year. Even Anna's health was worsening. Moura had taken her sister to a specialist, who had diagnosed her with the first stages of tuberculosis. She paid their medical fees, of course, and supported them financially. But it was not enough to guarantee them a decent life.

The consequences of Gorky's diminishing print runs in Europe didn't make matters easier for her. And the 1929 stock market crash was only worsening the situation. Not to mention the rise of Nazism in Berlin, which was making the city's atmosphere unpleasant. She would have to move elsewhere soon.

But where?

She dreamed of London. Gorky, however, dreamed of Moscow.

Would she come back to live there with him, with the friends from Il Sorito, as he had been asking her to?

She answered that she *couldn't* follow them, that she was still a *burzhui*, that she would be shot dead the minute she set foot on Russian soil. To which Alexey retorted that Stalin was his friend. And that he was negotiating Maria Ignatyevna's safety with him. That he would even make it a fundamental condition of his return. He offered to marry her if that would reassure her. Stalin would never dare touch Gorky's wife!

Moura sighed.

Once again, Alexey Maximovich was looking away and refusing to deal with unpleasant realities.

But the problem remained: if he returned to Stalin's land, what would become of her in Germany without him? The Epokha Verlag agency, which had been her bailiwick, would lose its raison d'être.

Time would tell. One thing at a time.

She finally picked up the phone and asked for her sister's number.

"Anna, my dear, can you hear me?"

The phone rumbled. As did the Kochubey's phone at the entrance of their modest two-bedroom apartment at number 17, avenue Émile-Deschanel.

Moura repeated herself, saying each word distinctly and carefully. "Listen to me: Alla needs to be hospitalized right away."

There was a pause at the other end of the line. Then:

"Is she cooperating?"

"No . . . I've called an ambulance. They're going to pick her up."

"You want to put Alla in an asylum . . . With the crazies?"

"In a clinic. To be treated for addiction."

"I believe, Moura, that you don't understand the situation properly: we don't have the means to care for Alla in a *clinic*!"

"Don't worry about that. I'm taking care of it. I'll figure it out. But she can't be alone here. She was in a terrible state. She's not eating anymore. She's not washing herself anymore. And she doesn't want to hear a word from me. She says I'm too young to deal with her. Too young to tell her what to do. But maybe . . . maybe she'll listen to you."

"Me?" Anna groaned. "She only visits me to complain to me! She drove us crazy back in Nice."

"I know."

"No, you don't know: you're never there! And in any case, why should you care, when you're fraternizing with the winners? It's so easy to play the revolutionary when you're basking in an Italian palace. You've sold yourself off to that idiot Gorky, who wants his bit of fame, as well: *Get out of the way so I can lie there*. He's just like all the other Bolsheviks! He's trash."

She couldn't get pulled into this rant, the same accusations Anna always made.

"Alla's state has nothing to do with my work. I simply need your help: it will take both of us to make her listen to the nurses. Papers have to be signed, documentation has to be presented. You're her twin, and you live in Paris."

"I don't want to see her anymore!"

"She doesn't mean what she says, Anna, nor does she mean what she does. She's sick."

"That's her own fault! She drove herself crazy with her rubbish . . . All those drugs she goes around buying God knows where . . . In seedy places! It's vile!"

"We need to pull her out. Otherwise she'll die!"

"Oh, good riddance to her."

"Don't say that, Anna."

There was silence on the phone again.

Then Anna spoke, more calmly:

"Is she still living in the same hole in the nineteenth arrondissement?"

"Yes. The same one. 1 rue Edgar-Poe. Eighth floor. Door 8."

"Very well."

"Wait, Anna . . . Be prepared for the worst."

"I don't harbor any illusions there."

"Thank you, my darling . . . See you soon. I'll wait for you in front of the building."

Moura hung up with a sigh.

In Alla's bedroom earlier, when she had talked about treatment for addiction, her sister hadn't said that she was "too young to tell her what to do": she had gone for her throat. She had tried to strangle her. There had been insults, screams, blows. Moura knew how this would play out: it wasn't the first time Alla had tried to knock her out. Alla was bigger . . . But, luckily, weaker.

Poor Alla. She had been on the brink for years. Morally, socially lost.

Mommy's intransigence, her constant withholding of love, had left her so weak that she was barely able to stand up on her own. The October Revolution had taken care of the rest, wiping out her fortune and all her stability.

She had gotten divorced, first in 1911 from Count von Engelhardt, the man Mommy had bought to legitimize her daughter, Kira. Her second divorce was in 1923 from the French journalist René Moulin, whom she had met in Saint Petersburg and found again in France at the outbreak of the Great War.

Her nobility and her beauty, however, had made it possible for her— early on in Nice—to be part of the circle of Princess Violette Murat.

The ultrawealthy owner of a palace on the Riviera, a high priestess at the altars of Sodom and Gomorrah, a fervent proselytizer when it came to drugs, Princess Murat initiated her into sapphism and opium.

The two women's relationship had been stormy from the start and had ended in scandal. There was an accusation of theft: Alla had filched a pearl necklace from Violette to buy a dose of morphine. Was it true or false? It didn't matter. Princess Murat didn't hesitate to get rid of her by accusing her publicly, dragging her in front of the courts.

This humiliation had destroyed what resistance Alla had left.

She was still beautiful, with her willowy proportions and her head of red hair. But she was adrift. And nothing anchored her, apart from her nostalgia for her youthful success beneath the chandeliers of Saint Petersburg's palaces. Alla, too, was living in the past.

And her third marriage in Paris, to an émigré by the name of Trubnikov—a morphine addict like her—only brought her new difficulties.

Their wedding reception, which Moura had attended in March 1925, had given her a glimpse of the excesses to come. The feast had merely been a succession of dramas and noisy apologies.

Alla's passion for Trubnikov ended just as it had begun: in tragedy. He died of an overdose in his Naples hotel room. In front of his wife. The couple was supposed to go down to Sorrento the next day to Gorky's residence: it would have been their first vacation at the Minerva boarding house. That was in October 1927. Moura had taken care of everything: handling the investigation by the Italian police and dealing with the delivery of her brother-in-law's body to Paris.

Moura had told no one about this trip back to France with Alla.

And after that, her sister had let herself go completely.

Over the last three years, Moura had managed to limit the damage and slow down her downfall. She had put her in a hospital in Orléans. Then in a sleep treatment in Berlin and Rome.

But to no avail. Alla escaped from everywhere.

How could Moura save her from the demons that made it impossible for her to live? How could she protect her from fear, laziness, envy? Moura asked herself the question for the umpteenth time. How could she get her off drugs?

And how could she shield Kira from her mother's turmoil?

From the outset, Moura had been intercepting the letters Alla sent to Kallijärv.

She had read them, and realized they were crazy. Too dangerous for Kira's sanity. The young girl didn't need to know that her mother was trying to reconnect with her. Alla had abandoned her at birth and hadn't started worrying about her until she was twelve. Alla's coming back into her life could only make the child more confused.

Micky, Uncle Sasha, the aunts, the whole family living by the lake had gotten the message: destroy every envelope that came from Paris. Better for Kira to forge her own way forward . . . Better for her not to know anything about the tragic fate that had befallen the woman who had given birth to her. Better for her to forget that she had even existed. And better for her to belong completely to the Benckendorff clan. Better for her to be Moura's own daughter, without question, like Paul and Tania.

That was even what Moura was telling Wells now, when he raised the question again about her lovers. She told him that Arthur von Engelhardt—whose name Kira bore—had been her first husband, that she had divorced him before marrying Djon.

By adding Engelhardt to the list of men she had slept with, Moura was making Kira the eldest of her children.

She always called Kira "my child."

A way of taking her in and protecting her. And a way of keeping the young girl's life simpler.

Kira never stopped wondering about her origins. She didn't know her father and had only ever seen her mother once, when Alla came and spent several days at Kallijärv during the Christmas of 1926.

During this visit, Alla hadn't shown any special affection for her. And Kira, who was seventeen years old then, had treated her as a stranger. There had been no connection between them.

Could it be that she really was Moura's daughter? Kira liked the thought.

She was now twenty-one years old and looking for work. Moura had brought her to Berlin. The two women lived in the tiny studio on the Koburger Strasse. And their relationship, in this narrow space, was starting to become strained. It wasn't serious. Living in close quarters was difficult for both of them, just as it would be for any other mother-daughter pair sharing the same room and sleeping in the same bed.

But Tania, who was alone back in Kallijärv, had just discovered something: a cache of letters from her aunt Alla. She told Kira about it. And Kira couldn't bear this realization. The idea that all these calls from her mother had gone unanswered, that she had been satisfied with both the love and the lies of her auntie-mommy, tormented her. She accused herself of being a coward.

This feeling of guilt about Alla would follow her for the rest of her life.

With a practiced gesture, Moura set her cloche hat on her head, walked through the café, and left. It was November, and the rain falling across Paris was icy. She made her way down the street to the building, where the ambulance was already waiting for her. Anna caught up with her just as she reached the porch. The two sisters insisted on going up alone.

Later on, answering the questions of the police who had been following Moura, the nurses said they had seen two tall women reappear, holding between them a third, who was even taller and thinner. That one wasn't wearing a hat. She was a redhead who was kicking and screaming.

They had to put her in a straitjacket. The nurses held back the other two, who refused to leave her in the van alone. Then the doors were slammed shut and the van started immediately.

Once the car had turned the corner, they saw that the two women hadn't moved. They were standing there, in the rain, holding each other tight in the middle of the road.

They were crying.

❖

Regular trips back to Kallijärv. Trips to Sorrento. Trips to Paris. Trips to London . . . Moura was unwaveringly faithful to those she loved.

Devoted to her children. Devoted to Gorky. Devoted to her sisters. Devoted to Lockhart. And now, devoted to Wells.

She was also constant in her shortcomings, in her disappearances and her absences.

Constantly frustrating and disappointing them all.

One thing was certain: nobody knew how to love like her.

And nobody knew how to wound like her.

Of course! How could she reconcile such deep, solid links, how could she build such strong attachments, with such an unwavering thirst for freedom?

How could she accompany her loved ones, support them, and protect them . . . all while sacrificing nothing?

Moura never allowed herself that question. She left, she returned. She didn't abandon anyone.

She was always welcoming. Always available. And always necessary.

But whereas Paul—like Kira—forgave her for their separations and only wanted to remember the happiness of their time together, Tania felt that she had grown up without her.

In her eyes, only Micky had any right to her affection, her gratitude, and her respect.

Her mother could care for them one month a year, could have the very best doctors looking after them, could have the very best professors teaching them, could send them to the very best schools, could invite them to Berlin every so often and perhaps set them up in London one day, she could claim to be offering all three of them "the best future possible."

But Tania—even at just fifteen years old—felt that Moura had betrayed them all.

◈

Wells wrote:

> *I was beginning to drop all pretense of wanting Moura to be "free." And my own "freedoms" were becoming more and more theoretical.*
>
> *. . . In 1931, Moura was knocked down by a taxi in Berlin and badly scarred on the forehead. She never mentioned it in any letter. "What was the good of worrying you about it?" she said, when I asked her about the scar.*
>
> *But that scar accused me. And I was growing more and more ashamed to be living on five or six thousand a year, while Moura lived in odd lodgings and wore old and cheap clothes.*

Wells's thoughtfulness, however, didn't restrain his pleasures. Odette and Moura weren't his sole conquests that year.

There was a change, however, a change that undermined his morale:

his body was giving out. His doctor had just diagnosed him with diabetes. It wasn't the end of the world: he would be able to live without insulin injections. But the implication was clear. He had to take it easy.

At sixty-five years old, he had finally gotten old.

Wouldn't it be nice to have a soul mate beside him? A woman, just one and always the same one, who he could get along with and have fun with? A woman who would take care of him, accompany him on his trips, see to his comfort, and share in his pleasures?

He was attached to the thought.

Odette, who understood this, loudly insisted on playing this role, wanting to leave their house at Lou Pidou and come to London, despite his protests. She said that she had come to learn how to be a nurse and care for him. She played the role of the other woman, pestering him with her jealousy, slandering Moura in every literary circle. It was a bad idea. In the end, Odette was nothing more than a mistress. Not a wife. And the pettiness of her gossip about this Russian aristocrat who had stolen her lover away was now making "Baroness Bedbug" notorious in England.

And Wells didn't bother to hide their affair anymore . . . because Odette knew about it. He introduced Moura everywhere as a very, very dear friend.

Baroness Budberg's respectable background, her charm, and her intelligence opened many doors.

He conceded:

All through those years of delay, I was slipping away from this deliberately careless attitude towards a complete fixation of my affections upon Moura. We were drawing closer to each other and she was becoming more and more necessary to me. Or perhaps I was only discovering my real reaction to her quality.

She began to haunt me when she was away from me so that I longed to come upon her round street corners in impossible places. One day, in breach of my treaty with Odette and when Moura was away in Germany, I went to an address she had once given me in Paris because of a vague craving that somehow she might be there (it was an hotel and they knew nothing of her).

. . . By the end of 1932, I was prepared to do anything and overlook anything to make Moura altogether mine.

That was when a new shock shook Moura's life. On November 2, Lockhart published the story of their struggles with the Cheka in 1918.

He had come back from Prague a ruined man. But his stylistic prowess and political acumen had secured him work with the most powerful press magnates in England. And his affair with Lady Rosslyn made it possible for him to run in aristocratic circles. He had dinners with Winston Churchill and played rounds of golf with the Prince of Wales.

His autobiography, titled *Memoirs of a British Agent*, described his adventures in Bolshevik Russia. He didn't explicitly say that he had wanted to topple the regime, but he did describe the efforts he went to in order to force Lenin and Trotsky to fight alongside the Allies. He described his connection with the Ace of Spies, Sidney Reilly, who was now rumored to have been assassinated by the Soviet intelligence services. He described the particulars of his own arrest, condemned the embellishments of the Lockhart Plot, and sneered at his death sentence in absentia. And, on top of that, he described his incredible love affair with a married woman . . . A splendid Russian countess who had risked so much for him.

He praised her courage during their imprisonment in the Lubyanka under Yakov Peters's thumb and rhapsodized about their passion during so much upheaval, their life together in Moscow. He even revealed that she had been ready to abandon her children to follow him to England.

And he named her.

In a matter of weeks, the book had become a best seller in London. And in Estonia, a drama followed that was far worse than anything Moura had feared.

With this memoir, the Benckendorff clan, her friends, her family—especially Micky, especially Kira, Paul, and Tania—learned that she had been lying to them this whole time. Mommy's illness, which had kept her back in Russia, unable to join Djon and their children at Yendel . . . Lies, lies, lies.

In all their eyes, she had become the monster that Uncle Sasha had extricated from the Narva Castle in 1921: a whore who had cuckolded her husband during the war.

But she had sensed that danger was imminent and had tried to limit the damage by asking to read the manuscript before publication.

Lockhart hadn't hesitated to send it to her. He was convinced that this ode to the glory of their love would delight her.

She wrote to him in June:

> *Dear Baby,*
>
> *Yes, I think the book is very good. I would change nothing. Except—and I am very sorry to have to say so—pages 69 and 104. The bit about the spying business gives it . . . a Mata Hari touch which is quite unnecessary for the book . . . and quite impossible for me.*

She was suffering terribly from her reputation as a spy, and couldn't help being alarmed by the grandiose role Lockhart had given her in the story of his liberation from the Kremlin.

He reacted by noting in his diary:

> *This morning I had a shock—a letter from Moura in which she requests me to alter the part in my book referring to her. She wants it made more formal. She wants to be called Mme Benckendorff all through. She is as conventional as a Victorian spinster. And why? Because I said that fourteen years ago she had waving hair whereas it is "flat as a Ukrainian's." Therefore, my description is shallow, false, etc., and this is obviously all that the episode meant to me! Therefore either the full love story or nothing. This will be very difficult. The book, however, will have to be altered. She is the only person who has the right to demand an alteration.*

He complied stingily. Too stingily to save Moura from family drama.

He had certainly taken care of the "Mata Hari touch." But he had left intact the portrait of the great lover and the adulterous woman.

"This man's selfishness . . . his boorishness is something else!" Tania declared as she singled her mother out viciously. "Doesn't his book bother you? Clearly not! You don't care about it! You haven't thought for a second about how much this little thing would hurt us all . . . You've only ever loved this Lockhart. We could all just go to hell!"

This time, Moura held back from putting the girl in her place. Tania was seventeen years old, and she was in a position to understand.

"No, my dear, I do care quite a lot. And you can't imagine how sorry I am that this book was published . . . I knew it would hurt so many people."

She sighed, with the combination of sadness and fatalism that was so typical of her in moments of crisis. "But what would you rather have had? Without the story of our affair, Robert Bruce Lockhart wouldn't have had such a resounding success. And he so needs glory . . . He so, so, so needs money!"

It was a justification that wouldn't satisfy the teenager at all, but that was perfectly phrased for the London elite.

In everyone's eyes, the Baroness was now a legend. She wasn't just Gorky's muse, not just Wells's companion, but also the passion of a famous adventurer in the service of England: the mad love of a man who had tried to topple Lenin and change the course of history. A heroine.

She had lived hand to mouth, had lost even the shirt on her back, and slept in small studios, but she was welcomed everywhere.

Lockhart ran in the same circles as Wells, those of literature, politics, and British estates, where high society invited them for the weekend. They had the same friends . . . And the same mistress.

Neither of them liked the other. Lockhart considered Wells fatuous and vain: a pretentious loudmouth. Wells called Lockhart a "contemptible little bounder."

But through them, the woman they both loved became London's sweetheart. And both men loved nothing more than her incredible popularity. As he watched Moura charm his friends, Aige-Gee thought about how this woman was exactly the right one for him. No question of it: she needed to be the third Mrs. H. G. Wells.

He wrote in his memoir:

I began to talk to her of marriage.

"Let us go on as we are," said she. . . .

"This is only the beginning of our life together," I said. "In a little while we will marry."

"But why marry*?" asked Moura.*

We began to dispute about marriage. "I will come to you anywhere," she said.

"But why go away?" said I.

"I'd be a bore if you had me always."

Astonished by this reluctance, he launched a new offensive. His proposition was nothing but to her benefit. He was offering her security. He was offering her fortune. And, most important: British nationality. Through his status as a great writer, he would be able to elevate her to the top of the social ladder. How could she not want to be his wife?

He got rid of Odette by leaving her the house at Lou Pidou and the angora cat . . . After the legal proceedings, he wanted some recompense. Making Moura his wife had become a fixation for him.

He complained:

What I wanted of her in that phase was, in the fullest sense, marriage, I wanted her to come completely into my life, to span my persona *with her own, as our bodies spanned each other, to launch upon a great adventure together.*

He couldn't understand why she wouldn't be interested.

The answer lay in a word he himself had pronounced so many times. Freedom.

Cherished freedom.

At the end of 1932, Moura left London to meet Gorky in Italy.

Gorky, her companion, her love, her Joy for nearly fifteen years now, was threatening to abandon her again.

CHAPTER THIRTY-SIX

One Suitcase . . . Just One

1932

All hands were on deck at Il Sorito. Alexey Maximovich was moving out. The Neapolitan exile was over. Everybody was going back home. His son, Max; his daughter-in-law, Timosha; Marfa and Darya—their two little girls, who were now seven and five years old—the Swiss nurse; the Nightingale; Pepekryu . . . In all, a dozen people who depended on the energy of their dear Tyotka to organize the voyage. And on her efficiency in packing up all the eight years they had spent at the home of the Duke of Serracapriola.

Their final return was planned for the next spring. They had made the decision without her, while Gorky had been celebrating forty years as a man of letters during his last stay in Russia.

This time, Stalin had outdone himself. This was probably the shrewdest of all his propaganda gestures.

He had gifted Gorky a villa in the Crimea—where the climate was better suited to him than in Il Sorito—as well as a splendid private mansion in Moscow and a dacha on the outskirts of the capital. Moreover, he had the city where Alexey Maximovich Peshkov was born stripped of its historical name and rechristened. Nizhny Novgorod would no longer be called Nizhny Novgorod, but Gorky.

And the outer suburb of Moscow, where Alexey's dacha was being erected, would also be called Gorky. And the largest park in Moscow would be called Gorky, as well. And the Moscow Art Theater would become the Gorky Theater, on Gorky Street. And many other streets in every part of the Soviet Union would be named after him: Gorky Avenue, Gorky Boulevard, Gorky Place. Not to mention the cities themselves, and the schools, and the factories. There would even be Gorky planes.

No nation had ever bestowed a living artist with so many honors. No power, no regime in the world had deified a writer to this degree.

And Gorky let himself be pushed around. Dazzled by his own glory, drunk with gratitude for his motherland, and mad with love for his people, he had lost what critical faculty he had left.

Now he accepted everything from the Party.

The illustrious Maxim Gorky, the only Communist personality to be beloved internationally, was now the defender of Stalinist Russia. The Little Father of the people and their standard-bearer.

But Stalin was suspicious. There was always the risk of this great man changing his mind: after such demonstrations of friendship, he couldn't risk Gorky withdrawing.

The director of the secret police, Genrikh Yagoda—even more cruel and far more corrupt than his predecessors—had been charged with ensuring his happiness, as well as the compliance of his coterie.

The result was that Il Sorito was now a nest of spies. And while Mussolini's Fascists were on the street watching the house's inhabitants coming and going, the Bolsheviks were informing the Soviet Union from the inside.

After 1922, the Cheka was called the GPU, and then the OGPU: these were acronyms the West understood as the State Political Directorate. Dzerzhinsky, its founder, was dead. Yakov Peters, in disgrace. As for Zinoviev, Gorky's old enemy, he had just been officially expelled from the Party. And replaced, appropriately enough, by Yagoda.

Dear Yagoda . . . Wildly in love with Timosha, Max's wife, who he loaded with gifts. Infamous Yagoda . . . One of the twentieth century's worst murderers, responsible for the deaths of nearly ten million people.

To please him—and out of curiosity—Gorky had gone to visit one of the forced labor camps Yagoda had established. In plain terms: a tourist visit to the gulag. It hardly has to be said that Gorky didn't see anything, didn't hear anything. All the worst-off prisoners had been moved out of sight, into the barracks that he was never shown. The tortured men, the exhausted men, the dying men—all hidden from view.

And so the gulag had struck him as a model of order, an institution of public utility for rehabilitating dissidents. He went so far as to congratulate the wardens on the camp's good performance!

Of course, nobody in Russia at that time had any idea of the horrific mistreatment the detainees were suffering.

And yet . . .

Gorky hadn't been born yesterday.

How could a man who had chosen exile rather than support the Revolution's atrocities be blind to this degree? And go so far as to be friends with this monster named Yagoda?

How could a man who had been courageous enough to condemn Lenin's lack of humanity, who had dared to fight Zinoviev's extortions, who had even defended a Romanov grand duke and saved dozens of *burzhui*—how could this man now claim that the regime's protesters should be liquidated? That the vermin had to be crushed?

How could a writer who had never stopped insisting on his freedom of thought and freedom of speech now claim that literature should only exalt the values extolled by the regime? That it was a propaganda tool that should serve only to educate the masses and celebrate only Work, the Proletariat, the Motherland, and Stalin?

The mystery of Gorky's incredible ideological transformation has troubled many generations of critics and intellectuals. Some insisted that his change of opinion was out of self-interest. Others attributed it to his habit of distorting reality to conform it to his vision, as per his old saying *You have to believe in it.*

He himself provided an answer of sorts:

The fact is that I hate with a passion the truth which for ninety-nine percent of the people is an abomination and a lie. I know that reality is miserable for fifty million who make up the masses of the Russian people and that men have need of another truth which does not debase them but which lifts their energy in toil and creation.

He added:

You say that you refuse to silence the facts that revolt you? Whereas not only do I presume to have the right to pass them over in silence, but I rank this skill among my most respectable qualities . . . What is important for me is to exalt the man who feels a great, healthy respect for life, the man who understands that he is building a new state, the man who lives not by words but by his passion for work and action. . . . You say that I am an optimist, an idealist, a romantic, and so on. Do as you wish; that business is yours alone.

Such a profession of faith justified all submission. It allowed him to support Stalin's rule and to further his prestige among intellectuals around the world.

❖

At Il Sorito that winter, Moura was seeing all the disorder of the Kronverksky Prospect days: the same atmosphere as in the waning weeks in Petrograd, the same war councils, and the same arguments. Each group was discussing its own future in private rooms before reviving the conversation under the Duca's aegis around the dining room table. And the whispers continued behind closed doors until dawn broke.

"The account books were catastrophic," Pepekryu sighed, leaning against the kitchen sink.

He had pulled Moura to the end of the hallway, as far as possible from Gorky and any other prying ears. He wanted to tell her one more time that returning home would only benefit them.

"Financially, we can't weather the storm anymore."

"I know," she replied. "It couldn't go on any longer. You're preaching to the choir."

While she was away, Pepekryu—Pyotr Petrovich Kryuchkov—had become Gorky's personal secretary and right-hand man. In fact, he had parted ways with the master's previous companion—the actress Maria Andreyeva—to marry a very young woman in Berlin. And since then, Gorky had sworn by him, loudly calling him *my very dear friend*. It wasn't that Gorky was grateful that he'd made Maria Andreyeva suffer; he didn't approve one bit of the fact that Pepekryu had abandoned her and left her unhappy. But Kryuchkov had known how to make himself indispensable and how to shrewdly, carefully establish his change in allegiance by going from the actress to the writer.

He had been rather thin and sympathetic when he was younger, but now, at forty-three years old, he only ever appeared in a banker's suit, his hair slicked back, his eyes steely behind his round glasses. He had gained weight, in every sense. The critic Korney Chukovsky, a pillar of the former World Literature and Moura's old friend, declared that Kryuchkov was unrivaled in arrogance and vulgarity.

Of all the State Political Directorate's informants at Il Sorito, he was the one closest to Yagoda. The two men had met in Germany, when Yagoda and Maria Andreyeva were working together to sell the artworks that had been seized from the *burzhui*.

Moura, too, had met Yagoda in Berlin in 1922.

These days, Kryuchkov worked directly for him. He chose Gorky's visitors, monitored his conversations, guided his answers, and stirred up his fanaticism.

An intelligent, effective, and zealous spy.

Moura had always gotten along well with him. They had the same perspective on practical decisions. And for years now, whenever she left or returned the passing of the baton had been handled smoothly and without any friction between the two. As for the matter of settling the master back in the Soviet Union, Kryuchkov still had some worries about how she would react. She was still Alexey Maximovich's companion and the lady of the house. Who knew whether she was hoping to keep him from cutting off all ties with Europe? Whether she wanted to ensure a fallback plan for him, such as keeping the villa in Sorrento? Tyotka's influence was considerable. Who knew if her arrival could mean a dramatic change in plans?

Kryuchkov was worried that she might oppose leaving Italy for good and even more concerned by the possibility of Gorky listening to her, and so he was trying to get her approval. An unconditional yes.

"Life here is too expensive. It's impossible to stay here at Il Sorito for much longer . . . While in Russia, Gorky would have a personal doctor, a live-in nurse, a car, a driver at his disposal. And an entire population at his feet, all the Russian people who love him and worship him!"

She sighed:

"In any case, his heart isn't in it. Alexey feels too unhappy abroad. He always has . . . He needs to go back, yes."

"So you fully approve of his decision?"

"He seems fixated on it. And when he gets an idea in his head, a feeling in his heart, he doesn't leave us any choice . . . His trips back to Russia have been so emotional for him." Then she added, sadly: "He wants to die up there. How can anyone say no to such a personal request? Even if I—"

Kryuchkov cut her off:

"Will you tell him that? Will you make sure he understands that you accept his decision? He needs you and your support so much! Will you say it to him, that you approve and that you support him? You would be reassuring him . . . Will you encourage him?"

"Yes, I'll do it, no matter what . . . I'll urge him. But the thought of separating from him, the prospect of leaving him . . ."

"Why leave him? You can come to Moscow anytime you like! Comrade Yagoda likes you very much. He'll give us all the visas needed for travel. And besides, Gorky will keep spending his summers in Italy . . . Those will be real vacations, for once."

She lit a cigarette, looked up, and blew the smoke toward the ceiling.

"Real vacations," she repeated. "Who knows?"

Her expression was vague, as it always was when she was trying to escape, and she gave a mysterious smile.

Was she being sincere in allying with him? He decided not to pursue the question and simply to play the same game she was.

"You're wonderful, Tyotka! You're going to give Alexey Maximovich exactly what he needs: peace of mind. And Russia will be indebted to you!"

❖

It was the end of an era.

The boxes were heaped up all the way to the bathroom. The massive library of books from Gorky's office, several thousand volumes strong, was being emptied out very slowly.

Of course, ever since the year Gorky had started thinking about returning—1928—he had been gifting his personal archives to the Push-kin House in Leningrad. Of course, everything touching upon his work was already there. He had even sent his manuscripts directly to Moscow. The rest would go to one or another of his three residences. On the right were the boxes for the private mansion; on the left were those for the dacha; and in the middle were those for the villa in Crimea.

There was still one matter to be resolved, which everybody had been discussing before Moura's arrival.

What would happen to his correspondence?

❖

The question had been tormenting Gorky for months.

The letters he had received before his exile—the "compromising letters" had come with him during his travels and been put in a safe deposit box at the Deutsche Bank in Berlin.

Maria Ignatyevna had the key.

The mail he had received since then—all the bags the mailmen had lugged to his front door every morning for eight years—was piled up in his office and everywhere in the villa . . . Letters from his readers, his colleagues, his friends, his enemies, letters from every level of Russian society, complaining to him about the regime and bitterly criticizing the Bolsheviks. Thousands of sheets of paper that told him what had been happening while he was gone.

And what should he do with the accounts written by White Russians who had emigrated to Paris, Berlin, and the United States?

What should he do with the stories told by touring actors, artists, scholars, and poets who lived back there but had gone to the trouble of visiting him in Sorrento?

What should he do with the notes he himself had taken during their conversations? Bits of their spoken words scribbled down in his notebooks, entire dialogues set down word for word?

Was he going to bring all this damning proof of betrayal back to Stalin? Any of these pages amounted to a death warrant. He knew that. And despite his change of feeling toward the Party, he was still keenly aware of the danger that the least of these papers represented for their authors.

Would he sentence all those who had trusted him with their words to years in the gulag or executions in the Lubyanka's basements?

But—if he didn't bring back these documents, what should he do, what *could* he do with them?

He was losing sleep.

While Maria Ignatyevna was away, he had discussed his crisis of conscience with his son and his coterie.

Everybody instinctively lowered their voices when the subject was broached. And each of them got up from their chairs often to make sure the doors were firmly shut. That neither the nurse, the cook, nor the gardener could hear them.

None of them, however, felt threatened or even concerned by these texts. They weren't afraid at all. All the more so because this little gang, as a whole, was on the Party's side.

But still . . . The presence of such condemnations of the Party under their roof worried them. They had never contemplated the risk these writings represented, not until Duca raised the issue. He had suggested entrusting them to his adoptive son, Zinovy Peshkov, who Max disliked.

Gorky's closeness with Zinovy, who he had known from his teenage years, was an old story. Zinovy Sverdlov, who, like Gorky, had been born in Nizhny Novgorod, was fifteen years younger than the master. A rebel and a roamer at heart, the boy had dreamed of becoming an actor. But he was Jewish, and the law forbade Jews from being onstage. And so Gorky had suggested that he convert to the Orthodox faith: he would be the boy's godfather, would adopt him and bestow his name upon him. And so

Zinovy Sverdlov had become Zinovy Peshkov. At that point he was nine-teen years old. Despite their difference in age, the two men were thick as thieves: they both believed in freedom. And they had fought together for freedom, traveled together for freedom, been imprisoned together for freedom—and they had fled together.

The Revolution had separated the two of them: Zinovy hated the Bol-sheviks' fanaticism. Unlike his own brother . . . the very commissar who had had the tsar and his family executed in Yekaterinburg. In homage to this massacre, the city now bore the name of that executioner: Sverdlov.

As he didn't want to serve the Reds or fight for the Whites, Zinovy had fought in the war of 1914 in the French Foreign Legion. A glorious war. He had lost an arm there but earned his stripes as an officer. It was the prelude to a brilliant future.

His last stay at Il Sorito was in 1927, just when Gorky was starting to sing Stalin's praises. It was a stormy conversation . . .

Despite their differences, Alexey Maximovich didn't doubt that Zinovy was the perfect man.

"He could take care of the papers . . . He's a man of honor. He'll keep the secret."

"No, no!" Max had declared at their last meeting. "Not Zinovy!"

"Certainly not him!" Kryuchkov had chimed in. "Absolutely out of the question."

He rarely stated things so categorically. His veto cast a pall over the discussion.

"Zinovy is a man of honor!" Gorky repeated, pounding the table. "And Zinovy is also my son!"

"I'm not arguing with that, Duca. I'm only saying that he's now a French national. And that he doesn't live anywhere. He's currently serv-ing in Morocco, and God knows where he'll be sent to fight tomorrow."

"And in service of who!" the Nightingale added. "Max is right. It's too much of a risk for papers as important as these to be delivered to some-one who's renounced Russia . . . Let's wait and see what Tyotka thinks."

"She does have good judgment," Gorky conceded. "We'll wait for Maria Ignatyevna."

But as soon as she arrived, she made a point of not getting involved in any of the community's decisions. She sorted, organized, packed up books . . . and when it came to the future, her only opinion was her agreement on the need to return. The only worry she expressed was her own sadness at the prospect of this separation.

On Christmas Eve, the problem still hadn't been resolved. Time was starting to run short. She would be leaving soon to enjoy the holiday at Kallijärv. Gorky dreaded that moment.

The children, as usual . . . The children. That was her argument for not following him. A pretext that still exasperated him.

That evening, he gathered together a full family council: Maria Ignatyevna, Max, Timosha, Kryuchkov, and the Nightingale. His tone wasn't joking. He chewed on his mustache, toyed with his cigarette holder, and smoked cigarette after cigarette. So many gestures that betrayed his tension. The other people's faces reflected the gravity of the evening. The butts nobody could be bothered to put out blazed in the embers.

Only Max seemed to be taking the situation lightly. With his leading-man figure, he bore no resemblance to his father. Even though he was thirty-five years old at this point, he still had his teenage sensibilities and his youthful reflexes. He loved nice cars, high speeds, and strong liqueurs.

"What are we going to do with all this counterrevolutionary muck?" he asked with a shrug of the shoulders. "It's pretty simple: let's destroy it all! I think we should build a bonfire in the garden."

"How dare you suggest something so stupid, Max!" his father barked. "Burning the writings of men as eminent as Shalyapin, Stanislavsky, or Bely? Those are just three geniuses, and there could be ten, or a hundred!"

"Oh, it'd be an amazing bit of pyrotechnics. People would be able to see it from Naples."

"Be quiet . . . And enough of these inanities."

"If you don't want to bring them back and you don't want to burn them, then what solution do you have in mind?"

"Leaving them with someone who isn't Zinovy?" Timosha said.

"But who?" asked the Nightingale.

"Well . . . I don't know . . ." Kryuchkov said, trying to think.

He didn't dare suggest that he take responsibility for them, since he was returning, as well. It wasn't that he didn't want to. A cache this large would be of great interest to the State Political Directorate. Such a hoard would especially be of interest to Yagoda and would put him in Stalin's good graces forever. Seizing this treasure now would be far easier than trying to recover it much later.

But it was impossible for him to make such an overt suggestion of this kind.

He thought out loud:

"What about Tyotka? She's going to be staying here."

"Tyotka?" Timosha replied. "Oh, sure!"

Everyone turned to look at Moura.

Gorky leaned forward to ask her:

"What do you think, Maria Ignatyevna? Would you be willing to keep these papers with you?"

She looked down and thought for a few seconds:

"I can't give you an answer, Alexey Maximovich. I have a vested interest in the whole matter. And if you don't mind, I'd rather not be involved in making a decision."

Without another word, she got up and left the room. This suddenness was so unlike her that everyone else was astonished. They were silent as she shut the door behind her, and then they started up again.

"She didn't seem very enthusiastic," Timosha remarked.

"That's an understatement!" Max said. "If I were her, I wouldn't want this pile of junk, no matter what. And I still don't understand why you refuse to burn it all . . . Your paperwork is a public danger, a powder keg. Keeping it here is like leaving a loaded gun on the table!"

"But I don't see any other solution," Kryuchkov said. "Maria Ignatyevna seems to be exactly the right person. The only one. She's been going through your mail for years, Duca. She knows all the details of your correspondence . . . She should keep it, she should keep all the papers!"

She already has the key to your safe deposit box at the Deutsche Bank . . . She should keep everything!"

"But would she accept such responsibility?" Gorky sighed. "Such a heavy burden?"

"That's your problem," Max snickered. "Because she won't deign to come with us back to Russia. Because she's abandoning you in favor of Europe . . . So you'll have to convince her!"

"Just between us," Kryuchkov added, "our dear Tyotka does owe you that much!"

❖

It had rained the whole day. The patio stones were slippery.

Leaning against the railing beside each other, Gorky and Moura admired the sunset over the Gulf of Naples one last time. They were looking straight ahead, their eyes fixed on the small lights of Castel del Mare and the hulking black mass of Vesuvius that they loved so much.

The damp and the chill had them shivering. But tonight, she wasn't thinking about protecting Gorky from that. Tonight, they were equals.

Equal in age, equal in illness. In how unknown their futures were.

All they could hear were raindrops pounding against the roof.

She had thrown Alexey's old housecoat over her shoulders, his mandarin, while he had on Yagoda's gift: a purple silk caftan embroidered in gold, exactly like the old one.

They were both thinking about their past. They recalled their first encounter during the meetings at World Literature, the difficulties they had shared. They recalled their happiest moments together. They were overwhelmed with that tenderness.

Alexey laid his hand on Moura's and stroked it gently. They had already said what they had to say, and now they were slowly sinking into the depths of despair.

Finally, he whispered:

"I want to thank you for accepting such a responsibility."

"How could I do otherwise, Alexey?"

"You could have acted otherwise. Prudently, for example. You didn't . . . I wasn't mistaken about you. I've often fought with you about small things, Maria Ignatyevna. But deep down, I've always respected you; I've always loved you. I've never forgotten that day, in my Kronverksky Prospect office . . . That day you confessed to me, at the risk of being thrown out, what Zinoviev was forcing you to do. You are still the greatest woman I have ever met. It is an honor to have known you."

The homage left her so speechless that she wasn't able to return the compliment.

"What should I do with all these papers? . . . With what's in the safe deposit box in Berlin and the boxes at Il Sorito?"

"You should place them somewhere safe."

"Where?"

"It doesn't matter where . . . Your estate in Estonia, your sister's apartment in France, somewhere in England . . . Wherever you'd like! What matters is that nobody know where you've chosen. Nobody, do you understand? I mean me just as much as the others . . . I don't want to know."

"But to hide your archives, they have to be moved somewhere. There are too many."

"Maybe we should read it all, sort it all . . . pack a few suitcases?"

"One suitcase. Just one."

"All right, just one . . ." He paused before adding: "Promise me you'll come see me in Moscow once I'm settled."

"I promise you, my Joy . . . I don't even know how I'll be able to live without you!"

"Promise me one other thing."

"Anything you want."

"Promise me you'll never bring this suitcase to Russia."

"Even if you ask me to?"

"Especially if I ask you to."

"Are you afraid of going back?"

"No!"

"Then why are you forcing me to make such a promise?"

He walked back inside without an answer.

CHAPTER THIRTY-SEVEN

Deny, Always Deny, Deny Forever, Deny Even Under the Guillotine . . . and After!

1933–1934

Moura's bed was a world unto itself. With its geometrically patterned quilt reminiscent of a Persian rug, it seemed to swallow up the room and float in the space.

The nights she spent there were fairly short, but she worked there every morning until lunch, lying down as she made her way through piles of books, heaps of manuscripts, numerous dictionaries and notebooks, along with fountain pens, tubes of lipstick, handbags, packets of cigarettes, and ashtrays. Her immense black Bakelite telephone, which rested atop a golden cushion, never stopped ringing. She talked on it for hours. When people weren't calling her, she was dialing number after number, flipping through her phone book repeatedly. At this point her address book was as thick as a Bible. The time when she had had internal monologues and self-doubt seemed long past.

London. She had finally made her dream come true. She was living in London!

It was exciting, yet difficult for her to settle in.

She had started by camping out in a tiny space not far from the British Museum . . . It had been dark. Then she had found two bedrooms, one above the other, at 98 Knightsbridge, a precarious duplex that she shared with her old friend Lyuba Hicks. No living room, no kitchen. Just a bathroom.

Lyuba, who was just as poor as Moura and now widowed, was fighting against poverty. She had lost her dear Hickie, the love of her life, to tuberculosis in Vienna. Upon her return to England in 1930, Lyuba had opened a small fashion boutique and was living off what she could make. She was still very pretty, and looking for a banker to marry.

The two women never ate at home. They went out every evening as guests at one meal or another. And if it should happen that they didn't have a cocktail party or a dinner planned, they would spend the whole evening talking as they drank their vodka.

At forty years old, they were living like bohemians.

But the perennial problem of money remained. Moura remained obsessed with her children's futures.

Kira seemed to be out of the woods. Thanks to Wells, Moura had secured her work as a secretary. Now her child was fending for herself. She had even fallen in love with a British doctor, a certain Dr. Clegg, who had just asked for her hand in marriage. The wedding was planned for the next season at the Orthodox church. All that had to be done was plan the party. Even without any money, Moura was in her element. All of London would go to the wedding of "her daughter," even though the young woman hated society life. That was Kira's only shortcoming, Moura thought: she needed to learn how to overcome her timidity. As for the rest, she considered the mission accomplished.

As for Paul, who was now twenty years old, he had never given her any trouble . . . Unlike Tania, who she struggled with each day.

Moura had gone to great expense to enroll Paul in a university in Shropshire, the prestigious Harper Adams Agricultural College. The curriculum would allow him to fulfill his ambitions to be a gentleman farmer. He was a calm, unperturbed boy of remarkable beauty. He had inherited the refinement, the tall stature, the regular features of the Benckendorff clan. Women flocked to him. He was just as attracted to them. He had long since lost count of his conquests.

Paul hated conflicts and avoided them almost as much as Moura did. He felt that she had done more than enough for him. He loved his mother.

But Tania and Micky were another matter. They still lived in Estonia, and Micky's health was poor. She had stomach troubles and a weak heart. One of the bigwig doctors Moura had taken her to see in Berlin had given her only six months to live. That verdict had been handed down three years ago. And Micky was still holding firm. She was still wearing the same skirts from 1900, the same small bun on top of her head . . . Micky might as well have been called the Eternal.

But she was still getting on in years. Moura was planning to bring her to England with Tania, as soon as the younger one had finished her studies.

Living in London was expensive. She only survived there through working for Gorky. She introduced herself as his agent for the international market, his translator, and his proxy. She made it clear that she controlled all his literary rights. Those books of Alexey's that she was able to get published in Europe brought her a substantial sum. But it wasn't enough.

And so she worked to promote contemporary novelists and poets, all the Russian authors, whether they were dissidents or apparatchiks, that she was able to market to publishing houses.

She harbored no illusions: Russia was her trademark. Nobody was better placed to represent the Slavic soul on British territory. Far from blending into the crowd, she played up her accent and emphasized all the clichés. Silly, lively, rowdy, overflowing with anecdotes of her successes at the tsar's court, of her adventures on the streets of Petrograd during the Revolution.

She embellished details shamelessly. Facts were irrelevant. History was only useful to the degree that it served to reinforce her persona.

Even with her most outlandish tales, she was still careful. She avoided touchy subjects. She didn't utter a word about what she really thought of the Russian aristocracy's behavior before the Revolution. Or during the struggle for power between the Reds and the Whites. She simply underscored that the atrocities committed by one side were just as terrible as those committed by the other.

Nor did she utter a syllable about what she really thought of the Bolsheviks. No condemnation of the regime. She simply stuck to Gorky's writings and followed the writer's preferences.

Once again, her ease in living between two worlds was to her advantage. She never offered the least criticism and never proffered the least value judgment.

But she didn't see herself as a hypocrite who was wearing a mask; at heart, she did not sacrifice her internal truth. Even when she was putting on a show, she was still the same Moura as always. Fickle yet faithful. Seductive yet sincere.

Her connection with Wells, however, led people to believe that she had chosen his side and that she, like him, had socialist leanings. For those who tried to make sense of her affiliations, she made it clear that she was leftist. But she refused to glorify or attack any party, apart from the Nazis.

On that point, she was unambiguous: her heart didn't waver between the Fascists and the Communists. Between Hitler and Stalin, she would choose Russia. And so she ended up embodying the motherland: in London, Moura Budberg *was* Eternal Russia. She symbolized all of Russian literature for the West.

It was that role, intermediary between Soviet writers and British intellectuals, that the State Political Directorate took great interest in.

Yagoda was well positioned to know about all the old connections between *Mrs. B.* and the men in the Cheka. He had even met her himself in Berlin, when he was working there alongside Maria Andreyeva and Kryuchkov.

It was the latter who had informed him that Gorky hadn't sent all his archives back to Russia. That his companion—this same Mrs. B., a former informant for Yakov Peters and Zinoviev—had kept the most compromising letters with her, and that she was safeguarding them somewhere.

Such news could only attract attention from the top. They had let the baroness lie dormant for more than a decade. The time had come for her to prove her love for the motherland and her loyalty to the Party.

They awaited her arrival.

In Moscow, Alexey Maximovich kept begging her to join him. He claimed that he had secured all the necessary passes and permits and visas from Yagoda. Stalin could guarantee her safety. She could leave again when she pleased.

Gorky left Sorrento once and for all on May 8, 1933. He had gone with his clan to Naples, in four hansom cabs and two cars. From there, the whole group had gotten on the steamboat headed to Odessa via Istanbul.

Once their train arrived at the Moscow station, it had been overwhelmed by a jubilant crowd. The factory workers had borne Gorky from the platform to his car triumphantly. It was an incredible welcome, the scale of which Moura wouldn't have been able to imagine had she not seen the images on newsreels at the theater. It was a "spontaneous" welcome—planned and carried out by the secret police.

Gorky's departure had resulted in his bank accounts being closed in Italy. Hitler's nomination as chancellor in January had, furthermore, set off a massive anti-Bolshevik campaign in Germany. Moura had therefore been forced to hurriedly empty the safe deposit box she had a key for at the Deutsche Bank. She had left its contents in the nearest location she could: Estonia.

At that point, the pre-exile papers were stashed beneath her bed in Kallijärv.

The other portion of the correspondence had been sorted and reduced to a single suitcase's worth. As planned. She had taken it with her after her final stay at Il Sorito, in April 1933.

That suitcase was hidden under her bed at 98 Knightsbridge.

The truth was that even though she was able to enjoy herself in London, she chafed at being away from Gorky. He was her conscience. Her soul. Her history. In a painful, almost unspeakable way, he symbolized the Russia she knew . . . Her lost Russia. Her beloved Russia. She considered him the best part of herself.

She missed him. But she didn't dare say more than that, apart from her promise to make the trip. Someday. Soon . . . Hopefully.

She wrote him:

Of course I'll come to see you. But that won't be enough, and I am also insatiable. You do understand I'm a deeply torn being, and it's not only to do with me setting everything up for everything and everyone. But let's not talk about that just now.

. . . For now, she had to go and get dressed. She was late, as usual.

Aige-Gee was coming in five minutes to pick her up in a cab. He was taking her to lunch at Quo Vadis, one of the chicest restaurants in Soho. He had booked her a little something.

Notwithstanding his tyranny and his demands, Wells personified life as she wanted it. He embodied action, surprise, whimsy, inventiveness. She loved how close they were.

She jumped out of bed and ran into the bathroom.

Her thinness from the years when she had been starving was long gone. Under the black silk of her kimono, her thighs were thicker than ever before.

And although the shapeliness of her ankles still charmed Lockhart, even though the thinness of her wrists still delighted H. G. Wells and excited Konstantin Benckendorff, she seduced them most overtly with her curves, her rounded shoulders, and her heavy breasts.

The lady the friends at World Literature had described in 1919 as "a slender sphinx" was now, in London, as powerful as a caryatid, as fully fleshed as a Maillol statue.

❖

"We need to get married soon," Aige-Gee declared just as she climbed into the cab. He stroked her hand with a sensuality she had seen only when they had been in bed together. His fingers worked their way from her wrist to the hollow of her elbow. "Before our trip to America. It's imperative!"

"Why is it imperative?"

"If we sleep together while we're not married, it'll be the stuff of scandal over there. I don't want to deal with rumors like the ones our friend Gorky set off in New York when he shared his hotel room with Maria Andreyeva!"

"Oh, that was in 1906, Aige-Gee. Things have changed."

"Not in Yankee Town: they're still puritans down there."

"There's plenty of time between now and next April."

"So do you agree that we should marry?"

"Why are we starting this conversation up again, darling? Haven't we already talked about all that?"

"I just want to make sure that you'll accompany me to the United States . . . And then I should go and interview Stalin in the USSR. And I want you to come with me to Moscow."

"I can't set foot there, you know that perfectly well."

He insisted: "We'll see Gorky there."

The prospect of Wells and Gorky in the same room made her shudder.

It was one thing to love the two men, and love them wholeheartedly. It was quite another to handle this love when they were both present. Being as selfish and jealous as they were, they would immediately realize that they were rivals, which neither of them would be able to bear.

And she couldn't bear that, either. Gorky ruled out Wells. Wells ruled out Gorky.

The idea of seeing Alexey Maximovich in Moscow . . . as a lover, as the wife of H. G. Wells!

She couldn't help pulling her hand away. She repeated:

"I can't return to Russia, Aige-Gee, you know that!"

"With me, you can."

"No. The minute I cross the border, the State Political Directorate will arrest me. And they'll very likely put me in front of the firing squad."

"Not if you're my wife! And that's exactly why you need to become that. Besides, everybody agrees. And our friends are waiting for us right now to toast our marriage."

She stared at him.

"You aren't serious."

"I am. They're at Quo Vadis . . . I've booked a private dining room for us. Then we'll all meet at my house for a small concert in your honor. I've asked your cousin, the harpist, Konstantin Benckendorff's wife, to come play an aubade for us."

"Aige-Gee, you didn't!"

"Didn't what? Invite the best of London society to our wedding? Of course I did. I've told everyone that we tied the knot this morning at the town hall. And I've invited Lady Cunard, Lady Lavery, Harold Nicolson, and Max Beerbohm to our wedding feast . . . Not one of them said no. And I haven't said a word about all the telegrams, the flowers, the gifts they've sent us."

The cab stopped in front of the restaurant.

When she stepped out, Moura was ashen. Not a bride but a ghost.

Fury wasn't an emotion she was familiar with, and she wasn't able to control it. The welcoming cry of "hurrah!" as she entered petrified her.

How could he have played such a trick on her? Put her in such a position where everything was already said and done? It was such a childish thing to do.

"All our best wishes, dearest Moura."

"We're so happy for the both of you!"

"You make such a beautiful couple."

People kept kissing her, congratulating her. She tried to smile. Wells flitted around in evident delight.

What sort of rabbit was he hoping to pull out of this hat? Did he really think he'd managed to corner her by forcing her to deal with the approval of London's high society?

She was filled with embarrassment and rage. She was going to have to make a speech, explain that this was just a joke, a pretext to put together a lovely lunch, a party far better than any other . . . Far more original.

And so she did. She stood up, raised her glass, and airily declared that she was toasting to everyone's good health, but that there was no wedding on the agenda. It had just been a sly joke to liven the party.

Standing next to her, Wells had to pretend to laugh with her and play along as if he'd cooked up the idea with her. It was the only way for him to keep his head raised high and avoid disgrace.

But not a person in the room was fooled. They all knew he had tried to force her hand. And this was how she had gotten her comeuppance.

Some of Wells's close friends were convinced Moura had agreed to marry him, but then changed her mind at the last minute. That very morning? Or in the cab? No matter what the particulars, they didn't take well to how she'd handled the matter.

Others had a sneaking feeling that she had set up this whole rigmarole on her own and had been intent on embarrassing him. They weren't very forgiving of her, either.

But she had been so kind to her companion for the entire day, so gracious to everyone present, that most of the people in that room were won over.

Another guest there rounded out the story by adding that the couple was going to spend their "wedding night" at his Sussex estate, just as Wells had planned. One witness to this "honeymoon" recalled Wells saying, with a sigh, "We act a fool when we're old, and when we're madly in love with a young lady . . ."

He had retorted: "You could have realized that much sooner, my dear fellow!"

And Moura had simply winked.

❖

If she was mad at him for that trap, she didn't show it. No scenes. No reproaches.

Wells, however, complained about her act endlessly.

He started to see that she had other dreams, other interests, other affections that were perhaps stronger than their love. That she still attended to family matters and remained part of a network established in her past. He didn't want to know anything, but, despite himself, he discovered that she hadn't only grown up amid the high society they moved within together. She also belonged to a world of rootless people. She saw friends who were in need, a whole crowd of Russian exiles, explorers, politicians, who she helped survive and who she held some sway over. For all of them, she was their "marvelous Moura." And she took pleasure in this role, which Wells considered too businesslike.

She liked to be useful, she liked to support and save people. She liked to give things, to give of herself: he deemed her "generous," he admitted she was "adorable." But he would rather have had her all to himself.

That Moura's life was filled with this horde of émigrés, press correspondents, and shadow diplomats, not unlike her Lockhart, exasperated him. A whole motley crowd that, as Wells put it, saw politics as only a set of backroom deals and handshake agreements, a clause here and a story there.

As for what he considered to be the only adventures worth taking—a trip to America to meet President Roosevelt as the wife of H. G. Wells; a trip to Russia to interview Stalin with him—Moura refused to change her mind. Aige-Gee tried to broach the topic again, but to no avail: no, she would not accompany him to Moscow. She explained that it wasn't that she didn't want to. But after more than a decade, ever since she had left for good, she had known she couldn't return without risking a lifetime sentence in the gulag.

She was persona non grata there.

Whenever he tried to press the question, she became so worried and so brusque that he soon had no choice but to let her have her way.

He also came to see that she was developing habits he had no say in. She dawdled in bed until noon, she gossiped with Lyuba the whole night, she changed her plans at the last minute over and over, she was always late . . . And she never stopped drinking.

In his confession *Wells in Love*, he wrote:

Whenever she found life a little dull or perplexing, whenever she felt the onset of doubt or indolence, she drank brandy. If life remained dull and perplexing, she drank some more. I did not realize how much her failure to adapt herself to my needs and respond to my appeals was assisted by this ready consolation.

I began to be exasperated and jealous.

She went off to Estonia for Christmas; she explained that that was imperative, and I could not see the pre-eminence of that claim. "But I have always spent my Christmas in Estonia!" she said, and returned after three weeks.

What Wells could not imagine, what he could not even conceive of, was that on the tarmac of the Tallinn airport, Moura had changed planes.

She was the only passenger aboard a small Aeroflot machine.

And from there she flew to Moscow.

❖

Which of Gorky's prayers had she finally answered?

Had their separation become too painful for both of them?

How did she manage to overcome her fear of being arrested? And accept this risk of a bullet to her head that had haunted her for such a long time?

No matter how many guarantees Alexey Maximovich gave her, no matter how often he swore that Yagoda was his nearest and dearest friend, that nobody in Russia would dare to touch "Gorky's wife," she was still an émigrée and a *burzhui*.

What reckless wish, what crazy impulse drove her to do this?

Whatever the answer, her love of Gorky turned out to be greater than her fear of death.

What pleas did she relent to?

What order did she accede to?

It was a quick trip.

Just four days: Yagoda's gift to his dear Gorky for Christmas in 1933.

The latter man had been willing to be locked in a gilded cage. He had even traded Italy for Crimea, willingly giving up his summer in Europe, the month Kryuchkov had already planned for him to spend there with Moura.

In August, Gorky had done him one better. He had taken the head of a delegation of writers he ran to the inauguration of the White Sea Canal, in Stalin's presence. This immense edifice, which was designed to connect the White Sea and the Baltic Sea close to Leningrad, had been carried out by the political prisoners sentenced to forced labor. A construction project that had resulted in the deaths of nearly thirty thousand of them. Gorky had sung the praises of this project, going so far as to say that these men were gaining freedom through their work—an idea the Nazis were all too happy to seize when they erected Auschwitz.

He deserved to be repaid by being allowed to spend the holidays with his companion.

Yagoda had gone to receive Baroness Budberg at the airport in person. There had been a red carpet and a bouquet of flowers . . . He had taken her in his Rolls-Royce with tinted windows to the writer's dacha on the city's outskirts.

She had insisted that her arrival be kept a secret. It was a mandatory condition. Nobody in England or Estonia could know she had crossed the border. If anybody learned about it, all the doors would be shut to her in London and Tallinn: she wouldn't be able to move freely in Europe anymore.

And Yagoda was determined that she remain so, so that she could move easily among the circles of the White emigration, among the British politicians and intelligentsia. All the milieus she had access to.

He had respected her insistence on discretion, ensuring the secrecy she had made a condition. The dacha was surrounded by walls, hemmed in by hedges, and guarded by the police. Consistent with her wish, she did not leave the park and did not see anybody apart from the writer's family.

While Yagoda didn't have any plan to broach the subject of "the suitcase" right away—it was too soon to alarm her and worry Gorky—he was still determined to interrogate her thoroughly on other topics. The spirit of the times, the famous personalities, the rumors that were circulating across Europe. What were people in Churchill's circles saying about the

USSR? How was Stalin seen by the Foreign Office? What did everyone think of Hitler? What were Great Britain's intentions toward Germany?

Those were just the first of many questions to come.

Moura would never mention this escapade. Not a single word about the emotions she felt upon seeing Gorky again. Nor anything about her sentiments upon seeing her dearly loved Russia again. She was absolutely silent about what she had seen. What she had done. What she had felt.

There was no trace of this brief encounter, apart from a single paragraph in the two letters she wrote to Gorky upon her return to England.

The first was dated December 27, 1933:

> *What vivid, varied impressions I felt during even those four short days [with you]—and how glad I am to have come. Everything has somehow become very simple and good.*

And the other, February 1934:

> *Above all I would like to be with you, and I know that, despite the immense joy of my stay in Moscow, it would be difficult for me to live there. . . . But nevertheless I'll of course come . . . to see you. And a little later, I hope, simply to stay.*

It was quite a plan, which the British counterintelligence services were swift to note down in their reports. And to forward, via the French ambassador in London, to their colleagues at the Deuxième Bureau in Paris.

It was a confirmation of what they had suspected for twenty years.

Only an informant of the highest rank, a spy hired directly by Stalin, could have entered the Soviet Union in this way. Entered, and left, without any of her comings and goings appearing on her passport. No visa. No stamp.

At this point, it wasn't enough to just follow her. Her phone was bugged and her mail opened.

The MI5 agents had plenty to do.

◈

Fate brought her to the dacha deep in the countryside again much more quickly than expected. Fate—or rather Yagoda—struck Gorky in the spring.

His son, Max, had died in three days from a sudden bout of pneumonia. It was May 11, 1934, during Wells's trip to America. Max was thirty-seven years old. Moura learned the news in London through a telegram from Kryuchkov.

He knew her well enough to know that she wouldn't hesitate a second. That she would take the first plane via Berlin to come support Alexey at such a terrible moment. It was out of the question, for her just as much as for him, not to go through this ordeal together. Kryuchkov wasn't wrong. She came immediately. In tears.

Officially, Max had fallen asleep by the shores of a lake after having had too much to drink during an outing in the countryside. He had caught a chill while he was asleep. The illness had taken hold in his lungs. Even the greatest doctors hadn't been able to save him.

The young man's relatives and widow were the only ones to believe this fable, one of various versions that circulated around this sudden death.

None of them was aware that in Moscow, Max's pneumonia went by the name of Yagoda. The head of the State Political Directorate often ordered these sorts of executions. He had long since lost count of how many had fallen victim to poisoning. It was a technique that allowed his police to rub out anybody who was troublesome without the bother of an arrest and the farce of a trial. He was well known for presiding personally over experiments with toxic substances in Stalin's research labs.

All that remained to ascertain were his motives.

Max had not seemed to pose any danger to the regime. He was reputed to be not very intelligent, a good boy, athletic, useless . . . He had always been supportive of the Party, and spoiled by its leaders. The Prince of the Soviets, his father had called him.

Ideologically and morally, he was unimportant. But he was an unimportant man with a stunning wife who was almost as lighthearted as he was.

For six years now, Yagoda had been madly in love, thoroughly obsessed with Timosha. He might be the most powerful man in Russia after Stalin, but he couldn't have her. And that—not being able to have a woman he lusted after—was an unfamiliar experience. He wasn't an Adonis by any means, but he had something else. A sly sentimentality that was a kind of charm. He knew how to talk, how to complain, how to beg. Foreigners and blind people even found him touching, welcoming, gentle. Like most of the Party's leaders—Stalin included—he came across as an honest man. An idealistic, pure man.

The truth was that with his toothbrush mustache, his flat hat, and his chaps and boots, he bore more than a passing resemblance to Hitler. And he had the chancellor's eloquence.

Timosha flirted with him, laughed with him, dined with him. She accepted his gifts, let him charm and flatter her. But she kept insisting that she was married and that as long as she was Max's wife, she would remain faithful to him. And she lived with her father-in-law. It was impossible for Yagoda to take her under Gorky's roof without the writer—or Stalin—knowing.

As for having her somewhere else . . . Max was wary.

The couple didn't get along well. Yagoda was certain that if she was freed of Max, Timosha would run into his arms.

This tragic story of a husband, a wife, and a lover was likely compounded by other motives that were more political and that called for the death of Gorky's son. As well as that of the writer. After this hardship, Gorky was devastated.

Max was buried hurriedly the day after his death. Those present recalled that at the cemetery, nobody was able to look directly at the poor father, so unbearable was the scale of his grief.

When Stalin embraced him and expressed his sympathies for the hundredth time, Gorky interrupted him: "There's nothing to say. Enough!"

Had he finally heard the rumors?

And once again, Moura did not share her impressions with anyone. She came the day after the funeral and claimed to have missed the ceremony.

It was enough for her to be there, beside the crying man she loved and whose grief she shared. She only had to think of Paul to imagine what he felt.

Did she, like the dead man's relatives and widow, remain unaware of Yagoda's role in Max's death? She wouldn't say anything about the silence and the tears of those who had loved him. Nor about the loud declarations of love from the others.

Nor about Gorky's despair.

And least of all about the mournful atmosphere of the dacha, the uniformed shadows that haunted Gorky's private mansion in Moscow, a residence that had once belonged to the richest banker. An art nouveau palace of unmatched opulence: a temple of modern style that the Soviet workers had renovated and transformed into a temple of vulgarity and bad taste.

Not a word, not even to her confidant Lockhart, on this descent into the shadowy waters of the Peshkov House kept under Yagoda's thumb.

This time, however, the head of the State Political Directorate did say a word to her about the archives. The next time she came, she would have to bring them. Gorky was asking for them. He needed them for his work. They would be grateful for her assistance here.

If the suitcase turned out to be too heavy, they could send someone to London, a "messenger" who would take care of it for her.

She got off the plane just in time to welcome Wells back from his sojourn to the United States. He arrived at the Waterloo station on May 20.

She was waiting for him, smiling, on the station platform.

❖

"My meetings with Roosevelt have reassured me that a rapprochement is possible between the United States and the Soviet Union," Aige-Gee said as he joined her. "I can be the go-between."

He was talkative and excited as he took her arm, making his way swiftly through the crowd to avoid the journalists.

"On top of that, as president of the International PEN Club, I can push Stalin to grant freedom of thought and speech for all Soviet writers. Gorky will support us."

"I don't think so. He's changed his mind on that point."

"All the more reason for you to come help me convince him. I need you beside me in this battle, Moura! You should be my English interpreter with Stalin. The same way you were for the Soviet Congress in 1920. Remember? You kept the official interpreter from putting words I would never think in my mouth. Without you in Russia, I'll be useless . . . Deaf, mute, blind! While with your eyes . . . You helped me to discover your country fourteen years ago. Why do you refuse to do so now?"

"Aige-Gee, you're the man I love! And you can't imagine how much I would love to come with you. But do you really want me to end up with a bullet in my head deep in a basement in the Lubyanka?"

It was simply too dangerous if Moura didn't marry him.

I went with my son Gip in July 1934.

I arranged to fly to Moscow, and, a week or so before I was to depart, we agreed that she should go to Estonia. Then I would come back from Russia and stay with her at her home near Tallinn and tell her all about the changes that had occurred there. I saw her off from Croydon. We parted very tenderly.

I remember her face peeping, smiling, from the aeroplane window as the machine taxied off.

That was the last I ever saw of my dream of Moura as a probable collaborator in a great political adventure.

❖

The truth was that Moura changed planes at Tallinn once again: a small Aeroflot plane, chartered specifically for her, took her to Alexey.

It was her third time . . . A few days stolen with him, a few days to share his sadness, to try to console him.

Their friend Yagoda had arranged a cruise that would take them down the Volga over several days. He wanted to distract the family from their mourning and to pull them out of the morass of their grieving. The family? Max's widow and their two little daughters; his mother, Peshkova; his father, Alexey Maximovich. Their confidant Kryuchkov. And Moura, who had come the day before they set sail.

Contrary to Yagoda's instructions, she had come back to Moscow without the suitcase. But she hadn't returned empty-handed. She brought him bits of documents. Letters she had received from Gorky during his years of exile: letters where he talked about money or business. But also his love letters.

The NKVD—under Yagoda's leadership, the State Political Directorate had changed its name—could be satisfied with this. The mass of documents made for a nice sheaf. She had added photos from Sorrento, where visitors whose comings and goings Yagoda already knew about could be seen. And the correspondence of artists his men had already executed.

As was her style, she had given him bits and pieces, not all of them real. Like the notebook she had invented for Yakov Peters so many years earlier.

For the week and a half of the cruise, Gorky was locked away in his cabin. She stayed there with him, crying. That summer in 1934, the heat on the water was unbearable.

She returned to Kallijärv as quickly as she could, on July 21, fleeing just as Aige-Gee was landing in Russia.

The postcard he sent her from Moscow should have given her a taste of the problems awaiting her:

Returning via Estonia as planned. Coming at the start of August at ten o'clock, on the Aeroflot plane . . . Which you're familiar with, I believe?

HG

Bad.

The tone and the form: bad.

Without her usual intuition, she didn't catch the implication and overlooked the threat that this prophetic note portended.

But she would find out soon enough . . .

She was wholly absorbed in the business of organizing the ball to celebrate Paul's coming of age.

In August 1934, she was waiting at Kallijärv for the entire Benckendorff and Budberg clans. Not just the families, but also all the friends. Her children's friends . . . and her own. *All* their friends. They were coming from Tallinn, Helsinki, Berlin, Naples, and London. She would be receiving Princess Galitzine, Lyuba Hicks, Ed Cunard . . . Even one of her latest fans, an outrageously wealthy British widow by the name of Molly Cliff, whose son was a very close friend of Paul's and a besotted wooer of Tania.

Not to mention her lover Count Konstantin Benckendorff, who had announced that he would be visiting with his daughter—his wife would stay home.

The only invitees unable to attend were Lockhart, who had been blacklisted, and the lawyer Carlo Ruffino, who had been detained in Italy by the Fascist police.

H. G. Wells would be coming three weeks before the others. As a guest star.

So much revelry went against every single one of Moura's principles.

It had been a long time since life had struck her as a train with sealed compartments. It had been a long time since "the Kallijärv car, with Micky and the children"; "the London car, with Lockhart and Wells"; and "the Sorrento car, with Gorky's group."

Had the appearance of a new train car—"the Moscow car, with Yagoda"—done away with all her other secrets?

No matter what the reason, she was now daring to take the risk of celebrating all the time she had lost and all the time regained. For her son's twenty-first birthday, she dared to bring together all the levels of society and realms of experience that made up her existence . . . Just as during her golden days at Yendel.

It was quite the about-face in her long career as a divided woman. A revolution!

But that was nothing compared to what awaited her when Aige-Gee stepped off the plane.

❖

Their embrace was icy. Not a look, not a smile, not even a question. She could sense the tension immediately. A state of fury that went far beyond all his usual reproaches.

She pretended not to notice. She was smiling, friendly, tender as always as she welcomed him just the way he loved. She even took a step back the better to admire him. She looked him in the eye and said, innocently:

"You look so tired, my dear."

"Exhausted. I don't like your new Russia."

"Come get some sleep at the house. You're going to rest at the spot by the lake . . . I'll take care of you! The train for Kallijärv doesn't leave until five o'clock, unfortunately. I thought we might put your bags down at the club here and have some lunch at a small restaurant just outside the city. Come with me. I'm borrowing my brother-in-law's car."

She slipped her arm through his and pulled him along. She was so happy to see him again.

She was charmed by his elegance, his impeccably cut white-linen suit, his silk tie of the same material as his pocket square, and his tailored Panama hat. He was still so English! She loved his body. Wells's profile, despite his weight, wasn't the least bit heavy. It was a compact, energetic physique full of promises and vigor.

But today, Aige-Gee wasn't himself. He stood stiffly, his eyes fixed straight ahead on the road. He didn't unclench his jaw. This silence wasn't a good omen at all. She chattered, bombarding him with stories about preparing for the gala.

They sat down at one of the tables by the water, under the massive trees. He set his hat on the table and pulled out his case and his cigar cutter, as if he were unburdening himself. She ordered crawfish and a bottle of wine for him, a small, fresh white wine just like he always enjoyed sipping in the sun.

It could have been a lovely afternoon. But once Wells had been served, he went on the offensive:

"I heard a very odd rumor about you in Moscow . . . That you had just been there."

She laughed.

"Is that so? It's incredible that they remember me over there . . . Who told you that?"

He exploded:

"Moura, you're a liar and a whore!"

She was shocked, but kept her calm.

Wells's high-pitched voice carried a long way. His cheeks were ruddy as he continued:

"Who told me? Just you listen! I came out of my interview with Stalin. I was taken to the dacha of your friend Gorky . . . stuck between the tour guide, who never left me alone, and the interpreter. They asked me how I was getting back to London. I said I was going by way of Estonia, where I would be staying with a friend: Baroness Budberg. And then the inter-preter said this astonishing sentence: 'She was here last week.' I couldn't help but yell, 'But that's impossible! I got a letter from her eight days ago when I was in London, mailed from Tallinn.' Then the guide yelled at the interpreter. They started shouting at each other in Russian. The inter-preter shut up like a clam, and all he said was: 'I must have been wrong.'"

"Well, he was wrong."

"Wait for it, Moura, wait for it: I'm not done yet! So then I sat down with Gorky, and I told him that my interpreter from years ago wasn't present. He asked me who I was talking about. '. . . Moura.' He replied: 'She came here three times this year. You've just missed her.'"

"How could he have told you that? Gorky doesn't speak English!"

"The interpreter translated it for me." Trying to keep his temper in check, he drank his glass of wine and then set it down violently. "I'm waiting for your explanation."

Acknowledge the truth? That was out of the question.

The trip to Moscow that July? That would already be one confession too many. But what else could she do?

As for the other points . . .

Aige-Gee was a gossip. If he told other people in England that she was visiting the Soviet Union as she liked and that she was able to leave at will, she would either be forced to move there permanently or never be able to go back.

She would lose Wells, she would lose Lockhart. Or she would lose Gorky.

It was an impossible decision.

And she had to be careful not to contradict herself. Hadn't she told Wells that she'd never slept with Gorky? She had said that a hundred times.

But if Gorky had only ever been a friend to her, how could she justify to Aige-Gee that she had taken not just one but three risky trips?

And the last problem: the secret of the suitcase with the letters.

If she should somehow mention the existence of those papers to Wells, he would end up telling every reporter he saw. The press all over the world would try to seize them. Not to mention the British spy services, which were perennially interested in what Soviet citizens had to say about Stalin.

As for the rest . . . Aige-Gee's words were a guillotine blade threatening to cut her head off.

Deny, her sister Anna had told her. *Always deny!* A survival instinct she had harbored ever since childhood.

"Don't get yourself worked up, Aige-Gee, darling. Not over such idiocy . . . I'm going to explain. My visit was at the last minute, the day after I came here. Tania knows about it. Micky knows about it. Everybody knows about it. They'll tell you everything . . . Let's have lunch now, my dear. You're very tired."

Wells poured himself more wine.

The habit of being happy with this woman was so deeply ingrained in his being that he was almost able to forget what had kept him awake for so many sleepless nights.

When he was with her, he wanted to be at ease, alive. Her presence was always so reassuring. He loved the feel of her skin, the curve of her breasts in her low-cut summer dress.

But she was merely a mirage.

She was looking back at him. She wanted to be happy the way he did. She loved their conversations. She loved his honey-scented skin. She loved his blue eyes that she knew so well as they smiled and frowned. She took such great pleasure in his presence. She wanted to tell him that.

But it was hard. She felt as if she had been flayed alive. He was a thousand miles away from her. Any word she uttered would unleash a storm.

She had to be quiet. She had to wait. She had to hunker down until the worst had passed.

He launched yet another attack, this time from a different angle:

"If this trip was as unexpected, as unimportant as you say it was, why didn't you wait until I came to Moscow?"

"Because nobody could know that I was in Russia. Nobody. My presence would have put Gorky in such a dangerous situation vis-à-vis the Party . . . And you, too, if you had been seen in my company. My presence beside you would have put you in serious, serious danger with Stalin. You would never have been able to get the interview you had come for."

"But we could have seen each other in private!"

"The walls have ears over there . . . And I had to return to Kallijärv as quickly as possible. I needed to ready the house for you."

"So you only went to see Gorky once, one time, last week?"

"Yes. Ten days ago: a quick trip . . . it was set up at the last minute. When I was already here. You must have been told that he lost his son this spring. Max's death undid him. It's still unbearably painful for him as he mourns. He asked me to come. He planned out everything with the commissar of foreign affairs . . . I wasn't able to say no to him. I have a debt of gratitude to him, Aige-Gee. He was a friend, a very dear friend. He saved me from certain death."

"So you haven't been back to Russia in some fifteen years?"

"Not even once."

"That must have been a very interesting visit . . . What did you think of it?"

"I was disappointed."

"By what?"

"By Russia, by Gorky, by so many things."

"Moura, why are you still lying to me? You went to Russia *three* times in the last eight months! First at Christmas . . . Then when I was in America . . . And the last time was right before I came to Moscow."

"No."

"Gorky himself told me."

"You've misunderstood, or the interpreter didn't translate it correctly."

"I want to believe you! Unfortunately, in my eyes, you are the worst strumpet ever to walk this earth. And I'm putting it nicely . . . Because you're also a spy, a cheat, not to mention Gorky's mistress. Now I understand why you refused to marry me . . . When I'm holding you close, *you're working*! You were planted in my circles from the very beginning: the very day we met. Were you already informing your little friends at the Cheka about what I was saying, what I was thinking, what I was doing, from our very first night together in Petrograd? You must have just loved toying with my scruples on Kronverksky Prospect when, out of consideration to Gorky, I refrained from fucking you. Yes, you must have been having a great laugh as you snared me for your own professional advancement. You sleep with Gorky, you betray me to Stalin, you've been fooling me this whole time . . . And I was stupid enough not to realize any of it!"

She was at a loss for words. Wells's attack was so vicious that she had to look down and close her eyes for a minute to regain her composure.

She had to return to the slow rhythm of her breathing.

She gave herself a few seconds.

"I'm not a spy. I'm not Gorky's mistress. And I only went to Russia once."

She was talking calmly, driving home every one of her assertions.

The warmth of her timbre, the intonations of her Russian accent, belied her peacefulness and made her seem strangely vulnerable. She seemed both categorical and self-assured. And the victim of immense injustice.

Her composure stunned Wells. This combination of self-mastery and passion was her in a nutshell.

In the face of such aplomb, he started to doubt himself. Could he have misunderstood, after all? Or had Gorky been tricking him?

When they had sat down to dinner together, they had just finished a debate about freedom of speech and artistic creation at some PEN Club for the USSR. They had been at loggerheads every step of the way.

Thinking back on the matter, Wells decided that his old friend had been dishonest and that he hadn't been welcomed in good faith. Gorky had been icy from the very beginning, and his coldness had been unvarying for the entire interview. Did he know about the ties that bound him to Moura?

She could claim that Gorky was impotent—that prospect appealed to Wells—but he had certainly been in love with her. And his decision to return to Russia while she chose to stay in England might have signified a break for him.

Was his murderous little line—*you just missed her*—the revenge of a scorned, jealous lover?

Wells found himself unsure of what he thought, what he felt.

In meeting Moura, he was certain he had found his soul mate. Discovering her duplicity had crushed that feeling. She was attacking his very existence. His feelings, his intuition, his certainties. She threatened them all.

In realizing that he didn't know this woman and that she was still wholly foreign to him, he had realized just how fragile he was, and he hadn't been able to bear the shock.

His first act had been to run to the British embassy in Moscow and rewrite his will so that Moura would not receive anything. It was a symbolic gesture that was meant to write her out of his life.

But now, as he watched her, he was lost.

Was he being jealous, cruel, insensitive, by not listening to her?

Had he been wrong to accuse her?

"When we're back at the house," she was saying, "we can call Moscow. We can call the interpreter. And Gorky. They'll clear up this misunderstanding . . . You're the man of my life, Aige-Gee. The only one."

"Yet another lie!"

The two of them took the train to Kallijärv together, and Wells described the stay in his autobiography.

I went to her home with her and that night she came to my room. . . . We made love—but we had the canker of this trouble between us. . . .

No lucidities came through from Andreychin and yet there was a good telephone service to both Leningrad and Moscow. . . .

She stuck to it stoutly that she had been to Moscow only once. I had misunderstood or Andreychin had misunderstood. . . .

"I've put my cards on the table with you, Moura, long ago; put your cards down. Come to me. Or am I nothing more to you than an adventure—one of a jumble of adventures?"

"You are the man I love," she said.

"That I had supposed—and it has been something tremendous to me."

She said she would get the matter of the misunderstanding cleared up. She had never been anything to Gorky but a friend; a great friend because he had done wonderful things for her when her life was in danger. Everybody knew—she threw in the information—that Gorky had been impotent for years. She had had only four days in Russia. . . .

I was jealous of the son, of her visitors, of the Estonian house, of Russia. Above all of Russia. . . .

I tried to put things right by talking, but instead we walked through the woods quarrelling. . . .

She came to see me off at Tallinn—like a lover, like the only lover in the world. For she loves partings and meetings; she does them superbly.

We lunched at Tallinn and went to the Stockholm hydroplane together. At the last moment she declared her intention of joining me in Oslo.

And that was exactly what she did the day after Paul's birthday.

Wells wrote in his memoirs that she ignored all her friends—Konstantin Benckendorff and the others—to fly and be with him. And after that she had been affectionate, tender, and tenacious, returning to England with him. And that no matter how much he interrogated her, insulted her, tortured her, she did not confess a thing.

———

But his discovery of a Moura beneath the Moura he knew had cost them their happiness. They were no longer lighthearted adventurers.

While Wells conceded that he didn't entirely believe that she was tangled up in a network of spies, he still refused to stop interrogating her on her activities and second-guessing her doings. Gorky and Russia had become taboo topics. There would be hell to pay if she hinted that she wanted to see one or the other again.

She did her best to reassure him. But it was a lost cause: he was wary of her from then on.

He didn't ask her to marry him anymore, but he kept on making scenes, acting like the suspicious husband. It was impossible for her to escape his watchful eye, and she had to invent yet more lies to avoid the drama. She schemed, feinted this way and that, sneaking away to see Lockhart again, to visit her sisters, and to spend time with Alexey Maximovich in Moscow once or twice a year.

But how could she get a week of freedom from Wells? She went so far as to tell him that she was pregnant and had to go away for an abortion.

Moura's duplicity in this relationship had no limits anymore.

And yet she was still devoted to him . . . She didn't let him go.

He wrote later:

> When all is said and done, she is the woman I really love. I love her voice, her presence, her strength and her weaknesses. . . . In this sort of love, the rights and the wrongs of the case are interesting but they do not alter the deep primary fact to any material degree. . . . Even when I have let my vexation with her take the form of an infidelity, or when she has behaved badly to me and driven me to anger and reprisals, she has remained still the dearest thing in my affections. And so she will remain to the end. I can no more escape from her smile and her voice, her flashes of gallantry and the charm of her endearments, than I can escape from my diabetes and my emphysematous lung. My pancreas has not been all that it should be; nor has Moura. That does not alter the fact that both are parts of myself.

CHAPTER THIRTY-EIGHT

Checkmate

1936

"Yagoda's messenger came to my place yesterday," she said.

"And?"

"He's got a filthy face."

Seated in the darkness of a small Russian cabaret in London, Lockhart and Moura were whispering their endless secrets into each other's ears.

The owner, in traditional boots and tunic, had rushed up to lead them to their table. They were beloved regulars. The musicians were playing their favorite melodies, the same Gypsy songs they had heard at Strelnya, when Queen Maria Nikolayevna had broken their hearts with her words of love.

Now the balalaika and the violins' quavering only served to hide their words.

"What did he want?"

"Take a wild guess . . . It was to get his hands on Gorky's correspondence. Just like Peshkova and Timosha when they came to see me here last year."

"Well, what did you tell him?"

"That I'd brought everything I had to Moscow already."

"You're crazy, Moura! Gorky's two ladies were nice enough. But those NKVD guys aren't idiots, you can't pull the wool over their eyes . . . You're going to end up dead!"

They were back to the familiar banter of olden days, back when they had been working, along with Hickie and Sidney Reilly, to keep the Brest-Litovsk treaty from being signed.

When they were together, they were absolutely inseparable. Their relationship had survived everything, even time's relentless passage. She would tell him in her letters:

I know nothing can tear us apart. Isn't it so strange, Baby? We've only been living together a few months, but it's for life.

At forty-nine years old, Lockhart was still a catch. He had the same sparkling blue gaze, the same smile, the same physical force, even though he kept complaining about his health.

As he had gotten bulkier and snobbier over the years, he had traded his bow ties for silk ties. But he still had that same old love for parties, that same old sense of humor, that same old intellectual curiosity. He was still an adventurer who could pull off almost anything when he wanted to. Or when he was in love.

Moura still adored him: that he knew. And the reverence was mutual. On some evenings, when she got him too drunk, their passion led them to her bed in Knightsbridge. And in the fall, their trysts took place amid the wall hangings of her room in Cadogan Square, in the apartment she had just invested in with Lyuba and their coterie of emigrants. Lockhart happily came there several nights in a row. But nowadays, the flame was flickering. He would only take her to bed every so often.

But if Moura was bothered by that, she didn't show it. With Wells, Gorky, Benckendorff, and others as well . . . she was often busy with others elsewhere, just as he was.

She insisted:

All the same, I love you the same way I did fifteen years ago, that is: wholly. And it's wonderful to love you that way.

She had told him about her disputes with Wells, shared the secret of her trips to Russia, that whole matter of Gorky's archives, and the fear that was eating away at her.

Lockhart was still the only man she felt comfortable baring her secrets to.

And he, too, told her everything. He told her about his career, asked her advice on which paths to take and which choices to make. She was his co-conspirator, his mentor, his unwavering support. He didn't hesitate to drive her crazy by telling her about his passion for one conquest or another.

She was told everything, she had to understand everything: that was the price to pay for maintaining her influence.

Even though he couldn't bring himself to be monogamous with her, he acknowledged that she was first and foremost in his heart.

And so Moura had triumphed on that front: she had had a remarkable recovery. She was, and she remained, the woman of Lockhart's life.

But it took two to tango.

"I'm not joking, Moura: you're going to end up dead."

"What do you want me to do? I can't give them those papers and send a hundred men to the gulag. And that's being optimistic! Gorky's correspondence includes more than nine thousand letters."

"But then why did he send his wife and daughter-in-law to get them from you?"

"Timosha is Yagoda's mistress now. And Peshkova—who doesn't suspect a thing—has always been connected to the Cheka. Yagoda is manipulating them. Gorky is more or less under house arrest. He can't take a single step without Kryuchkov telling the NKVD. You can't imagine, Baby, what it's like to see him shackled hand and foot, unable to move forward or backward . . . That's what they've done to him. They trot him out like an old bear for the May Day parades around Lenin's mausoleum, even though he's got a ring through his nose and a chain holding him in place."

"When you met him last time, he begged you to bring those papers, didn't he?"

"Yes, but while pointing at the wall . . . He was making it clear that we were being listened to, that there were microphones. I had to use my hands to ask him if he was actually thinking that I shouldn't. And he nodded."

"It's impossible for you to get out of this, Moura, unless you obey

Yagoda! His men can break your door down and go through your room anytime. Remember what happened to Kerensky's archives in France. They burgled his apartment and took the boxes they were looking for. And that's not to mention the fires that broke out at various dissidents' homes after!"

"I've sorted the documents and hidden the most dangerous ones someplace safe."

"When the NKVD goes looking for something, it finds it."

"I know, Baby, I know . . . Do you think I'm not afraid? I have no doubt they'll get their hands on the suitcase at some point. The same way they got Alexey to come back."

"The same way they killed his son . . . the same way they'll shoot him dead once they don't need him anymore. I guess his time hasn't come yet, but all the same . . ."

"Hush!" Her voice was barely perceptible now. "He suspects Yagoda's role in Max's death. And their communications have broken down. The result is that his visa application to come to the Congress of Writers in Paris was rejected. Stalin is saying that his absence is due to exhaustion."

"Pardon my French, Moura, but Gorky is screwed. He's not going anywhere. And you'd do best to keep your distance and forget him!"

In hearing Lockhart dismiss Gorky so uncaringly, the image of Alexey Maximovich's long body, bearing the weight of his years, his doubts, his torments, surged forth in her mind: a face that was more anxious than ever, a mustache he was chewing, hands that shook as he spoke. She was still under his charm and distressed to think of him so vulnerable.

"I can't just forget him. And I can't just keep my distance. I'm in deep. He made me swear, in Italy, never to give him the suitcase."

"That's enough, Moura! You know better than anyone else the price of life. Yours is worth far more than this show of honor."

She laughed. "You're saying the opposite of what Aige-Gee does. He lectures me every day, trying to convince me that it's better to be dead than to be alive but having compromised oneself thoroughly."

"Wells is a scribbler; the worst thing he's ever had to face has been his diabetes. He doesn't have the faintest idea what the horrors of a revolution are like. He has no clue what it's like to risk your own flesh. He's the pleasure-seeker I've always known him to be, and he'd sell out his own parents to live just one more day, one more hour, one more second."

"Don't say that!"

"Believe me, between betraying the authors of those letters and dying, your Aige-Gee wouldn't think twice."

"But for me, that would mean sacrificing a hundred people . . . And Gorky, as well. Should Stalin read his notebooks, take in the conversations he's reported in his notes . . . If he lays hands on Gorky's diary, the man will be dead in a matter of hours."

"Listen to me, Babygirl, listen to what I'm telling you: you're going to give them this darned suitcase and you're never going to go back to Russia. You've put everything into surviving this long. You can't just let yourself be shot dead over a pile of papers!"

❖

She wrote him the following morning:

Dear Baby, do forgive my bad mood yesterday. I do believe I'm exhausted. And so I'm feeling down. You know that's a rarity for me, and that I'll be quick to recover. Don't worry too much . . . I promise you our next evening out will be far happier.

But above all do not repeat to anyone what I've told you.

Fear consumed her completely. The truth was that she was paralyzed by it.

Lockhart had merely put into words what she already thought: the threat of her murder at the moment Gorky was no longer able to protect her. And that time had now come. Her visitor from yesterday would be back.

So what new lie would she come up with to get rid of him?

She couldn't think anymore. She couldn't move anymore. She was losing sleep, and her panic stubbornly refused to dissipate with the rising sun. Dawn found her with tense muscles, a mind drained empty by anguish. She still lay in bed until noon, but she wasn't getting work done anymore. The phone kept ringing, but she didn't pick up. She didn't even think about lighting a cigarette.

She started feeling dizzy.

She was starting to think that fate, this chess game where the other side's pawns kept gaining ground, was betraying her. Not only was her entire side not advancing anymore, but they—the king, the queen, the bishops—were surrounded. The same way as when, at Khlebny Lane, she had hesitated to give the men behind the Lockhart Plot Lockhart's notebook and the proof that Yakov Peters needed. The same way as when, at Kronverksky Prospect, Zinoviev had forced her to spy on and betray Gorky.

Moura knew this feeling of impotence well. She had already run up against the same brick walls. She could survive by letting the man she loved be executed. Or she could save him by having her own throat slit.

Back then, she had found a way out every time.

But she wasn't so sure she could this time.

She was outflanked. Caught, as Yakov Peters was so fond of putting it. No way out.

She had only told Lockhart about a fraction of the pressure she was under. In fact, she was receiving messengers not only from Yagoda but also from a dozen other emissaries, sent by Gorky. And it wasn't just the suitcase they were after. They had come to give her a new mission: to meet, in Alexey's stead, the French Communist authors who were planning to attend the Soviet Writers' Congress in Moscow that June . . . André Gide, Louis Aragon, Elsa Triolet.

They had come to the first congress, two years earlier, and had outdone themselves in singing Stalin's praises alongside Alexey.

Gorky had known them for ages. He had encouraged Elsa Triolet to write her first pieces after she had made the trip to Germany to meet him. She had sent him the Russian translation of her companion Louis Aragon's writings. He had appreciated them and had told André Malraux, who had come and spent several days with him in Crimea, of his admiration for Aragon.

For two months, Gorky had bombarded them with letters, even though neither of them had bothered to reply.

Why?

Gorky didn't understand.

His spokespeople needed Moura to meet them soon in Paris. She had to tell them in person that he was expecting them at his place the minute they arrived in Russia. That he had essential information to share with them. Vital information. That he wanted to talk to them *before* the congress.

His impatience was a form of panic. And Gorky's worry ended up throwing Moura into bouts of doubt. What did he want to tell his foreign colleagues, what could be so serious?

She wasn't unaware that Stalin was trying to get rid of Lenin's old collaborators. That he was laying the groundwork for their trials. The pioneers of the Revolution were an affront to him: he was looking for evidence of their "betrayal" to give some sense of legitimacy to their executions. Most of them had been friends of Gorky. They had corresponded with him over the course of their careers, and their letters could be found in the Sorrento suitcase. Was Alexey trying to save them by alerting the French Communist Party and influencing international opinion?

Rounding off these questions was, in Moura's eyes, the most important one: Were Gorky's ambassadors really coming on his behalf? They could also have been obeying the NKVD . . . Like Peshkova and Timosha. Was all this a trap that Yagoda had set in order to ensnare her in France?

Did Yagoda know that she had taken a portion of the correspondence to Paris?

She had already given him the most neutral letters in small batches. As was her wont, she had only given him half-true ones. A wealth that she had hoped would be enough for him.

The problem was that Kryuchkov knew just how immense those archives were.

And so she had divided them up.

The contents of the Deutsche Bank safe deposit box had stayed in

Estonia. She had broken that up into several parts, which were kept at Kallijärv, Tallinn, and Tartu.

The Sorrento archives had been hidden in two other places: under her bed in London, and under Alla's bed on the rue Edgar-Poe. It was a place where she was certain nobody would think to look.

Because, in Estonia just as in England, everybody thought Alla was dead.

That was yet another of Moura's lies.

Working with Anna, she had sent around the rumor that their sister had committed suicide, that the poor woman had been unable to bear the loss of her husband Trubnikov. Alla's death had been so painful for them that they had chosen not to broadcast her descent into hell.

Neither the Benckendorffs nor the Kochubeys nor the Zakrevskys nor anyone else was supposed to know about the tragedy of her downfall. It was unthinkable to tell anyone that Alla, who had been so gifted at the piano, Alla, whose beauty had been so extraordinary, was now a drug addict begging for money on the streets of Paris in order to buy her next dose.

It was a family secret.

Alla, however, didn't know that her family believed she was dead. Especially not her daughter, Kira. And she had no idea about the story of the suitcase beneath her bed.

On this front, Moura never stopped fearing the worst. She harbored no illusions whatsoever: if Alla ever realized that those letters existed, she would sell them off to the highest bidder so she could buy more opium.

That hiding place, therefore, could only be temporary. How could she abandon such important papers on the rue Edgar-Poe?

But then again, who could she trust with them?

Here, too, she kept running up against a brick wall: back to square one . . . To the first conversation she had had in Sorrento about the fate of those archives.

Who could she trust them with?

A name kept coming up in her thoughts: that of Alexey's adoptive son. Zinovy Peshkov.

Moura had met him in Germany and at Il Sorito. He seemed to be a ladies' man. She barely knew him at all. And he hadn't been particularly taken with her: her charm hadn't worked on this Russian man who had become a Frenchman.

But Zinovy's affection for Gorky, his hatred of the Bolsheviks, his courage, his discretion, all made him the only possible choice.

How could she reach him?

Zinovy Peshkov was currently on a diplomatic mission in the Levant. Was there any way to lure him back to Paris?

There was no way out.

❖

Wells wrote:

At the end of May 1936, a particular malaise came upon Moura. She had storms of weeping, a thing strangely unusual in her. She was seized with a desire to go off alone to France.

The shadow of the coming change of life lay upon her. Her generally invincible self-assurance deserted her for a time. She couldn't talk to me about it; she couldn't talk to herself about that phase; she wanted to be alone.

The British intelligence services—MI5—were swift to note in their reports that Baroness Budberg had left. And the French counterintelligence services were just as swift to maintain notes on her arrival.

The agents noted that she spent three days at the Hotel Continental between March 17 and 19, 1936, and again, at the same hotel on the rue de Castiglione, between May 9 and 12. That she received no mail or visitors during that time.

She only went to see Mrs. Vasily Kochubey, who lived in a modest family boarding house at 3 rue Duret in the sixteenth arrondissement, and Mrs. René Moulin, the widow of a certain Trubnikov, on the rue Edgar-Poe. Those two people didn't have files on them, even though the husband of one of them, Vasily Kochubey, seemed to be a pro-German agitator.

Given this lack of information, a conclusion seemed clear. She was summarized in two lines:

Madame B. is such a dangerous woman that her relatives and her connections provide no evidence of her true attachments.

The men of the Deuxième Bureau, however, had missed the most important detail: the name of the person staying in the room adjacent to Mrs. B.'s place on the rue de Castiglione. Had they bothered to look through the registers of the Hotel Continental, they would have seen that Mrs. B.'s neighbor was a hero of the war of 1914, an officer in the Foreign Legion in Morocco. Who was now stationed in the Levant. A soldier on leave.

A certain Commander Peshkov.

❖

The transfer of "Alla's suitcase" across the hallway, from one room to the other, had gone seamlessly. Moura knew she was being monitored and didn't dare to dawdle. She didn't contact the French Communists.

She rushed back to London, taking care to warn Aige-Gee that she was coming back. She took advantage of the fact that he thought she was in France to visit Konstantin Benckendorff on his property in Suffolk.

A week of secret love. A bit of magic, a bit of joy and lightheartedness!

She had barely gotten back to her apartment on Cadogan Square when a telegram came to her from Kryuchkov. Gorky's health was worsening again. Alexey Maximovich was calling her to Russia.

The telegram was followed by a phone call: Kryuchkov again. He didn't want to worry her, but he wanted Maria Ignatyevna to come as soon as she could . . . He had booked a ticket for her on the plane to Berlin the next day, June 5, with a return planned for the twenty-fourth.

Unnerved by his tone, she didn't hesitate. Wells thought she was in Paris. She could go to the Croydon airport without risking his wrath.

She said yes.

———

Just as she was stepping into the cab, she had a moment of dread. Lockhart's line came back to mind: "You're going to give them this darned suitcase and you're never going to go back to Russia!"

Would she ever return to England?

She decided to go into the lion's den. She went in knowingly. Without the correspondence. And without bringing Yagoda her usual offering of a few letters to suggest that she had spent time looking for what he wanted and that she was cooperating to the best of her ability.

Would this decision—to fly to Moscow today—mean the end of all her connections with Europe? Would it mean the sacrifice of all those affections that bound her to England? Who knew if she would be allowed to return to London? If she would see Aige-Gee again someday?

Notwithstanding all their arguments, she loved him deeply.

And her children! Would she ever see her children again?

But how could she abandon Alexey now? He knew he was a prisoner. During their last conversation, she had seen just how lonely, how desperate he was.

The way Kryuchkov had made it sound, Gorky had caught a chill on the train on the way back from Crimea. The doctors had first diagnosed him with a cold that complicated his respiratory problems. But his condition had worsened with each passing hour, and now he was sick with pneumonia.

If Alexey was going to die, as everybody sensed he would, she would never forgive herself for not having been at his bedside during this final struggle.

She couldn't let him fight alone.

Nor could she let herself be led to the slaughter!

As she thought over Kryuchkov's words again, a thought that she hadn't put into words yet paralyzed her. The "pneumonia" that Alexey was suffering from sounded strangely like Max's. The same circumstances, the same symptoms, even the same treatments. The similarity between the father's state and that of the son left her terrified.

She stayed there, on the sidewalk, in the middle of the London crowd, her massive black bag hanging from her arms. She was unable to get into the cab, but she was also unable to pull away and return home.

The driver's horn brought her back to reality.

She finally decided to get in, but she did not ask him to drive her to the airport immediately. He needed to make a stop at Regent's Park, right by 13 Hanover Terrace, and put a note into the box for "Wells" that she was currently jotting down in her lap.

Darling, dearest mine,

Don't be alarmed at this letter—it may be all nothing but I thought I would like to tell you that if anything happens to me, I am going away with a last thought of you and all that you have been to me.

There is nothing but gratefulness and tenderness in my heart and love and if I have not always been what you wanted—it is only through clumsiness.

Be good to Kira, Tania, and Paul—they'll miss me and you too, perhaps.

Moura

This farewell—three sheets torn out of a notebook, written in pencil, with no date and no postmark—terrified Wells. He saw in it the signs of suicidal depression that he had sensed, and he immediately called Tania. At the time, she was living at her mother's place.

She was twenty-one years old and had been told to hide the fact that Moura was in Russia, and not in France, as he believed.

Her diary entries, on June 10, 1936, were telling:

Pestered by H. G. all week; how is it I don't know the name of the nursing home!? Hate having to tell all these lies.

June 11th: dined H. G. (Antony & Flora R.)

M. rang from Moscow middle of the night. Told her it would be much better to tell H. G. the truth now . . .

June 13th: Good M has 'phoned H. G. from Moscow telling him she's left the nurs-
ing home and flown to Moscow as Gorky was dying and has asked for her.

Thank goodness no more lies required.

Still have to pretend I knew nothing of all this till today. Fed up being interme-
diary every time. Makes me look a complete fool . . .

June 18th: Gorky died. M. staying for funeral. Sad.

❖

What Moura had feared for seventeen years had finally happened. Alexey Maximovich was lying there, in front of her, his nose pinched, his cheeks hollow, on a bed of flowers.

Up to the last moment, she had believed he would hold out. He had overcome tuberculosis and so many other infections. A force of nature, a rock, despite his respiratory difficulties. Just two days ago, a camphor injection had gotten him back on his feet. It was an astonishing recovery that had surprised even Stalin, who had come to the dacha to mourn him.

This recovery had been attributed to Gorky's great joy at seeing his friend, the Little Father of the Peoples, raising a glass to his health.

Just after the Party's leaders—accompanied by Timosha and a horde of doctors—had left, Moura was alone in the room with him for a minute. The air still smelled like camphor, an odor that had filled the entire house.

Ever since Gorky had become bedridden, his faithful nurse, the care-takers hired by Kryuchkov, and his various doctors had been standing guard at his bedside. Whispers, prognoses, and consultations: all around him, the ballet of caregivers had been ongoing.

It was their first moment alone in days.

Alexey had called her to come be with him. She had held his hand, leaned over, wanted to kiss him. He had let her do so while whisper-ing something in her ear: to remove the document that he had taped to the bottom of his nightstand drawer. His diary for the past few months. A batch of several pages comprising his political last will and testament.

Gorky's gaze hadn't left her as she had slipped the document under her belt buckle. He was still perfectly lucid at that point.

It was impossible to imagine that the following night, for no clear reason, he would be suffocating again . . . And that twenty-four hours after they had gotten to share a moment alone, on June 18, 1936, at eleven o'clock in the morning, he would cease to exist.

He was sixty-eight years old.

Yagoda, who had set up shop in the house at the first sign of Gorky's illness, had kept his office and his papers sealed away. For the eighteen days of his illness, Kryuchkov had been busy "tidying" his office behind those closed doors.

The second Gorky took his final breath, a dozen agents had taken away the boxes.

His funeral ceremony had been planned out far earlier, down to the smallest details. Immense garlands, sprays of flowers, flags, crapes, processions of people in uniform, orchestras and choirs that would be singing "The Internationale," cannons, bells: everything was ready.

The very day of his death, they had made his death mask, photographed his face from every angle, and taken his corpse to Moscow for the wake.

There wouldn't be an autopsy. His brain would be embalmed, his body would be cremated the next day. The urn containing his ashes would be set on a dais that the regime's highest-ranking dignitaries would bear on their shoulders down Red Square. Stalin himself would lead the march. His arm, bound by a black armband, would hold up the remains of what he anointed that day as *his dear, only friend*.

Gorky would be playing the role assigned to him again.

Over the preceding months, he had tried to push back, but at this point he was the symbol of Bolshevik Russia again: a vase buried between two bricks in the walls of the Kremlin. That would be June 20, 1936, less than forty-eight hours after his death. The beatification of Alexey Maximovich Peshkov, a hero of the Russian people, was only beginning. The character of Gorky, the name of Gorky, the work of Gorky—all that was Gorky—was now Stalin's forever.

But on the evening of his death, his body, his memory, and his soul had not yet been stolen from those who mourned him.

In the Hall of Columns in the House of Unions, all that could be heard was the whir of the cameras filming the guard of honor—Stalin, Khrushchev, Mikoyan—and the slow, uninterrupted murmur of felt soles: the footsteps of the working classes filing past his deathbed. Over the course of the night, the sobbing populace had come to pay homage to the writer who had been able to give them a voice.

The physiognomy of each of these mourners had been carefully chosen to appear close-up on screens over the entire world.

There were the faces of workers reduced to skin and bones, women ravaged by grief, children in tears: the incarnation of the Russian proletariat had come from every corner of the Soviet Union to pay their respects to the friend of the working class, to the fighter for Communism.

The family, behind a velvet rope, was seated. Most of the silhouettes were female. The only male relative—Zinovy Peshkov, adopted son of the deceased—had not come. He had refused to ally himself with the regime.

Gorky's three companions were in the first row. Kryuchkov, who knew all the man's darkest secrets, had taken care to keep the three perennial rivals separate: between Peshkova and Maria Andreyeva, he had seated the last "wife," Maria Ignatyevna.

The British intelligence services trying to decipher the images had spent many hours examining this layout. Baroness Budberg's presence beside Stalin and the leaders of the Party raised more than a few questions in the West.

None of the three women showed any despair on their faces. Not even Timosha and the two granddaughters, Marfa and Darya, who held their handkerchiefs in their hands. This official mourning was such an experience that they could not simply wallow in feeling. They were frozen under the light of the projectors, and all of them felt like they were on display. They kept their heads up and their eyes fixed straight ahead on the replica of their Duca who they had loved so dearly.

Among all Gorky's kin, Moura had been the only one present at the end.

The anguish of losing him had transformed into a stupefaction of sorts for her. She was wholly unmoving. Those who saw her that day said she seemed just as rigid as he was and that she hadn't been able to look away from the mummified face.

After so many days and nights fighting for Alexey's life, the descent into death had been so painful that she was shell-shocked. The body lying there wasn't her Joy. What was there bore so little resemblance to him!

The transfer of the body to Moscow hadn't brought her out of her torpor. She was apart from the world around her.

All she dreamed about was Alexey's final moments, his despair at the thought of leaving *The Life of Klim Samgin*, the massive novel he had dedicated to her, unfinished. Of all his fears, that of dying without having finished his book had cut most deeply to his core. It had upset him down to his final moment of consciousness. In it he saw the symbol of his failure as a man, as well as his failure as a writer. He had left his work incomplete; he had left their love at loose ends.

Their love?

She scolded herself for not having done a better job of resisting his wish to leave Italy. She had taken his desire to return to Russia as an inarguable fact. She should have pushed him not to make such a definitive gesture.

If he had stayed in Sorrento, would he have been able to keep his illusions, his faith in that better future he so needed to bring about?

The night of his death, she asked herself the questions that she hadn't dared to ask herself back then. Four years . . . A century.

She accused herself of not having defended him. She blamed herself for everything she had allowed to happen. And everything she had failed to do.

She hadn't met any of his expectations.

She hadn't even gone to the trouble of meeting the French writers in Paris who he had been so determined to see. They—André Gide, Louis Aragon, Elsa Triolet—had just landed in Russia for the congress they were supposed to attend. Kryuchkov had deemed it necessary to underscore the extraordinary coincidence of their arrival the very day of Gorky's death.

But that was a lie, just like everything else touching on Alexey in his gilded cage.

Aragon and Triolet had come three days earlier, but they had been asked to visit Leningrad. Gide, however, had been asked to delay his flight by forty-eight hours. The result was that none of them heard what Gorky had to tell them.

Stalin arranged for Gide to give the eulogy in Red Square, so that Alexey's words would be stifled.

And she would never be able to forgive him for that, either.

Watching him as he lay dying, never letting go of his hand, had been the one act she was still proud of.

He had insisted on dictating his perceptions as a dying man. Things growing heavier, the room suddenly feeling much smaller. Gorky remained himself to the last breath: a writer who wanted to bear witness to what he saw, what he felt . . . Recording unto death.

She had remained his companion, the woman who had written down his final words.

For him, she had written:

It's the end of the novel. The end of the hero. The end of the author.

For her, it was the end of the Russia she had known and loved. The Russia she had considered the best part of herself. She knew that, with Alexey gone, she would never return. Presuming that she could leave.

As day broke, her instincts returned, including her old instinct to survive.

How could she negotiate her return to England with Yagoda? She realized that she had nothing to offer him. Apart from the most compromising of the documents he lusted after . . . The personal diary of Gorky's last days.

After everything she had done and promised, was she going to betray the trust of the man she loved by handing this text over to the NKVD? When all was said and done, would she save her own skin by betraying Alexey?

She tried to contemplate the consequences of such a surrender.

If Stalin should discover the criticisms that her dear friend had burdened her with, if he should learn that Alexey Maximovich had compared him to the most disgusting of creatures, a flea that had grown a thousand times bigger, he wouldn't continue glorifying Gorky as a national hero. But he wouldn't be able to seek revenge. He wouldn't dare touch his family. It would be impossible for him to get revenge on Timosha and the grandchildren. As for Peshkova and Maria Andreyeva, they were so wholly part of Gorky's public image that sending them to the gulag would be a mistake far too great for him to consider committing.

While he was alive, Alexey had been killed in seconds. His death and sanctification sheltered him.

If she delivered these notes to Yagoda, what would happen?

The notes only described Gorky's political vision. It was his and his alone—a form of a last will and testament that underscored the man's wishes for a triumphant Communist Russia, without Stalin. What it expressed was his disappointment and sadness in front of the man's monstrosity.

In all likelihood, Stalin would keep anybody and everybody from reading such an indictment. He would deem it "top secret." And at worst, he would destroy it.

She kept this bargaining chip and, this time, held up her side of the agreement. She would give the police chief the trophy he could deliver to his master.

Yagoda, in turn, was kind enough to reimburse the costs of her trip. And those of her previous six visits to Russia.

In the wake of Gorky's death, Wells recalled:

After that first telegram I heard no more from Moura, and I thought that Russia had swallowed her up.

I came back from the weekend at the Holdens on Sunday night and, about one o'clock in the morning, Moura, the incorrigible, unchangeable Moura, who manifestly I love by nature and necessity, rang me up—as if she had never been away . . .

Aige-Gee could be happy. For as long as he lived, Moura would never return to Moscow. Fate had done away with two of his rivals in one go: Gorky and Mother Russia.

CHAPTER THIRTY-NINE

Freeze Frame

On this late September afternoon, the light was already reminiscent of fall. Two silhouettes in the rain, a man and a woman, were making their way out of their cabs in front of the London branch of the Warner Brothers studios. They crossed the distance from the cars to the entrance in a single step.

There was no need for either of them to introduce themselves to the receptionists. The women had already picked up their phones to alert the higher-ups:

"Baroness Budberg and Mr. Robert Bruce Lockhart have arrived."

They took off their hats at the same time and kissed each other fondly. They were as tall as each other, equally powerful, equally indifferent to onlookers.

"How are you doing, Babygirl?"

"How are *you* doing?" She looked him over quickly before declaring: "You're so handsome right now. You're just perfect . . . So yes, Babyboy, I'm doing well!"

That was how they always talked to each other. They were miles away from the usual British standoffishness.

But there was something exaggerated, something vaguely artificial and tense about their hellos today. As if their declarations of adoration were a ritual, a safeguard.

Two boxers in the ring sizing each other up, shaking hands before the fight.

The producer meeting them rushed out of the elevator with alacrity, hurrying to welcome them in and roll out the red carpet.

The Warner Brothers were playing for high stakes. Everybody here was playing for high stakes: Baroness Budberg had come for a private screening of the film inspired by her relationship with Mr. Lockhart during the Russian Revolution. The fate of a multimillion-dollar venture lay in her approval.

The film had included Lenin, Trotsky, the founders of the Cheka. Hundreds of extras . . . Moscow, the Kremlin had been rebuilt in the studio lots. It was one of the biggest budgets in the history of Hollywood since the shift to talkies. It was the first American epic to describe the Communists' ascent to power.

The screenplay had been drawn from *Memoirs of a British Agent*, Lockhart's best seller, and the man himself had been involved in writing the script.

The author hadn't forgotten that two years earlier, just as the book had been headed to publication, his heroine had insisted on edits and forced him to cut several passages from his manuscript.

And now, as the film had come together, he hadn't shown her a thing. He had been wise enough not to warn her. In a few minutes, he would be showing her the fruit of his labors.

He hoped against hope that she would love what she saw!

And now the hour of reckoning had come . . .

What would Moura's feelings be as she saw her character, a spy in the Bolsheviks' pay? Such an interpretation of her actions would make life quite difficult for her in England.

Spy. The word was a threat to her status as an emigrant. In the wake of this film, she could be expelled. And be forcibly deported to the USSR. At best.

In Los Angeles, nobody at the top of Warner Brothers had given any thought to that problem. And Lockhart had been careful not to raise questions. Dramatizing history, creating the screenplay, had meant making her an influential member of the Cheka. It had been a necessary liberty to take . . . The prospect that such a depiction could be detrimental to Moura's life hadn't held him back.

But now he was wondering: how would she react to this image of a Mata Hari, an image she very likely refused to think of herself as embodying?

He was hoping against hope that she would love what she saw!

She would be foolish to complain. The film had been made by one of the most prestigious directors alive: Michael Curtiz. As for the cast, it was splendid. The star Kay Francis embodied Elena Moura, the *passionaria* working for Lenin. The thoroughly aristocratic Leslie Howard, who would go on to play Ashley Wilkes in *Gone with the Wind*, was playing the role of Lockhart: on the screen, the character's name was Locke.

Even the names had been virtually unchanged. And the greatest triumph of the production was that the two actors had managed to evoke the true personalities of their models. In their height, their looks, even the shapes of their eyebrows and the color of their hair: they were carbon copies. Interchangeable . . . as if the human truth, the historical truth, had been respected.

The resemblance between the two actors on the poster and the two guests making their way down the halls of the Warner Brothers office was so striking that even the receptionists weren't sure if they were looking at the actors or the real characters.

The couple sat in the second row of the screening room. Their heads met in the shadows cast by the backlight.

They were offered something to drink, a packet of cigarettes, an ashtray, everything they might need for their comfort. Then the producer and his assistants stepped away. As planned, the hero of the film would be watching it without saying a word.

Lockhart—who had already seen it multiple times—had slipped his arm through Moura's. He had to cajole her, seduce her, lull her. Make it so that all she felt was his presence beside her. That alone: his unflagging affection. Nothing else.

As the lights went down, he whispered in her ear: "You'll see: it's incredible!"

The truth was that he was afraid. She was, too.

———

The screening started off badly, with a mistake . . . Instead of opening with the credits, the projectionist began with the film's trailer.

To the tune of screeching violins and pounding bass drums, the taglines came in swift succession:

Told against a Background of World-Rocking Events . . .

Moura stiffened.

A Story that Reveals Every Love . . .

She straightened up.

Every Secret . . .

She pulled her shoulder away from Lockhart's.

Of the World's Most Beautiful Spy.

She let go of his hand. He didn't try to hold her hand again. He didn't try to pull her in. He understood. It was turning out exactly as he feared. The taglines kept coming, each one worse than the last:

Her Love Was a "One-Way Passage to Ruin."

She wasn't moving anymore. She was reading those lines, which he himself had written or allowed to be written.

Was that what he thought of their story? Was that what he had kept of their eternal love?

Each image showed her a distorted, monstrous, utterly disfigured reflection of what had been their passion.

The worst part was that it wasn't entirely wrong. She recognized bits and pieces of their conversations. She had indeed said some of those lines. But she had said them elsewhere, in another tone, in completely different circumstances from what was playing out in front of her eyes.

The film lived up to the promises of the trailer. It was so much treachery.

As the scenes played out on the screen, wholly disconnected from the facts, from her own emotions, the pain and shock became hallucinatory for her. Lockhart had deformed the fundamentals of her memories.

This betrayal by the man she had sacrificed everything for, shown so starkly, with such cruelty, left her paralyzed, unable to respond.

He had been successful on that one front. She didn't protest. What could she possibly have said?

❖

In the darkness, she sat straight up. All alone. She had lost what mattered most: the very sense of her own life.

But she still had a battle to fight.

There was an hour and a half left to go—the running time that Lockhart had decided on—to fight against betrayal and forgetting. An hour and a half to revisit her past, to reexperience her history. To reconquer the memory that had been destroyed.

❖

She couldn't look at the screen anymore, she couldn't look at her double anymore, at this spy in a leather waterproof. The uniform of the Cheka's torturers.

She had to seize upon what still belonged to her: the images, the smells, the noises, all the traces of her journey across this earth.

She had to return to Ukraine, to the time when Micky had woken her up in the middle of the night at Berezovaya. She had been led to the other end of the manor, into laughter and light.

She had to see the four chandeliers of the dining room again, and all the Venetian glass shimmering. She had to see herself again perched atop the table among the guests. She had to listen to herself reciting the lines of the poem dedicated to her grandmother, "The Testament":

And when in freedom, 'mid your kin,
From battle you ungird,
Forget not to remember me . . .

She had to recall the joy she had felt as a child amid the applause.

She had to reach into herself to find the Moura of the past, the Moura of her origins, the Moura of her childhood, of the time when love had a thousand faces. And who knew? By the grace of that being, she might be able to triumph over Lockhart's renunciation. She might be able to win that impossible battle. Overcome death and survive.

❖

The producer hadn't waited until the film was over to run in.

As he opened the screening room door, he immediately understood, from the expression on Lockhart's face, the scale of the disaster.

Baroness Budberg hadn't liked the film one bit. She was going to rip it apart and destroy all those years of work. She was a powerful woman: Gorky's secretary, Wells's companion. She knew everybody who mattered in London, everybody who mattered in France, even in the United States, through the International PEN Club. Everybody in literary circles, political circles, and press circles. The biggest papers would fall over themselves to offer her endless column inches. There would be no better person than this Russian aristocrat, who had been part of the events in question, to write a review of the film. If she wrote that it was a welter of inaccuracies, *British Agent* would be dead in the water before it even came out in theaters.

Who knew if she'd find a way to block it?

She was a very close friend of the Soviet ambassador. Often seen with Duff Cooper, the financial secretary to the treasury, one of the personifications of British political power.

The producer, however, couldn't keep himself from asking the suicidal question that had been making his heart pound as he sat in his office during the eighty-one minutes of the screening:

"So, my dear, dear baroness, did you like it?"

She gave him the most magnificent smile she had ever smiled and kissed his cheeks warmly. "I loved it!"

Lockhart, shocked, squinted at her.

Despite being taller than the producer, her chin was thrust upward, with that sphinxlike expression that revealed nothing . . . Apart from her authority and the miracle of her kindness.

She went on: "There's nobody like you Americans, *nobody* at all, to understand the winds of such an era! You alone were able to put the atmosphere of the Russian Revolution on the screen."

And then, suddenly, Lockhart understood. He guessed what she had realized.

This film made her—Moura the Bolshevik *passionaria*; Moura the spy working for Lenin, who chose the West out of love—an international star.

Of course, of course, the end—which showed the heroine on the train with her lover, Locke, leaving for London in 1918—would have struck her as bitterly ironic. But this denouement was far more brilliant, far more glorious than her being abandoned to fear and famine in Petrograd.

With all the intelligence she had, with her love for dramatization and her sense for publicity, she was turning a setback that could have destroyed another woman into a resounding success.

Slipping his arm through hers, Lockhart led her outside. The rain had stopped. They took a few steps on the sidewalk in front of the Warner Brothers building.

As they hailed the cab that would take them to the Gypsy cabaret to round out the night, he couldn't help but ask her the same question:

"Really? . . . You really liked it?"

"You're going to be a hit."

"*We're* going to be a hit. You and me, Babygirl! Both of us . . . together."

She burst out laughing, with a bluntness that was wholly unlike her:

"Oh, fuck you, Babyboy!"

But, Darling, That's Adventure!

What Happened to Them
Moura's Thousand Worlds

Wells, Lockhart, Micky, Paul, Tania, Kira, Alla,
Anna, and Kallijärv

As a myth and a legend, the character of Baroness Budberg hardly changed.

She refined some features of herself, altered others, played up some details, increased some aspects to the point of caricature. However, her looks didn't change one bit. She was a well-lettered Russian aristocrat, the provocative muse of two geniuses, a great seductress who was devoted to her loves, faithful to her friends, a bit of a spy, a bit of an artist: the incarnation of Slavic charm.

And, ultimately, the picture of an unworthy old woman.

After having uttered so many half-truths and sidestepped so many questions, she had been reduced to a representation of herself, a trick of shadow and light, a baroque decoration, a body whose noises hid her silences. She was slipping out of sight.

But she no longer suffered. She was no longer torn; her inner conflicts seemed to have been appeased. She had found her remarkable serenity.

❖

Moura would remain Lockhart's lover and Wells's companion to the very end.

After the worldwide success of the film *British Agent* and the death of

Gorky, she would become one of London's most renowned celebrities. As a woman of influence, she would hold a salon and each day, at six o'clock, receive the best of British society.

Her table would be open for more than thirty years.

A risky proposition, as she was still penniless and kept on refusing marriage proposals that could have provided her with financial security and material comfort.

How would she survive among the rich and powerful when she had nothing?

In 1938, her friend Lyuba Hicks would solve the problem by leaving their solitary confines at Cadogan Square to take up with a rich engineer who had retired.

And so, true to her nature, Moura would find a new roommate: Molly Cliff, the widow of a landowner from Yorkshire, who financed her receptions. Timid, reserved Molly would be charmed by Moura's kindness, energy, and joie de vivre. She would also be thoroughly fascinated by all the elite characters Moura introduced her to.

Molly would insist that she stay at her home, in a marvelous Edwardian-era building at 68 Ennismore Gardens. In the heart of the most elegant neighborhood in London, the apartment had five bedrooms and numerous dining rooms. Two maids, one who always looked after Molly, the other who would look after Moura, tended to their comfort. Rumors would swirl that the two ladies paid attention only to Moura. She would decorate her floor of the house with wall coverings and icons. She would live in her bed there, amid all her cushions, her books, and her papers piled up everywhere . . . Her mess was all to be expected. She would only arise at lunchtime to tend to her busy outside life.

The baroness's profile, her immense coat fluttering in the wind, her black bag dangling off her arm—an immense bag full of manuscripts— would become a common sight in the London streets. She would always be in a hurry, always late, always climbing out of cabs to run into the grand halls of every embassy and the lobbies of every theater. Her friends loved nothing more than her voice, with its accent that would grow more hoarse, more Russian with every passing year, along with

her perennial laughter and her warm embrace each time she greeted
them.

❖

During the war, she would deal with the bomb raids and the Blitz with
her typical courage: she wouldn't flee London. She would work for the
Frenchman André Labarthe, who had founded the paper *La France libre*.
This work would come her way thanks to Lockhart, who at the time was
in charge of British propaganda.

No matter how much Moura hated de Gaulle, who she was certain
was a dictator in the making, she would support Labarthe in the magazine's editorial work. In the eyes of her detractors, Labarthe was a Soviet
agent affiliated with the NKVD: his friendship with Baroness Budberg
would do nothing to help defray the rumor that Moura was a spy.

In any case, they would share the same dream of a civilization rooted
in freedom.

As she became one of the pillars of *La France libre* alongside Raymond
Aron, she would turn it into a well-respected, intellectually rigorous outlet. Her sheer wealth of contacts would make it possible for her to commission articles from renowned writers, including H. G. Wells, of course,
but also such men as George Bernard Shaw. The paper would argue
for *la résistance à la défaite* with such success that in the summer of 1943,
Churchill would order the Royal Air Force to drop a special edition of
it over France. Moura would also turn out to be the first editor to recognize the talent of a French pilot by the name of Romain Gary, whom
she would support every way she could by helping to get his *L'Éducation
européenne* published in English translation before it had even come out
in Paris.

❖

Wells, for all his bluster, would never leave her. She would remain his
great love, the woman who stayed with him until his death in 1946. At

that point he would be nearly eighty years old. And she, in turn, would only be fifty-three.

As with Gorky's death, she would be at Wells's bedside during his final days, and she would never let go of his hand.

The loss of Wells, after two decades together, would shake her to her core and leave her more reclusive than ever. He would leave her some money, of course, but not enough for her to live as she once had.

❖

After the war, she would work for Sir Alexander Korda, the renowned British producer of *To Be or Not to Be*, *The Third Man*, and *Anna Karenina*. Their meeting, their friendship, and their collaboration would open all of cinema's doors for her.

Moura's circles of writers, journalists, and politicians would be rounded out by yet another circle, that of directors and actors. She would spend time with Laurence Olivier, Vivien Leigh, and Peter Ustinov, whose father, of Russian extraction, was working for the British secret service.

She would go on being suspected of being a double agent until her death. Her telephone lines would be monitored, her mail opened. These presumptions would never be borne out by any concrete proof.

In the archives of MI5, the United Kingdom's intelligence services, her folder would include more than four hundred pages: the story of all her investigators' shadowings, all their reports and suspicions.

Europe's mistrust of her wouldn't keep her from gaining British nationality in 1947 and from returning to the USSR starting in 1958, at the behest of Peshkova, Alexey Maximovich's first wife. The two women would remain close, and Moura would come to Moscow again in 1965 for the funeral of her dear friend. She would return five other times, in 1961, 1962, 1963, 1968, and 1973, just before her own death. Each time, she would be an official participant in the annual celebrations of Gorky's birth and death.

―――――

After the deaths of Wells and Konstantin Benckendorff in 1959, she would suffer the despair of seeing Lockhart, the man she still loved, declining. No matter how many other lovers she had, he would remain the singular passion of her life.

Lockhart's career, which had been full of highs and lows, would flatline after 1938. During the war, he had been the director general of Political Warfare Executive, responsible for leading anti-Fascist propaganda. He would be conferred the Knighthood of the Order of Saint Michael and Saint George in 1943: *Sir* Robert Bruce Lockhart. As he was divorced from the mother of his son, it would be his secretary who he finally chose to bear the title of Lady Robert Bruce Lockhart.

During their nuptials in 1948, he would insist that this new alliance was a marriage of convenience, a "companionship" that would allow him to continue seeing Moura.

And he would keep spending time with her—they would dine together regularly—over the following twenty-two years preceding his death. But starting in 1965, he would start suffering from cerebral arteritis and lose his intellectual faculties. His death would come on February 27, 1970, the day after Moura's visit to his nursing home in Sussex. He would be eighty-two years old at that point. She would have been one of the last people to kiss him. His ashes would be scattered by his wife and son in Scotland during a ceremony that the family would not invite Baroness Budberg to.

She herself would not want anyone to see her in her grief.

She would receive permission from her friend Anthony Bloom, a Russian Orthodox bishop in the United Kingdom, to hold a twenty-four-hour funeral service at the Russian Orthodox church in London, a vigil to thank the Lord for this mad love that had brought light into her life.

The few chairs set out at the end of the nave would remain empty. And under the massive Byzantine Christ, the plank of wood wouldn't creak. The doors would remain shut and the aisles deserted.

Amid the scents of lilies and incense, she would be alone with her dear Babyboy.

Alone with her memories. Alone with their Creator.

Dressed in her long black coat, her head wrapped in a white head-scarf, Moura would evoke all the babushkas of Eternal Russia.

She would bend down and cross herself three times in front of each of the apostles that rounded out the chorus. She would kiss the icons and press her forehead against a sacred image. She would shut her eyes. She would pray. And she would cry.

She would give no thought to the fact that she had never stopped to apply the principle of the gilded letters running across the vault above her head: *Thou shalt not judge but save.*

❖

After this long vigil was over, she would feel decades older. Without Lock-hart, existence would no longer matter.

But she would be wrong to think that. She would still be *the unrepen-tant Moura, the incorrigible Moura* that Wells had described late in his life: "Moura is Moura as ever. Human, faulty, wise, silly, and I love her."

Her fascination with the world around her would remain limitless. There would be so many encounters that still excited her.

Despite being a bad mother, she would become a magnificent grand-mother who delighted the little ones with her kindness, her modernity, and her excesses. She would go on drinking too much, eating too much, smoking too much. And while age would put a damper on bodily plea-sures, she would remain every bit the seductress, the risk-taker.

And on that point, too, she would never change.

She always loved nothing more than taking a chance and slipping through the cracks.

But what could a stout lady who was nearly eighty years old do to keep her life full of adrenaline?

One idea was for her to steal utterly useless gifts, absolutely ridiculous trinkets, for her friends. She would make them smile. And she would feel like a daredevil. Two birds with one stone.

But where should she strike? An eye for an eye, as her sister Anna had once been fond of saying . . . In the most sumptuous, most heavily patrolled shop in all London: Harrods.

The only problem being that Moura's profile with her immense black umbrella, which she would stash her goods in, wasn't the sort to go unnoticed.

To the policeman who caught her in flagrante delicto, she would brandish a cake server, a champagne cork, and a vodka glass. When he interrogated her and expressed shock at the things, which she had the means to buy for herself, she would laugh in his face and declare, regally: "But, darling, *that's* adventure!"

The adventure, however, was drawing to its close. That much she knew. Two bouts of breast cancer had forced her to undergo a double mastectomy. She would describe the drama to a sympathetic friend with panache: "It's so much tidier with nothing there!"

She would never stop declaring that she wanted to die in Italy. But not in Sorrento. Maybe in Tuscany, where her son, Paul, had just settled.

Her determination to be close to him again would dismay her London friends. They all dreaded her departure. One of them would dedicate a poem to her: "Moura Budberg: On Her Proposed Departure from England."

> *Yes, age deserves*
> *Some quiet, as had youth—*
> *Or so you've told us.*
> *Is that the truth?*

In her dreams, she would return to Il Sorito, to the marvelous garden of the Serracapriola dukes, to the summer of 1925, which she had spent with Gorky, Kira, Paul, and Tania.

And with Micky.

❖

Micky would pass away in 1938, at the age of seventy-four. At Kallijärv. Without Moura.

Moura had made many trips to care for Micky. But she would learn of her death in London, by phone.

Thirty years later, she would still find herself crying over her death. The idea that Margaret Wilson could die alone, and be buried alone in Estonia, would still upset her.

Just as the fate of her two husbands' families would continue to upset her.

The German-Soviet Pact would offer the Baltic countries to the madnesses of both Hitler and Stalin. Estonia, which had fought nearly to its last breath for its independence, would become a martyr.

In 1939, a terrible letter from Uncle Sasha's wife—Aunt Zoria Benckendorff—would inform Moura that the aristocratic families had to abandon what remained of their properties and go into exile. They would have three days to get on German boats and flee to Polish lands, whose owners had been massacred by the Nazis.

It would be just the beginning of the Yendel Benckendorffs' descent into hell.

Once the Soviets had chased the Nazis out of Estonia, they would deport the remaining Estonians to Siberia, on the pretext that they had collaborated with the Germans.

Later, much later, Moura would find a way to bring Zoria to London. And this aunt would come to rest beside her at Chiswick Cemetery.

As for her own children, it would be by sheer luck that Moura was able to get them out of Estonia and bring them to England *before* the war.

None of them would ever see Kallijärv again before the collapse of the Soviet Union in 1991.

❖

The day after his twenty-first-birthday ball in August 1934, Paul would receive his diploma in agricultural engineering and move to Yorkshire to tend to the farm of his friend Tony Cliff—his sister's lover and the son of Molly, who his mother had grown close to. Twelve years later he would marry an Irish woman, whose little boy, Simon, he had adopted. His wife would be named Angel. She would bear him twins in 1947. At that point, the five Benckendorffs would be living on the Isle of Wight and leading a bohemian lifestyle. After that, they would move again and live in Italy.

❖

Tania, to her brother and mother's great disappointment, wouldn't marry Tony Cliff, as she was more interested in a brilliant British lawyer by the name of Bernard Alexander. The young couple would settle in a village not far from Oxford, where Moura and Wells retired on the weekends during the Blitz in London.

Tania would take after Moura. She would reveal her ferocity, her fire. And in her professional career, she would also take after her mother. Tania would work for publishing houses at first. Then she would translate several plays from the Russian, including Chekhov's *The Seagull* and Gorky's *Vassa Zheleznova*, which would be staged at the Greenwich Theater. She would also be involved in adapting a version of *Uncle Vanya* for the screen, directed by Anthony Hopkins.

Her first book, an autobiography that described her childhood and bore witness to her life in Estonia between 1918 and 1936, would be a genuine masterpiece. The intelligence, sensitivity, and honesty of the narrator would make *A Little of All These*—later published under the title *An Estonian Childhood*—a marvel.

Tania would go on to have three children, raising them partly in Switzerland when her husband was hired away to the United Nations.

Her relationship with her mother would remain mercurial, a mix of admiration and frustration, a resentment that time finally wore down. Moura's devotion to her grandchildren would assuage so many of their grievances.

❖

As for Kira, she would marry the doctor Hugh Clegg in 1933; the two would live together in North London, where they would rear two children. Dr. Clegg would become one of the editors of the prestigious *British Medical Journal*. He would die in 1983, twenty-two years before Kira. And she, in turn, would pass away in London in August 2005, at the age of ninety-six.

She would see the birth, in 1967, of her grandson, Nick Clegg, the future leader of the Liberal Democrats and deputy prime minister of the United Kingdom, and would remain very close to her two cousins, Paul and Tania. When her own daughter, Helen, was married, her auntie-mommy would organize the reception after.

Moura, a matriarch as always.

Their relationship would remain close and warm, notwithstanding Kira's anger at Moura for having cut her off so sharply from her own mother.

❖

Alla would lead a tragic life until her death in 1960. Whether out of anger or indifference to Kira, she wouldn't name her only daughter in the only will she left behind, a handwritten letter saved at the rue Edgar-Poe in 1942. She would leave what little she had—the few furs that remained— to her niece and goddaughter, the daughter of her sister Anna, who had the same name as her. It would fall to "the second Alla" to take care of her dog, the only being she seemed to care about.

It was a twist of fate that Alla would often be saved and cared for in Paris by her half sister, Darya Mirvoda, the actual daughter of Senator Zakrevsky with his mistress from Berezovaya Rudka.

Darya, who had been the Viper's frequent target back in Ukraine, had married a French doctor in 1898. She was every bit as elegant as the twins and had been lucky enough to settle in France before the Russian Revolution. And to claim her dowry before their father's death. The result was that after a terrible childhood, she had been able to enjoy a comfortable life that was far more pleasant than those of the three other Zakrevsky daughters.

❖

Anna, who was always at the mercy of poverty and fear, would die of tuberculosis at the Bligny sanatorium in Essonne in 1941. She would be fifty-four years old. On her deathbed, she would ask that Alla not be brought to see her until after she had exhaled her last breath. Her husband, Vasily Kochubey, and their three children would survive her.

Another twist of fate was that her daughter—"the second Alla"—would marry the son of Count Ignatyev in France, the son of the very man who had judged Moura and Lai Budberg during their Ehrengerichts in Tallinn in 1921 and 1922.

◈

Lai Budberg, having been divorced from Moura since 1925, would go on living in São Paulo while teaching bridge. He would remarry and die in Brazil in 1972 at seventy-six years old. During the half century that he was away from Moura, he would keep on corresponding with her. Their marriage had been a sham, but their friendship would last. As was usual for Moura, who never abandoned the men she loved and would always remain faithful to them in her own way.

All the same, he would be one of the men she never saw again.

Gorky's Archives
Yagoda, Kryuchkov, Peshkov

A year after Gorky's death, the people who had watched his final hours would be accused by Stalin of having murdered him. And of having also murdered his son, Max.

The weapon: poison.

The murderers: Yagoda, Kryuchkov, and the doctors.

The ones to order the murder: the Western powers, which wanted to take away the USSR's crown jewel, the singer of the Russian proletariat.

Of course, nobody would be unaware of the true murderer's name: Stalin, who was getting rid of all his henchmen.

Yagoda would be arrested on March 28, 1937. His dachas and his apartment in the Kremlin would be searched, revealing just how much he had stolen and how much money he had. A cellar filled with hundreds of fine wines, a collection of more than ten thousand objets d'art, fur coats, women's lingerie, high-end perfumes: all the spoils of his countless victims. He would be executed on March 15, 1938, after a trial that would be nothing more than a farce. Rumor would have it, however, that the NKVD was secretly keeping him alive, referring to him under the number 102 rather than his name. And that he was still being interrogated about his old folders until January 31, 1939, the day he would be deemed definitively dead.

In front of his judges, Kryuchkov—the kind Pepekryu of Kronverksky Prospect—would accuse himself of having killed Max in order to seize the rights to Gorky's work. An absurd self-criticism: with Max killed, Kryuchkov still wouldn't have received the rights. But even so, he would acknowledge the role he'd played in administering the fatal substance that killed both father and son.

And so he, too, would be executed on March 15, 1938. His young wife and Yagoda's wife would join the two men in their graves in the following months.

As for the doctors, two of them would be killed by firing squad, and the last sentenced to twenty-five years in the gulag.

Gorky and Moura's old enemy, Zinoviev, had already been executed in 1936. And Yakov Peters would face the same fate in April 1938.

Just as Moura expected, Stalin didn't attack Gorky's family. None of his three "wives" had to worry. Maria Andreyeva would celebrate her eightieth birthday at the House of Scholars, which she had run since 1931, and would pass away in her sleep in 1953. Peshkova would die the same way twelve years later.

Only Timosha would suffer any setbacks. The man she chose to replace Max and Yagoda would meet just as dramatic an end as his predecessors.

His name was Ivan Luppol. He was a linguist, and had been very close with Gorky. He had succeeded the writer to the role of head of World Literature. In August 1940 Luppol was arrested, because his correspondence and his personal diary had been discovered in a suitcase hidden in a house in Tartu, Estonia. The Soviet troops had broken and entered in July 1940 as part of their occupation of the country.

After the NKVD examined these papers, Luppol would receive a death sentence, later modified to twenty years in the gulag, and he would not resist, but rather die shortly after.

At that time, H. G. Wells wrote of Moura:

> *Something very bitter, I cannot tell the ugly particulars now, has hurt her heartbreakingly—in her pride and in her affections.*

Had she just learned that Stalin's men had come across a part of Gorky's archives?

She would say later that the documents had burned during the Nazi bombardments on Kallijärv. But no bomb ever fell on the house by the lake or in the woods of Yendel.

The mystery of these documents still unnerved the researchers of Gorky's work. Most of them were certain that Moura Budberg had given the full set of manuscripts still in her possession to Yagoda in 1936. And that this betrayal had been the cost she had to pay to get out of the country after Gorky's funeral, and to be able to return in the 1960s.

The day after Gorky's death, Yagoda and several other Party members read Gorky's diary, where he compared Stalin to a monstrous flea. And then it disappeared completely.

Nobody ever saw it again.

This diary, as well as the writer's compromising letters, would remain classified as top secret in one of the storage rooms of the NKVD's future incarnations.

But Wells would insist that Moura had kept her word and had never given up what Gorky had entrusted to her. And God knew just how often he had accused her of being a liar and a cheat!

He would write:

> *She did certain obscure things about his papers that she had promised to do for him long ago. I think there were documents that it was undesirable should fall into*

the hands of the [State Political Directorate] and that she secured them. I think
there was something she knew and that she had promised to tell no one. And I
believe that she kept her promise. In such matters Moura is invincibly sturdy.

But if Moura had handed over *all* the papers, as researchers now claim;
if Gorky's correspondence had been *completely* handed over to Stalin, then
what explanation could there be for the scene that the French writer and
resistance fighter His Excellency Monsieur the Ambassador Francis Huré
would describe at the French embassy in London sometime between 1955
and 1962?

A friend and biographer of Zinovy Peshkov, Monsieur Huré would
recall that the ambassador at the time—Jean Chauvel—had set up a
summit between Baroness Budberg and Gorky's adoptive son at the French
residence.

General Zinovy Peshkov was a well-respected figure at that point. He
had followed de Gaulle starting with the Appeal of June 18, and fought
brilliantly. He was now an ambassador, and he had received a Grand
Cross of the Légion d'honneur.

For Peshkov's talks with the baroness, the French ambassador had set
aside an office to the right of the entrance. Francis Huré's description
would be precise. He would say that Peshkov locked himself in there with
her for nearly an hour:

> *They discussed the archives Gorky had left in Italy, and the letters that Zinovy*
> *had kept in his suitcase. The thought of parting with them was upsetting. And*
> *yet . . . Mara [sic] was insistent. That was why they didn't get along.*

What could be presumed from those lines?

Only that Zinovy Peshkov still had a suitcase full of documents connected to Gorky's correspondence. That this suitcase still existed in the
1950s or '60s. That he hadn't handed it over to the woman he had met
with. And that in all likelihood, these papers are still in France, where
Peshkov died in 1966.

Forget Not to Remember Me
Moura: Memories in Ashes

After her final trip to Russia, Moura would make up her mind: she would join Paul in Tuscany.

He had just bought a farm not far from Arezzo. The house wasn't ready for her yet, but he had booked a small room for her at the hotel a few miles away. The village was called Montevarchi.

Everybody knew she was going there to die.

She would bring with her eleven tightly sealed boxes of papers. She would refuse to be separated from those boxes at any point. She would burn everything else in her London fireplace. "Nothing important," she would say to the friends who had come to say goodbye to her in August 1974.

By the time she set her boxes down on the platform of the Montevarchi train station after five transfers, she would have known she couldn't hold out much longer. But the worst wouldn't be over for her yet: her lodging at the hotel would turn out to be an order of magnitude too small. So Paul would have the boxes all stored for her in a trailer parked in the garden. The establishment's owners would have a power line strung between the main building and the trailer, which she would use as both an office and a personal library.

And that would be how catastrophe befell her: on a stormy night, while Moura was lying calmly in her room, the bare wires would short-circuit. The trailer would catch fire. And the eleven boxes of papers would go up in smoke.

Or so Moura and her children would insist.

Nothing would remain of her memories but ashes.

Did they include letters from Wells, and Gorky's mysterious correspondence? In which case, the disaster would have been immeasurable. A loss rivaled in the history of literature only by the burning of the Library of Alexandria.

But then what should be made of the fact that no conflagration was recorded in the archives of the Montevarchi firefighters in the months of September, October, and November 1974?

In any case, Moura wouldn't survive. Less than two months after she had come to Italy, she would die peacefully on October 31, 1974, in Paul and Tania's care. She would be eighty-one years old.

A detail stranger than all Moura's own fictions was that even her death would be a lie.

Italian law required that any death in a hotel result in the owners' shutting it down for three days, and so Paul would be forced to sneak out his mother's body, set it in his car, drive it to his own home, and then declare her death while she was on his farm.

Moura's corpse would be sent to London for an elaborate ceremony at the Russian Orthodox church. Four years after her vigil in Lockhart's memory, she would be mourned in turn beneath the apostles and the iconostasis. But this time, the nave wouldn't be empty. All London would attend her funeral. The ambassadors would sit in the first row, flanked by the British aristocracy and the exiled Russian aristocracy. The hordes of her friends would overwhelm her children and grandchildren.

Everyone would pay their respects. The London *Times* would publish a long obituary glorifying her. A laudatory eulogy. Exactly what she would have wanted to hear. The article's author would describe her as one of England's intellectual leaders for nearly half a century . . . Tongues would wag that perhaps she had dictated the whole thing before leaving the country.

Moura Budberg now lies at Chiswick Cemetery, in the section reserved for Orthodox Russians. Her family has had her tombstone engraved with the name Marie, which Djon had given her. And two Russian verbs, in the imperative: *Save and Preserve.*

Save and preserve life: a phrase that sums up her entire existence.

Her epitaph, too, could sum her up in a single paragraph: the first impression Lockhart had had of her at the outset of their adventures.

Where she loved, there was her world, and her philosophy of life had made her mistress of all the consequences. She was an aristocrat. She could have been a Communist. She could never have been a bourgeoise.

By Way of Postscript

My investigation has taken me to the sources of all the rumors that have swirled around Baroness Budberg. I've tried to disentangle them, to ascertain their origins, and to interrogate them systematically. Allow me to say here that of all the heroes whose lives I've retraced in my books, Moura has aroused for me the most passionate affection and the most enduring respect. While other researchers have been frustrated by her weaknesses, I haven't felt that way at all. Each one of my discoveries made her a more sympathetic, more endearing personality in my eyes. When all is said and done, I have to agree with Wells's summation: "Moura is Moura as ever; human, faulty, wise, silly, and I love her."

Even though it would probably have been more exciting to present her as a spy, my obligation to the truth forces me to underscore that her actions as a secret agent remain hypothetical. Even if numerous elements suggest that she worked for several intelligence services, none of the archival documents I was able to see have provided any confirmation. Not in the four hundred pages of reports kept in the Kew Public Record Office of the National Archives in the United Kingdom, not in the folders bearing her name kept in Tallinn or at the Château de Vincennes: nothing has provided definitive proof that she was the instrument of one nation or another. As she was followed and watched everywhere, her sphere of action was in any case restricted. And so the question remains unanswered.

But there is no doubt that she was an informant who described what was being said and thought in the social circles she so easily frequented. She served as a go-between for the British secret services during the War of 1914 in Russia. And for the Soviets when she was in Europe. But the possibility that she was part of a network, that she was paid to denounce people or spirit away state documents, seems unlikely to me.

And equally unlikely is the prospect that she was the mistress of Alexander Kerensky, the leader of the provisional government in the months following the 1917 Revolution, as their detractors insisted. I have gone through Kerensky's archives in the United States and found no evidence of a relationship with Moura Zakrevskaya Benckendorff.

It's true that Moura is never found where she's expected to be. And that in the future, new documents may come to the fore that illuminate her life in a completely different way.

One thing is certain: she did everything she could to hide her traces. And better still, she erased them with an irrefutable argument: the remnants of her time on earth no longer exist. Her memory was destroyed by fire. According to her, Gorky's archives burned in Estonia in 1940 during the war. And her own archives caught fire in Italy in 1974.

It was a formidable way to nip in the bud all attempts to find the truth.

What could be more effective, indeed, than spreading the word of a wholesale destruction at a woodlands fishing lodge in Lääne-Viru County and in a lost village deep in Italy where no tourists bother to go?

The conservator of the small Benckendorff museum in Yendel—now Jäneda, a specialist in the history of the region, confirmed that no bombs ever struck the estate.

And similarly, nobody remembers a fire at a hotel in Montevarchi in 1974. *La Nazione*, the only local paper, makes no mention of it. None of the five inns in the village seems to have suffered any such catastrophe. Apart from the Hotel Vapore, which has a garden big enough to hold a trailer.

The former owners, who I interviewed, recalled that there was indeed a fire near their place at that time. And there had been smoke in the hotel. But there was no damage: the problem was in a shared apartment. No short circuit, just a small gas canister that exploded. The same thing was said in a nearby village by the name of Terranuova, which was closer to Paul's farm, in a place called La Cicogna . . . Nothing: not a single conflagration that could have been called such in the fall of 1974.

As always with Moura, the details are probably half-true and half-false.

Fundamentally, however, there is one constant: she refused to let anybody take too close a look at her story. She turned away all the publishers who hoped to bring out an autobiography by her. She tricked all the authors who wanted to describe her life. And she told her kin to burn all the papers she might have left behind once she died.

But this desire for a clean slate doesn't necessarily mean that she intentionally destroyed valuable manuscripts.

She herself was too devoted to literature, too aware of the historical value of the letters of Wells and Lockhart—not to mention Gorky's correspondence with all the great minds of his time—not to have preserved them and protected them with every ounce of her being.

As for me, after three years of following her traces across Europe, Russia, and the United States, I have no doubt that these treasures remain, if only as fragments, somewhere. And that they'll resurface someday. But where? And when?

That remains a mystery.

Others might be just as certain of that fact.

In 2015, Vladimir Putin, retaliating against the Brussels sanctions, disseminated a list of undesirable personalities in Russia. Included was the former deputy prime minister, Nick Clegg. His banishment, according to the British paper the *Independent*, had to be due to his kinship with Baroness Budberg, whom the Russians accused of being a spy in service of the British. Nick Clegg is indeed her great-grandnephew, the grandson of Kira. According to Mr. Putin's advisers, the baroness tried to kill Lenin in 1918, during the Lockhart Plot. Consequently, her family is not welcome in Moscow.

How could anyone not smile at seeing how, even in the twenty-first century, Moura still appears to be everything and its opposite? She was called a Russian spy in England, and a British spy in Russia. A remarkable footnote in history: forty-one years after her death, she still controls the fate of her descendants.

The motive of the sanction that Russia invoked against her relative seems so absurd that one has to wonder what reality it disguises. Does this measure have some connection to Alexey Maximovich's papers, which the Gorky archives and museum are still trying to recover? Or do Putin's secret services have some information still unknown to the rest of us?

Perhaps the story of the elusive Moura Budberg is only beginning. . . .

Appendices

Several Historical Details

Saint Petersburg

The city was known as Saint Petersburg until 1914; Petrograd until 1924; Leningrad until 1991; and Saint Petersburg again from 1991 onward.

Political and Secret Police in Russia

Okhrana under the Czarist regime

Cheka between 1917 and 1922

GPU, then OGPU (State Political Directorate) between 1922 and 1934

NKVD between 1934 and 1946

MVD, NKGB, MGB between 1946 and 1954

KGB between 1954 and 1991

FSB and SVR from 1991

Russian Calendar

Dates in the Russian calendar (the Julian calendar) are thirteen days behind the rest of Europe.

As such, the February 1917 revolution corresponds to the dates of February 23–28 on the Russian calendar, and to March 8–13 for the rest of Europe (on the Gregorian calendar).

Similarly, the October 1917 revolution corresponds to October 25 on the Russian calendar and November 7 on the Gregorian calendar.

Lenin aligned the Russian calendar with Europe's in February 1918. In Moscow, January 31 was followed by February 14, 1918.

Estonia

The history of Estonia remains complicated, as the country has been victim to a succession of invasions.

It was conquered in the thirteenth century by the Livonian Brothers of the Sword, an order of German warrior monks; then annexed by the Swedish in 1595; then seized by the Russians in 1710; then occupied by the Germans in 1918. Estonia finally won its independence in 1921 and held it until 1939.

Once the German-Soviet Nonaggression Pact was signed, Estonia was immediately occupied by the Nazis, then recaptured by the Soviets. It remained in the heart of the USSR from 1944 to 1991, when it regained its independence. Even today, the country is still threatened by Russia's proximity.

In 2004, Estonia joined the North Atlantic Treaty Organization and became a member of the European Union.

List of Characters

MARIA (*MOURA*) IGNATIEVNA ZAKREVSKAYA (1893–1974)

The Zakrevsky Family and the Benckendorff Clan

IGNATY PLATONOVICH ZAKREVSKY (1839–1906): Moura's father

MARIA NIKOLAYEVNA BOREISHA (1858–1919): Moura's mother

MARGARET WILSON (*Ducky; Micky*) (1864–1938): governess to Moura and her children

DARYA MIRVODA (1875–1976): Moura's half sister by her father

PLATON IGNATIEVICH ZAKREVSKY (1880–1912): Moura's older brother

IVAN (*Johann; Djon*) ALEXANDROVICH BENCKENDORFF (1882–1919): Moura's first husband

ALLA IGNATIEVNA ZAKREVSKAYA (1887–1960): Moura's elder sister (twin of Anna)

ANNA IGNATIEVNA ZAKREVSKAYA (1887–1941): Moura's elder sister (twin of Alla)

NIKOLAI (*Lai*) ROTGER VON BUDBERG-BÖNNINGSHAUSEN (1896–1972): Moura's
second husband

KIRA ARTUROVNA VON ENGELHARDT (1909–2005): Moura's niece (Alla's daughter)

PAVEL (*Paul*) IVANOVICH BENCKENDORFF (1913–1998): Moura's son

TATYANA (*Tania*) IVANOVNA BENCKENDORFF (1915–2004): Moura's daughter

The British Ambassador's Coterie

MYRIAM ARTSIMOVICH (?–?): Count Artsimovich's stepdaughter; Moura's friend

SIR GEORGE BUCHANAN (1854–1924): British ambassador in Moscow from 1910
to 1918

MERIEL BUCHANAN (1886–1959): British ambassador's daughter; Moura's friend

CAPTAIN FRANCIS CROMIE (*Crow*) (1882–1918): British naval attaché in Petrograd;
Moura's friend

EDWARD CUNARD (?–?): secretary to the ambassador in Petrograd; Moura's friend

CAPTAIN DENIS GARSTIN (*Garstino*) (1890–1918): writer responsible for British propaganda in Russia; Moura's friend

WILLIAM HICKS (*Hickie*) (?–1930): specialist in counterattacking chemical weapons;
Lockhart's friend

GENERAL ALFRED KNOX (1870–1964): British military attaché in Russia

ROBERT HAMILTON BRUCE LOCKHART (1887–1970): consul in Moscow, diplomat,
and journalist; Moura's lover

SIDNEY REILLY (1874–1927?): spy in the service of England in Russia

The Gorky Clan

MARIA FYODOROVNA ANDREYEVA (1868–1953): actress, commissar of theaters and
public shows in Petrograd; Gorky's official companion between 1904 and 1921

ALEXANDER ALEXANDROVICH BLOK (1880–1921): famous poet, considered one
of the greatest geniuses of the early twentieth century

KORNEY IVANOVICH CHUKOVSKY (*Chuk*) (1882–1969): translator, literary critic, and children's book author; Moura's employer at World Literature and the Studio

ANDREY ROMANOVICH DIEDERICHS (*Didi*) (1884–1942): painter; husband of Valentina Khodasevich; friend and colleague of Gorky

MAXIM GORKY (*Alexey Maximovich Peshkov*) (1868–1936): writer and political man; Moura's protector and companion between 1919 and 1936

MARIA ANDROVNA HEINTSE (*Molecule*) (?–1927): medical student taken in by Gorky

VALENTINA MIKHAILOVNA KHODASEVICH (*The Merchantess*) (1894–1970): painter; niece of the great poet Vladislav Khodasevich

PYOTR PETROVICH KRYUCHKOV (*Pepekryu*) (1898–1938): Maria Andreyeva's lover; later, Gorky's secretary, accused of his murder

MAXIM ALEXEYEVICH PESHKOV (1897–1934): Gorky's son

ZINOVY ALEXEYEVICH PESHKOV (1884–1966): Gorky's adoptive son, born Sverdlov; hero of the Foreign Legion; French general with the rank of ambassador.

YEKATERINA PAVLOVNA PESHKOVA (1878–1965): Gorky's wife and his son's mother; close to Dzerzhinsky and representative of the Political Red Cross in Moscow

IVAN NIKOLAYEVICH RAKITSKY (*The Nightingale*) (1883–1942): painter taken in by Gorky

VARVARA VASSILYEVNA TIKHONOVA (1884–1950): Gorky's mistress

The Men of the Russian Secret Police

FELIX EDMUNDOVICH DZERZHINSKY (1877–1926): founder and president of the Cheka

YAKOV KHRISTOFOROVICH PETERS (1886–1938): Dzerzhinsky's right-hand man and vice president of the Cheka

GENRIKH GRIGORYEVICH YAGODA (1891–1938): vice president of the State Political Directorate, then director of the NKVD

GRIGORY YEVSEYEVICH ZINOVIEV (1883–1936): president of the Petrograd Soviet and president of the Communist International between 1919 and 1926

Author's Acknowledgments

The writing of this book would not have been possible without the support, kindness, and trust of a long chain of friends.

I want to express my gratitude here to the descendants of the Zakrevsky family, who very generously welcomed me into their homes all across Europe. My visits with each of them were hearty encounters. It is my hope that Mr. John Alexander and Mr. Nicholas Clegg, who received me in England; Mrs. Catherine von Tsurikov, in Germany; Mrs. Colette Hartwich, in Luxembourg; Mr. Basile Kochubey, Mrs. Janine Lansier, and Mrs. Francine Olivier-Martin, in France, all know how grateful I am for their warmth. It was their stories that allowed me to take full measure of the wealth that was Moura, this woman they loved so dearly. In their willingness to share their knowledge and their memories with me, they gave Moura her depth and all her humanity.

I also want to thank Danielle Guigonis, who supported me all the way through this long adventure. Without her devotion and her skill, I would never have reached the end.

I would also like to thank Jean-Yves Barillec, Delphine Borione, Frédérique Brizzi, Brigitte Defives, Carole Hardoüin, Frédérique and Michel Hochmann, Vincent Jolivet, Serge and Catherine Sobczinski, and Martine Zaugg, my perpetual victims who I tortured all over again for three years, by sending them snippets of a thousand versions of my manuscript. The patience they showed, their valuable comments, and their honesty continue to amaze me. I hope they all know just how thankful I am for their affection and their valiance.

I would like to tell my Russian friends just how indebted I am to them for having guided me through the labyrinths of Russia's archives and libraries. I especially want to mention my Russian translator Marina Chernykh-Lecomte, who unfailingly answered my questions and broke down for me every single publication about Moura Budberg in Cyrillic characters. It is due to her work and her patience that I was able to summon up the feelings at the heart of the letters that Moura and Gorky wrote to each other. A warm thanks is also due to Claire de Montesquiou, who helped me decipher Moura's handwritten messages to Lockhart while he was imprisoned in the Kremlin. I also want to acknowledge the support of Prince Nicolas Tchavtchavatzé, my mentor in the Russian world.

May the curators, the librarians, the archivists, and the researchers whose assistance I've asked for in American institutions know how grateful I am for their helpfulness. Most especially Dmitry Ahtyrsky and Tanya Cheboratev at the Columbia University Library in New York; Susan Floyd and Rick Watson at the Harry Ransom Center of the University of Texas at Austin; Carol Leadenham and Ron Basich at the Hoover Institution Archive of Stanford University in California; Kristina Rosenthal of the Tulsa University MacFarlane Library in Oklahoma; Denis Sears of the University of Illinois; Cherry Williams at the Lilly Library at Indiana University in Bloomington; and Kellyn Younggren at the Special Collections of the University of Montana.

Immense thanks are also due to Emily Dezurick-Badran and Frank Boyce at the Cambridge University Library in Great Britain; the staff of the British Library in London and the Public Record Office in Kew; the staff of the Centre Historique des Archives de Vincennes in Paris; Phil Tomaselli, the author of several works on genealogy and espionage; and Dottoressa Rossella Valentini of the Biblioteca Comunale de Montevarchi in Italy, all of whom were invaluable in their support of my research.

My gratitude also goes to Professor Richard Spence of the University of Idaho at Moscow in the United States, a specialist in British espionage in Russia at the beginning of the twentieth century, for our long conversations over Skype and for his generosity in willingly sharing with me the unpublished manuscripts he held in his archives, most especially those of the late Gail Owen, a scholar who had spent long years investigating the role Moura played in the Lockhart Plot. Thanks are also very much due to Dee Owen, who made all this possible.

I was especially touched by the very warm welcome I received in

Estonia. My days at Yendel and in Tallinn, accompanied by Georgi Särekanno, a historian and collector of Benckendorff family relics and a curator at the Yendel museum—Jäneda Mõis—remain in my memory as a special stretch of happiness and sharing. I can never forget the moment when Georgi offered me an original piece of Moura's letterhead paper, which he himself had found in the woods of Kallijärv. I also have to thank Enno Must, the director of Jäneda Mõis, who welcomed me at the mansion and the Kallijärv estate with boundless kindness. How could I recall these memories and not also think of Mairé Taska, the current owner of the lodge on the lake's shores, who took great care in setting out the books and documents that might be of interest to me? I have no words for just how much these days spent at Yendel, in the company of such hosts, revived the magic of the place.

I'm also deeply indebted to Bernard Paqueteau, the cultural counselor at the French embassy in Tallinn, and to his wife, Dominique, who arranged a succession of meetings with various Estonian academics focusing on the history of their country between 1910 and 1939. Most especially Professor Olev Liivik, president of the Association for Germano-Baltic Culture; Reigo Rosenthal, a specialist of espionage in Estonia between the two wars; Märt Uustalu, a genealogist of the Baltic nobility, who I was able to meet in Tartu; and Mari-Leen Tammela, who was completing a thesis on Communism in Estonia and who guided me through all the archives. My thanks also go to His Excellency the Ambassador of France in Estonia, Monsieur Michel Raineri, who assisted me in my endeavors.

I have a very tender thought toward my parents, Aliette and Dominique Lapierre, for their unfailing trust in my work. As well as toward Rosie Yangson, who has been a steadying presence around all of us.

It is my hope that Frank Auboyneau and our daughter, Garance, who stoically beared my passion for Moura over the course of all these years, accompanying me on her tracks in my faraway trips, and editing the manuscript each day, know that this book owes every bit of its existence to their love.

May my editor Teresa Cremisi, and all her collaborators at Flammarion in France, know just how keenly I've felt them to be at my side all along.

Finally, I want to offer my warmest gratitude to Atria Books and its fabulous team, Rakesh Satyal, Loan Le, as well as Jeffrey Zuckerman who sustained this project with tireless work and enthusiasm.

—Alexandra Lapierre

Translator's Acknowledgments

The translation of such a wide-ranging tome has been an incredible challenge and a wonderful privilege, and it is thanks to Alexandra Lapierre's passion that this fiery book first came into being, and now has a second life in English.

My utmost gratitude goes to Rakesh Satyal at Atria Books for ever so slyly convincing me to take this on; to Loan Le, who has been the editorial cheerleader every translator dreams of; and to the many other brilliant folks at Atria—Lourdes Lopez, Samantha Hoback, Vanessa Silverio, and Alexis Minieri—for the invaluable roles they played along the way. The research involved in finding English-language equivalents or sources for many quotations and historical details was made immeasurably easier by my time at the Columbia University libraries while translating this novel, as well as by the assistance of my dear colleagues Heather Cleary, Meghan Forbes, Marissa Grunes, Noah Mintz, Kaija Straumanis, and Megan Ross.

It has been a pleasant surprise to realize just how many Russophone friends I have, and I am above all indebted to Julie Hersh, whose research in Russia, Estonia, and the United Kingdom—and whose extensive experience as a copy editor—have made her a perfect colleague to pester endlessly while working on this book. And a large portion of the letters between Moura and Gorky, drawn from the Russian collection of their correspondence, owe their accuracy in English translation to Sean Gasper Bye's patient attention.

Last but not least, I'm grateful to Margaux Baralon, who I consider a dear friend, for her advice, her insights, and her perennial sense of humor, all of which were invaluable to crossing the finish line at long last.

—Jeffrey Zuckerman

Bibliography

Throughout the years of my search for the traces of Baroness Budberg, some thirty books never left my side. Their full details may be found in the general bibliography in the following pages. But I would also like to pay my respects to the memory of these authors, who, over the course of time, became both my guides and companions.

First and foremost, Senator Zakrevsky's "ward," Darya Mirvoda, Moura's half sister, who recounted in her dotage—under the title of *Mania* and the pseudonym of Mania Otrada—the cruelty of her childhood at Berezovaya Rudka. Moura had just been born at that point, and the two sisters barely knew each other. But it was through this deeply touching account that I was able to evoke the atmosphere of the estate and the descriptions of the Viper, Bobik, Anna, Alla, and their father. Then the memoirs and incredible autobiographies of Meriel Buchanan, which I quoted from in chapters 10, 11, and 12: *Petrograd, the City of Trouble, 1914–1918*; *Recollections of Imperial Russia*; *The Dissolution of an Empire*; and *Ambassador's Daughter*. As well as the writings of Count Charles de Chambrun: *Lettres à Marie, Pétersbourg–Petrograd, 1914–1918*; those of the French ambassador in Saint Petersburg, Joseph Noulens: *Mon ambassade en Russie soviétique, 1917–1919*; and Louis de Robien's notes: *Journal d'un diplomate en Russie, 1917–1918*, quoted as well in chapter 12. For the Russian world, I cannot understate the importance of Chukovsky's *Diary*, published in Russian by Elena Chukovskaya and translated into French by Marc Weinstein and into English by Michael Henry Heim, which I quote in chapters 24, 25, and 27. And for the world in which Maxim Gorky lived, I drew upon the extraordinary edition of his nearly twenty-volume correspondence published in Moscow by the Gorky Institute, most notably volume 16, which includes his correspondence with Moura Budberg and which I quote from in chapters 26, 30, 31, 33, and 37: *A. M. Gorkiy i M. I. Budberg: Perepiska, 1920–1936*. The credo that Gorky declares in my chapter 36 regarding the need to not tell the entire truth, and even to hide it for the sake of a greater truth, is published in his two letters to Yekaterina Kuskova: the first in *Noviy Zhurnal*, number 28 (1954); the second in the Gallimard Pléiade volume of *Oeuvres de Maxim Gorky*. The quotation concerning General Zinovy Peshkov's meeting in London with Baroness Budberg in my epilogue is drawn from the book *Portraits de Pechkoff* by His Excellency Ambassador Francis Huré: a magnificent testimony to the nobility and immensity of Gorky's adopted son. The text by Pavel Malkov from which I quote in chapter 17 is drawn from his autobiography: *Notes of a Commandant of the Moscow Kremlin*, republished under the title *Reminiscences of a Kremlin Commandant*. I first read the poem "Moura Budberg on Her Proposed Departure from England" in the archives of Andrew Boyle, held at the Cambridge University Library. This archive covers the wide-ranging investigation that Mr. Boyle had undertaken in hopes of writing the biography of Moura. He amassed many documents, most notably his interviews with Moura's nearest and dearest, after her death. Upon realizing the scope of his subject, he ended up abandoning the project. But his research contains a wealth of information and is invaluable for anybody curious about Baroness Budberg. The poem, which I quote in my epilogue, was by a close friend of Moura, the journalist, writer, and poet Michael Burn, who published it in his collection *Out on a Limb*. For the majority of the information about the connections between Moura and Robert Bruce Lockhart over half a century, I am, of course, indebted to the pieces he wrote about them in his brilliant tomes, which I quote in chapters 13, 16, 17, 19, 32, 34, and 35 and in my epilogue—most notably *Memoirs of a British Agent*; *Retreat from Glory*; *Comes the Reckoning*; *Friends, Foes and Foreigners*; *The Two Revolutions*; and the two-volume doorstop edited by Kenneth Young: *The Diaries of Sir Robert Bruce Lockhart*, vol. I, 1915–1938, and vol. II, 1939–1965. I also want to pay my respects to the utter masterpiece of introspection that is H. G. Wells's confessions of love, edited by his son G. P. "Gip" Well: *H. G. Wells in Love, Postscript to an Experiment in Autobiography*, which I quote in chapters 27, 34, 35, 37, and 38. Not to mention Andrea Lynn's remarkable book, *Shadow Lovers, The Last Affairs of H. G. Wells*, which I quote in chapter 37.

Finally, I want to express my respect and admiration to Tania Alexander, Moura's daughter, who drew a deeply vivid portrait of her mother in *A Little of All These*, later republished with the title *An Estonian Childhood: A Memoir*, which I quote in chapters 29 and 38.

Last but not least, the text around the trailer for the film *British Agent*, which I quote in chapter 39, a film adapted from Lockhart's book and directed by Michael Curtiz in 1934, comes from the archives of Warner Brothers Pictures.

❖

ALEXANDER, Tania. *An Estonian Childhood: A Memoir*. London: Faber and Faber, 1987.

ANDREW, Christopher. *The Defence of the Realm: The Authorized History of MI5*. London: Allen Lane, 2009.

ARON, Raymond. *Memoirs: Fifty Years of Political Reflection*. New York: Holmes and Meier, 1990.

ARTSIMOVICH, Beulah. "Our Escape from the Bolshevists," *Chicago Daily Tribune*, July 30, August 6 and 13, 1922.

AUCOUTURIER, Michel. *Un poète dans son temps: Boris Pasternak*. Paris: Éditions des Syrtes, 2015.

BABEL, Isaac. *Chroniques de l'an 18*. Arles: Actes Sud, 1999.

BAINTON, Roy. *Honoured by Strangers: The Life of Captain Francis Cromie CB DSO RN 1882–1918*. Ramsbury: Airlife, 2002.

BARANOV, Vadim. *Baronessa i Burevestnik*. Moscow: Vagrius, 2006.

———. *Bezzakonaya Kometa: Rokovaya Zhenshchina Maksima Gorkogo*. Moscow: Agraf, 2001.

BARING, Maurice. *Letters*. Selected and edited by Jocelyn Hillgarth and Julian Jeffs. Norwich: Michael Russell, 2007.

———. *The Puppet Show of Memory*. London: Cassell Biographies, 1987.

BAVEREZ, Nicolas. *Raymond Aron*. Paris: Flammarion, 1993.

BELONENKO, Alexander, and Galina Panova. "Le mystère de 'l'Affaire Zakrevsky' et ceux de l'affaire Dreyfus." Collection Colette Hartwich.

BENCKENDORFF, Constantine. *Half a Life: The Reminiscences of a Russian Gentleman*. London: Richard Press, 1954.

BERBEROVA, Nina. *C'est moi qui souligne.* Arles: Actes Sud, 1989.

———. *Histoire de la baronne Boudberg.* Arles: Actes Sud, 1988.

———. *Les Dames de Saint-Pétersbourg.* Arles: Actes Sud, 1995.

BERELOWITCH, Wladimir. *Le Grand siècle russe d'Alexandre Ier à Nicolas II.* Paris: Gallimard, 2005.

BOUNINE, Ivan. *Jours maudits.* Translated by Jean Laury. Lausanne: L'Âge d'Homme, 1988.

BROOK-SHEPHERD, Gordon. *Iron Maze: The Western Secret Services and the Bolsheviks.* London: Pan Books, 1998.

BUCHANAN, George. *My Mission to Russia: And Other Diplomatic Memories.* London: Cassel and Company, 1923.

BUCHANAN, Meriel. *Ambassador's Daughter.* London: Cassel and Company, 1958.

———. *The Dissolution of an Empire.* London: John Murray, 1932. Reprint, New York: Arno Press and *New York Times*, 1971.

———. *Petrograd, the City of Trouble, 1914–1918.* London: W. Collins, 1918.

———. *Recollections of Imperial Russia.* London: Hutchinson and Co., 1923.

BURN, Michael. *Out on a Limb.* London: Poetry Book Society, Hogarth Press, 1973.

CALDER, Angus. *The People's War: Britain 1939–45.* London: Granada, 1971.

CARRÈRE D'ENCAUSSE, Hélène. *Les Romanov: Une dynastie sous le règne du sang.* Paris: Fayard, 2013.

CARS, Jean des. *La Saga des Romanov de Pierre le Grand à Nicolas II.* Paris: Plon, 2008.

CHAMBRUN, Charles de. *Lettres à Marie, Pétersbourg-Petrograd, 1914–1918.* Paris: Plon, 1941.

CHENTALISKI, Vitali. *La Parole ressuscitée: Dans les archives littéraires du KGB.* Paris: Robert Laffont, 1993.

CHUKOVSKY, Kornei. *Diary, 1901–1969.* Edited by Victor Erlich. Translated by Michael Henry Heim. New Haven: Yale University Press, 2005.

CHURCHILL, Winston and Clementine. *Conversations in times: 1908–1964.* Translated by Dominique Boulonnais and Antoine Capet. Paris: Tallandier, 2013.

CLARK, Barrett H. *Intimate Portraits: Being Recollections of Maxim Gorky, John Galsworthy, Edward Sheldon, George Moore, Sidney Howard and Others.* Washington: Kennikat Press, 1951.

COOK, Andrew. *Ace of Spies: The True Story of Sidney Reilly.* Stroud, UK: History Press, 2004.

CRANKSHAW, Edward. *The Shadow of the Winter Palace: Russia's Drift to Revolution 1825–1917.* New York: Da Capo Press, 2000.

CRÉMIEUX-BRILHAC, Jean-Louis. *La France libre, I: De l'appel du 18 Juin à la Libération.* Paris: Gallimard, 1996.

DUKES, Paul. *Red Dusk and the Morrow: Adventures and Investigations in Red Russia.* London: Williams and Norgate, 1923.

FANGER, Donald, ed., trans. *Gorky's Tolstoy and Other Reminiscences: Key Writings By and About Maxim Gorky.* New Haven: Yale University Press, 2008.

FEIGEL, Lara. *The Love-Charm of Bombs: Restless Lives in the Second World War.* New York: Bloomsbury Press, 2013.

FERNANDEZ, Dominique. *Transsibérien.* Paris: Grasset, 2012.

FERNANDEZ-AZABAL, Lilie de (Countess Nostitz). *Romance and Revolutions.* London: Hutchinson and Co., 1937.

FISCHER, Fritz. *Germany's Aims in the First World War.* New York: W. W. Norton and Co., 1967.

FOOT, Michael. *H. G.: The History of Mr. Wells.* Washington: Counterpoint, 1995.

GARSTIN, Denis. *Friendly Russia.* London: Fisher Unwin, 1915.

———. *The Shilling Soldiers.* London: Hodder and Stoughton, 1918.

GONCHAR, Valentina Vassilievna. "The Zakrewski Manor and Park, Crowning Glory of Architecture and Landscaping in the Province of Poltava." *Our Heritage.* Russia, n.d.

GORKY, Maxim. *A. M. Gorkii i M. I. Budberg: Perepiska, 1920–1936.* Gorky Archives, vol. 16. Moscow: Gorky Institute, 2001.

———. *Letters.* Moscow: Progress Publishers, 1966.

———. *Maksim Gorky: Selected Letters.* Translated and edited by Andrew Barratt and Barry P. Scherr. Oxford: Clarendon Press, 1997.

———. *Oeuvres.* Edited by Jean Pérus and Guy Verret. Paris: Gallimard Pléiade, 2005.

———. *Vie de Klim Samguine (Quarante années).* Paris: Les Éditeurs réunis, 1949.

GRABBE, Paul. *Windows on the River Neva.* New York: Pomerica Press Limited, 1997.

HASTINGS, Selina. *The Secret Lives of Somerset Maugham.* London: John Murray, 2009.

HEWISON, Robert. *Under Siege: Literary Life in London 1939–45.* London: Weidenfeld and Nicolson, 1977.

HIPPIUS, Zinaïda. *Journal sous la Terreur.* Paris: Éditions du Rocher, 2006.

HOBSBAWM, Eric. *Interesting Times: A Twentieth-Century Life.* London: Abacus, 2002.

HURE, Francis. *Portraits de Pechkoff.* Paris: Éditions de Fallois, 2006.

IVINSKAÏA, Olga. *Otage de l'Éternité: Mes années avec Pasternak.* Paris: Fayard, 1978.

JEFFERY, Keith. *MI6: The History of the Secret Intelligence Service 1909–1949.* London: Bloomsbury, 2010.

JUNKER, Ida. *Le Monde de Nina Berberova.* Paris: L'Harmattan, 2012.

KAUN, Alexander. *Maxim Gorky and His Russia.* London: Jonathan Cape, 1932.

KERENSKY, Alexander. *Kerensky's Memoirs.* London: Cassell, 1965.

KESSEL, Joseph. *Les Nuits de Sibérie.* Paris: Arthaud, 2013.

———. *Tous n'étaient pas des anges.* Paris: Les Belles Lettres, 2012.

KETTLE, Michael. *Sidney Reilly: The True Story.* London: Corgi, 1983.

KLEINMICHEL, Marie. *Memories of a Shipwrecked World.* London: Brentano's Limited, 1923.

KOESTLER, Arthur. *Le Zéro et l'Infini.* Paris: Calmann-Lévy, 1945.

KROSS, Jaan. *Dans l'insaisissable: Le roman de Jüri Vilms.* Translated by Jacques Tricot. Paris: L'Harmattan, 2001.

KRUUS, Oskar. *Parunessi pihtimus.* Tallinn: Faatum, 2004.

LABARTHE, André. *La France devant la guerre: la balance des forces.* Paris: Grasset, 1939.

LEGGETT, George. *The Cheka: Lenin's Political Police.* Oxford: Clarendon Press, 1981.

LEVIN, Dan. *Stormy Petrel: The Life and Work of Maxim Gorky.* New York: Schocken Books, 1986.

LOCKHART, Robert Bruce. *Comes the Reckoning.* London: Putnam, 1947.

———. *The Diaries of Sir Robert Bruce Lockhart: 1915–1938.* Edited by Kenneth Young. London: Macmillan, 1973.

———. *The Diaries of Sir Robert Bruce Lockhart: 1939–1965.* Edited by Kenneth Young. London: Macmillan, 1980.

———. *Friends, Foes and Foreigners.* London: Putnam, 1957.

———. *Memoirs of a British Agent.* London: Putnam, 1932.

———. *Retreat from Glory.* New York: Garden City Publishing Co., 1938.

———. *The Two Revolutions: An Eye-Witness Account of Russia, 1917.* London: Bodley Head, 1967.

LOCKHART, Robin Bruce. *Ace of Spies: Story of Sidney Reilly.* London: Hodder Paperbacks, 1967.

———. *Reilly: the First Man.* New York: Penguin Books, 1987.

LODGE, David. *A Man of Parts.* London: Vintage, 2012.

LYNN, Andrea. *Shadow Lovers: The Last Affairs of H. G. Wells.* Oxford: Perseus Press, 2001.

MALAPARTE, Curzio. *Le Bonhomme Lénine.* Paris: Grasset, 1932.

MALKOV, Pavel. *Reminiscences of a Kremlin Commandant.* Honolulu: University Press of the Pacific, 2002.

MCDONALD, Deborah, and Jeremy Dronfield. *A Very Dangerous Woman: The Lives, Loves and Lies of Russia's Most Seductive Spy.* London: Oneworld, 2015.

MCFADDEN, David. *Alternative Paths: Soviets & American 1917–1920.* Oxford: Oxford University Press, 1993.

MESHCHERSKAYA, Ekaterina. *A Russian Princess Remembers: The Journey from Tsars to Glasnost.* New York: Doubleday, 1989.

MEYERS, Jeffrey. *Somerset Maugham: A Life.* New York: Random House, 2005.

MILTON, Giles. *Russian Roulette: A Deadly Game: How British Spies Thwarted Lenin's Global Plot.* London: Sceptre, 2013.

MONTEFIORE, Simon. *Sashenka.* London: Corgi Books, 2008.

———. *Stalin: The Court of the Red Tsar.* London: Weidenfeld and Nicolson, 2003.

———. *Young Stalin.* New York: Vintage, 2008.

MOSSOLOV, Alexander. *At the Court of the Last Tsar.* London: Methuen and Co., 1935.

MOULIN, René. *L'Année des diplomates 1919.* Paris: Librairie Félix Alcan, 1920.

NICOLSON, Harold. *Diaries and Letters, 1907–1964.* London: Weidenfeld and Nicolson, 2004.

NOULENS, Joseph. *Mon ambassade en Russie Soviétique 1917–1919,* vols. 1 and 2. Paris: Plon, 1933.

OKSANEN, Sofi. *Les Vaches de Stalin.* Translated by Sébastien Cagnoli. Paris: Stock, 2003.

———. *Purge.* Paris: Stock, 2010.

OTRADA, Mania. *Mania.* Paris: Éditions Notre Famille, 1963.

OWEN, Gail. "Budberg, the Soviets and Reilly." 1988.

———. *The Career of Sydney Reilly 1895–1925.* n.d.

———. "Moura Budberg's Spying and Allegiance." Unpublished manuscript, collection of Professor Richard Spence, University of Idaho, Moscow, n.d.

PALEOLOGUE, Maurice. *Le Crépuscule des tsars: Journal (1914–1917).* Paris: Mercure de France, 2007.

PANOVA, Galina. "L'Histoire génétique et la transmission des traits de caractère à travers Émigration et Revolution. L'exemple des Zakrevsky." Master's thesis, Saint Petersburg State University, 2013. French translation furnished by Colette Hartwich.

PARKHMOVSKI, Mikhaïl. *Fils de Russie général de France*. Paris: Albin Michel, 1992.

PASCAL, Pierre. *En communisme: Mon journal de Russie, 1918–1921*. Lausanne: L'Âge d'Homme, 1977.

———. *Mon journal de Russie à la mission militaire française, 1916–1918*. Lausanne: L'Âge d'Homme, 1975.

PASTERNAK, Boris. *Le Docteur Jivago*. Paris: Gallimard, 1958.

PERUS, Jean. *Romain Rolland et Maxime Gorki*. Paris: Éditeurs français réunis, 1968.

PIERRE-BLOCH, Jean. *Londres: Capitale de la France libre*. Paris: Carrère/Michel Lafon, 1986.

RABINOWITCH, Alexander. *The Bolsheviks in Power: The First Year of Soviet Rule in Petrograd*. Bloomington: Indiana University Press, 2007.

REED, John. *Dix Jours qui ébranlèrent le monde*. Brussels: Tribord, 2010.

REILLY, Pepita. *Britain's Master Spy, or the Adventures of Sidney Reilly*. London: Harper and Brothers, 1931.

ROBIEN, Louis de. *Journal d'un diplomate en Russie, 1917–1918*. Paris: Albin Michel, 1967.

SALZMAN, Neil V. *Reform and Revolution: The Life and Times of Raymond Robins*. Kent, OH: Kent State University Press, 1991.

SAYN-WITTGENSTEIN, Catherine. *La Fin de ma Russie: Journal 1914–1919*. Paris: Phébus, 2007.

SERGE, Victor. *Mémoires d'un révolutionnaire 1905–1945*. Montréal: Lux Éditeur, 2010.

SERVICE, Robert. *Trotsky: A Biography*. London: Macmillan, 2009.

SEYMOUR, Miranda. *Ottoline Morrell: Life on the Grand Scale*. London: Hodder and Stoughton, 1992.

SHERBORNE, Michael. *H. G. Wells: Another Kind of Life*. London: Peter Owen Publishers, 2010.

SMITH, Douglas. *Former People: The Final Days of the Russian Aristocracy*. London: Macmillan, 2012.

SOLJENITSYNE, Alexandre. *L'Archipel du Goulag*. Paris: Fayard, 2014.

SPENCE, Richard B. *Trust No One: The Secret World of Sidney Reilly*. Los Angeles: Feral House, 2002.

THOMAS, Gordon. *Inside British Intelligence: 100 Years of MI5 and MI6*. London: JR Books, 2009.

TOMASELLI, Phil. *Tracing Your Secret Service Ancestors*. Barnsley: Pen and Sword Books, 2009.

TROYAT, Henri. *Gorky*. Paris: Flammarion, 1986.

———. *La Grande Histoire des Tsars: Paul Iᵉʳ, Alexandre Iᵉʳ, Nicolas Iᵉʳ, Alexandre II, Alexandre III, Nicolas II*. Paris: Omnibus, 2009.

———. *La Vie quotidienne en Russie au temps du dernier tsar*. Paris: Hachette, 1959.

TYNAN, Kathleen. "The Astonishing History of Moura Budberg: A Flame for Famous Men." *Vogue*, October 1, 1970, 162, 208–211.

USTINOV, Peter. *Dear Me*. London: William Heinemann, 1977.

USTINOV, Nadia Benois. *Klop and the Ustinov Family*. London: Sidgwick and Jackson, 1973.

VAKSBERG, Arkady. *Alexandra Kollontaï*. Paris: Fayard, 1996.

———. *The Murder of Maxim Gorky: A Secret Execution*. New York: Enigma Books, 2007.

VALLENTIN, Antonina. *H. G. Wells, ou la Conspiration au grand jour*. Paris: Stock, 1952.

VASILIEVA, Larissa. *Kremlin Wives: The Secret Lives of the Women behind the Kremlin Walls—From Lenin to Gorbachev*. Translated by Cathy Porter. New York: Arcade Publishing, 1994.

WARNES, David. *Chronicle of the Russian Tsars: The Reign-by-Reign Record of the Rulers of Imperial Russia*. London: Thames and Hudson, 1999.

WELLS, H. G. *Experiment in Autobiography: Discoveries and Conclusions of a Very Ordinary Brain*. London: V. Gollancz and Cresset Press, 1934.

———. *H. G. Wells in Love: Postscript to an Experiment in Autobiography*. Edited by G. P. Wells. Boston: Little, Brown and Company, 1984.

———. *La Guerre des mondes*. Paris: Calmann-Lévy, 1917.

———. *La Russie dans l'ombre*. Paris: A. M. Métailié, 1985.

———. *Les Chefs-d'oeuvre de H. G. Wells*. Paris: Omnibus, 2007.

———. *L'Homme invisible*. Paris: Paul Ollendorff, 1901.

———. *L'Île du Docteur Moreau*. Paris: Mercure de France, 1901.

———. *Machine à explorer le temps*. Paris: Mercure de France, 1895.

———. *Monsieur Britling commence à voir clair*. Paris: Payot, 1918.

———. *Russia in the Shadows*. New York: George H. Doran Company, 1921.

———. *Une tentative d'autobiographie*. Paris: Gallimard, 1936.

WEST, Anthony. *H. G. Wells: Aspects of a Life*. London: Hutchinson, 1984.

WILLIAMS, Robert C. *Culture in Exile: Russian Emigrés in Germany, 1881–1941*. London: Cornell University Press, 1972.

WOLFE, Bertram D. *The Bridge and the Abyss: The Troubled Friendship of Maxim Gorky and V. I. Lenin.* Stanford: Hoover Institution, 1967.

WORTMAN, Richard S. *Scenarios of Power: Myth and Ceremony in Russian Monarchy from Peter the Great to the Abdication of Nicholas II.* Princeton: Princeton University Press, 2006.

ZAMIATINE, Evguéni. *Le Métier littéraire.* Lausanne: L'Âge d'Homme, 1990.

ZEEPVAT, Charlotte. *Romanov Autumn: The Last Century of Imperial Russia.* Phoenix Mill: Sutton Publishing, 2000.

About the Author

Alexandra Lapierre is a novelist and biographer whose many bestselling books have been translated into multiple languages throughout the world. *Fanny Stevenson*, her biography of the American pioneer, romantic muse, and wife of writer Robert Louis Stevenson, garnered the most prestigious literary prizes all over Europe. *Artemisia*, her portrait of the first Italian Renaissance woman painter, was voted Book of the Week by the British BBC and Best Book on the Seventeenth Century by Sorbonne University.

The Woman of a Thousand Names was published in France to rave reviews. The press described its author as the only French writer able to bring back to life, with heart and soul, the most captivating women that history has disparaged or forgotten. Alexandra Lapierre has been nominated a Chevalier of the Order of Arts and Letters by the French government. French by birth, yet educated in the United States, she is a graduate of the Sorbonne and the University of Southern California. She is based in Paris, but lives around the world, wherever her heroines take her.